Trisha Telep is the editor of the bestselling Mammoth romance titles, including *The Mammoth Book of Vampire Romance*, *Love Bites*, *The Mammoth Book of Paranormal Romance* and *The Mammoth Book of Time Travel Romance*.

Recent Mammoth titles

The Mammoth Book of Body Horror
The Mammoth Book of Steampunk
The Mammoth Book of New CSI
The Mammoth Book of Gangs
The Mammoth Book of SF Wars
The Mammoth Book of One-Liners
The Mammoth Book of Ghost Romance
The Mammoth Book of Best New SF 25
The Mammoth Book of Jokes 2
The Mammoth Book of Horror 23
The Mammoth Book of Slasher Movies
The Mammoth Book of Street Art
The Mammoth Book of Ghost Stories by Women
The Mammoth Book of Best New Erotica 11
The Mammoth Book of Irish Humour
The Mammoth Book of Unexplained Phenomena
The Mammoth Book of Futuristic Romance
The Mammoth Book of Best British Crime 10
The Mammoth Book of Combat
The Mammoth Book of Quick & Dirty Erotica
The Mammoth Book of Dark Magic
The Mammoth Book of New Sudoku
The Mammoth Book of Zombies!
The Mammoth Book of Angels & Demons
The Mammoth Book of the Rolling Stones
The Mammoth Book of Westerns
The Mammoth Book of Prison Breaks
The Mammoth Book of Time Travel SF
The Mammoth Quiz Book
The Mammoth Book of Erotic Photography, Vol. 4

The Mammoth Book of

ER Romance

Edited by Trisha Telep

RUNNING PRESS
PHILADELPHIA · LONDON

Constable & Robinson Ltd.
55–56 Russell Square
London WC1B 4HP
www.constablerobinson.com

First published in the UK by Robinson,
an imprint of Constable & Robinson Ltd., 2013

A copy of the British Library Cataloguing in Publication
Data is available from the British Library

UK ISBN: 978-1-78033-037-2 (paperback)
UK ISBN: 978-1-78033-042-6 (ebook)

1 3 5 7 9 10 8 6 4 2

First published in the United States in 2013 by Running Press Book Publishers,
A Member of the Perseus Books Group

Books published by Running Press are available at special discounts for bulk purchases
in the United States by corporations, institutions, and other organizations. For
more information, please contact the Special Markets Department at the Perseus
Books Group, 2300 Chestnut Street, Suite 200, Philadelphia, PA 19103, or call
(800) 810-4145, ext. 5000, or e-mail special.markets@perseusbooks.com.

US ISBN: 978-0-7624-4811-1
US Library of Congress Control Number: 2012942535

9 8 7 6 5 4 3 2 1
Digit on the right indicates the number of this printing

Running Press Book Publishers
2300 Chestnut Street
Philadelphia, PA 19103-4371

Visit us on the web!
www.runningpress.com

Printed and bound in the UK

Contents

COPYRIGHT

INTRODUCTION

There's something incredibly sexy about the Hippocratic oath.

Hospitals can be intensely emotional places. In the ER, that is virtually guaranteed. Victims of all stripes find their way into Emergency Rooms across the country, fleeing hurricanes, fires, and other natural – and not so natural – disasters. Reading through the heady mix of medical romance on offer in *The Mammoth Book of ER Romance*, it's easy to see why so many readers and writers believe that medical professionals make better lovers. If it's passion you're looking for, then you've surely come to the right place. You'll also get drive, dedication and determination thrown into the bargain for good measure with the men and women you'll find in these pages. If that's not a recipe for emotionally charged super romance, I don't know what is. And isn't it good to know that even if Cupid's arrow causes some damage – which Cupid's arrow is wont to do – they can always prescribe a little something to help with the heartache?

Falling in love at work is a hazard. Try organizing your love life between broken bones and surgical sutures and you'll see how easy it is. Even transferring to a hospital halfway across the country won't save you. You'll only run into the ex-love of your life, the handsome, young doctor you never quite got over, and your heartbreak will start all over again. Shy residents lock eyes across lonely cafeterias in the dead of the night, both on their fifth cup of coffee during their third back-to-back shift. A doctor and a policewoman who meet frequently in his ER decide to take the next step while she guards a crucial wounded witness. A famous surgeon, back to woo an old flame, almost gets burned in the process.

It's a chronic case of life and love, doctors and nurses, and those who adore them. If you're already a lover of medical romance, you know it's totally contagious and completely incurable. If you're just taking a look at medical romance for the first time, you're in for a comprehensive seventeen stories by way of introduction. Firmly in the foreground of many of the stories, and quietly in the background of others, the ER and the wider world of the hospital, all play a central part in these romantic stories. All feature heroes and heroines who have made medicine their business, and who must juggle medical responsibilities, and the odd romantic inclination, each and every day.

So call a code – for love!

THE NURSE IN CHARGE

Wendy S. Marcus

Chapter One

The call came in at 8.42 p.m., two hours after Ruby Kendell – charge nurse in the Frost Community Hospital Emergency Department – had arrived at work for the third of three back-to-back twelve-hour night shifts she'd agreed to cover.

She returned the receiver to the console. Her heart stopped beating. Her lungs stopped breathing. The world stopped spinning. Snippets of her life flared up, taking over reality.

The most joyful day: When she'd given birth to her son Dillon.

The most emotionally painful day: When she'd watched Dillon's dad, her first love, pack up and leave after choosing life on the road with his band over her and their infant son.

The most difficult day: When she'd left her six-week-old baby boy in the care of strangers at a daycare center for the first time – a single mother forced to return to work.

"You're white as the walls," the unit secretary noted. "What's wrong?"

"Call the operator," Ruby instructed, doing her best to remain calm. "Tell her code red."

Pat's eyes went wide on hearing the code for a major external disaster with a large number of casualties.

In a state of shock, she wondered how she'd look back on today – the day a tornado touched down at the local elementary school during bedtime stories with the principal, when students from kindergarten through third grade – her five-year-old son among them – gathered with their sleeping bags and favorite stuffies to listen to their beloved principal read to them.

Dillon had been so excited to attend.

Ruby pictured the large windows of the All Purpose Room shattering under the force of the high winds, turning shards of glass into lethal projectiles, impaling anyone in their path.

Ruby picked up the phone again and depressed the intercom button. "I need all staff at the desk. Code red." All staff for a Friday night shift in their small hospital consisted of three nurses, one nurse's aide, one doctor and one unit secretary. They were about to be overrun.

As her staff assembled, the operator's voice came over the PA system. "Code red. Code red. All non-essential staff to the Emergency Department, stat."

"What have we got?" Dr Johnson asked.

At least if she had to run a code red, she had a young, energetic, excellent clinician by her side.

"A tornado touched down outside the elementary school during an evening program," she said, trying to keep her voice even, her tone moderated. She swallowed her fear, tamped down the desire to run to her car, speed to the scene and rescue her son. "Estimated fifty to seventy-five casualties." The contents of her stomach started to churn. No one knew for sure how many children were in attendance and how many parents had remained on site. It'd be hours before all school staff, students and parents were accounted for.

"My God," Sandy, one of the nurses said. "This is New York. We don't get tornadoes here."

Not big ones, no. But the occasional small tornado could still do plenty of damage.

Ruby took a deep breath. "The bridge over the river is inaccessible due to fallen trees and downed power lines—" making the next closest hospital unreachable by road "—and Stat Flight is grounded due to high winds. So we're it."

"Ruby," Pat said from beside her. "Molly just called. Honey, you'd better sit down."

Molly, Dillon's best friend's mother, had taken both boys to the school that evening. Ruby felt the blood drain from her body. She grabbed on to the counter for support. "Tell me."

"Her son is in a full-blown asthma attack and they're on the way to the hospital." Ruby waited for the rest. "When the storm hit she got separated from Dillon. She said she tried to find him but—"

Ruby stopped listening. Visions bombarded her. Dillon, all alone in the dark, scared and cold on this frigid November night, maybe hurt and in pain, maybe dying, maybe hidden beneath a pile of rubble where no one knew to look for him. Suffering. Crying out for her.

A burning ache, like nothing she'd ever felt before, seared her heart.

Staff from other departments converged on the ER, and stood waiting for direction. From her. A mother in crisis. The nurse in charge. Which would take priority at this particular moment in time?

Luckily her disaster preparedness training kicked in. She looked at the night administrator. "I need a nurse on triage in the ER waiting room. Can you get me someone from pediatrics to help out?" She turned to the security guard. "Set up visitor screening in the main lobby. No one gets in until we call for them." Luckily the nurse's aide on duty tonight happened to be an EMT. "I need you on the radio, Jack," to coordinate the ambulance arrivals, alert the staff about what to expect, and get Dr Johnson for in-transit consult if needed.

Maintenance got to work lining up extra stretchers and wheelchairs, which staff from housekeeping wiped down and covered with sheets.

"I paged respiratory therapy to be here for your friend's son," Pat said. "Now I'll go down the on-call sheet and staff roster to see who I can get in here."

"I'll help," a young unit secretary offered, hurrying behind the desk.

They'd all been trained to pitch in, go where you're needed, and do what you're told.

As everyone began to disperse, Ruby climbed onto a chair. "One more thing," she yelled loud enough to get everyone's attention. "If anyone comes across my son – Dillon Kendell, five years old, short dark hair, wearing Spider-Man pajamas – I want to be told immediately."

One of the nurses sucked in a breath and brought her hand to her mouth. "Dillon's there?"

All Ruby could do was nod. Helpless tears collected in her eyes. She blinked them away. A breakdown would not help Dillon or the dozens of patients who would soon be arriving.

Everyone stood still, watching her, waiting. "I have to believe he's fine. And if he's not, I have to have confidence that the school staff and our emergency responders will look after him and take good care of him. Just like all the other parents have to trust we're going to take good care of their children when they get here. Now everyone get back to work so we're ready. I'm in charge. All questions and problems come to me."

As if on cue, the ambulance radio squawked to life with information on the first casualty en route. ETA – estimated time of arrival – six minutes, which didn't give Ruby much time.

As she carefully got down from the chair, she said to Pat, "I need two minutes alone." Then she hurried into the head nurse's office and closed the door. Yes, she trusted the school staff and emergency responders to do their best. But Dillon needed someone on site to look for him and make sure he received prompt medical treatment if necessary.

And in her absence, the only person she'd trust with that responsibility was Brady.

Because in the year of their friendship turned kind-of relationship, he'd been reliable and supportive, caring and understanding, thoughtful and sweet, affectionate and . . . loving. A wonderful father figure for Dillon. A man Ruby never thought she'd be lucky enough to find – one who'd gotten her to let down her guard, one she could talk to for hours and trust with her son, one she loved in a best-friends-who-have-sex kind of way, one she could have maybe, possibly, at some point in the future, love in a till-death-do-us-part kind of way . . . at least she'd thought so until five days ago, when he'd gone and decided to do the one thing she feared most.

And, in true grown-up form, she'd been avoiding him and ignoring his attempts to contact her ever since.

Ruby picked up the phone and dialed his mobile with shaky hands. Would he even take her call?

As soon as he answered she blurted out, "It's Ruby. Please don't hang up."

"I'd never hang up on you, Ruby," he said quietly. So laid-back. So calm. The perfect counterpart to her high-strung, obsessive worrier.

"I know you're busy packing."

He said, "Packing was quick and easy and I'm done." But instead she heard, *Deciding to go was quick, leaving you is easy, and I'm done trying.*

Could her heart handle any more devastation tonight? She'd agreed to switch from day shift to cover three nights in a row so she'd be too tired to think about him, too busy to track him down to beg him to stay, and too far away to watch him walk out of her life for good – in eight short hours.

Focus on Dillon. "I know whatever we had is over and—"

"I don't want us to be over," he said calmly.

No. He wanted her to sit at home with Dillon while he traveled the country with his band as the opening act on a national tour. He wanted her to wait for him, for four months, to dream about him and yearn for him to return to her. When she knew he wouldn't be back.

Having spent the better part of her eighteenth and nineteenth years as a groupie on the concert circuit, she had intimate knowledge – intimate being the operative word – of what went on off-stage during tours. She understood the allure of that life, the strong pull. Heck, she'd already lost one love to it.

Falling for another musician was just plain stupid. Had she learned nothing from the heartbreak of loving Dillon's dad? Apparently not, because once again, Ruby had allowed herself to be sweet-talked by a smooth voice, to fall under the spell of a song written and performed just for her, to get caught up in the creativity and talent and nights watching her man on stage. So cool, carefree and confident.

In her defense, the Brady she'd first met worked as a firefighter paramedic with county EMS – Emergency Medical Services, specializing in search and rescue. By the time she'd found out about his love of guitar and bi-weekly Saturday night gigs in local bars, she'd been too into him to think with a clear head. But all the clues had been there – the dark, wavy, chin-length hair and the way he dressed, his love of rock music, his excellent singing voice and expert knowledge of all the lyrics to songs on the radio.

She'd been distracted by his wit and kindness, by his body, his deep brown eyes and large hands. And the things he could do with that talented mouth and tongue of his . . .

Stop! "I didn't call to talk about us. I need your help. Dillon needs you."

"What's wrong?" Mention of Dillon seemed to slap the calm right out of him. "What happened? Where is he?"

By the time Ruby finished explaining the situation, tears streamed down her cheeks and her breath came in choppy gasps. "And he's . . . all . . . alone. And I'm . . . at work . . . and can't leave." She fought to catch her breath. "Oh God . . . Brady. What if he's—"

"He's not," Brady said, so sure. Ruby wanted to believe him. "I can be at the school in five minutes." A door slammed and he sounded like he was running. "Don't worry, honey. I'll find him."

Honey. "I know you will." Because in all the time she'd known him, Brady always did what he said he'd do. Yet when he'd promised he'd be faithful, and call her every night, and return to her as soon as possible, she just couldn't bring herself to believe him.

"You should probably wear your uniform or you won't be able to get close to the school," she said.

"I know everyone on the police force and in the fire department," he said, breathing a little heavier. "If I don't find him outside, I'll get inside. And I will not stop looking for him until you tell me that he's with you or I have him with me."

Ruby inhaled a shaky breath. "Thank you."

"There's no need to thank me." Another door slammed, an engine turned over, and music started to play. "You and Dillon are the most important people in my life," he said. "I'd do anything for you."

Except stay.

An ambulance siren sounded. Someone knocked on her door. She told Brady, "I need to get back to work."

"Try not to worry," he said. "Dillon and I will see you soon."

His confidence gave her hope.

But when forty-five minutes passed with no word from him, Ruby's hope started to fade. She considered calling him but talked herself out of it. He'd call when he had a reason to call.

"Ruby," Jack yelled for her.

She hurried back to the desk where he sat, his face tight with concern. Her lungs contracted.

"Ambulance on its way in with a young boy," he said. "Crush injury. Unresponsive. Severe head and facial trauma. Unrecognizable." His eyes met hers. "Short dark hair, wearing Spider-Man pajamas."

Ruby's world went quiet, her vision narrowed and she reached out to steady herself.

"You okay?" Jack's words brought her back.

No. "Yeah." He started to stand and she held up her hand to stop him. "I'm fine. Knowing is better than not knowing, right?" And Spider-Man pajamas were pretty popular which meant there was 50–50 chance it wasn't Dillon. "Let's put him in trauma two, bed one." No matter whose little boy he turned out to be, Ruby would take good care of him.

She went from room to room until she found Dr Johnson talking to a group of parents. Ruby waited in the doorway and as soon as he finished she pulled him aside. "Major trauma on the way, I'd like you to take it."

Other doctors had arrived to help, but she knew Dr Johnson and trusted him.

"Is it your son?" he asked.

"Not sure." But as the ambulance's siren grew louder, Ruby ran to meet it.

Chapter Two

Brady Rodger cradled Ruby's son on his lap in the front seat of the ambulance, his little body enveloped in Brady's jacket so entirely that not even his feet were showing. He held him close to stabilize him against the bumpy road, to warm him, and comfort him as the wind howled outside and rain pelted the windshield.

Dillon let out a weak moan.

"Hang in there, champ," Brady said, maintaining pressure on the bandage covering the boy's forehead laceration. "We're almost to the hospital where your mom is waiting for you." Probably going out of her mind with worry, since due to the weather and widespread power outages he hadn't been able to get a cell signal to call her.

Dillon moaned again, turned his head toward Brady's chest and vomited. "It's okay." He shifted Dillon in his arms to elevate his head and tilt him forward so he wouldn't choke. "It's going to be okay." He wiped Dillon's mouth with his sleeve.

"Good call not waiting around for another ambulance to return," his buddy Tyler said as he drove. "That's three times. He's got a concussion for sure."

Please let that be the worst of it. Please don't let there be an intracranial hematoma or hemorrhage or irreversible damage to the brain. He dropped his head back and closed his eyes. God help him, he'd turned into a worrier, just like Ruby. Her words echoed in his head, *That's what happens when you become a parent.*

No, he wasn't a name-on-the-birth-certificate parent, but no father could care more for his child than Brady cared for Dillon. And no father could love the mother of his child more than Brady loved Ruby.

And even though she'd never said the words and insisted on referring to their relationship as nothing more than best friends who have sex, he knew she'd grown to love him, to depend on him and value him as more than a friend. Unfortunately, not enough to overcome her fear that at some point he would leave her and never come back. Not enough to let him spend more than a few hours in her bed or to participate in a discussion about a more permanent arrangement like them living together or getting engaged or married.

And at thirty years old, Brady had lived alone long enough. He wanted more than snippets of family life by invitation only.

Tyler turned into the hospital's parking lot. "Good thing they have power."

Damn good thing.

As Tyler maneuvered to back into the ambulance bay, Brady caught a glimpse of Ruby, pacing on the sidewalk. "There's your mom," he said to Dillon. "Wake up, Dill Pickle." He gently shook his boy bundle.

Dillon moaned.

"You got him?" Tyler opened the door, no doubt in a hurry to assist in the unload of the critical patient in the back.

"Yup. Go do what you have to do." Brady then turned his attention back to Dillon. "You need to talk to me." He patted the boy's cheek. "Wake up and talk to me."

Dillon kept his eyes closed and said, "No."

It was a response. And thank God for that.

Brady made sure he had a good hold on Dillon before he opened the door and climbed down, expecting Ruby to charge in his direction. Only she didn't. And when he walked to the back of the ambulance, he found the sidewalk empty. So he carried Dillon to the electric doors, made it through the first set but was stopped from entering the Emergency Department by a huge security guard who stood in front of the second set of doors. "You can't come in here." He pointed down the walkway. "All patients need to be triaged first."

"Please get Ruby Kendell." He held up Dillon. "Tell her Brady's here and her son needs medical attention."

"Light hurts," Dillon said, burying his face in Brady's chest.

"Nice try," the guard said. "Ruby's son was just brought in. Now if you'd—"

"No I won't," Brady said. "Ruby," he yelled as loud as he could.

"Ow," Dillon whined.

"Sorry, champ," he apologized and yelled again. "Ruby, I have Dillon." The guard took a threatening step forward. "Don't." Brady stood tall and used his six-foot-two-inch height and solid build to threaten him right back. "There's obviously been a mistake because I am holding Ruby's son in my arms. If you'd just get her . . ."

"Brady?" Ruby stood frozen in the hallway behind the security guard, her dark bangs and shoulder-length hair framing her pale face, her green eyes staring up at him.

He imagined what he must look like, filthy from searching through rubble, sopping wet from the rain, stained with blood and vomit, holding Dillon's limp body in his arms. "He's got a head wound. He's lethargic but arousable." Brady gave her the most important information first.

"That's Dillon?" She glanced over the guard's shoulder. "You're sure?"

He nodded. "I found him with three other children up on the stage. A rack of musical instruments fell on top of them.

Questionable loss of consciousness," Brady said, keeping his voice calm, taking a step around the security guard. "Sensitive to light. Complained of head pain twice. Vomited three times."

With tears in her eyes and her fist clutched to her chest, Ruby whispered, "He's alive."

"Yes, honey. He's alive. But he needs a CT scan and some stitches and a good once-over by your best doc." He tapped Dillon's shoulder. "Wake up and show your mom you're okay."

"Mom?" Dillon asked, his hoarse voice little more than a whisper, but enough to jolt Ruby into action.

"Yes, sweetie." She hurried forward and bent over to kiss Dillon's cheek. "Mommy's right here and I'm going to take good care of you." Carefully she lifted the dressing covering Dillon's laceration.

"Brady found me," Dillon said quietly.

"I knew he would," she said with a smile and a look of appreciation he'd never forget.

A woman in a colorful top and navy scrub pants that matched Ruby's came up beside them. "Private three is open and ready."

Ruby turned to the woman. "Would you cover for me in trauma two, bed one? I was on my way to get warm blankets."

"Of course." The woman hurried away.

"That poor boy," she mumbled then looked up at Brady. "I thought he might be Dillon. Same pajamas." She started to cry. "Thank you." She threw her arms around his neck. "Thank you so much." She jumped back. "You're soaked and freezing." She looked down. "Because you gave your jacket to Dillon. Come." She put her hand on his lower back and guided him to a room. "Sit." She pushed down on his shoulders. "Let me get you both some warm blankets and dry clothes."

"Don't worry about me," Brady said. "Take care of Dillon." Dillon had to come first, had to be okay.

Gently she set her palm to his cheek. He leaned into her touch, had missed her so much these past five days. Going on the road without her was going to be brutal. "You know I am quite the proficient multitasker," she said. "And I can take care of both of you just as easily as I can take care of one of you." This was his Ruby, so caring, so capable. She pressed her lips to his in a kiss filled with tenderness and love. "I'll be right back."

If he didn't have his arms filled with Dillon he would have used them to pull her close, to remind her of the months of love they'd shared, of what she'd given up so easily.

Fight for me. Fight for us.

But his arms were full, so all he could do was sit there as she stepped back and left the room.

He gave Dillon's shoulder a shake. "Wake up, buddy."

Dillon responded with a moan.

"Not good enough. Talk to me. What's your name?" he asked, trying to determine his level of orientation.

"You know my name," he mumbled.

"I know I know it, but do you know it?"

"Dill Pickle," he said with a tiny hint of a smile.

Brady smiled too. "That's right. You're my Dill Pickle." He hugged the boy he'd grown to love as his own, and sent up a prayer that his plan would work, that not having Brady readily available would force Ruby to recognize how much a part of their life he'd become. Hopefully she'd miss him and find a way to conquer her fear of relationships so they could be together, a real committed couple, when he came home.

And he planned to make good use of his time away to prove he'd follow through on his promise to call her every night. Hopefully, nightly phone sex would convince her she was the only woman for him. But, most of all, he wanted to show her that when he gave his word he'd come back, he'd come back.

In typical organized, efficient Ruby style, it didn't take her long to return with her arms loaded down with towels, a pair of scrubs for him, warm blankets, a suture kit, an electronic thermometer and a laptop. A man in blue scrubs and a white lab coat followed right behind her.

"Dr Johnson, this is my . . ." She hesitated. "My . . ."

"Her boyfriend," Brady finished her sentence for her because in his heart that's what he was. A little disagreement, or even a big one, or a couple of hundred miles of distance between them, wouldn't change the way he felt about her. "I'd shake your hand but . . ." He looked down at Dillon.

"I understand you were a paramedic with the fire department," Dr Johnson said while he examined Dillon's head.

"I am a paramedic with the fire department." He looked up at Ruby who looked away. "I took a leave of absence to help out some buddies of mine, but the town is holding my job for me. The woman I love is here. I will definitely be coming back."

Dr Johnson looked back and forth between them. "All righty then. Let's get him up on the stretcher."

Brady stood, carried Dillon to the stretcher, and carefully put him down. "Wake up, Dill. Doctor's here to take a look at you."

Dillon tried to open his eyes then squeezed them shut and winced. "Hurts."

Brady shielded him from the overhead light while he gave Dr Johnson his report, informing him of everything that happened from the time he uncovered Dillon under a pile of band instruments to his arrival at the hospital. The doc did a very thorough exam – under Ruby's watchful eye he'd be a fool not to. Dr Johnson asked Dillon questions and gave him commands to which the boy responded and moved appropriately.

And Brady finally started to relax.

"Let's get him over for a CT scan and then I'll stitch him up," said Dr Johnson, using a stylus to enter information into his laptop. With a smile and a "nice to meet you", he left the room.

Someone knocked on the door. Ruby opened it. An older woman stood there. "I'm sorry to bother you but Jack has a cardiac arrest on the way in and we're out of beds. A few parents are creating problems in the waiting room and we're out of suture kits."

Ruby looked back at Dillon, obviously torn between staying by her son's side and doing her job. "Go," Brady said. "I'll stay with him. Any change and I'll find you."

"Thank you," Ruby said, closing the door behind her. A few seconds later it opened and Ruby stuck her head in. "I forgot to mention." She looked him up and down. "There's something oddly attractive about a man covered in vomit who's so concerned about my son he doesn't care that he's covered in vomit."

Brady smiled. "The strangest things turn you on, woman." One of the many reasons he loved her.

With a wink she ducked back out. And it felt like nothing between them had changed. Like she hadn't pushed him away, like he wasn't leaving, like they had a chance. It felt damn good.

Chapter Three

After shuffling around some patients to make a trauma room bed available for a fifty-four-year-old male in cardiac arrest, then sending the night supervisor on a mission to track down more suture kits and matching another ten children with their parents, Ruby glanced down the hallway leading to CT scan. Still no sign of Brady or Dillon. What the heck was taking so long? She checked the time. They'd been over there close to an hour. What if the tech found something? What if Dillon had a seizure or lost consciousness or stopped breathing?

She couldn't wait another minute. "Pat, I—"

Words failed her at the sight of Dillon rolling toward her, sitting up, with the head of his stretcher fully elevated, wearing sunglasses and sipping on a straw stuck inside a can of ginger ale.

Ruby rushed to meet him. "Hey, honey." She kissed Dillon's head then looked up at the handsomest stretcher pusher ever. "I was starting to get worried."

Brady responded, "Tell her what happened, Dilly Vanilly."

"I threw up again," he said.

Ruby should have been there to take care of him. Dillon was her son, her responsibility.

"Stop," Brady said as if he could read her thoughts. "I'm very capable. I got him cleaned up and changed all by myself."

Of course he did, because he was the best fill-in daddy ever.

"What's with the shades?" Ruby asked Dillon.

"My head is spinny."

Brady went on to explain. "I thought if he opened his eyes and focused on something the dizziness might go away."

"But light hurts," Dillon added in.

"So I borrowed a pair of sunglasses from Betty in Radiology."

"And are they helping?" Ruby asked.

Dillon gave a small nod then had to catch the oversized frames as they slid down his nose.

"Not sure if it's the glasses or the ginger ale but he seems to be feeling a little better."

Ruby managed a deep breath for the first time in hours. "Thank you for taking such good care of him."

"I already told you," he said, walking toward her. "You don't need to thank me." He put an arm around her waist, pulled her up against him, and leaned in so close his lips brushed her ear. "But a nice big kiss before I leave would be very much appreciated."

The electronic doors behind them opened. And if course, Ruth, the stern, professional, ethics-enforcing, policy-and-procedures obsessed head nurse of the Emergency Department, would choose that exact moment to arrive.

Ruby jumped away from Brady. Lord help her. Getting caught in a very public display of affection, while on duty, in the middle of a disaster she was in charge of managing.

"I'm sorry," Ruby said, sliding her now clammy hands into her pockets. She liked this job, needed this job. Frost Community was the only hospital for miles. She had a great little apartment five minutes away. Dillon loved his school and his teacher.

"No," Ruth said. "I'm the one who's sorry." She looked at Dillon. "How are you feeling, little man?"

"My head hurts," Dillon said. "And I'm tired."

"Please take him back to his room," Ruby instructed Brady. She turned to Ruth. "He just came back from a CT scan. I admit, having Dillon here as a patient got me a bit distracted, but I'm doing everything I need to do, handling every crisis as it arises, putting forth my best effort . . ."

Ruth put her hand on Ruby's arm. "You always put forth your best effort," she said. "But after you give me report and bring me up to speed, you are officially done."

"Done?" As in fired? As in unemployed? "But . . ."

"Done as in off duty," Ruth clarified.

"But there are still so many patients that need to be seen. My boyfriend is with Dillon." Funny how, as the evening progressed, referring to Brady as her boyfriend became easier. "As long as I have someone I trust to take care of Dillon I can do my job, no problem." What would she have done tonight if Brady hadn't answered her call for help? What would she do in the future with Brady gone?

"I know you can," Ruth said. "But you don't have to. You told me from the start that being a mother is your top priority." She walked toward her office, speaking over her shoulder. "Now come give me report so you can focus all of your attention on that precious son of yours."

Ruby followed with mixed emotions. Surprise. Relief. Thanks. Dread. Because now that she no longer needed Brady to stay with Dillon, he'd have no reason to stick around. And she wasn't ready to say goodbye.

Twenty minutes later she dragged an extra visitor's chair into Dillon's room, slid it up beside Brady's stool and sat down.

"What's up?" Brady asked, leaning over to bump her shoulder with his.

"Ruth took over so I can focus my attention on Dillon," who lay sound asleep on the stretcher. She fiddled with a pack of gum, looking down at it flipping between her fingers. "I guess you'll probably want to get going." It was, after all, close to midnight, and as per one of his many messages that she hadn't responded to, he needed to be on the road by 5 a.m. to make his New Jersey rendezvous with the tour bus.

Brady wrapped his strong arms around her and pulled her onto his lap. "Are you kidding me? This is the first opportunity I've had to hold you and actually engage in a two-way conversation about my leaving since you went berserk-o crazy on me five long miserable days ago." He hugged her. "Not that my holding you is in any way intended to restrain you." He nuzzled her neck then kissed her. "As long as you don't try to escape, that is."

She didn't want to escape and couldn't muster up a decent rebuttal to the "berserk-o crazy" reference because as soon as he'd mentioned going on tour and leaving her she had gone a little nuts. Okay, a lot nuts. Insisting he should go and enjoy himself and not give her a second thought. Lying that she'd been wanting to take a break anyway because things between them had gotten way too serious. Telling him how much better life on the road would be without the burden of a woman waiting for him at home. Talking fast and not letting him get a word in before noting the time and reminding him she had to be up early the next morning, and physically dragging then pushing him out of her apartment so he didn't witness the total, hysterical breakdown that occurred within seconds of her closing the door behind him.

Because once again she wasn't enough, once again she would be left behind. Discarded.

Wait a minute. "Miserable?" she asked, looking up at him.

"Didn't you listen to any of my messages?"

Every single one of them, over and over, mostly to hear his voice. "You sounded more frustrated and angry than miserable."

"Okay." He smiled. "I'll admit to equal parts all three." He smoothed some hair off her face, his hands rough, his touch gentle, so nice. "You wouldn't take my calls. You didn't answer your door. You purposely changed your routine so I couldn't meet up with you. You shut me out of your life. I didn't like it."

She'd cut him loose before he could do it to her. It was the very opposite of mature. "I'm an idiot."

He lifted her chin and stared into her eyes. "No. You're not. You're scared of history repeating itself. Which, I have to tell you, is a huge insult considering Dillon's piece-of-shit father."

"I don't think you're like him."

"You do," he said. "If you think I'd enjoy life on the road more than life with you and Dillon, and if you think I'd pick up and leave you and never come back, without giving you a second thought, then you think I'm just like him."

"I'm sorry," she said, meaning it more than any other apology she had given in her life. Brady had been nothing but kind and supportive and loving to her and Dillon. He didn't deserve to be lumped in with her ex and the roadies and musicians she'd come in contact with all those years ago.

"I've told you over and over how much I love you and want to be with you, but you still don't believe me."

She said nothing. As much as she wished his words weren't true, they were.

"So I'm doing the only thing I can think of to do," he said. "I'm leaving to prove with my actions rather than my words alone that I can love music and performing and still love you. I can spend time away and not forget about you and still be faithful to you."

She wanted to point out that since he'd be in another state she really would have no way of knowing if he was faithful or not, but he didn't give her time.

"I'm leaving so I can come back to you, so I can show you that when I say I'm coming back, I am, in fact, going to come back. I'm leaving so I can prove to you I'm a man of my word, a man you can trust."

What? "Let me get this straight," she said. "My biggest fear is history repeating itself and the man I love leaving me. So you're doing exactly what Dillon's – to quote you – 'piece-of-shit father' did and leaving me to show me that you're a man of your word and I can trust you?" If he hadn't been with her for the past few hours she would have wondered if he'd had too many cold ones.

"I'm not doing exactly what Dillon's father did because I'm not leaving for good. And I'm going to call you every single night."

She looked away. "I'd rather you don't make promises you won't keep."

He cupped her chin and turned her to face him. "I will call you every night," he said. "And after my lips touch yours in the amazingly memorable goodbye kiss you're going to give me, my lips will not touch any part of a woman's body until I'm back in your arms, because I will return to you."

That remained to be seen.

"And when I do, you'll have to stop grouping me in with all the losers from your past."

He was so much better than all of them. "You're certainly putting forth a lot of effort." For her.

"You're worth it. But for the record," he said, still staring into her eyes, "when I told you the band asked me to join them, I was looking for an excuse not to go. I'd kind of hoped you'd beg me to stay."

Ruby sat up straight and crossed her arms over her chest. "Then you don't know me near as well as you thought you did because I never beg. For anything."

He smiled. "There were a few times . . ."

"Don't." She covered his mouth with her hand. She remembered those times in vivid, spectacular detail, when he'd had her so aroused she had, in fact, begged him to touch her. Based on that little tingle between her legs, her body remembered them, too.

In yet another example of how well he could read her, Brady whispered, "Straddle me," and lifted her off his lap.

She wanted to. Oh boy, how she wanted to. But, "I can't." She tried to twist from his grip. But Brady was pretty darn strong. And maybe she didn't try as hard as she could have. Even so, her responsible, rational side felt it necessary to mention, "I may not be on duty but I'm still at work. And anyone can walk in here at any time. And Dillon could wake up."

"Just for a minute." He coaxed her legs apart and eased her onto his lap. "I need to feel you," he said, palming her butt, maneuvering her right where he wanted her, which coincided nicely with right where she wanted to be.

Through the two thin layers of scrub material separating them she felt him harden, which was so totally inappropriate, considering where they were, yet so wonderful at the same time. He ground up against her. "My God, you feel good."

Tears filled her eyes and she dropped her head to his shoulder. "What am I going to do without you?"

He rubbed her back. "I'm kind of looking forward to lots of hot phone sex."

She slapped his chest. "I'm serious. I'm going to miss you so much."

"Hopefully I won't be gone for the full four months," he said.

She jerked up. "What? There's a chance you could come back sooner?"

"If you'd have given me the chance to explain the situation fully, I could have clarified that four months is the longest I'll be away. That's how much time is left on the tour. I'm only covering for Bart whose mom recently got diagnosed with cancer and is going in for major surgery. If all goes well he could be back in a matter of weeks."

Truth be told, after Ruby had heard "leaving", "going on tour" and "four months" she'd stopped listening and lurched into self-preservation mode. "I hope she makes a speedy recovery."

"Me, too," Brady said, and with a rather firm hand at the back of her neck he directed her in for a kiss. When they broke for air he said, "While I'm gone, I'd like you to think about us getting engaged."

Ruby reacted on instinct, as she always did when he brought up the subject of getting married, and tried to pull away. Boyfriend–girlfriend was one thing. When the split came and he decided to move on, like every other man in her life had done before him, sure, it'd hurt, but things wouldn't get messy. Add in an expensive ring, legally binding documents, and joint assets, and splitting up got complicated. And she had Dillon's feelings to consider.

Unlike all his past attempts to discuss marriage, this time Brady didn't let her go. "No more refusing to talk about it. I love you and I want to marry you. I want you and me and Dillon to be a family. And maybe, if you're up for it, we could have a couple of more kids."

Ruby felt her body stiffen.

"Hey," Brady said quietly, reassuringly, as he caressed her arms. "Give me a chance. All I'm asking is for you to take some time to think about it while I'm away. No pressure."

She started to relax a bit. Just think about it. Toss around the idea. Get used to it. "I can do that. I will do that." He loosened his hold, allowing her to move back onto the chair beside him. And not a moment too soon, because with a quick knock, Dr Johnson opened the door and walked in, followed by another doctor she didn't recognize.

Reinforcements? Why had Dr Johnson felt the need to bring in another doctor with him? Was he a specialist? A neurologist or neurosurgeon here to deliver the bad news? Ruby grabbed for Brady's hand.

"CT scan's negative," Dr Johnson said.

Thank God. A huge breath of air she didn't know she'd trapped in her lungs whooshed out of her mouth.

"This is Dr Stevens," Dr Johnson introduced the man beside him. Ruby stood to shake his hand. "He's a plastic surgeon. While I'm happy to stitch up Dillon's forehead, I thought Dr Stevens is probably a better choice. I want my favorite nurse to have the best care available for her son."

"Thank you." Ruby was touched by his sincerity. "I'm happy to assist, Dr Stevens."

"Absolutely not," Dr Johnson said. "I've been given strict instructions that you are here in a mommy capacity only. I'll find another nurse."

She bit her lip to keep from making a request.

"Would you like a say in who I choose?" he asked with a teasing grin.

Yes, she would, because while she liked most of her colleagues, she respected the skills of some more than others. "If Sandy has a few minutes I don't think she'd mind."

An hour later, after lots of tears and even more bargaining, Dillon – the soon to be new owner of the Lego toy of his choice under twenty dollars – had eleven, tiny, meticulously placed, evenly spaced stitches and was ready for discharge home.

Brady returned from driving her car to the curb, leaving it running to warm it up. "I found a ride back to the school to get my truck."

Ruby's insides felt hollow. This was it. She couldn't look at him so she occupied herself by wrapping Dillon in a blanket instead. "So I guess this is goodbye."

He leaned in close. "Then you'd guess wrong," he whispered. "Leave your door unlocked for me." Then he picked up Dillon. "Come on, pal. I'll carry you to the car."

Chapter Four

Six weeks later

Brady set up his laptop, looking over his shoulder to make sure the wall behind him would not clue Ruby in to his actual location, and logged on for their scheduled video chat.

"Hey." Her beautiful, smiling face filled his screen.

"Hey, yourself, gorgeous. Love the outfit." The silky, low-cut baby doll negligee he'd mailed to her from Las Vegas.

"You told me to wear it tonight, so I'm wearing it."

"Where's Dill?" he asked.

"Next door at Tammy's. They're having some super-secret movie party."

According to plan. Thank you, Tammy.

"So you're alone." He stripped off his shirt. "And I'm alone."

"I swear," she groused. "We have more sex now that you're away than we did when you lived downstairs."

He smiled. "You love every minute of it."

She smiled back. "I do. But it's not the same. I want the real thing. I want to feel your naked body on top of me." She leaned back on the couch, exposing her skimpy, matching panties. "I want to feel you here." She touched herself.

Brady was rock hard and ready. Damn she had a knack for video chat sex and phone sex. But tonight he was after some real sex with the woman he loved.

"The other night you said that if I wanted to know what you'd decided about marrying me, I'd have to get down on one knee and ask you." He pushed the coffee table back to make room and got down on one knee.

"In person, you loon." She laughed. "And with a ring."

He glanced at the jewelry box beside the computer. For the last few weeks Ruby had been talking much more positively about marriage, even dropping a few hints that she'd be ready for a proposal once he got home. Well, Brady had no intention of giving her the chance to change her mind. So within two hours of receiving Bart's call that he'd be back in time for tomorrow night's show, Brady had taken the opportunity of a travel day and hopped a flight home.

He looked to the side, pretending something had caught his attention. "Shoot. Baby, someone's at the door," he lied. "Give me a minute." He closed his laptop and stood.

Brady picked up the ring, shoved it in his pocket with one hand while he grabbed the bottle of champagne with the other, and ran out the door and up the stairs to Ruby's apartment. Without waiting to catch his breath, he knocked.

A few pounding heartbeats later, the door flew open and Ruby launched herself into his arms. "Oh my God," she screamed. "You're here. You're really here. Please tell me you're home for good."

"Is that how you answer the door?" he asked, looking up and down the hallway, shielding her lingerie-clad body from onlookers – of which there were none, thank goodness.

"It's how I answer the door for you," she cooed, jumping up, locking her long, bare legs around his butt, and her arms around his shoulders.

"And how did you know it was me?" He carried her inside.

"Peephole." She kissed along his cheek to his ear and down his neck while thrusting her fingers in his hair. It felt so damn good. "God, I've missed you."

He'd missed her, too. More than he'd ever imagined possible.

She rubbed her upper body against his chest and Brady almost forgot that sex was not his main reason for traveling thirteen hours on three planes and a taxi to get to her. "Wait." He let go of her.

She clung to him like a baby koala.

"Please." He pulled at her arms. "I need a few minutes of your time first."

"Uh-oh." She climbed down and stood before him, her arms clamped over her belly, looking concerned. "This sounds serious."

"It is." He set the champagne down behind his leg, trying to keep it from her view. Then he reached into his pocket, went down on one knee, lifting and opening the ring box in one smooth motion.

She brought the tips of her fingers up to cover her mouth.

"Ruby Kendell, I love you."

She stared at the ring, her eyes glistening with tears.

"I've been away for thirty-nine days and nights, I have met hundreds if not thousands of people, and you're still the only woman for me. I wake up thinking about you and go to bed wishing you were with me."

She nodded and kept on nodding, seemed entranced by the pear-shaped diamond.

He watched her. "Why are you nodding?"

"Yes," she said from behind her fingertips in a voice just above a whisper.

"Yes, what?"

She moved her eyes from the ring to him. "Yes, I'll marry you."

"But I haven't asked you yet," he teased.

"Well, that's where all this—" she moved her hand back and forth between them "—is headed, isn't it?"

"I won't be rushed," he said. "I want to do this right, because you deserve it."

"Okay," she said. "I appreciate that. Just keep in mind Dillon will be home in two and a half hours. And if we want to have any real, in-the-same-room fun at all, we need to get a move on."

He laughed. "Ruby Kendell, will you marry me?"

She looked down at him, her expression serious. "You said you'd call me every night, and you did. You said you'd be faithful to me, and I believe you have been. You said you'd come back to me and you're here. I trust you, I love you, and I'd be honored to be your wife."

And with those words she made him the happiest man alive.

She held out her hand and Brady slipped the ring onto her finger. A perfect fit.

He stood and pulled her in for a kiss. "I've been traveling for hours, but I couldn't wait to see you so I haven't taken a shower and I probably need one."

She flicked open the button on his jeans. "You can take one here." She unzipped them. "And what would you like to do after that?" She slipped her hand inside and cupped him and Brady went so hard so fast it hurt, but in the best possible way.

"Then my sweet fiancée—" he squeezed the tight bud of her nipple between his knuckles "—I'm going to spend the next two hours making you beg." He kissed her chin. "Over." He kissed her jaw. "And over." He kissed that sweet little cove behind her ear. "And over again."

ON THE ROAD AGAIN

Fiona Lowe

Chapter One

Day One

"What do you mean you're not coming?" Dr Felicity Hamilton-Smith's voice rose in a combination of disbelief and panic as she pressed her phone hard against her ear. "Jessie, this entire gig was your idea."

"I know and I'm so sorry," Jessie wailed her disappointment, wobbling down the line. "I've been looking forward to this cycling trip for months. I can't believe I sprained my ankle tripping over the cat."

"I always told you dogs make better pets," Felicity said dryly, stepping out of the long line of people and pulling her backpack with her. "I'll see if I can grab a ride back to Melbourne."

"No," Jessie said firmly. "We've been planning this trip for ages and just because I'm a klutz, it doesn't mean you have to miss out on this trip."

You've been planning it. I've been dreading it. "Really, I don't mind—"

"You need this, remember?" Jessie's tone became stern. "It's a total change for you, a week in another world and a way to forget all the recent crap in your life."

"I'm sure a week at a spa would do it just as well," she said wryly.

"You know that's not true," Jessie rebuked mildly. "*That* Felicity vanished a very long time ago."

And she had. It had been years since she'd indulged herself in any form of pampering. It had been so long, in fact, that it felt like another lifetime lived by a completely different person. Drew would barely recognize her.

She abruptly shoved the thought sideways, furious at herself for allowing a memory of him to sneak in. Eight years had passed since she'd watched in disbelief as he'd walked away from her without a backward glance. Eight long years, during which she'd worked hard at forgetting him and had instead focused on establishing a very successful career in A & E. Along the way, she'd proved many people's preconceived opinions of her to be very wrong.

Your private life, however, isn't quite so triumphant.

She closed her eyes against the thought. The current nightmare of her personal life was the reason Jessie had chivvied and cajoled her onto this ride where they'd combine some cycling with volunteering – a big adventure. Now Jessie was bailing on her and the thought of spending eight nights alone in a tent after cycling anything from sixty to one hundred and ten kilometres a day had her pining for those heady days of old when pampering ruled. "It's not going to be any fun without you."

Jessie laughed. "There are four thousand people for you to meet so of course you're going to have fun. Besides, you have that lovely new carbon fibre bike you won to ride. It's so light it will practically glide up the hills on its own."

She wasn't convinced. "Jessie, I can ride it another time when you're better."

"You have to go," Jessie instructed. "It's bad enough that I'm dropping out at the last moment. The medical care team can't afford to lose both of us."

And as much as Felicity wanted to stop before she'd even started, values and ethics got her every single time. She'd made a commitment to the medical care team and she had no choice but to honour it. "Okay, but seeing as I'll be pitching the tent on my own every night, I want you to book me a motel room for the rest day."

Jessie laughed. "Wimp."

"Damn straight."

After telling Jessie to ice and elevate her ankle, she ended the call and slipped her phone into the back pocket of her cycling jersey. Mustering all her strength, she lumbered up the truck's narrow silver stairs and half-threw, half-dropped her twenty-kilogram pack onto the massive pile of luggage.

The salt of the sea filled Felicity's lungs as she climbed a punishing hill, which led out of the pretty coastal town of Lakes Entrance. With each spin of her pedals, she left behind the fishing boats, the circling Pacific gulls and the glistening Tasman Sea and she headed inland to the rolling hills of Gippsland. Black and white Friesian cows dotted the lush paddocks and the grass was still green from spring rains, yet to be burned brown by summer heat. It wouldn't be long though – the forecast was predicting hot weather on the ride.

Today, however, was perfect. No headwinds, no rain, just the joy of the road helped along by a friendly tailwind. School groups passed on her right, calling out, "Enjoy your day," and she smiled. Already she could feel the stressors of work and home slipping away, and if day one was anything to go by, Jessie was right – she was enjoying herself. With a touch of sadness she realized this was as close as she'd come to happy in a very long time.

A couple of hours later, she cycled into the tiny town of Bruthen and found the show grounds, which were being converted into a city of dome tents. She located her luggage truck, found her bag, pitched the tent, had a shower and then pulled on her bright blue volunteer polo shirt. The cheerful volunteer at the gate had told her that today the travelling medical centre was in the football club rooms so she crossed the oval and walked inside the building. Her eyes took a moment to adjust from the bright sunshine to the dimmer conditions, and at first she could only make out silhouettes.

"Hi, I'm Dr Felicity—"

"Hamilton-Smith."

Her heart stalled in her chest. Even after eight years, she instantly recognized the deep vibrato voice. Blinking rapidly, she forced her eyes to focus so she could check that her ears hadn't deceived her. Slowly, six feet two of sheer male perfection came into view. She soaked in the sight of short golden hair, a thick, strong neck, broad, square shoulders, a washboard-flat stomach and solid, toned thighs. Her body leapt at the memory of being held in his muscular arms and she immediately battled it, hating how fast her body could betray her.

"Drew."

She swallowed a groan as his name came out on a soft, wavering breath instead of the crisp, professional and utterly detached tone she'd been aiming for.

"Flick." Intelligent eyes, the vivid blue of an outback sky – eyes that had once glowed with love for her – scanned her face coolly, seeming to miss nothing.

His mouth flattened. "This has to be the last place I ever expected to meet you."

The slight hint of derision in his tone brought the past rushing back so fast it was like eight years had vanished and time had stood still. Only it hadn't. Time had passed, things had changed – she'd changed and she refused to wear his out-of-date opinions.

A slow burn of indignation glowed deep down inside her and she picked up the large medical emergency pack that had her name on it in large print. "Well, expectations are not often met. I'm here to work."

And then it hit her. So was he. Her nine days in another world – her week to escape her life – had just been blown into a thousand pieces.

Chapter Two

Drew Baxter had only recently come out of Afghanistan. He certainly hadn't expected his first job after the army medical corps to take him into another war zone, however the tight expression on Flick's beautiful face left him in no doubt that time had not healed a damn thing. Why the hell was she even here? Felicity Hamilton-Smith belonged in five-star luxury, not camping on a physically challenging bike ride.

He'd immediately regretted his terse greeting, but meeting her here was beyond unexpected. Her image, which had been burned on his brain all those years ago, was now out-of-date. Her once-long, chestnut hair that he'd loved burying his face in was now cut into a short bob that stroked her chin when she moved. She was thinner than he remembered and there were faint lines around her eyes. Some things though didn't change at all and she still radiated the same glow that had always called to him.

It was calling to him now and he fisted his hands by his sides, steeling himself against the pull that promised – should he give in to it – the joy of holding her against him and feeling her body mould perfectly to his.

He'd spent years trying hard to forget her and he refused to give in to the unreliable memories that hammered him hard and fast, urging him to catch her around the waist and kiss her. Recollections that conveniently forgot all the bad stuff that had destroyed them as a couple.

What did you say to your ex-fiancée after an eight-year gap? He swallowed, clearing his throat. "You look good."

Her shaped brows rose as if she didn't believe him.

"Drew, Felicity," Becky, the nurse, called out to them, "we've got a dislocated shoulder that needs treating and a head lac that needs suturing."

"Looks like we're on," Felicity said, swinging the medical pack over her shoulder.

Drew didn't miss the relief that shone stark and clear on her high cheekbones. Neither of them wanted to be here in the same room, but if they had to work together, at least the universe could help by keeping them busy.

Day two of the ride dawned clear and cool. Felicity, having faced the long breakfast line, packed up her tent and hauled her gear onto the truck for transport to the tiny Victorian town of Briagolong, no longer had a valid reason to delay meeting up with Drew.

Now he stood before her in tight-fitting, black leather motorcycle gear, looking for all the world like the devil, tempting her with burnished hair and piercing eyes. Her stomach flipped as the traitorous girl deep down inside her – the one who remembered exactly what it was like to be wrapped around his amazing body – squealed with insatiated lust.

He left us, remember? She bit the inside of her mouth, welcoming the distraction of the pain.

"Hey."

"Hey." Drew handed her a large disposable cup. "Two shots and skim milk."

"Thanks." She tried hard not to read anything into the fact he'd remembered exactly how she'd taken her coffee eight years ago. "These days I've cut back to one shot."

"Me too. The palpations got to me." He grinned, dimples carving deep into his stubble-covered cheeks. "The joys of being thirty-something, eh?"

She hadn't found much joy in being thirty-two. "If you say so."

A slight frown marred his forehead and questions filled his eyes, but when he spoke, his voice was all business. "So it looks like the roster has us riding the emergency motorbike up and down the route today and every alternate day after that."

She nodded, not telling him that she'd learned that bit of information last evening and it had kept her awake half the night. "So what do I do with my bike?"

His gaze took in the state-of-the-art bike with its distinctly different spoke configuration, electronically controlled gears and glossy Italian paintwork. His face hardened. "Still buying the best and the most expensive toys, Flick."

She opened her mouth to tell him she'd won the damn bike in a raffle that was raising funds for disadvantaged children, but she promptly closed it. There was no point wasting words trying to disabuse him of his opinion of her. It hadn't worked eight years ago and she doubted it would have any effect now.

She tilted her chin. "A girl has to be comfortable."

He grunted. "Hey, Phil," he called out to one of the volunteers, "can you put our bikes on the trailer, please?"

"Sure thing, doc. Have a good day out there."

"Thanks." Drew downed his coffee and turned to look at her. "Ready?"

To be pressed up hard against Drew's broad back for hours on the motorbike? Not at all. "Sure."

As she slung her leg over the gleaming machine, she wondered what she'd done in a past life to deserve this.

* * *

"There! Up ahead on your left."

Flick's urgent voice in Drew's headset broke the spell that her breasts and the rest of her delicious torso pressed up tightly against his back were working on him.

He looked in the direction of her instructions. A male cyclist in a bright yellow jersey stood on the wrong side of the road frantically waving them down.

He pulled over. Flick was off the bike and running with the medical kit before he'd killed the engine. He turned to the cyclist who'd flagged them down. "What happened?"

"It all happened so fast." The guy, who looked to be in his mid-forties, was wringing his hands. "One minute she was talking to me and the next she was going straight over the handlebars. It was terrifying."

Drew's experienced eyes took in the scene. "Speed and gravel make for a lethal combination. Have you called 000?"

The worried man nodded. "Yes, straight after I called you. Her mother – my wife – is going to kill me."

"No, she'll be thankful you're here with your daughter and doing all the right things. Stay here to flag the ambulance and we'll take good care of her."

Drew gave the stressed father's shoulder a squeeze before kneeling down across from Felicity who was doing a head injury check on their patient.

"Pupils equal and reacting," she said briskly in her "doctor's" voice as she tucked her penlight back into its slot in the medical kit. "Erin, this is Drew, another doctor."

"I'm sorry," the teenager said, grimacing as she moved her head.

"No need to be sorry, Erin, these things happen." He started to examine her, keeping her flat on her back in case of spinal damage. "In fact, it happened to me once when I dumbly applied the front brakes first. I hit the road, broke a few bones but I'm fine now."

Felicity's eyes widened and he caught a flash of concern before it was instantly buried under her professional demeanour.

Erin started shaking violently. "My shoulder's really killing me."

"Top to toe?" Felicity said, already starting her examination at Erin's feet.

"Good idea." Drew's experienced fingers examined Erin's shoulders and arms and quickly found the telling lump on Erin's clavicle. "You've got a classic, high-impact cycling injury, Erin. A fractured collarbone.'"

"Is that ba-bad?" Erin's voice struggled to stay steady.

"Only that you don't get the glory of a plaster cast." Drew smiled, wanting to reassure the scared teen as he continued his examination down her torso.

"The good news is that your legs aren't broken," Felicity added. "However, you've got a big rip in your bike shorts and you've taken off some skin on your left thigh and calf. We'll dress them and they'll heal up. No problem."

Felicity pulled out the green whistle from the kit and met Drew's eyes. He nodded his agreement, immediately recognizing her unasked question.

Memories of working with her during their intern year flooded back fast, filling him with both warmth and regret. They'd always shared a simpatico – an ability to pre-empt each other and work as a tight team. Sadly they hadn't been able to replicate that unity outside of work.

"Erin," Felicity said, handing her the green whistle. "I want you to suck on this. It will give you pain relief from the fracture and the skin damage."

"Really?" With shaking fingers Erin took the whistle and raised it to her mouth, sucking it deeply.

"Really." Drew said. "Originally it was an Australian invention for the defence forces to use with injured soldiers. Now we're selling it around the world for emergency pain relief."

Felicity fitted a triangular bandage on Erin's arm, supporting her elbow and using the weight of her arm to pull the clavicle into alignment. When it was in position, she tucked a space blanket around the girl.

"Cool, silver." Erin giggled; the methoxyflurane already working its magic. "You're really cute, Drew. Don't you think he's cute, Felicity?"

Felicity's hands halted on the space blanket and she gave a strangled laugh. "When he was younger he was."

"Hey," he said with mock chagrin. "I'm right here."

Her eyes met his, their chocolate brown depths swirling with mixed emotions. "I'm very well aware of that."

The husky words hit him in the solar plexus, bringing with them memories of the heat that used to flow between them like a living, breathing entity.

His pulse kicked up. Who was he kidding? Used to flow – it still did.

Chapter Three

"One fractured elbow, one femur and two clavicles," Felicity said, finishing off her report for the day and signing out of the computer.

"That's hills and inexperience for you." Drew gave a wry smile. "We've worked hard and we're off duty. Can I buy you a drink at the Bike Bar?"

No. Not a good idea. But the thought of wandering off to have dinner alone wasn't enticing. She'd enjoyed working with him today and she'd managed to survive hours pressed up against him on the motorbike. Sharing a drink in a crowded bar would be a walk in the park.

Needing to keep her now-wavering distance she said, "How about we go Dutch?"

A deep crease formed across his brow and his wide mouth, which could smile so broadly, flattened into a thin line. "I can afford to buy you a drink, Flick."

She sighed. Money was the bane of her life – it could achieve great things and just as quickly destroy others. It had destroyed them. They may have just shared a working camaraderie today but it appeared nothing else between them had changed.

She headed towards the brown tent. "If it's so important to you then I accept."

"Champagne?"

Her head jerked up, expecting to see mockery on his face but all she saw was genuine concern that he was buying the drink she wanted. She shook her head. "Sauv blanc, please."

Surprise shot across his cheeks at her change of beverage but he didn't comment. A couple of minutes later he returned with the drinks, sat down and held up his plastic souvenir glass.

"Cheers."

She nodded. "Are you still in the Army?" The question that she'd held simmering on her lips for two days finally came out.

He shook his head and leaned back in his chair, a vision of relaxed male beauty. "Nope, I'm done. Eight years of service repaid for six years of medical training. The Army no longer owns me. My life's mine again."

Eight years of service she'd pleaded with him not to give. "You could have had your life back years ago but you chose not to."

A muscle in his jaw twitched. "You paying my tuition debt would have meant you owned me instead of the Army."

The steel in his voice told her nothing had changed, and it torched years of cooling anger. She gripped the stem on her plastic glass so hard she was surprised it didn't snap. "Still finding it impossible to be loved, Drew?"

Familiar shutters fell across his eyes, closing down all emotion. "Love has nothing to do with it."

His words slapped her. "No, Drew, love has everything to do with it. There is no accounting in love, only you don't seem to understand that."

"'No accounting?'" His voice rose. "That's rich, Flick. When we were together, you organized everything. You booked and paid for our holidays, you bought my clothes, you owned the apartment we lived in and you did everything without consulting me on any of it because it was your money."

She fought against his interpretation of their life. The same old emotions of betrayal flew to the surface. "It was our money, but you resented it from the start. I was only trying to create the life we wanted."

He shook his head. "You had the money to live the life you wanted. Me? I was like your prince consort tagging along one step behind."

His stony words sliced into her and she railed against them. "Don't be ridiculous. If you were so unhappy why didn't you say anything? Why just pack up and leave one day when I wasn't even home?" She heard her voice rise and she couldn't do anything to stop it. "You left me for the Army, Drew. You left me and you finished our engagement with a note."

Haggard lines pulled around his mouth. "I tried to tell you how I felt several times, Flick, but you never heard me."

She trawled her memory for clues. Their intern year had been the happiest year of her life. She'd been exhilarated with the joy of being able to share everything she had with the man she loved. She thought they'd been blissfully content and excited about their future together. Surely she'd have noticed if he was miserable?

Drew traced the outline of the coaster with his finger, letting the silence roll out between them. There was no point rehashing the day he'd left her. He wasn't proud of the way he'd gone about it, but that didn't change the fact it had been his only choice.

"What are you going to do now?" Felicity asked, finally breaking the impasse.

He shrugged. "Probably A & E. After years on the front line I think general practice will be far too mundane." Shut up, now. "Sorry, I didn't mean to offend you."

"I don't work in general practice."

Astonishment lit through him. First her hair, then her change in drinks and now this – he was starting not to recognize her at all. "But you always said you wanted to go into general practice."

"That was when I thought I was going to be juggling a marriage, a career and babies."

The animosity in Flick's voice hit him in the chest. He hadn't meant to hurt her. God, he'd loved her more than anyone, but he knew that if they'd stayed together they would have destroyed each other. "You can still do that."

Her brows rose sardonically. "I did that."

He sighed, hating the way that every conversation vibrated with their past and everything that had changed between them. "I meant with someone else, Flick."

Her brown eyes fixed on his face. "So did I."

The quietly spoken words whipped him so unexpectedly hard that they stole the breath from his lungs and he struggled not to cough. It shouldn't bother him at all that she was with someone else. He shouldn't care.

You left her. His rational mind accepted that after eight years Flick being married to someone else was both reasonable and expected. Only, every other part of him recoiled violently at the idea and bile hit the back of his throat.

"You're married?" Despite a desperate attempt, he couldn't hide the shock from his voice.

She sucked in her lips. "Divorced."

Relief rushed into every cell and he reached out his hand, covering hers. "I'm sorry." Only he wasn't sorry one little bit.

Her warmth seeped into him. His palm registered the soft and wondrous touch of her skin against his and it sparked a visceral craving that filled him to overflowing. He wanted to pull her hand up to his mouth, kiss each fingertip, trailing his tongue down its length, tasting her salt and the tangy hint of grapefruit body butter. He wanted to do what he'd done so often years ago when he'd had permission to touch her at any time.

She abruptly pulled her hand out from under his, the action starkly reminding him he'd forfeited any claim to her.

"No need to be sorry. I made a mistake." Her beautiful, lush mouth twisted. "Something I seem to do with men."

Ouch. His heart beat with guilt and he hated this angst-filled atmosphere that cloaked them – it was exhausting. "Flick, it's been eight years. Can't we leave our past behind and be friends?"

Her eyes hardened with the legacy of betrayal. "Friends? Seriously?"

The day he'd ended their engagement loomed large in his memory. *We're not going to work, Flick.* "Fair call." Being friends was a ridiculous long shot. '"How about a truce then, so we can enjoy the ride? When it's over, we go our separate ways."

Her intelligent forehead crinkled the way it always had when she was deep in thought. "Well, this was supposed to be nine days in another world for me to recharge, and we're colleagues so . . ." She gave a wry smile and raised her glass. "To a ceasefire."

He welcomed the relief that flowed through him. He'd spent a large amount of the last eight years being on tenterhooks in war zones and he didn't want to bring that level of anxiety into his civilian life. "Thanks, Flick."

"You're welcome." He was unprepared for the kick of heat her throaty words generated.

Chapter Four

Sixty-one kilometres an hour. Felicity glanced at her bike odometer and grinned. She was freewheeling down the other side of an incredibly steep hill, savouring the wind in her face and the exhilaration that exploded in her chest – the addictive adrenaline charge of speed. Despite the momentous physical effort of climbing an inexorable hill, she'd discovered she loved flying down the other side more than she disliked the climb.

"Flick!" Drew shot past her with a wave, his weight giving him extra speed. "Meet at lunch?"

"Yes," she called out to his back.

She caught him up on the flat and they rode into the lunch spot together. Lake Glenmaggie sparkled in the sunshine and, after having their lanyards scanned and being presented with chicken and avocado wraps, cheese and biscuits and fruit by the smiling volunteers, they carried their haul to the pebbly beach.

Felicity sat and squirted hand sanitizer into both their palms. "I've never eaten so much food in my life."

Drew grinned. "Carbs and protein are the food of cyclists." He bit into the wrap and gazed out at the lake. "When did you take up cycling?"

His tone said, *What else about you has changed.* "Technically, I haven't. I won the bike and Jessie railroaded me onto this trip. I did some training rides and rode the Punt Road hill every morning so I'd be fit enough for these hills."

"It worked. I'm impressed."

She tried to squash the ridiculous glow that his praise generated. *What he thinks of you is immaterial.* "The cycling is the easy part. Coping with camp life and those plastic box showers is another thing entirely."

"Have you ever camped before?"

"In Africa." She shivered at the memory.

He laughed. "I meant real camping, Flick, not glamping in a game park in a tent with a wooden floor and a double bed with 1,000-thread count Egyptian cotton sheets."

The automatic spark of indignation flared and she opened her mouth, the cheap shot teetering on her lips. She swallowed it, forcing it back down where it belonged – unspoken. If they were to have a real truce, she needed to tell him about her life.

She raised her head and met his gaze. "I lived and worked in a refugee camp for two months. This bike trip is utter luxury compared with that."

Drew felt like he'd been hit over the head by a plank. He'd always known she was a caring doctor, but he'd never seen any examples of altruism outside of her working hours. She'd always liked the good things in life. The expensive things – things he'd grown up never knowing. "Which aid agency did you go with?"

She chewed her lip in prevarication and he didn't understand why. "Flick?"

Picking up a handful of the coarse sand, she let it trail through her fingers. "Mine."

He must have misheard. "Sorry?"

She squared her shoulders as if she was preparing herself for battle. "I turned my trust fund into a charity. We provide medical aid in Africa."

"That's . . ." Every word on his lips dried up as the full impact of her words soaked into his brain. He stared at her blankly as shock, surprise, delight and a thousand other emotions rocked him.

Her brows rose and her mouth twitched. "Unexpected?"

"No. I . . . yes." There was no point denying it. "You never mentioned doing anything like that with it when we were together."

"No." The quietly spoken words carried a weary gravitas. "Back then I didn't realize my money was such a problem to either of us."

He wanted to know more. "When did you start it?"

"A year after you left. Most of the time our work is village specific but after a massacre in the Congo, we responded to a call for medical aid in a camp. It was the single most difficult job I've ever done." Her face filled with anguish. "Part of me's still there."

He thought of Afghanistan – the fear and the pointless carnage. "You see stuff that nothing in Australia can ever prepare you for."

Appreciation filled her eyes. "You'd have seen it on the front line."

"Yeah." He didn't like thinking about it – moving forward was the only way to survive trauma like that, but there was an understanding on her face that pulled at him. She'd seen awful and life-changing things too and he had an unusual need to share. "I was fine until the day a six-year-old child was brought in."

He sucked in a fortifying breath, trying not to let the memory reduce him to a sobbing mess. "He'd stepped on a mine."

Her hand slid into his – her fingers curling around tightly. "The kids undo us."

"Every single time."

He downed his electrolyte drink, keeping his eyes fixed on the horizon, watching the way the towering gum trees turned the sky a pale shade of purple, which contrasted with the lake's vivid blue. The peace of it slowly seeped into him, along with the supportive touch of Felicity's hand. He could stay here forever.

Not a good idea.

"Come on then." He jumped quickly to his feet. "The Glenmaggie hill awaits."

She groaned. "But it's so nice sitting here."

He grinned. "That attitude won't get you into camp. It's only a hundred-metre climb and then you've got the reward of working in the clinic until eight. Just think of all those sore knees waiting for us."

She rolled her eyes. "Oh, well, when you put it like that . . ."

He tugged her to her feet with a strong pull and she rose, laughing.

The momentum carried her into his chest and her body brushed his from his sternum to his toes. Muscle memory exploded and every cell moulded to hers with a need so strong it threatened to knock him over. Her scent of apples and cinnamon filled his nostrils and he wanted to bury his face in her hair and breathe her in.

Scratch that. He wanted to bury his lips against hers and revisit her mouth, rediscover her taste of mint, coffee and the quintessential flavour that was Flick. He ached for the scorch of the heat he knew burned there and he wanted to experience again the most sensual kisses he'd ever known. He wanted to lose himself in a place that had once been his sanctuary.

Her huge brown eyes widened at the touch of their bodies and he caught surprise in their depths, followed quickly by a desire that matched his own. Her tongue flicked, licking the bow of her plump top lip.

He groaned as the final thread of his fraying restraint, which had barely held him in check for three days, gave way and he lowered his head towards her lips.

"Hey, doc," a male voice called out.

Felicity spun out of his arms so fast she could have been auditioning for a job as a ballroom dancer.

His body moaned in monumental frustration as it lost the glorious touch of her.

"Phil," Felicity said. "How's the eye?"

"Great, thanks to you, doc. I can't thank you enough."

The cyclist seemed oblivious to the breathlessness in Flick's voice. Drew quickly stepped in behind her because, damn it, Lycra bike shorts hid nothing.

What the hell had he been thinking, trying to kiss her surrounded by a thousand cyclists?

Chapter Five

Day Four

Lightning lit up the sky and thunder rumbled around the hills of Tarra Bulga National Park. The massive tree ferns bowed low, heavy with the weight of the rain, which had fallen continuously since 7 a.m., turning a gravel road into muddy slush and cycling hell. The tops of the towering mountain ash trees disappeared into a thick grey fog that cloaked everything, reducing what should have been spectacular views of old-growth rainforest and the distant coastline down to less than a metre of visibility.

Felicity was working in the first-aid tent at the rest stop and she took a moment to flick yet another leech off her leg. She'd been flat out, dealing with cuts and grazes caused by falls on gravel for the last hour, but she wasn't complaining. Being busy gave her welcome relief from the continuous dialogue in her head. Yesterday she'd almost kissed Drew.

When Phil had interrupted them, half of her had wanted to throttle him while the other half had almost hugged him because he'd just stopped her from doing something she knew she'd regret. Something that would create problems, not solve them.

Drew wanted to kiss you too.

And that confused her the most. He'd been the one to walk away from her all those years ago. He'd been the one who'd betrayed her trust, broken her heart and turned her life upside down. *We're not going to work, Flick.*

So why now? Why after all this time and eight years of radio silence did he want to kiss her?

"Excuse me. My friend's really cold and she's gone all weird.'"

Felicity instantly spun around and focused. A tall, skinny, teenage girl was slumped against her friend, shivering violently.

"I'm Felicity. What's your name?"

The girl didn't reply.

"She's Jamie and I'm Pippa. We stopped to eat some food and she said she was sleepy. I'm really worried."

"You've done the right thing." She guided Jamie to a chair. "Sit down."

The shivering girl stared at her as if she didn't understand her.

Felicity put one hand on Jamie's shoulder and another behind her knees, making her sit. "I'm going to take your temperature."

Jamie barely nodded as Felicity placed the digital infrared thermometer into her ear. It quickly beeped: 34 °C. Mild hypothermia. "Pippa, can you help me get Jamie out of her wet clothes?"

A horrified expression crossed her face. "But it's kinda public."

"I know, but we need to warm her up and right now this wet gear is causing more harm than good. Do either of you have anything dry on your bikes?"

Pippa shook her head. "No."

Felicity sighed, hauling her polar fleece off over her head whilst giving thanks she'd seen the weather forecast and worn her thermal top. Together, she and Pippa pulled three layers of wet clothes off Jamie before putting the polar fleece over her head and wrapping her in a space blanket. "Pippa, are you cold?"

"A bit, but I'm okay."

For now. Pippa, unlike her skinny friend, was a healthy weight, which gave her more protection against the wet and cold. Felicity grabbed an umbrella and thrust it into Pippa's hand. "Can you go to the coffee cart and buy two hot chocolates for Jamie, please."

"Sure."

The moment the girl left, another three teens arrived, all shivering with cold. Every one of them had temperatures hovering between 33 and 34 °C and she could see more likely patients walking across to her. The makeshift medical tent was no longer able to cope with demand and it offered scant protection against the elements. She made an executive decision.

Addressing the friends of the cold teens, she said, "I'm going to need your help. We need to relocate everyone to the information centre down the hill and out of the rain. Then I need two people to go and buy ten hot chocolates." She pulled a fifty dollar bill out of her wallet, passing it over to a young man who'd raised his hand in an offer of assistance.

The teenagers all rallied around and, within ten minutes, Felicity had all the cold students grouped together, wrapped in space blankets and all with a buddy sitting next to them. She'd instructed them to talk to their friends to keep them awake and to report back to her any change in conscious state.

Drew, who'd been called away earlier to treat two girls with hand injuries after they'd ridden too close to each other, appeared with water cascading off the hood of his waterproof jacket. His forehead was creased in a frown. "I've got six people in the café across the road with mild hypothermia and probably another six will have appeared in the time it's taken me to walk here."

Felicity bit her lip. "I've got more than triple that here and we're running low on space blankets. I'm really concerned about two kids who I think should go to hospital."

"This weather's a bastard and the radar's showing rain for another couple of hours."

Felicity swallowed a sigh. "That will make eight hours of rain and we're fast running out of ways to warm these kids up."

"I know. They're soaked, the volunteers are soaked and we're not doing much better. We're on top of a mountain, the ambient air temperature's 6 °C, visibility's almost zero and the road down is so slick it's beyond dangerous. It's time to pull the pin."

"How?" she asked.

"I'm calling it in to the police and requesting they close the road. With so many students on the ride, it's now a duty of care issue and we're going into a full-blown evacuation." He pulled out the sat phone and made the call.

In the short time it took for the police officers to arrive, Felicity had diagnosed another five cases of hypothermia, including two adults. She was triaging everyone, tagging them with numbered wristbands. The most urgent cases got a red tag with a number one printed on it.

"Flick." Drew's hand touched her shoulder and she turned to face him, seeing worry in his eyes. "I think the best solution is that you go down the mountain on the hospital bus and I'll stay here to treat any of the stragglers who need it."

"Sure, that works."

"Good." His fingers tapped a fast tattoo on his head and she recognized the action. He'd always done that when he was thinking fast. "The police have closed the course down the mountain and the sag wagons are now picking up all cyclists who are still riding to the summit. There's an estimated five hundred people and bikes to be transported down to Traralgon."

"At least three and a half thousand people got through. Still, won't that take hours?"

"Yup." The left side of his mouth tweaked up wryly. "It's going to be a long day."

A police officer walked over. "Dr Baxter, the café owner's worried about one of the kids."

"Tell her I'm on my way," said Drew.

"Will do." The officer turned away and spoke into his walkie-talkie.

Drew picked up the remaining space blankets. "Text me when you've wrapped up your end of the day."

"Sure thing."

"Have fun." He leaned in and brushed her cheek with his lips in the exact same way he'd always said farewell to her when they'd been a couple.

As he pulled back, she caught the expression in his eyes. She didn't know which of them was more shocked at the automatic kiss.

Chapter Six

In cab now. Five minutes from camp.

Drew smiled at Flick's text as anticipation spun through him. It was 8 p.m. and he'd been back for an hour, having left the mountain on the last bus. He'd been in contact with the hospital and of the twenty people Flick had transported down only two had been admitted. The rest had recovered swiftly once in warm clothes and filled with hot food and drink. The potential for a mass disaster had been averted and now the camp was full of cycling war stories and the excitement of a rest day tomorrow.

He walked towards the gates of the park to meet Flick's taxi. The satisfaction of a job well done glowed warm inside him and he was keen to dissect the day with her.

You always enjoyed doing that.

For the first time in a long time he didn't bother denying the thought.

Today, as they'd swung into disaster mode on the top of the mountain, it was like they'd never been apart. Hell, working with her had felt so good, so normal in fact that he'd automatically leaned in and kissed her goodbye. When he'd realized what he'd done, the shock of it wasn't enough to bring the expected regret. It had merely reinforced what he wanted.

He wanted her.

For now? Or forever?

His mind baulked.

Just for tonight.

As the cab pulled up, Felicity saw Drew walking towards the vehicle carrying two packs. He gave her a wave and spoke to the driver. "Strzelecki B & B, please."

A minute later, after hefting the packs into the trunk, he slid in beside her.

She scanned his face for clues. "What's going on?"

He smiled. "You've worked twelve hours, you're still in wet clothes and I thought you deserved to have a hot shower that wasn't in a plastic box, enjoy a meal that wasn't eaten off a plastic plate and have the joy of stretching out and sleeping on a mattress rather than a thin camping mat."

She stared at him, trying to work him out. "That's a lovely thought, Drew, but what happened to the man who always said luxury was an overindulgence?"

He frowned. "Did I say that?"

She nodded. "Once or ten times."

Contrition crossed his high cheeks. "That was before I'd experienced life in a war zone. Can I make a caveat? There are occasions when you need some home comforts to re-energize and today's one of them."

The cab pulled up in front of a Victorian weatherboard workman's cottage, meticulously painted in heritage green and cream. A picket fence surrounded the front garden, which was entered through a central gate. Standard iceberg roses in full bloom lined the path to the front door and chickens and ducks ran around the garden. After the close confines of the camp, where the tents were pitched less than thirty centimetres apart, it looked like heaven.

Drew paid the cabbie and then opened the car door for her before following her up the path, carrying their packs.

Felicity took in the white cane furniture on the veranda, the immaculately swept and polished boards and glanced down at her muddy shoes and wet clothes. "I can't go in like this."

"Of course you can. I've spoken to Helen, the owner, and she's running you a hot bath as we speak. Just ditch the shoes and the socks here." He opened the door.

Thoughts bounced around her head, trying to align this Drew with the man who'd argued long and hard about wasting money on five-star luxuries. Granted, this cottage wasn't five star but after four nights in a tent and a day of mud and leeches, it seemed blessedly luxurious to her.

A woman in her fifties welcomed them. "Come in, come in, doctors. You both look exhausted."

Within ten minutes, Felicity was ensconced in an enormous claw-foot bathtub savouring both the warmth and the fragrance of the water. There were times in life when the simple things she took for granted suddenly seemed like miracles, and today was one of those times. Forget champagne and chocolates, forget marble bathrooms and gold plated taps. All a girl needed was a hot cup of tea and a bath.

And Drew.

She sank under the water, trying hard to push the increasingly strident thought away. Her body was only craving something it remembered. Nothing had changed between them and falling into bed with him would only lead to more heartache.

It doesn't have to. It could be just tonight.

She sat up fast, water sluicing off her. Could she do that? Could she take him for just one night and walk away? It wasn't like he'd want anything more than that either.

Heat curled deep inside her, reminding her of how great they'd always been together in bed. *Yes, please.*

A knock sounded on the door, making her start.

"Flick, may I come in?"

She opened her mouth to say, "just a minute," so she could grab the plush towelling robe, but "yes" came out instead.

Chapter Seven

Drew opened Flick's door and stepped into the room. He glanced towards the canopied bed, expecting to see her sitting there but all he saw was a pristine duvet. His gaze swung to the bay window and the claw-foot tub.

Her ankles were crossed gracefully and her feet were extended over the end of the bath – the only parts of her body out of the water. If there'd been bubbles in the bath to start with, they were now long gone. Absolutely nothing hid the full length of her glorious and naked body.

He was instantly hard.

She raised a lovely, toned and tanned arm and waved at him with a wide smile. "You were quick."

His throat convulsed, unable to form words as his brain fought for the remnants of some blood to give the speech centre some oxygen. He swallowed. "Habit." The word came out so husky it was barely recognizable.

"I guess the Army doesn't lend itself to comfort." She rose gracefully, water pouring off her body until she stood in front of him – his own Aphrodite – blissfully and divinely beautiful.

An ache consumed him from head to toe.

God, I've missed her.

He stared at her – hardly able to believe this visual gift – soaking her in as his gaze revisited the body that he knew as intimately as his own. Her breasts were still generous and firm. The left one slightly and deliciously larger than the right.

The sweet curve of her waist and the intoxicating roundness of her hips made his hands tingle with the memories of the thousand times he'd moulded his palm around them. His gaze swept lower to the small triangle of chestnut curls at the apex of her thighs. He'd never forgotten those.

"Drew."

He jerked his head up fast and met dancing eyes and a wicked smile on her lips. "I don't want to break a leg getting out of this tub. Can you give me your hand?"

"Sure." The hoarse word hung in the air as he stepped forward and raised his arm.

Her hand slid into his, gripping him hard. Keeping her eyes firmly on his face, she stepped over the high side of the bath, and the next moment she was standing right in front of him. The delicious scent of coconut and lime spun through his nostrils and he wondered if she tasted as good.

"You're wet," he said, picking up the plush towel.

"I am."

Her throaty voice sent every pulse point in his body into overdrive, throbbing with glorious anticipation. He threw the towel around her shoulders and, pulling each end slowly back and forth, he dried her back and then her breasts. Next he focused on the backs of her legs and then her behind.

Throughout it all, she stood silent and perfectly still, her expression one of delicious taunting – *I'm here and I might be yours.*

When most of her skin was dry, he brought the towel up between her legs, moving it back and forth.

Her eyes widened into pools of liquid chocolate and her slightly detached aura vanished as her head fell back and a soft moan escaped her lips. "You're not playing fair."

He laughed and pulled her into his arms. "A man has to do what works. You're as beautiful as ever, Flick."

She wriggled her nose. "I have stretch marks."

"They're beautiful too. I plan to kiss them soon."

Felicity wrapped her arms around Drew's neck, as his mouth plundered hers. The earthy taste of him filled her mouth, streaking through her fast and waking up every single cell in her body. Her tongue met his, desperate to touch, taste and feel him and fill the void that had been part of her since he'd left.

Her heavy, tingling breasts pressed against the soft cotton of his shirt and ached to touch skin. She pulled back.

His glazed eyes tried to focus. "What?"

"One of us is overdressed." Her fingers undid the snap on his shorts and reached down under the waistband.

He shuddered against her and, with a daring smile, brought his hand up to cup her breast. "Two can play at this game."

She wrapped her palm around the silky length of him and almost cried at how right it felt. "Is that so?"

His thumb brushed her erect nipple. The pleasure-shock rocked through her and she dropped her hand, sagging against him. "You remembered."

He stroked her hair behind her ears. "I've never forgotten."

His words thudded into her but she didn't want to think about what that may or may not mean. She kissed him hard and fast, letting desire take over and making her blessedly deaf to everything except the raging need that burned so brightly, consuming her.

He staggered backwards towards the bed, taking her with him as he kicked off his shoes, shucked his pants, and then he pulled them down together. Their bodies sought each other, knowing exactly what the other needed and fitting together like two pieces of a puzzle. He entered her, vanquishing the empty feeling she'd lived with for so long and she cried out in a combination of relief and joy. With arms around each other, they moved together as one until their rhythm drove each of them beyond the other to that place of sheer and utter bliss.

Chapter Eight

As Felicity caught her breath, she tried not to think about the fact she hadn't experienced mind-blowing sex like that since the last time she and Drew had been together. In fact, she tried not to think about anything other than the residual pleasure that lingered in her veins like sweet caramel sauce.

The only thing the sex had meant was that both of them had given in to memory. She was calling it "farewell sex" – the sex they'd never had because he'd left her without a word.

Drew's arm reached out and she allowed herself to roll into him. He pressed a kiss into her hair. "Thank you. I wasn't expecting it."

She dug him gently in the ribs and laughed. "You are so transparent, Drew. Of course you were expecting it."

His face sobered. "Actually, I wasn't certain. I hoped it might happen, but if it did, I thought I'd have to wait until at least after dinner."

"It's your lucky night then." She moved her head off his chest, disconcerted by the rhythmic and reassuring lub-dub of his heart and how good it sounded. She couldn't risk letting herself want more than tonight. "Talking about dinner, I'm starving. It's been hours since I ate anything."

Drew's fingers trailed through her hair. "What do you fancy? There's Thai, Indian, Italian or the greasy spoon down the road."

She sighed. "I'm famished, but I don't have the energy to get dressed and leave this bed."

"No problem." He reached for his phone. "We'll find a place that delivers."

Day Five

Drew couldn't remember the last time he'd felt so relaxed. Last night had been amazing. After he and Flick had consumed a massive amount of pad thai and a huge amount of chicken satay, they'd made love again before falling asleep. He'd woken this morning with her arm across his chest and her hair in his face but instead of his chest cramping and his body readying to flee, he'd smiled and kissed her because it had felt so good. So . . . right.

Now, they sat under the shade of a huge gum tree in the park, with a feast of dips and cheeses, a baguette, baby spinach, organic tomatoes, summer sausage and a chocolate éclair, all purchased from the farmers' market.

He spread pâté onto the bread. "I thought you would have wanted to eat in a restaurant today rather than picnicking like we do every day on the ride."

Leaning back against the tree, she sipped the pinot noir he'd chosen. Her brow furrowed. "I enjoy being outside. I always have, even when we were together."

He tried to align the statement with his memories. "We never picnicked."

She sighed. "We worked seventy hours a week and lived in inner-city Melbourne. When we had time to go out it was usually with friends at restaurants. You do the maths."

Was that why he associated her with silver service? He could only remember feeling ill at ease at restaurants "du jour" with hoity maître d's who refused his booking but on hearing Felicity's surname always accepted hers.

Thinking about that made him ask, "How are your parents?"

"They're well. They're pretty much living at Portsea full time now."

He recalled the holiday house, which was four times the size of the house he'd grown up in and that was before he factored in the swimming pool, tennis court and the half-sized polo field. "I can't imagine your father slowing down."

She smiled. "He's serving on a few boards and both he and Mum have raised a lot of money for Africa through the charity."

He felt the tightness at the edge of his smile. "Ladies who lunch?"

"Get over yourself, Drew," she said wearily. "My parents may be rich but they use their connections for good."

"You're right; my bad." He accepted her rebuke and determined there and then never to make another cheap shot. He was a different man now and secure in himself. The Hamilton-Smiths were good people and they'd always welcomed him despite his lack of a private school education and his then obvious lack of funds. The problem of him feeling inferior had nothing to do with them and everything to do with him.

"What about your family?" Genuine interest shone on her face.

"Dad's retired from driving trains and he now drives the little motorhome they bought. He reckons they can live more cheaply on the road than in the house. Shelly's married with two little girls and Evan's doing medicine at Melbourne Uni."

"Wow, little Evan's going to be a doctor." Her eyes glowed with affection. "That's great."

"Yeah." He cut a big slab of his favourite runny Brie, which he'd paid a ridiculous amount for because he'd wanted it and he could now afford it. It was Flick who'd introduced him to the world of European cheeses and wine all those years ago. His family had never had the money to afford such luxuries. "I'm helping Evan out financially while he studies so he can avoid the Army."

Her relaxed aura vanished and she leaned forward, her jaw rigid. "And he's accepting your help? Tell me, how is that any different from what I offered you?"

The past hit him as hard as the butt of an assault rifle. "He's my baby brother, Flick, and he shouldn't have to work in a war zone when I can afford to help him. I'm just doing what family does."

The moment the word "family" left his lips he wanted to grab it back. Instead he was faced with watching it land on her ears. Like a scud missile, it exploded in front of him.

Incredulity streaked across her face. "And as your fiancée, I wasn't family?"

Her rising voice, filled with pain and anger, speared him hard. There was no easy way to answer her question so he went for the truth. "I loved you, Flick, but I needed to pay my way. I needed you to understand that."

She shook her head as if she didn't understand at all. "But Evan doesn't have to pay his way?"

"He does. All I'm doing is giving him an interest-free student loan."

"And what? You thought that as my husband you'd never be contributing to our income?"

He sighed, hating they were back to this again when it only touched on a small part of why he'd left. "It was more complicated than that and you know it."

"I don't think I do, given you never explained any of it to me."

"I tried. God, Flick, I really tried."

She bit her lip. "I'm sorry I didn't hear you."

His guilt burrowed deep and he reached for her hand. "I'm sorry too. If I had my time over, Flick, I would have told you in person that I was leaving."

She blinked rapidly and moved just out of reach. "Is that supposed to make me feel better?"

"No. Yes." He ran his hand through his hair. "I never meant to hurt you. We were at an impasse that was widening every day. You wouldn't marry me if I joined the Army and I couldn't marry you if I didn't. I thought by leaving I was doing us both a favour because with the way things were, I truly believed we couldn't be happy."

"Because of my inheritance?"

"No."

The disbelief on her face launched him into the explanation he should have given her so long ago. "Sometimes the money made me feel uncomfortable, but it was the seven years of university that had left me in limbo. I didn't feel at ease in your world, but as much as I railed against that at times, mine no longer suited me either. I was a stranger in my own life and I had no clue how to fix it except to do something that separated me from the two worlds I was straddling."

Two furrows appeared at the bridge of her nose as if she was trying to work something out. "Did you feel you belonged in the Army?"

He shrugged. "The Army's world is one of following orders. I didn't have to think, I didn't have to question who I was, I just did."

Her intelligent gaze didn't waver. "But it doesn't suit you any longer?"

He shook his head. "I've changed. Some might call it growing up, but all I know is that for the first time in a long time, I'm at peace with who I am. I know what I want."

"And what's that?"

You. I want you.

The thought crashed through him, bringing with it the clarity of crystal. It illuminated everything – who he was, what he wanted and what was important.

He held his breath, waiting for the fallout – for the fear, for the sense of dislocation, for the crushing weight of obligation – for all the reasons that had driven him away years ago.

None of it came.

Four days ago, if she'd asked him what he wanted, he would have said a job in A & E and an apartment in Lygon Street, but that was no longer enough. Nowhere near enough. He wanted her in his life.

I love you.

He loved her. The thought didn't terrify him.

He'd always loved her, even when he'd believed they couldn't be happy together. Over the years, as much as he'd tried, he'd never stopped loving her. Being with her again this week had energized him in a way he hadn't enjoyed since their intern year, and last night, she'd rocked his world to its foundations, reminding him of everything he'd lost when he'd left her.

She was generous and caring and she made him laugh. She understood the horrors he'd seen overseas having witnessed trauma herself. Now, for the first time since he'd walked away from their engagement, he felt whole again.

You need her.

The thought of not sharing his future with her was too awful to contemplate.

This time he picked up her hand and laced his fingers between hers. "I want you, Flick. Marry me?"

Her face paled to white on white. "This isn't a very funny joke, Drew."

He shook his head so fast that her face went out of focus. "It's no joke. I'm deadly serious."

Her body stiffened and she seemed to shrink away from him. "We had sex and now you think everything is back to the way it was years ago?" She tugged her hand out of his. "It doesn't work like that."

"It can if you want it to."

"Wanting has nothing to do with it. I can't trust you."

Her words slammed into him and he moved to reassure her. "This time things will be different."

"Really? Why would I believe that?" Her sharp words jabbed the air. "Ten minutes ago you were taking a cheap shot at my family."

He threw out his hands, the gesture imploring. "And I apologized. Please don't do this. Eight years is a long time, Flick, and we both know we've changed. We're different people than we were then and we're leading different lives. We've got wiser, we've learned about life, about ourselves and what's important. We've learned about love.'"

She flinched. "Have we? I got divorced and you're still single because you think love is an obligation and you hate owing anyone anything." Her voice cracked. "Despite everything you've said, I have no guarantee that you're not going to walk away from me the first time we hit a hurdle in our relationship." She struggled to her feet.

Panic simmered in his veins at her leaving. "Flick, I promise you, no matter what, I will always talk to you and I will never walk away again."

The lack of faith in her eyes terrified him, but it was her words that stole all hope.

"I'm not prepared to risk it, Drew. Not ever."

Chapter Nine

Day Six

Sweat poured off Felicity as she climbed a never-ending, five-kilometre hill. Humidity hung in the air like a cloak, clogging her lungs and draining her energy. Her legs felt like porridge and she couldn't find her usual rhythm.

The irony wasn't lost on her that within forty-eight hours the weather had gone from hypothermia-causing to heatstroke-inducing. Surrounded by cyclists who pushed on slowly up the nemesis that was another section of the Grand Ridge Road, she'd never felt so alone.

Silver spots danced in front of her eyes and she moved off the road, grabbing her bottle of electrolyte drink. Despite feeling nauseous, she chugged half of it down in one hit, hoping to stave off dehydration. She adjusted her wet necktie, trying to cool her body. So much for an enjoyable ride on her off-duty day – she'd rather be working. She should have been working, but she'd convinced Becky to swap with her so she could avoid Drew.

Drew had ruined everything. Again.

What should have been wild sex for the last four days of the ride, companionship and finally a sense of closure on their relationship had instead turned into the ripping open of a festering wound. How could he say that he loved her? He'd said that once before and then he'd left her, stealing part of her heart. It had taken her a very long time to recover from his leaving.

When she and Geoff had divorced, she'd got through the dark days more easily. Although she'd been sad that they'd failed, deep down she'd always known that they didn't really belong together. With Drew, she didn't have that reassurance. He was her soul mate. But she didn't dare believe it when he said that he loved her this time because if he left her again, she knew she'd go under and she might not survive.

She couldn't risk that happening. Sure, her life wasn't exactly what she'd hoped it would be, but she had a good job, she had her charity work, good friends and that was enough. It had to be enough.

She gave herself a shake and ate a muesli bar for much-needed energy. She was about to get back on her bike when she realized she needed to pee. Well, at least she wasn't dehydrated. Rising to her feet, she ignored her postural hypotension and wobbled towards a grove of trees.

Grass brushed her legs and she immediately regretted her decision. It was snake weather and this long grass was perfect snake habitat. But she really needed to go. Stamping her feet to make the ground vibrate, she kept walking, trying to shake off her woozy feeling. God, she hated humidity.

She noticed that in a few feet, the land dropped away in typical Gippsland steepness. Ever cautious, she carefully took a couple of steps so she was just out of view of the passing cyclists but far enough from the incline to be safe. Seeing the perfect spot, she quickly turned towards it. Her vision blurred, her feet stumbled, a rock moved and dirt and gravel gave way under her. She threw her hands out to grab at the tree but missed. Then she was falling – tumbling over and over, gaining terrifying speed with every roll. She screamed, unable to stop her slide despite frantically grabbing at trees and rocks and trying to push her feet into the earth, anything to stop herself.

Pain seared her.

Everything went black.

Sunlight penetrated Felicity's eyelids.

Where am I?

She tried to sit up, but everything hurt, so she took the path of least resistance and opened her eyes. Oh, God. She instantly closed them again and tried to breathe slowly against her panic. She was balanced precariously on the edge of a mighty drop and the only thing between her and certain death was a shallow-rooted sapling.

A sob rose in her throat, but she cut it off, biting down hard on her lip. Her body vibrated in pain as she fought-forced air into her lungs.

You've fractured ribs.

Again, the blackness seeped into the edges of her mind, calling her to close her eyes and to go willingly into that dark place. She could let go of everything and forget the red-hot pain. Forget the fact she was thirty-two and alone, forget that she'd never known a successful relationship.

I was a stranger in my own life and I had no clue how to fix it.

Drew's words hammered her with guilt. She'd had no clue he'd been struggling so much and instead of helping, she'd made it all about her.

I love you, Flick. I promise you, I'll never leave you.

The memory of his voice – words she hadn't believed yesterday – called her back from the brink of darkness. She forced her eyes to stay open, knowing that she wanted the chance to see him again. Wanted the opportunity to explain her culpability. She wanted to see her parents and friends and her patients. She wanted a better version of her life.

She had no clue how far she'd fallen, but her survival depended on her not having punctured a lung or internal bleeding, and not moving a millimetre. She could only control one of those scenarios.

"Coo-ee." The Aussie call to find a lost person, floated in the air above her.

"Coo-ee. Felicity. Felicity Hamilton-Smith." Voices called her name.

People must have seen her bike and read the tag. "Here," she tried to yell as burning hot pain stole her breath. "I'm . . . down . . . here."

"Don't move. Medics are on the way."

She glanced up at the escarpment. How they hell were they going to reach her without risking their own lives?

Chapter Ten

"Flick."

The abject fear in Drew's voice penetrated her semi-conscious brain. She mustered a breath against the red-hot poker of pain that sliced through her. "D . . . Drew?"

"Hang in there, sweetheart. I'm almost there. The helicopter's on its way."

A spray of small rocks hit her and dread clawed at her. "No." She had no more breath to say, *It's too dangerous. Don't come, you could die.*

More scree filled the air and then he was kneeling beside her, his large and capable hands running all over her body – assessing, reassuring, loving.

His anguished face stared down at her. "What do you mean, 'no'?"

Tears welled in her eyes as fury and relief duelled inside her. "You . . . could . . . have—" she tried to get some air into her lungs "—gone over . . . edge."

"I'd go beyond the edge for you every single time. I love you, Flick."

The man had just risked his life, sliding halfway down a cliff to reach her. Her heart quivered at the apprehension and fear that burned brightly in his eyes. Fear and concern she knew that went way beyond professional concern. Feelings that matched her own for him. "I need you, Drew."

"I'm here and I'm not going anywhere."

* * *

Felicity opened her eyes and Drew squeezed her hand. "Hey."

"Hey." She only had flashes of memory – of brutal pain and of being winched into the helicopter strapped to Drew. She'd passed out when he'd inserted a chest tube and woken again to the sting of an IV cannula going into the back of her hand. She recalled the scream of the ambulance and arriving at the hospital and being greeted by the rushing of staff. Now it was dark outside. "What time is it?"

"Just past midnight."

Dark rings circled his eyes and deep lines scored his mouth. Her heart hiccupped at his exhaustion. "You should get some sleep."

He shook his head, his expression firm. "I told you, I'm not going anywhere."

She wanted to hug him but all the tubes kept her resting on the pillows. "You catching some sleep and coming back here for breakfast, isn't leaving me."

Hope shimmered in his vivid blue eyes. "What are you saying, Flick?"

"I know yesterday I said I couldn't trust you, but when a girl almost dies, she does some serious thinking. I do trust you, Drew." She traced her finger along the back of his hand, needing to explain. "The thing is, all those years ago, we both made a mess of us. I wanted to blame you implicitly because you walked away from me. I thought it was about the money, about you being ridiculously independent and seeing my love as an obligation, but it wasn't about that at all, was it?"

"No."

The quietly spoken word, so full of emotion, made her throat tight. "I let you down, Drew. I was so happy with you that I didn't want to believe that I was part of your misery. I didn't realize you felt like a stranger in your own life, feeling like you didn't belong anywhere. I hate that I contributed to that by not giving you the chance to be the man you needed to become. By not compromising. I'm sorry."

"We both did things we regret." He raised her hand to his lips and kissed it. "But we're older and a hell of a lot wiser. We know that neither of us is happy without the other, so where does that leave us now?"

She pressed her palm against his jaw. "More than anything else in the world, Drew, I want to make us work."

"So do I."

His heartfelt words filled her with elation. "It means you telling me how you're feeling in the good times and the bad, and me listening and vice versa."

He nodded. "It means being a team and consulting each other before making any big plans."

She gave a wry smile. "I'm not a trust-fund girl any more, Drew. I live off my income so it means budgeting, saving for big things and some camping holidays."

"Some camping in the great outdoors sounds fabulous, although I've been quite successful on the stock market so we can afford the occasional splurge." He grinned. "Come to think of it, we might need a pre-nup."

She laughed and then flinched at the pain of her ribs. "Are you proposing to me?"

His eyes twinkled. "Are you?"

She picked up both his hands. "Drew Baxter, will you spend the rest of your life with me?"

"I've already started."

Tears pricked the back of her eyes. "I love you, Drew. I always have and I always will."

He leaned in and captured her lips in a kiss so gentle and so filled with love that joy rushed her.

After all these years, she was finally where she belonged – back with the man she loved, with the man who adored her and wanted to spend the rest of his life with her.

She kissed him right back.

TIME OUT

Lucy Clark

Chapter One

"That's your locker there."

Amy Pendelton smiled at Sarah, one of St John's Hospital's theatre nurses, who had shown her around the department.

"Thanks, Sarah. I appreciate your help." Amy stood in the theatre's female changing rooms, mingling with the staff who were either changing back into their clothes after a long stint in theatre, or getting into scrubs, about to start their shifts. She noted their moods, the way they brushed their hair, and how they disposed of their dirty scrubs. One blonde woman walked into the changing rooms and simply grabbed the top set of scrubs from the trolley by the door without even looking. Any one of these women could be a suspect, and it was her covert mission to find out whom.

"Ah, this is Louise." Sarah called the blonde woman over. "She'll be the anaesthetist for Dr Wow-Wow Whittaker."

Amy chuckled at the doctor's nickname as she shook hands with Louise.

"It's what a lot of the female staff are calling the new acting head of general surgery because he is hot." Louise fanned her face with her free hand before casually tossing the scrubs onto a nearby chair and starting to undress. "He only started two weeks ago and already he has half the women in theatre salivating when he walks by."

"Do you think he's a good surgeon?" Amy asked Louise, stowing her handbag in her locker, as Sarah and the other nurses left to start their shifts.

"He is, actually."

"Flawless techniques?"

"There is that, but he also cares about his patients. On his second day here, we lost a patient on the operating table and he didn't like it." Louise pulled on her scrubs. "Of course, there are times when you can't save everyone, especially when the injuries are just too extensive. But of course you'd know that, being a surgical registrar."

"Yes." Amy started changing into her theatre scrubs, clearly noting the way Louise had paused slightly. Did she have a speech impediment? Had she lost her train of thought? Or was she hiding something?

Amy had been sent on this mission because as the Defence Intelligence's leading surgical expert, it was up to her to gather as much intel as she could about two suspicious deaths at this hospital, both taking place within the last month. The patients in question had been known mercenaries, news of their deaths creating unrest in several countries. Many governments wanted answers, and, as yet, Defence Intelligence hadn't much to give them, especially when both bodies had been removed from the hospital's premises before medical examiners could perform an autopsy. False paperwork had replaced the real reports, stating both bodies had been cremated. Something was very wrong and it was her job to figure out what it was.

Once they were changed, they headed to Theatre Five where Louise took over from her anaesthetic registrar. Amy headed to the scrub sink where she'd hoped to meet Dr Wow-Wow Whittaker before the surgery, but by the time she was gowned and gloved, there was still no sign of him. She rolled her eyes as the surgical team waited for his arrival. He may be "hot" and make women go weak at the knees but that meant little to her when he was late.

Part of her wanted to begin the surgery, especially given she was a fully qualified general surgeon. But, as she was undercover as a registrar, and as this was her first day, she didn't want to draw unnecessary attention to herself. The other reason she was itching to start this particular procedure was because of the patient, Mr Naki Devneeta. Another mercenary, whose unknown whereabouts since his arrival in Australia three days ago had caused her department to explode in a frenzy of activity. To have three known mercenaries – two already deceased – not only arriving in Sydney, Australia within weeks of each other, but ending up in the same hospital, was far too much of a coincidence. She'd gone to great lengths to secure her presence in this theatre and now the lead surgeon was late. Her impatience increased.

"Sorry," a deep male voice announced a minute later, as a gowned and gloved figure entered the theatre. He walked to the table, hands upheld. With his theatre hat, mask and facial shield securely in place, the only part of him Amy could clearly see was his eyes.

They were the most perfect shade of blue, like the sky on a summer's day. As he moved with ease into position by the operating table, his gaze met hers. He seemed to study her for a moment, looking directly into her eyes without a flicker of doubt. Oh yes, those bluest of blue eyes were clearly the main reasons why the women here called him Dr Wow-Wow.

"Who are you?" he demanded, his brisk tone snatching her off the cloud she'd been on since he'd walked into the room. A frown puckered her brow. Given all he could really see of her was her eyes, how could he tell she was a different registrar from the one scheduled to assist with the surgery?

"'Dr Pendelton, sir. Dr O'Hara had a family emergency and asked me to switch shifts." Amy made a point of swallowing, as though she were uncomfortable with his scrutiny. She stared at him across the operating table, the anaesthetized patient between them.

His answer was to growl at her, clearly indicating he wasn't at all happy about the last-minute change. "You'd better be able to pre-empt my every move, Dr Pendelton, or your time here at St John's will be short lived."

"Yes, sir," she replied.

He moved on to address the rest of the theatre staff. "Patient is Mr Naki Devneeta. Multiple lacerations to the abdomen and lower back region; perforation of the large intestine and spleen. The urological surgeon will be in after us to patch up the bladder rupture and check the kidneys, so let's get our job done, people." He looked across at the anaesthetist. "Ready?"

Louise nodded back. "Very ready, Dr Whittaker." There was a firm confidence in her words. Amy glanced towards the patient's head where Louise was busy monitoring the man's vital signs. She noted the absence of the anaesthetic registrar. Perhaps he'd been needed in another theatre?

She heard Dr Whittaker exhale harshly.

"This isn't a good beginning, Dr Pendelton," he growled. He held out his hand for the scalpel.

"Sorry, sir," she replied, focusing on doing her job, which was to ensure that Mr Devneeta survived this surgery so Defence Intelligence could take him into custody. Devneeta was a valuable source of information about the underground mercenary networks in India. Although she might personally despise the man – wanting him brought to justice for his crimes – his intel could help save lives. He was a necessary evil she had to endure.

The surgery proceeded nicely. "You can let the urology team know that we're almost finished here," Dr Whittaker announced to the scout nurse who nodded and quickly went to the phone.

A second later, an alarm sounded. "Myocardial infarction," Louise called, urgency in her tone. She was frantically trying to stabilize the patient.

"No!" Dr Whittaker began to remove the instruments they were using, Amy instantly calling for the crash cart.

"Charge paddles," Amy stated.

"Oxygen saturations still decreasing," Louise called. "Respirations—"

Her words were cut off as a flatline sounded.

"No!" Dr Whittaker's tone was adamant. "We're not losing him. Paddles." The theatre sister handed him the paddles. "Clear," he called and thrust the paddles onto Mr Devneeta's chest. Still the flatline reigned.

"Again."

Amy looked around the theatre, trying to take everything in, trying to notice what others might not. It was what she'd been trained to do. As Dr Whittaker continued to attempt to revive the patient, she couldn't see anything out of the ordinary. She tried to take snapshots with her mind, to recall every detail possible. Who was in the theatre? What instruments were on the trays? What type of gel was being used on the paddles? This would be the third mercenary to die on the operating table with treatable injuries.

"Pupils fixed and dilated," Louise called a moment later. Everyone in the theatre turned to look at Dr Whittaker. He stood there, motionless, staring down at the deceased patient. When he lifted his head, his gaze bored into Amy's.

"Call it." He thrust the paddles at the theatre sister and stalked out. Amy did as she was told, leaving the late Mr Devneeta to the care of the experienced theatre staff. She knew it was imperative to report this latest turn of events to her superior – stat.

She de-gowned and headed quickly to the female changing rooms to retrieve her phone from her locker. As several staff were in the changing room, Amy went into the corridor, ducking inside a nearby maintenance closet to make her call.

"General? He's dead."

Amy winced as the General blustered, the sound fiercer than Dr Wow-Wow's growling. "I want a full report on my desk within the hour, Major. I'll send a crew to collect the body from the morgue."

"Yes, General."

Amy sighed and rested her head against the cupboard, unable to believe the turn of events. The myocardial infarction had happened quite suddenly and very quickly, with little warning. She needed to get her hands on those case notes, to copy every single piece of paper in the file, especially Dr Whittaker's operation report. Had he been involved somehow? She'd been assisting him quite closely and she couldn't recall him doing anything out of the ordinary. However, his efforts to save the patient had seemed quite desperate. Perhaps he was like that with every patient who dared to die on his operating table? Once Louise had announced that the pupils were fixed and dilated, Dr Whittaker's response hadn't been one of defeat but, rather, annoyance.

Pocketing her phone in her scrubs, she carefully opened the door when she hoped the coast was clear. No one was around, so she slipped out.

"Going somewhere?" a deep voice growled. Amy instantly spun around to find none other than Dr Wow-Wow, in all his de-gowned glory, leaning against the wall on the other side of the closet door, as though he'd been waiting for her.

She placed a hand to her heart and smiled brightly. "Oh, Dr Whittaker. You startled me."

Amy took a quick inventory of him without his theatre garb. His hair was blond, cut in a short-back-and-sides fashion, which suited him. His nose was slightly longer than she'd expected, and his chin was firm and square. He lifted a sardonic eyebrow, and it was only then she realized she'd been caught staring. Deciding to use the situation to her advantage, she made a point of touching her hair, not surprised to find some of her unruly brown curls had escaped her low bun. She blinked a few times, as though dazzled by his presence, and tucked the curls behind her ear.

"What were you doing in the maintenance closet?"

"Er . . ."

"It's not a difficult question, Dr Pendelton."

Amy cast her glance downward, noting they both still wore the protective theatre booties over their shoes. "I was using my phone, sir."

"You keep calling me 'sir'." He took a step towards her.

"I'm only trying to be respectful."

"Most staff would reply 'yes, doctor' rather than 'sir'."

"My father was in the military." Amy lifted her eyes to meet his for a second. "It won't happen again, doctor."

"I don't care about that," Dr Whittaker said. "I do care about why you were in the closet." He walked past her and opened the door. "No one else is in here so you couldn't have been meeting anyone for a quick kiss. Therefore, Dr Pendelton, I'll ask you one more time. What were you doing in there?"

Amy slipped her hand into the pocket of her scrubs and slowly withdrew her phone. "I was calling my mother's neighbour."

He seemed clearly surprised by her reply but Amy had been taught years ago that when you were fabricating a story, the more specific you were, the more people tended to believe you. "Why?"

"My mother's been sick. She has early onset dementia but she's as stubborn as anything and refuses help. Well, she's on antibiotics at the moment, to clear up a bad leg-ulcer infection, and last week I found out she'd been forgetting to take her medicine. Her neighbour's agreed to help me and—"

"And so you high-tailed it out of theatre, after the sudden death of a patient, to check on your mother?" he interrupted, his tone a little incredulous.

"Yes, sir . . . er . . . doctor." She held her phone towards him. "You can call my mother's neighbour if you like, to confirm." When he showed no interest in taking her phone, she quickly tucked it back into her pocket. "I'm sorry, Dr Whittaker. I know we're not supposed to use cell phones in theatres but—"

"This is your first day, Dr Pendelton," he remarked, once more cutting her off. "And this is your first and last mistake. If you put one foot out of place again, you'll be dismissed. Understood?"

Amy swallowed and nodded eagerly. "Yes, doctor," she said with just the right amount of meekness in her tone. When one of the theatre sisters came over to talk to him, she took the opportunity to escape.

When she arrived back at Theatre Five, she looked for Devneeta's case notes, but wasn't able to find them. No doubt Dr Whittaker still had them. She'd have to search his office later. For now, though, she needed to get changed and start writing up her report. The General was counting on her and she wasn't going to let him down.

Amy walked with a purposeful stride through the quiet hospital, knowing the best way to not attract attention was to pretend as though she owned the place. She was dressed in dark trousers and a burgundy shirt, her wayward curls pulled back into a simple ponytail, her hospital identification badge and pass-card hanging from a lanyard around her neck.

She'd had one of her tech colleagues tweak her hospital pass-card to allow her access to any room in the hospital, and as she walked through the now deserted department of general surgery – the administration staff having gone home at midnight – Amy headed straight for Dr Whittaker's office.

After she'd emailed her report to the General, she'd received a phone call from their operatives sent to collect Devneeta's body from St John's morgue.

"It's not here," they'd told her.

"What!"

"The body's gone missing, just like the other two."

Amy had thought quickly. "Any paperwork?"

"Says he has no family. Completed autopsy confirms death by natural causes and a transfer order to the crematorium."

"You've checked the crem—"

"Yes. Their paperwork says the body was cremated half an hour ago."

Amy had thumped the desk. "That's far too quick. All the i's dotted and all the t's crossed?" She'd shaken her head, frustrated. "There's more than one person involved in these deaths. No one person could do all this."

"Agreed. Do you have the operation report?"

"I couldn't get hold of the case notes but I'll find them tonight. Keep me informed of any new information."

"Yes, Major."

Amy paused outside Dr Whittaker's office for a moment, looking around to make sure no one was watching, and then swiped her pass-card over the sensor. She'd already provided her defence colleagues with the names of all the staff who had been in the theatre at the time of Mr Devneeta's death and had received extensive dossiers on half of them so far. "A little light reading for when I'm finished here," she murmured to herself as she slipped into Dr Whittaker's office, closing the door quietly behind her.

She flicked on her torch and walked over to his neat desk. She was surprised. Usually doctors, especially hectic surgeons, had desks covered with papers, folders and case notes. Perhaps James Whittaker was excessively good at both surgery and administration. Seriously, the man seemed too good to be true. It wasn't fair he should be perfect at his job as well as perfectly good-looking. He had to have some flaws, but she knew she probably wouldn't get the chance to find any of them out. Once she'd finished gathering intel here at the hospital, she would be transferred out, off on her next mission.

She tried the drawers on his large mahogany desk and found them locked. A good sign. As she quickly picked the locks, she couldn't believe how exhausted she felt simply thinking about rushing off to yet another assignment. It felt like an age since she'd had any sort of time off. As the General always said, "National Security never takes a vacation, Major."

It wasn't that she didn't like her job, she did. But what she'd been craving for some time now was just a few weeks of a normal existence – to work at a hospital like this one, to see patients, to do surgery, to chat with people without looking for ulterior motives in everyone around her.

"Ahh." She felt the first lock click and slowly opened the drawer. There, inside, were Mr Naki Devneeta's case notes. "Excellent," she remarked, putting them on the desk and using her cell phone camera to take photos of every page. She was just finishing up, and was about to email the information to the General, when there was a sound to her left. A second later, the room was flooded with light and there, in the open doorway, stood Dr James Whittaker himself.

"Something I can help you with, Dr Pendelton?"

Chapter Two

Amy didn't take her gaze off him. She quickly pressed "send" on her phone before pocketing it. Next, she closed the case notes and slipped them back into his drawer, thinking quickly. The easiest solution to this situation was to have James Whittaker read into the mission details. That, of course, would require his cooperation, but she'd learned from experience that where national security was concerned, people were usually willing to help.

"Calling your mother's neighbour again? Checking if he needs copies of those files in order to assist your mother in her dementia?" He stalked slowly towards his desk.

Amy pasted on her brightest smile and tucked a stray curl behind her ear. "Dr Whittaker. I can explain." She held her palms out, face up, showing him she wasn't about to cause trouble. Carefully, she moved out from behind his desk, keeping her distance from his advancing presence.

"Perhaps you'd like to discuss your position here at St John's? Not satisfied with the treatment we're giving our patients? Needing to check over my work?" He folded his arms across his chest and stopped on the opposite side of the room. He indicated the two chairs between them. “Perhaps we should sit down, discuss this situation calmly. Generally, I don’t take too kindly to new staff members breaking into my office and photographing a patient’s case notes.”

He sat down in one of the chairs, indicating she should do the same. “I’m not threatening you, Dr Pendelton, if indeed that is your real name. I’m simply trying to open a dialogue, to calmly and quickly rectify this situation in a manner that is beneficial to both of us.”

Amy gave him a quizzical look. “You sound as though you read that in a counselling manual.”

He smiled at her then, a full-on blast of that gorgeous mouth. She instantly understood why the female staff melted. She was finding it increasingly difficult to ignore the wayward thump-thump of her heart. He really was a devastatingly handsome man. When he turned on the charm, he became lethal. Amy wet her dry lips, caution pulsing through her.

“I did. ‘How To Manage Staff 101’. Although they didn’t really provide specific protocols for this sort of situation, I’m sure we can muddle through.” He indicated the chair again. “Please sit.” His tone was calm, not antagonistic at all. That alone was enough of a reason for Amy to keep her guard up.

She knew she needed to remain calm if she was going to garner his cooperation. Inclining her head slightly, she acquiesced and sat in one of the chairs, ensuring there was still distance between them.

“Comfortable?” Again, there was that smile, as though he was lulling her into a false sense of security.

“Yes. Thank you.”

“OK. Let’s start from the beginning. Ever since I walked into my operating theatre this morning, I’ve found your behaviour very . . . odd.”

“I see.”

He spread his palms wide. “That’s it? ‘I see.’ You wouldn’t care to explain a little more?” He paused. “You might want to start with just how you ended up in my theatre, then move on to who you were really calling in the maintenance closet, and end with why you’re breaking into my office and photographing classified medical information in the middle of the night." His tone had changed now, his words direct, clipped and brooking no argument. "I don't care how long it takes. I want the truth."

Amy nodded, wondering if it was still possible for her to keep her cover intact. It might require some inventive thinking but she could at least give it a go. "I was in your theatre this morning because Dr O'Hara asked me to change shifts with her."

"Why?"

Amy looked downwards, as though trying to recall the facts. "Um . . . something about an emergency at her daughter's school, I think. She'd received a call from the school and was told to come immediately."

James Whittaker eased back in the chair and studied her for a long moment. "Liar."

"I beg your par—"

Before Amy could finish her sentence, he had lunged forward sharply, his hands coming towards her throat. Reacting purely on instinct, Amy grabbed his arms, hunched her back and, within another moment, had flipped him over her head. She jumped up from the chair and stared down at him, lying flat on the carpet.

"What did—?" She glared at him, but when he expertly flipped himself back to a standing position, Amy's eyes widened in surprise "Who are you?"

"Ahh good. We're getting closer to the real you."

He lunged again, his hand slicing through the air towards her head. She blocked it as effectively as she did the next blow, countering with her own as they shifted around his office. Amy kicked at his thigh, hoping to topple him. She'd fought bigger guys than him before but James's technique was flawless. Trained . . . government trained?

"Who are you?" she demanded, but her curiosity only allowed him to land a blow at the base of her ribcage. She coughed and breathed through the pain, ducking to avoid his arm, managing to punch him in the solar plexus. He sucked in a breath and shot her a daggered look.

"I could ask the same question." Before she had time to regroup, he'd levelled her with a hefty kick. The force was so great, Amy was knocked off her feet and lying flat on her back before she could blink. He moved fast, pinning her down, straddling her body. Amy stared at him, noting the skin near his eyebrow was split and bleeding, making him look menacingly handsome.

As her breathing slowly returned to normal, she became all too aware of her predicament. James was sitting on her, intimately so, and whereas she'd been fighting for her life a second ago, she was now fighting her wayward hormones.

"You're well trained. I'll give you that, but who trained you and why are you at St John's?"

Amy swallowed, demanding her body stop reacting to this man. "Why are you at St John's?"

"Did you have anything to do with Devneeta's death?"

"Did you?"

His eyes widened perceptibly at the question and he leaned forward a little, his chest hovering over hers. Amy licked her lips and tried not to stare at his mouth, only inches from her own. "Something's got to give if we're going to . . ." His gaze left hers, resting momentarily on her parted lips before returning to her eyes. ". . . move forward.'"

"Yes," she breathed, and, taking advantage of his shifted weight, she braced her body and raised her right leg sharply to whack him in the back of the head. It was enough to loosen his hold and she immediately twisted free of his grasp, leaving him once more sprawled out on the carpet. She clambered to her feet, breathing heavily. "So? You go first."

James sat up, rubbing the back of his head. "Australian Intelligence Service. You?"

"I don't believe you."

He gingerly stood and then reached into the back pocket of his trousers, bringing out his official identification. Amy glared at it, still not willing to let down her guard.

"Come on, Dr Pendelton. Share." When she still didn't move, he shrugged and exhaled sharply. "Or we could continue to fight." He grinned at her and waggled his eyebrows. "I can go all night along."

Amy's eyes widened in shock at his double entendre. He'd been tough enough to resist when he'd been just another handsome general surgeon, even more so when she'd noticed he was firm and dictatorial . . . But now? Having him flirt with her? Tease her? She parted her lips and tried to gain some control over her senses. It didn't help when he tugged his shirt out of the waistband of his trousers and pulled off his tie.

"Wh— what are you doing?"

He grinned maddeningly. "Perhaps I'm getting ready to torture the information out of you? Tie you up." He ran his necktie through his fingers, his tone suggestive. "Find a way that's mutually beneficial to both of us to entice you to talk." He slowly advanced towards her, and as a multitude of scenarios flooded through her mind, each and every one of them more erotic than the last, Amy quickly held up her hands to stop him.

"All right." With an audible sigh, she retrieved the identification from her pocket. James looked at the badge.

"Major Amelia Pendelton? Defence Intelligence? What on earth do you want?"

The answer to his question became apparent six hours later, as he sat in an AIS briefing room across the table from Major Pendelton, the two of them watching as their respective bosses, General Lowry and AIS Director Malcolm yelled at each other.

"Defence is required to inform AIS of undercover operatives," Malcolm demanded.

"As is AIS. Protocols are in place for a reason – to be followed," the General countered.

"Spoken like a military man," Malcolm sneered.

The General straightened, squaring his shoulders. "Do you have a problem with the military, son?"

"Son?" Malcolm laughed without humour. "Don't be so condescending."

"The defence forces of this country have been in place far longer than your little spies." The General stabbed the table with his index finger and Amy winced. She'd seen her boss riled up before but never like this. He was a man who liked order and this debacle was far from it. She got to her feet.

"If I may, General?" She pointed to the paperwork she'd managed to pull together. At the nod from the General, she proceeded. "Naki Devneeta was under suspicion for selling sensitive defence information. We'd been watching him for a few months, noting his connections with both Rishwood and Mei-Soong."

"Those were the other two deaths at St John's," James added. "We'd been watching Mei-Soong for suspected mercenary activity but didn't have anything concrete on him."

"We do." Amy handed Director Malcolm another file. "This highlights his history as far back as thirty years ago. That's where we found the connection between the three of them. All were in the Amazon jungle." Amy opened another folder and pulled out copies of old photographs. "They attacked many of the native villages, slaughtering and killing not only the indigenous people but also American and Australian scientists who were researching in the area. Turns out it was the research they were after. They simply killed the natives for fun. After that, it was difficult to place the three of them together. If they ever met face to face, it must have been done covertly because we have no intel on it."

"What were the scientists working on?" Malcolm asked.

"A new cardiotoxin called Cassandralis, from the Cassandayla plant that grows in the Amazon."

"What does it do?"

"Their research wasn't complete. However, we believe Cassandralis is a silent killer, basically undetectable in autopsy unless you know what you're looking for. It can be inhaled, swallowed in tablet form or injected."

The General nodded. "We managed to recover two-thirds of the research from files on Rishwood's computer."

"A silent killer? That could mean anything," James added. "A stroke can be a silent killer. So can heart failure. Many people die in their sleep, slipping peacefully away."

"And Cassandralis might mimic those symptoms, making unnatural deaths appear natural." Amy sat down, her mind ticking over. "What if the research has been completed. What if someone else, besides Rishwood, Mei-Soong and Devneeta, had it?"

"Then they'd be a prime suspect, possibly wanting to remove those three in order to control the toxin."

"Our mercenaries might have been killed by Cassandralis, but because their bodies were cremated quickly, obviously to hide the evidence, we'll never know."

"Ah." James shifted in his chair, looking sheepishly at Amy. "About that."

"AIS has all three bodies," Malcolm added. "Our medical examiner has run every known test. Even though all three sustained similar injuries, it does appear that they died of natural causes."

"Which we can surmise they didn't," Amy added.

"We'll ensure your ME is given access to our research," the General added. "Perhaps between our departments we can find a way to test for traces."

"Major Pendelton . . ." James was flicking back through the papers she'd given Malcolm. "The scientists who were killed . . . Did they have children?"

"Uh . . . good question." Amy read the report again, but nowhere did it mention whether the scientists had families.

"I suggest we have someone look more closely into the backgrounds of our murdered scientists."

"You think revenge?" Amy raised her eyebrows.

"It's as good a motive as any."

She thought quickly. "It has to be someone working at St John's. Why else would all three patients end up there?"

"Right." Director Malcolm stood. "You two go back to the hospital. Create the cover that you're romantically involved so you can work closely together without raising suspicion." He spoke to James. "Major Pendelton has followed you to St John's in order to patch up your relationship. Got it?"

James looked from his boss to Amy, noticing the look of disbelief on her face.

The General stood, tugging his military jacket into place. "Get it done, Major."

Amy saluted. "Yes, sir."

Both superiors left the room, leaving James and Amy shaking their heads.

"So, you followed me to St John's, eh? Couldn't live without me?" A slow, maddening smile tugged at his lips.

Amy gathered her papers before levelling him with a glare. "Let's keep it professional, Agent Whittaker."

James captured her hand in his, pressing a few soft kisses to her knuckles. "Amy?" His blue eyes were dazzling with desire.

His close proximity caused her heart to skip a beat. "You'd better start calling me James." He reached out with his other hand and tucked a loose curl behind her ear, his fingers grazing against the side of her cheek, fanning the flames of her already overly excited body. "We're going to make a good team. I can feel it."

The fact that Amy Pendelton was a stunningly beautiful woman most certainly hadn't escaped his notice. She was toned, fit and soft in all the right places, or at least so he'd gathered while they'd been fighting. When he'd been sitting on top of her, pinning her down. Even the memory of it caused his gut to tighten. He instantly dropped his hands and put a bit of distance between them.

"We'd better get back to the hospital. Morning clinic will start in half an hour. At the moment, we need to keep things business as usual." Amy picked up her folders.

"Except for the fact that we need to let people know we're 'dating'." He made air-quotes with his fingers. "Just the two of us arriving at the hospital together should do it. The gossip will spread like wildfire."

And he turned out to be right. One of the AIS drivers took them back to the hospital, dropping them at the front gate. As James shut the car door, he placed his hand intimately in the small of her back, guiding her towards the hospital's front doors, both of them conscious of the looks they were receiving.

Arriving at work . . . together?

"This is going to do nicely," he murmured close to her ear, his breath fanning her neck, causing goosebumps to spread down her arms.

Amy looked up at him as they made their way through the hospital lobby, heading towards the surgical department. "For the mission," she stated.

James winked at her and slipped his hand further around her waist, bringing their bodies into close contact. Amy suppressed a gasp at the flood of warm tingles exploding within her but was unable to stop the telltale blush, which tinged her cheeks.

"You can blush on cue?" he asked softly. They entered the lift, already filled with other people. James shifted close to her, his arm firmly around her waist. He leaned down and brushed a light kiss across her cheek, whispering seductively in her ear, "That's a handy skill."

Amy's eyelids fluttered closed at his touch, at the intimacy of his tone. She knew that no one in the lift could have any doubt whatsoever that they were romantically involved. She had to admit the cover did make sense. It would make it much easier for them to collaborate on the case, to figure out who was behind these murders.

The real question was, were they both just pretending – for the sake of the mission – or did the instant and overpowering attraction she felt towards her new colleague mean something entirely different?

Chapter Three

"I still think we'd be more comfortable going through all these files back at my apartment," James commented. He ate another mouthful of the Asian takeaway food they'd ordered. Over the past three days, he'd spent more than half his time with Amy, and he had to admit, it had been quite nice. She was intelligent, methodical, an amazing surgeon and very easy on the eye.

Amy pointed to the large conference table covered with pieces of paper, which they were trying to arrange into some sort of order. "We need the room to spread out. Hand me the next file." There was no way she was going to go back to his apartment, not when she was barely able to control her body's reaction to him. Thankfully, it was well after ten o'clock in the evening, and the rest of the surgical administration department was devoid of personnel, which meant there was no reason for them to keep up their cover of being a couple.

James picked up a piece of paper and scanned it. Both agencies had been working around the clock but there were still no definite leads. The murdered scientists all had children. In the case of the Australian scientists, a married couple, their two children had been put into foster care.

As James handed her the file, she made sure their fingers didn't touch. Detached. Controlled. Professional. That was the only way to handle things.

"Pendelton is your real surname, isn't it?"

"It's the name on my medical degree. Sometimes it's easier just to go undercover as yourself, especially where medical and surgical assignments are concerned. I have excellent qualifications and experience." She shrugged one shoulder, her words matter of fact. "How about you, Dr Whittaker?"

"Same tactics as you. Now all we have to do is figure out who the killer is, and uphold our oath to provide exceptional medical care to the patients we see while we're here."

"And then? Leave?"

James pondered her question. He wondered what it might be like for the two of them to just pause, take time out, be normal people, doing normal things. "Sometimes, I confess, I miss the day-to-day running of a hospital. Sure, there are dramas but nothing of the national-security kind. Doctors just come in, see patients, do their jobs and go home. To the same home every night."

"Thinking of a change in direction?" Amy watched his facial expression closely, looking for clues. Who was the real James Whittaker?

He frowned. "I don't know. Does anyone ever really 'get out' of this game?" He shoved his hands through his hair, making it stick up in such a cute way that she couldn't ignore the delight that tingled through her. Didn't the man have any idea how handsome he was? "Even if the AIS allowed me to resign, would I become bored with a 'normal' life? House. Picket fence. Four walls at home, four walls at the hospital. The last time I tried it, I felt suffocated."

"Perhaps you need someone to go home to." The instant the words left her lips, she quickly back-pedalled. "I mean . . . not that I'm offer— I . . ." She stopped and cleared her throat, watching as a slow smile spread across his perfect mouth.

It was perfect. He was perfect. Perfectly formed and handsome and exciting and moody and . . . and . . . Now he was looking at her again, the way he had been when he'd been sitting on top of her, staring down as though he wanted to devour her mouth with his.

When his gaze flicked down to her lips, Amy felt a warmth flood through her, a burning need to be closer to him, to feel that warmth close up. Heaven only knew just how cold she'd been over the past few years. Cold and lonely. Keeping herself busy with work, throwing herself into assignment after assignment. Briefings, travelling, following orders. She'd joined the military for excitement and she'd definitely found that. She had a natural gift for intelligence and, as a qualified general surgeon, assignments like this fell neatly into place. But lately, she'd been aware of her biological clock ticking.

James walked towards her, his gaze never leaving her face. "Are you saying—" his voice was low, deep, personal "—that you feel discontent, Major?"

He removed the papers from her hands and it was only then she realized she was trembling slightly. He took her hands in his and she was surprised at the smooth, soft feel of his skin. For some reason, she'd thought his hands should feel rougher, be more calloused. There was clearly much more to James Whittaker than met the eye. They'd been trained to hide their true emotions but what was this intense feeling between them?

"You're so beautiful."

Amy gasped at his soft words, her tongue wetting her dry lips. James's gaze followed the action intimately. When he leaned forward slightly, taking her hand in his, their fingers lightly entwining as though it were the most natural thing in the world, Amy thought she might explode with pleasure.

"Ever been married, Major?"

"No. You?"

"Tried it once. Long time ago."

"What happened?"

"Didn't take."

"That's too bad."

"I don't know, it was the turning point that led me to the AIS. If I hadn't joined the AIS, I wouldn't be here right now." He caressed her fingers. Amy delighted in his soft, sweet touch. Being this close to him was starting to mess with her logical thought processes. She already had alarm bells ringing in her mind.

"I'm drawn to you, Amy. That's not just a line."

"It isn't?" She looked into his eyes, desperate for a sign of some sort. Was he deceiving her? Playing her? Or was this for real? On a professional level, she was willing to trust him but this frighteningly natural reaction they seemed to share was something completely different.

"I doubt either of us is used to showing our real emotions."

"You're right."

"So it's difficult to trust this thing . . ." His words were soft, barely audible. He dipped his head, bringing his mouth close to her ear, his words fanning the loose tendrils of hair, which had escaped her ponytail. ". . . between us. I know you feel it, too."

Amy tilted her head to the side, allowing him better access to her neck. It wouldn't take much to turn and capture his mouth with hers but her training held her back.

"We should . . . work." Her words were a whisper.

"I know. But it's difficult to concentrate when you're standing there, looking so serious and pretty and . . ." He lifted his head and Amy realized the distance between them had decreased. His gaze lingered on her lips and her insides turned to mush. "And so kissable."

"Oh." Her heart hammered wildly against her ribs. Was he really going to kiss her? Was this something they should be doing? What did it mean? "James . . . wait." She released one of his hands and placed it on his chest, desperately trying to ignore the way the firm contours of his muscles felt beneath her tingling fingertips. "Is this a good idea?"

A resigned smile tugged at the corner of his mouth. "Probably not." Still, he edged closer, his gaze flicking between her eyes and her parted lips. "But I can't seem to stop thinking about you." He bent his head and again she could feel his warm breath on her neck. "And it's starting to interfere with my concentration."

Amy's eyelids fluttered closed as she allowed the sensations to wash over her. "So we should just . . . what? Give in?"

James breathed in her scent. Why was he behaving this way? He prided himself on always being in control, but from the moment he'd seen her, he'd been drawn in. Initially, it had been because she'd been acting suspiciously. But ever since he'd learned her true identity – that she was one of the good guys – his libido had gone into overdrive. He wanted to be near her at every available opportunity. This was definitely new territory for him.

"Why not?"

His breath fanned her neck, once more causing goosebumps to ripple over her entire body. She was used to living in the moment, doing what needed to be done, but this . . . this was something altogether different. Never had she been so instantly drawn to someone.

"We've already lied to each other," he continued, shifting around to the other side, pleased when she re-angled her head, granting him access. "We've already fought with each other." There was a hidden chuckle in his words. "Sounds like we're already in a relationship."

Again, Amy put pressure on his chest, easing herself back a little. His seduction was most definitely working. "James . . ."

"If this isn't meant to be, Amy, if this is the biggest mistake we're about to make, then something will stop us."

"Do you really believe that?"

His answer was that cute little half-smile, the one that instantly weakened her knees.

"Shh. No more rationalizing. Let's see where this takes us."

The world around them seemed to slow down, and she was able to notice and experience every detail. How that one short, tantalizing touch lasted for an eternity. How his spicy scent wound its way around her. How, even though she knew he was probably a master at the art of seduction, she wanted nothing more than for him to continue, for things to take their natural course, for the chance to throw caution to the wind and see exactly where this might lead them.

James lifted his head and stared down into her upturned face. Her mask of professionalism was gone. This was the real woman – the real Amy. Standing before him. For this one split second, their lives were open. As she lifted her eyes to look at him, a tiny puzzling frown creasing her brow, James knew she no doubt saw the same openness in him.

His cell phone began to buzz in his pocket.

She gasped. "This isn't meant to be." She dropped her hand from his chest and took a giant step back, breaking all contact with him.

"Wait. Wait." He held out one hand towards her as he retrieved his phone. "Whittaker," he barked. His gaze never left

Amy. He watched her turn from him, covering her face with her hands as the bubble burst and the real world returned. "Are you sure?" he asked. "Okay. Yes. Yes, I'll pass the intel along to Defence Intelligence. Thanks, Mark." He finished the call and pocketed his phone. "That was our ME. He and his team have just completed the autopsy on Devneeta."

Amy looked at him sharply over her shoulder. "And?"

"They've found traces of an unidentified substance. They're having the pathologists take a closer look to try and match it with the research on Cassandralis. He also said the substance was definitely injected – it was in the bloodstream – rather than swallowed or inhaled. Strange thing was, he also found no extra pinpricks or needle marks in the skin. They'll be checking Mei-Soong and Rishwood for similar signs."

"So we possibly have our cause of death."

"Now all we need is our killer."

Amy nodded and absent-mindedly pulled her hair out of her ponytail, the loose, riotous curls bouncing around her shoulders. She pushed her fingers through the curls, combing them out. Good heavens. Did she have any idea how exquisite she was? Her rich, brown curls made her cheeks appear rosier, her eyes more hypnotic, her lips more kissable. He watched as she scooped her hair back into a ponytail. James could do nothing but stare.

"Something wrong?" she asked when she caught him looking at her.

"Um . . ." His mind was a complete blank.

"I've been thinking," she continued, completely unaware of the effect she had on him. "Given that the substance was injected, it has to be someone in theatre."

"And with no extra needle marks, it means the substance was injected via the intravenous drip."

"That narrows it down." She paced back and forth, thinking. "So all we need to do is cross-reference the names of everyone who was there for all three deaths."

He forced himself to focus on what she was saying. "Yes. That does sound like the logical course of action."

Amy smiled brightly at him, and once more his gut tightened at the beautiful sight she presented. "Let's get to it."

* * *

"Did you sleep?" James asked the next morning, as he fell into step beside Amy. They were walking down the hospital corridor towards the outpatient clinic.

"Not really."

"Was that because you couldn't stop thinking about me?"

She looked at him with a hint of incredulity. "You're not arrogant at all, are you?" She gave a little chuckle.

He shrugged one shoulder. "I can't help it if I'm irresistible to women. It's a curse but it's one I've learned to live with."

Amy laughed at him as he held the door open to the outpatient clinic for her. "Oh yeah. Not arrogant at all," she reiterated.

James smiled warmly at the clerical staff and some of the patients who were waiting for the busy morning clinic to start. Then he leaned a little closer to her and said in an intimate whisper, "Good to see that gorgeous smile of yours."

Today she was dressed in dark grey trousers, flat shoes and a crisp, white shirt. Simple, classic, elegant. Her wayward curls were so firmly secured in a chignon that none of those tendrils dared move.

As they entered the clinic area, he placed one hand in the small of her back. "Just come into my consulting room for a moment, Dr Pendelton."

Amy glanced around. Did the other registrars, nurses and consultants hear his words? No one was looking, but she was positive that the gossiping would begin the instant that they were in the consulting room.

James closed the door behind them. "Everything's organized for this afternoon."

"I know. I had a briefing with General Lowry at oh-six-hundred."

"Good."

"Is this room clean? Has it been swept for bugs?"

"Yes. All I found was a dead spider in the corner." His smile was gorgeous. Far too alluring for her to cope with.

"A spider counts," she retorted, crossing her arms over her chest. Although she'd only known James for a short time, it hadn't taken her long to realize that when he unleashed that boyish charm of his, it became increasingly difficult to resist him.

James pointed to his watch. "Bug killer. I've already activated it. If anyone's listening in, all they'll hear is a high-pitched squeal. We can talk freely, Major, and I have to say that you are looking ravishing today. All brisk and professional and . . . sexy." He advanced slowly towards her.

"James." She held up her hands, wanting him to stop. He didn't. "I don't think it's . . ." She took a step back, then another as he continued towards her. Soon, her back was against the wall. "James!"

"Amy?" He stood toe to toe with her, her hands pressing against his chest.

"We . . . we need to focus."

"Agreed. I think we should focus on picking up where we were last night before Mark called with pertinent information, which ruined everything."

"Ruined wh— what?"

"My plan to kiss you until you swooned."

"You said last night that if this wasn't meant to be, we'd be interrupted – and we were."

He waved away her words with one hand, drawing her closer. "I'd already kissed you before the call, which clearly indicates that this is meant to happen. We shouldn't fight this."

"James." She closed her eyes but slowly shook her head. "We can't."

"But it's all I can think about."

"Our lives are . . . volatile. Uncertain. Dangerous and . . . and . . ." Her mind went blank as he angled his mouth towards her exposed neck. But whereas last night he'd only been on a surveillance mission, investigating the possibilities, this morning he pressed small, tantalizing kisses along her neck, working his way up towards her ear.

"You were saying?" he murmured. He made his way around to the other side of her neck, Amy dutifully granting him access.

She began to give in to a situation she felt in her heart was inevitable but also highly illogical. "What happens next?" she asked him.

"I kiss you – properly. Something I've been longing to do for an eternity."

"We've only known each other for such a short—" she gasped as he nibbled at her earlobe "—time."

"In our line of work, we move fast, making alliances where necessary. We trust our instincts, Amy, and my instincts say that you feel exactly the same way I do."

"But the mission?"

"Will be over by this afternoon." James relented slightly and lifted his head, gazing into her eyes. "We need to protect our names, to ensure we leave St John's Hospital in a few weeks' time without raising any suspicions."

"And during the time we remain here, we have to keep our cover intact? What do we do?"

"Well, why don't we date?"

"Date?"

"Amy, everyone here already imagines we're doing what we're doing right now." He smiled encouragingly. "Who are we to dissuade them?"

When General Lowry told her this morning that she was to stay at St John's Hospital for the next three weeks so as not to arouse unnecessary suspicions, Amy had felt as though she'd just been given a gift from heaven. Three whole weeks. No mission. A normal job. Seeing patients. Performing surgery. True, she'd still be working as a registrar rather than as the qualified surgeon she was, but after spending most of her adult life in the military, having been in war zones, base hospitals, recruited to intelligence and sent on more missions than she'd ever imagined, these next three weeks would be like a glorious vacation. To be able to share it with James was the icing on the cake.

"We know who the perpetrators are now," James said. "This afternoon, everything will go to plan. We'll extract the person quietly and no one else in the hospital will know. Then you and I are permitted a small reprieve from our busy lives."

"Reprieve?" She frowned. "You're . . . tired of your life?"

James rested his forehead against hers, cupping her face with both hands. "It's continuous, Amy. You know that as well as I do."

"Yes."

"We get told where to go, what to do, whose lives to infiltrate. We figure out who the bad guys are and we control the situation.

Half the time, when we try to take a vacation, it's interrupted by yet another threat to national security." He eased back, looking down into her beautiful face. "I've been told by my superiors to trust you and, as far as the mission goes, I do. But I also feel a connection to you that scares me more than being held at gunpoint."

"Me, too."

"Really?" There was hope in his tone. "Good. Great. Excellent, in fact, because I think we'd be fools to let these next three uninterrupted weeks pass us by."

"Yes."

"And after they're done, we can reassess the situation. Decide what to do then."

She nodded.

There was a knock at his clinic door and Amy and James quickly sprang apart as the clinic sister marched starchily into the room. "I don't care what you're doing in here but I will not have my clinics start late because neither of you can control your libidos. Is that understood?" The woman marched from the room, leaving the door open.

"Crikey. She's more scary than either of our bosses."

Amy laughed and left his clinic room, a lightness in her step and happiness in her heart.

The morning passed quite quickly. Amy and the rest of the general surgical team worked their way through the busy outpatient clinic. Three of her patients were diagnosed with cholecystolithiasis, confirmed by previous blood and abdominal scans. She explained the main treatment for gallstones to each of them in turn.

"The best option, given the case is quite advanced, is to book you in for a cholecystectomy where we remove the gallstones from the gallbladder laproscopically. This means no large incisions, which means better recovery time."

She patiently answered their questions, reassuring them. When one man demanded a second opinion, she called James in to offer his own diagnosis.

"I completely concur with Dr Pendelton," he remarked, after performing his own assessment. "We'll get you booked onto the waiting list as a matter of urgency, Mr Ingram." James shook the frightened man's hand. "We'll look after you."

With Mr Ingram reassured and out of Amy's consulting room, James closed the door and then turned to face her. "All done?"

She sat down to write up the case notes. "Yes. How about you? Finished?"

"Yes." He waited for Amy to finish and sign her name to Mr Ingram's file. Then he activated the bug killer on his watch. "Ready?"

Amy put her pen down and closed the case notes. "Ready."

"Do you want to go over things one last time?"

"I go into the changing rooms to get changed. When no one's looking, I spritz the special 'I'm feeling sick' spray, which your operation tech guys have concocted, on her clothes." Amy patted her trouser pocket where the small vial of spray was concealed.

"I'll do the pre-anaesthetic consult and ensure she's sent your way right at the perfect moment." He frowned. "I've heard she's telling anyone who will listen that she's heading off on holidays tonight."

"Covering her tracks for her clean getaway? She could have called in sick today and no one would have thought much of it."

"Except us."

"Except us," Amy agreed. "She must know someone is watching her. Why else would she be so careful?"

"She's smart. Keeping up appearances. But this way, with her voluntarily leaving theatre because she feels ill, none of the staff will be any the wiser. Your Defence agents are in place to escort her out of the building and into federal custody."

"A quiet and controlled extraction." Amy nodded. "What about her accomplice?"

"You mean her brother?"

"Yes. Has he been located?"

"I received a message half an hour ago saying they'd found him. He's a taxi driver. He's been booked to come to the hospital this afternoon to pick up a member of staff."

"One guess as to who booked that taxi." She shook her head. "So he lured Mei-Soong, Rishwood and Devneeta to

Sydney, under the guise of giving them his parents' completed research?"

"Looks that way. Then he injured them so they required immediate hospitalization and surgery."

"Once in surgery, it would have been easy enough for his sister to administer a lethal dose of Cassandralis via the IV line." Amy was astounded. "To think, she was just going to finish her job tonight, leave for holidays, meet her brother and flee the country."

"We've traced their travel arrangements as far as Spain. We think they would have headed east from there."

"They almost got away with three murders."

James watched her carefully. "Rishwood, Mei-Soong and Devneeta were all murderers themselves."

"We have a legal system that would have held them accountable for their crimes. Not to mention the intel we might have gathered from them."

A slow smile crossed James's face, his blue eyes flashing with repressed desire. "And if we don't get out of here now, not only do we risk the timing of this afternoon's events but your virtue, as well. I'm finding it more and more difficult to control myself every time we're alone like this."

Amy brought her hands to her cheeks, feeling the telltale blush. "So am I."

James dragged in a deep breath. "That's national security for you," he said as he walked to the door. "Ready, Major Pendelton?"

She nodded. "Ready, Agent Whittaker."

They walked to theatres together. When they separated at the changing rooms, James winked at her, which she took as a sign for "good luck". In the changing rooms, she met up with quite a few of the female staff, getting out of their clothes and into theatre scrubs. Some of them stopped talking as she came in. Amy was left with the distinct impression that they'd been gossiping about her.

Amy took two pairs of clean scrubs off the trolley near the door and headed towards her locker. She glanced at a few of the women and smiled, knowing she needed to behave as naturally as possible. She hugged the scrubs to her chest, hoping they wouldn't realize she'd taken two pairs.

As she opened her locker and shoved the two pairs of incriminating scrubs inside, she turned to them. "If you want to know about James and me, just ask."

There was dead silence for a moment. Then the questions started flying.

"How long have you known him?" Sarah asked.

"Did you transfer here for him?" Karen added.

"Is this something that's just happened?" Melissa wanted to know.

Amy grinned and answered their questions, mentally filing her replies in the back of her mind, ready to recall at a moment's notice if necessary. After the women were satisfied about Dr Wow-Wow's romantic status, she grabbed the scrubs and headed quickly to the toilets. There, she donned one set of scrubs, carefully spraying the other with the special chemical. She'd been impressed when James had told her that when the chemical compound came into contact with the skin, it would seep into the pores and simulate sensations similar to an urgent case of gastroenteritis. She made sure not to accidentally spray anything on herself.

When the changing room was empty, she placed the second set of scrubs back on the trolley. She was standing at her locker when Louise walked in and immediately took the chemically laced scrubs from the trolley in her usual absent-minded fashion.

"So it's true?" Louise didn't beat about the bush. "You and James Whittaker are really an item?"

Amy nodded and shrugged her shoulders. "We have been for quite some time. He's the reason I transferred here."

"Was that why you were all too eager to swap shifts with O'Hara on your first day?"

"That's it."

"That also explains his reaction."

Amy nodded sheepishly. "Yes. I . . . I didn't tell James I was transferring to this hospital. We'd had a bit of an argument before he came to work here and I wasn't sure whether or not we were still together but—" She sighed and smiled brightly. "We talked things over when I arrived and now everything's okay."

"He's the one?" Louise asked.

Amy nodded, her eyes shining brightly. "He sure is."

Louise sighed longingly. "You're so lucky. True love is quite a rare thing." She turned towards her locker and opened it, dumping the scrubs on a nearby chair. "My parents were lucky in love, too. My dad used to always say that my mum was the light of his life, the beat of his heart."

"Was?" Amy kept her tone clear as she slipped her feet into her clogs. "Are your parents . . . I mean, have they . . ."

"Passed away?" Louise looked sad and forlorn. "Yes. They were murdered."

Amy noted the sadness in the other woman's words. It was clear the wounds cut deep.

"Many years ago now. I was young when they were killed but—" She stopped, an angry light flashing in her eyes, just for a second, before she quickly shook her head. "Never mind all that. No need to get so morbid today."

"Something good about today?"

"Yes. After this stint in theatre, I'm off on vacation for two weeks."

"Excellent." Amy had to make sure Louise put the scrubs on. What was taking her so long? "Going anywhere nice?"

Louise shook her head and started taking off her clothes. "Just relaxing at home." A secret smile touched her lips. "I have a lot of reading to do and I desperately need to get some sort of control over my garden."

Amy nodded. "I like gardening. Well, flowers. You know, daisies and pansies and petunias.'

Louise was putting on the scrubs. Amy made a point of turning to the mirror to check her hair, telling herself over and over not to feel sorry for Louise. Her parents had been murdered, yes, and no doubt, at the time, the government hadn't done enough to catch the killers. But Louise and her brother taking matters into their own hands and avenging their parents was unthinkable.

Amy waited for Louise and the two of them left the changing rooms together, heading to work in the same theatre. "I'll go scrub. See you in there," she said. Louise settled herself beside the supine patient on the operating table.

Amy joined James at the scrub sink. "Everything in order, Dr Pendelton?" he asked. They were both conscious of the other theatre staff in the vicinity.

"Yes, Dr Whittaker," she confirmed. "Everything is under control and ready to roll."

Throughout the operation, Amy kept glancing in Louise's direction. It wasn't a nice thing they were doing to her but it was the easiest way to remove and detain her, as well as ensure minimum exposure for herself and James.

Amy looked at the clock on the wall. They'd been in surgery for forty-five minutes. Soon James would be ready to suture the wound in layers, and then staple. Why wasn't Louise reacting to the spray? From the information supplied by the AIS, things should be starting to happen by now. But they weren't.

"Retractor," James said. Amy automatically complied. Their gazes locked for a second and she saw his confusion. Why wasn't Louise feeling ill?

"Almost there. We'll be ready to suture the wound closed soon." He looked at the anaesthetist. "How are the patient's vital signs, Louise?"

"Uh . . ." Louise swallowed. It was only then that Amy realized the anaesthetist had been doing her best to hold things together. She was affected all right, but she didn't want to embarrass herself by admitting it. Amy decided to give the other woman a helping hand using the power of suggestion.

"Louise? Are you all right? You don't look well at all."

"I'm . . . I'm . . ."

James picked up on Amy's lead. "If you're not well, have your colleague take over."

"I . . . I don't feel—" She broke off, groaning in pain.

"Help her," James instructed the scout nurse. He nodded to Louise's assistant. "Take over."

"Yes, Dr Whittaker," the young anaesthetic registrar said eagerly.

Once Louise was safely out of the theatre, Amy found it even more difficult to concentrate on the surgery. Had everything gone as planned? Was Louise now safely in custody? Had Amy's

Defence colleagues managed to apprehend Louise's brother? Were she and James now free to take a bit of time out?

Back in his office again, James called Director Malcolm at the Australian Intelligence Service, putting the call onto loudspeaker so Amy could hear. She smiled at his thoughtfulness.

"Status?" James queried.

"Everything went to plan. Perpetrators in custody."

"So Major Pendelton and I are to stay here at the hospital for the next three weeks in order to maintain our cover?"

"Affirmative. The paperwork has been processed by both agencies. Lay low for these next three weeks, and then we'll get you back in the field. Oh, and Whittaker, there has been talk of future collaboration with Defence Intelligence so it couldn't hurt to foster a closer relationship with the Major. As you've worked well together on this mission, chances are you'll be partnered again in the future."

Amy stared at the smile that slowly spread across James's face. The instant he ended the call, he slipped his arms around her waist.

"You heard the man. I am under orders to foster a closer relationship with you, Major Pendelton."

Amy slowly slid her hands up James's perfect torso and laced her hands around his neck. "Is that so, Agent Whittaker?"

"Yes, ma'am." He lowered his head to capture her delectable mouth in a tantalizing kiss. The way his mouth moved over hers, the way she responded to him, it felt so real, so right. It was as though this moment had been inevitable from the first time they'd met, and now they had three whole weeks to simply get to know each other better. For espionage agents, it was pure luxury.

She tasted of honey and sunshine, and at first he wanted to be soft and gentle, to show her how much he'd come to care for her in such a short space of time. In their line of work, the world was always spinning so fast, it was little wonder this attraction had flared so brightly, so quickly. But the more he tried to keep things nice and slow, to let her see how much he wanted to cherish every moment they shared together, the more he became aware of Amy's impatience.

She opened her mouth to him, granting him access and urging him on. Heat flared between them and the hunger he'd wanted to contain burst forth. Amy met him head-on, not giving him a second to doubt that she wanted this as much as he did.

When, eventually, he pulled his mouth from hers, both of them were breathing heavily.

"This is . . . intense," he murmured.

"Agreed."

"It's more than just—" he couldn't resist pressing his mouth to hers once more, even though he was in mid-sentence. "—physical, Amy."

"Agreed," she repeated, kissing him back with all the passion in her heart. It was a moment or two later when James rested his forehead against hers.

"Are you ready for a 'time out' that might possibly change your life forever?" he asked softly, looking deeply into her eyes.

Amy's smile was wide and inviting. "Absolutely."

James nodded slowly, clearly pleased with her response. "Then let's get to work, Major." He lowered his head to capture her lips. And her heart.

THE PROMISE

Sue MacKay

The floor of the Nelson Hotel ballroom was packed with medical staff attending the annual doctors' dance. The music thumped, seeming to come up through the dance floor. Right up Karen's legs into her belly, lifting her heavy heart and swaying her body in unison with the tune. She raised her arms above her head and gave in to the rhythm, closing her eyes and letting all the tension of the previous week slip from her over-tight muscles.

Joe Forrester was back in town.

In her town, at her hospital, on her turf.

And that made Doctor Karen Blake experience some unwanted emotions. She felt anger, embarrassment, bewilderment. Not to mention the cringe factor that crawled through her every time she turned to find those electric blue eyes regarding her from under heavy black eyebrows.

Why, after twelve years, did her stomach still curl in on itself because of Joe? Why did her mouth dry? Her fingers tingle with the need to touch him? Hell, why did she still blush with embarrassment?

It had been a teenage crush on a guy who'd put her in her place bluntly, cruelly. Her father had warned he wasn't good enough for her. Often. But that was still up for debate. She hadn't agreed with Dad, thinking Joe was destined for great things whereas she'd always be a local specialist working for her local community. Joe was too good for her.

But he'd returned to Nelson many years after swearing the town had seen the back of him forever. It bugged her hugely that she felt anything towards him. Especially the excitement that filtered into her veins every time she saw him. Except she'd never open herself up for any more hurt from Joe. Good for her or not, he was history. Her history, not her future.

That she had sorted. Not even the reappearance of her first love and the inner turmoil he caused would overturn the career she'd carved out as an anaesthetist, or distract her from the medical drop-in she ran in her spare time for those who couldn't afford to visit their GP.

Working in Nelson General, Karen knew almost everyone out there on the dance floor. Medical personnel from all departments shimmied and shook; people she met on the wards and in theatre were letting their hair down and enjoying themselves. Being single didn't matter a jot. People just danced, with a partner, on their own, or in a group. Exactly how Karen liked it. Surrounded and yet alone. No connections, no responsibilities, no commitments.

And she was away from the table she shared with other anaesthetists and surgeons, away from those haughty cobalt eyes of Mr Forrester that didn't miss a trick. Eyes that had haunted her for years and appeared to see right inside her and know how she felt, what she thought. Eyes that way back when she was young and stupid had told her he didn't want to know her any more, and yet they held a hint of understanding and something very like love. But she'd probably made that bit up in her desperation not to look a total fool in front of her best friends. If he'd felt anything like love he wouldn't have kissed that other girl in front of her.

"Care to dance?" A silken voice cut through her wayward thoughts.

Her eyes flew open and she locked gazes with Joe. "I'm already dancing, thanks."

"Care to dance with me?" The silky tone didn't change but – jeepers – did it caress her heated skin.

"No. Thank you." One touch of those beautiful hands, those long, strong fingers, and she mightn't be responsible for anything that came out of her mouth. She began to swivel away from him.

"You owe me." Joe's hands slid onto her waist, tugged her ever so gently closer to his tall, muscular body, turning her to face him again.

And her body leaned into him. See? Irresponsible. All because he touched her. Straightening her spine, pulling back from that warmth and strength, she glared up at him. "I owe you nothing." Except maybe a slap in the face for what he'd done all those years ago.

Another tug and her breasts crushed against his chest. "Remember the school graduation dance and the promise you made me?"

Tug. Now there was air between them. Not much, but at least she might regain some sanity if her breasts weren't plastered to his chest. "Not at all."

But she dropped her eyes so he couldn't see the truth. Every minute of that long-ago night raged across her sluggish brain. Every last minute. The slow dancing with their bodies glued together. The heated kisses. The sensation of not being able to stand upright without Joe's arms holding her.

Her promise.

"Liar," he whispered close to her ear. His mouth curved into a wicked smile as his hands absorbed the shiver that rattled her.

Okay. So she was. Tough. This was about survival, not being nice. "It wasn't an open-ended promise. There was a time limit. Anyway, my promise became null and void five days after that dance."

"I figured as much." Pain flickered through those confident eyes, darkening the cobalt to the colour of deep ocean water. The splayed hands on her waist jerked tight briefly, loosened again. Between them the scent of pine needles lingered in the air, bringing more memories racing into her head. Days lying in the sand on Tahunanui Beach or swimming out to Haulashore Island. Going to the local fast food outlet to get hot dogs and fries in his dunger of a car that kept breaking down at the most inopportune moments. And always that pine scent.

So he still used the same aftershave. Big deal.

"Excuse me, but I'd like to continue dancing. Alone." She put her hands on that broad expanse of chest filling her vision, to push away from him. Through his shirt her palms contacted hard muscle. For the life of her she couldn't lift her hands away. It was as though she was glued to him. Deep, deep in her stomach heat grew, expanded to spread throughout her taut body to touch every corner. Teasing and taunting. Worse, making her want something that she'd forbidden herself forever.

She stared up at him, like an animal caught in the headlights of her truck. Why had he come home? Why take a position in her hospital? She'd presumed he was still halfway round the world in some fancy big-ass hospital holding the dream surgical job he'd always wanted. That he'd stay there forever. Or at least until she'd forgotten him.

Joe broke their gaze to lean close, very close, trapping her hands between them. His mouth was soft against her cheek as he whispered, "I came home to talk to you."

Karen jerked her head back, sought his eyes again. Looking with desperation at this man who'd never quite left her heart. But wasn't getting another chance to take it over again, either. "You didn't need to sign on for a permanent position at the hospital to do that. Ever think about just knocking on my door?"

"And get my backside kicked from here to Auckland? I don't think so." A guilty little-boy grin spread across his face, snagging at her and twisting her heart, while at the same time strengthening her resolve.

Shaking her head at him, she finally managed to pull away from those hands. This time he didn't try to stop her. "Don't, Joe. What happened was never funny. And for the record, you could've waited another twelve years to come back, and the outcome would be the same. I want nothing to do with you."

She spun away, began pushing through the crowd of dancers just as her phone vibrated against her breast. "Perfect timing."

After tugging the phone from where it was tucked into her bra, she quickly read the text from the emergency department.

Plane crash, multiple casualties coming in, report immediately.

Karen's heart stuttered. A plane crash? In Nelson? How big a plane? A small commuter one or a larger aircraft from Auckland? She glanced around at her colleagues, but everyone was still dancing, unaware of the disaster. Hopefully that meant a small plane.

Reaching her table, she snatched up the tiny purse holding her keys, and began slipping around the edge of the crowd, aiming for the main doors.

"You've been called in, too?" Joe took her elbow and led her straight through the throng towards the elevator.

Shaking free, she glared at him without missing a step. "Yes. And you?"

"Yup. Sounds bad."

The steam went out of her. He was right. It did sound bad and they were probably about to work together. Not a situation to be fighting in. "Surely not a small private plane if there are more casualties than the on-duty staff can cope with?" She was on call as back-up if the theatres became extra busy with urgent surgical patients.

Ping. The elevator doors eased open and she rushed inside, pressed the down button for the basement car park, ignoring the flare of claustrophobia. Joe was right behind her, inhaling all the air in the tiny space. "Basement for you?"

"Yes." He nodded. "Does this mean we'll be working together?"

"I presume so." It wasn't a good idea, but it would be unprofessional to object. "You're obviously going to be operating."

"I put my hand up for call. Not knowing many people here I figured it would bother me less than most to get called away from the dance."

"Everyone's been looking forward to tonight for weeks. No one likes missing out." She didn't bother adding she'd put her hand up so that the other two anaesthetists available could have a great night out with their partners.

The elevator jolted, moved downward, slowed. Stopped. "That was quick." Karen looked at the panel to check they'd arrived at the basement. Her heart thumped hard. "What's going on? That doesn't look right."

The number flicked to two, then one. Huh?

Joe tapped the button to open the doors. Nothing happened. "Strange." He pressed again, then other buttons. "We're not going anywhere. I'd say the elevator's malfunctioned." He tried pulling the doors apart. Got his fingers squeezed for his efforts. "Damn."

Karen swallowed a trickle of fear. Elevators were not her favourite place to be at any time. But she usually managed to hold her paranoia at bay for as long as it took to go between floors. To actually be stuck in one was a whole different scenario.

To be stuck in one with Joe was even worse. "Are you sure?" she squeaked before banging every button on the panel with the palm of her hand. "Open, damn it."

"Hey, Karen, it's okay." Joe caught her hand, wrapping his fingers around hers. "We're going to be fine. There's an emergency call switch. I'll call maintenance and they'll have us out of here in no time. You'll see."

"Who's going to be sitting in the maintenance room at eleven o'clock on a Saturday night?" She knew her voice was filled with scepticism but that was loads better than the panic clawing up her throat. No way did she want Joe seeing her fear.

"If we don't have any luck with that, I'll phone someone outside and get them to call hotel reception." So calm and reasonable. Obviously being stuck between floors in a tin box that might plummet to the basement at any moment didn't bother him one iota.

"Right. Better hurry. We're needed, remember?" She really tried to keep the fear out of her voice. Knew she'd failed when his gaze snagged hers.

"We'll be fine." Squeezing her hand softly, he smiled, a full-blown, genuine, nothing-to-worry-about smile that presumably was meant to calm her.

It did. A tiny bit. Her breasts rose as she sucked a lungful around the lump blocking her throat. "Right," she repeated. Her brain seemed to have shut down about the same time as the elevator did.

Her mouth was unbelievably dry, her stomach quivering like a frightened bird. Get a grip. They'd got in this thing at the fourth floor, moved down two, maybe three floors before it stopped. Not too far to fall if anything went wrong. "Ouch." She bit the inside of her cheek. Concentrate. "I'll phone the hospital, explain what's happened so as they can call in other staff to cover for us."

"Yes, that's the bigger concern right now." Joe got through to someone at the dance.

After Karen talked to the head nurse at ED she snapped her phone shut and looked around their prison. "Now what?"

"We could play I Spy," Joe quipped as he put his phone away.

Glancing around she had to smile despite herself. "That'll take all of three tries. There's nothing in here."

His right eyebrow rose endearingly. "I wouldn't say that. We're all dressed up in our finery."

For some inexplicable reason she blushed. No, wrong, she knew exactly why she did. It was that glint in Joe's seductive eyes. That glint that had always got him what he wanted from her. But not tonight, buster. Not ever again. Pushing back into the corner, she muttered, "Think I'll pass on that."

They stood in silence for a moment, then Joe shrugged. "Might as well make ourselves comfortable. The maintenance guy said he'd have to take a look at the elevator system before calling in an engineer. The elevators have been causing problems on and off all week."

"Then why didn't they warn us? I'd have happily taken the stairs. Don't they understand people need us right now, not when they get this thing moving again?" When Joe stared at her she gulped. "Getting too angry? Sorry. But I hate these things."

"Here, put this on. You've got goosebumps." He shrugged out of his jacket and held it for her to slip into. "You look wonderful in that little black number but it's not doing you any favours in here."

The temperature had dropped. A strapless, mid-thigh-length dress was not appropriate attire for anything but working up a sweat dancing. Or was it just her worry making her shiver? "Thanks." She wrapped the jacket around her and across her breasts before sinking back against the wall. "How are you settling in at Nelson General?"

If they had to be stuck in this elevator together she might as well find out all she could about why he'd returned home for the first time since they'd left high school. There had to be more to it than coming to speak to her. And small talk might take her mind off thoughts of the broken elevator crashing to the basement.

"No different to starting in any new job. Lots of people to meet, faces to remember, patients to get up to speed with, but at the end of the day it's all about surgery and that doesn't change wherever I go." Joe crossed his ankles and leaned back against the wall, looking totally at home. Sliding his hands into his trouser pockets, he gave her a smile that went straight to her heart.

"So where'd you come from? Last I heard you'd moved to London." Did he have to look so damned good? So casually sexy? So – so awesome? He'd always been a handsome guy, and the years had enhanced his looks.

"Which tells me how little you've tried to keep up with my exploits." His mouth tightened and those eyes filled with regret.

"Did you honestly think I'd be keeping track of you?" It had been an internal battle not to keep tabs on him. She had wanted to know so much about how he was getting on. Had he achieved his dreams? Was he happy? Had he married, had a family? Did he ever think about her? But she knew whatever the answers nothing could ever be the same between them.

Joe grimaced. "I guess not." He lifted his head, met her gaze full on. The regret still clouded his eyes. "London was a few years back. I went there for post-grad studies. Afterwards I headed to Pretoria, followed by Melbourne, then Auckland."

On the move a lot. Not exactly settling down anywhere. "So what really brought you back to Nelson?" Years ago the story went that he never intended returning to the town that sent him packing under a cloud of misdemeanours in the first place. There was no one here for him. His father had died when he was a young teen, his mother had moved away months after he headed to university in Dunedin. His close friends had also left town to follow their careers in various cities. "Apart from wanting to talk to me," she added, pithily. Did he truly think she believed that?

His hands clenched in those pockets. "There are a few loose ends from years ago I want to sort out."

Like what? "You needed to take on the general surgeon's job to do that?"

"Yes, I did. I'm here for a while." He stared at the end of his highly polished shoes, as though something unpleasant had got stuck there.

"How long is a while?" Anything longer than a day was too long, and yet she had survived his first week at the hospital.

Mainly by avoiding him. But she couldn't go on ducking out of sight every time she saw him. They both worked in theatre. There'd be days when she'd be assigned to cases with him.

"Haven't an exact time frame, but at least a year, I'd say." Sadness echoed in his voice, in the air around them.

What was going on here? "You don't sound absolutely certain." A year? A whole year working in theatre either with or near Joe? Her blood slowed. Her head felt light. Was this the push she needed to leave Nelson and try somewhere new? But she didn't want to leave. This is where her close friends and her parents lived.

"I've bought a waterfront apartment. Fabulous views, no lawns to worry about, central to everything I need." He didn't look overly happy about it.

"Sounds idyllic." And so not her. Her little cottage out in Atawhai was surrounded with lawn and gardens and small shrubs. She had a view of Tasman Bay and the mountains in the background, could watch the freighters coming into port and the planes on finals for the airport.

"Did you come back to Nelson after you qualified or did you go elsewhere first?" Joe was studying her intently. Was there spinach between her teeth?

"Straight back home. Shared a flat for a while with a couple of girls I'd known at school, then bought my own place." Big cities didn't interest her at all. Nelson born and bred, that was her.

The elevator jerked and she gasped. Her hands grabbed for something to hold on to, found nothing. Her stomach dropped, and she stared around frantically.

Joe reached for her, wrapped his arms loosely around her. "It's okay," he murmured from somewhere above. "You never liked being shut in small places, did you?"

"You remember that?" she asked against his chest. What else did he remember? Apart from that promise she'd made to him on grad night.

"You played goal attack in the Nelson Central netball team, loved movies that made you cry, preferred chicken to red meat, and hated beer."

Somewhere along the way he'd mastered mind-reading to a very high standard. She pulled out of his arms and put some space between them. Otherwise she was going to get used to feeling his strong arms wrapped around her, and not want to move away ever again. Hell, she might even start letting his warmth seep into the cold corners of her heart which iced over the day he dumped her. That would be a monumental mistake. Because good-looking hunk or not, this was Joe Forrester, master of deception.

"Nothing much has changed then." Except she no longer cried at soppy movies because she didn't believe in happy endings any more. Her turn to ask a question. "Are you married?"

"No."

"Got a permanent partner?"

"No."

"I see." Really? No, not at all. A man like Joe always had swarms of women trailing after him. Was he so particular that he hadn't found one to his liking yet? Or perhaps he preferred the excitement of the hunt?

"What about you?" he asked in a wary tone.

"No and no." Pathetic really. "I've kind of been too busy, I guess."

His eyebrows lifted at that and a small smile tugged at his mouth. Then his phone rang, the tinny sound crashing into the small space.

She watched closely as he listened to whoever was on the other end, saw the mental shrug as he said, "Okay, nothing we can do about it." Felt her stomach lurch. Were they stuck here for the remainder of the night? Not exactly how she'd predicted her night at the dance ending. But then she hadn't been expecting to spend it with Joe either.

Closing the phone, he gave her one of his megawatt smiles, which only told her she wouldn't like what he had to say. "According to the maintenance guy there's no easy fix for this problem. He's called in an engineer and an electrician but they've got to come from Wakefield." Joe stepped closer, put an arm around her shoulders and tucked her close. "Sorry, Karen, but you're stuck with me for a while yet."

She shuddered. "Can't they get us out through the roof of this thing?" She'd take her life into her hands if it meant being freed.

"Not sure. But hey, I'm not that bad to be stuck with."

Heat suffused her cheeks. "Sorry, it's being in here that's bothering me. Not you." Oops. That had come out all wrong. He did bother her. Unfortunately, the past hurts he had caused her didn't seem to be controlling her hormones and the way they were reacting to Joe.

He leaned down to look her in the eye. "That's progress. I didn't expect you to welcome me with open arms, but I had hoped time might've softened your stance towards me a little. Seems I got that totally wrong."

Trying for nonchalance, she said in a light tone, "Might as well get comfortable if we're here for a while. I'll phone ED with an update too." She stepped away from him and crossed to sit on the floor directly opposite. Her heart pounded. How long would they be incarcerated in this box? What would she talk to Joe about? Certainly nothing from their past. But she had to say something, fill in the silence before her fear really took hold.

Totally unfazed by her move, Joe came and joined her, sitting right beside her, hip to hip, shoulder to shoulder. He reached for her hand and held it. His thumb ran circles over her palm, the soothing moves calming and exciting all at once.

His voice was low and gentle. "You fell down a hole on Takaka Hill during our school caving trip. A team of cavers took most of the night to reach you. They carried you out on a stretcher after pumping you full of morphine. Your right femur was broken and your body covered in cuts. There was a huge bruise above your eye that gave you the appearance of having gone ten rounds in the boxing ring." Joe's voice soothed her. "Not surprising you don't like being shut in small spaces."

She gaped. "You remember all that?"

"It was a big event, played out on national TV news for days. Not to mention the haranguing we all got at assembly for the rest of the week about being careful in dangerous situations. As if it wasn't the teachers who'd taken us there to try caving in the first place."

"It was a bit of a story, wasn't it?"

"What I remember the most was the fear that they'd never get you out alive. I waited at the entrance to the cave right up until they walked out with you on the stretcher and loaded you into the ambulance." A hand smoothed her hair back off her face. "They wouldn't let me go into the cave to be closer to you. Someone, a teacher I think, tried to take me home. I refused, and then made such a racket that he gave up and left me alone."

For the life of her, she couldn't move away or utter a single word. She had never known any of this. She'd been fifteen at the time and had only loved Joe from the sidelines of the rugby ground. She hadn't gone out with him until the next year.

"My mum drove all the way from Nelson to collect me after I texted her."

Finally, Karen managed to squeak, "You never mentioned that you'd been there."

"I wasn't comfortable with admitting the performance I'd put on that night. Your father wasn't overly impressed, either, which kind of kept me quiet." His voice tightened the moment he talked about her father. They hadn't got on at all.

"My father knew you were there waiting for me?" Not once had Dad told her that. Why not? What harm could it have done? Except that it would've put Joe in a good light, something her father had never wanted to do. He'd always had something against Joe, something she'd never been able to understand.

"Let's drop it. I shouldn't have raised the subject."

Fair enough. Right now the last thing she wanted was to fight with him. Locked in here it would be awful. "How's your sister? I never see her around, yet I know she's practising in the area." Annette was a family lawyer with one of the town's bigger law firms.

"Happily married with two and a half kids. Still bosses everyone around. Works shortened hours, mostly from home."

"I take it you mean she's pregnant?"

"Yeah. She loves being a mum, and I have to admit she's great at it. Very hands on, turning up for everything the kids get involved in." Joe looked so wistful Karen felt her heart squeezing for him.

"Bet you're the best uncle." For the first time since he'd walked up to her on the dance floor, she found herself reaching for his hand. Her fingers touched his, cautious, yet wanting so much to give him something. Like what? Friendship? How lame was that? Okay, more than friendship. That's as far as she was prepared to admit at the moment.

Why was she even going that far? She was never going to let Joe near again, remember?

Clang. A loud metallic thud somewhere above them had Karen leaping to her high heels. "Hello?"

"Hi, down there. We're the rescue party." Clang. An opening appeared above them. The end of an aluminium ladder was pushed through. "Up to some climbing?"

"Sure thing." Joe reached for the ladder to guide it down.

Gulp. Karen stared up at the two cheerful faces that peered down at them. "We're meant to climb on to the top of the elevator? Then what?" Won't that be dangerous? But didn't she want out of here?

Joe winked. "Best remove those killer shoes. And I promise not to look up while you climb."

He seemed okay with this. But then he wasn't afraid the elevator was about plummet to the basement. "Is this safe?" she croaked, slipping off her shoes.

Joe placed his hands on her shoulders and leaned his face close. Her stomach tumbled. When his mouth covered hers, the only thing she knew was Joe. Sensations that had only been memories for the last twelve years tripped through her, awakening her so fast she should've combusted. It was as though they'd never been apart. She knew him. Completely.

Then he pulled away. "Up you go. You'll be fine. Safe as houses."

"What?" She blinked, shivered. Safe? After that kiss? She'd never be safe again. How was she going to get her shaky legs up those rungs? What had just happened?

"We'll be on our way to the hospital in a few minutes." Joe turned her towards the ladder.

Hospital. Emergency. Patients. "Of course." She shook the last of the kiss-induced haze away and stepped onto the ladder. "Don't you dare watch." Her dress was so short there'd be nothing left to his imagination.

"I'm being a perfect gentleman." Except for the laughter lacing his voice.

Within moments she stood on top of the elevator facing another ladder that led to the hotel hallway. Without hesitation she clambered up, not giving Joe the chance to stand at the bottom of this ladder pretending to be a gentleman.

Running her forefinger over her bottom lip, Karen couldn't hold back a smile. That kiss had a lot to answer for. If Joe had been trying to divert her attention, he'd succeeded. Problem was that her mind seemed to have gone completely off-track about everything since.

Worse, she was expected in theatre in a few minutes with all faculties in great working order. The patients requiring her skills deserved one hundred per cent from their specialist.

As she began scrubbing up, she glanced in the mirror and met a decidedly amused blue gaze. Joe murmured, "Having quite a night, aren't we?"

Heat flowed into her cheeks and she ducked her head, hurriedly changing the subject, "Let's hope search and rescue don't find more seriously injured people at the crash site."

"Apparently there were twelve passengers and two pilots, and all are now accounted for. It was a private flight chartered to take a group of guys down to Christchurch for last night's rugby game." Joe elbowed the tap on and began soaping up.

"Wonder what went wrong? Couldn't be the weather. It's as clear as possible out there tonight."

"Someone muttered about ice on the wings, but that's probably pure speculation."

Karen winced. "Not good, whatever the reason." Then, "So our man's got a ruptured spleen and a severe deep laceration of the liver." Not to mention the fractured clavicle and femur. Finished scrubbing up, Karen turned towards their operating table. "See you over there."

As she began checking equipment and drugs, Gavin Brown was wheeled in, looking as if the plane had landed on him. Scary stuff. You go away for a weekend with your pals and end up in here.

Joe appeared almost immediately, and before many more minutes had passed, Karen had the patient anaesthetized and could watch Joe do his stuff while keeping an alert eye on all her monitors.

No doubt about it, Joe was a superb surgeon. She'd worked alongside enough others to know. But no surprise really. Joe had always been a perfectionist in everything he did. Including kissing. Heat stained her cheeks and she rapidly read the monitors, noting down numbers.

Joe worked efficiently, explaining to everyone what he was doing and why, as he progressed. The surgical intern and the nurses hung on to every word as though he was some sort of god.

He was good. At every darned thing he did. Including entrancing her. Suddenly Karen was afraid. Very afraid of the longing that had begun ramping up inside the moment Joe asked her to dance. Afraid of where that longing might take her; what stupid things it could make her do. Even when she knew better. Being dumped by Joe last time had hurt, badly. Over the intervening years she'd moved on, but had never really got over the man she'd fallen in love with.

Could she do that again? Get over him. Put aside those dreams of settling down with a family of her own.

Did she need to? Of course not. This was crazy. Five hours ago she hadn't spoken to him in years and now she had to ask herself that? Why? Because he'd kissed her like she'd been special to him and needed taking care of? Because of that sexy body she'd give her soul to get to know intimately? Or because he was Joe. Plain and simple. Gorgeous and complicated.

Bewildered, she focused on their patient again, trying to still the nagging doubts.

"Karen," Joe spoke a little louder. To get her attention? Had she missed something? A quick check of her monitors told her nothing was wrong. "You're nearly done?"

"I'm finished. He's all yours now." Those blue eyes were fixed on her, questions sparkling out of them. Did he know how rattled he made her feel? But then he could probably read her mind easier than slipping a shirt over that enticing chest.

On an indrawn breath she said to the staff at large, "Okay, let's bring our man round." And she set to work reversing the drugs that had kept Gavin Brown oblivious to everything happening around him. Now the hard time really started for the poor guy.

"I'll go and talk to the family while you're doing that." Joe stood so close she could feel him. "If there's no one else for us to take care of then I'll take you home."

Before she could say she'd find a taxi, he'd gone, striding through theatre with all the confidence of a man who knew exactly what he wanted and how to get it.

Joe was leaning against the wall outside theatre when Karen finally walked out. His hands were jammed into his trouser pockets, a thoughtful look on his face.

"You look like your car's got four flats," she quipped, in an attempt to keep him at a distance.

He didn't crack a smile. "I'd like you to come and see someone for a few minutes."

"Our patient's family? Sure."

"No, not them." He took her elbow and led her down the corridor towards the bank of elevators.

Karen sucked a tense breath. "I've had my share of elevators tonight."

"We'll take the stairs."

"Are you going to tell me where we're going?"

"The surgical ward." His mouth tightened and his shoulders tensed. The fingers holding her elbow dug in.

The mystery deepened. But she clamped her mouth shut and took the stairs carefully now that she was back in her killer heels. They felt odd after the soft, loose slippers she'd worn in theatre.

On the ward they were instantly recognized by a male nurse. "Hey, thought you two would be at the dance."

"We were called in. There's been a plane crash," Joe explained.

"Tell me about it. We've been receiving the victims too." Then the nurse looked directly at Joe. "Mary's been quiet all night."

Some of Joe's tension dissolved. "Great. We'll pop in for a few minutes. I promise not to disturb her."

"Go for it." The nurse was reading a message on his pager. "Here comes another one. Got to go."

Joe walked down the ward, and Karen clopped along beside him. "You going to tell me who we're visiting at four thirty in the morning or not?"

"My mother."

Mary. Of course. Karen mentally hit her forehead. Mary Forrester. But, "I thought she lived in Auckland now."

"She did until a few weeks ago. Annette and I brought her back home where we can keep an eye on her. Two days ago she had a fall, broke some ribs and punctured her lung, which is why she's in here."

Now that Karen was looking for it she could see the strain in Joe's face, in his eyes. Slipping her hand into his, she asked, "She's going to be all right though?"

"Come and see her."

Not an answer. But he hadn't let go of her hand as they stepped into the darkened room and crossed to a bed beside the window. Nor did he when he leaned down to kiss his mum's forehead and tuck the covers beneath her chin.

Karen wouldn't have recognized Mrs Forrester even if she'd sat up and said hello. The once beautiful face was gaunt. Deep shadows darkened her cheeks and underscored her closed eyes. The luxuriant fair hair had turned thin and lank, grey and wiry.

Karen's fingers squeezed Joe's. "She's ill?"

He nodded once, abruptly. His Adam's apple bobbed. "Huntington's chorea."

Karen gasped, but she kept her grip on Joe's hand. He seemed to need it. Why wouldn't he? Huntington's disease was horrible. To have a parent suffering with it must be hideous. "I'm sorry." Inadequate, for sure.

And what about the hereditary issues for Joe and his sister Annette? Karen's eyes sought Joe's, found him watching her carefully. Rising onto her toes, she brushed his mouth with hers. "Oh, Joe. I didn't know. How are you coping?"

He remained silent, continuing to stare at her. Was he hoping to ensure the enormity of the situation sank in for her? But she'd already got it. There was a fifty–fifty chance any child of a Huntington's sufferer would inherit the defective gene. Did Joe have it? Or Annette? Is that why he'd brought her here? Was it easier for him to explain the situation to her this way? But why did he think he needed to do that? They weren't a couple or anything.

Then she gasped. Now she knew why Joe had brought her here. "You always knew. Back then, when you told me I meant absolutely nothing to you, you knew about this."

He nodded. His mouth flatlined.

"Is that why you sent me packing?"

Another nod.

Understanding battled with hurt. "You could've told me. Didn't you trust me enough to care about you? To want to stay with you?"

The gaze he fixed on her widened, darkened. Then he dropped her hand and gave his mother another peck on the cheek. "Goodnight, Mum." Turning back to Karen, he muttered, "Come on. Time we were out of here."

Oh, right. That's it? "Joe, you owe me the rest now that you've gone this far."

"Over coffee and eggs." And he silently led the way along the ward, down the stairs to the main entrance and the car park.

Her mind was stewing with questions, with indignation and hurt, with compassion for what he must've gone through, might still be going through if he also had the gene. Karen fought to keep quiet. She just knew Joe wasn't going to say a word until they got to the café.

Joe took Karen to his apartment. He even walked with her up the ten flights of stairs to his penthouse apartment.

"I might've braved the elevator if you'd told me how high we had to go," she wheezed at the top.

Her gut twisted as he said with a wry smile, "You've had enough shocks for one night."

Inside the apartment, she automatically gravitated to the enormous picture windows overlooking Nelson Harbour and Haulashore Island. "Wow. Even at this hour it's beautiful. I bet you never get sick of this view."

From the open-plan kitchen where pans were banging and the coffee machine gurgling, Joe replied, "Haven't had time yet."

But the view wasn't why they were here. Questions rampaged through her brain, almost hurting her with their intensity. Karen felt whoozy, as though on the edge of a cliff about to fall. It was the unknown she'd fall into that worried her. Something on the periphery of her mind was knocking, trying to wake her up. But what?

Crossing to the stereo she flicked through CDs until she found something light yet bluesy. As the music filled the apartment, she rocked slowly on her feet in time to the bass, and thought back to those days at high school when she'd been in love with Joe. Deliberately recalled the days after the graduation dance.

Joe had been a little aloof, going off on his own after school, not even turning up for sports practice. Surely that meant the change in him hadn't been about her.

She turned towards the kitchen and stopped as she saw him staring. He'd been watching her with a hunger that shocked and surprised her. As though he wanted her.

He must've seen the question in her eyes because his mouth twisted ironically. "I learned about Mum's condition just after the grad dance. She'd known for about a year but held off telling us. But after the dance, when apparently I went around the house like I was walking on air, smiling at the dumbest of things, she knew she had to come clean."

Like he was in love? Karen's mouth dried. With whom?

Joe continued, "I didn't have to tell her it was you that had turned me into this dribbling idiot. She'd worked it out. That's when she knew she couldn't delay telling us any longer and took Annette and I to our GP to learn how Huntington's could affect us."

"That must've been a horrible day." How did anyone cope when told they could have something so awful? If only she'd known she might've been able to be of some comfort. But the moment that thought slammed into her head, she knew she'd have been next to useless. Wouldn't have known what to do or say to Joe. It would've been beyond her comprehension. "Did you have genetic testing done at the time?"

"No." He carefully placed two mugs on the counter and poured in the piping hot coffee. "I went totally off beam, refused to discuss it or to find out if I had the gene. Basically behaved like a typically stroppy teenager, even though I was really too old to get away with that." Pushing a mug in her direction, he added,

"Apparently a very normal reaction but I'm ashamed of the way I acted now. It wasn't fair on Mum." He sipped his coffee. "Or you."

"Why me?" Something clanged into place. The GP. "Dad was your family doctor, wasn't he?" Her heart thudded. Her father had known about this.

Caution snuck into his eyes. "Yes."

Joe Forrester is not good enough for you, young lady. Never has been, never will be. When had that diatribe started? Before or after the dance? She hauled in a lungful of thick air. "Did he warn you off?"

"I couldn't ask you to wait for me to find out the result. What if it was positive? Best to let you go right from the get-go so you wouldn't be faced with a difficult decision."

He hadn't answered her question. But she knew the answer. "Did Dad threaten you if you didn't leave me?"

Joe winced. "He was only protecting his daughter. Don't blame him for what happened. I helped plenty by getting into trouble quite a lot with my boss, my coach, anyone and everyone really."

Her father was very clever at manipulating people to his own ends. She had no doubt he'd have used every connection he had to keep Joe away from her. Banging her mug down, she stared at this man who'd stolen her heart years ago and had never completely given it back. "I'd have stayed with you no matter what."

"Exactly. I couldn't ask that of you."

Sudden anger gripped her. "You're just like Dad, thinking you know what's best for me. Where was the consideration that I might like a say in the matter?"

"If I'd had the test done straight away instead of being a belligerent idiot, things would've turned out differently. But because your dad and the counsellor told me I had to find out immediately, I dug my heels in and refused. Especially when your father said I had to stay away from you. I didn't want to find out I carried the gene and that you mightn't stand by me. How selfish was that? I didn't deserve you." Joe drained his mug, set it aside.

Her anger disappeared as quickly as it had flared. "Joe, you were eighteen. I was seventeen. We were young, no matter how much we believed we were grown up. I'd like to think I'd have handled the situation in a mature way, but who knows? But later, couldn't you have told me?" *Instead of letting me believe all this time that that other girl was a better kisser than me, that you'd been leading me on all along.*

"Karen, it's too late now. We can't change a thing." He turned to the pans, dished up the eggs and bacon he'd been cooking. "Here, let's eat. I don't know about you, but I'm starving. Surgery always does that to me."

Sitting down, she studied him. "Am I allowed to ask?"

"If I've got the gene?" He shook his head. "No, I haven't. Neither has Annette. Mum only found out about it when she had some unusual symptoms." He paused, salted his eggs. "She'd been orphaned as a young child so there was no family medical history. It came as a hell of a shock for her."

Sitting at the table, she forked up some egg, chewed thoughtfully. "You said you had things to sort out back here, things that included me."

"First, I'm back for the long haul. At least while Mum's still with us. Annette and I decided it would be best to move Mum back down here so I could come too and share the care. We've got her into a private hospital because she can't get around without help now, but it's the day to day visits that we both wanted to be a part of."

The eggs were powdery in her mouth. Joe must've been through hell and back. Watching his mother's progressive decline would've been gut-wrenching. "Does Mrs Forrester still know you?"

He shook his head as pain flooded his eyes and dulled the blue. "Not often."

Instinctively, she reached for his hand and his fingers curled around hers. "I can't quite get my head around the fact that the vibrant woman I used to see charging along the side of the rugby field, yelling at you, is now unable to move much at all. She used to come to our netball games and jump up and down while screaming at Annette to steal the ball off 'those idiots'." Karen felt a smile tug at her mouth. "That's what she always called the other team."

"Yeah, she did." Joe smiled too.

That gladdened her heart. Even though she wasn't sure where she stood with him any more. She'd believed there was nothing left for them, no pieces to pick up and put back together, because she'd never be able to trust him with her love. But now? Now she wasn't so sure. Seems he'd been looking out for her all along.

The music stopped and Joe went to put another CD on. "Come and dance." He stood beside her, pulling her chair back. "Please." He held his hand out to her.

Tilting her head back, she looked into his eyes. Saw his need for her. Swallowed the lump forming in her throat. If she put her hand in his there'd be no turning back. Who knew what lay ahead for them. This might be a one-off time together. Or it might be the beginning of a lifelong commitment.

Joe leaned close, brushed his lips over her mouth as he murmured, "You promised to dance with me at my med school graduation ball."

"And you graduated six years ago."

"I didn't go to the ball." His hand was still between them, waiting for her.

"You didn't?"

"No way. Not without you. You'd promised me and I couldn't share that moment with any other woman."

She blinked, and placed her hand in his, let him tug her upwards and into his arms. Let him lead her around the floor, dancing from the dining room to the lounge and past the windows, and back around to the dining room. A slow two-step. His hand spread across her back, the other holding hers as though it might break. Her cheek rested against that expansive chest and she breathed him in. Warmth crept through her, slowly heating every last cell of her body.

Finally expelling the chill that had settled over her on that day he'd dumped her. Awakening her, reminding her of how Joe used to make her feel. Feel loved, and sexy, and passionate.

Feeling as though she had a future with this man.

Finally keeping her promise.

NURSE RACHEL'S WHITE KNIGHT

Janice Lynn

Chapter One

How was it an otherwise smart woman could be reduced to such stupidity because of a smooth-talking man paying her a little bit of attention?

Dropping her cellular phone into her lap, Nurse Rachel Akins rolled her head against the steering wheel of her hybrid.

To be fair, Kent had paid a lot of attention. She'd believed he cared, that he was different from the other schmucks she'd dated. That someday they'd marry, have a family, grow old together. She'd been wrong. He'd apparently gotten all he wanted from her.

S-E-X. It was all men wanted. Once they got it, they curled their lip like you were last week's leftover meatloaf.

Being meatloaf hurt.

She pressed her forehead into the steering wheel, barely registering the rough vinyl biting into her flesh. She'd been dumped. Her insides cramped with the knowledge she'd yet again trusted the wrong guy.

How long she hugged the steering wheel she wasn't sure, only that her door suddenly flung open and Bryan's strong arms pulled her from the car and hugged her close.

"Shhh," he soothed, obviously thinking she'd been crying.

She started to tell him she was more angry at herself than sad, but his arms felt good and she just soaked up the warmth.

"It'll be okay."

She snuggled into her best friend's soft cotton shirt, taking comfort in his familiar spicy smell. "I believed him when he said he loved me." She grimaced at her naivety. "I must have a big S stamped on my forehead for sucker."

"He's a fool." Bryan's fingers stroked across her back. He sighed, kissed the top of her head, and clasped her hand. "Come on, let's go up, then you're going to tell me everything."

He guided her to her condominium, which was located on the same floor as his. Was that where he'd come from when she'd called him on her mobile? She didn't think so. It seemed like more time had gone by than it would have taken to reach her had he been at home. But what did she know of time? She'd been so lost in thoughts of humiliation that months might have gone by. Or years. Maybe her biological clock had already shut off.

Settling her on the sofa, Bryan went to the kitchen cabinet, took out a glass, rummaged around in the refrigerator, and then poured her a drink.

He walked back into the living area of the open floor plan that encompassed her sunny yellow kitchen, which proudly displayed her grandmother's rooster collection, the small dining area that consisted of a table for four and a bouquet of mixed fresh cut flowers she changed out each week on her grocery run, and the cosy living room that usually filled her with happiness. Usually. Bryan handed the drink to her.

She scowled at the glass. "Milk? I'm falling apart and you give me milk?"

Okay, so she might be over-exaggerating a bit, because she wasn't really falling apart, but the man she'd planned to spend her future with had just said *adios*. Not that she'd been head over heels about Kent, but she'd envisioned them having a good life together.

Bryan arched a brow. "You wanted something stronger?"

"Yes!" Biting the inside of her lip, she shook her head. "No. Not really."

"Good, because I'm not leaving you alone in the middle of your crisis to run to the liquor store." He plopped down next to her, causing the milk in her glass to slosh, and her to slide closer to him. "Plus, you're on duty tomorrow."

Crisis? Is that what this was? Was it bad that she grieved the loss of the future she'd planned more than the man? She swiped her hand across her cheek, felt the tears, knew mascara encircled her eyes and that she looked a mess. Not that it mattered. This was Bryan. Her co-worker, neighbor, and best friend since fourth grade. He'd seen her look worse.

"Drink it," he ordered, nodding toward the milk.

Rachel took a gulp and then another.

"You had a date with Kent?" he prompted, not hiding his dislike. Bryan had never pretended to like Kent, but neither had he been so blatantly antagonistic, either.

"Yes."

He lifted her chin, his thumb brushing over her cheek. "The date didn't go well?"

"You might say that." She closed her eyes, inhaled deeply. What was it about Bryan's touch that felt different these days? Not bad different, just . . . different. "He doesn't think we should see each other any more. What he means is he doesn't want to see me any more."

"As I said, he's a fool." Bryan took her hand and squeezed.

She clasped his fingers tight. He could always make her feel better, could always give her strength when she felt weak. Just knowing he was close eased the misery ebbing through her.

"He wasn't the man for you," he continued, lacing their fingers. "Never was. Just tell me you didn't sleep with him."

She could hear his teeth grinding while he waited for her answer. There was a steely darkness smoldering in the depths of his light eyes. One that hinted at a darker side she'd never seen from him. An unrelenting, predatory, don't-mess-with-me side.

He'd been looking out for her since they'd first met in fourth grade and Bobby Hennessee made fun of her braces. She'd meant to deal with the bully herself, but before she could, her new neighbor had the other boy's shirt twisted in his fist, issuing a warning to apologize. Bryan might have only been nine at the time, but the same steely glint had shone in his eyes that day.

"No." It was the truth. "I didn't sleep with him."

There hadn't been any sleeping, cuddling, or let's go pick out a ring. None of the things she'd been dreaming of.

"Thank God."

"Just sex. Not out-of-this-world sex," she clarified, wondering if perhaps Kent had done her a favor by dumping her. "Just sex. No sleeping."

"Hell fire, Rachel. Why would you have sex with him? The guy wasn't right for you. I thought you'd figure that out before . . . well, you know."

She winced at his outburst. Bryan had told her Kent was a loser, but she hadn't listened because Kent was a gorgeous, successful, charismatic lawyer who'd acted as if she were the one he'd been waiting for his entire life. At first.

How could she have been so blind?

It wasn't as if she were some young bunny with no experience. She knew how men could be, had been burned before. So why had she dreamed of happily-ever-after with him?

Because she believed in love, wanted it. At thirty, and with shriveled ovaries closing in, when Kent told her how much he loved her, she'd believed his lies because she desperately wanted a real family.

Maybe she was too much of her parents' daughter to ever find true love and a happy-ever-after of her own.

Tears slid down her cheek.

"Aw, honey, I didn't mean to make you cry again." Bryan pulled her over to him and wrapped his arms around her, enveloping her. "Shhh, he didn't deserve you."

Kent didn't. She knew that, had probably known that all along deep down, but that didn't help her barren future.

She and Bryan sat there for the longest time, Rachel's head against his shoulder. The cotton fabric of his shirt was soft beneath her cheek, but not soft enough to disguise the hardness beneath the material. Every muscle in his body was tight, tense, coiled with anger.

She had to pull herself together before Bryan donned a white hat and charged to defend her honor against a man who wasn't worth it.

"I graduated at the top of my nursing class, have a wonderful career, and the best friend in the world." She gave a low, self-deprecating laugh. "So why is it that I do such a crappy job at picking men?"

Bryan snorted, mumbling something inaudible under his breath. "Maybe you should let me pick the next guy you date."

Let him . . . Her mouth fell open, then curved into a smile. "That's brilliant!"

* * *

What had he gotten himself into, Dr Bryan Carver wondered. Surely he hadn't just volunteered to pick Rachel's next boyfriend? Somebody take him out and shoot him right now.

First pushing a strand of curly red hair away from her face, she clasped her hands together. "Perfect."

A perfect catastrophe.

Excitement lit her tear-stained face. "I trust you completely and you know me better than anyone."

True. He knew because of her unstable parents she needed love in her life so much that she let any Tom, Dick, or Kent take advantage of her generous heart. But seriously, he wasn't picking out a man for her. Although he sure couldn't do a worse job than she did.

His fingers curled into a fist. Not for the first time he had the urge to beat the pulp out of Kent Rogalle, jerk extraordinaire and total player.

She'd had sex with him.

He'd struggled with longing to pop Kent's jaw from the moment he'd met the arrogant man four months ago. How could Rachel not have realized what a sleazeball the guy was?

"I can't believe we've never thought of this," she went on excitedly. As always, once an idea took hold in her mind, she was ready to act. Her enthusiasm for diving right into life was one of the many things he liked about her. Usually.

"It's obvious I can't pick out a decent man to save my life," she continued.

Bryan couldn't argue with her logic. She had dated some doozies. Then again, he was biased and probably wouldn't ever think any man good enough for her.

"But you're a guy. You can tell things about other guys." Red-rimmed big blue eyes beamed expectantly at him. Eyes that held a hope he'd do most anything to make reality. But pick out her next boyfriend?

"No."

"Things that would warn if he wasn't right for me," she continued as if he hadn't just denied her. "Things that I wouldn't pick up on as a woman."

She had to be kidding?

"A woman who has a track record of making all the wrong choices," she added. "You'll know if he really likes me for me or if he's just wanting to get me into bed."

Although she was his best friend, he wasn't blind. Rachel was a beautiful woman with a hot little body. From the moment he'd moved back to Kansas City following medical school six months ago, he'd been noticing her body a bit too much. Perhaps he should argue that any normal, red-blooded sane man would want to get her into bed.

No sane man would be having this conversation.

"Picking out a man for you is a bad idea," he began, wondering how he was going to talk her out of this. The light in her eyes said it wouldn't be easy. That she hung on to her idea like a lifeline. Had she cared that much for the womanizer she'd been dating? Sometimes he thought she purposely picked guys who would never work out.

"It's a good idea. An excellent one," she insisted. "I always end up with the wrong guy. You're my best friend and have seen right through the men I've dated. Don't think I didn't notice that you've never liked any of my boyfriends. Kent in particular." She cast her eyes downward.

Seen right through them? More like he'd been playing the role of overprotective big brother and wanted the guys to get away from his best friend. Particularly Kent because Rachel had fallen for the man's lightly spoken promises. She'd dated before, but Kent had been different. Apparently, she'd reached a point in her life where she wanted to meet her Mr Right and would have gone down the aisle had Kent had the brains to ask. She'd have expected Bryan to be right there with her, too. Probably standing in the maid of honor's spot.

"Hell no."

She retrained her baby blues on him, steely determination shining brightly. "If you pick out someone who you think is good enough, I'll know he's the right one."

"Finding you a man isn't in my job description."

The only positive to their conversation was that focusing on her hare-brained scheme seemed to be distracting her from her breaking heart. Her tears had stopped and her eyes glowed with a plan. A plan he wanted no part of.

"Job description?" Doing another pass beneath her eyes with a tissue to remove any remaining traces of streaked mascara, Rachel laughed softly. "You sound as if being my friend is a chore."

"Isn't it?" he teased, warming at her low laugh. Being with Rachel, seeing her smile, meant more to him than anything any other woman could offer. Always had. Which was why when Rachel had called, he'd abandoned his date with a promise of a redo the following evening.

"A chore?" Rachel's gaze narrowed and she gave him a serious look. "I hope not, Bryan. I sincerely hope not, because that really would break my heart."

Her expression was so earnest that he laced his fingers with hers. "You're not that bad."

"You're not so bad, either." She scooted closer and flashed an overly bright smile. One that said she hurt but would move forward because that's who she was. "Do you have someone special in mind?"

She innocently stroked her finger over his chin, easing the tension from his clenched jaw, strumming the rest of him into a tight bow. Probably was just the surge of testosterone at wanting to smash his fist into Kent's face that had his body humming at her touch. Probably.

"Because," she continued, "I refuse to sit around the house moping over Kent. I'll give myself tonight to whine, and then so be it. The best way to get over a bad relationship is to find someone new. That's what everyone always says. Let's find me someone new."

She really wanted him to find her someone new.

"Maybe you should slow down, take time to think about what it is you want," he suggested slowly.

"Slow down?" Her forehead wrinkled. "Kent's already got a new girlfriend. That's why he dumped me. Can you believe he was seeing someone else while he was still dating me? He's been seeing her for almost two months." Her blue eyes darkened with the spunk Bryan so admired. "I refuse to let him think I'm devastated."

Bryan took a long drag of air, praying for strength. "This isn't about Kent, Rachel. This is about you. All about you." He cupped her face, making her look at him. "Promise me?"

She gazed at him with her wide, trusting eyes. "Anything."

If only. He'd have her promising to join a convent and stay away from men altogether. Certainly, his life would be simpler. He wouldn't have to worry about her and then perhaps he could focus on his own relationship issues.

Like his inability to date any woman for more than a few months due to his getting bored and his preferring to spend time with Rachel. He had more fun with Rachel, enjoyed how they could look at one another and know exactly what the other was thinking without saying a word, enjoyed how warm and cuddly she felt in his arms at this very moment.

A wave of protectiveness washed over him. Rachel had been special from the moment his fourth-grade eyes had first beheld her. She brought out the white knight syndrome in him and he didn't doubt that he'd gladly spend the rest of his life slaying her dragons.

Only someday she'd meet her Mr Right, would have someone else to play that role in her life, and she wouldn't need him any more. He'd never really thought of that until Kent.

"Don't jump into another relationship any time soon," he heard himself saying, not liking the acidy feel to the back of his throat at the prospect of some guy sweeping her off her feet. What was wrong with him? He wanted Rachel to be happy, to meet a man who would treat her right and make her dreams come true. Only, he admitted he hadn't liked how much time she'd spent with Kent. He hated that she'd had sex with the bastard. Teeth clenched, he swallowed back bile. "Take time and figure out what it is you want out of life, out of a man, before you start something new."

"But . . ."

"Promise me," he repeated with a sterner voice. He knew how she was, that somewhere during the time he'd been away at medical school, she'd gotten into the habit of dating all the wrong men. Well, as of six months ago, he was back and he wanted her to see that she was a strong woman who deserved to wait on the right guy rather than settling for any Joe Blow who came along. He wanted her to see the woman he saw.

A bright beautiful woman who was amazing, fun, witty, kind, smart, hard-working. No woman he'd ever met held a candle to her.

She laid her head back against his chest and snuggled her tight little body up against him, sighing her contentment and making his very male body react with anything but satisfaction.

"Fine," she whispered. "I promise. For now."

Chapter Two

First checking on her one-month-old patient's oxygen level, Rachel sent a reassuring smile to the worried parents eyeing the croup tent and monitors as if they were torture devices designed to keep them away from their baby.

"Are the levels okay?" the mother asked, her eyes weary with worry.

Rachel nodded at the Fanns. Austin was their first child and, like most new parents, they were nervous. In this case, they had a right to be. She smiled sympathetically, wishing she had the ability to make her tiny patient all well. It was an ability she often found herself wishing for in the pediatric intensive care unit where she worked.

"His oxygen saturation is slowly improving," she reassured her. "Dr Carver has ordered another breathing treatment. That should open Austin's airways even more."

Austin's mother nodded, her gaze settling on her tiny son. "How long will he have to stay in the tent?"

"He is doing better, but it'll probably be a few days before he will be out of the croup tent."

Austin's mom nodded. "His breathing isn't as noisy as it was last night when he was admitted. He went from being stuffy to not being able to breathe in just a matter of minutes." Fear entered the young woman's eyes. "His skin was blue."

Rachel listened to the baby's wheezing chest. Bilateral crackles sounded and his body worked hard to pull in each breath.

"RSV is a nasty virus," she said, cleaning her stethoscope with alcohol then draping it around her neck. "Austin has a particularly bad case."

"That's what the Emergency Room doctor told us," the baby's father admitted. "What exactly is RSV?"

Rachel continued to check her patient while she explained the virus to the worried couple. "Respiratory syncytial virus is actually a very common illness. Around ninety-eight per cent of children check positive for antibodies by age two, meaning they've been exposed. Although common, the virus can be dangerous, especially when contracted by premature infants."

Austin had been born at thirty-five weeks.

The tired-looking young mother sighed. "Did we do something wrong? Is that why he got sick so fast? I keep thinking there must have been something I did wrong."

"No. Just make sure you always follow good health protocol and do things like hand-washing prior to picking him up or feeding him." The baby wrapped his fingers around Rachel's thumb and let out a hoarse cry. "Speaking of feedings, I think this little guy wants his mom."

The couple exchanged worried looks.

"The last time I took him out of the tent the alarm went off." His mother's gaze went to the machine beside Austin's isolette.

"His oxygen level was dropping due to the congestion in his chest. I understand your concerns, but he needs to nurse." Rachel's gaze lowered to the woman's swollen chest. "And you really need to nurse. Have you pumped your breasts today?"

Mrs Fann winced. "No. I was going to earlier, but my mother came by and I never did. Austin didn't act hungry and I wasn't sure about taking him out of the tent again."

Rachel nodded. "You should pump some milk off prior to feeding Austin due to your breasts being so engorged. It'll make it easier for him to nurse. I can put the milk in the freezer for later use."

"Thank you." But she still looked afraid to take her baby out of the croup tent.

"Why don't you have a seat in the rocking chair and pump a few minutes. I'll go check another patient, then come back and stay with you while Austin feeds?"

"Could you really?" The woman gave a relieved smile. "That would be wonderful."

Rachel helped Mrs Fann get settled and made sure everything she needed was within reach. Her husband leaned against the hospital room wall, looking helplessly between his anxious wife and his ill baby. Poor man.

Still, barring any complications, Austin should recover without any long-term effects of his illness.

Rachel loved her job. Loved being a pediatric nurse. Taking care of children had always been her dream. From the time she was old enough to tell anyone what she wanted to do when she grew up, she'd wanted to be a pediatric nurse.

How many times while growing up had she and Bryan played doctor with ragged ACE bandages and his pediatric nurse mom's old stethoscope? She smiled at the memories.

Stepping out of Austin's room, she caught sight of Bryan talking with one of their co-workers, a pretty dark-haired, dark-eyed nurse whom Rachel had grown close to over the years they'd worked together at Kansas City Memorial.

Angela gazed at Bryan with admiration. No wonder. He was as good-looking as they came with twinkling brown eyes, sun-kissed brown hair, and an easy smile. With a heart as good as gold and a medical degree hanging in his office, he was quite the catch. Always had been. Even in the fourth grade when they'd first met, all the little girls in their class had chased him around the playground. Fortunately, Rachel had never fallen under his spell like so many of the women they knew.

Fortunately, because Bryan went through women like a cop went through doughnuts. A dozen at a time.

But unlike the men Rachel ended up with, Bryan didn't lie to the women he dated. He didn't declare love and promises of a happy-ever-after. From the word go, he told his dates he wasn't looking for anything serious.

She knew this because several of his exes had come to her for advice. As Bryan's best friend, she'd done her duties, warned them he wasn't the settling-down type, comforted them as best she could when things didn't work out, and sent them on their way.

"Why are you looking so sour?" Bryan interrupted her thoughts when she came over to stand by him and Angela at the nurses' station.

"Sour?" She huffed, flashing a big smile. "I'm not sour."

"Sure you're not," he teased, and then with concern in his eyes, he bent closer and asked, "How are you holding up? Better?"

She nodded. "Better."

During the long night, she'd alternated between tears and humiliation over her foolishness. She tried to figure out why Bryan made her promise to take things slow, and she plotted on ways to get him to choose her next boyfriend. Oddly enough, she really did feel better this morning.

"Good."

"Okay, quit whispering or I'm going to think something's going on between the two of you," Angela warned, giving them an accusing look that said she already thought it.

Something between her and Bryan? Yeah, right.

"Not on my most needy day," she snorted to her friend. She hooked her arm with Bryan's and they headed down the hospital hallway. "Have you given any thought to what we talked about last night?"

When he didn't answer, she glanced at him. His forehead furrowed deep in a scowl.

"Bryan?"

"I haven't and I won't." His words were clipped. "'Not on your most needy day', huh?"

"Of course not. You'd only break my heart."

"I thought we agreed you should take it slow? And who's to say you wouldn't break mine?"

"We both know who the heartbreaker in this duo is and it's not me. Besides, I'm not asking you to pick out a husband for me, Bryan. Just a boyfriend."

But they both knew she wanted a husband. With thirty knocking on the door and her ovaries ticking time bombs, how could she not want to meet a nice guy and start the rest of her life? She wanted kids, a family. Bryan wouldn't understand because he'd always had family. She'd only had her grandmother and her absent parents.

"I'm not picking out your boyfriend."

She frowned. "I'd do the same for you."

"If I ever ask you to pick out a boyfriend for me, you have my permission to say no." His lips twisted with wry humor.

She rolled her eyes and tugged on his arm, still hooked with hers. They resumed their walk down the pediatric unit hallway. "You're funny, but I'm serious. I gave this a lot of thought last night. I want you to pick out my next boyfriend."

"That's not a good idea."

"Because?"

"I'm a man. What do I know about picking out boyfriends?"

"We've already covered this," she reminded him. "You care about me. You have my best interests at heart and you know what I like in a guy."

"No way in hell would I pick a boyfriend like the ones you typically date."

The trace of anger in his voice had several nurses glancing their way, reminding Rachel they were officially at work. Not the best time or place to be having this personal conversation, but she couldn't let go.

Waving her fingers at her co-workers, she flashed a bright smile at Bryan and whispered, "Then you agree that I have no taste when it comes to men and I need serious help before becoming involved with someone new?"

"You need help all right," he muttered.

"As my closest friend—" she beamed at him "—don't you feel obligated to give that help? To steer me in the right direction so I won't make all the same mistakes yet again?"

"I know where you're going, Rachel, but it's not going to work. I've already told you what I think. You need to take time to figure out what it is you want, not jump straight into another relationship."

"I already know what I want," she insisted. "Don't you think it's a man's duty to help keep his friend from making really bad choices?"

Angela looked at them like they were crazy. They tended to get that look from her a lot. "What are you two talking about this time?"

"Haven't you been listening? I think Dr Carver should pick out my next boyfriend."

Angela laughed, a deep laugh that rolled out of her heavy chest and snorted from her nostrils. "Oh, absolutely. This I gotta see." Angela turned her dancing eyes, full of mischief, on Bryan. "Who is the lucky guy?"

Bryan's gaze darkened to molten lava as he glared at Rachel. "We will discuss this later and, for the record, it is not up for debate or a vote from the nursing staff. I am not doing this, Rachel. End of discussion."

He pulled his arm loose from both nurses and headed toward Austin's room to check on his patient.

"Can you believe him?" Rachel asked Angela, waving her thumb at Bryan's retreating back. "You'd think he'd be jumping for joy that I'm asking him. After all, he's the one who has to listen to me cry when I make bad choices."

"Why is that?" Angela gave a probing stare, one that said she already knew the answer, but seriously doubted Rachel did.

"What do you mean?" Everyone at the hospital knew she and Bryan were best friends and had been for years. "Isn't that what friends do?"

"Yes, but dig deeper. Why is Bryan there for you every time you crook your finger? Maybe you should give that some thought before you jump into another relationship." Angela headed off to a patient's room.

Rachel stood in the hallway, watching her go. Just what had her co-worker meant by that? Bryan was there for her every time her life fell apart because that's what friends did.

She'd do the same for him.

Not that his life ever fell apart. He was always the one breaking women's hearts, not the other way around. Still, if his heart ever were to break, she'd be there for him.

And she'd punch the nose of whomever the woman was who hurt him.

And scratch out her eyes.

Shave her bald.

Tattoo "LOSER" on her forehead.

With a smile at her overreactive silliness, Rachel checked on a six-year-old who'd had her appendix taken out that morning. After assuring herself the little girl was doing as expected and didn't need anything, Rachel headed to Austin's room.

Bryan smiled at the anxious young couple, and then quickly examined Austin. When he'd checked on Austin first thing that morning he'd looked over the emergency room admission notes. Austin had been in acute respiratory distress upon entering the

ER. Fortunately, the little fellow had responded to the medication treatments.

One of the hardest parts of Bryan's job was when his patients became seriously ill. Or when they died. He felt personally responsible that each one remained healthy and vibrant.

Austin hadn't been healthy or vibrant last night. Wasn't now. But the infant was on his way to recovery. A few more days and he should be strong enough to return home with frequent follow-ups in the clinic.

"Does everything sound okay?" Austin's mom asked from where she adjusted her shirt and the baby blanket covering her chest. She'd been discreetly pumping her breast with a small handheld breast pump when he'd knocked on the door. He'd advised her to finish while he examined Austin.

Austin had been grunting, even letting loose with a whimper when he smelled his mother's milk. A good sign. Breast milk was the best for Austin if he'd nurse. Rachel's nurse's note reported that he'd been unable to earlier in the day.

Rachel. Had his friend lost her mind? Pick her out a boyfriend? Not during this lifetime.

He carefully lifted Austin from the crib, taking care not to tug on the IV and monitor lines.

"Shhh, little guy, I'm giving you to your mother," Bryan assured. The baby fussed a moment, and then quieted in his arms.

"Maybe you shouldn't," Mrs Fann said nervously.

"His lungs are clearer than they were earlier and he'll do better if he nurses," Bryan advised as he handed the precious little boy to his mother.

With worried, love-filled eyes, she smiled at her son and stroked her finger over his cheek. Automatically, Austin rooted toward her. Her husband moved behind her to stare in amazed awe at his son.

Perhaps he could understand how Rachel so desperately wanted this, to have a baby, a family of her own. Perhaps.

As if his thoughts conjured her, Rachel knocked on the door and then waltzed into the room, smiling at Mrs Fann holding Austin.

"I'm so glad you're attempting to nurse again." She smiled reassuringly at the family. "Austin needs to have his mother's arms around him and feel your love. Knowing you're here will help him."

Mrs Fann covered herself with the baby quilt for privacy, adjusted her top beneath her soft blue cotton shield, and then helped Austin to latch on to her nipple.

"He's nursing," she sighed in relief, as the sweet sound of a suckling babe filled the room. Austin's breathing was still congested, still noisy, but he greedily nursed. A very good sign.

Bryan and Rachel's gazes met and they shared a smile. One that said so much without words.

His chest tightened and he gulped back the emotion welling within him.

She wanted him to pick her out a boyfriend. So she could experience this.

Since meeting her, had he ever been able to deny her anything she wanted?

Chapter Three

"Hey, do you have anything you need washed?" Rachel asked Bryan after he'd finished his rounds that evening. They stood at the nurses' station. He had just entered new orders on Austin. "I'm doing laundry tonight."

"Do I ever not have laundry?" The corners of his mouth lifted in a grin. "I'll cook dinner while you do the wash. Deal?"

The tense knot in her stomach uncoiled. She hadn't realized how little time they'd spent together in recent weeks due to her relationship with Kent. Doing things with Bryan had been difficult when she'd known how much he disliked Kent. That alone should have warned her Kent wasn't right for her.

"It's a deal." She hated to cook. Bryan hated to do laundry. It was a swap they'd often made in the past. "We could watch some bad TV."

"Sounds great. Wait, I can't." Bryan snapped his fingers. "I forgot that I have a date."

Hiding her disappointment, she rolled her eyes. "What's this one's name?"

"Mandy." He picked up a lab slip from the counter, glanced over it. He'd already read the contents. Twice. "I'll cancel if you need me, Rachel."

Cancel. Please cancel. "Don't be ridiculous. I'm just doing laundry."

"I meant if you didn't want to be alone."

"I'm fine. Already getting over what's-his-name," she lied. She'd wanted Bryan with her because she felt better when she was with him. If he came over, she'd smile and laugh. "Do I know Mandy?"

"Nope," he answered without lifting his gaze. He must be putting the lab report to memory. Or not wanting to tell her about the latest woman in his life. Which made her all the more curious.

"Where did you meet her?"

"The gym."

"What's she like?"

"She's nice."

"You don't date nice girls. What's she really like?" she asked, wondering why he was being so evasive. Was there something different about this girl?

"What is this? The inquisition?" He shook his head in mock chagrin and dropped the lab report back into the bin. "You're worse than my mom."

"Your mom is a good woman and raised you better than to pick up stray women at the gym," Rachel scolded, only half-playing.

"Yeah, but I'm my father's son." His grin dug dimples into his cheeks as he winked at her. "He pats me on the back and says, 'That's my boy'."

He did a fair imitation of his dad. She could hear a proud Wayne Carver saying just that. After her parents' divorce, she'd spent more time at Bryan's than at her home. She loved his parents dearly.

Smothering a smile, and the odd twisting in her gut, Rachel rolled her eyes again. "Drop your laundry off before you go. I'll add it in with mine and you can pick it up later."

Rachel finished her shift and headed to the break room to collect her things, but was distracted by thoughts of Bryan's date.

What was wrong?

Bryan went on lots of dates. Why was this one bothering her?

Because she'd wanted to spend the evening with him.

Doing laundry.

Okay, so she couldn't blame him for opting to go on a hot date rather than cooking dinner for a whiny friend while their laundry ran, but jealousy bit her.

Not romantic jealousy. Never that. Just jealousy that some other lucky woman had his company for the evening.

Which drove home something that had been nagging her since Angela's comment.

Bryan was always there for her. What was she going to do when he no longer was? When he met someone and fell in love?

No woman in Bryan's life was going to put up with another woman occupying so much of his time. Rachel wouldn't blame her one bit.

A few of his girlfriends had complained in the past, but for the most part their friendship hadn't been an issue because Bryan changed girlfriends so frequently. Despite the girlfriends who'd come crying on Rachel's shoulder, she was pretty sure none of them had really liked her.

For that matter, none of her boyfriends had ever liked Bryan. Which always surprised her since he was such a great guy and everyone at the hospital adored him. He was just one of those guys everyone liked.

Except her dates.

Kent had hated him with a passion, had even accused her of sleeping with Bryan. Did camping in her backyard when they were kids count?

"You're looking thoughtful," Angela said, gathering her jacket and purse from the break room. "Something on your mind? Or someone perhaps?"

Rachel was standing, her bag and jacket in hand, staring blankly ahead. No wonder her friend thought she was mooning over Kent.

"We didn't get a chance to talk, but you probably figured out from my conversation with Bryan. Kent dumped me last night."

"The fact you asked Dr Carver to find you a boyfriend clued me in. As far as you and Kent being finished – good," Angela surprised her by saying. "You should have dumped him months ago because he didn't deserve you. Never did."

Rachel sighed, clutching her purse tighter. "That's what Bryan said."

"I've said it before, but it bears repeating, you're really lucky to have him."

"Bryan?"

"Well, I'm sure not talking about the lawyer." Angela grabbed her belongings then faced Rachel. "Good riddance to Kent, I say."

Angela hadn't ever said she didn't like Kent. They'd gone on a double date with one of Kent's partners, but it hadn't worked out. Angela had a four-year-old little girl and not every man was willing to become involved with someone who was a package deal. Angela hadn't seemed to mind, had said she was used to the reaction when men discovered she was a mother, rather than a hip single woman looking for a good time. A real shame. Her daughter, Gabriella, was a little darling.

"Yes." She decided to ignore Angela's attack on Kent. Kent was a big boy and could defend himself. Or not. "Bryan is a good friend."

"Nothing more?"

"Nothing more," she assured Angela.

"Too bad," Angela sighed, giving Rachel a look of disappointment. "He's a great guy."

"A great guy who has a hot date tonight."

"Great guys usually do have hot dates," Angela pointed out. "When did Dr Carver tell you Kent didn't deserve you?"

"Last night," she answered, wondering where her friend was going with this. Was Angela interested in Bryan? Maybe she should mention it to Bryan and see if he was interested. Play matchmaker. Then again, she'd hate to see her friend hurt when Bryan moved on to the next woman. She dismissed the idea.

Regardless, the look Angela was giving her wasn't the look of a woman who was interested in Bryan herself. "Hmm, didn't Dr Carver say something about having a hot date last night, too?"

Rachel's mouth dropped. She'd forgotten, but Bryan had mentioned a date yesterday when they'd talked after rounding on his patients. She'd blocked it from her mind. "He did."

"About what time did he come by to console you after Kent's abrupt departure from your life?" Angela's black brow rose with a knowing arch.

"I called him about eight thirty or so." Right in the middle of his date. Great. She really was a horrible friend.

"Guess his date was barely started," Angela needlessly continued. "Is he taking the same girl out tonight or someone different?"

"I don't know." She didn't normally ask much about his dates. For the most part Bryan's dates were a long string of faceless women, and Rachel preferred keeping it that way.

Angela toyed with her purse strap. "Have you ever thought about asking Dr Carver out?"

"I asked him over tonight." At Angela's surprised look, she quickly added, "To do laundry."

"To do laundry?" Angela shook her head and sighed. "You are so blind. You should ask him over to do you."

Fire burned Rachel's face and her jaw dropped. "He's my best friend! Nothing more."

"Well, if you ask me, he should be something more. You go out with all the wrong men, and yet you have a gorgeous hunk at your beck and call." Angela tapped her finger thoughtfully against her cheek. "Let's think about this a moment. You already adore him, he already adores you. You're single, wanting to date someone who's a great guy. Dr Carver definitely fits that description. Why not him?"

Later that evening when Bryan rapped at her door, Rachel couldn't look him in the eyes. Not with the heat rushing to her cheeks. She couldn't get Angela's words out of her head.

Why not him?

He'd laugh if she told him about Angela's suggestion. The two of them dating. It was the most ridiculous thing she'd ever heard. So why couldn't she bring herself to tell him so they could share a laugh and move on?

"Here." She reached for his half-full laundry basket. "Give me that. You go. With Mandy."

"You're talking in monosyllables." Staring at her with an odd expression, Bryan let her take his basket. "Are you okay?"

"Fine," she mumbled, still not meeting his eyes and gripping the basket as if she clung to it for dear life. "I want to get a load started so I can finish. You know how I am."

He didn't look convinced. "You could have done yours without waiting for mine," he said, following her into the apartment.

"I could have, but that would be wasteful as I don't have enough whites for a full load and I'd already offered to do yours and would have had to do yet another load if I'd started mine." Her words ran together in a mumbled mess and, mentally prying her fingers loose, she dropped his basket to the floor with a thud that echoed around the tiny utility room.

"Am I missing something?" he asked. He leaned against her dryer, and watched her.

"Nope." She began sorting his clothes. Jeans into the color stack. Socks into the whites. Boxers into . . . She was holding Bryan's boxers. She'd held them before and never thought about it. Never thought about the fact that he wore them, probably looked like a calendar pin-up in them. Would Mandy be seeing him in pin-up mode before the night ended?

As if they seared her skin, she threw his boxers into a pile.

Why in the world would she think about Bryan's date seeing him in his boxers? He liked women and was no saint. No doubt lots of women had seen those boxers, touched them, slid them down his narrow hips and . . . She gulped.

"Start talking, Rachel, because apparently I've missed something and I'm not leaving until you tell me what's going on." Still leaning against the dryer, arms folded, he stared expectantly at her.

"Your date is the only thing you're going to miss if you don't get a move on." Had that been sarcasm in her voice? What was wrong with her? She felt . . . She wasn't sure what she felt. Only that she needed him to quit hogging all the oxygen. Because she was definitely struggling to breathe.

What was wrong with her?

She flashed a fake smile in an effort to take the edge off her tone and went back to sorting, flinging more of his boxers into the color stack as if touching his underwear was no big deal. It wasn't. She'd been helping do his laundry since grade school. No. Big. Deal.

"That's it." He grabbed her arm, forcing her to face him by lifting her chin with his other hand. "What's wrong? And don't tell me 'nothing' because we both know something's bothering you."

"Noth—" She stopped at his raised eyebrow. "I'm just cranky. I am allowed to be cranky on the night after my boyfriend dumps me, you know."

She sure sounded cranky. Enough so that she almost apologized. She wanted him to leave so she could breathe normally and figure out what was wrong with her. Maybe she was coming down with a cold. Stress could have lowered her resistance, be making her think all these odd thoughts. That must be it. She was getting sick. Illness would explain the odd fluttery feeling in her belly when Bryan touched her.

"Being rid of Kent is cause for celebration, not crankiness," he muttered, not letting go of her chin. His grip grew lighter.

"That's another thing." She moved her chin out of his hold. "Maybe things would have been better between Kent and me if you'd liked him. He knew you didn't like him, which made it difficult for him to come here when he worried he was going to bump into you."

"Made it difficult?" Bryan gave a sardonic laugh. "The jerk made a point to talk loudly outside your doorway so I'd know he was with you when he'd bring you home."

No way. Kent had done that? "Why would he do that? I never let him stay at my place."

"You'd have to ask him," Bryan practically snarled. "I never knew kissing could be so loud."

Loud? She and Kent hadn't been loud. Had they? She barely recalled kissing him outside her doorway. Then again, Kent's kisses weren't that memorable. Yet another clue that should have told her he wasn't the man for her.

That and the fact she hadn't been willing to have sex with him at her place. In hindsight, she had to admit that was strange, but she hadn't wanted him in her bed.

"I won't be asking him anything. I'm no longer on speaking terms with him and am unlikely to ever be again."

"Thank God."

"See what I mean?" she accused, bristling at his tone. Or maybe it was her own thoughts upsetting her and making her feel so contrary. "You didn't like Kent."

"I never claimed to."

"He was my boyfriend. You could have made a little more effort to be nice."

"I put unbelievable effort into remaining civil." The tic in his jaw confirmed just how much effort.

"That's just it. You don't like any of the men I've dated, and they haven't all been losers." At his look she amended, "Okay, so in your eyes most of them were losers, but not all. I wanted things to work with Kent."

Bryan's face remained stony.

"So you didn't like him, I did." Hadn't she?

"You like the idea of being in love," Bryan corrected.

Was that a bad thing? She didn't think so. Just look at his parents, in love and happy for over three decades. She wanted that.

"Of course I like the idea of being in love. Don't you?"

"Not particularly," he commented wryly.

"Be sure to let Mandy know up front you're a cynic."

Now why had she brought up his date again?

"I always do." He stared at her, his expression shifting to amusement. "Cranky or not, you're acting strange." He leaned toward her, staring intently. "Here, let me check your pupils. Maybe you bumped your head and don't remember."

Tossing a narrowed-eyed glare his way, she attacked the laundry, sorting the rest of his load in record speed.

"I did not fall and hit my head. I'm doing laundry." She twisted the knob to wash, starting the water to fill the basin.

He whistled. "You are cranky, aren't you?"

"Hello." She scowled, getting more and more flustered with the flutters in her belly when she looked at him. "Boyfriend dumped me. Best friend abandoning me for hot date."

Oops, she hadn't meant to say that last part.

"Abandoning you?" Looking somewhere between amused and concerned, he straightened up, his shirt stretching over his broad chest.

Why was she noticing his chest? Darn Angela for putting such thoughts into her head.

"I left Mandy at the restaurant last night when you called, paid for a taxi to take her home so I could come straight to you. I think I owe her a decent meal tonight, don't you?"

Guilt hit her. Last night she hadn't considered where he was, what he was doing. She'd wanted him and she'd called. Not once had she considered that he wouldn't come. Bryan was always there for her. Always. She liked him being there, counted on him to be there, couldn't imagine life without him being there.

"If I asked you to stay with me tonight, would you?" she perversely asked, thinking herself a fool for testing their friendship that way. But, despite her guilty conscience, she had to know, had to ask. A fever rose in her blood, forcing events into motion that she wasn't sure she liked or could control. Events that felt odd and unfamiliar.

Bryan stared at her, golden eyes intent, jaw set, hands crammed deep in his jean pockets. "Are you asking me to stay, Rachel?"

What was she doing? This was Bryan. Her best friend. Not a boyfriend for her to act jealous or proprietorially over.

"No." She sighed, frustrated with her thoughts. "I guess I'm out of sorts over Kent. Sorry. I shouldn't keep you from your date two nights in a row."

Without thought, she reached up and placed a kiss on his cheek. She'd kissed his cheek hundreds of times in the past. Not once had her belly auditioned for the Olympic gymnastic team with dozens of perfect somersaults when she did it.

Not once had she wanted to push him back on the washer and share the spin cycle with him.

Until tonight.

Hello, my name is Rachel Akins and there is something majorly wrong with me because I just had the most impure thought zip through me in regards to my best friend.

Turning so he wouldn't see her scalding face, Rachel fled the laundry room.

"Have fun on your date. Don't forget to pick up your laundry," she called breathlessly over her shoulder as she disappeared into her bedroom. "I'll be waiting for you to come home."

* * *

Battling with his thoughts, Bryan left Rachel's and picked up his date. Mostly he'd left for fear he'd say or do something he shouldn't. Like pull her to him and demand to know what she'd been thinking when her cheeks went red.

No matter how much he tried to focus on Mandy, he couldn't get his conversation with Rachel out of his head.

I'll be waiting for you to come home.

Had she been requesting he come home? To her?

Her soft lips pressed to his cheek had fried his brain, and he was imagining the subtext of her comment, the trembling in her fingertips when she'd touched him. She'd have told him flat out if she wanted him to stay.

Why did the feel of her lips against his skin keep playing through his mind? Why had his breath caught at the innocent kiss?

By the time he dropped Mandy at her apartment, it was after midnight. Driving home, his thoughts continued to run wild. Had he imagined the difference in Rachel? More than likely she was still upset over Kent. She'd thought she was going to marry the man. Bryan's insides twisted into a gnarled knot. If he'd had to endure their marriage, their becoming parents – no, he couldn't have done so. Not even for Rachel.

He and Kent had formed an instant dislike for each other.

His shoulders tense, Bryan hesitated outside Rachel's apartment. Was she awake? She had to be at work before seven. He didn't want to wake her if she was asleep.

He reached for his keys, planning to go into his apartment and catch her later. Rachel's door flung open and she pushed his laundry basket toward him. She was dressed in sweats and one of his old baseball T-shirts she'd confiscated years ago. "You're late."

Without another word, she slammed her door shut. Loudly.

Bryan ran his hand over his jaw.

Rachel had been dumped before, mostly because she chose guys where the possibility of things actually working out was next to nil. But she'd never acted like this.

Had never avoided his eyes like she just had.

Had never slammed a door on him.

Had never . . . Oh hell. Bryan's stomach plummeted and his blood ran green.

Maybe she had really been in love with Kent after all?

Chapter Four

The next day, Rachel suctioned Austin Fann's lungs, pretending Bryan hadn't just entered his patient's room. Fluid had built back up on the baby's lungs overnight and his breathing had become labored. Throughout the day he'd gotten worse. Rachel had called Bryan.

"How's he doing?"

"His O_2 is still too low, but hopefully this will help." She finished the suctioning, watching the baby closely. "I wasn't expecting to see you until after you'd finished in the office."

"I had a cancellation and wanted to check on Austin," he explained. "Your call worried me."

"I'm keeping a good eye on him," she promised.

"Where are the Fanns?" he asked, looking around the empty hospital room and noticing Austin's parents were missing.

"I sent them down to the cafeteria to get something to eat. They look exhausted. I'm not sure they've stepped outside this room in over twenty-four hours."

"They're worried about this little guy." Bryan checked over the baby, watching as Rachel finished suctioning him.

"I owe you dinner," he said from right beside her. Too close.

"You don't owe me anything." She withdrew the tubing from the baby's lungs and took a step back.

"Sure I do."

Why was he looking at her like that? Like he was trying to read her thoughts? Like her denial worried him?

"You did my laundry last night and I was supposed to cook for you. That's the natural order of things."

"You don't owe me dinner," she repeated, staring at the suctioning device in her hands.

"I do and I'm paying up tonight."

Why was she acting like dinner was a big deal? Why wasn't she smiling, joking with him like she normally would?

She took a few moments to consider her response, and then faced Bryan. "Look, I just wanted you to know that I'm okay with it if you wanted to take Mandy out again tonight. I don't need you babysitting me."

His smile faded. "Huh?"

"I acted selfish last night, wanting you to stay with me to distract me from my grief over losing Kent, and I was just as selfish the night before when I called you away from your date." She smiled weakly. "I've been taking advantage of you for a long time. I'm sorry."

"That's what friends are for."

"Yeah, but you never need me the same way, Bryan. When it comes to need, our friendship is one-sided." Something else she'd been thinking about thanks to Angela pointing it out. Bryan was a hot guy with a life to live and Rachel had treated him like he was hers for years. When she needed him, she just assumed he'd be there, no questions asked.

How fair was that to him?

Bryan stared at her, confusion in his eyes. "You think I don't need you?"

"You don't. I'm always the one calling, crying on your shoulder." Unable to face his golden brown eyes in case he could see her total confusion, she averted her gaze, and in the process found herself staring at the strong pulse beating at his throat. "When have you ever had to do the same? To cry on my shoulder?"

"You want me to cry on your shoulder?"

She shook her head.

"That's not it." Why was everything she said coming out wrong? Why was the beat making her stare? Why did she want to reach out and touch that beat?

"Just because I don't cry on your shoulder doesn't mean I don't need you, Rachel." He stroked his fingertip over her face in a soft caress. "Or that I don't view our friendship as important. I enjoy the time we spend together."

"Why?" she asked, truly wondering, battling with simultaneous urges to turn into his touch and to turn away. "What do I ever do for you?"

"Sometimes I wonder," he mused in a teasing tone, but when Rachel refused to smile, he frowned. "Aw, come on.

You're a good friend and if I ever needed anything you'd be right there."

"That's just it, you don't ever need anything. Not from me."

"I need you all the time and you give without even realizing."

"Like when?"

"Like when you did my laundry last night."

"Laundry doesn't count."

He thought a moment. "Like when my grandmother passed away last spring and you dropped everything to drive me to Huntsville. You stayed with me, protected me from my crazy family, and even went to the funeral with me."

"That was an easy one, Bryan. I didn't just go for you. I wanted to be there for your parents during their time of loss. Especially your mom."

"She appreciated you being there, Rachel. We all did. Which is my point. You are there for me when I need you. I could name other times – like when I had the flu our sophomore year of undergrad and I thought I was going to die. You nursed me back to health even when it meant exposing yourself to my germs. Then there was that time I was having trouble with Comparative Literature and you tutored me through it and . . ."

Biting back a smile, as he'd no doubt intended, she rolled her eyes. "I suppose."

"Suppose all you want, but I know." He brushed her chin with his knuckle, his fingers lingering near her lips, lingering long enough that her stomach flip-flopped.

Her gaze met his and she swallowed. Bryan looked . . . looked . . . like he wanted to kiss her.

She jumped back, bumping into the isolette, startling poor Austin. She reached in, patted the baby's back, and spoke a few soft, soothing words. Other than whimper, Austin didn't make another sound, just drifted to sleep, exhausted from the tolls of his illness.

"He is so precious, isn't he?" Rachel said. "I could bundle him up and take him home with me."

"You'll be a good mother," Bryan said.

"Thank you." Heat burned her cheeks. "I'd like to think so, but these days I think I'm never going to know. Biological clock and all that."

Bryan froze, staring at her as if she'd lost her mind. "You've got to be kidding me. You've got a good ten years left before you have to be worried about your biological clock."

"Not really. I'm almost thirty, Bryan. After a few more years, I'll become high-risk just due to my age," she sighed. "I really need to meet a nice guy."

"If this is your way of hinting that you want me to find you a boyfriend—"

"It's not," she assured him, suddenly feeling tired. "Just the reality that I'm not a spring chicken any more."

"Spring chicken?" He rolled his eyes. "Okay, it's official. You have totally lost it. You are not old."

"I'm being serious, Bryan." She shoved against his arm. "I know I'm not old, but I'm not as young as I used to be. That's all I'm saying."

"None of us are."

She sighed with exasperation. "You don't understand."

"Then tell me because something is eating at you and I'm not buying that it's crankiness over Kent."

"I thought Kent and I would marry and I'd someday have his babies," she said, wondering why the thought almost seemed repulsive now.

"Don't remind me," Bryan growled.

She straightened the croup tent, checked Austin's monitors, and then frowned. "How did we get on the topic of Kent? Let's talk about something else."

"Gladly. What was wrong with you last night?"

She didn't prefer that topic any more than she did Kent. "What do you mean? What about last night?"

"When I picked up my laundry."

"Nothing was wrong." Nothing except everything, because during the long hours of the night she couldn't stop thinking of him. And not in a sisterly way. Now when she looked at him, all she could do was wonder what his mouth tasted like.

"You threw my clothes at me."

She waved her hand dismissively. Better than throwing herself at him, as she'd done in her dream when she'd finally drifted into sleep. "I was tired."

"You didn't have to wait up."

"Yes, I did."

"You did?"

"I had your clothes."

"I could have gotten them later."

"I wanted to give them to you last night. To get them out of my way," she added, fidgeting back and forth. Why couldn't one of them get paged? Why didn't the Fanns come back? Anything to rescue her from this conversation.

"You folded my socks and boxers," he reminded her.

"So?"

"Since when do you fold my underwear?"

Her cheeks burst into bright red flames that matched the big hearts on her scrub top. "I didn't want your stuff to wrinkle."

"Thanks, but wrinkled jockey shorts and socks don't bother me."

"Well, they bother me. So does this conversation." Before he could stop her, she practically ran from the room.

But she'd barely gotten out of the room when Austin's monitor starting buzzing. She hesitated only half a second, wondering if Bryan had messed with the monitor to intentionally draw her back, but she wouldn't risk it.

When she got back into the room, she saw that this was no joke.

Austin was blue, and Bryan had lifted him out of the bed to perform cardiopulmonary resuscitation.

"Call a code," he ordered.

Jumping into action, she picked up the phone, punched in the appropriate numbers, and then announced the code so a nurse would come with the crash cart. She grabbed an airbag, and gave Austin two breaths.

While Bryan compressed Austin's little chest with two fingertips, Rachel gave him breaths at the appropriate intervals.

The Fanns arrived at the same time Angela did with the crash cart. She pushed the cart to Rachel, and then turned back to the baby's parents.

"What's going on? No!" Mrs Fann cried out, realizing what was happening.

Angela pulled the parents to the side, keeping them back so that Rachel and Bryan could focus on trying to save Austin's life.

While Bryan compressed and gave air, Rachel hooked up the defibrillator leads, then waited for Bryan to give her the all clear signal.

He placed Austin back into the isolette. "Now."

Rachel hit the button that delivered the electrical shock to Austin's tiny body, then immediately gave the baby a breath of air.

Never had she felt such relief as when Austin's heart monitor gave a low beep, then another, and another.

"Thank God," Mrs Fann cried, rushing over to the isolette to stare down at her baby.

Knowing Austin was far from out of the woods yet, Rachel glanced at Bryan, giving a breath with the bag and waiting for him to tell her what he wanted done next.

"He's not breathing right. I'm going to intubate him."

Rachel nodded and started grabbing equipment. Austin was alive, but not stable. His tiny lungs needed help. Help Bryan would give.

Rachel met his gaze, knew what he was thinking – if they hadn't lingered in Austin's room, if Bryan hadn't been right there to start CPR almost immediately, the baby would have died.

Thank God he'd been there.

Thank God he was always there.

In that moment, she knew she always wanted him to be there, and she knew exactly why.

"You've been here ten minutes and you've barely said a word." Bryan didn't turn to face her, which left her staring at the backside of his jeans and his light-blue button-down shirt. Nice. Something she'd seen him in dozens of times.

Yet had she ever really seen him?

And he was barefoot.

The man hated shoes. Kicked them off the moment he got home and only put them back on under protest.

She liked his feet. Strong, masculine. Not too long. Not too wide. Nails clipped straight across and clean. Just right.

She liked Bryan's feet?

Rachel rubbed her temple, trying to ease her drumming thoughts. No wonder she hadn't wanted to come tonight, had tried to beg off on his dinner invitation. Because over the past couple of days she'd had a few too many revelations.

"You still worried about Austin?" he asked, glancing over his shoulder for a brief second before putting his attention back on their dinner. "I called and checked on him just a little while ago. He's holding his own."

Chewing on her fingernail, she leaned against the countertop, watching him deftly add the finishing touches to their meal.

"I'm glad to hear it. He scared me today."

"Me, too."

Taking a deep breath, she glanced around his kitchen. "You didn't need to go to all this trouble. We could have gotten takeout."

"I'm not whipping up anything gourmet. Just a chicken casserole and salad. Nothing fancy."

"Oh."

He turned, met her gaze. "Did you want something fancy?"

"Not really." What she wanted was for this unfamiliar awkwardness to go away. This was Bryan. Her best friend. The man she'd shared everything with. He knew as much about her as she knew about herself. She shouldn't be nervous.

She shouldn't be noticing his feet.

Or how good he looked in his jeans.

How delicious his voice was.

How even over the aroma of dinner, she caught the scent of his soap from the shower he'd had before she arrived.

How she'd like to touch the dampness lingering at his nape.

She shouldn't be noticing any of those things.

Yet she was.

Darn Angela's comment for making her so aware of him!

Darn her own heart for falling for a man who loved her like a sister.

"I bought that new Bruce Willis movie when I stopped by the store on my way home from the office. You want to get it ready to watch?"

She'd do anything to escape from his nearness. Including tackling the numerous gadgets in his living room that provided what he called a "sweet entertainment experience". Mind reeling, she left the kitchen and found the action movie he'd bought and peeled off the plastic cover.

"I'm almost done," he called, causing her to jump. "You want to eat at the table or in front of the television?"

Why would he ask that? She couldn't recall the last time they had sat at the table. They were two friends having dinner together. Not a date.

A date? Why would she think that?

Panicking at how her pulse quivered inside her arteries, she called, "In front of the television."

"I thought you'd say that," he said, coming into the living room with a tray containing two plates of salad. He'd already put just the perfect amount of her favorite dressing on hers. Returning to the kitchen, he came back through with two glasses and a bottle of sparkling wine. Not their usual fare.

"Wine? I thought you said we weren't doing fancy."

"We're celebrating."

"Celebrating what?" she gulped.

"The end of your relationship with Kent."

Great. Back to her biggest mistake. Or perhaps it had only been a distraction from her feelings for Bryan himself? Because how could she ruin their friendship by letting him know that somewhere along the way she'd developed feelings for him?

"Okay." She allowed him to pour her some of the sparkly white liquid. Nervousness filled her. A nervousness she had to get rid of. Or at least disguise, before he suspected her thoughts. Not too much alcohol though, she warned herself, because she needed her senses about her.

"And to you finding me a replacement so I can quit being a bother to you," she added, acknowledging to herself that it really didn't matter who he chose because no man could ever live up to him. Not in her eyes. She chinked his glass and took a small sip.

Bryan didn't lift his glass.

"You're not a bother, Rachel." His eyes met hers. "You promised to give yourself some time before rushing into another relationship, remember?"

It wasn't that she wanted to rush into another relationship, not really. But she needed something to distract her all-too-female thoughts about Bryan. Stat.

"I'm not going to rush into another relationship, but I don't want to sit around waiting for life to happen to me, either. I want to find someone to share my life with. What's so wrong with that?"

"Nothing." He studied her for a long time, and then started to speak but stopped. He finally said, "You're not going to give up on the idea that I'm going to pick your next boyfriend, are you?"

"No." Because ever since Angela had asked, "why not Bryan?", her heart – and libido – had been nagging. Why not Bryan?

There were thousands of reasons as to why not Bryan, but just in case she forgot them all, she needed someone else to focus her obviously raging hormones on. Pronto.

Bryan was her best friend. He wouldn't appreciate her developing other feelings for him.

If he figured out that when she looked at him she now saw so much more than just her best friend, he might shut her out. She could never bear losing him. Much better to buy herself some time, and figure what action to take to make sure their friendship survived.

"Then it isn't too soon for this." He'd slid closer to her on the sofa, and now he took her into his arms, and kissed her.

Then he rocked her entire world.

Or perhaps Kansas City was experiencing a major earthquake.

Her eyes closed and her lips parted, granting him entrance to her mouth, granting him access to whatever he wanted.

Because his kiss was unlike anything she'd ever experienced. Mind shattering. Body exploding. World rocking.

Dear sweet heaven, he had a delicious mouth.

Her fingers found their way to his nape, toying with the damp hair she'd wanted to touch earlier. Her mind reeled at the thought this was Bryan she was touching. A man so familiar to her, yet suddenly a stranger as they trod unknown waters.

One kiss and already she felt as if she were drowning.

One kiss and everything within her craved more.

Lots more.

Everything.

He pulled back, stared into her eyes, and then grinned. "You never told me you could kiss like that."

"Like what?" she asked, wondering at how hoarse her voice sounded.

"Like you're sugary sweet and spicy hot all at the same time."

"Oh, that. You never asked," she somehow managed to respond, loving the grin that spread across his handsome face. She felt her insides start smiling, too. "Now what?"

"Now, I pick out your next boyfriend because you deserve the best in life, Rachel. You deserve the fairy tale and that's what I want to give you." He bent forward, and then whispered, "I choose me."

"You want to be my boyfriend?" Dare she hope it could be true? That he'd been harboring feelings for her, too?

"How else am I going to keep you from ending up with the wrong guy again?"

The balloon of hope inside her deflated. "That's why you choose me? To keep me from going out with the wrong man?"

His fingers nudged her chin, forcing her to look into his eyes. "Rachel, honey, haven't you figured out yet that any man who's not me is the wrong man?"

"But . . ." she gazed at him in wonder. "I didn't know."

He hugged her close. "I'm a blind fool, Rachel. When I think back, I've been half in love with you since the moment I first laid eyes on you."

"You have?"

"Not that I acknowledged it, but yes. I guess I was waiting for us to grow up, for us to be ready."

"Ready for what?"

"The rest of our lives. Together."

Much later, Rachel lay on top of Bryan on the sofa, kissing him thoroughly and deeply.

"You're my best friend, you know. If this doesn't work out, it's going to be really bad."

"I know." He smiled up at her. "But I should warn you, if this doesn't work out, you're going to have to listen to me whine over and over about the girl I love with all my heart and how much I need her by my side."

Rachel's insides melted.

He placed his palms on each side of her face, and smiled up at her. "But I'm not worried, because you've always been there for me when I need you, and I'm going to need you for the rest of my life, so this one's a no-brainer."

He was right. Too bad she'd been too blind to see what was right before her eyes for so long, but maybe he was right. Maybe they hadn't been ready, had needed to grow up, figure out who they were prior to starting this next phase of life.

"You're mine, Rachel. Now and forever. I won't settle for less than everything with you."

"You won't ever have to."

"Neither will you."

And they didn't.

NIGHT SHIFT

Karen Elizabeth Brown

Chapter One

"Code ninety-nine, ER, room eighteen. Code ninety-nine, ER, room eighteen!"

Jessie McGreevy sighed as he crossed through the double doors of the Emergency Room. He watched the staff hurry to room eighteen, pushing and carrying the special resuscitation equipment. It looked like the ER was going to be swamped tonight. He hated working nights. The twelve-hour shifts left him bleary-eyed and sleepy on his days off, but he didn't have enough seniority to move to days without taking a pay cut that he couldn't afford. Even though nurses were in short supply in southern Oregon, he was a single income household, carrying the weight of supporting both of his elderly parents.

Jessie slipped into a seat with the other nurses gathered in the ER break room. They were talking about the code and how they would be going into the lions' den just when it was time to change shifts. Jessie blinked in surprise at the newcomer sitting across the table from him.

"Don't I know you?" he said, his heart racing with expectation.

The dark-haired nurse, who wore blue scrubs and a light blue sweater, sat writing out her schedule.

"That's original," she said. She didn't look up from her paper to see Jessie flush bright red at the snickering from the other nurses.

"I only meant that I'm sure we've met somewhere before."

Groans could be heard all around the table. Jessie clamped his mouth shut as his attempt at conversation went from bad to worse. That is, until the charge nurse interrupted them by introducing the newcomer.

"This is Margaret Wilcox. She's new to the ER and to Good Samaritan, so make her feel welcome."

Margaret finally looked up from her paper, wary eyes staring across at Jessie. "My friends call me Maggie."

After hearing her name, Jessie was certain he knew where they'd met.

"I remember now! You were in nursing school with me."

But Maggie frowned. "I still don't remember you. I'm sorry."

Great! That's just fantastic. What Jessie remembered most about Maggie was that he'd had a huge crush on her. All the way through school, her luscious brown eyes and saucy smile had won his heart, but he never had the courage to tell her.

What had happened to her since school? Was she married? He wanted to ask her all sorts of things but now wasn't the time. The charge nurse was handing out assignments and starting the tape recorder that held the day shift's report.

So, instead, he and Maggie exchanged glances throughout the narration.

The ER was divided into different work assignments. The triage area; the exam rooms; and the nurses' station, where the nurses did their charting on the computers and sent orders to the rest of the hospital, like the lab, pharmacy, X-ray and the blood bank. Jessie figured with his luck, he and Maggie would be assigned to different areas and wouldn't see each other all night. But the charge nurse, Eva, had a different idea.

"Maggie, I'm going to have you shadow Jessie tonight, so you can see how our ER is set up and how we work."

Maggie glared at Jessie. "Thanks. I'm sure I'll figure it out. But who's going to show Jessie what to do?"

The studious silence in the room was broken up with guffaws and laughter from the other nurses as Jessie tried to think of a witty response. But he ended up silent and red-faced again. Eva stood up, indicating it was time to relieve the day shift. As they entered the nurses' station, there were sighs of relief from all around the room.

"We've had an avalanche this evening," said the charge nurse from the day shift. The day nurses gave a final report on each patient and said their brief goodbyes. Jessie led Maggie to the triage area where they would work together tonight. He took a clipboard from the front desk and read the list of names and complaints.

"We have someone who just came in, complaining of chest pain. Would you care to check him in?"

Maggie grimaced. "You don't have to be so polite. Just tell me what to do, okay?"

Jessie drew in a deep breath and smiled. He believed in being kind and polite. But he wondered what had happened to Maggie to make her so jaded. He had a feeling it would be a long night.

The night shift started at 6 p.m. and ended at 6 a.m. The hospital ran on military time, so their shift started at 1800 hours and ended at 0600 hours. New patients kept coming into the ER until around 0200 hours and, all the while, Jessie followed Maggie with his eyes. He wasn't watching what she was doing, he was watching her. She was still as beautiful as he remembered. He knew she was aware of his silent speculation, and it seemed she was enjoying teasing him. Finally, Jessie and Maggie were relieved for a late dinner. Sitting alone together in the break room, Maggie put her sandwich down and clamped her lips together.

"Well?"

Jessie looked down at his scrubs to see if he'd dropped food on them and then looked back at Maggie. "Well what?"

"Aren't you going to tell me how I'm doing tonight? After all, that's how it goes with newbies. They get evaluated by their peers and it's reported back to the supervisor. I'd rather hear it from you first."

"No one asked me to evaluate you. If they did, I'd only say that you seem awfully defensive about something."

"What are you talking about? Me? Defensive?"

"Exactly. What happened to you, anyway? You used to be the sweetest, kindest person I'd ever met."

Maggie stuffed her sandwich back in her sack, unfinished. "That's what you get for going on assumptions. And what's with you? Why do you care anyway?"

"Maggie, I'm only trying to understand you."

"Well, don't try. It's none of your business."

Jessie clenched his jaw shut and counted to ten. Then he took in a deep breath and growled to himself. Her attitude was trying his patience. From what he remembered of Maggie's school life, she had been the center of her social scene. While he had to work and go to school, she was off to parties on the weekends. During the holidays, she flew to vacation spots around the world. But during those same holidays, Jessie had to take care of his parents when he wasn't working.

After a few more minutes of strained silence, Jessie couldn't contain himself any longer.

"You know, if you'd get down off your high horse for a minute and think of someone besides yourself, you'd realize that I was interested in you. Maybe I care about you."

Maggie burst out in a sardonic laugh. "Me? You're interested in me?"

Jessie's face paled as he slid down in his seat. "Yes. I like you." He whispered the last part, but was sorry he'd said it as soon as the words escaped his lips.

"Don't bother liking me."

But Maggie was the only girl he had ever imagined loving, even if it was from afar. Was this why she was pushing him away now? Confused, he looked at his watch and signaled the time.

"It's time to go back to work."

"You sure you still want to work with me?"

She wasn't going to let up, even when he'd tried to give her a gracious way out. But two could play at this game.

"Are you sure you want to work with me? After all, I told you I liked you."

Her eyes narrowed. "No, I'm not sure. But I don't have a choice, now do I?"

Chapter Two

At 0300 hours the triage area was finally deserted, so Jessie and Maggie cleaned and restocked the shelves, preparing for the next onslaught of patients. Maggie was exhausted, she'd never worked in such a busy ER department. As much as she tried to keep her distance, she could feel the heat of Jessie's body whenever she happened to brush by him. She remembered him from nursing school now – the shy, cute, quiet guy who kept to himself. She would have liked to get to know him better then but she was caught up in her own stupid little world of parties and having fun. She should've known none of that would last.

And now she'd run into Jessie again. Small world. He was still shy and cute and quiet. But now she wasn't sure that she could open herself up to get to know him. After everything that had happened to her, she was battered and bruised. Did she still have anything to offer Jessie? She wasn't sure if she did, but she couldn't help that her skin tingled in anticipation of his touch. Although she had pushed away Jessie's earlier advances, she found him transparent and genuine. That was something she hadn't experienced in any other man before.

So, they played their silent game until the night supervisor floated out of the elevator and into the ER. Norma Jean had worked for Good Samaritan Hospital for as many years as the place had been in existence, Jessie had told her. Starting out as a monitor technician, watching heart rhythms in ICU, she worked nights and went to school during the day so she could become a registered nurse. She'd told Jessie that if you wanted something bad enough, you'd get it somehow.

"Good evening, you two." Norma Jean nodded to them both.

"How's the house census tonight?" Jessie asked.

"We have some room for admissions, but only if they're necessary. Jessie, can I speak to you for a moment?"

Maggie watched anxiously as Norma Jean took Jessie by the arm and propelled him through the door of an empty exam room.

"What's up?"

"Tell me how Maggie is working out. And be honest." Norma Jean had her hands on her hips.

Here it was. The evaluation Maggie had been talking about.

"Norma Jean, you've caught me a little bit off guard. I'm not prepared. I didn't know I would be evaluating Maggie tonight."

"But that's what I want. An unbiased opinion that isn't prepared. Tell me: does she work well with others?"

Jessie paused. "Yes, once you get to know her."

"How's her attitude?"

If he told a lie, his credibility would be shot. But if he told the truth, she might get fired.

"When I was about twelve years old, my father and I found a seagull in our front yard. It had a broken wing. My father wrapped its wing and we kept it in a cage until it was well. My job was to feed the bird. Every time I got near the poor thing, it would ruffle its feathers up and try to peck me. It was frightened to death."

Norma Jean shook her head. "What's your point?"

"That's what I see in Maggie. She's like a wounded bird that needs some kindness."

Norma Jean patted Jessie's arm as she gathered her papers and turned to leave. "Well, I guess it's your job to soothe the wounded bird."

"But . . ."

"No buts, I'll make sure you are assigned as a pair this next week and we'll see how it goes."

At 0500 hours, a familiar face appeared in the ER. Jessie ran over to greet Sharon Wheeler. She was a gaunt, pale woman who wore a turban over her thinning hair. She was pushing a walker, and wore a multicolored gown that hung down to her pink, fuzzy slippers. He noticed that Maggie watched him intently.

"Hi, Sharon. Is it time again?"

"Yes, the doctor wants me to stay. I'll get chemotherapy and then he's planning some tests, too."

"This is Maggie." Jessie gestured Sharon towards Maggie. "She'll take your vital signs and finish your paperwork."

But Maggie's face had suddenly turned pale, as if she'd been struck by lightning. Although she had performed her nursing duties exceptionally well on their shift that night, sweat poured from her brow and her hands shook, Jessie noticed, while she took Sharon's blood pressure. Jessie frowned. Sharon must have felt the tension, too, because she tried to make small talk with Maggie.

"Are you new?" Sharon asked.

"Yes."

"Aha! I've got more hospital time here than you do. Maybe I rate a timecard?" Sharon chuckled, all the while watching Maggie carefully. Then, after watching her hands shake even more, Sharon reached up and touched Maggie's wrist. "Cancer isn't catching, Maggie, so relax. I know I do."

Jessie was going to step in and take over when Maggie's head snapped around and she stared into Sharon's eyes. "My mother died of cancer."

Jessie inserted himself into their conversation quickly.

"Are you going to come and visit me tonight, Sharon?" Jessie carefully pushed the IV needle into her arm.

"If I'm feeling up to it, I wouldn't miss it for the world."

Jessie noticed Maggie's bewilderment. The girl appeared lost as she looked between the two of them. When she finally spoke, it was in the timid voice of a little girl. "What's tonight?"

Sharon smiled and held her free hand up in the air. "Another day!"

Maggie and Jessie watched the techs take Sharon away to her room in the cancer wing. After she was gone, Jessie saw Maggie grab a piece of paper that Sharon had been absently scribbling on while she waited for them to take her to her room. Jessie looked at the words of Sharon's poem over Maggie's shoulder as she read, smiling to himself.

Another day is gone again
Another day to make a friend
Another day to laugh out loud
Another day to make you proud
Another day to breathe sweet air
Another day to lose more hair
Another day to know I'm leaving
Another day to watch you grieving
Another day to help you mend
Another day until the end

Reading Sharon's poems gladdened his heart. She was always leaving little inspirational scribbles all over the hospital. She was an amazing woman. It was painful to see the cancer waging its war on her.

But Maggie dropped the paper on the desk as if flames were licking her fingers.

"Are you okay?" Jessie asked.

"My mother died of cancer. Since she died, I've have felt so guilty that I couldn't save her. We tried every experimental treatment we could but it didn't help. I just . . . can't be around cancer patients."

"But these people aren't your mother; they just need a little patience and understanding. They are going through a lot of pain and turmoil inside while they deal with their own mortality."

"I can't . . . I just can't do it. That's all. Please don't try to make me."

Maggie's eyes filled with tears, but before they could escape, she wiped her hand across her face and set her mouth tight. Her lips were hard and she dug her nails into the palms of her hands.

"It's okay to cry, Maggie." Jessie touched the top of Maggie's hand, but she snatched it away.

"Why? So everyone can feel sorry for me?"

"Is that what it's all about? You can't let anyone close to you?"

"Of course not. It's just that . . ." Maggie was afraid and the tears began to well up.

"Go ahead and cry. Let out the angry feelings that have been bottled up inside and are making you miserable."

Maggie glared at Jessie and turned her back to him. As many times as Jessie tried to start up a conversation with her, she was silent for the last half-hour of their shift. When it was time to leave, she didn't speak to him at all.

Chapter Three

Jessie made it home by 6.30 a.m., just in time to feed and clothe his parents. After the dishes were washed, he sat in the living room with his mom and dad to talk with them about the day. Then they would watch television and he would head for bed after putting their lunch in the refrigerator. While he was walking down the hall to his bedroom, the doorbell rang. His mother answered the door before he had a chance to.

"Jessie? There's a young lady here to see you," said his mother.

Jessie froze. A bill collector? He didn't think they owed any more bills. He turned around and huffed back down the hall, already getting angry at whoever was interrupting his precious sleep. He pulled the door away from his mother and stopped short.

Standing in front of him was a vision of loveliness. He flushed when he realized he was staring.

"Maggie? How did you find me?"

"I looked you up in the computer at work. It's amazing what you can find out if you know how." Maggie batted her eyelashes at Jessie playfully. "Is this your mom?"

"Yes, sorry . . ." Jessie stumbled over his words, flustered, as he introduced Maggie to his mother. His mom kissed him on the cheek and gave him a knowing wink before disappearing back into the living room to join his father watching TV.

"What can I do for you?" Jessie was dumbfounded. What was she doing here? What would she think of the fact that he took care of his parents? He wanted to crawl into a hole and hide.

"How about inviting me in?"

Jessie hesitated, but then his manners won out. "Sure. Come on in."

As they walked past the living room on their way to the kitchen, Jessie was suddenly embarrassed by his elderly parents sitting in front of the television. His mother had potato chip crumbs all over the front of her sweater. His father was laughing at a dumb sitcom.

Maggie nodded to his parents and smiled. She didn't seem bothered. Maybe this wouldn't be so bad after all?

Jessie led Maggie through an old-fashioned swinging door into a breakfast nook beside the kitchen. He made a fresh pot of coffee and poured two cups for them. They sat down at the long wooden table.

"So . . . here we are. Why are we sitting at my kitchen table when we both should be sleeping?" Jessie asked, smirking.

"I . . . um, had a good cry."

Jessie noted that her eyes were bright from past tears. They were a beautiful color. A light green and gold. "Okay. That's a start."

"I wanted to ask if you'd like to go out with me sometime?"

"When?"

"We have the same days off this week, so how about Friday night? I figure I owe you an apology and I'd like to treat you to a night on the town. Come on, say you'll go."

Jessie thought he was dreaming. But before he could pinch himself, Maggie reached over and gave him a quick kiss on the lips. He started to kiss her back, but as he did, Maggie jumped up out of her chair and ran for the front door, giggling.

"I didn't say I would go!" Jessie called after her, finally making it to the open door as she bolted out into the sunlight.

"Yes you did!" She turned around and blew him a quick kiss, still racing for her car.

"When?!"

"When I kissed you, you kissed me back! In my books, that's an undeniable 'yes'!"

Maggie turned, laughing, and he had to steady himself against the door frame suddenly when his knees threatened to buckle. Her eyes were shining and her smile lit up her face – he was utterly, head over heels in love with her.

Had she truly gotten rid of the memories she was carrying? Or was this just a temporary reprieve?

Jessie's parents sat watching the action from the living room. He caught his mom peeping out of the curtains as he turned to head back into the house. This was definitely much more exciting for them than the television.

His mother grinned as he passed her on the way to finally heading to bed for some sleep.

"You kissed her back. That's a yes," she said with a chuckle.

"Yes, Ma, I did."

As he fell into bed, he licked his lips, reliving their brief kiss. He could taste the lipgloss she was wearing. Strawberry.

The day was looking better already.

But the next few days at work were like a bipolar nightmare for Jessie. One minute Maggie would be elated and happy, and then some small thing would set her off. For the most part, the cancer patients were her worst challenge. Jessie knew that she needed more than a good cry.

One day, Jessie asked Norma Jean to sign them up to attend a session of the cancer center's "Dealing with Death" seminar. But when he told Maggie about it, her beautiful eyes grew large, as if she'd seen a ghost. She wailed and complained for a good hour. Who was this person? She wasn't the girl he had fallen in love with, that much was for sure. All he could do was try to calm her down. Jessie knew this would be the best thing for her.

"I don't want to go!"

"It's part of our training here and we get paid for going."

"I don't care if it's part of my arm. I don't want to go!"

"If you don't get it over with now, you'll still have to do it within your first year of working here."

"But I've dealt with death. Isn't that enough?"

"This is from a different perspective. It's from the viewpoint of the person dying and those surviving them."

"That's two different viewpoints."

"True. We deal with patients and their families."

"You sound like you've already taken this seminar."

"I have. But it's excellent and it wouldn't hurt me to refresh my perspective."

"You're only going because I'm supposed to go."

Jessie's face turned pink. "Well, I . . ." Why was he so nervous to admit that? So what if she knew that he would do anything for her? Was that so terrible?

But just when he thought it couldn't get any worse, Maggie leaned in and brushed her lips across his cheek.

"I think that's sweet."

Jessie faced Maggie, shocked at her sudden about-face. "Then you'll go?"

"Yes, I'll go."

Jessie twirled her around the triage area, laughing. He panicked, however, when the elevator opened. Norma Jean, making her rounds of the hospital. She wouldn't be thrilled to find out that two of her nurses were getting romantically involved. In truth, she had fired nurses for less. It wouldn't do to get caught at this stage in the game.

Sharon Wheeler emerged from the elevator as well. She pushed her walker with one hand and pulled an IV pole along beside her with the other. Jessie smiled and waved to Sharon, and then approached Norma Jean when she waved him over.

"I hear you and Maggie are attending a seminar next week?"

"Yes, we're signed up, but it'll put us into overtime. Is that okay?"

Norma Jean nodded. "That's no problem. I'll sign for it."

Meanwhile, Maggie screwed up her courage to greet Sharon. Leaving Jessie and Norma Jean talking at the nurses' station, she strode over to the cancer patient, determined to keep the smile on her face, even though she was feeling like she just wanted to run and hide.

"Hi, Sharon. Can I help you?"

"I came down for a visit. Jessie always likes to have visitors when it's not overloaded with patients down here. Are you busy?" Sharon looked around the waiting room, to see only three people.

"No, they've already been checked in." Maggie struggled not to look away. She said brightly, "So how are you doing today?"

"Oh, I can't complain."

They both felt the awkward silence, which was suddenly punctured by the piercing beep of Sharon's IV. The blue box that monitored the fluid into her arm had stopped running. On instinct, Maggie jumped into action, pressing the silence button and checking the line for obstructions.

"What's the problem?" Jessie came up behind her just as the machine went off for the second time.

"Darn thing is plugged up, I think," Maggie said, working diligently on the line. She could feel Jessie's eyes on her as she worked. She hoped he'd been pleasantly surprised that she'd been talking to Sharon. She would get over her fear if it was the last thing she ever did. In a minute, Maggie had the line clear and she punched the run button. The IV was running perfectly again.

Jessie turned to her, smiling. "That was fast. Where did you get your experience on IV machines?"

"On my last job. I also got quite good at it when my mom . . ." Maggie grew quiet again and Jessie knew he'd hit another nerve. Maggie excused herself.

"Did I say something wrong?" Sharon asked.

Jessie shook his head. "No. It's not you." He watched Maggie aimlessly stock the already full shelves and look for things to do that didn't involve sitting with them.

When it was time for the day shift, Sharon left to go back to her room. Maggie returned and sat next to Jessie.

"I'm sorry. I really am. I just . . . couldn't do it. Memories of my mother . . ."

Jessie took her hand. "I know you're sorry. Don't worry."

When Jessie touched her, she felt everything was going to be all right. He seemed to lift a tremendous weight off her heart. For the first time, Maggie didn't pull her hand away.

Chapter Four

Friday morning after they'd finished their shift, Jessie drove to Maggie's apartment. She'd invited him around for breakfast before their date that night. He sat outside in his car for a few minutes, looking at his trembling hands. Why was he so nervous?

When he reached the front door, the smell of bacon and eggs escaped from an open window and his stomach growled. Smiling, he rang the bell. Maggie answered the door with a spatula in one hand.

"Hi! Wash your hands and get ready to eat."

"Yes, ma'am!"

Along with the bacon and eggs, Maggie served sourdough toast and blackberry jam. They ate and laughed and didn't talk about work.

"How did you get to be such a good cook?" Jessie asked.

"Come on, it's only bacon and eggs. Anybody could do this."

"Not true. There's something special about these particular bacon and eggs."

Jessie grinned and watched Maggie sit down at the table. She still had luscious curves. He reached out and grabbed her, unable to resist any longer, pulling her to his lap. He kissed her neck but then she jumped up right away.

"Time to do the dishes."

Soon, they were washing the dishes, throwing soapsuds at each other whenever possible.

"You keep snapping me with that towel and I'll make you pay!" Maggie laughed.

Jessie scooped up a mound of soap bubbles and blew them into Maggie's hair.

"Okay, I give up," Jessie shouted when Maggie threatened him with a bubble-loaded spatula.

Maggie allowed Jessie to nudge up against her while he dried soap bubbles out of her hair. This was the closest she'd really ever allowed him to get to her. She turned her head so their lips met and Jessie pressed his lips against hers. They leaned against the kitchen sink, entwined, until Maggie pulled away with a smile.

"Why don't we make ourselves comfortable?" She led Jessie into the front room and they sat down on a beige, overstuffed sofa. Jessie leaned in next to Maggie and sighed.

"Ahh . . . comfortable."

"I'm glad you like it."

"Not the couch, you!"

Maggie whacked him on the shoulder and they did a little play fighting. It ended with Jessie snuggling next to Maggie, his hand caressing long strands of her hair, while he lavished her with kisses. Jessie couldn't remember when he'd had such a happy time. He pulled Maggie close to him. It felt like all his dreams were coming true. Rays of sunshine peeked in through the window as the day progressed. Their eyes closed sleepily after their long night's work.

They slept together on the sofa until Maggie shifted next to Jessie and woke him up.

"Let's sleep in the bedroom," she whispered, groggy. "Much more comfortable."

Jessie didn't argue, and followed her down the hall. They slept until 4 p.m. when Jessie's watch alarm suddenly went off.

He jumped up, panicking, almost knocking Maggie off the bed.

"I have to go." Jessie was pulling on his coat, which he'd left on the floor.

"Is it your parents?"

"Yes. I have to make them dinner."

"The play starts at eight. Are you still coming with me?"

Jessie thought for a moment. It had been years since he'd been away from his parents for an evening when he didn't have to work. At the hospital, he checked in with them constantly, making sure everything was all right. He felt guilty leaving them and going out on a date. But why? It's not like he did it often, right? And Maggie was special – he deserved to go out and have a nice time with her, damn it!

He smiled and kissed her on the lips, shaking the sense of guilt out of his head. "Sure, of course. I'm looking forward to it."

"Pick me up at seven?"

"I'll be here."

As he walked to his car, Jessie's feelings of guilt, deep down in his gut, overwhelmed him. He shut his eyes, and concentrated on getting home to his parents. He'd make them a nice dinner, lay their clothes out for bed, and then he'd have a good time tonight. That was his number one priority. He deserved it!

The play was performed in an outdoor theatre, on a stage that was designed to imitate an original Elizabethan stage. For as long as Jessie had lived in southern Oregon, he'd never driven to Ashland and taken in a play before. Tonight would be his first one. And how appropriate – *Romeo and Juliet*. He snuggled into Maggie's shoulder as they watched the drama unfold.

Driving back to Maggie's apartment afterwards, Jessie's thoughts turned to his parents. Were they okay? Had they gotten to bed all right?

"Where's your head?" Maggie asked.

"It's late . . . I should be getting home." Jessie had gone so far as to not even check in with them this evening, resisting the urge to call them all through the play.

"Your parents manage on other nights. This isn't any different."

Just then, Jessie's cell phone rang. He pulled over, stopped the car and answered.

"Is this Jessie?"

"Yes, who's calling?"

"This is Norma Jean."

"Hi. I'm actually out tonight so I won't be able to work. Is it possible to call someone else in?"

"Jessie, that's not why I'm calling. I wish it were that simple. Your parents were brought in to the hospital tonight. It seems there was a fire in your home."

Jessie barely remembered the rest of the conversation. When he pulled into the hospital parking lot, he didn't park in the employee lot, but sped right down in front of the Emergency Room's double doors. As he rushed through the sliding doors, Norma Jean met him.

"Take it easy, Jessie, your parents are in ICU. There was a lot of smoke, so you know what kind of damage that means."

"Can I see them?"

"Let me check with the doctor. I think he's still here writing orders."

Norma Jean disappeared quietly, leaving Jessie standing there, his knees ready to buckle. He staggered over to a chair and dropped down into the plastic seat. It was then that he became aware of Maggie standing next to him.

"Maggie . . . I'm sorry. I should have taken you home." Jessie sat, wringing his hands, mesmerized by the highly waxed floor of the waiting room.

"Are you kidding? I want to be here for you." Maggie sat in the chair next to Jessie. They waited in silence for another fifteen minutes. Finally, Norma Jean appeared with a doctor that Jessie had seen on occasion when he floated to the intensive care unit.

The doctor approached Jessie. His name tag identified him as Dr Brandenburg.

"I'm not going to sugar-coat it for you. Your mother received a fair amount of lung damage from inhaling smoke and your father was burned extensively when he tried to put out the fire. Both of their conditions are extremely guarded. And I may have to put your mother on a ventilator."

"Why?"

"If she can't breathe deeply enough for herself, I'm concerned that pneumonia will set in and that could kill her. By helping her breathe, we might keep her lungs clear enough to keep that from happening."

"Can I talk to her?"

"You'll want to talk with your father first, however. He's been calling for you and won't allow us to give him any medicine until he sees you. He needs to have the burns debrided and eventually skin grafts, but right now, it's touch and go to see if he's going to fight off the infection."

"Does anyone know how the fire got started?"

Dr Brandenburg sighed. "Your mother decided to make a meal and a dish towel caught fire. From what I can gather, your father stopped your mother from being burned and it was then that your mother thought to press her emergency response pendant."

Jessie couldn't look Dr Brandenburg in the eye. The emergency buttons they wore were supposed to save their lives. But if they didn't get pushed early enough, what good were they? And why was she cooking in the first place?

"I left their dinner in the refrigerator. All they had to do was heat it up in the microwave." Jessie's voice was hoarse and he turned away from Dr Brandenburg, anger building inside. He'd done everything he could think of to take care of them. The one day he tried to go out and have a little fun, they almost killed themselves. The guilt was a silent rock weighing him down.

"Jessie?" Maggie put a hand on his shoulder. He shook off her hand by stepping away. Tears welled in his eyes. He knew it was ridiculous to blame her, but it was difficult to stop the anger. Had he not been out with her, his parents would be safe at home, and not dying in ICU.

"Not now, Maggie. I can't talk now."

Jessie followed Dr Brandenburg into ICU.

It was a difficult visit. Both his mom and dad just wanted Jessie to take them home. They had no idea why he simply couldn't.

Maggie watched Jessie follow the doctor into the ICU. Her heart was breaking for him, but there was nothing she could do. Norma Jean appeared next to her in her familiar ghostly way and flipped through some papers on her clipboard.

"I don't have anyone to replace Jessie Saturday and Sunday night, so you'll be working on your own in the ER. Are you comfortable with that?"

"No problem."

Maggie walked into the ICU waiting room and curled up on the couch. She would wait there for Jessie. She wanted to be the first friendly face he saw after visiting his parents. Closing her eyes, she figured she'd get a little shut-eye in case she didn't get home before her morning shift. Jessie might want to stay by his parents' bedsides all night, and she wanted to be supportive of him, no matter what decision he made. If she didn't make it home before work, she'd just change into some scrubs and get to work.

Maggie punched the couch cushion and buried her head into it. She took in a deep breath and drifted off to sleep, amidst the sounds of the hospital in the background.

Chapter Five

Working the rest of the weekend in triage by herself left Maggie with the feeling that she was an outcast. The other nurses were polite, but distant. Sharon came down Sunday night to visit and Maggie actually welcomed her.

Sharon shook her head and pursed her lips in thought. "It's too bad about Jessie's parents. I hope he's doing all right?"

"I haven't seen him, so I don't know anything." It was true. Jessie must have walked right past her as she slept on the couch in ICU yesterday morning. He hadn't woken her up. He had just abandoned her. She would have been a little angry if she hadn't understood why he did it. He must be walking around in a daze right now.

Maggie looked directly at Sharon. "Do you know something I don't?"

When Sharon began to hem and haw, Maggie pressed her. "C'mon, Sharon. Spill it."

"Well, the hospital scuttlebutt is that his mother passed away last night, and his father isn't expected to live much longer. But that's only what's going around on the floors."

"Damn it!" Maggie turned away from Sharon, tears springing into her eyes. The hospital grapevine was usually amazingly accurate. "I wish I could help Jessie, but I'm not sure how. I mean . . ." Maggie wasn't sure what she meant. She wanted to wrap her arms around him and protect him from all this.

Sharon waited while Maggie struggled with her thoughts.

"How do you cope?" she finally asked Sharon, but then she blushed. She was embarrassed for the prying question. "I'm sorry. I didn't mean to . . ."

"It's okay. I've already been through my screaming and accusing stages. That includes bargaining, pleading and all the rest."

"But you don't act like you're just sitting around waiting to die, either." Maggie wiped her tears away.

"Of course not. Do you remember the poem I scribbled out for you the first day I met you?"

"It was called 'Another Day', I think. It drove me crazy because I knew it came from someone who was . . . I mean . . ."

"Say it. I'm dying. As much as they keep trying new things, I'm losing ground and I'm going to die. But as long as I have breath in my body, I want to make these days meaningful and worthwhile. I don't consider them wasted days because I'm in the hospital. I'm visiting with you, aren't I?"

Maggie suddenly understood the significance of the poem. How important each day was and how each smile was important. That's how she could help Jessie. One small thing at a time. She reached over and wrapped her arms around the frail lady before her, pulling her close for a big hug.

"Thank you, Sharon."

Sharon smiled. "Actually, this is a warm-up for Monday's seminar. I'm going to be one of the guest speakers."

"Really? Jessie and I are supposed to attend. At least, I am. I don't know if Jessie is up to it right now."

"I hope he goes. It will be good for him. Well, I need to go back to my bed and get some rest. I'm feeling a little worn out."

"Let me send you up in a wheelchair, so you can save some steps."

"Heavens, no! Not unless I can't walk at all."

So Sharon pushed her walker and IV pole ahead of her into the elevator and Maggie waved goodbye. The hospital was in the grip of the eerie quiet that regularly descended on it at 0300 hours. The elevator door closed on Sharon. Maggie silently wished her a pleasant sleep.

* * *

Maggie was waiting for the day shift to come to the triage area when Jessie appeared over her counter. His eyes had dark circles around them, his hair was messy and he had a slight beard. His forced attempt at a smile failed, but his hoarse voice was what caught Maggie's attention. This was the first time she'd seen him since the day of the accident.

"Are you still going to the seminar today?" he asked.

"Absolutely. What about you?" She was overjoyed that he was still thinking of going.

"If I can get cleaned up in time, I'll go, I guess."

"I hope you do." Maggie locked eyes with Jessie and willed him to go. "We'll sit together."

"My father passed away this morning," Jessie whispered. He had tears forming in his eyes.

"I'm so sorry." Maggie pressed his hands between hers. She started to get up, to circumnavigate the counter and hug him, try to soothe his pain.

"I'll see you in a while, okay?" Jessie turned and headed for the men's locker room before she made it to the other side of the counter.

Maggie saw him again at the lecture, though. Just as she was entering the room, Jessie stepped up by her side, clean-shaven and in pristine scrubs.

"Hi. Mind if I sit with you?" Jessie's eyes were red. He didn't smile.

"Of course not. I'm so glad you're here." She touched his shoulder tenderly. They sat together without any more conversation.

The woman at the front of the lecture hall waited for the room to quiet down.

"Thank you all for coming. Unfortunately, one of our guest speakers is unable to be with us."

Maggie's stomach tightened.

"Sharon Wheeler passed away this morning from advanced cancer."

Jessie put his face in his hands and quietly shook his head. Maggie knew this would be a tremendous blow to him in the midst of everything else that was happening. She tried to comfort him but he didn't seem consolable. She felt completely useless.

"Let's get out of here," Maggie whispered into his ear. She grabbed his hand, determined to get him out of this atmosphere of crisis and death. It would kill him. He needed some fresh air, some sunshine. He needed to smile again.

After a quick stop with Norma Jean, she pulled him outside the hospital doors, into the bright sunshine.

"What's going on?" Jessie asked.

"We're going to the beach."

"Are you kidding? That's a five-hour drive."

"And I want you to sleep the entire way so you'll enjoy the view once we get there."

"What about work?"

"I've already taken care of that. You need a holiday and that's exactly what you're going to get!"

Jessie gave a half-hearted chuckle as she ordered him into the passenger seat of his car. As she started the engine, he lay back in the seat and closed his eyes. As the car roared out of the parking lot, Maggie noticed with some satisfaction that he had quietly dozed off, completely drained.

Jessie woke up when the vibration of the car ceased. He smelled salt air and heard the crashing waves of the ocean. Seagulls called overhead. Sitting up, he looked around to see where they were.

"Good afternoon, sleepy head," Maggie said. She gave him a peck on his cheek.

"Bandon? I've never been out here before. Are we staying here tonight?"

"Yep. I called ahead and we have a room overlooking the ocean. Right now, we have a little shopping to do."

Maggie led Jessie through a nearby outdoor fruit and vegetable market where she bought an assortment of fresh veggies and a bag of basmati rice so she could make a stir-fry for them that night. When they got to the room, his jaw dropped. The ocean view was fantastic. They sat at a small breakfast nook and watched the sea lions and gulls on the boulders while they ate dinner that night. Jessie smiled at Maggie's imitation of a sea lion and he was overwhelmed by all her efforts to cheer him up. It was working. He realized, tearing up, that she had helped him through the worst day of his life.

"You want to go for a walk?" Maggie asked after dinner.

Jessie reached out and took Maggie's hand. As they walked together down the beach, the sun was dropping into the ocean. The beauty of the sunset made his heart glow.

Back in the room, Maggie snuggled up to him on the sofa.

"Do you like the room?"

"Yes. It's wonderful."

"Jessie, I do remember you from school, you know."

"But I wasn't in your circle."

"You were so shy. You never gave anyone a chance to get to know you. Now I know it was because you had so many responsibilities at home. Will you give me that chance to get to know you now?"

Jessie knew Maggie wanted to help. And as much as he wanted to open up, he couldn't let go. When it was time to sleep, Maggie invited him to lie down next to her. He lay still, caressing her hand in his. But even though they slept in the same bed that night, Jessie couldn't make love to her. A cloud floated over him. One that he needed to deal with.

All the way back from the coast, Jessie couldn't relax.

"Do you want to come back to my place? We could have a drink and I could make some dinner?" Maggie asked when they got back to town.

"I have to go home. I'm supposed to call about our insurance and . . . all that."

"Why don't I come with you?"

Jessie locked eyes with Maggie. "Well, okay. If you want to."

They drove in silence to Jessie's street – an out-of-the-way side street with older homes lining each side. They pulled in the driveway. Jessie could see the black sooty footprints from the firemen leading right up to the front door. They got out of the car, breathing in and out through their mouths to avoid the scorching smell. When they opened the front door, Maggie commented that the rug was wet.

"Yeah, it's water damage," Jessie said. "I'm going to have to replace it."

"Do you have insurance?"

"They're coming out today to appraise the damage."

Maggie felt the couch and chairs but Jessie already knew what she'd find out. Wet. Everything was wet. He walked around in a daze, just like the first time he'd come back to have a look at what was left of the place. He became totally unaware of Maggie, until she came over to him and put her arms around his neck. Tears fell freely down his cheeks.

"If only I'd been here . . ."

"Jessie, you didn't kill your parents. You couldn't be here all the time."

Jessie leaned his forehead onto Maggie's and he tried to speak, but no words would form.

"Gather up your things and bring them to my apartment. You're moving in until all this gets sorted out, okay?"

Jessie blinked at her in surprise. "Thank you. That helps. I know I can't stay here any more. This was my parents' home, not mine. I'll fix it and sell it, I guess."

Jessie padded through to the hall closet and retrieved two suitcases and a backpack. He carried them to his bedroom and filled them with essentials and all his important papers. When he was finished he returned to the living room to join Maggie.

As Jessie crossed the threshold of the house, probably for the last time, he stopped abruptly and returned to grab a silver-framed picture of his mom and dad from the mantelpiece. He stowed it in his backpack for safe-keeping.

"Let's go." Maggie kissed him on the forehead.

He closed and locked the front door. He knew he'd never live in that house again.

Chapter Six

"Put your things in the spare bedroom."

Jessie stood in Maggie's front room, weighed down with all his belongings. He turned full circle and looked around the small apartment. But Maggie pointed beyond the familiar beige sofa towards the hall.

"This apartment doesn't look big enough to have two bedrooms."

"It's down the hall on your left, across from the bathroom."

She followed Jessie as he carried his suitcases into the spare bedroom and dropped them inside the door. The room had a twin bed, a dresser, a bookshelf filled with books and a laundry hamper. It was painted a soft green and had a window with blinds covering it. She hoped he found it to his liking.

Jessie opened the blinds and sunlight spilled into the room. But the glare only made him frown so he pulled them shut, plunging the room into semi-darkness.

Maggie came up behind him and wrapped her arms around his waist. "Of course, you won't be spending much time in this room." She nipped his neck playfully.

But Jessie pulled away from her kiss as if he'd been stung by a bee. He turned around to face her with a scowl. "Maggie . . ."

"Listen, Jessie. When my mom died I thought it was the end of my life. But all that it meant was the beginning of another life. A new beginning." Maggie stood silent, waiting for him to respond.

Jessie took the silver-framed picture of his parents out of his backpack and set it on top of the dresser. Tears began to form in his eyes again.

"This was their wedding picture."

Maggie gave him a small smile. "I have a similar picture of my parents in my bedroom. But it doesn't hurt to look at it any more."

She could feel her heart breaking for him. He looked so lost and alone. She wanted to hug him to her, but she knew he wouldn't allow it. Not at the moment. He stood erect, with dead eyes, holding himself away from her.

"I need some time, Maggie." His voice had a rough edge to it.

"What can I do to help?" She was there for him, she wanted to show him she wasn't going anywhere. She was there for the long haul. When she reached for him, though, he pulled away, stiff and unrelenting.

"I don't want you to do anything. Don't you understand? Please leave me alone and let me sort this out."

The silence between them was deafening. Maggie sighed, frustration growing at his stubbornness.

"Go ahead, Jessie, turn into stone if you choose. But remember that it wasn't your fault." And with that, she turned on her heel, hoping Jessie would come to his senses and follow her. No such luck. When he didn't move, she walked out of the spare room, closing the door behind her, leaving him alone with his demons.

Since Jessie and Maggie weren't talking at all, work became unbearable. Except for necessary – and brief – work communications, they hadn't really talked for two weeks. Even Norma Jean felt the temperature of the triage area plummet when Jessie and Maggie were working.

"Okay, what's going on down here? I've been getting some pretty strange reports. Now I know there have been some extenuating circumstances, but if your attitudes don't shape up, you're going to be put on report."

"Could I get a transfer?" Maggie asked. Jessie wouldn't talk to her at all. So after five days of fruitless pleading, she'd given up completely. If that's the way he wanted it, fine. If he was just going to wallow in self-pity and shut her out, fine.

"Why?"

"It's the job . . ."

"Explain. Is it too difficult? Do you not like the challenge?"

"No. It's who I'm working with." It even seemed to Maggie that he had started to blame her. She had caught him looking at her sometimes with an awful, sour look on his face. She guessed he thought that if she hadn't asked him out, none of this would ever have happened. She just couldn't take it any more.

"Maggie, Jessie is easy to work with. If you can't get along with him, I find it unlikely that you'll get along with anyone else."

Maggie looked at the ground, torn. This wasn't something she could confide to Norma Jean, though she wanted to. Norma Jean frowned on relationships at work. "Yes, ma'am."

Norma Jean glanced between the two, standing at opposite ends of the room, and huffed. "You got involved with each other outside work, didn't you? And now you're angry and can't work together? Do you see why I don't like it? I should fire you both right now. But instead, I'm giving you a warning. Learn to get along with each other. I'm giving you one week."

The night supervisor turned and headed for the elevator, shaking her head and mumbling to herself. Jessie and Maggie watched the elevator close, and then Jessie turned to her.

"So. Either we get along or we get fired. Which is it?" he asked.

"I don't care whether I keep this job or not!"

"Well, I do. I've worked here for eight years and I don't want to have to start over somewhere else with a reference that says I got fired. So I don't know about you, but I suggest we make this situation work."

"And what about after work? You can't just waltz into my apartment every morning, pretending we're good buddies when you won't even speak to me."

"You're right. As soon as I can find a place, I'll move out."

Then Jessie gave a curt nod in Maggie's direction and went to check in their newest arrival in the Emergency Room. Maggie fumed. How dare he. Of course, he was blaming her. It was written all over his face!

The new arrival was a sixty-five-year-old gentleman, whose breathing sounded shallow, his face was cold and clammy and his left arm ached. Jessie didn't want to, but he knew he had to call Maggie over to help.

"Get Mr Pointer's vital signs and let's get him in a room."

Maggie took the man's blood pressure. Her heart raced with alarm. When Jessie returned with a wheelchair, she wrote down the results on the triage report.

"Jessie, take a look at this."

She pointed to the 220/126 blood pressure and the 100 pulse.

"Notify the doc while I get his EKG done," Jessie said. Even if they couldn't stand each other, Maggie thought, they made a great team in the ER.

While Jessie ran Mr Pointer's EKG, Maggie stood by with Dr Brandenburg, who was on call in the ER. When the machine spit out the EKG results, Jessie handed it to the doctor and glanced at Maggie.

She looked at the results as the doctor read over them. She'd seen those rhythms before. And it wasn't good.

Dr Brandenburg spoke quietly with Mr Pointer and explained his situation. "You need to be in the cardiac care unit, so we can watch you."

"Am I having a heart attack, doc?" Mr Pointer wheezed out his words as he sat back on the gurney.

"Yes, it looks that way."

But just as Mr Pointer received his answer, he collapsed on the bed, his arms flailing at his sides as he gasped for air.

Dr Brandenburg checked Mr Pointer's heart to see if it was beating. After thirty seconds, he said, "Call a code."

Jessie pick up the nearest phone and dialed the operator. "Code ninety-nine, ER, room twelve. Code ninety-nine, ER, room twelve!"

Code 99 meant that Mr Pointer's heart had stopped beating. In less than two minutes, the room was filled with doctors, nurses, someone from the lab and X-ray. Outside were more nurses ready to run for supplies. They worked as a team, the doctors pumping his heart and inflating his lungs with air. Jessie and Maggie started an IV on each arm so medicines could be injected as the lead doctor called out what he wanted. Another nurse stood by with the crash cart, charging the paddles in case his heart needed to be shocked into a restart. Another nurse wrote down everything that transpired, minute by minute, medicine by medicine. Then, after seven minutes into the code, Dr Brandenburg shouted, "I've got a rhythm!"

The doctor pumping his heart stopped and they waited to see if Mr Pointer's heart would continue to beat.

"Okay, let's move him to CCU."

The whole room evacuated to CCU with Mr Pointer, except for Jessie and Maggie, who stayed behind to clean up the mess.

The room was silent as they went about their cleaning. But then Maggie couldn't be silent any longer. She missed him. She needed him. Maggie cleared her throat, and then asked Jessie what his thoughts were about Mr Pointer.

"Do you think he'll make it?"

Jessie shook his head, blinking away tears. "It's hard to say. He's in a very guarded position."

"Jessie?"

Jessie turned his head to her. "What?"

"Are you okay?"

Jessie froze in the middle of picking up the trash off the floor. When he stood up, tears rolled down his cheeks. "I can't help thinking of the family that's worrying about Mr Pointer right now."

"Just the family?"

Jessie hung his head and threw his handful of trash into a plastic bag. He turned to face Maggie, his eyes swollen with tears.

"I don't think I can do this any more."

"Do what? Be a nurse? Pick up trash after a code? Or maybe feel like everyone you love has died and gone away?" Maggie waited for his answer, feeling that this might be the one and only time she could get through to him. If they didn't start talking soon, it would all be over between them. And that wasn't what she wanted. She didn't think Jessie wanted that either.

"I can't be around all this tragedy," Jessie answered.

"What about working in the labor and delivery unit? Women having babies can be very uplifting . . ."

"I . . . I need a change. Something's got to change." Jessie wiped the tears off his face and quietly went back to work. They didn't speak any more until the room was cleaned up and it was time to relieve the floating nurses who'd come to the ER to fill in.

"Thank you, ladies," Jessie said to the two nurses. "We appreciate your help."

"We just got the word," said one of the nurses. "Mr Pointer is settled in CCU. His family is on their way in right now. I thought you'd better have the heads-up, since they usually come here first."

"Thanks. We'll be on the lookout," Maggie answered for both of them, when Jessie stayed silent.

Five minutes later, a blond-haired man, a younger version of Mr Pointer, came rushing into the ER. Jessie was sitting at the desk, finally composed and ready for work.

"Excuse me. I'm looking for my father, Edward Pointer. They said he was in the emergency room, having a heart problem."

Jessie motioned for the man to come to an empty examination room. He told the man to bring his wife and daughter, too. Somehow, Jessie wished Maggie was there for this talk. But she was in another exam room and hadn't returned yet.

"I'm sorry, Mr Pointer, but your father had a heart attack. He was taken to the critical care unit just a short time ago. If you'd like to talk to the doctor who . . ."

"Oh, God!" Tears streamed from the younger Mr Pointer's eyes. "We had a fight and I refused to say I was sorry. He tried to make up with me, but I was so stubborn. I wanted him to feel bad for a few days. But now . . ."

"Mr Pointer, your father is alive," Jessie said. "And please know that when he came in here, he wasn't feeling angry or upset."

"Of course not. That's his way. Listen, if you have anyone you're angry at, make sure you settle it." The man wiped away his tears. "Don't let something like this happen to you."

"Yes, sir." Jessie thought of Maggie and what a fool he'd been. It wasn't her fault that his parents died. She kept telling him it was an accident. Of course it was. He couldn't hold her responsible. He longed to tell her how much he loved her. He had to do it today.

It was then that he realized Mr Pointer was still talking to him.

"I'm sorry, Mr Pointer, but what you said really hit home. I haven't heard another word you've said, I'm afraid."

"Did you have a fight with someone?"

"It's a long story."

"Of course it is. But the ending is short and easy. Just say 'I'm sorry'."

"Yes, sir." Jessie felt a great weight lift from his chest. He breathed deeply for the first time in weeks.

"Now where is that doctor you wanted me to talk to?"

Jessie found Dr Brandenburg and introduced him to the Pointer family. Then he went in search of Maggie. He found her at the front desk in the triage area, swamped with admissions.

He couldn't wait any longer. "Maggie, I need to speak with you, please."

"Right now?"

Jessie looked at the clipboard and saw that none of the patients were urgent. They could all wait another minute or two. He pulled Maggie by the arm into an empty exam room, slid the door shut and pulled the curtain. Looking at her, face to face, he smiled and shook his head.

"I'm sorry. I've been such a fool. I love you very much. I don't know what's come over me these past couple of weeks."

Maggie was quiet for a full minute. Jessie wondered if he was too late. Had she already decided to wash her hands of him?

"Well?" Jessie asked.

"Is that all?"

"No, it's not. But I thought I'd wait for a more romantic spot to ask you to marry me."

Maggie smiled. "This is romantic enough for me." Maggie reached up and stroked his cheek.

He took her hand and kissed her palm. "Will you marry me, Maggie?"

"Yes, I will." She rushed into his arms and he finally held her like he should have all along. The ER never heard such a shout as when Jessie finally kissed his bride-to-be, and put the past firmly behind them.

WOUNDED HEART

Cassandra Dean

Chapter One

The shrill beep of the Accident & Emergency pager split the air.

Ruefully, Matt looked down at his half-full coffee. He'd splashed out on a proper coffee from the specialist coffee shop next to Royal Flinders, stupidly thinking he'd have more than five minutes to relax. He should have known better.

Exhaling, he threw his coffee in the trash and strode from the A & E break room. Chaos surrounded him.

A & E bustled, staff preparing the trauma rooms for the influx of patients. As Consultant to A & E, he was responsible for providing and coordinating the care of the emergency patients who came into his hospital. Primarily, he stabilized the patients for handover to the surgical registrars, where required. Some nights it was quiet. This wasn't one of those nights. His shift wasn't even half over and already they'd had an emergency appendectomy, a motorcyclist who'd come off her bike and tore up her arm and side, and a man complaining of chest pains that had turned out to be the onset of a heart attack.

And now . . . God knows what they had now.

Reaching the nurses' station, he forced a smile, pangs of the lost coffee break still swirling. "Hey, Veronica."

Veronica looked up from the computer, an apology on her face. "Dr Ripley. Hey. Sorry to interrupt your break, but we've got a call come through."

"Not a problem, Veronica, it's what I'm here for. When did the call come?"

"A couple of minutes ago. Paramedics are on the way." She looked at the computer screen. "One patient, multiple gunshot wounds."

Familiar adrenaline ran though him as part of his mind started cataloguing what needed to be done. "Which room?"

"TR One. But there's more."

"Oh?" He needed to be on fire to go a tussle with gunshot wounds.

Veronica looked up from the computer. "It has something to do with a drug bust. Drugs Task Force and Major Crimes are travelling."

That stopped him. A kind of excited churn began in his stomach, distracting him from thoughts of the incoming patient. If the Drugs Task Force was involved then perhaps Detective Constable Hicks was among them.

Annoyed at himself, he forced his stomach to calm. Now was not the time to think of messy brown hair, liquid dark eyes and a fleeting smile that made him want to trace her lips with his tongue. *For Christ's sake, Ripley. Bleeding people would soon be here.*

"Right," he said, forcing his thoughts from Detective Hicks. "Shall we?"

Veronica nodded, and they made their way to Trauma Room 1.

While Veronica updated the team already in TR1, Matt made his way to the sink and washed his hands, then pulled on gloves and a disposable gown. One of the junior nurses, Meg, stood by the whiteboard, already writing down what information she had and what Veronica had just told her.

Matt scanned the board as, in the distance, he heard the arriving ambulance cut their sirens. Arnold Simmons. Thirty-two-year-old male, multiple gunshot wounds. Mentally, he ran through again what needed to be done. Check patient response, ensure airways were clear. Control blood flow. Ensure circulation was functioning. Emergency theatres had been notified, but it was up to him and his team to deliver the patient, stabilized and prepped for surgery.

A moment later, Mr Simmons was wheeled into the trauma room on the paramedics' stretcher, an oxygen mask over his face, an IV already in his arm. The paramedics started detailing their handover report as Veronica slipped the PAT-slide beneath Mr Simmons, and Matt listened with half an ear, knowing Meg was writing up any and all information presently being relayed.

"Transfer on three," he said. A moment later, Mr Simmons was on their examination bed, ready for their attention.

Betty, the anaesthetist, was talking to Mr Simmons, calling his name. No response. Matt wasn't worried, not yet. Betty was an outstanding anaesthetist, and she'd get the patient on track. As it was, she was checking their patient's drip, ensuring replacement fluids to give Mr Simmons the best chance possible, given that he'd already lost a lot of blood.

Eric, one of the best A & E nurses Matt had worked with in a long time, was already listening to Mr Simmons's chest, performing observations as Veronica checked the patient's blood pressure.

"BP is low," Veronica reported.

"Pupils equal and reacting to light," Eric added.

Matt looked down at Mr Simmons. "Cut his clothing," he said. "Cross, type and match bloods."

Veronica and Eric undertook his directions, quickly and decisively, Veronica cutting and removing the patient's clothing while Eric took his blood.

"Oxygen saturations within normal limits," Betty said.

Matt nodded to acknowledge, his gaze cataloguing Mr Simmons's injuries. "So we have gunshot wounds to the left shoulder, left hip, left upper thigh and right abdomen. Eric, check the wound in his hip."

While Eric did so, Matt assessed Mr Simmons's shoulder. The wound went straight through the fleshy part of the shoulder, and appeared to be of little concern. "Eric," Matt said. "How's your wound?"

"Through and through, Doctor."

"Right. Pack them and bandage." Matt glanced at Veronica. "Veronica, confirm the femoral artery hasn't been hit, although I'm sure it hasn't otherwise this guy would already have bled out."

"On it," Veronica said.

"Eric, let's deal with the abdomen." Matt glanced at the whiteboard where Meg had written down the last lot of vital statistics the team had called out. "Clean and debride. We need to find that bullet."

Eric pre-empted Matt's every move as they flushed the wound to give them a better view of the area.

"Retractors," Matt said and, almost before he'd finished speaking, Eric had the skin retractors in place.

"Angle that light a bit more for me, will you?" Matt asked, and again his instructions were followed, quickly and efficiently. He put his fingers into the abdomen, feeling around, needing to find that foreign body, needing to remove it if they were going to give Mr Simmons any chance of survival.

"Femoral artery intact. I'll clean, pack and bandage the wound," Veronica reported.

"Oxygen saturations still within normal limits," Betty added. "BP still low."

"Thanks." Perspiration beading on his brow, Matt continued to search for the bullet. Where was the bugger? "Ah. Found it. Angle the light." He held out his hand. "Forceps." After the instrument was placed into his outstretched hand, Matt carefully removed the bullet, holding it up to the light to check it was completely intact. "Kidney dish." The dish was placed before him, and the bullet clattered into the metal bowl. "BP?" he asked.

"Still low," Betty said.

Matt nodded. "Let's find the bleeder," he said, more to himself than to Eric. He carefully checked the area, Eric mopping up the excess blood with gauze.

Ah. There it was. Matt lifted his hand, palm up. "Locking clamp."

Eric placed the instrument into his hand.

"Femur packed and bandaged," Veronica said.

Matt clamped the offending artery. "Eric, clean the area. We need to see if there are any others."

"Yes, Doctor." Eric mopped again, gauze staining red.

The area now cleaned, Matt noted with satisfaction they'd patched any and all bleeders.

Glancing away from the monitors, Betty said, "BP improved. We're out of the woods, Matt."

Matt nodded. "All right, let's put a temporary suture in and alert emergency theatres their patient will be with them shortly."

Matt glanced over his shoulder at Meg who was still writing all information on the whiteboard. "Who's the surgical registrar on call?"

"Dr Willis," Meg replied, not looking away from the board.

"Good choice." Matt looked at Eric. "Okay, let's pack and bandage and get him off to theatres. Betty? You satisfied?"

Betty nodded. "He's a tough one. Should be fine to survive surgery."

"Excellent. Veronica, call the radiologist in to take some nifty photographs of Mr Simmons so Dr Willis can see exactly where those bullets are."

"On it."

The radiologist made it to the trauma room in record time. As Matt and Eric finished tidying up Mr Simmons's abdomen, the radiologist set up the portable, digital X-ray machine. Satisfied he'd done all he could, Matt stood back from the table, noting Eric did the same. "Eric, notify the orderlies they can whisk Mr Simmons away to surgery as soon as the X-rays are done."

"Will do, Doctor."

Adrenaline still running high, Matt breathed in slowly. Pulling off his gloves, he surveyed his team, the best A & E staff a consultant could wish for. "Thanks, everyone. Outstanding work as always. Mr Simmons will live to see another day, unless those boffins in surgery muck it up."

Huge grins on their faces, his staff laughed. He knew well what they felt. It was an amazing feat, to cheat death.

He looked at Veronica. "What's next?"

Chapter Two

"You can't be here, Detective Constable Hicks."

A frown creased her brow but Ella Hicks didn't turn from the A & E staff working on the witness. "I need to stay with the witness."

The nurse exhaled. "Detective, you cannot be in A & E right now. Medical staff only."

Annoyed, she turned to regard him. He wore an implacable look, but she'd seen a similar expression in the mirror. "I understand that, Nurse—" she looked at his ID badge "—Dobson, but this patient can identify an extremely sensitive person of interest. I will not be letting him out of my sight."

He didn't look convinced. "Be that as it may, Detective, the patient is in the trauma room and only medical personnel are permitted in A & E. You were only allowed in here due to concern regarding the blood on your clothing. You're endangering his life and the lives of other patients by remaining."

Glancing down at her bloodstained clothes, Ella could see why they'd been worried. However, the blood staining her shirt was all the witness's, gained when she and another officer had tried to stop the bleeding by putting pressure on the wounds.

Drawing her jacket closed to cover the bloodstains, Ella opened her mouth to respond but a woman in nurse's uniform pushing a trolley containing medical equipment brushed past her. Ella danced out of the way, but it didn't stop the nurse from throwing her a scowl as she continued past.

Shoving a hand through her hair, Ella exhaled. Well, she couldn't argue with what Nurse Dobson had said, could she? Especially when she clearly was in the way. "Which doctor is attending Mr Simmons?"

Nurse Dobson smiled, but it didn't quite reach his eyes. Clearly, she was annoying him by refusing to leave. "Dr Ripley."

Tension drained from her, somewhat startling in its sudden absence. Dr Ripley. A memory of him flashed though her mind, his dark hair askew and a grin on his face.

Thank God. If Dr Ripley was attending, then she could be sure her witness was in the very best of hands. "All right then. Is there somewhere I can observe?"

"Unfortunately, there's only the waiting room," Nurse Dobson said, and his tone was polite but firm. "We will let you know as soon as the patient is stabilized."

Frustrated but knowing there was nothing she could do, Ella started for the waiting room. The nurse followed her, holding the door open as she went through. "We'll let you know, Detective."

She exhaled. "Thank you."

He nodded and let the door go. It swung into place and, just like that, she was separated from A & E.

Making her way to the moulded plastic seats lining the wall, she sank into the nearest one, without sacrificing a full view of the A & E doors. Only this morning, she'd been focused on the upcoming police operation and her part in it, and now she was in Royal Flinders A & E, blood staining her clothing. Her unit had been planning the drug bust for over a month, acting on information gleaned from three separate informants. It was supposed to have been an exchange between low-level Collier group underlings, facilitating distribution of 120 kg of uncut cocaine. They'd locked the targets down, no problems, taken them with little fuss. However, then one of them had declared he could identify the leader of the Collier group himself – Nick Collier.

Collier was a ghost. No one had seen his face, or if they had, they didn't live long enough to tell anyone about it. In every interview with every Collier underling, they spoke of him in hushed, fearful tones, but not one of them could give even a vague description of the man. But all that was about to change. The man under triage in A & E, the man riddled with four gunshot wounds, was currently the most important personage to Australian Federal and Local police.

The events of the past five hours – hell, the past five weeks – crashed over her. Shoulders slumping, she dropped her head into her hands. Somehow, Simmons had seen Collier's face. He'd been quick to claim such, throwing his hands to the sky when the SWAT team had burst into the warehouse, and screaming he would talk, that Collier himself was among those who'd run from the crime scene. They'd barely had time to verify his claim before one of the other Collier men had broken free and put four bullets in Simmons. Chaos erupted, but they'd managed to get Simmons to the paramedics and then to the hospital. Now, it was her task to ensure he survived and, further, that he talked.

And there was no way in hell she was going to screw that up.

Scrubbing her hand through her fringe, she leaned against the wall. She'd been the one who should have protected Simmons. She'd been the one to collar him, had him in her cuffs, but the next thing she knew, he had four bullets in him, and three cops were subduing the suspect who'd somehow pulled a gun and fired. Now, her sergeant – Detective Sergeant Matheson – had given her a chance to redeem herself, to make her screw-up right. She'd stay here until Simmons woke, and then she'd get the description of Collier. There was no other option.

"Detective Constable Hicks?"

Tired in her bones, she removed her hand from her eyes and focused on the two uniformed constables standing straight and tall before her, hats tucked under their arms. "Yes?"

One of the constables stepped forward. "I'm Constable Ayres, and this is Constable Taylor. We're here to protect the patient," he said.

"Good." She nodded towards the A & E door. "The patient is currently in an A & E trauma room, and we will be informed of any developments." Her cell phone buzzed. Pulling it from her pocket, she said, "You two stay on point, make sure no one enters through that door who isn't supposed to be there."

The uniforms nodded and stationed themselves at the swinging doors. Never taking her eyes from them, she pressed "accept" and raised the phone to her ear. "Hicks."

"Detective Constable, how is the witness?"

At the sound of her sergeant's voice, she straightened. "Sir, he's currently in A & E. The nursing staff will inform me the moment we're allowed access."

"Good." Matheson exhaled. "Christ Almighty, Hicks, this was a royal fuck-up."

"Yes, sir." Again she saw the chaos of an operation gone bad. Simmons spinning like a top, an almost comical surprise on his face. Delayed reaction from the police surrounding him. The blood. God, the blood.

Pushing the horror aside, she focused on work. "Sir, is there any update on the situation?"

"They're still searching for Collier, but no one is hopeful of a capture." Matheson exhaled again. She could almost picture him, lines cut deep into a careworn face, tired eyes speaking of his concern as his words never would. "We're reliant on that witness. He better fucking hope to whatever God he prays to he can identify Collier."

"Yes, sir."

"Make sure you get him to talk, Hicks. Don't fuck up." His tone implied "again".

Guilt turned her stomach to knots. "I won't, sir."

"Good. Report in one hour." The phone went dead.

Slowly, Ella lowered the phone and replaced it in her pocket. Pushing to her feet, she started towards Ayres and Taylor.

The A & E doors swung open and a doctor strode through, his gaze searching the waiting area. Ayres and Taylor straightened, sharp eyes assessing the situation but there was no need. This doctor she knew.

Ripley.

His chocolate-brown hair was askew, probably from his surgical cap, and a shadow of beard darkened his jaw. The white jacket did nothing to hide his lean form or broad shoulders, and the green of his shirt somehow highlighted the flecks of green in his hazel eyes. As he looked at her, the beginnings of a smile quirked his sensuous mouth, before settling back into lines of concern.

Gritting her teeth, she forced herself to focus on work. Just work. She was responsible for the safety and interrogation of a witness important to both federal and local police. She wasn't going to allow her attraction to a doctor whose first name she didn't even know distract her.

Squaring her shoulders, she nodded a greeting. "Dr Ripley."

"Detective Constable Hicks," he said solemnly. Even as his eyes twinkled. "Good to see you again."

"You too." Her heart raced and she was distinctly short of breath. Damn it, she had to focus. Focus! "Terrible reason for it, though."

"Yeah." Brows drawing, he scrubbed a hand through his hair. "The patient is stable, though he still needs surgery. He's being wheeled in now."

"Right." Heart smoothing to something approaching a normal rhythm, she crossed her arms. "How long do you think the surgery will take?"

"At least a few hours. The registrar will see you when it's finished, update you." He looked at the chairs lining the wall. "You comfortable here?"

Abruptly, her shoulder ached. Shifting her weight did nothing to ease it. "Yeah, I'm good."

"Right. Right." He scrubbed at his hair again. "I'd stay, but my shift won't be over for another four hours."

"Hey, no problem at all, Ripley." Rubbing her shoulder, she smiled. "You got work to do, same as me. Besides, Constable Ayres and his partner are here. We've got it covered."

"I know, but it's always easier when you've got someone to pass the time with."

Something warm flared in her chest. How was she to ignore him when he said such sweet things? "Seriously, I'll be fine. Stop by when you're free if you want."

"Yeah." He shifted, and then a grin flashed across his face. "Yeah. Well, I'll see you."

The warmth flared into heat. "Okay," she managed.

With one final, quick smile, he disappeared into A & E.

She watched him go. She'd known Dr Ripley for just over a year, by her reckoning, and they'd become friends of a sort. More often than not, they ended up together, passing the time as she waited for test results or recovering patients or a coroner's report. She knew he loved being the consultant to A & E, that he unwound at night with beer and football, and that his eyes looked flecked with gold when he laughed.

Shaking herself, she forced him out of her mind. Ripley was a complication she didn't need right now.

Straightening her shoulders and ignoring the burn in her muscles, she made her way to the A & E doors. The constable who'd spoken – Ayres – straightened at her approach. She nodded to him and his partner and took up a place beside them.

A nurse pushed past her, the door swinging wide as she entered A & E. Ordered mayhem greeted her, the A & E team working on the next patient. She could see Dr Ripley amongst them, his expression calm as he directed the chaos.

The door swung closed. Leaning against the wall opposite, she stared at the door. No more thoughts of Ripley. She was here for the witness, and she wouldn't move until Simmons did.

Chapter Three

Pulling on his jacket, Matt strode down the ward corridor. His shift finally over, all he wanted was a cold knock-off beer, the replay of the football game he'd set to record earlier and perhaps forty-two-point-three seconds of sleep before having to drag his arse back to work to do this all over again tomorrow.

Rotating his shoulders, he nodded to hospital staff as he passed. What a day. The gunshot victim had been the worst of it, that's for sure, but he'd still had a carpenter who'd bashed his fingers with his hammer, a six-year-old who'd fallen from a slide and needed seventeen stitches, and paperwork. God, the never-ending paperwork. He was exhausted. Beer, football and sleep would fix that.

As he neared the ICU, his steps slowed. As exhausted as he was, it wouldn't be too much out of his way to check on the gunshot victim. The man had been out of surgery for two hours and by all accounts was recovering well, stationed in a private ICU room with his protective detail flanking the door. He knew all about what had happened after the patient had left his A & E, knew the surgery had been a success, and that Ayres was the handsomer of the two constables on guard – all thanks to gossip. If you ever wanted to keep something secret at Royal Flinders . . . Well. You couldn't.

A frown troubled his brow. Mr Simmons had been a tricky one. The three wounds to the upper thigh, shoulder and hip were bad enough, but the abdomen wound had given him real concern. He'd done the best he could, removing the bullet and patching the torn flesh, but at the end of the day, his skills were focused on stabilization – keep the patient alive, prep him for surgery, pass him on. However, it behoved him to discover how the man's surgery had gone.

Besides, Detective Hicks had said he should stop by after his shift.

Turning on his heel, he strode into ICU. With a smile and a nod for the duty nurse, he made his way to where the man was recovering. At the end of the corridor, away from the other patients and with only one access point. The room was flanked by the two uniformed officers, just as reported. There was no sign of the nurse to special Mr Simmons, but then it was possible the nurse devoted to his care was behind the closed door, checking the patient's vitals.

And to the side, slumped in a chair that didn't look any more comfortable than the ones in the A & E waiting room was Detective Hicks.

His heart stuttered in his chest. Even tired, she looked gorgeous. Her light brown hair was a tumbled mess, tied back with a band that seemed to be losing the battle, and her sensible coat and comfortable trousers could probably do with a press, but she was the best sight he'd seen all day.

As he neared, the familiar awkwardness stuttered his steps, blanked his mind. Jesus, Ripley, you've operated on thousands of patients, saved countless lives. *Get it together.* "Detective Hicks?"

Dark, liquid eyes regarded him from under straight brows and hit him like a punch in the gut. Heart lurching, heat rushing through him, he struggled to something approaching a smile.

She blinked, shook her head as if to clear it, and with that small motion, she broke the spell her gaze always cast. Oh look at that, he could breathe again.

"Sorry, Ripley. I've been sitting here for so long, I've become a part of the seat." A wan, rueful smile teased her mouth.

"No worries." Seating himself beside her, he relaxed into the chair. "How's things?"

"Oh, great." She rubbed the bridge of her nose. "I'm really enjoying waiting for a criminal to wake up."

"Yeah, I can see how that would be awesome fun times." Lines of tiredness cut deep furrows in her brow. He wished he could wipe them away. "Coffee?"

She made a face. "From here? No way."

Horror filled him. "God, no. There's a place next door. Great coffee. Almost enjoyed one earlier today before your call came in."

A smile tugging at the corner of her mouth, she glanced at him. "Is that right?"

He held his forefinger and thumb apart. "This close, my friend."

She laughed, lines of tiredness melting away.

A thrill warmed him. He loved this time with her, sitting and waiting and talking, learning each other as they did so. She came to the hospital often, escorting injured victims or suspects, and they'd struck up a friendship, though one that hadn't left the hospital. Every time he saw her, she wore those lines of tiredness. It gave him such a kick to see her face light with a laugh or a smile, to know he'd distracted her from her worries for a moment or two.

Leaning her head against the wall, she sighed. "I better give the coffee a miss. I'm already jittery, I don't need to add caffeine to it."

"Cool." Relaxing into the seat, he leaned his head against the wall as well.

Sighing again, she glanced at him. "How's things with you?"

"Good. Got my paper on A & E procedure accepted by *New Australian Medical Journal*."

Delight lit her face. "Really? That's great!"

A warmth started in his chest at her enthusiasm. "Yeah, it's pretty good. Probably mean longer hours, though. They want me to do a follow-up."

"Don't talk it down, Ripley. That's awesome, and they want you to do a follow-up as well? Congratulations."

"Ah, yeah. Thanks." He told himself the heat in his cheeks was because of a suddenly malfunctioning hospital air conditioner.

Smiling still, she studied him. "You know, the registrar said if it weren't for you, they would have lost the patient."

"Yeah, well." He was good at his job. He didn't think much of it. It had to be done, so he did it.

She shook her head. "Sometimes you're so Australian, you make me sick. Stop being so modest."

"I will if you will." He'd thought that would make her blush – and look, it totally did.

But only for a moment. A cheeky glint lit her eye. "Bit different from a big shot A & E consultant who has a paper in Australia's premier medical journal, though."

"Not different at all, Ms Super Cop."

She hiccupped a laugh. "What?"

He grinned. "Oh, I don't know."

They smiled at each other for a long while. Feelings welled inside him, feelings that made him feel full to the brim. The sort of feelings he wasn't yet ready to identify.

Finally, she looked away. "So, you'll just have to keep taping the football, hey?"

Thank God she'd broken the tension. "Yeah. I do enjoy seeing the game seven hours after everyone else. And when I'm busy at the hospital, it's so easy to avoid the results."

Suddenly he really wanted to touch her. Just brush her cheek, trail his fingers lightly over her skin. Her lips. Then, maybe, he would kiss her.

An orderly pushing a trolley rattled past, snapping him out of his reverie. Clearing his throat, he returned his thoughts to where they should be. "That guy in there should be okay. The patient."

She looked towards the door, her brow furrowing. "The registrar seems to think so."

Following her gaze, he frowned at the door. "I can check his chart if you like."

"Nah." Turning her head, she shrugged. "He'll wake up at some stage." She rubbed the bridge of her nose again.

Concern twisted in him. She looked so tired. "How long has it been since you slept?"

She exhaled. "I don't know. Yesterday?"

Brows creased, he glanced at the door. "Are you going to be okay to watch this guy?"

"Of course."

Surprised at the sharpness of her words, he looked at her.

A scowl marred her features. "What are you saying?"

"Nothing." Confused, he rubbed his thigh. "You look tired is all."

"Oh." Her face softened. "Well, my sergeant wants me to watch him."

Of course. She loved her job with a passion. Who was he to question that? Besides, he shouldn't lecture her. He practically lived at the hospital.

Exhaling, he rubbed his neck. "Want some company?"

Her brows shot up. "Really?"

Shrugging, he let his hand fall to his lap. "Nothing better to do."

A smile played about her mouth. "But the football was on today."

"It can wait. Besides, I already know who won."

She laughed. "Damn spoilers."

Chapter Four

"And then he turned to me, absolutely saturated with fake blood, and said calm as you please, 'I don't think that was a real kangaroo, Hicks.'"

Holding his taut stomach, Ripley was laughing so hard tears streamed down his face. "Oh God, Hicks, you've got to stop. It hurts."

Ella held up her hands. "Hey man, I only report the facts."

Still hiccuping with laughter, he wiped his eyes. A warm, bubbly kind of satisfaction filled her at the sight. She loved to see him laugh like that, and know she was the one who had caused it.

His amusement settled into a wide grin. "Then what happened?"

"Then? Then nothing. We went home. Got a kebab on the way, though."

"'Course you did. Covered in fake blood?"

Cocking her head, she lifted a brow. "Best time to get a kebab."

"Oh yeah, and I'm sure you didn't freak them out at all."

"Nah. Those guys are used to it."

He shook his head, still chuckling.

Smiling, she leaned her head against the wall. The fake kangaroo was one of her best stories and always got a chuckle. In fact, it was kind of weird she hadn't told it to him before. They'd spoken of so many things. Making him laugh distracted her from just how tired she was. And from the nerves twisting her stomach.

She cursed herself. Why did she have to remind herself of that? She had been going along nicely, chatting with Ripley, enjoying his company and, if she were truthful, sneaking glances when he wasn't looking. He had this way of stretching so his T-shirt rode up, displaying the golden skin and muscles of his abdomen. Every time, her mouth would go dry and she'd lose whatever thought was in her head. Then she'd lick her lips and all manner of inappropriate thoughts would flood her mind.

It was a pleasant sort of distraction.

He was doing it now. Stretching. She watched as his T-shirt separated from his jeans and a thin sliver of golden flesh appeared, the muscles of his abdomen contracting as he stretched.

Her mouth went dry.

Fascinated, she stared as he stretched further. He probably knew she was watching, was probably doing it on purpose, but she didn't care. Maybe it was time. Maybe they should see each other somewhere outside Royal Flinders, somewhere that wasn't lit by fluorescent lights and didn't smell of antiseptic. Maybe they should—

A loud bang echoed through the corridor.

She frowned, and then looked in the direction of the sound. Had someone dropped something? It hadn't sounded like that—

A second bang. Another.

Christ Jesus. That was gunfire.

Launching to her feet, she drew her weapon as she shoved Ripley behind her. Ignoring his protest, his confusion, she scanned the corridor. Nothing obvious. No sign of a weapon, or the assailant wielding it.

She turned. Ripley stared at her, pale under his olive skin. "Hicks, what—?"

"Are you okay?"

"Yeah. Yeah, I'm fine. Was that . . . God, Hicks, was that . . ."

She gripped his shoulder. "Stay here."

He looked around. "But what was that?"

"Ripley." She squeezed.

His gaze flew to her.

Meeting his eyes, she said, "Stay here."

Shoving a hand through his hair, he nodded. "Yeah. Yeah, okay."

With a final squeeze to his shoulder, she rose and in two strides was at Simmons's door. Three neat holes perforated the wood. Amazingly, all three had missed Constable Ayres who stood before the door, his weapon drawn and his stance tense. God, what had happened? She knew Ayres had been standing to the side of the door, but what had happened when the shots were fired? She'd been looking at Ripley, had been distracted . . .

She shook herself. Now was not the time for recriminations.

Placing her hand against the door, she pushed it open. The other constable stood inside, his weapon drawn and his skin green. The duty nurse crouched beside Simmons's bed, face pale but hands steady as she checked the man's vitals.

"All okay?" Ella said

The constable looked at her, his gaze sharpening as he regained composure. "Missed."

She nodded, and backed out of the room. "Guard the witness," she said to Constable Ayres as she strode down the corridor.

All around, people were in a panic. Three women huddled behind a hospital trolley, clutching each other, while others tunnelled down the corridor, cries and screams rending the air.

Gun drawn but lowered, detachment settled upon Ella, as it always did. She wove through staff and patients, scanning the area for any sign of the assailant. As she passed the duty station, a nurse looked at her gun, her badge and then pointed frantically down the corridor towards where it turned to the east.

Following the direction, Ella slowed as she came to the turn. Shoving back against the wall, she edged a glance around. Clear.

As she pushed down the corridor, people scurried past her, half bent and hands curled around their heads. Paying them little mind, she took note of the elevator, the door to the stairwell. At the end of the corridor, a doctor performed CPR on a man lying prone. Heart attack, stroke, something brought on by shock. No wound.

Ella stopped. The stairwell.

Reversing her direction, she hesitated a moment before bracing herself to bust the stairwell door wide. Barely noticing the ache in her shoulder from the hard contact with the door, she checked the corners. Glanced over the edge of the stairwell. Nothing.

She proceeded down a flight, gun lowered but ready. Then repeated this again. Checked the corners. Glanced over the edge of the well.

Still nothing.

"God damn it!" She hit the wall with a closed fist. She'd lost him, she'd fricking lost him. The assailant had waltzed right up to the witness's room and shot at him without her notice, and she'd lost him. Goddamn it. Goddamn it.

"Hicks?"

Quick as a flash, she whirled and levelled her weapon.

Ripley took a step back, his hands rising into the air. "Hicks, it's me."

She lowered her weapon, and an unholy rage consumed her. "What are you doing here? I told you to stay put."

Hands still in the air, he didn't move. "Yeah, you did."

"So what are you doing here?"

"I came for you."

As quick as it had flared, the anger abated. For her? He'd come for her? But he could get hurt. The assailant could still be here . . .

No. He was gone. She'd let him go.

The strength went out of her legs.

Ripley caught her as she slumped. "Hicks? Hicks, are you hurt?"

"No." Her voice sounded off, as if it came from far away. "He got away, Ripley."

"It's okay. You're safe. It's okay." She felt a shudder go through him.

"But he got away, Ripley. I didn't get him." She felt cold. Was she cold?

Ripley hadn't seemed to notice. His hand cupped her jaw, his thumb tracing her cheek. "It's okay."

"No, you don't understand. It was my responsibility. I should have got him."

"Hicks . . ."

She shook her head. "I should have got him."

"Jesus, Hicks, you could have been shot. Think about that, would you?"

She looked at him intently.

Eyes wild, he was pale under the olive tint of his skin and, for the first time, she noticed that the hand on her cheek was shaking. "You could have been shot and there would have been nothing I could have done about it."

Covering his hand with hers, she stopped his shaking. "But I wasn't."

He laughed, and the sound of it was harsh. "Oh yeah. That makes me feel a ton better." He closed his eyes, swallowed. "Fuck."

She'd never heard him swear before. "Ripley . . ."

Exhaling, he looked down. "Jesus, Hicks."

Curling her other hand around his upper arm, she gripped his bicep tight. "I'm fine."

His gaze met hers.

"Ripley. I'm fine." She willed him to believe her.

His eyes flickered. Abruptly, she became aware of the heat of his palm against her cheek. How close his mouth was to hers. Less than a breath.

Her fingers curled into his biceps.

A moment passed. Another. Her chest felt tight, her breath strangled in her lungs. His hazel eyes darkened, his gentle fingers tunnelled into her hair as he drew her to him.

And then, he kissed her.

Passion exploded, fuelled by fear and worry and him. Heat tore through her as he moulded to her lips, the tip of his tongue coaxing hers to part. Rising to her toes, she wrapped her arms about his neck. His hand tightened in her hair, his other clutching the small of her back and pulling her into him.

This. This is what she'd wanted. When they'd talked of his studies. When they talked of football and kebabs and exploding fake kangaroos, she'd wanted to feel his mouth, his body, his arms holding her tight. She wanted all of this, and so much more.

He turned her so the wall was against her back, the length of him pressing against the length of her. His lips trailed over her cheek, her temple, before travelling to her ear. She gasped as he licked her neck, felt his smile against her skin. Tugging his head back to hers, she kissed those smiling lips.

Something buzzed in her pocket.

Frowning, she ignored it, focusing on the taste of him.

It buzzed again.

Belatedly, she realized what it was. Her cell phone. Buzzing.

Pulling herself from him, she pushed against his chest and shook her head. She felt thick, heavy.

Ripley blinked at her, his lips red from hers, and his eyes heavy with passion.

She leaned towards him.

No.

Pushing against his chest, she turned from the tempting sight of a passion-drenched Ripley and, shakily, drew her phone from her pocket to hit "accept".

"Hicks." God, her voice sounded so hoarse.

"You didn't check in, Hicks."

Her spine snapped straight. Shoving Ripley from her, she put distance between them. "I'm sorry, sir. There's been a situation."

Her sergeant exhaled. "I know. What I want to know is why you didn't inform me?"

"Sir, I pursued the assailant and was unable—"

"Did you apprehend him?"

"No, sir."

Another exhalation. "I'll be there in an hour, Hicks. I'll expect you to brief me on the situation."

"Yes, si—" She pulled the phone from her ear and stared at it. Already dead.

Inadequacy crashed over her, remembered and fierce. He was right. She should have apprehended the assailant – hell, she should have prevented him from firing – but she'd been distracted. She'd been looking at Ripley, at his abdomen of all things, and she'd allowed someone to attack the witness. Christ, she'd almost messed up again.

"That was your sergeant?"

She looked up. Ripley stood, his hands awkwardly at his sides as if he didn't know what to do with them.

She replaced the phone in her pocket. "Yes."

Taking a step towards her, he raised his hand to her shoulder. "Hicks . . ."

Sidestepping, she looked past him. "We should go."

"Right." He dropped his hand. "You know, we didn't do anything wrong."

She said nothing.

Scrubbing his hair, he said, "I like you, Hicks. You know that, right?"

"I . . ." She shook herself. It didn't matter. "I can't do this now."

He stared at her.

She stared back. Detachment made it so no emotion crossed her face, not even when he scowled.

"All right. But, Hicks—" hazel eyes bore into hers, "—we will do this soon."

Again, she said nothing.

Frustration darkened his scowl. Exhaling, he made for the stairwell door.

"Ripley." He turned as she called out to him. "You can't go anywhere. You're a witness."

He nodded sharply and strode from the stairwell.

Silent, she followed him.

Chapter Five

Drumming his fingers against the out-of-date magazine resting on his thigh, Matt stared down the corridor. Hicks sat beside him, unusually quiet. They both awaited the arrival of her sergeant at the A & E nurses' station – she, to make her report, and he, because he'd had the goddamn bad luck to be a witness to the shooting. The ICU was cordoned off to anyone bar police and ICU staff. They both sat and waited. They hadn't spoken since the stairwell.

Gaze focused steadfastly down the hall, he clenched his hands. After a year of wanting, he'd finally had her where he wanted – in his arms and flushed with passion. That kiss had damn near blown his head off, had left him weak at the knees, as clichéd as that sounded, and she'd treated it as if it were nothing. She'd removed herself, refused to talk or even acknowledge there was something between them, something that warranted exploring. Instead, she'd turned cold, told him he was a witness, and that had been that. As if his opinion didn't matter. As if the last year of talking and laughing and thinking she was the most beautiful woman he'd ever met was nothing. She'd turned on a dime, changed from a warm, passionate woman into a cold, detached police officer. Detective Hicks. Goddamn it, he'd wanted to shake her, yell at her, do something to get her to react, but she'd looked at him with that detached look on her face and told him he was only a fucking witness.

Christ.

Exhaling, he looked down at the magazine. He needed to calm down. Anger would get him nowhere.

Stretching his fingers, he went over the events in the stairwell for the fourteenth time. It had been . . . awesome. Her mouth had been soft beneath his, her skin silken against his fingers. He'd felt all of her against all of him, and he'd wanted more.

He could still taste her.

Then, she'd gotten that phone call and it was like a wall had come down. From that moment on, it had been like she was a different person, someone he'd never met before. He knew she was stressed. Hell, how could she not be? Her operation had gone south, her witness had been close to death, and she'd gotten a phone call from her sergeant that had obviously not gone well.

And there'd been the shooting.

Holy hell. The shooting.

Fear came upon him, remembered and intense. She could have been shot, so easily. She'd pushed him behind her, her first instinct to protect him. Christ, she was half a foot shorter than him. He should have protected her, should have held her to him and assured himself she was well. Instead, he'd stood in shock while she'd checked on Mr Simmons and then taken off after the shooter, putting herself in even greater danger.

Oh God. His chest hurt.

Rubbing at the pain, he focused on his breathing. What would he have done if she'd been injured? Shot? Or . . . worse?

"What new fuck-up is this, Hicks?"

Beside him, Hicks tensed. Flanked by constables in uniform, a rumpled-looking man wearing a bad suit and too-big trench coat scowled down at them.

Hicks rose to her feet, her back almost impossibly straight. Cautiously, Matt rose as well.

"So?" The man could only be her sergeant.

"Sir," she said. "At approximately 12.47 a.m., an unknown person fired three low-calibre rounds at the door to the witness's ICU room. Three shots perforated the door. All three shots missed the intended target, which we can assume was the witness himself. After assessing the safety of the witness, I placed Constable Ayres and Constable Taylor on protective duty and pursued the assailant. I lost him in the stairwell."

The sergeant's frown intensified. "And?"

Hicks's back went, if possible, straighter. "I've assigned Constable Taylor to interview witnesses furthest from the patient's room, and Constable Ayres is to remain on protective duty. I've also retained Dr Ripley, who was with me at the time of the incident and can perhaps offer further insight."

"Right." The sergeant raked Matt with his gaze. "Dr Ripley. That would be you?"

"Yes." He ignored the urge to shift his weight.

The sergeant's gaze narrowed. "What were you doing with Detective Hicks?"

Even if it killed him, he would not react. "We were talking. I'd finished my shift and thought to keep her company."

The sergeant's eyebrows shot up. "Did you?"

Matt crossed his arms. "We've done so before."

"Hmm." The sergeant rubbed his chin, his gaze never leaving Matt. He lowered his hand. "How would you describe what happened?"

Expressionless, Matt. Don't let him get to you. "Detective Hicks and I were talking. There was a loud bang, then two more. Before I knew what had happened, Detective Hicks had assured herself of my safety, the patient's, and then took off after the shooter. After a while, I became concerned and followed her."

The sergeant's brows drew together. "Then what?"

Expressionless. "I found her in the stairwell. She was upset she'd lost the shooter's trail. We . . . talked, and then you rang her cell phone."

"Thank you." The sergeant turned his attention to Hicks. "Detective Hicks, why did you allow a civilian access to a potential crime scene?"

Hicks looked at the sergeant unhappily. "Sir, I—"

"This doctor should not have followed you, and you should not have allowed him to remain once you discovered his presence. You've failed in your duties, Detective."

"Sir—"

"Detective Hicks did not fail." The sergeant's ire-filled gaze snapped to Matt. Hands tightening on his biceps, Matt scowled back. "She took off after a shooter, to apprehend him and protect hospital staff and visitors. She had no control over my actions. If I was in the wrong, I apologize."

The sergeant's eyes narrowed. For the longest time, he studied Matt. "Dr Ripley," he finally said. "This is no concern of yours. Detective Hicks is under my command, and if I believe a subordinate under my command has been derelict in their duties, I will tell them." And so dismissed, the sergeant turned to Hicks. "Hicks, deal with this. You get that witness to talk. Don't fuck up."

"No, sir."

With a final look, the sergeant turned and strode down the corridor, the uniforms trailing after him.

As soon as the sergeant cleared the corner, Hicks rounded on him. "What are you doing?"

He blinked. "What?"

Fury wrote her face. "How dare you talk to my sergeant like that? I don't need you to defend me."

Anger that hadn't diminished flared anew. "You need someone. Why do you let him talk to you like that?"

"He's my sergeant. How else is he supposed to talk to me?"

"With respect. You're damn good at your job and he should acknowledge that."

"And he does, but he was also right. I fucked up."

Goddamn it. "Hicks, you can't control my actions. I followed you to the stairwell—"

"I'm not talking about that. I'm talking about . . ." Abruptly, she sat.

Cautiously, Matt lowered himself into the seat beside her. Staring at her hands, she remained silent.

"Hicks." He covered her hand with his, entangling their fingers. "What is it?"

She didn't look up from their entwined hands. "I screwed up, Ripley."

"What?" He frowned. "When?"

"Today. Yesterday. Whenever. After the operation was over." Her fingers tightened on his. "I was responsible for the witness. He'd revealed himself to us, and I got him shot."

Now that he couldn't believe. "What do you mean?"

"One of the apprehended suspects shot him. They managed to get a gun and . . ." She shook her head. "I should have protected him."

"How? With your body?"

She said nothing, but she didn't have to.

Horror chilled him. "No. No, Hicks. Just . . . No. You give everything, but you don't have to give that."

She averted her eyes. "It's my job."

"To throw yourself in the path of a bullet? You're going to give away your life for some scumbag turncoat?"

"No." Finally, she looked at him. "To prevent another scumbag importing and distributing drugs."

Speechless, he stared at her. How could he argue with that? He wanted to, though. He wanted to yell and punch the wall and get her to admit her life was precious. Precious.

"Do you know why the witness is so important?" she said.

Unable to speak, he shook his head.

"He can identify a drug lord. Not just a drug lord. *The* drug lord. He can give us the scumbag of scumbags, all wrapped up in a bow. That's worth a life."

Finally, he found his voice. "But not yours."

"Yes, mine. The sergeant's. All of our lives. This is what it is, Ripley. This is my job." She smiled faintly. "Want to talk about us now?"

He couldn't talk about that now. He couldn't talk about that when she had just said she would lay down her life for her job. "How can you say that as if it's nothing?"

She looked away. "I don't."

"You do. You're saying it like your life is nothing, that using it to protect another is all it's good for."

She exhaled. "Of course I don't mean that, but I'm a police officer. A detective. This is me. This is who I am, who I've chosen to be. You know this."

"I know this? Is this what I know?" He heard the panic in his voice. Taking a breath, he forced himself calm. Well, calmer. "I've just . . . never seen it so close before."

She said nothing, but then, what was there to say?

"I have to go," she finally said. Pushing to her feet, she hesitated before starting down the corridor.

That snapped him out of it. He couldn't let her leave, not without sorting things out. Catching up with her, he said, "Where are you going?"

"Back to the ICU." She glanced at him. Her shoulders slumped. "I can't do this right now, Ripley."

No. Of course she couldn't. God, why was he insisting on this? This could wait. He would wait. For her. "Can I help?"

She stopped. "Really?"

"This is my hospital. It doesn't make me glad that some thug thinks he can endanger the lives of my patients."

A tentative smile teased at her mouth. The old warmth warmed his chest. "I . . . enjoyed what we were doing. Before the . . . incident. You know. The talking."

He pushed his misgivings and his worries aside. "I can do that."

Her smile bloomed full.

Well, that decided it. He would help her get through this. And then, when they were both calmer, more rested, they would talk.

They had time.

Chapter Six

"The patient has regained consciousness."

Ella looked up through gritty eyes to find a blurry registrar standing before her. She blinked, and the registrar – Dr Willis – sharpened. "Sorry?"

"Your witness." Willis crossed her arms over the patient chart she held. "He's regained consciousness. You can interview him now, if you're up to it." Brows drawing in concern, she said, "Maybe you should rest first."

"Nah, I'm good." Wearily, Ella pushed to her feet.

Dr Willis looked past Ella. "Ripley, can you get her to rest?"

He didn't look up from the year-old woman's magazine he was perusing. "I reckon she knows her mind better than I do, Willis. If she says she's good, she's good."

Willis sighed. "Well, in any event, the patient is prepped and ready for you. Mind you go easy on him. Four gunshot wounds and surgery would sap anyone of their strength."

Rubbing her forehead, Ella nodded and, with a final concerned look, Willis left.

Staring at the door, she ran over again how she was going to approach Simmons. A strange sense of calm slid over her. She'd interviewed hundreds of suspects. She knew what she was about. She wouldn't screw this up.

After taking a step, she hesitated. Then she looked back at Ripley.

Magazine lying forgotten in his lap, he met her gaze. "I'm not going anywhere."

At his words, she felt . . . steadier. A tremulous kind of smile pulled at her.

In return, a gentle smile lit Ripley's face. "Go get him."

She nodded. Outside the door, she stopped, regarding the constable on guard. Ayres straightened, immediately alert.

"Get the sketch artist here as soon as possible," she said. Ayres nodded, and bent to his radio.

With one final breath, she turned the door handle and pushed.

Simmons sat propped up on his bed, wires and tubes running from him to the surrounding machines. Though his skin was pale and he looked tired, she could tell by the set of his jaw and his narrowed eyes this would not be easy.

She exhaled. When was it ever easy?

Proffering her badge, she entered the room. "Mr Simmons, I'm Detective Hicks."

Crossing his arms, he scowled. "Yeah, I remember you. You were at the bust. You cuffed me, didn't ya?"

Taking up position at the foot of his bed, she arranged a pleasant, non-threatening smile on her face. "Yes, I apprehended you."

"What's the story? Why didn't that other copper make sure Chapman was unarmed? How did he get a gun when you guys should have— " Simmons descended into coughing, holding his abdomen.

Dispassionate, she watched him splutter. She should feel something at his obvious pain. Did it make her a monster that she didn't care? Simmons was a criminal of the highest order, a drug trafficker who thought nothing of the consequences of his actions. Sure, he was a cog in a larger wheel, but he still helped the machine run. If not for the information he possessed, she would have been happy to have never seen him again.

So who was the greater monster?

Finally, Simmons recovered and sidled her a glance. "So what do you want?"

"Mr Simmons, you claim you can identify Nick Collier."

"And I can." Simmons wiped his mouth. "What are you going to do for me in return?"

Forcing herself to disguise her revulsion, she said, "I've been authorized to offer you immunity."

"I want protection. I tell you, and I'll have everyone and his son after me."

"We can speak to the Federal Police about that, but we have to know your information is good before we can proceed."

Setting his jaw, he crossed his arms again. "I'm not saying anything without seeing a deal in writing."

She needed a different tack. Clearly, detached and business-like wasn't going to cut it. She needed something more.

Drawing her features into something approaching compassion, she took the seat at the side of his bed. "I understand, you know."

He didn't respond.

Brows drawn in false compassion, she said, "You're scared. I would be too, if I had Collier after me."

He stared at her a moment, then looked away.

She continued, the gentle smile she forced wearing her thin. "The thing is, it doesn't matter what you tell us. Collier's going to assume you're a rat, and that's all she wrote."

He flinched. She'd touched a nerve there.

"It's unfair, isn't it? That he'd assume such a thing."

Finally, he looked at her, and she could see his fear written in his eyes. "You don't know what they'll do to me."

"No. But I can imagine." She adopted sympathy, in her tone, her look. "Must be hard, always looking over your shoulder."

"Never being able to settle in one place." His arms tightened, holding his stomach. "Sleeping light, in case they get you."

"God," she said. "I can't even imagine how horrible it's been for you."

"It's not what I signed up for, that's for sure."

That gentle smile pulling at her, she silently encouraged him to talk.

"I don't even know how it happened. One day, I'm dealing a bit of bud, thinking about upgrading to party pills, you know, ecstasy and the like. The next, I'm in a warehouse with a fuck-load of coke, reaching skyward as the cops come storming in." Disgust, at himself, the situation, or something she couldn't fathom, turned his features sallow. He shook his head. "It's not worth getting shot. Not even once, let alone four times."

Trying to hide her rising excitement, she kept the compassion on her face. He was going to talk. She could feel it.

"Those bastards deserve to swing. Collier's going to have me killed anyway? Well, I'll take the bastard with me." He looked at her direct. "I'll tell you. I'll tell you everything."

At his words, the door opened and the sketch artist edged into the room. Ah, conscientious Ayres, with perfect timing

Simmons looked at the artist, wiped his hands against the blanket covering his legs. He looked at her.

Ella smiled encouragingly. Gaze flicking back to the artist, Simmons took a breath.

Then he started to talk.

The out-of-date magazine open in his lap, Ripley still sat in the moulded chairs outside Simmons's room.

Ella watched him for a moment. He didn't turn the page, didn't move, just sat there staring at the same page.

Warmth filled her, and a kind of elation. He'd waited.

"Hey, Ripley," she said.

He looked up, and the bright smile he gave her made his handsome face beautiful. "Hey."

Her step light, she walked towards him, stopping short of his seat. "So, what celebrity gossip did you learn?"

Momentary confusion dimmed his smile. "What?"

She gestured at the magazine.

"Oh. I have absolutely no idea." Placing the magazine in the chair beside him, he stood. "How did it go?"

"Good." She couldn't stop the smile spreading across her face. "I got the description."

This time, his smile was blinding. "You did? That's great!"

"It is, isn't it?" Happy to the point of giddiness, she hugged herself. It was great. It was goddamn fabulous, is what it was.

His smile turned tender. Mouth going dry, she watched as he closed the distance between them, so there was less than a breath. "So I guess that means—"

"Sorry. Detective Hicks?" Blinking, she turned her head to find Ayres, trying to look at everything but them. "Do you have the Chief Inspector's email address?"

"The Chief Inspector's?" Why on earth would he ask that? "Why?"

"He wants a copy of the artist's impression."

Bewildered, she drew her brows together. "I sent it to Detective Sergeant Matheson."

"I know, but the Chief Inspector . . ." Ayres shrugged.

Damn it, one more thing she had to do. "Right. Leave it with me."

He nodded and disappeared back into the ICU room.

Exhaling, she looked at Ripley. "I have to . . ."

"I know," he said.

"Sorry."

"It's okay."

She got her phone and pulled up her email, feeling his eyes on her all the while. Her internet failed. Stupid phone.

Finally, the internet bars glowed green and orange, and her email was sent to the Chief Inspector. Putting the phone back in her pocket, she looked up at him. "Sorry."

"Hicks, it's okay." He touched his jaw. "I'm sorry I was such a dick."

"When?"

"Before. About your job. I shouldn't have had a go at you."

She shrugged. "It's okay."

"No, it's not. It's your job. Your choice. It's only . . . I'll worry." He ran his hand through his hair. "From now on, I'll worry. It's never been so close, the danger. I haven't seen it before, you know?"

"I know."

"So I'll worry. And I'll be a dick, but just tell me when I'm being one. I'll stop, I promise."

"Okay." Silence fell between them. "So what does that mean?"

"It means . . ." He smiled ruefully. "I don't know what it means."

"Is it something you won't . . . Can you . . ." She took a breath. "I really liked what happened. In the stairwell."

His smile turned wolfish. "Me too."

A shiver went through her at his blatantly sensual look. "Will my job affect that?"

The sensual look bled from his features. "What?"

"My job. Will you . . .?"

"God. God, no." His expression sobered. "I'm so sorry I even made you think that. I will just . . . worry. About the danger you're in. I can't help it."

"Not all the time."

"No." He exhaled. "It just . . . It will be there. The worrying."

"I know."

He scowled. "And your sergeant's a dick."

Amusement tugged at her. "Nah, he's just stressed."

His look clearly stated he didn't agree with her. Then, a lopsided smile shaped his mouth. "So . . . Maybe we could go hang out in a stairwell a bit."

A laugh bubbled inside her as she arched her brow. "Just hang out?"

Smile widening, he shrugged. "Maybe do a bit more. A repeat, if you will."

"Sounds good to me." She wrapped her arms around him. He rested his chin on her head. Never, in all her life, had she ever felt as good. As safe. As . . . loved?

Finally, she pulled back. "Maybe we could hang somewhere that isn't here." Mustering her courage, she said, "Maybe get that coffee?"

"I reckon that would be a good idea." Ruddy colour lit his face. Awkwardly, he held out his hand. "I'm Matt."

Heat bloomed in her own cheeks. How was it they didn't know each other's first name? Feeling kind of stupid, she placed her hand in his. "Ella."

They shook.

A bright, shining grin spread across his face and she felt an answering one tug at hers. "I'm free now. Off duty."

His thumb caressed her skin. "Then let's go."

He held her hand all the way to the coffee shop.

IN THE BLINK OF AN EYE

Lynne Marshall

Chapter One

One Good Deed Deserves Another

"Adam, can you help me in procedure room two?" The words staggered out of Dr Ellen Deeds's suddenly dry-as-dirt mouth.

It had taken every last ounce of nerve to ask for help, especially from Adam. Of all the people to be stuck working in the Emergency Room with this Saturday. But who could fault Dr McGregor for wanting to be by his wife's side during labor? Adam had filled in last minute. Until today Ellen had managed to work opposite shifts from him since she'd asked him to leave after nearly eight years of marriage.

He glanced up in the middle of suturing a patient. His dark eyes enquiring, and his unshaven jaw looking more sculptured than usual. Had he lost more weight?

"I'll be right there."

Even though things had gone dead between them, he never would have left if she hadn't kicked him out almost six months ago. Her stomach knotted with unwanted memories. She rushed back to her patient, the young lady with breast cancer who needed fluid removed from her lung.

If it weren't an emergency, she'd never ask for his help. "Veronica." On her way back to the patient, Ellen rounded up her favorite RN to help. "Can you prepare the patient in procedure room two for a thoracentesis?"

"Sure thing, Dr Deeds."

She glanced inside at the frail thirty-seven-year-old woman on the gurney, and her heart sank. Quiet as a cat, she entered, not wanting to disturb her more than necessary.

"Jasmine," Ellen whispered, approaching the dozing woman who was hooked up to oxygen and fighting for each breath. "We're going to take out some fluid, help you breathe. You'll be feeling a lot better soon." She took the woman's hand and Jasmine's cool, bony fingers squeezed the slightest bit.

Veronica barreled into the room pushing a stainless steel procedure table with several sterile packages on top. So much for peace and quiet, but that was never really the case in an emergency department. Ellen checked the heart and blood pressure monitor, which had just finished taking Jasmine's vital signs. They were low but stable.

She slapped the X-rays, fresh from radiology, onto the reading box, turning on the lights just as Adam came in. Heat radiated from his tall frame when he stood behind her, and she smelled the final hint of his spice and sandalwood aftershave lingering on his scrubs. On an inhale, hoping to build some confidence, she turned. From the looks of him, he hadn't shaved since yesterday evening, and his hair hadn't seen a single tooth of a comb today. Messy and unkempt, he still coaxed an unwanted reaction from her.

They'd been dividing their shifts. She took days, and because he didn't have the responsibility of their daughter, he worked nights, until today's double shift. Tired or not, Ellen knew Dr Deeds was the king of challenging thoracenteses. She was pretty darn good herself, but the X-ray showed a small, hard-to-reach pocket of fluid, and she didn't want to risk puncturing Jasmine's lung while trying to get it out.

"This is the area we need to fix," she said, not bothering to look again at Adam. "Right here."

"Got it." His low voice hummed over her ear and she brushed away the quick twinge she felt.

Ellen walked toward her nurse, Veronica, lowered her voice and said, "Make sure we have a set-up for pneumothorax, too."

"Sure thing, Dr Deeds." On her way out, Veronica approached Adam. "Dr Deeds, do you need anything while I'm collecting equipment?"

"That should cover it, Ronnie. Thanks," he said.

Adam went to the patient. "We'll get this fluid out of your lungs and have you breathing as good as new." He spoke softly yet with confidence. Jasmine gave a wan smile.

Ellen had missed hearing him talk like that. She'd especially missed seeing him play with Bailey, and conspiring in hushed tones with her about how best to sneak up on Mommy, or how he would soothe their daughter's hurt feelings after a particularly tough playground incident at school. But those days were over. From now on they'd share Bailey – one weekend with Daddy and the rest of the time with Mom. It was just the way it had to be.

A light grip on her shoulder made her jump. "I'm sorry," Adam said. "Didn't mean to scare you."

"That's okay." How many times had he said I'm sorry over the last year? She'd lost count. "What do you need?"

"Do we have a consent for pleural aspiration?" He didn't remove his hand, and his body heat seeped through her doctor's coat and across the thin scrubs to her shoulder. When was the last time she'd been touched by a man? By Adam?

She nodded, unable to stop the soft tingle crawling up her neck from his point of contact. Now, all soft and bedroom brown, his big, thick-lashed eyes stared into hers. She made a dry swallow, and fought back the impact of his total attention. That was hard enough. When he ventured to smile, she had to look away.

"Good. As soon as Veronica gets back, we'll get started," he said. She heard disappointment in his voice, but she didn't think she could ever smile for him again.

As much as she missed their shared life – and lately the physical craving for him had come back with a vengeance – she had to move on. It was over. They were over. Their little family would never be the same again.

After the procedure, meticulously carried out by Adam, where she'd watched every movement of his long, nimble fingers, and remembered how they'd once felt on her bare skin, Ellen snapped back into work-mode. She stepped outside the room and ordered a portable X-ray for Jasmine to double check the fluid was gone, and that they hadn't punctured her lung.

From the way the patient rested comfortably on the gurney, vital signs and oxygen all within normal limits, she was sure the pleural aspiration had been a success. For now, anyway. Until the fluid built back up again.

The charge nurse strode across the department heading straight for her. "The resident needs assistance with a subclavian line in room one." Her deeply creased face showed concern.

"I'm on my way," Ellen said, before she could thank Adam for helping her out. "What's up?"

"The patient has been on long-term antibiotic therapy for abdominal abscesses after a gunshot wound. All his veins are shot, and now the PICC line has occluded."

Ellen entered the room where the young man with a buzzed head and loads of tattoos lay flat on the gurney, the head of the bed slightly lowered to enhance filling of the central veins for easier cannulation. She opened a sterile package and donned a gown, facial mask, and gloves, and then stepped forward to assist the new resident. The skin preparation had been completed.

"Have you checked the guidewire?"

The baby-faced resident nodded. In front of the patient, she didn't want to ask how many of these procedures he'd performed, assuming since he'd asked for assistance it wasn't yet enough to feel confident. Being a basic and frequent procedure in ER, she opted to talk him through it.

"Then go ahead and make your incision."

He nicked the skin over the ribs in the right upper quadrant. The introducer was already prepared with an attached syringe with a few ccs of normal saline inside.

"Now go deep towards the clavicle and aim for the sternal notch."

He followed her instructions, guiding the introducer toward the mark, without success.

"Withdraw and try again," she said.

The resident tried a parallel course, again without success.

Seeing beads of sweat forming on his brow, she stepped in and, keeping gentle continuous suction on the attached syringe, aimed the long needle of the introducer for the sternal notch. When a flush of blood appeared inside the syringe, they both knew she'd successfully entered the vein.

"Insert the guidewire through the introducer." She instructed the resident to stay involved in the procedure as she removed the syringe and he threaded the guidewire into the subclavian vein. She stepped back to allow him to do the next part.

"Remove the introducer and hold the guidewire stationary and close to the incision. Good. Now check your markers. Looks like you're there. Now advance the cannula over the guidewire. Good. Remove the guidewire. Be sure to keep that cannula in place. Great!"

She smiled through her mask at the resident, and she could tell by the tiny crinkles at the corners of his almost black eyes that he was smiling back.

"All you have to do now is suture it in place." She looked at the assisting nurse. "Is a portable X-ray ordered?" They'd need to check for placement before using the newly inserted line. The RN nodded.

"Is everything under control here, then?" The resident and nurse answered yes simultaneously.

Since Ellen's legs were tired and she hadn't eaten in several hours, she decided a cup of coffee and a snack were in order. After tossing her gloves and mask into the trash, she removed the sterile paper gown and threw it out too, and then informed the charge nurse she was taking a lunch break. Halfway to the cafeteria, she remembered she needed to take her packet of vitamins with food and now was as good a time as any. She headed in the opposite direction for the on-call locker room.

Swinging open the door she halted. Adam had his scrubs top half off, over his head. With his long torso exposed, thinner than she'd remembered, ribs and muscles on display, his chest dusted with brown hair, her breath caught. She wanted to turn and run, but her feet held firm to the spot. He removed the rest of the top and smiled at her, his thick dark hair pointing every which way, looking inviting as all hell, and his killer smile nearly stopping her heart.

"I realized I'd been wearing these clothes for over twenty-four hours, and thought I might reek by now, so . . ." he said, reaching inside his locker for a stick of deodorant and swiping it under his arms. She tried not to watch. "I thought I should freshen up."

Her mind suddenly fuzzy, she couldn't think of a response. She closed the door and leaned against it, waiting for her legs to start working again. Vitamins. Must get vitamins.

She missed watching him shower and walk around the bedroom with a towel wrapped around his waist. She missed turning toward him in bed at night, nuzzling her head under his chin. She yearned for the love they'd shared and, lately, she feared she'd never know that feeling again. Except with him.

But they were over. Well, she couldn't spend the rest of her life crying over what had happened. How their life had come crashing to a halt a year ago. How some losses could never ever be gotten over.

"I need to get my vitamins." She finally found her voice, and walked to her locker, which was several down from his. Thankfully. She fished in her doctor's coat for the key, coming up with several tissues, a dollar bill, lip balm, and finally the key. Her hand lightly trembled as she inserted the key into the lock. She hoped he didn't notice.

He came up behind her, still topless, and wrapped his arms around her waist, pulling her flush to his chest. His chin dug into her shoulder. "I miss you so much," he said, in a soft raspy voice.

She tensed. His nose nuzzled her cheek and soon his lips bussed the skin along her jaw. Stop it, she wanted to say, but her mouth didn't move. Stop it. Tingles and chills fanned across her neck and shoulders, and tiny fingers of pleasure danced along her scalp. Stop. Please.

He turned her towards him, dark desire in his eyes, and pressed his mouth firmly over hers; kissing her like she'd forgotten how it was done. On reflex, her arms reached around his neck and found the thick hair at his nape, digging into it, as she opened her mouth and kissed him full on. She'd missed him so much. So, so much.

His heavy, hot breath blew over her, and seemed to travel all the way down to her center, as if steam from a warm, inviting bathtub. He backed her toward the lockers and pressed his hips into hers, still kissing her. Damn, he was already hard and heavy against her middle. She should stop it before the kiss got out of control. But her desire wasn't to stop. Right now she wanted only to kiss him until her brain went numb, until she forgot everything else in life. And she was almost there.

He stopped. Her eyes popped open. She saw the look of no return in his heated gaze, as if he was figuring out the best way to tell her how much he wanted her.

Fully revived by his kisses, she'd stopped thinking rationally and wanted him, too.

He took her hand and led her to the adjoining on-call room with several bunk beds. She followed, tingling from head to toe from his attention. He locked the door to the darkened room and started toward one of the bunks.

Ellen stopped him short, instead pushing him onto the end of a wooden bench and straddling his lap. If she was going to break down and make love to her estranged husband, she would do it her way, not his.

Adam settled onto the hard bench, balancing himself with one hand behind him, loving the weight of Ellen across his lap. Thighs apart, she moved against his ridge, and he nudged back, wishing they'd magically become naked. He scrambled to remove her doctor's coat, and just as quickly yanked her scrubs top over her head. Her breasts were pushed tightly together by a bra that seemed a size too small. The sight of her like that, on his lap half naked, almost made him drool. Through the white of the bra he could tell her nipples were as tight as his. He touched her soft cleavage as he unlatched the front clasp, reverently removing the bra and releasing the most beautiful prize he'd seen in . . . how long had it been since they'd had sex?

Over a year. And five months twenty-six days since she'd kicked him out.

He took the weight of her breasts into his palms, savoring their feel, lightly running his thumbs over the nipples. He tasted and took first one velvety tip and then the other into his mouth, his tongue prodding and sucking, hardly able to believe they were this close again.

She arched her back and pressed her chest toward his mouth, so he tugged harder. Her wandering fingertips across his chest and the quiet moan escaping her parted lips made his erection tighten. More turned on by each passing moment, he inhaled the lingering scent of her lavender and vanilla body lotion. Damn, he needed to be inside her.

He untied and rolled the waist of her scrubs down toward her hips. She helped by raising up, feet on either side of the bench as he removed the fabric over her round hips, and he took great pleasure feeling the pliable curves of her cheeks as he removed the clothes as far as possible in this position. He clenched her hips with his fingers and planted a kiss on her stomach, loving the feel of her skin against his lips.

A jiggling on the doorknob, then a quick knock arrested his bliss. They both bolted to standing. He glanced at Ellen, half naked and ready for his taking, everything he ever wanted right within touch. He placed his finger over the soft pillow of her lips.

"I'm catching a nap," Adam said, voice firm. "Try the other on-call room." He pretended to sound perturbed that someone had interfered with his sleep. Everyone knew he was pulling a double shift.

Whoever it was must have left. He looked back at Ellen, who hadn't tried to put her clothes back on. A good sign. In a quick move, he yanked down the rest of her scrubs, untied his own and nearly jumped out of them in record time.

"Now, where were we?" he said, pulling her towards him, and easing back onto the bench. Her scent intoxicated him, making every single thing in the world spiral down to their one point of contact.

Within seconds she'd placed him inside her, and feeling her warmth and moisture tight around him was almost his undoing. He held her hips firm and she took the lead, wasting no time in taking the rhythm to the hilt. From zero to one hundred, like a racecar driver, she made it clear, this wasn't about making love. It was about release. Pure and simple.

He watched her every move, ran his hands over as much flesh as he could, while she drove him to his limit. By the look on her face, her eyes closed tight as she bit her lips and groaned, he knew she was right there with him.

He wanted to sustain this unbelievable pleasure all day, tattoo the vision of her writhing in pleasure on his mind. He wished he could record the throaty sounds she made with each thrust to be replayed whenever he needed cheering up, but he was too damn human, and she was forcing him to come too damn soon.

She beat him to it. He felt her tighten even more around him as she whimpered the final sound of ecstasy then gasped. Waves and spasms clung around him as her orgasm powered on. A thunderbolt shot down his spine, heading right to his erection as he gave up the fight and pumped inside her every last surge of energy he had until nothing was left.

Their sweat-slicked bodies clung together, the heat they'd created with their hasty sex more comforting than anything on earth. They were as they should have been for the entirety of last year – wrapped in each other's arms, mourning together, sharing their love and pleasure as man and wife.

She sighed over his shoulder. He lifted her sweat-matted light brown hair and blew across her neck. She stirred, as if coming to from a time-out-of-body experience. Her expression, the return of caution to her hazel eyes, her lips tightening into a thin line, alerted him that their moment was done.

Ellen pulled away from his chest and got off his lap. She stood and took a step backwards. Without a word, she quickly gathered her clothes and headed for the bathroom.

He sat there, rubbing his temples and covering his eyes, wondering what in the hell he should say to her. For that one perfect second after they'd made love, he'd wanted to tell her he loved her, but if he had she'd have shot out of the room as if a code blue had just been announced.

A flush of the toilet and the running of water, and a few seconds later she reappeared from the tiny bathroom. She'd dressed in fresh scrubs, splashed water on her face, and had pulled her long, straight hair back into a ponytail, looking young and vulnerable. All he wanted to do, after eight years of marriage, was take her into his arms and tell her he loved her.

"Forgive me?" was all he could muster.

As if a veil had slipped over her face, her expression changed from love-flushed to frozen. She slipped on her doctor's coat and reached for the door handle.

Without so much as a glance over her shoulder, she muttered, "I'm sorry, but I can't," and was gone.

Chapter Two

For Better or Worse

Under the yellow bug-resistant porch light, Ellen unlocked her front door. Clouds had been forming and thickening on the drive home, and she was glad to beat the impending rain. Dinner made by the housekeeper-nanny hit Ellen's nostrils full on, something warm and comforting for the chilly night. She was famished after her long day of work and the unexpected sexy encounter with her husband.

She dropped her keys into the ceramic bowl on the entry table.

"Mommy!" Bailey's squeal of joy made her spirits swell. The elfin six-year-old came catapulting across the living room, her favorite kids' show instantaneously forgotten. This was all Ellen lived for these days.

"Hi, Button," she said, as her daughter wrapped her arms around her thighs and hugged tight. Bailey's enthusiastic love never got old. Ellen smiled as she ran her hand over her daughter's silky, fine light-brown hair. She seemed to have lost most of her body fat in the last year, as she'd pined along with her parents after the tragedy.

"Mommy, I could read all the words in the story today at the library."

"That's fantastic." Ellen bent and kissed Bailey's forehead. "Did you eat yet?"

They walked together from the darkened living room into the bright and TV-noisy family room.

"Uh-hmm. We had macaroni and cheese and I ate my veggies, too."

Diana stepped out of the kitchen, drying her hands on the skirt of her apron. "Hello, Mrs Ellen."

"Diana, how did things go today?"

"*Bueno*. She busy at playground and library. *Muy* outdoor time."

Ellen rubbed her daughter's head. "Did you get lots of fresh air?"

"Yes. I played on the slides and swings and monkey bars . . ."

Ellen smiled at her daughter and her obviously loose front tooth as the little girl worried it with her tongue, wiggling it back and forth. How long did she plan to hang on to that tooth before letting Mommy pull it out? "Do you think the tooth fairy will come tonight?"

"No." Bailey snapped her mouth shut.

Not even the thought of a dollar under the pillow could coax her into letting Ellen take the tooth out.

"I have your dinner ready, Mrs Ellen."

"Thanks so much, Diana. You can go now. I'll give Bailey her bath after I eat."

"We had custard for dessert, Mommy."

"Flan," Diana quietly corrected, chuckling, on her way back to the kitchen.

"Sounds wonderful," Ellen said. She took off her jacket, tossed it across the leather recliner that used to be Adam's favorite seat in the house, and put her purse on the coffee table. She plopped down onto the multi-sectional couch that ate up so much of the family room. "Are you watching *101 Dalmatians* again?"

"It's my favorite!" Bailey flung herself into Ellen's lap. "Can we get a dog?"

How many times a week could a kid ask the same question. "Maybe next year. When you're old enough to take care of one."

"Daddy said I can get a dog and keep it at his house."

"He did, did he?"

"Uh-hmm. And I can name it, too. And I can walk it and feed it."

"And pick up the poop?"

"Yuck! No way."

"Well, when you're ready to clean up the poop, then you're old enough to get a dog," she said, thinking, I'll have a little talk with Daddy about that dog promise next weekend when it's his turn to keep Bailey.

Without warning her mind flashed back to the on-call room. Adam's taut muscles and solid body rubbing close against hers, driving her to orgasm in record time. Her face went hot and she swallowed against a parched throat, the erotic image growing ever more vivid. After trying to ignore the fact that he'd knocked her scrubs off today, she'd probably blush to her toes and stumble over her words when confronting him next. She prayed she wouldn't see him for a long time.

"I go now." Diana had taken off the apron and put on her coat, purse in hand.

Ellen stood, and Bailey rushed to her nanny to hug her goodbye.

"Thanks so much. We'll see you tomorrow, then," Ellen said.

"Yes, Mrs." The middle-aged Bolivian woman walked on sturdy, short legs toward the front door. Ellen and Bailey followed her, having gone through this routine since Bailey was a few months old. Diana didn't need anyone to show her out, but they always did.

"Take one of our umbrellas. You'll need it before you get home."

"Thank you." She grabbed an umbrella from the holder near the door, and then turned. "If you let your mother take the tooth, I bring you a surprise tomorrow."

Bailey shut tight her lips, obviously guarding her two front teeth with her tongue. She shook her head vehemently.

Ellen and Diana exchanged one last amused look before the nanny left.

Once Bailey went back to watching the *Dalmatians*, Ellen wandered into the kitchen, remembering how hungry she was since she'd skipped lunch today. It was almost seven now.

As she warmed her dinner plate of skinless chicken, rice pilaf and steamed veggies, her skipped lunch break and the incredibly sexy man who'd helped her "skip" it, came to mind again. How often had she thought about that hot and crazy scene all afternoon? More than she could count.

Unsure if the saliva forming in her mouth was over Adam's nakedness or the delicious-smelling meal, she swallowed and sat down to eat.

"I love this part!" Bailey called out and giggled over the house full of puppies running amok.

Ellen decided to take her plate over to the couch so she could share the movie with Bailey. She turned to her bright-eyed daughter. "Here, have more broccoli."

Completely swept up in the movie, Bailey opened her mouth without giving it a thought, and chomped down on the food.

She'd hoped that tooth might finally give way with the added chewing, but no such luck.

Once dinner and the movie were over, Ellen escorted Bailey to the bathroom and bathed her, all bony arms and knobby knees. The added task gave them some relaxing time together. They both squealed when a particularly strong clap of thunder broke overhead and a thunderstorm started outside. Ellen dried Bailey with a large, soft towel.

When Bailey was in her pajamas, Ellen read her favorite bedtime book, *Hazel's Amazing Day*, as the rain slapped at the windows. It felt extra cosy and warm as they snuggled together and mother love welled up in her chest. From the corner of Ellen's eye she could see Bailey constantly working on her tooth with her tongue. Back and forth. Back and forth, she moved it.

"Okay, Button, it's time to go to sleep. I love you." She kissed her daughter's forehead.

"I love you, too." Bailey wrapped her arms around her neck and squeezed tight.

"Sleep tight." Ellen put her child's favorite animal toy, an overstuffed bunny with crimped brown fur, by her side, and Bailey settled into her pillow. Fortunately, the thunder had moved on, but the rain still pattered on the roof.

Just as Ellen made it to the door, about ready to turn off the light, Bailey sat back up. "Here, Mommy."

Ellen walked to the bed and opened her palm under her daughter's outstretched hand. Out dropped one tiny white tooth. "How 'bout them apples!"

Ellen laughed, hearing Bailey mimic one of her dad's playful phrases. "Guess I better put a call in to the tooth fairy tonight."

"Yay." Bailey clapped her hands. "It didn't even hurt."

After putting the tooth in the special pink velvet sack with white silk ribbon ties under the pillow so it wouldn't get lost, Ellen closed the bedroom door. She thought about the new smile that would greet her in the morning from her daughter, reminding her to have the camera ready to go. She couldn't help but smile to herself.

Adam had missed it, another big day in their daughter's life. With an aching squeeze in her chest, as doubts piled upon doubts about her decision to ask him to leave, she made her way to her own bathroom for a long, forgiving shower.

Afterwards, making sure Bailey was sound asleep, she removed the tooth from under the pillow and put a dollar bill in its place. Then, with the stealth of a proud tooth fairy, she felt her way out of the darkened room.

Even with this fun distraction, there'd be no escaping it – every day was the same since last year. Once Ellen's head hit the pillow she'd weep about her little boy, and how she would never get to put him to bed again.

An hour later, hair wet and bathrobe on, Ellen headed for the kitchen to make some herbal tea. Maybe it would help her sleep – something she'd never struggled with until last year when her nights became living nightmares. Nights were now something to get through instead of something to look forward to for needed rest. Did she ever feel rested these days?

As she brewed her tea, an odd sensation came over her. She was relaxed. The hot shower had taken away the minor aches and pains from a long day on her feet, as it always did, but something new was evident. Her body was spent from the gift of one amazing and powerful orgasm, compliments of her husband. She'd almost forgotten how exquisite sex with Adam could be.

A firm triple knock came from the front door, startling her. And repeated. In thick, furry slippers, she padded across the hard wood to flip on the light and peep out the door window. At the sight, her heart clutched, shortening her breath, and her stomach threatened to revisit dinner.

It was Adam.

"We need to talk," he said, hair wet from the rain that had finally materialized after threatening all day. Droplets gathered on the shoulders of his jacket, like legions of rhinestones.

How could she tell her husband he couldn't come into the house he'd helped buy? She opened the door and gave him a wide berth. Even though they'd been buck-naked earlier that afternoon, she clutched her warm robe across her chest to cover herself. Or maybe it was to protect against her suddenly haywire physical reactions to him.

Tension marked his face and his nearly black eyes were narrow slits. She tightened the grip on her robe. He didn't bother to remove his coat.

"Haven't we said everything we need to say?" she ventured.

He shook his head. "We haven't talked about anything for almost a year. You shut down. I drank. We've avoided everything important."

"It wouldn't change things. What's the point?"

He turned on her, his expression twisted, agonized. "Don't you think I'd change that one instant if I could? I blinked. I messed up . . ."

Don't go there. Please. At the hint of where this conversation might lead, her eyes welled up, his face went blurry. "What's the point of rehashing this, Adam?" She glanced at her slippers rather than look at him another second.

He stepped closer, and though she wanted to back away, she stood firm. He cupped her arms, forcing her to look at him. "I've quit drinking. I'm living responsibly again." He searched her eyes for a hint of forgiveness, but the shield she'd built to protect herself had slipped into place. She'd needed it before, or she'd have fallen apart and been useless for Bailey. She needed it now, so she wouldn't drop to her knees and bawl at the mention of their twisted, messed-up existence.

"You know I love Bailey. Damn it, Ellen, I still love you." He gently shook her. She could feel his fingers digging through her robe into her skin. "You've got to open your heart and forgive me."

Her shield faltered, tears rushed down her cheeks. If he weren't holding her so firmly, she would have needed to sit down. Rather than look at him, she broke away from his grip, searching for a chair, using her bathrobe to wipe away what seemed more like a waterfall than tears.

"How can I love you when I can never trust you again?"

His hands fisted. He turned his head as if she'd delivered a physical blow to his cheek. He took a few moments to gain control. "I've always been trustworthy," he said in a tightly measured tone. "I'd proved it for years, until . . ."

Frightened and angry that he'd forced this conversation again, she struck out. "Your mistake killed our son."

She may as well have shot him in the heart. Pain and regret rippled over his features, she'd stripped him naked without shelter. He lifted his hands in surrender. "Can't you understand the torment I live and breathe every single minute? Every freaking day? If I could have exchanged my life for Ben's I would have. You know that."

No. She couldn't bear this. Please don't make her relive the moments that couldn't be taken back, the moments when Adam turned to answer his cell phone, leaving two-year-old Ben contentedly playing on the dock by the lake. That elusive second when Adam turned away to fish out the phone from his backpack, when their boy must have made a run for the water.

"I was on call. I had to answer the phone. I made a mistake by turning my back for one second . . ."

She grabbed her face, trying to rub out the scene she'd had to recreate in her mind, since she hadn't been there. Don't think about Benny in the water. The last thing she wanted or needed was to imagine her baby boy drowning. Oh, God, why did she have to go make sandwiches for lunch or put Bailey down for her nap that day? She knew Adam was in the water in a flash, diving and hunting for their son. She understood he'd done everything in his power to save the boy once he'd found him, but fate and the devilishly inviting water had been especially cruel that day – it had taken Ben's life.

"Stop it. Please, just stop it." Her voice gripped so tight in her throat, she hardly recognized the sound. "I can't go there again."

He stood before her, a broken man, the rain on his jacket looking like heavy tears from heaven. His dark hair was pasted around his face, torment implanted into his eyes. And regret. So much regret oozing out of him. His mouth a jagged line fighting with words demanding to be spoken. "When will you forgive me?"

"Go. Just go." She stared at her ridiculously fuzzy white slippers, because looking one more second at the despairing man she'd once loved with every fiber of her being would rip out her heart. "Please, go."

Why did he have to do this, to repeat this scene, almost exactly the same one as the day she'd kicked him out? They'd lived like robots for six months after Ben's death. Trying their best to carry on, failing miserably. They'd quit looking at each other, seeing each other, touching each other. What was the point of continuing?

She fingered the tiny tooth in her robe pocket and thought about telling him about Bailey, but that would be too normal, and nothing was normal between them any more.

His shadow covered her as he stepped forward. He lifted a lock of her hair, still damp from her shower, and played with the ends. She delved deep inside herself, refusing to let him draw her out. It was her only defense.

"I thought . . ." He needed to clear his tattered voice. "I thought, after today, things might be different."

She should never have let her body rule her brain. The release wasn't nearly enough to compensate for this rush of feelings, for the pain she'd unearthed by getting naked with Adam again.

She shook her head. "Nothing's different."

He knelt in front of her, forcing her to look into his eyes, his pleading gaze almost her undoing. "We can't bring Ben back. I just keep hoping you'll forgive me, so we can move on. That's all I'm saying. All I'm hoping for."

Her breakdown and keening surprised her. Every last ounce of pain came flooding out. She prayed her crying wouldn't wake Bailey. Adam gathered her into his broad shoulders and held her tight. She felt his chest rise and fall with his own swallowed cries. They held each other and wept, mourning for all they'd lost. He kissed her hair, her forehead, her jaw, until she felt drained of every last emotion and tear.

His mouth found her lips. She couldn't let him kiss her again. With trembling hands she gently pushed Adam away and wiped her face with the sleeve of her robe. Her lower lip twitched when she tried to speak. "I need more time. Just please go."

Truth was, deep in her heart, she still couldn't understand how answering a phone call could be more important than watching their child on the dock.

Backing away as if she was the most fragile item on earth, Adam gave her space. She drew a ragged breath, trying to keep it together. Before her, she saw a man recovering his dignity. Adam stood tall, refusing to give up. He gave her one last look before walking to the door, one last intense gaze that said almost as much as words. Life moved on and maybe it was time she did, too.

With his hand on the knob and his shoulders straight and proud, it seemed there was something else he wanted to get across to her. Was it hope that maybe someday she'd finally come around?

"I love you," he said. "I've never stopped." Then he disappeared into the pouring rain.

Chapter Three

Forgive but Never Forget

"We've got a F.O.O.S.H. in room three, Dr Deeds," the lanky male LVN with the full-throttle southern accent said, making the term sound like something you'd play with Wiffle balls in the park.

"I'll be right there," Ellen said, finishing up her orders for the combative middle-aged man in room seven. She understood that ER lingo must sound bizarre to the average visitor, but a F.O.O.S.H. – fall-on-outstretched-hand – wasn't her highest priority right now. "Kelly," she said to the fresh out of nurses' training RN, "can you get a Utox from seven, then give him some vitamin H."

From the total look of confusion on the young nurse's face she knew she'd have to stop using jargon and be more precise. "Please collect a urine test for drug screen from Mr Anderson, then give him 5 mg IM of Haldol. If necessary, we'll call security in on this. Take that burly medical assistant in with you when you go in the room."

Kelly's eyes registered the orders. Ellen predicted she'd be slinging ER lingo around with the rest of them in no time at all.

Breaking in over the intercom they all heard the announcement. "Attention, we've got a donor-cycle, I mean motorcycle accident with multiple fractures plus head injury on the way in. ETA twenty minutes."

The ER saw so many motorcycle accidents each week they'd changed the word to "donor-cycle", and the dark sentiment hadn't gone unnoticed by Ellen.

Fifteen minutes later, after examining the right wrist in room three, and hearing the story of how the young woman had lost her balance and fell forward down a short flight of stairs, Ellen ordered an X-ray to rule out what she was positive would be a Colles' fracture of the distal radius. Except, looking at the watch on her own wrist and hearing the ambulance siren in the distance, she soon realized she wouldn't be around to find out the results, or see the winners and losers from the latest installment of motorcycle versus motor vehicle.

The ER had been full all day with case after case, and the hours had sped by. Now it was time to hand off the patients to the next shift. Thank goodness her replacement had arrived on time.

"Can you take over from here?" Ellen asked Dr McGregor. "My nanny couldn't make it today and I've got to pick up Bailey from after-school care before six."

After giving the CliffsNotes version of ER rounds, and hearing the final shrill sounds from the arriving ambulance, Ellen bolted to the lockers to grab her clothes, then rushed into the changing cubicle. It was Adam's day off, so she didn't need to worry about running into him again, naked from the waist up and looking all sexy. Why was it men never seemed to use the changing rooms?

During the quick exchange of scrubs for street clothes, she glanced at her watch again. She only had twenty minutes to get to the school. There was no way she could stop at the market to pick up something for dinner first, which meant she'd have to deal with a tired and restless six-year-old while she shopped.

She dashed out the door and got to her car in record time. On the short drive to get her daughter her mind drifted away from medicine and toward her personal life. She always looked forward to seeing her daughter, loved seeing Bailey's excited face whenever she showed up at school. She understood that Bailey loved her dad just as much and missed him, too. Heck, she'd insisted on calling him first thing the morning after her tooth came out, telling him she wished she could bring it to his house for her next sleepover so the tooth fairy could come to her other house. Ellen almost decided to give her back the tooth so she could do it, too.

Devoted father that he was, every night since he'd moved out, Adam called Bailey without fail.

With the thought, Ellen's heart cracked like an antique teacup, spidering out in all directions. How long would the pain go on? She'd lost her son and now she'd lost her husband, too. Some days she'd get distracted with medicine and feel normal again. But with one lull in patient care, or a pause while being kept on hold on the phone, reality would come flooding back, assaulting her on every level. Her son was dead and she'd never have him back.

Think about Bailey. Think about Bailey . . . and Adam.

Since Adam's visit the other night, his pleading eyes had broken into her thoughts more times than she cared to count. They'd pierced into that numb spot buried deep in her soul, her single defense for survival. She'd loved him with all of her heart for years and years. As far as she was concerned, he'd been the greatest husband and father on earth . . . until . . .

Ellen parked in the closest space to the school door and hustled inside, not wanting Bailey to be the last child picked up, again.

"Hi, Mommy!"

There she was with her coat on, sitting on a bench in the entryway all by herself. Ellen's heart sank. She glanced around. One slightly impatient-looking childcare provider was putting the last touches on closing down the facility.

"Hi, Button. Sorry I'm late."

Bailey bolted to her and gave her signature hug around the hips. "I forgive you."

At what stage in life did people lose the ability to forgive and forget so easily?

Ellen smiled, greeted the care provider apologetically, and signed Bailey out. "Guess what," she said as they left the school.

"Did I get a present?"

"No." Did the child ever give up on surprises? "We have to stop at the market on the way home."

"Oh." After less than a second of looking disappointed, Bailey brightened. "Can I get a new cereal for breakfast tomorrow? Can we have cereal for dinner?"

"Yes and no."

After buckling Bailey into the large child car seat, they headed across town to the market closest to their house. They both knew the drill. Mom pushed the cart and Bailey's job was to hold on and stay nearby.

"Would you like some home-made chicken tenders for dinner?"

"Yum. Yes. Can I have cereal for dessert?"

Her daughter's single-mindedness never ceased to amaze Ellen. "Let's save it for breakfast, okay? That is, unless you'd rather not have frozen yogurt for dessert."

Bailey clapped her hands and jumped up and down. "Yay. My favorite!"

Knowing she'd have trouble with Bailey, Ellen left the final stop for last and turned down the breakfast cereal, crackers, and cookie aisle. Why did the store have to put the sweetest cereals at eye level for kids? Did they enjoy watching children throw tantrums while frazzled parents dealt with embarrassment, along with everything else?

"Oh, look at this one, Mommy. Can we get this?"

From the picture on the cereal box, the entire "cereal" seemed to consist of colorful mini marshmallows. "No, not that one."

"How about this one?" That one looked like little puffy chocolate balls.

Ellen hated to only say no, so she diverted her daughter's plea, "How about some snap, crackle and pop?"

"We got that last time. I'm tired of it."

Refusing to yield to defeat, Ellen reached for a more nutritious-looking box on the top shelf. Right about now she wished she were at least two inches taller. Even on her toes, she could barely reach the wholegrain with cinnamon and honey cereal. She'd play up the cinnamon and honey part when she showed it to Bailey. More determined, she tried to reach up again. On the third try, she finally snagged the box.

"Here," she said. "How about this one?" She glanced to where Bailey had just been standing nearly drooling over all the colorful and unhealthy cereals, but she was gone.

"Bailey?" Ellen looked up and down the aisle, but her daughter was nowhere in sight. Sudden alarm sent a flood of adrenaline throughout her system. She left her cart where it was and darted around the corner to the next aisle. "Bailey?" This time her voice carried over the store Muzak. "Bailey!"

Where had she gone? Why couldn't she hear her calling? Panic rooted in her gut as frantic thoughts took hold. Images of someone grabbing her child and running. Talking herself off the ledge, Ellen tried to be reasonable, knowing the odds of that actually happening were low. But what if Bailey were the unlucky one?

With her nerves snapping, her hands shaking, and anxiety escalating by the instant, Ellen charged toward the next aisle. "Bailey! Where are you?" Her voice had gone up at least three octaves. "Anyone see a skinny little girl with brown hair in braids?" The startled shoppers in this aisle shook their heads in unison, alarm registering in their eyes, which now darted up and down the aisle along with Ellen's.

Dear God, where had her daughter gone?

As if living an abduction nightmare, Ellen's pulse tripled in time. Dread beat at each nerve in her body, and filled her eyes with tears by stealing every last drop of saliva from her mouth. Hysteria took over, messing with her sight and muffling her hearing.

"Bailey!"

Where should she turn, which way should she go? Why would anyone want to take her child? The reason sent shivers down her already trembling spine. She could never forgive herself for letting Bailey out of her sight for one instant. Was bargaining over cereal anywhere near enough of a good reason?

If someone had taken Bailey – please God, don't let that be the case – they'd head for the exit, and she'd give them the fight of their life as she screamed for security.

"Bailey!" She let go a panicked wail as she ran to the last aisle in the flower section, by the automatic doors.

This couldn't be happening. If her baby was gone, she'd die right on the spot.

"Over here. She's over here."

Rounding the corner, those words from a familiar-sounding voice reminded her to breathe. Bailey wasn't gone, she was over there! When Ellen made it to the other side, she stopped dead in her tracks. There was Bailey hugging a man with his back to

Ellen, kneeling beside the little girl, wearing an overcoat. She recognized the broad shoulders and the thick waves of dark hair.

Adam.

An instantaneous blanket of relief enveloped her, but her body needed time to catch up.

Ellen prepared herself for Adam's reprimand as he stood and turned. She'd let their daughter out of her sight. Bailey had disappeared within the blink of an eye. Ellen reached for the display of potted plants to steady herself as her knees nearly buckled. Now she knew all the way to her bones how he'd felt that day. She'd just lived Adam's horror. He'd blinked, looked away for less than a minute, just long enough to lose their son to the water.

Ellen had done the same thing just now, but thank God in heaven Bailey had wandered into her father's arms instead of some stranger's. She could have lost their daughter, not by negligence, but by being human, by making that damn box of cereal more important than her daughter's safety. Just like that cell phone call had distracted Adam.

He'd lay down his life to redo that moment, he'd told her so time and again.

Myriad thoughts and fears wrapped in frazzled emotions came crashing over her. Her face twitched with the intensity of it all. She'd blamed Adam for their son's death. *How could you?* She'd never offered mercy or forgiveness, just condemnation. *How could you?*

Standing before Adam in the market, she saw the wise look in his eyes. He knew exactly what was going on with her, but instead of lashing out and blaming her for being a horrible mother, he remained silent. He'd let her stew in her own accusations, as he must have done when Benny got away, except she hadn't been anywhere near as gracious with Adam. When she'd found out what had happened, she'd laid into him, bashing her fists on his chest and cursing, calling him every despicable name she could think of for what he'd done. And he'd let her.

Oh, God, forgive me. Adam, forgive me for never forgiving you.

Now she knew, all the way down to her trembling toes, how it felt to lose a child by accident. She couldn't hold Adam hostage to her pain of loss another second. It wasn't fair. Everything was suddenly as clear as the shiny Mylar balloons on display. Ellen needed to forgive him.

Adam hadn't taken his eyes off of Ellen, though now he stood and tightly held Bailey's hand. Ellen finally understood how it felt and he'd picked up on it, and his all-knowing response sent a significant though silent exchange between them. There was empathy in his gaze as she nearly crumpled onto the grocery store floor.

Instead of giving in to her lashing emotions, with newfound strength, Ellen rushed to both of the people she loved. With a combination of relief and anger over Bailey slipping off when she'd been taught better, Ellen immediately forgave her. Bailey was here, in her father's arms, and the alternative was too gruesome to contemplate. Later, when things had calmed down, she'd reinforce to Bailey about never wandering off by herself.

Ellen bent to hug her daughter, tighter than necessary, happier than she'd ever been to see her since the day she'd been born.

"Why did you leave me, Button?" Ellen took Bailey by the shoulders and looked into her widened eyes.

"I wanted to skip. I saw the pretty balloons."

"I could have lost you."

"But Daddy was here." Bailey gazed back at her father.

"I wanted a roasted chicken for dinner, decided to grab the Friday night special," Adam said, cautiously observing her, his black overcoat and exceptionally good-looking features making him seem like a superhero. "Looks like my timing was impeccable."

With each parent holding tight to one of Bailey's hands, Ellen rose and looked into Adam's eyes. Her free hand reached for his broad shoulders, the very ones that had borne the brunt of her condemnation this past year.

Their eyes connected and she watched the deep brown turn darker as it sank in that she finally, really and truly, got it. Caution flickered in his eyes, like a man liberated from jail, and not quite believing it. Yes, she had just forgiven him for the biggest mistake of his life. Now all she needed to do was tell him.

She'd have a lot of trust to rebuild with Adam, and it was a gate that, she suspected, swung both ways.

Ellen reached for his face, touching the day's-end stubbles on his jaw, finally allowing her love to take over. She gave a tender thank-you-for-being-here kiss, and finished by gazing into his eyes and promising with her long overdue empathy that more would follow. But not now, not right here in this market with a crowd of people looking on.

"Can Daddy come to dinner with us, Mommy?"

Ellen passed a quick look of contrition toward Adam. "I'm only fixing something simple, but . . ."

He smiled and it nearly set her heart on fire. "I'll meet you there."

"Yay!" Bailey clapped.

Adam glanced at Bailey. "How about them apples?"

Ellen grinned at both of them. "Oh, I better get the cart."

Adam lifted Bailey as if she was a toddler again instead of six, and took Ellen's hand to fetch the grocery store cart, once again a deeply connected family unit. After all these months, it felt surreal.

Once they'd found the cart four aisles over, they checked out.

Adam insisted on paying the bill. Ellen didn't protest. Putting his wallet back in his pocket he smiled at Bailey, then gave a familiar smoldering glance toward Ellen.

"Let's go home," he said, and something stirred deep in Ellen's belly.

Bailey was finally in bed. Ellen hadn't seen her daughter so ecstatic since she'd won a stuffed bunny at the fair last year. For the first time in six months both her mother and father had kissed her goodnight. The child practically levitated over the bed with glee.

With the bedroom door closed on Bailey quietly murmuring about her amazing day to her favorite stuffed bunny, Ellen and Adam walked down the hall holding hands. They'd practically held hands all throughout dinner, too.

He'd put a log in the fireplace earlier and now it burned bright, emitting a rich hickory scent. They sat on the couch, Adam edging closer to Ellen the instant they both hit the cushions. He'd poured them both some wine already, and now handed her a glass.

"Thank you," she said.

Their eyes connected and held tight, so many thoughts and secrets sparking between them.

"Thank you for everything today," Ellen said.

He sipped the deep red wine, thoughtfully. If she could only read his mind.

Ellen took a quick sip then set the glass back on the table. A tiny adrenaline pop went off in her chest, knowing she couldn't put it off another second. "Adam, I owe you an apology."

His large hand gripped her wrist. Did he want her to stop? Her gaze drifted up his arm to his face. Pain still dwelled in his eyes. Some way, somehow, she needed to relieve it.

"After today," she said, "I understand how horrible things can happen in an instant." His fingers tightened on her skin. "I was the lucky one today. You were there, but it could have been completely different." She needed to clear her clogged throat where so much emotion seemed to have gathered. "The thing is, I know now what you went through, and I am so, so sorry." His features blurred to her vision as tears welled and spilled over her lids. "I'm so sorry. Please forgive me."

Adam was there in a flash, holding her, soothing her sorrow with warm wandering hands, kissing her hairline and jaw.

"Please forgive me, Adam."

He pulled back to study her. She'd always loved his strangely sensitive eyes, now accentuated in the dancing light from the fireplace. Come to think of it she'd always loved everything else about him, too.

"With all my heart," he said.

They smiled at each other, merciful, healing smiles. Then they kissed, soft caresses, lips opening, mouths welcoming each other. Warmth and moisture mellowed her body as her husband did what he did best – drive her crazy with desire for him.

There was much more to work through, but for now they were finally back on the right path. And right now that path led straight to the bedroom.

Once Bailey fell asleep, Ellen planned to spend the rest of the night in Adam's arms, making up, forgiving, moving on, focusing on the future, and never looking back.

Not long after their first kiss on the couch, they moved to the bedroom to the same bed they'd owned since their wedding night. After twelve long months, and one quickie in the on-call room, they took their time getting reacquainted. In the hushed and darkened room, they rekindled their love, making unspoken promises for a bright and enduring future as man and wife.

THE PHOENIX

Sam Bradley

Chapter One

Dr Quinn Pennington looked up. "He's a 'yellow'. He'll need suturing."

The man's injury needed care but it wasn't life-threatening. Nurse Jesse Harmon threw a bandage on the wound to keep the bleeding under control then turned to the firefighter-paramedic who had brought the patient in.

"Take him into Treatment Twelve, Jeff."

The tall man nodded as he and the patient moved off with the ambulance crew.

For the first time in over an hour, no patients were lined up to be triaged – the process of sorting injuries and illnesses by colored categories to determine those that needed immediate treatment versus those who could wait.

"How many does that make?" Quinn asked.

"Nine, I think," Jesse answered. "We should have two more coming."

Quinn nodded, pushing a stray strand of dark auburn hair behind her ear. "That accident must have been a real mess."

Jesse nodded. "We don't always appreciate what those firefighters deal with out on the streets."

Quinn nodded. "This job is anything but boring."

Jesse began cleaning up bandage wrappers and IV bag packaging. She looked up at the young physician. "Agreed, and it's only your fourth day. You know, you're already building a reputation as a 'shit magnet'."

Quinn grinned. She couldn't argue that point. In the last four days the trauma center had taken in patients from a refinery explosion, a multiple shooting, an outbreak of botulism poisoning from spoiled potato salad, and now this multiple patient vehicle accident.

Having Jesse by her side made it easy. Small in stature but with a big personality, the nurse very effectively managed the busy Emergency Room. She made sure the medics were quickly relieved of their patients, and that trauma teams worked at peak efficiency. Woe to the patient, doctor, or firefighter who tried to bully her. She had a soft spot for the firefighter-paramedics. As much as she was sometimes tough on them, she'd also be the first to listen to them vent after a tough call, and would defend them vigorously when an arrogant trauma surgeon chewed them out.

Quinn had been impressed with the paramedics she had met on "B" and "C" shifts, and today was meeting the "A" shift as they brought in patients from an eight-car pile-up on the freeway.

"Let me off of here!" Loud, slurred words followed the sound of the ambulance ramp doors opening and drew the attention of the doctor and nurse. A firefighter accompanied an ambulance crew and a patient who was restrained to a gurney with handcuffs. His arrival in the triage area was preceded by a strong odor of alcohol.

Jesse gave the crew a plastic smile. "Would we assume Mr Pleasant was the driver of the errant truck?"

Quinn looked at the tall, handsome firefighter with soft blond hair and ice blue eyes – Chris.

His smile was snide, but warm. "You would assume correctly, Jess."

"What's his complaint?" Quinn asked.

Chris turned to her. "His complaint is the fact that he's on that gurney and being transported against his will, even though I tried to explain to him that paramedics don't use handcuffs. That's a clue that he's under arrest. Police will be along presently to take him off your hands. The only significant injury we could find is a possible left tib-fib fracture."

Lower leg, Quinn thought. Why is it drunks survive with less injury than the innocent victims they traumatize in an accident?

She felt anger welling up. She'd seen seven patients come through the ER with moderate to serious injuries because of this idiot who decided to have beer for breakfast then drive an eighteen-wheeler on a busy freeway. The man wouldn't know until he sobered up how much legal trouble he was in.

The doctor took a deep, calming breath. Mindful of her expression and professional tone, she addressed the patient. "I need to do a quick physical assessment. Is that okay?"

The patient glared at her. "You touch me, bitch, and I'll sue you into next week."

Quinn felt her skin flush and her heart rate quicken. She leaned toward him and spoke in a quiet voice, "You call me bitch again, and you'll find a leprechaun with spiked shoes doing a little dance on your face." The man's mouth went slack then closed. Quinn turned to Jesse. "Who's handling the yellow area?"

Jesse grinned. "Dr Nasty . . . uh, Nasturtium."

A conspiratorial smile crossed the physician's face. "Perfect."

"Take him to Treatment Eight," Jesse said.

The ambulance crew moved off with their patient who launched into yet another rant.

"Remind me never to piss you off," Chris said dryly.

"Sorry – my Irish is showing."

"Chris Cavalari, this is Doctor Quinn Pennington, our new ER physician," said Jesse.

Chris took her hand. Quinn found his grip solid and his smile engaging.

"We call her Doctor Quinn," Jesse continued.

"Okay, I get it. As in the TV show, *Doctor Quinn – Medicine Woman*."

"Yeah," Quinn said, making a face. "I've been stuck with that moniker since I started medical school."

Chris laughed. "You'll have to meet our medicine man. He also has a bit of the Irish."

"Where is AJ?" Jesse asked.

"When we left he was still extricating the victim from the car that was hit first by the truck. They're coming in by helicopter."

Jesse nodded. "He's in good hands with AJ."

Chris turned to Quinn. "My partner's a good paramedic, but he's an extraordinary rescue technician. He's also an expert at mitigating difficult rescue situations. He gets extra points for this one. The cops noticed a green bumper in the debris that didn't match any of the identified vehicles. There was a car we simply couldn't find. AJ went inside the trailer of the semi and heard a weak voice. Turns out the guy's car was under the trailer and almost completely crushed. They had to cut through the floor of the truck, then the roof of the car, to get him out. Pretty delicate operation, but AJ pulled it off."

They turned to the sound of elevator doors opening behind the triage area. This particular elevator brought patients down from the helipad on the roof of the hospital. A yellow gurney with a patient emerged, accompanied by two nurses in royal blue jumpsuits, and a disheveled firefighter. Given the severity of the damage to his vehicle as related by Chris, the doctor, nurse and paramedic were surprised by what they saw. The young male patient was awake and being treated only with IV fluids, oxygen, and a sling on his right arm. The group stopped in front of the triage team.

"This is the guy who was crushed under the trailer?" Chris asked.

"The same," said the male nurse. "Our friend, Scott, definitely has some vigilant guardian angels."

Scott looked at AJ and held out his left hand. "And here's one of them. If it hadn't been for him, no one would have found me until I was officially a corpse."

AJ shook his hand. "Glad I was there to help."

"What are his injuries, Giovanni?" asked Quinn.

"Needless to say, lots of soft tissue trauma and a probable fracture of his right arm," said the nurse. "He has some belly pain, but it could be due to being bent up in a confined space for so long."

"Mind if I do a physical exam?" Quinn asked Scott.

"After what I just went through, you can pull out my guts and put needles in my eyes."

"That won't be necessary," Quinn said, as she pressed her hands over a number of places on his belly. She straightened and smiled. "No evidence of any active bleed. I'd like to have Doctor Mac or one of the other surgeons check his abdomen more thoroughly though."

"Mac's in Treatment One," Jesse said.

The nurses took their grateful patient to the next level of care.

Now that there was no patient to focus on, Quinn suddenly felt self-conscious. Chris was nice-looking, but a glimpse at his partner made her almost forget who she was. AJ was drop dead gorgeous, even with tousled hair and a dirty face. Chris had called him their "medicine man", which would suggest a Native American heritage, but his features seemed more Anglican than Indian. His large cerulean-blue eyes were mesmerizing and she was already lost in them. His light chocolate skin was framed by very dark brown hair with a hint of red. He had a strong, toned body and stood with perfect posture. That could easily be interpreted as arrogant or challenging, but she didn't sense either of those things about him.

Her eyes fell on a red bandana tied around his muscular bicep. Chris was staring at it as well.

"Is this a new part of your look, AJ?"

"Uh . . . no."

Quinn took a closer look. "There's blood under that bandana. Does that belong to the patient?"

He didn't respond.

"AJ?" Chris asked with a slightly admonishing tone.

AJ sighed. "It's fine."

Jesse had already donned a pair of latex gloves and pulled the bandana off. A nasty-looking laceration started bleeding. The nurse grabbed some 4 × 4 dressings and placed them over the wound.

"Nothing, huh?" Chris asked. "How did that happen?"

"I had to squeeze through a small hole in the car's roof and there wasn't enough room to wear my turnout coat. I snagged my arm on a piece of metal."

Chris shook his head. "Quinn, you need to understand that my partner has an aversion to being fussed over even when he needs care."

"When was your last tetanus shot, AJ?" Quinn asked.

"Probably yesterday, as often as he's in here," Jesse commented. "If it wasn't for suture material, he'd have fallen apart long ago." She looked at Quinn. "Perhaps you'd like the honor of sewing him up this time. You're the only doc in here who hasn't."

Quinn was cleaning up after AJ left when Jesse came in.

"Looks like things are back under control out there," she said. "Back to the regular flow of patients."

"Good."

Jesse grinned. "So, what did you think of our AJ?"

The picture of the bare-chested firefighter was indelibly embedded in her mind and would probably keep her up at night. His brown chest was beautifully sculpted without being too muscular, and he had a six-pack that morphed into an amazingly flat belly. She didn't dare look further south, but she'd already noticed his strong, slim legs and a tight ass she could stare at for hours.

How to answer that? *The man's body melted me into a dysfunctional puddle of raging hormones?*

"He's nice. Kind of quiet. I tried to engage him in conversation, but he didn't have much to say."

"AJ's the poster child for the strong silent type. He's a good man, though. Loyal to the bone. There's nothing he wouldn't do for someone he cares about or someone who needs his help. Problem is, he works pretty close to the edge sometimes, hence his frequent ER visits. He's almost illegally cute, don't you think?"

Quinn tossed a wad of bandage wrappers in the trash. "Jesse, if you're trying to sell me on him, don't bother. He's great eye candy, and I'm sure he's everything you say he is, but I have no interest in dating him or anyone else. Firefighters, in particular, are off the radar." Especially this one, if he puts himself in harm's way with such regularity.

Jesse grinned. "Okay. But what's your issue with firefighters?"

Quinn sighed. "It's a long story."

Chapter Two

Chris drove the fire department rescue unit through the intersection and made a left turn.

"So, did Doctor Quinn cause you any pain when she sutured you?"

"Didn't feel a thing," AJ answered.

"Interesting." Without looking, AJ could envision the grin on his partner's face. "Would you like a towel to wipe that drool off your face?"

AJ shook his head. "Fuck you."

"So really, what did you think of her?"

AJ remembered walking into the ER and seeing the new doctor for the first time. He'd heard they were getting a new trauma surgeon, but wasn't ready for a beautiful young woman with a body that he would love to wrap himself around. He'd felt like a fool when he got alone in the treatment room with her. She was trying to make conversation with him, and he was unable to form words.

She must think I'm a moron – or rude as hell.

"She's really . . . uh . . ."

Chris laughed. "Damn, you have it bad."

"Stop it. Okay, she's attractive." Attractive didn't begin to describe the good Doctor Quinn. A ponytail of long, dark auburn hair and an oval face with intelligent green eyes and the sexiest mouth he had ever seen. Although she wore a lab coat over her scrubs, it was obvious her slim body was very well toned. As she sutured him, he'd tried not to stare at her very firm, ample breasts. The memory caused a twitch in his cargo pants.

"So, maybe you should ask her out."

AJ shook his head. "I can't believe she doesn't have a husband or a boyfriend. Maybe both. If not, there's also a whole gang of 'B' and 'C' shift firefighters that probably have their sights on her."

"According to Jesse, Doctor Quinn is very single and, in her opinion, is smitten with you."

"And she knows this from an hour and a half in the ER? That woman is a master at meddling."

Chris made another turn. "She also has uncanny accuracy when it comes to her perceptions of people. What the hell? Ask Quinn out. You know you want to."

AJ expelled a long breath. "She's a doctor, Chris. She's extremely intelligent. She got through all those years of medical training and is still in her twenties. According to Jesse, her family has generations of doctors and plenty of money. I'm sure she has no interest in dating a half-breed, blue-collar firefighter with an AS degree."

"You don't know that." Chris's voice turned serious. "AJ, I hate that you think so little of yourself. I know you had a fucked-up childhood, but you've accomplished a hell of a lot as an adult. Think about all the lives you've touched and people who are alive because of you."

"That's my job, and I'm fortunate to have learned it well. Relationships with women . . . well . . . complete failure is an understatement."

"So, at twenty-nine you're just going to give up on any chance of marriage and family? Did it ever occur to you that maybe you haven't found the right woman yet?"

AJ glanced over at him. "That's blatantly obvious. Maybe I just need to quit having sex with them. It seems once I do, that becomes the focus of the relationship."

Chris grinned. "It's tough being such a stud."

AJ didn't smile. "I'd rather be bald and overweight and have a woman who cares about the man inside."

Quinn felt like Pavlov's dog whenever she heard the ambulance ramp doors open . . . especially on "A" shift days. Her heart rate accelerated when she saw Chris escorting an ambulance crew and an older woman on a gurney. They stopped at triage where Quinn was again assigned.

"Hey, Chris. What do you have?"

"Bessie had a bit of a sugar crisis. She has Type 2 diabetes and hasn't been very consistent with her meds. We gave her some IV sugar and she's feeling much better now."

Quinn asked the patient a few questions and sent her off to a medical treatment room.

"AJ will be along in a minute," Chris said with a wink. "He

never got to finish his first cup of coffee this morning so he'll be looking for some."

With no one in triage, she casually walked to the paramedic break room. The coffee pot was almost empty.

The more she got to know AJ O'Halloran, the more she liked him, and the more she ached to see him – the Native American man with the perfect body and the captivating Irish blue eyes. She hated that this man assumed control of her dreams at night and sent her to her battery-powered boyfriend with great regularity. It didn't help that she hadn't had sex for months. She hated the fact that she wanted him so badly. She had no room in her life for a man right now. And, worse yet, he was a firefighter.

Definitely off limits. What's a girl to do?

"Is this part of your job description?"

The sound of his sexy voice almost made her drop the pot of water she had just filled.

She ignored the tightening in her belly and smiled casually as she poured the water into the coffee machine. "Chris told me you missed your first cup this morning and I . . . I needed some myself," she lied. She never really liked coffee that much but drinking it had become a habit of necessity. AJ was a caffeine junkie.

She intentionally stood between the firefighter and the Styrofoam cups. Not to be deterred, he placed a hand on her shoulder and leaned over her, brushing against her. After retrieving a cup, he pulled back, their chests almost touching. The air was so full of sexual tension she thought her hair might catch fire, although the real heat flared much further down her body. They stared at each other for a tense moment. There was enough electricity between them to light up Las Vegas. She honestly thought he was going to kiss her and she wouldn't have stopped him.

"Quinn . . ."

Startled at the sound of Jesse's voice, she quickly dropped her hand from his chest. AJ pulled back and his cup dropped to the floor.

"Sorry," Jesse said, honestly apologetic. "They need some help in Trauma Ten."

* * *

The patient was a teenager with a laceration on his leg from a skateboard accident. Quinn went through the suturing procedure almost on autopilot. All she could think of was how close she had come to kissing AJ. Would he have kissed her if Jesse hadn't interrupted them? Her yearning to feel his soft, perfectly formed lips on hers was almost painful. She couldn't consider a relationship with him, but for the first time in a long time she'd found a man she really wanted to sleep with.

Minutes later, the young man was bandaged and released. A nurse accompanied him back to his parents in the waiting room.

The nurses disliked the fact that the young doctor insisted on cleaning up after herself rather than waiting for one of them or an ER tech to do it. In Quinn's opinion, the ER was too busy for ego trips. They were all part of the same team.

She was tidying up after her suturing job when a man entered the room, stopped inside the door, and gave her a cold stare. The warm feeling that AJ had left her with was suddenly replaced by cold foreboding.

Quinn was immediately uncomfortable with this man. He was tall, thin and had a shaved head. Covering his arms and chest was a multitude of tattoos . . . not the artistic kind, but the type seen on prison inmates with gang affiliations. Up until now, it hadn't bothered her that she was in the room alone. Now, she wished more than anything that someone would come in.

"Is there something I can do for you?" she asked, trying to keep her voice calm and professional.

He seemed confused for a moment, but began to walk toward her. Her level of discomfort rose astronomically as her brain began to process options.

Stay calm, Quinn.

She moved a few steps back, putting the gurney between her and potential danger. With her hands, she searched for the button at the head of the gurney that patients pushed to summon the nurses' station when there was a problem. There definitely was a problem. The man slowly continued to advance toward her.

"You need to stop," she said more forcefully. "What do you want?"

He was close enough now for her to see the tightness in his face. His glazed eyes also told her that he was high on some kind of drug.

Not good. Really not good.

She had no idea how he perceived her in his altered state – friend, enemy, or his next meal.

Her fingers finally found the call button and she pushed it.

Within a minute, Nurse Stephanie and Tim the ER Tech showed up at the door. They stopped, stared and seemed frozen in place for a moment. The man was still closing in on her.

Tim's face blanched white. "I'm sorry!" he said. "He was restrained and lying quietly on the gurney in Treatment Eighteen. I went to get Doc Eden. When I came back, he was gone. He broke through the restraints. He's also on a 5150."

This just keeps getting better . . . he's strong enough to break through leather restraints and he's on a psych hold.

"Well, I guess that's all academic now, isn't it?" Quinn said with a quaver in her voice.

Suddenly, the man launched. He grabbed Quinn, got behind her, and put his left arm around her neck. She grabbed at his wrist and pulled, but it didn't budge him. Panic welled up and her mind spun as she considered potential means of escape.

What the hell does he want?

"Heroin," he said, answering her unverbalized question.

The situation worsened as his right hand raised and she saw light reflect from something metal in his hand. Her heart rate maxed out when she recognized that the item was the scalpel from the suture set she had just used. He must have grabbed it from the tray.

She tried to think of something to say, but words were clearly useless with this man. She was also afraid of doing anything that might further provoke him. He was drugged, confining her movement, and could easily cut her throat with that scalpel.

Get a grip, Quinn, stay calm . . .

Chris grinned as he drained his cup. "So, you have a doctor making coffee for you now? Good trick. Maybe she'll make you cookies next time."

AJ laughed. "How did you know about that?"

"How do you think?"

"Jesse, of course. She also told me there was some serious magnetism between you two in the paramedic room."

"Let's get back to the station," AJ said. "We haven't even done a morning checkout yet."

As they passed through the ER, AJ looked around to see if Quinn was anywhere in sight. He saw Tim and Stephanie stop abruptly at the door to Treatment Ten. Something about their body language alerted him. Chris was still walking toward the ambulance ramp doors.

"Chris."

His partner stopped, gave him a curious look, and then returned to his side. "What's up?"

Now, a small cluster of ER staff, including Jesse, was standing in the doorway.

"Something's not right," AJ said.

The firefighters moved in the direction of Treatment Ten. Jesse turned, saw them, and locked onto them. AJ saw a look on the face of this salty old nurse that surprised and alerted him: fear. He increased his pace.

"What's wrong?" he asked when he reached her.

Jesse put a calming hand on his arm. Her voice was quiet but firm. "AJ, there's a man in there holding Quinn hostage and threatening her with a scalpel."

Before the words were completely out of the nurse's mouth, AJ had pushed through the crowd and into the room. His body tightened when he saw a scruffy, wild-eyed man standing behind Quinn, holding her in a headlock. In his right hand was a scalpel that he held close to her throat.

Both the man and Quinn turned to him. The man's eyes narrowed, as he appeared to assess AJ as a new threat. In Quinn's eyes he saw fear, hope and expectation . . . expectation that he was going to somehow mitigate this situation.

Shit.

"AJ!" She sounded like a scared kid.

"Stay calm, Quinn." His voice belied the anxiety he felt. He wasn't dealing with a victim who needed to be extricated from a vehicle or who was trapped in a confined space. Those situations were familiar and manageable. Handling this was much more delicate and the price of failure much higher.

AJ assessed the situation and the assailant who was threatening the woman he cared very much about. Glazed eyes . . . white . . . shaved head . . . tattoos . . . swastika . . . The man was most likely a skinhead.

Not good.

His top priority was to not put Quinn in more danger. Usually, the police had scenes like this under control before paramedics arrived. It also occurred to him that when the police did arrive, the presence of guns could push this man over the top.

"Jesse, get everyone out but Chris," he said without looking back. Jesse complied.

The firefighter's jaw was set and his body tense. He was prepared to do battle. "Let her go." His voice was stern and unwavering.

"No!" the man spat.

He knew he needed to divert the man's attention from Quinn. "What do you want with that white girl? She's just like you. Why would you want to hurt one of your own?"

He saw a flicker of confusion in the man's eyes.

Good.

"It's me you want. Look at my skin. It's brown. I'm an Indian. You like Indians?"

"No!" the man shouted again.

"Then come for me, asshole. You want a piece of this Indian?"

AJ could see anger on the man's reddening face. His plan was working. He just hoped Quinn wouldn't do anything to distract the man back to her.

"You can't touch me, white boy. Your people thought you got the best of us a long time ago, but you were wrong. We're stronger and smarter than any of you."

The man's eyes flared.

He heard Chris speak quietly from behind him, but didn't take his eyes off his target. "AJ, be careful, he's on PCP."

AJ felt a chill go through him. Game changer. Animal tranquilizer – angel dust. I could hit that man with a fire engine and he wouldn't feel a thing.

He glanced at Quinn and saw renewed fear in her eyes. It reaffirmed his resolve. In the seconds he made eye contact with her, he tried to communicate a message of comfort even though he didn't know what the hell he was going to do if the man actually came after him. It didn't matter . . . as long as this guy didn't hurt her.

Time to push this over the top.

"Come on, dirtbag. Come and get me!"

The man didn't move.

It's not working, AJ. You've got to come up with something harsher.

"How about I go and fuck your mother so she can have little brown half-breed babies like me?"

That did it. The man's face got even redder and his eyes all but bugged out of his head. Every muscle tightened and hate radiated from every pore. It seemed he just couldn't get his drugged-out body to take action.

Quinn stayed perfectly still as AJ tried to draw the man out.

My God, he's willing to sacrifice himself for me!

She heard Chris tell AJ the man was on PCP and her spirits fell. Not only was her assailant incapable of feeling pain, he was capable of wide mood swings. Worse, if he reached AJ, he could seriously hurt him.

Can't let that happen! Think, Quinn . . .

The man was very focused on AJ – enough so that if she moved quickly, she might be able to free herself from his grasp. Her timing had to be exact so she could get out of the way of the scalpel if he tried to slash her with it. Then, as if her stunned brain cells suddenly came back on line, an obvious solution surfaced.

Most people, when in a chokehold, will try to grab the assailant's arm and pull outward, but the assailant still has the mechanical advantage.

Instead, Quinn now grabbed the man's wrist from the inside and pushed down and out. In an instant, she felt his grip loosen just enough that she could duck under his arm and dash away.

If he slashed at her, she was unaware of it. In fact, the man didn't seem to care about her at all any more. He appeared totally fixated on the man across the room. It was AJ who was in danger now.

"Quinn, get out of here!" AJ said firmly.

"Hell, no!"

She surprised herself with those words, but there was no way she was going to leave AJ alone with that man.

But what the hell can I do?

The paramedics and the doctor were surprised at the speed with which the man charged toward AJ, the scalpel held high like a weapon of war. AJ, unarmed except for his wits, braced himself. As the arm with the scalpel started to come down, he grabbed it with both hands. For a moment he seemed to have the advantage, but not for long. Even though he was able to deflect the strike that was probably meant for his chest, he couldn't disarm the man. The skinhead pulled out of AJ's grasp, and the scalpel came down again. This time it cut through the firefighter's shirts and sliced into the skin of his upper arm.

I have to do something!

She looked at Chris and could see the same frustration in his eyes. What could they do that wasn't going to risk AJ further? She scanned the room, and then her eyes went back to Chris. She pointed. He nodded.

Chapter Three

AJ, undeterred by pain, fell to the ground and rolled, coming up to his feet again. The man may have drug-induced strength, but the firefighter was naturally more agile. Having been in a lot of street fights as a kid gave AJ an added advantage. He could feel blood running down his arm, but didn't lose his focus. He realized the only weapon he had was his body.

Charging toward the man like a bull, he butted him in the chest, forcing the skinhead backwards and off balance. The man fell into the gurney, which rolled and pushed into the tray that held the rest of the used suture set instruments. They fell to the floor with a huge clatter of metal and glass. The man, however, managed to struggle to his feet. AJ, unbalanced as well, scrambled to get out of his way.

He felt a sharp pain in his back. This pain was much more intense than that from the first slash and couldn't be ignored. He cried out, grabbed his shoulder, and fell to his knees.

Absorbed with the pain, he didn't realize his back was exposed.

The next thing he heard was the man crying out. He heard feet flying by him, then the sound of metal hitting tile.

Worried about Quinn, he looked up. What he saw wasn't close to what he expected, and a picture that would stay in his mind for a long time.

Chris was sitting on the man, who was now prone on the ground. Standing behind them was Quinn. A syringe with a large exposed needle was in her hand. Her eyes telegraphed anger and determination, and then her face morphed into a satisfied smile.

"I think you can get up now," she said. Chris cautiously removed himself from the man who was no longer fighting. Quinn held the syringe up with the pride of a victim who had prevailed against her assailant. "He'll be asleep for a while."

Police charged into the room followed by the gang of ER employees. The cops restrained the man, and then dragged him out. Only peripherally aware of the other activity in the room, Quinn's attention turned to AJ. He was still on the floor, clutching his shoulder. Chris and Tim helped him up and assisted him to the gurney. His shirts were cut off and Jesse pressed dressings onto the bleeding wound on his back.

Quinn disposed of the syringe, and then went to him.

"I'm okay," he said.

Chris shook his head. "AJ, you'd say that if you had a damned stake in your heart."

He groaned. "I almost did."

"Quinn, take a break," Jesse told her. "You've been through a harrowing experience. I'll find someone else to take care of him."

"Hell, no! The man saved my life. I'll take care of him." She gave the nurse a stern look.

"Okay, everyone out," Jesse said. "Let the doctor take care of her patient."

Quinn knew Jesse would assure their privacy, which gave her some relief. Now that the emergency was over and the adrenaline rush gone, she felt drained.

AJ was sitting up on the gurney. When she looked at him, she felt a shiver go through her that started at her toes and flashed through her entire body. She considered what could have happened. He looked back at her, and she could see he was having similar thoughts.

With no concern for protocol or appropriateness, she threw her arms around his neck. He put his arms around her waist and pulled her to him. They held each other for several minutes.

She pulled back and looked at him. "I can't believe you made yourself a target like that."

"I couldn't let him hurt you, Quinn." He gave her a quick smile. "Besides, my guardian spirits are always with me. They protect me from serious harm."

She shook her head. "I'm serious, AJ. Why do you take so many chances, press your luck like you do?"

His expression dissolved into seriousness. "Quinn, I work with a man who has two kids. If something happened to me—" he shrugged and looked down "—it really wouldn't matter."

Her fingers wove into his thick hair and he looked up at her again. She searched his eyes. The pain she saw there had nothing to do with his wounds. Unbidden, tears began to fall down her face.

"You're so wrong."

AJ put his hand on her face and used his thumb to wipe a tear from her cheek. They both smiled self-consciously. Her heart was captured by a sea of blue that now showed profound appreciation. He slowly leaned into her. His lips tentatively touched hers. Quinn felt an explosion of sensation radiate from her core to every nerve in her body. Her psychological trauma and his physical injuries were momentarily forgotten.

AJ sat in his favorite booth in the corner of Houlihan's Irish pub. He nursed his second beer and watched the comings and goings of other patrons. This was a common hangout for off-duty cops, firefighters, and medical personnel so he often ran into people he knew. Tonight, though, he wasn't in a social mood nor was he looking for companionship. He generally didn't drink on the night before a shift, either, but tonight he desperately needed a diversion.

Quinn Pennington had completely consumed him. When he'd found her in danger, the warrior in him came out and he was willing to battle to the death for her. He'd never felt that way about a woman. When he kissed her in the ER, his emotional fate was sealed. She seemed to care about him, yet the relationship hadn't moved forward as he thought it would. It had been a whole week and nothing. He felt like a child who had been given a taste of fine chocolate only to have it jerked away, never to be enjoyed again.

Loud, young female voices accompanied the sound of the opening door. He knew before he saw them that the voices belonged to Katie and Sherry, two EMTs from the ambulance company. Katie had been after him for months, most likely to add another set of firefighter balls to her collection. He wasn't interested in her anyway, but since meeting Quinn, he had no desire to be with anyone.

It was only minutes before Katie, drink in hand, sidled in next to him. Shy she was not. He assumed it would become quickly apparent that he wasn't up for idle chatter, but no. She started into a complex story about people at the ambulance company he couldn't care less about. She talked; he pretended to listen.

The door opened again and he almost choked on the drink of beer he was taking. In snug Levi's, boots, and a red sweater that showed every delicious curve, was Quinn. Stephanie, the ER nurse, accompanied her. He had never seen either of them at the bar before.

It seemed every male in the place stopped what they were doing to stare at Quinn. AJ's belly filled with acid.

Stephanie and Quinn sat at a table facing him. Quinn immediately caught his eye and smiled warmly, then the smile quickly faded and she looked away.

What the hell? Crap . . . Katie. The girl was still chattering on. *Quinn probably thinks she's with me.*

He was considering what to do when a clearly inebriated man appeared and invited himself to a chair next to Quinn. AJ recognized the man as a cop from across town. He wasn't close enough to hear what the guy was saying, but he watched Quinn's body language. She responded to him a couple times with a sharp retort, but he didn't back off. He then put a hand over hers and she jerked it away. Quinn looked up and caught AJ's eye. They had become good at non-verbal communication. The message was clear.

AJ quickly made his way across the room and stood between Quinn and the cop. He looked down at the man and glared. "I think the lady wants you to leave."

The man returned his stare, although much more glassy-eyed, and his body stiffened. He stood and faced AJ, posturing with typical cop bravado. The firefighter was taller, stronger and outweighed him by fifty pounds. Without another word, the man turned and left, presumably to find safer prey.

His task done, AJ started to move away.

"AJ, where are you going?" Quinn asked. "Oh, sorry . . . your date."

He'd forgotten about Katie. He saw her at the bar talking to another firefighter. "She's not my date."

Quinn stood to face him. "Good, then we need to talk."

She took his hand and led him outside. The night air felt good – so did her warm hand in his. She stopped next to a blue Toyota FJ Cruiser.

"Yours?" he asked.

"Yeah."

"I'm impressed. I was expecting a BMW or Mercedes."

"Shows how little you know about me."

He gave her a sly smile. "I'm sensing a little attitude."

She exhaled a frustrated breath. "Maybe. What's up with you, AJ? You're obviously attracted to me. You're willing to save my life and even kiss me in the ER, but you've never asked me out. I don't get it."

He was uncomfortable and a little confused. This was the woman that had made it clear she didn't want to date a firefighter. But he also had his own issue.

"You and I are very different people, Quinn. You're intelligent, well educated and have money. I'm a half-breed Native American born in poverty on a small reservation. I was raised by an apathetic grandmother and an uncle who reminded me frequently how worthless I was. Except for my talent as a firefighter, he was right."

She gave him a long look. "Are you trying to say you don't think you're good enough for me?"

He looked her directly in the eye. "Yes."

She gave him a look of defiance. "Well, you're wrong, and I'll decide who's good enough for me. AJ, 'good enough' has nothing to do with money or education. It has to do with character. Rich, well-educated guys are pompous asses, and boring enough to put me to sleep in minutes." She poked him in the chest with her finger. "You, Fire Boy, are honest, loyal, intelligent, and talented. That and—"

AJ kissed her, drowning out her words. His tongue slid past her lips, tasting, exploring, teasing, and creating a sensual rhythm that brought a moan from deep in her throat. She wound her arms around his neck and molded her body to his. He crushed her against him and his kiss became deep and needy.

She could feel his erection between them and warmth spread throughout her body. The few drinks she'd had only increased the feeling.

She broke the kiss and whispered in his ear, "Take me home and make passionate love to me."

She felt a change in his demeanor. He pulled back to look at her.

"No."

She shook her head in confusion. "No? You don't want to have sex with me when you've been kissing me like this?"

His voice was soft but his expression serious. "I didn't say that, Quinn. I want to have sex with you more than any woman I've ever known. I want to make love to you until the sun comes up. But, I won't have a one-night stand with you. I respect you too much for that, and I value the professional relationship we have. I don't want to screw that up."

"AJ . . ."

"Quinn, I need to know there's something more. If there isn't, then that was our last kiss." His thumb traced a line down her cheek and tried to ignore the fire in his loins. His lips closed in on hers again. "Do you still want to come home with me?"

She looked at the expectant expression on his handsome face and the anxiousness in his eyes. Desire sparred with reluctance.

She answered him with a kiss.

* * *

The heat between them was instant and intense. His clean, woodsy male scent assaulted her senses. As soon as they were in his bedroom, she pulled his polo shirt over his head. It fell to the floor, revealing his beautiful strong brown chest. She ran her fingers over his skin, then into his thick hair. She touched her lips to his, softly nibbling and teasing. He cupped the back of her head with his hand and kissed her deeply while her hands caressed his back.

He removed her sweater and bra then moved his hand to cup a breast. She gasped softly when he touched her. She closed her eyes and moaned; her breathing quickened. Her hands ran down his sides until they reached the border of his Levi's. She unbuttoned them.

In moments, they were naked and lying together on his bed. His hands ran down the length of her from her face to her breasts to her thighs. She trembled with need. She writhed, wanting him, but he clearly wasn't ready. He was in control. A small cry escaped her lips. He lightly bit her neck and her world disintegrated into pure sensation.

She kissed his mouth and his neck. His moans told her she was giving back every exquisite experience that he was giving her. She arched her back and cried out, feeling as though she would explode if he didn't take her.

"AJ, please!"

He had been kissing her slowly and seductively, but now captured her lips with a kiss that was desperate and hungry. Warmth spread through her entire body. Each touch to her sensitive skin sent sparks throughout her body.

His own fever was driving him now and when he entered her, she responded with a small cry of ecstasy. Her body slowly opened to him. Tenderness was now replaced by the voracious hunger that consumed them both. They feasted on shared passion fueled by months of sexual tension and drought.

"AJ!" She gasped as pure sensation engulfed her. He had reached a place inside her that had never been touched, and was his alone. Fulfillment finally cascaded into hot pulsating waves. Her nails dug deeply into his back as he cried out. She held his head and kissed his neck. He was dizzy from the intensity of the experience and physically spent. His head fell next to hers, his hair, face and body wet with sweat.

After taking a moment to recover, he raised up to look at her. He took her face in his hands and kissed her lightly, and then smiled.

"I love you, Quinn."

This woman had captured him, mind and soul, long before giving him her body.

Quinn blinked at the sunlight that assaulted her eyes. Opening them slowly, it took her a moment to realize where she was. She felt profound warmth when she remembered how AJ had made love to her – all night – as promised. The man was an incredible lover.

Reality suddenly smacked her in the head and she sat up, searching for a clock. She found one on the bedside table that said 09.57. She relaxed when she realized she had a few hours before her swing shift at the hospital.

It was then she realized she was in AJ's bed. Alone.

Shit, he had a shift that started at 07.00. He had probably gotten up moments after she had fallen asleep in his arms.

Shower . . . I need a shower to clear my head.

She went into his bathroom and was impressed with its neatness and cleanliness. She found the clean towel and washcloth he had left for her. The water was hot and felt great on her aching body.

Coffee had never been a requirement for her, but she needed some now. In the kitchen downstairs she found a fresh pot that was still hot. A clean cup sat on the counter, and under it was a note. It was written with AJ's left-handed block letters:

> Quinn, thank you for the best night of my life. I hope I gave you everything you needed. I meant what I said when I told you I loved you. You're the first woman to hear those words. I hope it isn't more than you can handle. Call me when you're ready.
>
> AJ

She sat heavily on a stool by the breakfast bar. This man was amazing. She'd just had the best sex of her life. His body could grace the cover of a romance novel. He was intelligent, honest, thoughtful and neat. And he loved her. She had to be the luckiest girl in the world, right?

Why, then, did she feel such a sense of discomfort?

Before he took her home with him he'd made her promise that this was more than just a one-night stand.

I didn't exactly promise . . .

But she had come home with him, so the agreement was understood.

This was a huge burden to bear.

She could never hurt him, but panic welled up in her.

I feel strongly for him, but is it love? Do I love him but can't bring myself to admit it? How did he feel when he told me he loved me and didn't hear those words from me?

And there's the issue of his being a firefighter!

The ER was fairly slow. Quinn was happy with that. She had been put in charge of the ER for only the second time, which was an awesome responsibility. She told herself she needed to get AJ O'Halloran out of her head and concentrate on her work.

That lasted as long as it took for him to bring in the first patient. When he'd completed the patient turnover, she was waiting for him at the coffee pot. She handed him a cup when he walked in.

He grinned. "How did you know?"

"I heard someone kept you up all night."

"That's true, but it was well worth it." He leaned into her as close as he could without being inappropriate. She put a hand on his waist.

"Funny, you smell like the soap from my bathroom. Irish Spring, of course."

Her face sobered. "AJ, I feel like I didn't give you everything you needed."

He smiled warmly. "It's okay. I know you have an issue with dating firefighters. I don't understand it, but it's something you have to work through . . . or not. I'm not going to pressure you, Quinn. I want you to come to me freely – when you're ready."

An old feeling of angst presented itself as a lump in her stomach.

I owe him this.

"AJ, before I left for medical school, I had a boyfriend who I'd been with all through high school. Being a firefighter was all he wanted to do. I loved him desperately. We planned to get married. For a while, we were both members of a volunteer fire company."

AJ's eyebrows rose.

"We rarely got big fires, but one day an industrial complex went up. Mike and I, with others, were ventilating the roof."

She stopped. AJ must have perceived how hard this was for her. He also likely knew what she was going to say. He took her hand and squeezed it.

"The roof opened up and Mike and another firefighter fell through to their deaths. I was right on the edge. If it wasn't for a guy with quick reflexes and a strong arm, I would never have met you."

There was a moment of silence as she relived the moment.

"I'm so sorry," he said softly.

"Mike fell face up, and the look on his face was almost . . . apologetic. Like he'd made a mistake that was going to ruin my life. In essence, it did. I never went back to firefighting. I had a complete meltdown and almost flunked my med school entrance exams. As it turned out, a complete immersion in school gave me a great excuse to avoid dating."

She met his eyes and felt tears well in hers. "I swore I would never love another firefighter and risk watching him become critically injured or die like that. It would be too painful to go through that again. Even worse would be the stress of always worrying about when it's going to happen."

He touched her face. "I understand."

She gave him a light smile. "And you're the worst of the lot when it comes to taking chances!"

He smiled back. "Don't you know they call me 'the Phoenix'? I get hurt sometimes, but I come right back – and I heal quickly."

She poked him in the chest. "The Phoenix, the mythical bird, would burn himself up so another could be reborn. I hope you're not going to do that!"

"No," he laughed. "I have great guardian spirits, but even they have limits."

She looked into his beautiful eyes. "You're so easy to love, AJ. I'm trying. Just give me time."

He pushed a lock of hair behind her ear. "Quinn, life is risk. If you never take a risk, you don't live."

"AJ." Chris's voice broke into their moment. "Come on, we have a rescue."

Quinn went back to work, glad she'd revealed her fears to AJ. It was hard to believe he was so patient with her.

She checked the triage area, and then conferred with the nurses on the status of patients in the treatment rooms. Activity in the ER was pretty routine at the moment.

She was at the triage desk completing some paperwork when Jesse came out of the radio room. The base station radio allows direct communication between ER staff, and paramedics in the field. She was alerted by the strangely uncomfortable look on the nurse's face. Jesse took her arm and looked at her in a way that felt ominous.

"Come with me," she said. It wasn't a request. Jesse led her to the empty paramedic room, stopped, and then turned to her. "We have a trauma coming in by helicopter."

"Okay," Quinn said, confused. There were several of those every day. "Has the trauma team been notified?"

"Yes."

Quinn struggled to understand the sense of urgency that she read in the nurse's face. "Is AJ bringing the patient in?"

Jesse sighed deeply. "Quinn, AJ is the patient."

Chapter Four

Quinn felt the blood drain from her face and acid rise in her gut.

"No, I just talked to him!" The familiar feeling of overwhelming terror squeezed the breath out of her.

Jesse took her arm and gripped it hard to ensure she got her attention.

"Quinn, we only have minutes. Right now, you're in charge of his case. You have to decide right now if you're capable of taking care of him. If not, I need to find another surgeon."

The doctor swallowed hard and reeled herself in. "I owe him my life, Jesse. Of course I'll take care of him."

The nurse's eyes burned into hers. "Not good enough. Can you divorce your emotional attachment to him and give him everything he needs?"

She felt nauseous, but from somewhere deep within, she summoned the strength.

I couldn't help Mike, but I'm sure as hell not going to lose AJ!

"Yes!" she said adamantly. Give me a patient report."

Jesse exhaled a breath and nodded. "They were rescuing some boys from an abandoned warehouse. The building started to disintegrate and AJ fell through the second-story floor. Quinn, AJ has an active belly bleed and they're having a hard time holding his blood pressure."

Quinn took a minute to absorb the information. "We know his blood type. Order six units and have more on standby. Make sure the team has the surgery suite ready. We're going to push him through the ER as fast as we can."

AJ was conscious even though he had been chemically paralysed. It was frightening not being able to move or breathe, even for a few minutes. Giovanni deftly inserted the endotracheal tube into his airway. The tube felt suffocating even though its purpose was to ensure oxygenation to his brain and vital organs. He also knew it was there in case he quit breathing. It reminded him just how critical his situation was. A moment of raw terror seized him. He could feel his heart pounding in his chest, trying to keep up with the loss of fluid from his damaged organs.

I don't want to die! Especially now . . .

He thought of the conversation he'd had only hours ago.

I'm sorry, Quinn.

The stretcher bumped as he was loaded into the helicopter. As the air ambulance took off, he stubbornly held on to consciousness, but was too weak to respond with more than a plaintive look at Giovanni. A wave of pain engulfed him. He would have cried out, but the tube prevented it.

"Okay, AJ, we're going to take a fast ride and we'll have you at the trauma center in short order," the nurse said. "Right now, I'm going to give you something for your pain."

In a few minutes the medication started to calm him and relieve the worst of his pain.

He was sedated enough to fall into a light sleep during the flight, lulled by the whish of rotor blades. It was the jolt of the skids hitting the helipad on the roof of the hospital that woke him. His body felt heavy, like he was still paralysed. He couldn't even summon the effort to open his eyes.

All the sounds around him seemed muffled and surreal, yet he recognized voices, especially one.

"Stay with me, AJ. I need you to stay with me."

He heard the elevator doors open as they made their way to the ER. The medication was wearing off and the pain in his belly, left arm, leg, head and chest came back with a vengeance. He tried to draw up his legs against the restraints of the backboard straps. He was very agitated until a firm, warm hand clutched his, and he heard her voice again.

"I've got you, AJ. I won't let you go."

Things became fuzzier as he was taken into the bright lights and frenzied activity of the ER. "Trauma One," he heard someone say. That's where the most critical cases went.

I wonder how many people have died in this room?

He was surrounded by indistinguishable voices as the trauma team poked, prodded and pressed on his body. A male, Dr Mac, he thought, shouted orders for labs and X-rays. He groaned and pain shot through him when the doc pressed on the left upper quadrant of his belly. He felt a firm grip on his shoulder.

"Hang on, AJ. I know it hurts."

He felt a needle in his arm as the lab tech drew blood, heard the beep of the cardiac monitor, and the tone of the X-ray machine.

"It looks like a splenic injury. That's probably where the bleeding's coming from. Let's get him prepped!" Quinn said.

Cold sweat ran down AJ's face and his mind was numb. He was cold, so cold. Even his strong survival instinct was failing him now. He wanted so much to quit struggling against the pain.

"His respiratory rate just dropped," the respiratory tech said. She took control of his breathing.

AJ's mind floated. It was so much easier to let someone else breathe for him. He was beyond exhausted. He was beyond caring. It would be so easy to just let go, to fall into the sweet oblivion of sleep.

The beep of the cardiac monitor slowed. AJ's consciousness became greyer.

"Dammit to hell, he's crashing!" Mac's voice played at the fringes of his consciousness.

"His blood pressure's dumping!" Jesse shouted.

Mac's voice raised above the others, "Squeeze that blood in and let's get him upstairs, now!"

AJ felt detached from his body. Grey was turning to black. The last thing he heard was Quinn's voice, and then he felt her cool hands on his face.

"AJ O'Halloran, don't you dare die on me. I love you!"

The door opened quietly and Jesse stepped into the surgical waiting room.

Chris sat with his head in his hands. Jesse walked over to the small couch and sat next to him. He looked up when she put her hand on his arm.

"There's nothing more you could have done, Chris. You had limited options of supplies and equipment, and had no control over the fact you were trapped in there for a while. You gave him fluids. That was critical."

Chris slowly shook his head. "All I did was turn his blood into Kool-Aid. Normal saline wasn't carrying oxygen to his brain."

"But it kept his pressure up long enough to get him here alive."

Her expression begged for acknowledgement. He nodded, and then looked back down at his hands. "I can't fathom losing a partner after nine years. How long is this going to take?"

"As long as the surgeons are in there, AJ is still alive. You know they're the best in the county, and many of them are the best in the state."

Her cell buzzed, and she walked across the room to answer it. "Okay," was all she said before returning to Chris. "I have to go back to the ER. It seems we're short a doctor down there."

"Who?"

"Quinn."

Chris considered the implications. Besides Jesse, he was the only one who knew that the relationship between AJ and Quinn had become serious. Maybe AJ being so seriously injured was more than she could handle.

Jesse put the phone in her pocket. "It seems Doctor Nasty had an ego attack and refused to work on AJ because he felt he was too unstable. Mac insisted that immediate surgery was the only option if AJ was going to survive. Of course, Nasty wouldn't agree with Mac if he told him his hair was on fire."

"What does that have to do with Quinn?"

"Mac needed another pair of hands. She is a surgeon, and quite a good one, I understand."

"But . . ."

"Yeah, I know. He needed her, Chris. She needed to be there for him. She won't let him down."

Last night he was inside her, making love to her in a way that was fresh, sincere, and intense. Today, she was inside of him, desperately trying to save the life of the man she finally admitted she loved. She watched as Doctor Mac removed the last of AJ's destroyed spleen.

"Get that bleeder, Quinn," he said.

Quinn reached in and cauterized a small artery.

It had been dicey for a while. AJ's blood pressure was barely holding. Not caring what the other surgeons thought, she started talking to him. She had read studies that provided evidence that patients, even deeply under anaesthesia, could understand and respond to a doctor's voice.

"I know you're tired, AJ, but it's important that your blood pressure stays above eighty. Can you do that for us?"

It stabilized. The other surgeons were amazed. This man was fighting to survive. Once they had gotten inside of his abdomen they found the problem right away. The spleen, a solid organ that's filled with blood, had been shattered. All that blood was spilling into his abdominal cavity. Fortunately, one can live without this organ. There was a small amount of liver damage as well, but it didn't require surgical intervention.

"You close, Quinn, and we'll start working on these fractures," Mac said.

Quinn started the laborious task of suturing the multiple layers of AJ's abdomen. The top layer of skin would be stapled.

Her thoughts wandered to when she would be able to run her fingers over his surgical scar. He had told her he loved her, something she knew wasn't easy for him, and she shut down like a drug deal in a police station.

What the hell, Quinn? Did you think if you told him you loved him, that you'd jinx him? Well, you didn't tell him, and this happened anyway. But he didn't die like Mike. He'll have another chance at life and you'll have another chance with him.

AJ's last words came back to her. "Quinn, life is risk. If you never take a risk, you don't live."

It was time to live.

So drained she could hardly hold her eyes open, Quinn sat by AJ's bedside in recovery. She was waiting for the effects of the anaesthesia to wear off. He moved occasionally and then would fall back into a drug-induced sleep.

The tube had been removed from his throat and he was breathing well. His lower left arm was casted and lay on a pillow. His lower left leg was also casted and elevated. A bandage around his head held a dressing where a laceration had been sutured. A blanket partially covered his lower body, but she could see the bandages that protected the surgical wound on his abdomen. She'd put them there with special care.

AJ's groan pulled her attention. His eyes fluttered open for a few seconds, then closed again. She glanced at the monitors that measured his heart rate and rhythm, respirations and blood pressure, and took comfort in the fact that he was broken, but alive and stable.

She felt a hand on her shoulder, and then looked up into Jesse's smiling face. Despite the obvious elation following the news of AJ surviving surgery, the nurse looked as tired as Quinn felt.

"I thought I'd find you here," she said. "Have you had any sleep?"

Quinn shook her head. "He's starting to come out of the anaesthesia. I want the first person he sees to be me. I can sleep later."

"And you want to make sure he's . . . intact."

Quinn's expression tightened and she nodded. "His blood pressure dropped so low, and the hemoglobin that carries oxygen to his brain was diluted by the fluids Chris and Giovanni had to give him."

Jesse faced the young doctor. "You held it together and were able to perform a major role in his survival. You should be proud of yourself. Dr Nasty did you a great favor when he refused to scrub in."

Quinn exhaled a long, tired sigh. "That's true. I'm obviously relieved AJ survived, but if he's unable to do his job, it would be worse than death for him."

Jesse nodded. "What if he does have some brain impairment? What will you do?"

"Take care of him," Quinn answered without a moment's hesitation.

"Because you love him, or because you feel obligated?"

Quinn narrowed her eyes. "You know the answer to that."

Jesse smiled warmly. "Yes, I do."

Quinn felt the pressure of AJ's hand squeezing hers, followed by a groan. She looked down and saw that his eyes were open.

"Hey, welcome back to the land of the living."

His voice was hoarse and his speech groggy. "If living is this painful, I'd like to consider the alternative."

Both women smiled.

"Nothing wrong with that brain," Jesse said.

"I think the better alternative is for me to get some pain meds for you." Quinn gave the order to the recovery nurse making notes on his chart. The medication was injected into his IV.

"What's wrong with me, Quinn?" AJ asked.

"Well, you have a plethora of soft tissue trauma in a lovely shade of purple on your left side, several stable fractures, and the absence of a spleen in your belly. Nothing that will keep you from a full recovery, though."

He gritted his teeth as a wave of pain hit him, but Quinn could see the medication was beginning to relax him.

"Do you remember what happened, AJ?" Jesse asked.

He closed his eyes. "Rescue . . . falling . . . more pain than I've ever felt in my life . . . Chris talking to me . . . Giovanni in the helicopter . . . the ER – lights, voices, pain . . . not much else." He opened his eyes, but seemed to have trouble keeping them open. He looked at Quinn. "Are you my doctor now?"

"Well, Doctor Mac is your physician of record, but I'll be your doctor, your nurse, your physical therapist, your hygienist, even your maid if you need me to be."

He blinked several times. "You will?"

"Yes. I love you, AJ. I'm sorry it took this long to tell you."

"You told me . . . in the ER."

Jesse and Quinn both looked stunned.

"That's impossible," Quinn said. "You were crashing and deeply unconscious."

His words were slurred and his eyes barely open. "The last sense that goes is hearing. I was tired, so tired. I had nothing left. The pain was unbearable. I just wanted to sleep. Then I heard your voice. You told me . . ." His eyes closed.

Chapter Five

The late-afternoon sun came through the living room window near where Quinn sat on the floor reading her novel. The lights were off so AJ could sleep. Sensing something, she turned to look toward the couch. He was watching her. She smiled.

"I miss you," he said.

"How can you miss me? I've been with you at least ten hours a day."

"No, I miss you," he repeated, changing the inflection of his words. She went to him and knelt beside the couch so she could look at him. He was lying on his back with his head on a pillow. He reached up and ran his hand through her long loose hair. She read the need in his eyes.

"Oh."

He put his hand around the back of her head and pulled her to him, kissing her deeply. Her body responded immediately and profoundly, but she pulled back, kissing his face lightly. "No, baby, it's too soon. I'd be afraid of hurting you."

"Hurting me? Not being able to make love to you is killing me. We've only had one night together and that was weeks ago."

"Have you forgotten the fact that half the bones in your body are broken?"

"Not half. Besides, the most important one isn't broken."

"That's not a bone, AJ," she said, with mock seriousness.

"Look again!" He grinned.

She sighed. He was wearing only light scrub pants and the "bone" to which he referred was clearly evident. She felt a warm tingle run through her body. She needed him as much as he needed her.

"Okay, if we can get you to the floor without you falling apart, maybe we could make this work." She helped him move onto his back on the carpet and put the pillow under his head. He winced and bit his bottom lip.

"AJ . . ."

"It's okay." He pulled her to him and kissed her again. His tongue dancing with hers fueled the fire of unmet need. She gave in to the feeling.

His voice was husky and hot. "Make love to me."

Electricity surged through Quinn's loins at the idea of making love to him. As they kissed, his hand reached under her shirt.

She pulled off his pants, leaving him naked except for the casts and bandages.

Smiling, she straddled him. She moved onto him slowly so they could both enjoy the feeling. She locked her legs around his and leaned forward to kiss him. His moans became so loud she was concerned she was hurting him, but if there was any pain, it was masked by ecstasy. She loved that she was driving him crazy. She leaned into him and he kissed her again. She loved his kiss. Everything he felt was communicated in his kiss.

These last few weeks had focused solely on his healing. Without sex to get in the way, they had been able to learn about each other, understand each other's fears and dreams, and generally strengthen their relationship. He had accepted that she really wanted him, and she had decided he was worth any risk.

He was breathless. "Thank you, baby."

"Well, it wasn't all for you," she said, grinning. "You know, you're an amazing lover even when you're incapacitated." She moved to lie beside him and put her arm over his belly.

He gave her a long, lingering look. "I want you to stay with me," he said, brushing her hair with his fingers.

"I am staying with you."

"I mean, after I'm healed. Move in here with me."

"AJ, we haven't talked about this . . ."

"We're talking about it now. Better yet, why not just marry me?"

Her eyes registered surprise, and then an impish grin grew on her face. "No."

His eyes widened. "No?"

"This isn't how you propose to a girl, post-coital, lying naked on the living room floor."

He fell silent for a minute and then smiled. "Go to the left side drawer in the entertainment center and look for a small wooden box."

She retrieved the handcrafted box and looked at it, impressed with the grain and detail in the dark wood. When she came back, he was sitting up against the couch.

"I made it," he said. "I love to work with wood. That's one thing you don't know about me." He reached for her hand and she sat next to him. "I know we still have a lot to learn about each other." He opened the box and took out a turquoise and coral ring that also looked handmade.

"This ring was made by an artist on my reservation. It belonged to my mother who died when I was three years old. It's one of the few things I have of hers." He looked at Quinn in a way that made her heart melt. "Quinn, I'm serious when I say I want to marry you. Not today or tomorrow, but when we're both ready. There's no question that you're the woman I want to spend the rest of my life with." He took the ring out of the box and extended it toward her. "This can signify a promise rather than an engagement. I want you to wear it. I want it to remind you every day how much I love you."

Tears fell down her cheeks. She felt a sense of comfort, security, respect and adoration that was almost overwhelming. This beautiful, amazing man was offering himself and a real life, new adventures, and even risks. She held out her left hand and he slipped the ring on her finger.

She rose to her knees, touched his face lightly and kissed him.

NO PLACE TO GO

Dianne Drake

Chapter One

She was stuck in that moment, somewhere between breathing and not breathing. That instant where a person's head would go light and the room would start to spin. Only it wasn't the room spinning. It was simply several seconds of oxygen deprivation wreaking havoc on her body. Cerebral hypoxia – her brain wasn't getting the oxygen it craved.

Ducking into Room 302, Anna finally took that breath. Finally, with blessed oxygen flushing through her system, the tingle that had spread all the way down to her toes disappeared.

"Did you bring my urinal?" the old man in the bed by the window bellowed. "I called for it ten minutes ago and, so help me God, if somebody doesn't get me a goddamn urinal pretty soon, I'm going to pee in the bed."

Trying to regain her wits, Doctor Anna Craig turned to the man, and smiled. "How about I call the nurse? Urinals aren't—"

"I know, I know!" he snapped. "Urinals aren't in your job description because you're a high-and-mighty doctor. But let me tell you something, young lady. Someday you're going to be in my place, can't get up and walk to the bathroom to have a decent pee, and some handsome young doctor's going to come into your room and refuse to help you. Then see how you feel about it." He yanked at the call button dangling over the side of his bed, pulled it up through the half expanse of bed rails, and pressed frantically at the red "nurse" button. "Then when you go in the bed and they have to come in and clean you up, I hope to hell you're embarrassed, because you deserve to be."

And this is what she'd struggled through medical school for.

"Yes, Mr Longworth?" the nurse on the other end of the call button responded.

"Urinal!" he screamed at her. "Bring me a goddamn urinal."

"Here's your urinal," Anna said, grabbing it from the bathroom and taking it over to him.

She glanced out the door to the hall, and instantly she was right back where she'd been. Couldn't breathe. Couldn't move. No, he wouldn't recognize her because they'd never met face to face, and she'd never been photographed in this face. But it didn't matter. Of all the places in the world to be accepted for her residency, it would have to be where he was working. Half a country away. One big, terrible coincidence.

"I said I'm done," Mr Longworth said. "Get this thing away from me."

Anna glanced down at the man, and let her breath out. "I'll get a nurse." Then figure out whether or not she could stay here.

"Sure you will," he complained. "And I'll be stuck with this contraption for the next hour."

Better than being stuck in hell, Anna thought to herself as she headed out the door.

Doctor Sam Cooper sat himself down on the cracked vinyl sofa and propped his feet up on the rickety coffee table someone had scrounged from a Dumpster for reuse in the doctors' lounge. Maybe he wasn't supposed to be on for three straight shifts, but that's how it had turned out. Blizzard outside, ER busting at the seams inside. Why was it that more people got sick during a blizzard? Or that critical emergencies doubled with the first foot of snow, tripled with the second? For some reason he didn't quite understand, it always seemed to work out that the more emergencies coming through his doors, the fewer staff members he had available to return to duty. He wasn't sure why. Maybe it had something to do with them having real lives outside the hospital, which was something he didn't have for himself. In fact, he owned a condo adjacent to the hospital parking lot so, technically, his whole world was about a third of the size of a Walmart. One of the old Walmarts, too, not a new superstore.

"Apartment fire," Elliott Clark said, poking his head through the door. "Sixteen casualties on the way."

"We don't have room. Have Cassie divert them to Northwestern, or Mercy. Hell, get them sent to Stoger's."

"Cassie said to tell you Mercy's diverting them to us. And no way in hell an ambulance is going to get through to Northwestern, let alone any of the Stoger's various ERs. Not with the way the wind is blowing that white shit down on us. So that means it's us, buddy. You and me, together again. Now get up off your lazy ass and get back to work."

"First thing I'm gonna do is call security and have your sorry butt hauled back down to the morgue where it belongs. Then second thing I'm gonna do is take a thirty minute nap."

"In your dreams."

"Exactly." Sam knew that for Elliott to be there, fatalities were involved. No other reason for Lakepointe's chief pathologist to be in the ER. And that was the somber note that set Sam's mind to working, trying to figure out where sixteen more patients were going to go. Halls were already lined, all rooms full to capacity and then some. The waiting room, maybe. Or even this underwhelming dump of a lounge? He glanced around, took a quick measurement, figured they could get four in there easily. Maybe even five. "You don't know how many of those sixteen are fatalities, do you?" He hated to hell that he had to ask.

Elliott shook his head. "Communications are shutting down all over the place. Dispatch can't get through, all the lines are jammed up." He grinned. "Remind you of the good old days?"

The good old days where they'd spent their residencies together in an understaffed, underfunded, undersized charity hospital? How could anybody forget days like those? "Then I guess I'll prepare for sixteen, and hope your services aren't needed."

"Me too, man. Me, too."

Elliott and Sam had been best friends from pre-med days but Elliott had always been the noticed one. A handsome man with perfect ebony skin and effortless six-pack abs that turned heads. Sam had suffered with a bit of acne in pre-med, which thankfully cleared up by the time he was in med school, and his six-pack came with lots of effort. He matched his best friend in height though – both a couple inches over six feet. And it was said he didn't look half bad in his scrubs.

But Sam had always felt that he was in Elliott's shadow. Even now, as chief of emergency services, he still felt it. Because Elliott had it all – beautiful wife, beautiful daughter, beautiful home. Oh, and the perpetual single friend as a guest during the holidays, of course. Sam always came alone, bringing a bottle of wine for the adults and some sparkling grape juice for Chauntal.

And he had . . . his work. It kept things uncomplicated, and that's how he liked them. Except right now, when he really needed thirty minutes off his feet – an hour would have been preferable – and there was no way he was going to get it. So he pushed himself back up off the sofa, plodded to the lounge door, where Elliott slapped him on the back, and the two of them plodded shoulder to shoulder to the double doors that would give them access to Lakepointe Medical's Emergency Room. "You sure you want me coming over for Christmas?" Sam asked as they entered. "You and Althea and Chauntal have never had a Christmas to yourselves. This year I was thinking about taking a double or a triple here so you could have some family time."

"She bought a goose, man." The expression on Elliott's face showed his own disgust. "You know how you're always telling her Christmas isn't Christmas without a goose. So, you've got a damn goose this year."

"Seriously? For me?" Turkey was fine, ham was fine, but he loved goose. Hadn't had it for years.

"No way in hell we're eating that nasty thing. So all I can say is, the woman bought you a goose. Better think twice about working a triple because you know what she'll do with that goose if you don't show up."

"I'm going to owe you a lot of holidays . . . someday, when I get myself settled."

"Ain't holding my breath on that one, man."

And that was precisely the problem. Neither was Sam.

Chapter Two

"ER briefing in two minutes," Boyd Lawson, chief of pediatric surgery shouted in passing. "I've got a case on deck, can't get down there myself, so Anna, you're on."

"Are there pediatric casualties?" she called after him.

He spun around to face her but didn't stop running. "Don't know. If you need back-up . . ." He shrugged, then turned back and disappeared around the corner.

It wasn't the medical duty that scared her. She was a year away from completing her residency and was looking forward to venturing out where, hopefully, the higher-ups weren't always looking over her shoulder. And she was good. Otherwise she wouldn't have landed here at Lakepointe so easily, especially after transferring midway through her residency. Normally, late slots were rare.

Most of the time you earned your way up, but she'd had a delay. More than a delay. A major life setback that knocked her out of her residency slot in San Francisco. So the position here was a godsend. Being the only pediatric surgeon in the ER didn't scare her as much, however, as being recognized by Sam Cooper.

The thing was, she trusted her looks now. Nobody would recognize her, least of all Mark's brother, she hoped. He'd said some pretty awful things back then. Grief did that, of course. But the accusations weren't justified. So after a change of hair color, new nose and a little redo of the cheekbones – thanks to his brother's temper – there was no way her former brother-in-law would see through all that. Then taking on her grandmother's name . . .

"Sixteen casualties," Sam shouted to the group of five residents and seven med students all running through the ER doors at approximately the same time. "Don't know what's coming in yet, but that's going to change in about one minute. So . . ." He pointed to two "long coats", the medical vernacular for full-fledged doctors as opposed to med students, who wore short coats. "Each of you grab a med student and make yourself useful in triage. Treat everything up to critical and pass the criticals off to . . ." He pointed to Anna, didn't bother looking at her, though, other than a fleeting glance. "And the rest of you, circulate. Make yourselves useful wherever you're needed, unless I tell you otherwise. Oh, and sixteen may be a conservative number. Usually is. So if you're not wearing comfortable shoes . . ." He shrugged. "Too bad."

Well, faith in the Cooper family was restored. Sam had the same bad attitude as Mark. Only Mark had a charm to go along with it. That's what had drawn her in to begin with, and kept her there much longer than she should have stayed. "Where am I supposed to work?" she asked Sam.

"Wherever you can find the space," he said, still not looking at her. "Hell, clear the waiting room and use that if you have to."

She'd have preferred fading into the woodwork right about now, but the wailing of approaching sirens, more of them than she could discern, told her there was not going to be any fading anywhere, any time soon. So, grabbing her stethoscope from her pocket, she headed to the incoming door, and waited along with about a dozen other hospital staff.

Then it started. The pneumatic door opened, and in gushed a blast of frigid air, an avalanche of blowing snow and two paramedics stomping their boots on the black rubber mat while wrestling their stretcher through the awaiting crowd.

"He's serious, not critical," the shorter of the two medics said, then looked around to see who amongst the waiting medical staff was going to spring forward to accept the patient.

"Mine," Anna said, spotting the patient's respiratory distress immediately.

"I said you get the criticals, Red," Sam shouted over the growing ruckus of another two stretchers coming in the door. "Step back."

"Not a chance," she said almost under her breath then gathered up her courage and shouted over the crowd, "that's Doctor Red, and . . . screw you." That last said under her breath as she motioned the paramedics into the first open ER cubicle. Sam had always been the more handsome of the two. Older than Mark by two years, he was the epitome of success and family pride while Mark had flunked his med school exam, failed to get into dental school, and couldn't even get a job as a pharmaceutical rep. Tall, broad shoulders, sandy hair, green eyes, Sam was the complete opposite of his brother, whom most would have described as swarthy.

* * *

"She's got a temper," Elliott said, catching up to Sam, who was assessing some broken ribs. "You heard what she said, didn't you? And that's after she dressed you down royally."

His patient, an inebriated young man, had had no problem with jumping out of the second story window, except he hadn't anticipated the landing, or the brick wall underneath the snow. And, while the firefighters would have simply led him down the back stairs since the fire was on the other side of the building, he'd decided to take the leap. And now, here he was, lucky his broken ribs hadn't punctured his lung. "Didn't hear a word. Why?"

"Too bad. Because you deserved it."

"Deserved what?" he asked, as he scribbled orders on the patient's chart then handed it to the nurse.

"What she said." Elliott grinned. "But since I don't tell tales out of school . . ."

"Like hell you don't," Sam said, waving over the next stretcher. Pregnant woman. Very pregnant. Very miserable looking, too.

Elliott parted the cubicle curtains and headed out. "It seems my services aren't going to be required down here so, for now, I bid you adieu, and . . ." An even bigger grin crossed his face. "'Screw you'!"

Sam glanced over. "Seriously? That's what she said?"

"But with venom, man. So much venom. It's like she knows you."

"Contractions, every couple of minutes," the woman panted as she was settled onto the exam bed by the paramedics and a nurse. "I can feel it."

"Who's your obstetrician?" Sam asked, heading to the end of the bed to get himself into position to have a look.

"I'm just visiting here for Christmas. Don't have one. Oh, oh . . ."

"Don't push," he warned her as she started to bear down. "I need to . . ."

"Got to push. Can't stop it . . . oh . . ."

Now, she was panting. Pushing, panting, and trying to pop that baby out. Something that became apparently clear when he got himself into position to take a look, and saw . . . "Obstetrics kit, stat. And get someone down here from obstetrics, and peds. We need a pediatrician." He glanced up over the woman's belly, saw that she was squinting, getting ready to bear down again. "How far along are you?" he asked, as he snapped on a pair of gloves, in prep to deliver the baby.

"Too far," she grunted. "Too damn far!"

Anna stepped out of the way of two paramedics pushing a gurney down the hall. "We need a doctor here!" one of them shouted. "Now! We need a doctor, stat!" That from a rotund little paramedic who was so short of breath he was wheezing. "Inhalation casualty."

"I can see that," she said, taking a look at the firefighter stretched out on the cart. Immediately, her fingers went to his pulse.

"Ninety-eight, blood pressure one-sixty over ninety, temp normal. Bilateral wheezing," the more physically fit of the paramedics said.

Anna looked into the firefighter's eyes. "Do you know where you are?"

"In heaven, and you're my angel," he choked out through his mask.

She laughed. "How much smoke did you take in?"

He shrugged. "More than I should have. Not enough to kill me."

"Any respiratory problems other than the obvious?" she asked him, as she placed a stethoscope to his chest.

"Nope. Healthy as a . . ." Gasping, he went into a paroxysm of coughing, shoving Anna's stethoscope away so the sound wouldn't be amplified in her ears. "Horse," he finally managed, once the coughing subsided.

"Not right now, you're not," she said. "Look, I want to get some chest X-rays, have some lab work done, get you started on an IPPB treatment in case you inhaled any soot or other particulates into your lungs . . . a pneumonia preventative."

"Then I can't get back out there? I'm their chief, I need—"

She smiled and laid a sympathetic hand on his arm. "I'm sorry, but not tonight. You wouldn't do them, or yourself, any good. So I'm afraid the only place you're going right now is up to the ward, to a bed, where you're going to get some good treatment, lots of rest, and maybe by morning . . ." She glanced over just in time to see the rotund paramedic collapse on the floor. Instantly, his partner dropped to his knees to assist, but Anna shoved him aside. "Call a code," she whispered, as she felt for a pulse in the man's neck. Found none.

"Hang in there, Gary," his partner – a man named Doug – said, as he stood and ran to the ER desk. Seconds later, the code was called, and the hall was swarming with medical personnel, all ready to jump in to save Gary's life. And Anna, who'd already started chest compressions, was surrounded.

"Let's get a monitor on him," she shouted, but it was already in the works. So was the intubation – the breathing tube that would be stuck down his throat. IVs were going in as well, as Anna continued pumping the man's chest. Then, when everything was in place, that hall in the ER went still for a moment as the whole team pulled back to look at the tracing blipping its way across the heart monitor. "V-fib," she said. The heart was quivering, not beating. "I want blood gases, stat. And let's get him hooked up with some epinephrine." A drug used to stabilize the heart. "Also I want chest X-ray. Oh, and about Chief Malloy, my smoke inhalation patient, please get him a chest X-ray, too . . . somebody!"

Another check of Gary's heart rate showed he was still in V-fib, so Anna called for the defibrillator, and delivered an electrical shock to his heart. This time the heart rate came back, and after several more minutes of scurrying to get preliminary tests done, then stabilizing him for transport to the Cardiac Care Unit, Anna finally leaned back against the wall to take a breather.

"And the evening is only just beginning," Sam commented, handing her a cup of hot chocolate. "Didn't know what you liked in your coffee, didn't know if you liked tea, but on a cold blustery night like this, everybody likes hot chocolate."

In truth, she hated coffee, only liked her tea iced, and loved hot chocolate. But did he know that, or was he only guessing? Actually, she wasn't sure Mark had even known that about her, and even if he did, it wasn't the kind of thing he'd tell his brother. Still, it gave her an eerie feeling and, as she lifted the steaming paper cup to her lips, her hands started to tremble.

Did he recognize her, or think he did? This was too close. She had to leave. Not just the proximity, but the area. Chicago. Even the state.

Except getting another residency wasn't that easy. So, what were her alternatives? "Thank you," she said, keeping her head turned away from him.

"Look, Anna." He emphasized her name. "I just got a call that there's at least another four over the original sixteen on the way in. No place to go."

No place to go was certainly a feeling with which she could identify. "Do you really think we can manage?"

"We'll be fine. All we have to do is . . ." The rest of his sentence went unspoken as the trauma inflow began for real. Four patients in at one time, followed by another two, then by another three. These were the nights Sam dreaded the most, and loved the most – the reason he'd gone into emergency medicine. That and because of Mark, who'd died in an ER hall before a doctor or nurse even had a chance to see him.

Chapter Three

"You're holding up well," Sam remarked in passing. Anna was holding up better than pretty much anybody on shift, and it surprised him because the past six hours had been grueling. Not to mention that now that the worst of the storm was over, they were completely snowed in, couldn't leave even if they'd wanted to.

"Surgeons are like that, you know. We have endurance."

"Have I ever done anything to you?" he asked. "Offended you, dated you and didn't call you for a second date when I said I would? Disappointed you in bed? Because we've been doing some pretty good work together for the past several hours, but the air around you is colder than the air outside. So, did I say something, do something?" Normally by now, in the face of a crisis, people were hanging all over each other, friendly, glad to get through it together. The rest of his makeshift department certainly was, but she kept to herself. Didn't talk, didn't mingle. Didn't look comfortable in her own skin. And he couldn't figure it out.

"I like to keep it professional."

Again, another cool response. "Professional is one thing, but you're downright icy. Or should I call it hostile?"

"Not hostile, Doctor. But I don't like to get involved the way the rest of you around here seem to. I do my work, and I leave people alone, and I expect them to do the same with me."

"So if I asked you down to the cafeteria for something to eat, you'd refuse me?"

"Yes, I would."

"Because?"

"Because, like I said, I don't get involved."

"But have you eaten?"

"Not recently."

"Then taking a break to grab a sandwich seems a practical matter, not a social one."

"Why me?" she asked. "There are dozens of people down here working, so why pick on me?"

"Most people would consider taking a break a good thing. I certainly do, when I have the chance."

"Then, by all means, take a break. You're well covered here, and I'm sure your ER can get along without you for the time it takes to eat a sandwich, so . . ." She started to spin away from him. "Bon appétit, Doctor Cooper."

"You're losing it, man," Elliott said, coming up behind Sam, as Sam watched Anna practically run to get away from him. "I remember a time when the pretty ones would fall all over you. Now, look at what you're doing to them. You've got that one scared to death."

"But why?" Sam asked, totally perplexed.

Elliott chuckled. "Maybe she got to know you? Or heard rumors? You did used to have your way, you know."

That was true, especially when he'd returned from Afghanistan. Something about a doctor in uniform. Except, he'd gotten over that nonsense early on, gotten serious about his work, his new life, all the adjustments. Losing a brother the way he had tended to make a person take everything more seriously. "Well, it was just a sandwich," he muttered.

"And a blow to the old ego," Elliott quipped.

"That's what friends are for, aren't they? Rubbing salt into the wound."

"So she wounded you. Now, that's interesting. Pretty damned interesting."

Once out of his sight, Anna hid herself in a supply closet and let her nerves have their way. Her knees were shaking, her hands . . . even her lips. It was crazy, but Sam Cooper was a hero. He'd saved lives in battle, risking his own life, and he didn't deserve to know the truth about Mark. Nobody did.

But in that phone call after Mark's death, Sam had blamed her. Told her she was responsible. But that wasn't true and she didn't deserve his wrath, which was what awaited her. The thing was, right now, right this very moment, she didn't have many choices. Because if she walked away, or more likely ran, it would end her medical career. One start-over and second chance per person was all most people got, and she'd used hers up. Besides, she'd fought too hard to come back simply to walk away from everything she'd earned. No wishing upon a star, no magic genies to grant wishes. This was her future, the one she'd almost died to make happen, and somehow, some way, she had to make it work.

"He doesn't recognize me," she whispered, as she gathered her wits and laid her hand on the doorknob, ready to re-emerge into the frantic pace of the ER. "Or he'd have already said something." Or, more likely, thrown her out into the blizzard. "So that's a good thing."

But how good? She didn't know. She just didn't know, and that's what worried her the most, because she'd spent most of her marriage to Sam's brother not knowing either, and look what happened with that.

Chapter Four

"You did a good job for someone who doesn't normally work emergency," Sam commented, strolling into the on-call room like he owned the place. It was a tiny room with two beds, one of several like it in the hospital.

"You're not thinking of sleeping in here, are you? I thought one of the female residents . . ." Anna stopped, watched the way he shook his head, like he was enjoying her dilemma.

"We've got a lot of extra staff onboard right now, and sleeping spots are at a premium. No extra patient beds, no gurneys, not even a couch in a waiting room. So for the next couple of hours, you're stuck with me."

It wasn't like she'd never slept in the same on-call with other virtual strangers, male and female. When it was time to sleep, those distinctions weren't made because sleeping hours were golden when you were on call. But he was . . . her brother-in-law. And this wasn't right. Except, he didn't know that. So Anna merely nodded then turned away when he stripped off his scrub shirt, even though he was wearing a provocative, fitted white T-shirt underneath.

"I sleep in my boxers, if you don't mind," he said, not even waiting before he untied the waist drawstring, then hooked his thumbs into his scrub pants and started to tug them down.

"If I did?"

"Then you wouldn't be staring at my reflection in the window," he said, sliding down onto the bed nearest the door.

"I wasn't staring."

"Sure you were, but that's okay. I've been stared at before in less glamorous clothing."

"You think this is glamorous, parading around in front of me in your boxers?"

"I think it's necessary, if I want two hours of uninterrupted sleep. For that, I have to be comfortable." He stretched out on the bed, pulled the sheet up over him. "Oh, and so you'll know – at home, I sleep in the nude."

An image she didn't want in her mind, but which was firmly planted there now.

"And I meant what I said. You did a good job. Sorry it was so hectic, but that's something I can't control. So, do you sleep in the nude, as well?"

He was so impudent he was actually funny. "I sleep in a flannel granny gown. It starts at my throat and stops at my toes." In truth, she slept in panties and a T-shirt, but there was no way she was telling him that.

"Pity, because I wanted to picture you in the nude when I went to sleep, like you're going to picture me. But now all I see is . . . a granny."

"Good," she said, climbing into her bed, wearing a full, clean set of scrubs. "That way you'll be better rested when you wake up."

"Or worse for wear, if underneath all that granny garb I find you."

"Go to sleep, Sam," she said, turning on her side, her back to him.

"You don't snore, do you?" he asked.

"Go to sleep!"

He liked her. Wasn't sure why. Aside from some very impressive medical skills, she was actually nice to be around once you broke through her hard outer shell. Sure, he could have slept elsewhere. In his own office on the couch, actually. But there was something about Anna Craig that made him want to know more, and sleeping with her, even from the other side of the room, was facilitating that – a little. She did have a sense of humor. Very quick on the comeback, too. Both qualities he liked in a woman. Qualities that would definitely be at the top of his list when he decided he wanted permanence in his life. Which wasn't now.

Hell, he didn't want anything right now other than what he had, because he was burned out. Rode hard, put away wet. Whatever you wanted to call it. Between the last couple of grueling years of his residency and the first couple years on staff, and with all his family problems . . . Work had turned into his respite. Sure, there'd been an occasional night off, if that's what you wanted to call it. A few women in and out his door. Nurses, residents, and couple of hot med students.

But for him, once was usually enough, because if you went back for seconds you ended up like his brother – in a bad marriage with a demanding shrew who chewed you up and spat you out for sport. He'd heard the stories from Mark, how he couldn't please the bitch, that no matter how hard he tried, it was never enough. She wanted more, wanted bigger and better, wanted Mark to bend over backwards when she snapped her fingers. It had driven his brother to the brink, and there was nothing Sam could do at the time because he'd been in Afghanistan. And words weren't enough, not when your brother was dying in a dozen different ways.

So, no permanence for him. He couldn't stomach it. But he couldn't stomach those one-night stands, either. So it was better to do nothing, except work.

Still, listening to her quiet, even breathing across the room filled him with such a longing – one he hadn't expected, one he didn't think he had in him.

It would pass though, he thought to himself, as he rolled to face the wall, and put the pillow up over his ear to blot out the sound of her. But blotting out the sound of her breathing didn't in any way blot out his thoughts of her. And Sam found himself literally ticking off the minutes in his head. Every last one amounting to lost sleep. Two hours, minus twenty minutes, minus twenty-one minutes, minus twenty-two minutes . . .

Damn, he needed to sleep.

But damn, he'd sure tripped himself up this time. Because with Anna in the same on-call, sleep wasn't going to happen.

Giving in, Sam sat up, tugged on his scrub pants, gathered up his shirt, socks and shoes, and practically kicked the door open to get out of there. So, he was going to sleep in his office after all, and he'd lost thirty minutes of sleep to boot. In his world, sleep was a terrible thing to waste, but he had an idea that sleep was going to be hard to come by right now with Anna on his mind.

"Damn," he muttered, plodding down the hall. "Damn it to hell!"

Chapter Five

Day two in solitary confinement. At least, that's what it felt like, not being able to leave the hospital. She was a California girl by birth, loved the warm weather and beaches. Snow was for ski vacations, not for real. But this mess was for real, and she was going nowhere for a while. It wasn't that she minded the work, because that was the best. Being a doctor was all she'd ever wanted.

But not a doctor working side by side with a brother-in-law she was hoping to deceive.

And not one whose naked image had kept her tossing and turning for a good half of her time off last night. Four hours to sleep, two with Sam Cooper frolicking in her fantasies. She'd heard him leave, was glad to hear the door click behind him. But his images hadn't gone with him. In fact, after he'd gone, they'd intensified. Smacked her around, but in different ways than his brother had.

"I want you to stay in Emergency for the duration," Doctor Lawson, her department chief said. "They're still short-staffed, and since all but critical or emergency surgeries are cancelled until after the blizzard, we're sufficiently staffed here for whatever we have to do. But Emergency is still being bombarded, and because Doctor Cooper is impressed with your abilities, I've assigned you there until further notice."

Anna swallowed hard. If she protested, it would raise suspicion. Or cause animosity. Which she didn't need, since she'd been accepted into her position only by the skin of her teeth. So for now, she really didn't have a say in anything she did. But that was okay, because she was grateful for the opportunity to work as a doctor again. "Call me if you need me," she said, taking one last look at the snow from the third-floor pediatric ward window before she trudged her way to the elevator, then punched the down button.

Naturally, he was in the elevator. "Sleep well?" she asked, purposely not mentioning that she knew he'd left the on-call after only a few minutes.

"Like a baby," he said, folding his arms across his chest.

"So, are you out making the rounds, locating your minions for the day?" The elevator doors closed.

"From the tone of your voice, I take it you've already been told I requested you to be my minion."

"Yeah, well, it's not my choice. But you know that already, don't you?"

He laughed. "Did my images haunt your dreams last night, because you're sure grumpy this—" His words cut off when the elevator lurched, then came to an abrupt stop. At the same time, the light shut off. "Damn," he muttered, immediately pulling a penlight from his lab coat pocket and flashing it at the control panel, looking for the emergency phone.

"If you thought I was grumpy before this . . ." she said, drawing in a deep breath to steady her nerves. The only thing worse than being in an elevator, was being in one that was stuck between floors. Claustrophobia time. And being claustrophobic in the dark. Anna squeezed her eyes shut, hoping that when she opened them again the lights would be back on and the elevator would lurch back into motion.

It lurched all right but stopped again. And this time, Sam picked up the emergency phone, while Anna prayed to God someone on the other end would answer and come running. After all, this was Sam Cooper, and he had an emergency department to run.

"How long?" Sam asked.

Anna cosied up to him to see if she could hear the other end of the conversation, but Sam was too tall and the phone receiver was out of earshot. She did, however, like the feel of being pressed into his side. While it didn't stop the claustrophobia, it made her feel safe.

"Seriously? That long? Can't you hurry it up because I'm needed in Emergency."

"How long?" she whispered, not liking the sound of his end of the conversation.

"Too long," he said, more for the benefit of the operator than her. "I can't be trapped in here when I've got patients to see. So, what about getting us out through the emergency trap door?"

Anna looked up, but couldn't see it in the dark.

"OK, so the fire department?" he asked the operator. "Maybe if you told them that your chief of emergency services was trapped. Do you think that might get them here?"

She felt his body go from rigid to limp, and that was all the answer she needed. They were going to be staying here for a while. In the dark. The two of them together. Walls closing in.

"So?" she managed to whisper once he'd hung up.

"Hospital's totally without power, and the backup isn't kicking in. The surgery, emergency, nursery and intensive care units are on their own backup, and those are working, but the rest of the hospital is shit out of luck for God only knows how long."

"God didn't happen to tell you how long that would be, did He?"

"No, but the operator's betting on two hours, since they want necessary services up and running first."

"And you're not necessary?" she asked.

"Apparently not as much as I thought."

"So, in the mean time . . ."

"Make yourself comfortable on the floor."

Like she could. In fact, if anything, this was her worst-case scenario. Trapped in an elevator with a sexy, charming man she found so tempting she could almost forget all the reasons she couldn't, shouldn't, wouldn't get involved. Apart from the obvious that he hated her, he was Mark's brother, and it didn't take a genius to realize that the DNA that made Mark so utterly sexy and so utterly evil was the same DNA that made her want to cuddle up with Sam in the dark.

And no, she didn't like the bad-boy types. Hadn't known Mark was bad to the bone in the worst way until their six-month anniversary, when he'd failed his med school entry exam. Then all hell had broken loose. Smashed apartment, smashed face . . . He'd cried afterwards, told her he'd never do it again. Begged her forgiveness. Begged her not to leave him.

She hadn't. And true to his word, Mark hadn't hit her again for nearly three months, when he failed to get in to dental school. Next time was when she'd burned dinner. Then there was the time she hadn't filled up the car's gas tank. After that, she and her lab partner had worked late in the cadaver lab and she'd forgotten to tell Mark not to expect her home. The list went on, and every single time he cried, begged.

"You don't like the dark, do you?"

"Spent a lot of time in the dark when I was a child. Now I have more of a fondness for the light."

"Your parents didn't give you a nightlight?" he asked.

"They would have, if we'd had electricity. But we . . . we had an alternative lifestyle. Lived on beaches, in tents, when the weather was nice. Stayed in communes, too, and the ones my parents always seemed to find didn't have electricity, or it was in short supply. So, no lights, except candles, or kerosene lanterns."

"Good thing you got away."

"Not got away. I loved my lifestyle, and my parents were the best. They taught me well, loved me the way most children never get loved. It was an amazing childhood, and there were always so many adventures, so much to do." She sighed contentedly, as the fond memories embraced her. "Every child should have what I had. And sure, you might think of our lifestyle as odd. By most standards it probably was. But we were so . . . happy."

"And your parents? Where are they?"

"Gone now. My mom from cancer. And I think my dad grieved himself to death after she died. They were in love like I've never seen anybody in love before, and he just couldn't make it without her."

"I'm sorry," he said, his voice practically a whisper. "They sound amazing."

"They were. I was blessed." But along with that happiness came the naivety that plopped her into the middle of a destructive marriage because she'd really, truly never known people could be so cruel. And she'd married one of the cruelest. Now, here she was, sitting in a dark elevator, on the floor, with his brother's arm around her shoulder. Not minding it so much, either.

So, was Sam different from Mark? Because she thought he was. Or was that her naivety coming back to haunt her?

Chapter Six

"Why did you want to become a doctor?" he asked her. She still hadn't moved away from him, and he liked the feel of her pressed into his side. But to keep his sanity, he wondered if he shouldn't keep his distance, because the thoughts running through his head were pretty much the same ones that had sent him running out of the on-call room, like a sissy, last night. She was tempting and he was so damn tempted. Then, as now. And smelling the lemony scent of her shampoo wasn't helping matters any. Neither was feeling the softness of her skin. Or the roundness of the curves hugging his side.

And it would be oh so easy to brush up against the wrong curve. *Excuse me, I didn't mean to* . . . Hell, she'd never believe that, because a single accidental brush would never be enough for him. He had an idea it would become addictive.

"My parents taught me charity and love, and they were all about giving back in the world. Being a doctor seemed like the best way to do that. And to honor them. So, why did you?"

"My dad was an army doctor, my mom a nurse. My brother almost went to medical school . . . He got sidetracked." He felt her stiffen. Wasn't sure why. "But I made the choice when I was young, and never considered anything else."

"Always emergency medicine?"

"I'll admit I'm an adrenaline junkie. I like the rush you get from the fast pace."

Her voice sounded a bit strange now, and he wondered if the walls were closing in on her the way they were on him – and he wasn't even claustrophobic. Just hot. In more ways than one. And trying to fight back thoughts that would cause a boner, which would surely spring to life the moment right before the elevator's power surged back on. Like he really needed that kind of a reveal. So, he was the one who pushed himself away from her. "Getting warm in here," he muttered, focusing on remembering the names of all the bones in the body, starting with the toes. "Phalange, metatarsal, cuneiform, navicular, cuboid, talus, calcaneus," he muttered aloud.

"What?" she asked, pulling at her scrub top, which was clinging tightly to her.

"Just going over some basic anatomy. Keeps my mind off the fact that it's hotter than hell in the elevator." That much was true. "Electric's off in the whole damn building and people outside these doors are probably freezing to death, but this elevator must be hooked directly into a blast furnace somewhere because I think we're going to smother to death before they get this motherf— Excuse my language. This thing moving." He knew this was more about his emotions than the actual level of heat, but he couldn't control the way he was feeling.

"We're running out of oxygen," Anna gasped.

"There's plenty to breathe, don't worry."

"No, you don't understand. We're running out of oxygen. My logical mind knows that's not the case, but the rest of me can feel it happening. We're going to run out of oxygen before they get to us."

"We've been in here twenty minutes, Anna. We're fine, I promise you."

Suddenly, she bolted off the floor. Started pacing like a caged tiger. "I can't breathe," she choked. "Gotta get out of here. How, Sam?" she begged. "How are we going to get out of here?"

He couldn't see what she was doing, but he could hear her pacing, hear her heavy breathing. He imagined the look of panic on her face. "We wait until they come get us," he said, pulling out his penlight in the hope that a little light in the total darkness would make her feel better. "Look, Anna. You're obviously claustrophobic, but pacing isn't going to do you any good. So, come sit down. Try to relax."

"Can't relax," she said, plastering herself against the cool steel of the door. "I've just got to get out of here . . . now!"

He stood, and then moved next to her. Shone the light so he could see her face. "Listen to me. You're going to be fine. You're just having a panic attack, and once you realize that this car is well ventilated, you'll calm down."

"No," she gasped, shoving his hand away. "I'm too hot, can't breathe, can't . . . Sam," she practically begged. "Please, I can't do this. Please."

She lunged away from the door, straight into his arms, where he held her like he'd held no other woman in his life. Wanting to protect her. Wanting to kiss away her fears and never let go. More than anything though not wanting to take advantage of a situation that he probably already would have with any other woman. But Anna was different from any other woman. She was . . . good. Vulnerable and good. "Listen, sweetheart, you've got to calm down. As much as I would like to fantasize a moment like this – and trust me, you occupied most of my two hours of trying to sleep last night – there's nothing I can do except what I'm doing right now." And he did so enjoy the feel of her in his arms. But he knew he shouldn't. Not like this, anyway.

"I'm sorry, Sam. It's just that . . . I am claustrophobic. Severely."

"Because you're a free spirit who spent her formative years in nature?"

"No, because I was married to a bastard who locked me in a closet. A small closet where I could barely move, barely breathe. In the dark."

"What the hell?" he gasped.

Damn, she hadn't meant to say that. He loved his brother, adored him. So, as bad as Mark had been to her, there was no reason for Sam to find out. "Nothing. I didn't mean to . . ."

Rather than pressing her for more information, Sam simply held her even tighter to his chest. Didn't say a word. Just sat down on the floor with her and held her close, until almost an hour later, when the lights came on and the car lowered itself to the first floor.

That's where they parted. "Thanks," she said, sounding somewhat embarrassed. "Sam, I'm sorry for being such a baby."

"I think you have good cause," he replied. "And if that bastard ever shows up here, let me know so I can show him what it feels like to be locked in a closet. I mean it, Anna. Let me know."

She smiled, nodded, and practically ran away. They spent the next six hours working side by side, saying nothing to each other that wasn't hospital-related. At the end of that shift, though, what she'd told him was still on his mind. So was the fact that he wanted to protect her. That scared him because it was the first step toward permanence. Which, with Anna Craig, didn't seem so bad.

Chapter Seven

"We've got another influx," Sam warned his staff. It was going on to 10 p.m. of the second day, and people had wandered into the hospital in droves. Some were trying to find a place to stay warm or just be with people, others had weather-related conditions such as frostbite or broken bones from falling on the ice. Emergency had also received five heart attacks – people shoveling snow who shouldn't have been. "Roof collapsed at nursing home. Seven injuries." He glanced at Elliott, who'd wandered back down to the ER only moments before wearing a grim expression. "Hopefully no fatalities, but it's too soon to tell."

That added a somber note to an already somber mood, since there was, quite literally, no place to put any more patients.

"Heard you two had an elevator adventure," Elliott said, as the emergency staff went in different directions, their first assignment being to make room, come hell or high water.

"Not an adventure. More like a panic attack and a horny guy who blew a perfect opportunity."

"Sounds like true love to me."

"Sounds like you don't know what the hell you're talking about," Sam snapped.

Elliott took two steps backwards, threw his hands into the air in mock surrender. "Just sayin'. That's all."

"Sorry. It's just that . . ." He shook his head. "Doesn't matter. Blizzards have a way of bringing people together, but once we get through the next twenty-four hours, she'll be back where she belongs and we'll be strangers again."

"Is that what you want? To be strangers?"

Truth was, he didn't know. "Makes it easier that way."

"You know Althea would love to set an extra place for her at Christmas dinner. All you have to do is tell me to tell her to get out the plate, and I can almost guarantee a red carpet to go with it."

"You took the best one before I had a chance with her myself."

"I'm betting Doctor Craig would be another best one, if you weren't so damned stubborn."

"Maybe, but . . ." He shrugged.

"I know what happened to Mark affected you, but don't let it take over your life, or you'll miss all the good stuff. And you deserve the good stuff. Just like I've got."

"What I deserve is a kick in the ass for letting this distract me when we have more injuries rolling in."

"Well, I'll be glad to give you that kick, but it's going to be about the pretty doctor you're going to let get away if you're not careful." Elliott gave Sam a good jab in the arm, then headed down to the ambulance bay. Sam went the opposite direction, to roust everybody out of the overflow waiting room, the very last bastion of sanctuary his ER had to offer.

"Two hypothermias, three shocks, six with contusions and assorted minor injuries, three broken hips, a couple of concussions, one with unspecified internal bleeding. No fatalities." She drew in a deep breath, and then went on to the allocation list. "Two in surgery, two awaiting surgery, two on warming blankets with IVs, six being made comfortable in the waiting room, two on gurneys in the hall, under observation. And dietary called to say they're running out of food. Oh, and the blood bank is short on blood supplies, and they're soliciting in-house donations from anybody who wants to give." Anna offered Sam a weary smile. "Also, we're low on bandages and tongue depressors. Central supply is almost out of stock, and they're going to start rationing if a supply truck doesn't get through in the next eight hours."

"Impressive, Doctor. I think you missed your calling. ER's definitely your style."

"No way. You run a crazy house. I like the peace and quiet of the OR much better. Give me a little bit of soothing Mozart in the background, and everybody at his or her assigned station, instead of all the frantic running around you have going on down here. That's all I need to make me a happy woman."

"Anna," he said, turning serious. "What you said earlier, about your husband . . ."

She shook her head. "I don't want to talk about it. Didn't mean to say . . ."

"No, I'm not going to pry. But I do want to ask one thing. Are you still married to him?"

"No," she said. "I'm not. I got smart and divorced him."

"Good for you. And may the bastard rot in hell."

"I expect he is," she said, and turned quickly so Sam wouldn't see the tears brimming her eyes.

"Did you love him?" he asked before she could get away.

"It's complicated," she said. "Live and learn, right? Or maybe live and don't learn and get used to the consequences."

"Live and learn," he repeated, and then mulled the words for a moment before he spun away and exited the hall faster than Anna did.

Swiping at her eyes, she turned around to watch him leave, and realized what she'd done. She'd fallen in love with a man she could never have. A man with whom she could never be honest, unless she wanted to face his hatred.

"Live and learn," she whispered, and then headed off to the kitchen to figure out how she was going to get all the patients piled up in ER fed.

"How could I have been so stupid!" Sam shouted, pounding his desk.

"You're sure?"

"It's her eyes. Everything else is different, but her eyes. I told you I thought I knew her. Turns out I was right."

"Or wrong." Elliott was sprawled on the couch across from Sam's desk, his long legs, hanging off the end of it. "You wouldn't have fallen in love with the – and I'm just repeating what I've heard you call her – 'ball-breaking bitch' you believe is responsible for Mark's death."

"I know she's responsible. I know she's responsible!"

"So equate the ball-breaking bitch to Anna. How do they stack up side by side?"

"They don't, and that's just it. The woman Mark described to me was . . . horrible. Mean. Bad-tempered. Selfish. And Anna . . . She's none of those."

"One of these women is not like the other." Elliott sang the song from *Sesame Street*. "Which can mean only one of three things. Anna's not Mark's wife Marcie. Or she's completely changed. Or Mark . . . lied." He swallowed hard. "He was a little over the top at times. You'll have to admit that yourself."

"Because she drove him to it," Sam said, although his heart wasn't in the argument. That was evident in his voice. Because he truly didn't want to believe Anna could be all those despicable things.

"Was that before or after he locked her in the closet? Because you believed her when she told you that, didn't you? At least, that's what you told me."

It was Sam's turn to swallow hard. "It didn't sound like she was lying."

"So this is the part where you've got to trust your gut. Do you believe Anna, or Marcie, or whatever the hell her name is? Or do believe your brother? And think back on your history with him, man. I know you got along in your later years, but the guy pulled the wings off of flies, and fried ants with his magnifying glass. And how many times did he blame you for the bad things he did? Like the day he broke the windshield out of your dad's truck, blamed you and stood there while you took the punishment. Without flinching, man. You told me so yourself. Your brother didn't even bat an eye for that whole two months when you worked your butt off with extra chores to pay for what he'd done."

"But he grew up."

"And you're still defending him the way you always did. But that's going to cost you, man. This time it's going to cost you bigger than you can know if you're not careful."

"You're on her side, aren't you?"

"I'm on your side." Elliott spun around and stood up. "I feel the need for a nice, long conversation with my wife coming on. Think I'm going to go find me a quiet spot with good reception." He grinned at Sam. "And what I said a minute ago about going with your gut? I was wrong. And this is the only time in your whole worthless life you're ever going to hear me admit that. Don't go with your gut. Go with your heart." He crossed the room to his best friend, gave him a man-hug, and exited with the swagger of a very happy man. Because he was. Thanks to the love of a good woman.

Chapter Eight

She could feel him watching her. The goosebumps on her arms were rioting. But she wouldn't turn around and absolutely refused to give in to the feeling coming over her. "It's just a slight sprain," she explained to the wild-haired kid who clearly didn't want to be there. "X-rays were negative for a fracture, which makes you very lucky, considering the way you were trying to ride the blizzard. And while we could get an MRI, that's costly, and we won't be able to schedule it for several days due to the numbers of injuries that have come in. So I'm inclined to give you something mild for the pain, tell you to stay off your foot as much as possible, use crutches if you're comfortable with them, then wait until the end of the week and see if you're getting any improvement. If you're not, then we'll move on to the next round of tests."

By "riding the blizzard", as the kid called it, he'd been snowboarding down the street behind the snow plow, jumping over the cars parked along the side that were snowed under, first by the blizzard itself, then by the snow thrown off the plow blade. He claimed that made awesome mogul hills, and while maybe that was true, what wasn't so true was his ability to navigate. He'd cleared his very first car, but didn't see the one directly in front of it. By the time he'd made his mid-air correction, he'd come down, *thunk*, on what turned out to be a row of streetside newspaper stands. Got his ankle caught. He was lucky he didn't snap it in two.

"So I can't, like, get on the board again today?" he asked.

"No, you can't, like, get on the board again today. Or for another couple of weeks."

"But I'll be missing the best snow of my life."

"And avoiding another injury, possibly surgery." She really wanted to tell him that snowboarding in the aftermath of a blizzard wasn't the wisest choice but who was she to lecture him on wisdom? Just look at her life choices. "Look, I'm going to wrap it, and if you're good, which means if you stay off your foot for the next few days, maybe we can get you back out on the tail end of this snow. But, no promises."

"Tail end ain't no good, dude. Not when it's mushy."

"'Dude" is male, and I'm female, so that would be dude-ette. And hey, what can I say? You took the risk and it came back to bite you on the butt. Big time!"

"What kind of doctor are you, anyway?" the boy asked sullenly.

"Pediatrician."

"I'm not a kid!" he snapped.

"You're lucky that you don't have something worse than a sprain." She closed the chart. "Your choice, dude. Live and learn, or live and don't learn and get used to the consequences. Because one way will make you smarter about your snowboarding choices and the other way will wipe you out again and again, and that's a promise."

With that, Anna exited, almost straight into Sam's arms. "What?" she asked, seeing the brooding expression. "More casualties coming in?"

"Just one. And I'm not sure if it's a casualty or not."

Now she was curious. "I'm not sure I understand."

"Me neither," he said, pulling her off to the side of the hall. "I've got to make rounds, to see how my doctors are doing. Could you meet me in my office in thirty minutes?"

"If I'm not busy."

"Meet me, Anna," he said.

Something about the seriousness in his voice gave her a chill. "Why?" she whispered.

All he said was, "Meet me." Then he walked away.

Had she done something wrong? Misdiagnosed someone? Had someone died as a result of her error? That's all she could think of, unless . . .

"Why didn't you tell me?" he asked. Sam pointed for her to sit on the couch across from his desk.

"I think I'd rather stand for this," she said, feeling her heart sink. "It's too casual to sit while someone's giving you bad news."

"Whatever." He perched on the edge of his desk with his arms folded across his chest. Anna took up her own rigid pose against his closed door, her hands in the pockets of her lab coat so he couldn't see her balled fists and white knuckles.

"So?" she asked.

"So why didn't you tell me?"

"Tell you what?"

"That you're my sister-in-law." He looked her straight in the eye. "That you were married to Mark."

"My first response might have been to say it's none of your business why I didn't tell you. But I guess that's not good enough now that we've actually gotten to know each other." Now that she'd fallen in love with him.

"Are you at this hospital because of me?"

She shook her head. "That's a coincidence. I promise you, after your phone call that day, I wouldn't have come had I known you were here." She appraised his chilly look. "You don't believe me, do you? You think I'm here because I derive some perverse pleasure in watching you suffer over your brother's death. Or maybe I'm here to shake you down for some kind of settlement because, God knows, your family is wealthy enough and I walked away with nothing. That's it, isn't it?"

"I don't know what it is, Anna. Or should I call you Marcie?"

"Legally, I'm Anna now, and I'm not going back to Marcie. That's my past." A past she didn't want to relive. "It's my grandmother's name, by the way. Anna Elizabeth Craig."

"Anna Elizabeth Craig who didn't have the decency to tell me she used to be Marcie Cooper."

"Marcie Rhodes. I never took the Cooper name."

"Because it wasn't good enough for you? That's what Mark told me, when I asked him. He said, 'She wants my money, not my name.'"

"That's not true. My parents wanted me to keep the family name. It was a tradition. My mother kept her maiden name, so did my grandmother. Mark knew that and he was fine with it when we married." But apparently he'd lied to his family about it. And about her motives for marrying him. Now she wondered how many other lies he'd told. "But I'm sure you're not going to believe that, or anything else I tell you."

Sam flinched but didn't move away from the desk. "What you said about your husband locking you in the closet . . . Were you married to someone else before Mark? Someone who did that to you? Or were you setting me up? A sympathetic story you expected me to believe."

Now was the moment of reckoning. She'd have given anything not to hurt Sam, but this was going to hurt him deeply. But she couldn't lie to him because she loved him. More than that, she respected him, and out of the respect she would not lie. Oh, she wanted to though. She owed him that. All she could do was be honest, and then walk away knowing she'd done the right thing. "It never occurred to me to have a sympathetic story just in case I needed one. And Mark was my one and only husband."

"And he locked you in the closet?"

Now she saw the beginning of realization, and pain, in his eyes. "Yes, he did."

"Why, Anna? Make me understand why."

Did he believe her? That was almost too much to hope for. "I was late getting home from the hospital one night, and I'd forgotten to call him. It was the second time in a couple of weeks I was late. He accused me of cheating on him. Said he wasn't going to give me that opportunity again."

"Did you cheat on him?"

She shook her head. "No, never." Although Mark had cheated on her, but Sam didn't have to know about all that ugliness. She couldn't do that to him.

"How long . . ." He swallowed hard. "How long were you locked in the closet?"

"Two days. It was an old house, I wasn't strong enough to knock the door down, or kick it in. So I was there for two days before he let me out."

"What else?" he said, his voice suddenly hoarse. "Did he beat you?"

She nodded.

"And?"

"Does it matter? It's all in the past, and Mark's dead now. Can't we just let it go?"

"I have to know, Anna. I have so many questions."

She braced herself, but only because she loved him. And maybe he did have the right to know. It really didn't matter though, did it? Because since the first moment she'd seen him she'd understood what the outcome would be if he found out who she was. She would, once again, be moving. Starting over. Trying not to look back on her mistakes. Or, in this case, trying not to look back on falling in love. "Then ask. But Sam," she said, fighting back her tears, "I'm so sorry. So very sorry. This isn't what I wanted. None of it is."

He nodded. "It's not what I wanted either. So, what else?"

"It started when he flunked his medical entrance exams. He'd been drinking a lot, and he wasn't really studying the way he should have been. I tried to get him to slow down, at least until after the exams. But he wouldn't. The day he took it, he knew. In fact, he'd walked out halfway through. He came home, and while I was trying to comfort him, he . . . he hit me for the first time. Then apologized. It was the beginning of his pattern though. You know, beat me up, cry and beg me to forgive him, promise it would never happen again."

"And you always took him back?"

She nodded. "Something in the way I was raised. You know, eternal optimism, always look for the best in people. And Mark did have so much good in him. But he also had demons. Anyway, I kept thinking if I concentrated on those good things, and fostered that goodness, he would change." She laughed bitterly. "Which is so typical of a battered wife, isn't it? Give him one more chance and hope he changes. But once someone hits you, it never changes. And I should have left him that first time, but I honestly wanted to believe . . ." She swiped angrily at the tears streaming down her cheeks. "I wanted to believe."

"But you don't seem . . ."

"I don't seem the type? I'm not now. But back then I'd recently lost both of my parents, and I just wanted to feel connected again. And Mark was a charmer. He swept me off my feet when we met. And I was ready to be swept. I think he saw that. Used it. But for the first few months he gave me so much attention. At least, that's what I thought it was. Until I realized it was obsession. He wanted me as a possession and not as a wife."

"He told me that you called him home halfway through the medical exam, that you claimed it was an emergency, and when he got there your emergency was that you were lonely. That you were the one who was obsessed with having him at your beck and call."

"I was working when he took that test. Pulling a double shift."

"What about when he failed his dental school exam? He said you forced him to take it because you wanted to be married to a professional."

"It was his idea. I didn't think being a dentist would make him happy, but he wanted to . . . to keep up with you, probably even me, in some fashion, and I suppose he believed that was one way of doing it. As for his entrance exam, he was doing drugs by then. Pretty strung out that day, and I begged him to wait. But he wouldn't. Instead, he made a scene, and they kicked him out after just a few minutes. And he told you what?"

"You took the car and he was late getting there, so they wouldn't admit him to the exam."

"I went with him, Sam. Drove him. And I was sitting in the hall waiting, heard him screaming at the proctor."

"When did you divorce him?"

"After the closet incident, which came about a month after the dental exam incident. When he let me out, he beat me so badly, I almost . . . I was in the hospital for several days, and met a woman who helped me get away. There's an underground network for women who've been abused. They make you disappear, help you start a new life. Like witness protection, I guess. In my case, my face was so badly damaged I had to have several surgeries to put it back together, so they suggested I take a new name to go with my new face. It worked. I got a job working in a lab, not loving it, but the network was working on getting me back into a residency program somewhere. Here, as it turned out. But Mark found me before I moved.

"Apparently he'd been looking for months, and a friend of a friend tipped him off that they'd seen me." She shivered, and then wrapped her arms around herself, more for protection than warmth. "He broke the door down at my apartment. He was beating me when the police arrived. They grabbed him, he resisted, tried to get the gun away from the arresting officer . . ." Finally, the tears began to flow in full. "I tried to save him. They took him to the hospital, but the bullet had nicked his heart and . . . and he bled out before anybody could do anything. It's not how I wanted it to end. No matter what he'd done to me, Mark didn't deserve to die. I just wanted . . ." She sniffled. "I wanted to live my life without being hurt. He hit me so many times, and I kept taking it, and it got to the point that I didn't care if he killed me because that would have been the easiest way out. Then when I got away, I realized that while I was weak, it wasn't about me. Nothing he did was. And all I ever wanted was to be safe."

She swatted back her tears. "I never wanted you to know any of this. Never wanted your parents to find out, or your grandparents. They loved Mark. Knowing what I knew about him would have hurt them so badly. They'd lost a son already. They didn't need to lose his memory, too."

"We all believed him when he blamed you for everything that was going wrong in his life, Anna."

"I'm sure you would have. But it was my choice not to tell your family the truth. The police and hospital records would have backed me up. It would have been an easy thing to do, but I didn't plan on . . . on any of this."

"He called me the day before he died, told me you were stalking him, wouldn't leave him alone. That you'd been after him to take you back from the minute he left you. But you left him."

"I'm not a stalker. I wouldn't have . . ." Her body shook with a sob. "And I won't bother you here. As soon as my department head can replace me, I'll leave. It's only right."

"Nothing's right, Anna. Dear God, nothing's right."

She nodded, but didn't speak. After all, what was there to say? She'd loved and lost. Not Mark, though. Later, after the pain was gone, she'd realized she'd never loved him. More like, she'd been in love with the idea of love. With Sam, though . . . love. The real love. The only love. But a love she'd never have returned. "Maybe it's not, but after I leave you can . . . I suppose it's trite to say you can get back to normal, isn't it?"

"I can't get back to normal. Not after I fell in love with you, Anna. Not after I found out what my brother did to you."

He loved her? In a way, she regretted that he'd told her because knowing that he loved her and that she couldn't have him only made the pain that much worse. "I was afraid you'd recognize me at first. My face is different, but not so much. But when you didn't . . . How did you find out?"

"'Live and learn, or live and don't learn and get used to the consequences'. Mark used that expression all the time, since he was a kid. It came from my dad. I knew you looked familiar, too, even though I'd only seen you in photos. So, I put one and one together, and got, well . . . you."

"He kept me hidden from the family, Sam. That was part of his obsession, I think. I only met your parents once, and it was brief. And we lived so far away from them. But at the time I didn't know he was trying to isolate me. He kept telling me he wanted me all to himself, and I thought it was romantic."

"About that time I called you . . ."

She shook her head. "It doesn't matter."

"But it does. I told you to stay away from his funeral, that if you came anywhere near my family I'd physically remove you. And I accused you of . . ."

"Being responsible for his death."

He nodded, too choked to speak.

"I understood how you felt, Sam. He was your brother. You were grieving."

"I was wrong."

"You were loyal." The eyes staring at her now were so sad it was all she could do to look back at him.

"I'm not Mark," he finally said. "I knew he had problems, but I didn't know how deep they were, or I'd have . . ."

"It's not your fault," she whispered. "Just like it's not my fault. Mark knew what he was doing. That's why he always apologized and begged for another chance. Because he knew." She shut her eyes. "And my life isn't about Mark any more. I've moved on."

"But how far?" Sam asked.

"Some days as far away as I need to be, and some days not far enough. But it's good. I've got back the parts of me I wanted to get, and I'm not letting them go again." She smiled triumphantly. "Not ever."

"Then what happens to us?"

"Us?"

"You and me?"

"Love lost?"

"Or love found?" he asked. "If you trust me when I tell you I'm not Mark, that I'd never, ever hurt you."

"I know you wouldn't." She locked the door behind her and took two steps forward. "But I'd be lying if I said this doesn't scare me."

"Do I scare you?"

Shaking her head, she took two more hesitant steps, then flew into his open arms, and kissed him – his chin, his forehead, his nose, his earlobes – everywhere but his lips. Through his scrubs she felt his immediate erection, and that's when she traced his mouth with the tip of her tongue.

"Dear God," he moaned. He tried to suck her tongue into his mouth, but she refused him.

All too soon that was even more than Anna could bear, so she moved tighter into his body, darted her tongue into his mouth, but only for a second. She gently sucked, and then lightly nibbled on his lower lip, inviting him to return the favor. Which he did, masterfully.

"We shouldn't be doing this here," she said, her voice husky, as she totally disregarded her own words and started to strip down. "But in case I'm wrong about that, sit down." She pointed him to the chair opposite his desk, where he went willingly, waiting for her . . .

"So if I were to bring you home to meet the folks, chances are they wouldn't recognize you, right?" he said an hour later, as he tugged his scrub shirt on.

"What?" she gasped. She still couldn't believe it was true. The two of them. Everything.

"If we could work this out beyond, well, this, and I if took you home to my parents. You know, holidays, birthdays, those sorts of things. Because that's the traditional thing to do. You and me together."

"You can't mean it, Sam." Running her fingers through her wet hair, she looked out at him from his office en suite. Making love in the chair had been wonderful, but the second time, in his tiny stall shower . . .

"I can," he said. "But it's not going to be easy because you're right. They shouldn't know about Mark. Then once a grandchild or two happens, I think we'll be home free."

"What are you talking about?" she asked, scared to death to hear his answer because what he was saying was everything she wanted to hear. The dream she didn't want to lose.

"Well, it's not a marriage proposal yet, but I'm projecting into our future."

"Then you believe me? You really believe me?"

"I believe in my heart, and my heart believes in you."

"I love you," she whispered, still too stunned by the turn of events. "But I never thought . . ."

He smiled and opened his arms to her. She ran straight into them, barefoot, wrapped in a towel, water droplets still glistening on her skin. "I do have one rather important question for you. Actually, two. First one is, when I do propose, and if we do get married, are you going to be a Cooper or a Craig? Or even a Rhodes?"

Nestling in his arms she knew this was the only place she wanted to be for the rest of her life. "I'm Anna Craig now. Marcie Rhodes is gone, and she's not coming back, so I think Anna Craig will . . . hyphenate."

"Sounds good. So, next question. What are you doing for Christmas dinner? Because I have these friends who are already setting a place for you at the table."

"Will there be mistletoe?" she asked.

"You like mistletoe?"

"Find some for me, Santa," she said, removing the scrub top he'd just put on, "and see."

PLAYING WITH FIRE

Julie Rowe

Chapter One

The smell of smoke woke Dr Nora Callahan out of a sound sleep. It poked at the back of her throat, sharp and bitter, making her cough, but the alarms in her home stayed silent.

She slipped out of bed and headed for her bedroom door to investigate, but sirens going off outside pulled her to the window instead. She threw the curtains aside, looked out, then prayed she was still sleeping.

The street lamps glowed orange, backlighting the houses across the street. Light that danced with ribbons of smoke to a tune played off-key by shifting gusts of wind.

Fire, but where?

The house vibrated, a pounding that resonated through the walls, that could have only come from her front door. It convinced her she wasn't asleep and this wasn't a dream. The familiar chant – Please, no dead. Please, no dead – ran through her head.

She ran from her room, down the stairs and threw the door open before whoever was hammering on it could break it down.

Sheriff Jake Turner stood on the step, his fist raised, his face and uniform dusted in black and grey soot. The sheriff was a tall man, a couple inches over six feet. Though he'd only been sheriff in Dead End, North Dakota for a year, everyone knew he'd spent several years in the Army's Special Forces. No uniform could hide his broad shoulders and muscled body. He had all the single women in town, and a few married ones, panting after him, but the only woman he spent any time with was Nora.

It started with a couple of meetings. He brought coffee for them both and they kept it professional, but eventually the meetings progressed to working lunches and careful questions about her personal life, or the lack thereof. Very careful.

Obviously, some of the folks in town had told him a thing or two about her.

Doctor Nora doesn't date.

Doctor Nora's never had a boyfriend.

Doctor Nora runs at the first sign of masculine interest in her.

Poor Doctor Nora is going to die young.

They were right. Her lifespan wasn't going to be a long one.

Born with a congenital defect – no right pulmonary artery – meant something as common as pneumonia could kill her. She became a doctor knowing she couldn't save herself, but she could save other people. There was enough time for her to do that. But what she absolutely wasn't going to do was tie herself to a man and put him through all the pain of her dying young.

She told him that the day he'd asked her out to dinner.

She repeated it when he asked her out for lunch.

They argued about it when he asked her to have a picnic with him at the lake. He accused her of hiding behind what might happen. She told him she'd seen it happen to her parents. Her father had the same defect. He died when she was ten. Her mother died of grief six months later.

Jake had gotten even more careful after that.

But tonight, the look on his face was as far from careful as it could get.

He stared at her for a full second, his gaze sweeping over her. One eyebrow went up, but he didn't comment on the men's boxer shorts or tank top she'd worn to bed.

"Get dressed and get your gear," he said, stepping past her and into the house.

She shut the door and made for the stairs at a run. "Where's the fire? How many injured?"

He followed her. "It's everywhere. Wildfire started about ten miles west of town. With the winds as high as they are, the fire department thinks it could reach the western edge in the next two hours."

She paused in her rapid search for clothes and glanced at the window. "It's so bright. I thought there were houses already on fire."

"Not yet, but it's bad, Nora. We're on total evacuation order. The entire town." He ran a blackened hand through his hair. "It could take every building we have."

A cold shiver racked her body. She yanked out some jeans and a shirt and threw them on the bed. "What do you need from me?"

"I've got teams evacuating the residents. I need you to coordinate the evac of the hospital and seniors' lodge."

"Okay." She pulled out some underwear and turned to face him.

His gaze dropped to the lacy pink panties in her hands.

She glanced down then blushed. "Could you turn around so I can change?"

His gaze shifted to her face and she almost took a step back at what she saw there. Raw male desire with enough heat that she was surprised her panties hadn't gone up in smoke.

"You're playing with fire, Doc." His voice was a deep rumble, igniting a blaze in the pit of her belly.

Her breathing stalled for a moment then stuttered back to life. "I thought we were trying to avoid that."

"Maybe you were." His gaze grew impossibly hotter, and then he turned around slowly, giving her his back.

"Do we have a timeline we need to follow for the evac?" she asked as she tore off the boxers and jumped into the panties as fast as she could. She whipped off her tank top and snatched up a bra.

"Fast."

She hopped into her jeans, pulled on her shirt and grabbed socks. When she glanced up, Jake had turned around and was staring at her again.

"I'm beginning to think getting burned by you might be something to look forward to."

For the second time in two minutes she forgot how to breathe. "You know I can't . . . but . . ."

He smiled at her, a sinful temptation, and held out his hand. "Don't worry, Doc. I'm not going to do anything about it tonight."

A lunatic she hadn't known about inside her head took over her tongue and asked, "What about tomorrow?"

"Is that a yes?" His voice slid over her like dark chocolate, decadent and delicious.

What was she doing? Flirting with a man like Jake was dangerous. "Why haven't you dated anyone else?"

He took a step closer, his hand still out. "You're the woman I want."

She blew out a breath and put her hand in his.

He pulled her out of the room and down the stairs. "Grab your shoes. I'll drive you to the hospital."

She plucked her sneakers off the floor, and then grabbed her purse and the comprehensive first aid kit she left at the front door in case of emergencies and followed him outside.

His police truck was parked right out front of her house, the lights on, but the siren off. They jumped in and he drove toward the hospital. The road was crowded with cars, trucks and vans full of people. It looked like the entire town of Dead End was running for dear life, heading toward the highway.

"Where are all the evacuees supposed to go?"

"I'm telling everyone to head for Grand Forks. The sheriff there is coordinating food, shelter and medical care."

"Good. That's good." She blew a breath out. "You really think the town is in danger?"

"Yeah. It's been a dry spring and the winds are high. The two worst conditions for fighting a fire." He turned a corner, narrowly missing a minivan coming toward them too fast. He turned his siren on for a couple seconds, but didn't stop or change his course. "We've got water bombers on it, but it keeps jumping around. A couple of firefighters nearly got toasted when the fire jumped over them."

"Oh my God."

"The forest service has pulled all their people back. It's just too dangerous to fight it at close range."

"So it's up to the water bombers?"

"Yeah. We've got helicopters and more bombers coming in from Canada, but they won't be here until morning."

"Too late."

"Too damn late."

He pulled up in front of the hospital and handed her a radio. "Cellular service may or may not work. If the wrong tower gets knocked or burns down, it could bring the entire cell service to a halt for the whole area. Keep this with you and set on channel three. You call if you need help, got that?"

She nodded. "I will." She moved to open the door, but he grabbed her arm and pulled her back.

"Don't take any chances, Nora. I want a live doctor, not a dead hero."

"Heroine, Jake. I'd be a dead heroine, but I have no plans to martyr myself tonight."

"Good, because I do have plans for you and me."

She gave him a sad smile. "I'm not a safe bet, Jake." She wished she could be, but wishes wouldn't change a thing.

"And a sheriff is?" He grinned, leaned forward and pressed his lips to hers in a kiss that left her breathless.

He let her go and she escaped into a building that was almost more familiar to her than her house was.

Inside the doors was chaos.

People ran in several directions, the phone was ringing off the hook and the hospital administrator, Meredith, was calling out instructions.

"Dr Callahan," Meredith said as soon as she caught sight of Nora. "We're evacuating."

"Sheriff Turner told me. Where are we with the evacuation?"

"Nurses, nursing aids and even family members are getting the patients and resident seniors ready to leave. Can you organize things from here? I need to ensure our computer files are backed up—"

"Of course, go."

Meredith didn't hesitate. She ran.

Nora went to the main reception desk, activated the paging system and announced the general evacuation order. Then she added that all staff must meet in reception for a two-minute meeting.

As soon as she figured everyone who could come had arrived, she broke all of them up into teams and gave orders for each team to evacuate a specific section of the hospital. She also assigned team leads for the evacuation of the seniors' lodge attached to the hospital. As soon as everyone had their orders and were dispersing to their tasks, Nora called Jake on the radio.

"Sheriff, it's Dr Callahan. We're going to need transportation to get our patients out of here."

"Roger, Doc. I've got a couple of school buses that should be there any time. More are coming after that. Do you have anyone who absolutely needs an ambulance?"

She went over the patient list in her head. "No. Not yet at any rate."

"Understood. I'm going to keep the ambulance on standby for now. Let me know if anything changes."

"I will."

Staff and family members began to line patients up in preparation to go outside. One of the school buses pulled up in front of the main doors and she got a couple of nurses to start loading patients. The second bus arrived a few minutes later. A third ten minutes after that.

Nora kept the radio in her hand and listened to the back-and-forth conversations between Jake, the fire chief, and the Forest Service staff.

Evacuating an entire town was complicated. She was incredibly proud of the man who could keep his cool under such circumstances and keep all the details straight.

At the thirty-minute mark Jake called her on the radio. "Dr Callahan, can I get an update on the state of the evac from the hospital?"

She brought the radio up and pressed the talk button. "We're ninety per cent complete on our evacuation, Sheriff. The building should be clear in about ten minutes."

"Do you need additional transport?"

"I need someone to pick me up. I want to stay with emergency services until the entire town is evacuated."

"Roger that. Pick up in ten minutes."

Ten minutes later, Nora and Meredith were locking the doors when Jake arrived. He jumped out of his truck and ran toward the two women.

"We don't have much time. The fire is only a couple of miles from town," he yelled at them.

"Already?" Nora asked, coughing. Smoke lay thick and heavy in the air as if the streets had been taken over by ghostly party streamers.

"The winds are pushing it in a direct line toward us."

Another vehicle entered the drive and pulled up behind Jake's truck.

"That's my husband," Meredith said. "We're going to Grand Forks."

"Keep in touch with me," Jake said. "Let me know how our people are doing."

"Will do," she said with a hug for Nora. Then Meredith rushed over to her minivan.

Jake tugged Nora toward the passenger door of his truck and she got in.

The sudden quiet of the interior of the truck surprised her. She hadn't realized how much noise there had been. Between the emergency vehicle sirens and the town's public announcements siren, her ears were ringing. She coughed some more, but the air inside the truck was a lot more breathable than the air outside.

Jake got in, started the engine and pulled away from the now dark hospital.

"Have the water bombers helped at all?" she asked.

"Hard to say. The fire's moving so fast no one can keep up with it. Our only real option is to get the hell out of the way."

"The town's in real danger then?"

"Yeah." There was a bleak tone to his voice that made her stomach knot. "It's going to be bad."

"What's left to be done?"

"We're still rounding up a few people who've refused to leave."

"What?" This wasn't good news. "Who's refusing to leave?"

"Some of the older folks don't want to leave their houses."

"Stubborn fools."

"I can understand why they don't want to just cut and run at the first sign of trouble, but we're way past that."

"Can I help?"

"What I'd like for you to do is stick with the paramedics and the ambulance team. We may need more than the paramedics can handle and with the hospital evacuated and the staff gone, you're my backup medical plan."

"Okay, I can do that."

He nodded, and a minute or two later they were pulling to a stop at the outskirts of the eastern edge of town. Here was a phalanx of emergency vehicles with lights flashing, and people scurrying about in reflective gear.

Dawn lit up the horizon on what should have been a beautiful day.

"Okay," he said leaning toward her. "Keep that radio with you. I'm going to check on the western edge and make sure everyone is out in that part of town. Let me know if you have to leave this area."

"Got it. Thanks." She reached for the door handle, but he tugged on her left arm. She turned back. "Did I forget something?"

"Yeah, this." He leaned closer still and kissed her again. This time, however, it wasn't quick or safe. Her lips parted under his at the shock of his tongue tasting her bottom lip. He drove that tongue into her mouth, promising all sorts of illicit things. Taking up a life of crime seemed like the most desirable thing she could ever do.

He pulled away and she followed, wanting his taste on her lips again. "Nora, honey, let go. I promise we'll pick right up where we left off later."

She opened her eyes and realized she'd grabbed him by the collar of his uniform shirt with both hands and had a death grip on the fabric.

She pried her hands loose and tried to catch her breath, but between the smoke in the air and her combustible libido, she didn't think that was going to happen any time soon.

"Sorry, I didn't mean to, um, wrinkle you."

His grin looked eerily bright in contrast to the soot on his face. "Doc, you can wrinkle me any time you like. Except for right now."

"Darn forest fire."

"Yeah, when I catch up to the moron who started it, he and I are going to have words."

"Someone started this fire?" Dismay dampened the desire

heating her blood. How could anyone be so careless, so stupid, when they'd had so little rain this spring?

"That's what the fire marshal thinks. Stay with the ground crews here unless something changes, and keep in touch."

"I will." She hopped out of his truck, grabbed her first aid kit out of the truck's box and strode toward a cluster of men in firefighter gear. She recognized one of them as the town fire chief, Hank Walker. The expression on his face told her something else was wrong.

"Hank," she called out as she approached. "What's going on?"

"We're missing a couple of men. They're ten minutes overdue on check-in and I can't raise them on the radio."

She glanced at the rest of the men, but they had started to walk away toward an ageing fire truck parked on the shoulder of the road. "Send someone to look for them."

"I don't have anyone. Those guys—" he pointed at the men now climbing into their truck "—are going to try to keep the fire from crossing the highway and cutting off our escape route. I'd go, but someone needs to stay here to keep this evac from turning into chaos."

"I'll go."

Hank stared at her like she'd lost her mind.

"Give me a truck." She held up her hand. "I've already got a radio."

"The sheriff won't like it."

"Beggars can't be choosers, Hank. Got a truck I can borrow?"

He sighed, fished a set of keys out of his pocket and tossed them to her. "Do not get hurt. Understand?" He gestured with his chin at a white half-ton parked not far away.

"Yes, sir." She got in, tossing her first aid kit in the passenger seat and drove over to him. "Where am I going?"

"Down Southside Road towards the eastern edge of town. They'd gone to help Old Man Banner and his wife. Something about a downed tree. They radioed that they'd gotten the Banners on their way. That was the last contact I'd had with them."

"Names?"

"Pete and Ernie Ramsey. Brothers."

"I know them. They volunteer at the hospital." Both men were in their sixties and retired. They were in good shape; Pete and Ernie were black belts in karate and taught a fitness class for some of the seniors in residence. They'd been in the military for years, even rumored to have participated in some dangerous missions, but they always found a way not to answer direct questions about their time in uniform.

They were awfully friendly with Jake.

"I'll check in every ten minutes," she told Hank.

"See that you do." Hank smacked the truck a couple of times and she drove off.

The turn onto Southside Road wasn't far. When she finally got there and made the turn, she found herself staring into what looked like a solid wall of smoke.

Chapter Two

Pete and Ernie owned an old navy-blue truck they'd had for years. Nora watched for it as she drove east down the road. A few vehicles passed her going the other way, their lights flashing in warning. She waved and kept going. The Banners' place was a two- or three-acre lot on the edge of town. They had a sizeable garden, several apple trees and a large strawberry patch. She wouldn't put it past Mr Banner to be out watering his property in a bid to save it from the fire.

The smoke became heavier and heavier, making visibility a real issue.

She pulled into the Banners' driveway and found Pete and Ernie's truck. She got out, her first aid kit in hand, and started yelling, "Pete, Ernie, are you here?"

She listened for a reply, but didn't hear anything except the distant sound of sirens. Walking toward the house, she tried again, "Pete, Ernie!"

This time she heard something.

She took a deep breath and shouted, "Keep yelling so I can find you."

She listened and followed the shouts around to the back of the house. Several trees were down. Someone waved from beneath one of the trees. She rushed over.

Pete and Ernie were both under the tree, but only one of them was conscious. Pete.

"Are you all right?" she asked him.

"I think my leg is broken. Ernie hasn't woken up since the tree fell on us."

She ran around the tree to see how they'd been pinned underneath it. It was too big to shift by herself, nor could she drag them out. They were both tangled up in branches.

She was going to need a chainsaw.

Nora turned up the volume of her radio and depressed the talk button. "Sheriff Turner, this is Dr Callahan. I've got two injured men at the Banner place on the east end of town. They're trapped under a tree. I'm going to need a chainsaw to get them out."

She waited for a couple of seconds, then the radio crackled to life.

"Roger, Doctor. I'll be there in about five minutes."

"We're behind the house," she added. She turned to Pete. "The sheriff is on his way. How long ago did this happen?" she asked Pete.

"I don't know, maybe thirty minutes."

She checked the carotid pulse of Ernie first. It was slow, but steady and strong. She looked to see if there was an obvious head injury, but she couldn't find one. Until the tree was out of the way there was little she could do for him.

She turned to Pete. "Which leg?"

"The left. A little higher than my ankle."

The tree had him pinned to the ground across his chest, leaving his legs accessible. She felt along his lower leg starting from his knee and moving down. She found some swelling and Pete sucked in his breath when she gently touched the area just above his ankle.

"You're right, your leg is probably broken, but most likely just the tibia. I'm going to splint it. Any other injuries?"

"I'm not sure. Nothing that's bothering me."

"Okay, I'm going to work on your leg."

She pulled out two splints and a couple of triangular bandages and quickly stabilized the limb. Pete groaned a couple of times.

"How are you doing, Pete?"

"Not bad considering." He made it sound like he broke his leg every other week.

"Been through worse?"

"Sorry to say, yes."

She checked his pulse below the splints. Strong and steady. "What's worse than a broken leg?"

"Got shot in the ass once."

That made her laugh. "Really?" She moved over to Ernie. Running her hands carefully over all the parts of him she could reach, searching for swelling, blood or other signs of injury.

"Yep."

"When was that?"

"Can't tell ya."

"No?"

"Nope. Uncle Sam is real particular about who knows about his secret missions and other stuff."

"Secret missions, huh? Like military missions or are we talking about secret recipes?" Her fingers found a swelling on Ernie's clavicle, but she couldn't wiggle her hand further down his chest to check his ribs. They felt fine from the back, but if there was one broken bone, there could be more.

"Not telling, Nora."

The wind changed direction and a waft of smoke was shoved up her nose, causing her to cough violently. She sidestepped away from the men and the mangled tree so she wasn't coughing all over them.

"Nora!"

She turned toward the sound of her name and saw Jake heading toward her, chainsaw in hand. She waved at him.

"Are you okay?" he asked as soon as he was close enough to see her clearly.

Eyes watering, she managed to choke out, "I'm fine, but Ernie is unconscious and Pete has a broken leg."

"How bad is Ernie? Do we need the ambulance?"

She shook her head and managed to say, "Won't know until I can get at him."

Jake stepped over to the tree and looked at how it had the two men pinned. He glanced at Nora. "I'm going to start cutting off branches. Can you pull the cut pieces out of the way?"

She nodded.

He started up the chainsaw.

As branches came free, she grabbed them and tossed them aside. Soon the only thing holding the men down was the two-foot-diameter trunk of the tree. Jake cut through it in sections then helped lift it off Pete and Ernie. As soon as it was gone she was at Ernie's side, her hands checking for more broken bones.

She found a goose egg on his head, but other than his collarbone, couldn't detect any other injury. She put a neck collar on him to keep his head stable.

"Can you help turn him?" she asked Jake.

He helped her turn the older man onto his back.

Nora checked his pupils.

"His eyes are responsive. Let me do one last check and strap his left arm to his chest, then we can get the both of them out of here."

"I've got a gurney in the back of my truck," Jake told her, and ran off to get it.

They moved Ernie onto the gurney then, with Jake taking his head and Nora at his feet, they moved the man into the back of Jake's truck.

As they were jogging back to grab Pete, Jake said, "What are you doing here alone?"

"Hank needed someone to check on Pete and Ernie. I was the only person who could do it."

"You shouldn't be doing anything alone."

"So, I'm not capable of working unsupervised, is that it?"

"I'm saying that, with your health concerns, you should know better than to go off into heavy smoke without someone else with you."

"The smoke isn't that bad with the winds the way they are right now."

"You two want to save the argument for later?"

Nora and Jake turned to stare at Pete where he sat on the ground.

"I'd rather not wait for the fire to get here, if it's all the same to you."

"I'm sorry, Pete." Nora knelt next to him and pulled one of his arms over her shoulder. Jake did the same on the other side.

They stood, with Pete hopping on his good leg, and got him into the back of the truck next to his brother.

"I'll ride in the back with them," she told Jake.

He continued to frown at her, but didn't say anything.

She was tempted to stick her tongue out at him, but got into the back instead.

She checked Ernie as Jake got them on their way, thankful his condition hadn't changed or worsened.

Pete patted her knee. "He's a good man."

"Don't worry, I'm going to do everything I can for Ernie. He's going to pull through this."

Pete smiled and shook his head. "I'm talking about Jake."

"Oh." She blinked. "Yes, he's a very good sheriff."

"No," Pete said, his smile growing wider. "I mean he's a good man for you." He smacked her knee. "Stop pretending you don't know what I'm talking about."

She looked away. What he was suggesting couldn't happen. "It's impossible and you know it."

"Maybe I do and maybe I don't." He shrugged. "But I saw how he looks at you. He's not going to let you hold him at arm's length for much longer. Maybe not even for the rest of today."

"I'm quite certain I'm the last thing on his mind today."

"I wouldn't count on that if I were you. This kind of disaster reminds a man he's mortal, makes him think of the future. And you, you're a future kind of woman."

She snorted. "That's just it, Pete. I don't have much of a future."

He laughed, but the sound was tempered by the pain. "No one gets out of life alive. We're all running on a clock that will eventually stop. So what if yours is set for next week, or next month or next year? I could be gone tomorrow."

"So, what, throw caution to the wind? Is that what you're saying?"

"Yep."

She glanced through the rear window of the truck, her gaze meeting Jake's for a moment in the rear-view mirror. He gave her a quick smile, even though she knew he was still angry with her. "I don't want to hurt him."

"The only person I see you hurting is yourself," Pete said. "Besides, he's a big boy. You shouldn't be deciding what he can or can't handle. Let him decide for himself."

Jake slowed the truck and Nora glanced around the cab to see that they were coming up on the muster area just off the highway.

"Don't give Jake any funny ideas," she warned Pete as the truck came to a stop and the ambulance pulled up next to them.

"I think he's got plenty of his own," Pete replied with a strained smile.

"Starting to feel the pain now?"

"Oh yeah. It's hitting me."

She ordered an intravenous painkiller for Pete and gave orders to transport both men to Grand Forks asap. Ernie was going to need a CT scan and both brothers would need X-rays. She spoke to one of the trauma docs at the hospital in Grand Forks, so they'd know what to expect. Then she watched the ambulance leave, lights flashing.

"How are they?" Jake asked.

She turned and realized he hadn't moved more than a few feet away since he'd parked his truck on the shoulder of the highway.

He had his radio in his hand and she realized he'd been busy talking into it while she'd gotten Ernie and Pete settled in the ambulance.

"They're stable, but need some tests done to see if I missed any internal injuries or even broken bones. What's happening with the fire?"

"The wind shifted and it's holding about a half-mile from town. The water bombers are pushing hard to keep it there."

"Okay, so we have time to go back for Hank's truck."

Jake swore. "I forgot about it."

She grabbed his arm and pulled him toward the driver's side door of his truck. "Let's go."

"I've got a town to evacuate, a fire to fight and you want me to go for a drive so you can pick up a vehicle?"

She stopped and considered it for a second. "You're right." She yanked on his arm and dragged him around the front of the truck. "I'll drive, so you can talk to your people, give orders and generally be a badass sheriff." She gave him a little shove then ran around to jump into the driver's seat.

"Badass?" he asked her as he got in.

The radio went off with someone calling for the sheriff.

He didn't immediately answer.

"That would be you," she informed him, pulling away from the shoulder and heading toward Southside Road.

"I am not a badass," he said as he brought the radio up to speak into it.

Nora listened to Jake give directions to some incoming Forest Service people.

When he finished, she said with a smirk, "Badass and in charge."

He turned slightly toward her and asked, "Is that why you're scared of me?"

She sucked in a breath and glanced at him. "I don't know what you mean."

"I'm right. You're scared." He crossed his arms over his chest.

"I am not."

"Are too."

"What are you, five?"

"No. What I am is determined to show you why you don't need to be scared."

Chapter Three

"There's fear and then there's correctly identifying a dumb idea. I'm most definitely not afraid."

"Dating me would be a dumb idea?" He sounded insulted. Pissed off even.

"Okay, maybe I put that the wrong way."

She could see him shaking his head in her peripheral vision. "No. No, you're right, I've been an idiot."

He could admit it? Out loud?

"I've been treating you with kid gloves this whole time when I should have gone after you direct, like I wanted. But, no, the whole population of Dead End told me you'd cut and run if I did that. They said you'd faint at my feet if I wasn't really careful. They said you were timid around men."

"I am."

"No, you're inexperienced, but timid . . . no." He thrust his chin out. "You know what you are? You're a great big faker."

"I am not."

"You're not scared of me."

"I already told you that."

"You're scared of getting hurt by some jackass who doesn't know what a woman like you needs."

Now that was an interesting statement.

She was almost afraid to ask, but couldn't keep her mouth shut. "What does a woman like me need?"

"A commitment. A friend. A lover. Someone who appreciates how smart, kind and vulnerable you are."

"You make me sound like some Victorian virgin."

"That's what I thought I was dealing with, but you snookered me along with everyone else in town. You are a strong woman. I think you can handle me with one arm tied behind your back."

She pulled into the Banners' driveway behind Hank's truck and then turned to gaze at him, though she did keep one hand on the door handle, just in case. "I can't give you what you need, Jake."

"And what is that?"

"A commitment. A friend. A lover."

"Bullshit."

She sighed. "I'm going to die young."

"So you've said."

"I won't put someone I love through the emotional torture of—" she searched for the right word "—that kind of grief."

A smile spread slowly across his face. "You love me?"

"I . . . no . . . I mean, that's not what I meant."

"Ha! You love me." He leaned across the seat and kissed her. A full-contact, open-mouth, tongue-tantalizing kiss.

He ended it as abruptly as he started it and jumped out of the truck.

She was frozen in place for a moment before she opened the door and hopped out too.

He rounded the front of the truck and made straight for her, but she put out a hand, palm facing him.

"Don't you dare. We don't have time for . . . for . . . fooling around."

He laughed, cupped her face with one hand and rested his forehead against hers. "I'm willing to wait."

He had waited. For almost a year, even with offers from other women, he'd waited.

"Why?" she asked, terrified to know the answer, but needing to know it anyway.

"I knew the moment I met you that you were the woman for me. Smart, beautiful, funny. Sexy. You give until you don't have anything left, and yet you find a way to give even more."

"Jake, I don't know how to be with . . . you. You're not anything like a . . ."

"A what?"

"A tame man."

"There's something you need to know about me." He shifted closer. "There's not a damn thing I wouldn't let you do to me. Tie me up, tie me down, any damn thing at all."

All the air in her chest deserted her when she needed it most. "Oh."

"Now get in that truck and let's get the hell out of here. We can continue this conversation later. In private."

She swallowed hard. On one hand, the idea of discussing what she thought he wanted to discuss in private scared the crap out of her. He was no polite and retiring nice guy. He was an ex-military sheriff with a well-developed sense of duty and firm ideas on most everything. On the other hand, he was strong, thoughtful and gentle when the situation demanded it. Everything a smart woman wanted in a man.

This was not the time to play dumb. "Okay." That didn't sound too certain, so she said it again with a little more oomph. "Okay." Much better.

He let her go and she rushed to Hank's truck, got in and backed out after Jake. They turned on to the main road and headed toward the muster point.

The smoke was getting thicker and thicker, and her coughing resumed. A strong gust of wind rattled the truck hard enough that she had to fight with the steering wheel for a moment. She glanced in the rear-view mirror.

What she saw couldn't be right.

Nora looked again.

The fire had reached town. Worse. It was already eating the Banners' house.

She grabbed her radio and yelled into it, "Jake, the fire is right behind us."

"I see it," he replied. "The wind has shifted again. Keep up with me."

He started to pull away from her and she pressed down on the gas pedal, catching up then matching his speed.

The wind pushed them again, but this time the gust came with sparks, like a shower of fireflies. Ahead, she could see flames in the ditch on the left. It had crawled up a large tree.

Good Lord, the fire was traveling faster than they were.

Another gust blowing through was the only warning she got before the burning tree crashed to the ground just as Jake came abreast of it. It shoved his vehicle to the side, then rolled it into the opposite ditch.

Nora braked hard, fishtailing Hank's truck, leaving burnt rubber all over the road. She barely missed the tree and ended up in the ditch too, but on all four tires.

Jake's truck was still.

As soon as she got Hank's truck stopped, more or less, she dove out the door and ran to the other vehicle.

The smoke was thick now, acrid and dry, and she coughed and coughed until she was certain she was going to hack the lungs right out of her chest.

Jake. Where was Jake?

No movement from inside the truck.

That was bad. Bad, bad, bad.

"Jake!"

She ran around the vehicle to the driver's door. His head leaned against the window at an angle. Blood smeared the glass.

The door was stuck.

She yanked and yanked. Then screeched when it wouldn't open. She banged on the window, slammed it with both fists, beat it until the vibrations reverberated back through her arms and down to her soul.

"Goddamn it, wake up!"

Pushed by the wind, the heat, smoke and flames crawled

closer. She didn't have time to wait for him to wake. There wasn't time for much of anything.

She ran around the truck and managed to open the passenger side door partially.

"Jake," she screamed. "Jake." She squeezed inside, unbuckled his seat belt, all the while yelling in his ear to wake, to move, to live. Tugging at his body, she dragged him across the seat a few inches, but he was a big man and he weighed a lot more than she did.

A gash on the left side of his scalp had blood dripping down past his ear and onto his uniform. She felt around his neck, couldn't feel anything broken, so she tilted his head back and pried open one eye.

It reacted to light. So did the other one.

Good. That was good. Now if he could just wake up.

She shook him again and he groaned, "What?"

"Jake, you have to wake up. You have to move with me. If we don't get out of this truck right now, our goose is cooked. Literally."

He blinked at her a few times, coughed, then seemed to realize what was going on. "You have blood on your hands and shirt. Are you okay?"

"I'm fine. You're the one who's hurt." She tugged at his arm. "Come this way, your door is blocked."

He slid across the seat with her, then helped open the door a bit more so they could both tumble out. A few feet away, the tree was on fire, the flames getting dangerously close to the vehicle.

Nora dragged Jake to Hank's truck, pushed him inside and across the seat, then started the engine, revved it a couple of times and stomped on the gas.

They barreled out of the ditch in a move that would have made Evel Knievel proud.

"Put your seat belt on," Jake said as he fumbled with his. "It's the law."

She glanced at him incredulously. Okay, maybe he had a small concussion. "I promise to do it, just as soon as we're not in danger of being burned to death."

It was a distinct possibility. Fire now surrounded them on both sides of the road, the heavy winds pushing the flames rapidly east. If they didn't get out soon, they wouldn't get out at all.

She kept her foot heavy on the gas, watching the trees along the side of the road in case another one toppled over into their path.

Jake put his left hand on the dash and braced his arm, his head low as if he were thinking or possibly nauseous.

"Jake, you okay?"

His response wasn't the one she was expecting. "You know I'd give you a speeding ticket under normal circumstances, right?" He slowly turned his head to look at her and she thought she saw more awareness in his gaze. "A big one."

"Are you with me now?"

"Mostly. Give me a recap."

"Uh, we left the Banners' place, the wind shifted, a tree fell on your truck. It rolled. I got you out. I think you might have a concussion. We're trying to beat the fire to the highway."

He grunted. "Sounds like we're in trouble."

She had no time to respond as they came upon another downed tree. Nora had to drive into the ditch again to get around it, and some of that was on fire.

"When we get out of this," she said to him, "I'm never having a barbecue again."

"Here I was planning a big home barbecued steak dinner in a couple of days." He chuckled. "Party pooper."

The radio went off, Hank telling everyone to move clear out, as the wind had shifted and the fire was now entering town. Burning buildings, destroying livelihoods.

"We're almost there."

They approached the highway and, though the smoke remained heavy, she couldn't spot any flames in the ditches there. She turned the corner and saw the flashing lights of fire trucks and State Troopers who'd come to help. Some of the vehicles were pulling away, while others were still idling.

"Can you tell them we're here and that you're out of commission?" she asked Jake. "I want to take you straight to the hospital in Grand Forks."

"Am I broken, Doc?"

"I hope not."

He grabbed the radio and relayed all that, telling Hank he was in charge now.

Hank's response was short and to the point. "That damn fire is running the show, not me."

"Yeah, well, Nora thinks I've got a concussion. So you and the State Troopers are on your own."

"All we need is the National Guard and we can call this a party."

"Good idea," Jake said. "Call them."

"Goddamn it, Jake, I hate military music."

"And they hate country. Stop whining and get to work." He let go of the radio and put a hand to his head. "I've got the worst headache."

"Dizzy, sick to your stomach?"

"Yeah."

"You need a CT scan."

"Great, I did break something, didn't I?"

"Maybe bruised your brain."

"So, what, you're going to have to drill a hole through my skull?"

"Hopefully not."

"Hopefully?" He sounded irritated, confused or maybe sarcastic. "I sort of feel like I should offer you a can opener."

"Gave up using can openers on people in medical school."

"Heh, it's good to know you've ditched at least one bad habit."

She fought a smile. "I try so hard to be a good girl."

"Do not flirt with me now, Nora."

"I don't know, it seems like the perfect time to me. 'Cause you're the one who'll be saying, 'I can't, honey, I've got a headache.'"

"Evil woman."

"Wonderful man."

She waited for him to respond to her teasing, an easy smile on her face. But as the silent seconds rolled past, the smile dissolved into doubt. She glanced at him.

He stared straight at her, his jaw clenched tight.

"Jake?"

"Be sure, Nora. Be absolutely sure." He touched his head then looked at his hand and the blood smeared on it. "That knock on my head may have loosened a few things, because I thought I would be able to let you set the pace, let you step back when you needed to." He shook his head slowly. "I don't think I'll be able to do that any more. I've waited a long time for you. Too long. I've only kissed you twice, but I already crave to have my mouth on yours, your taste on my tongue, my hands on your skin like an addict craving his next fix."

Shock froze her lungs and forced her to focus on breathing alone, because the alternative was too raw, too dangerous to allow.

She wanted him just as badly, more than the need to eat or sleep.

Old habits tried to pull her into the safe path. The one that led to a lonely bed, a lonely life where all that existed was Nora Callahan, medical doctor.

She didn't want that life any more. Hank was right. Time to dig herself out of the grave she'd been living in for as long as she could remember. Sunshine would feel so wonderful on her face.

"I'm sure of one thing, Sheriff."

"Oh?" He didn't sound careful at all. He sounded like a man on the edge.

"I'm tired of sleeping alone."

"Fuck." The word came out of his chest like a gunshot.

"Exactly."

He groaned. "You're killing me."

"None of that now. This conversation is about living."

"Pull over."

"What? No. You have a concussion. Your health is more important than . . . sex."

"How long," he said between clenched teeth, "do I have to wait to have you in my bed?"

Chapter Four

"Until I'm sure you don't have a concussion any longer," Nora told Jake.

He grumbled something unintelligible.

"What?"

"Okay."

"That is so not what you just said."

"It was part of it. Sort of."

Nora sighed. "You're never going to be any kind of domesticated man, are you?"

"Is that a problem?"

She considered it. He'd been pushy, flirted with her, then took it way past flirting, but instead of feeling scared of him she felt . . . safe. "Doesn't look like it."

"How long until we can get that CT scan done?"

"Shouldn't be too long after we arrive at the hospital."

It wasn't. Only a couple of hours after they arrived at the hospital in Grand Forks, Nora was looking at the results of Jake's scans.

"Looks good."

"Then why is my headache so bad?"

"The swelling might not be bad enough to make your brain too big, but it's still bruised. I'm going to give you a painkiller that will help with swelling. That combined with lots of sleep should be all you need."

"Isn't sleeping with a concussion dangerous?"

"That's a myth for the most part. This baby—" she patted the CT machine "—is much better at detecting the kind of swelling that can kill than waking you up every hour or so."

"So I don't need anyone to check on me?" He sounded altogether disappointed about that.

"Not necessarily. You should still have someone with you in case the pain gets worse."

"I don't want to stay at the hospital. I'll never get any sleep here."

"How about I get a hotel room and you stay with me?" It was difficult, God knew, to stare into that handsome, hopeful face and not smile, but she did.

The grin that spread across his face at her suggestion promised sin of the most pleasurable sort. "Sounds like the best cure for my ills."

She wasn't going to let him get whatever he wanted that easily. She pointed at him with one indignant index finger. "Only if you follow your doctor's orders."

"I swear to God I will."

She laughed at his sincere expression.

She found a nice motel not far from the hospital and got a room with a king-sized bed in it. One bed. They entered their room without anything more than her fancy first aid kit and the smoky, soot-stained clothes on their backs.

She dropped the kit on the floor next to the door and toed off her shoes. "I'm so tired I could fall asleep right here."

"Shower first, then bed."

She nodded. "You first or me?"

"How about both?"

"I told you, no funny business until I'm sure your head is up to it."

He laughed. "I'm just offering to wash your back. I promise."

"Ha. Men have been promising that since the beginning of time, but you know what happens? They start with the front and never seem to get past that."

His smile slipped a little. "I need to touch you. I need to hold you and smell you and know for sure, for absolute sure that you're all right."

"But you're the one who got hurt."

"You're the one who risked her life to save me." He lifted a hand and ran the backs of his fingers over her cheek. "Please."

"You were scared for me?"

"Yeah." He shrugged one large shoulder. "It's part of the male DNA to feel like that when the woman he loves is neck deep in a burning tree."

She swallowed hard. Suddenly the room didn't have enough air in it.

Who needed air anyway?

"I'll start the water."

She went into the bathroom and started the tub filling, then stripped out of her clothes before she could chicken out and hide in the closet. She'd just stepped into the bathtub when the door opened and Jake came inside.

"How's the water?"

"Good. You coming in?"

"Try and stop me, darlin'."

She put shampoo in her hair and listened to him removing his clothes. She moved back under the showerhead to rinse the suds from her hair as he stepped into the tub. When she opened her eyes, she discovered him staring at her.

His gaze seemed trapped at chest level. It was the most intense stare she'd ever seen on his face. Ever.

"Jake?"

"You're gorgeous." His gaze finally met hers. "Perfect."

"Really? Because, well, I'm not . . . I mean I've never . . ."

His eyebrows rose so high they got lost in his hairline. "You're a virgin?"

"No, I've had one sexual partner, but it was in the dark and he couldn't see me any better than I could see him."

"When was this?"

"College. I thought I'd try it, you know, but it was disappointing. I figured I was just one of those women who can't achieve an orgasm."

"College kids rarely know what they're doing." He shifted closer and put both hands on her hips. "College guys are usually more interested in getting their rocks off than pleasing their partner."

"So maybe it's not me?"

His hands ran up her sides, his thumbs stroking the sides of her breasts, and he rested his forehead against hers. When he spoke, his voice came out like a deep rumble she could feel in the pit of her stomach. "When I make love to you, it's going to take hours."

"Hours?"

His hands moved to curve around her breasts, his thumbs brushing over her nipples in a feather-light caress. "Hours."

Already she felt more pleasure from just having his hands on her than she'd ever felt before. Her eyes drifted closed as he continued to stroke her, then he rolled her nipples between thumb and fingers and her eyes popped open. "You should stop."

Was that her out-of-breath voice?

"Why?"

"Because you have a concussion."

He whispered in her ear. "But you don't."

"You . . . you need at least twenty-four hours of total rest. No working, no talking on the phone, no stress of any kind."

"Sex relieves stress."

"Yeah, but it also raises your blood pressure. Please, as much as I want you to . . . do what you're doing, I'd rather we waited."

He sighed. "Okay. You're the boss." He pulled back and kissed her lightly on the lips. "You'll sleep with me."

It wasn't a question.

"Yes. I'll sleep with you."

"Good, I'd worry about you if you left."

She met his gaze. "I'm not going anywhere."

He smiled. "Hand me the soap. I'll actually wash your back."

Three days later they still hadn't done more than sleep together. After the twenty-four hour period was over, Jake went back to work, using the sheriff's office in Grand Forks, coordinating the flow of information to the victims of the Dead End fire. Most had ended up in Grand Forks, but some had gone to stay with relatives in other towns.

A quarter of the town had burned to the ground. Including the school, library and town hall. Everyone walked around in a semi-glazed state of shock. A state of emergency had been declared and the Federal Emergency Management Agency stepped in to help Dead End with the clean-up, removal of debris and emergency shelter for those that wanted to come back.

For some, Dead End was the only place they knew. Others never wanted to see the place again.

Nora spent most of her time at the arena where many of the town's citizens were staying. She provided on-the-spot medical care as well as helping with meal preparation and sorting of donated clothing and other items.

Dinner had just been served to the entire group when Jake walked in.

"How are things?" he asked as soon as he was close enough to talk.

In a place as public as this, he'd kept his distance and hadn't flirted with her as much.

"Good." She looked over the room, taking in the families eating together, the kids that were chasing each other around the tables. She realized things really were good. "Yeah," she said, turning back to him. "And getting better."

"Can you be spared for the rest of the evening? I have a meeting set up with some people and you're needed."

"Yes, I think so. Let me just tell the other volunteers I'm going." She told the women who were currently in charge that she was leaving, and then headed back to Jake. "Okay, I'm all yours."

He walked with her out to his new work truck, one donated to him to use until the town could get him another one, and opened the passenger door for her. He got in and he drove out of the parking lot.

"Where's this meeting and who's going to be there?"

"It's in our hotel room and it's just you and me."

"What about the people you mentioned?"

He grinned. "You and I are people."

Her heart started to pound. "So, what are we doing?"

"We're going to eat dinner in our room, then we're going to spend the rest of the night in bed." He glanced at her, his gaze an inferno. "Not sleeping."

Heat infused her face. "Oh."

"You okay with that?"

"Yes." She cleared her throat. "Yes."

His grin got wider.

The drive to their motel wasn't a long one and before she knew it she was in their room staring at a table set for two.

"Just give me a minute and I'll get the food," he said as he headed out into the night. Then he was gone and she was alone.

The bed looked awfully small for some reason.

She went to the bathroom to wash her face and hands and, when she got out, Jake was back with a bag full of takeout boxes.

"What is it?"

"Fried chicken, potatoes and all the fixings."

"Where'd you get that?"

"The owners of the motel mentioned a small family-run restaurant not far from here. I pre-ordered." He pulled out one of the chairs. "Have a seat."

She sat. He took the other chair and began dishing out the food.

"It smells really good."

They ate, Jake telling her about all the work FEMA and the State was doing to support the residents of Dead End.

"We should be able to turn the utilities on within the next few days," he said. "Then the hard work is going to start. Cleaning up and rebuilding."

"Some people lost everything."

"No one lost their life. That's important to remember."

She nodded. He was right, they'd lost material things, but not each other.

He stretched his hand across the table toward her, palm up. "Say yes."

She didn't pretend to be confused about what he meant. She put her hand in his. "Yes."

Jake stood, drawing her to her feet with him. Then he began a slow backward walk toward the bed. When his legs hit the mattress, he stopped, enfolded her in his arms and buried his face in her neck.

For several moments he did nothing more than breathe her in.

Her hands went around him and urged him as close as he could get.

"Sorry," he whispered. "I just need to hold you for a little while."

"I know. Me too."

Minutes later, his lips began a slow migration from her neck to her mouth. At first, his kisses were light, but they quickly changed into something more. A dessert she had no intention of passing up.

His hands roved her body, molding her ass, her breasts, cradling the back of her head as he took her mouth the way she prayed he'd take her body.

One of his hands found its way under her shirt and they broke apart to tear their clothes off. They came back together in a rush and fell on the bed.

Jake urged her onto her back and proceeded to kiss his way down her body.

Her fingers wrapped themselves in his short hair.

"Yes?" he asked. "You want something, darlin'?"

"You, I want you." Something on her face must have told him how much because his smile faded and he crawled up her body like a tiger on the hunt.

"You've got me."

"Wow."

The grin he gave her was all male pride.

He leaned over her and put his mouth next to her ear. "How long has it been?"

"Um, a few years."

He groaned. "I'm going to lose my mind."

She managed to choke out as he ravaged her with kisses, "People appreciate the things they work hard for."

He pushed against her and made her crazy with want. "More. I need more."

"Darlin', more is what you're going to get, but slow."

"I won't survive slow," she said on a gasp.

As he drove deeper, her orgasm hit her without warning, smacking her into a place she'd never experienced before. The pleasure rolled outward in a wave from her core; she could no more control the scream that roared out of her throat than she could've stopped the pleasure from overtaking her.

She came back to earth, muscles shaking. "Wow."

Jake started to laugh. "Still think it was you?"

"Nope. I've discovered that all my girl parts are fully . . . functional."

He laughed, a deep body-shaking sound that was the last piece of the puzzle that was Jake.

She turned her head to look at him. "I love you."

His eyebrows rose as his laugh turned into a grin. "Yeah? Already?"

"You think I just love your penis?"

That got him laughing again and he pulled out of her slowly.

"I love your calmness, your persistence and intelligence. You're funny, tough and brave."

He tilted his head at her. "Those things take a while to grow on a person."

"I've been watching you for a long time. I know who you are, but even if it scares you, understand this: I'm done playing it safe. You were the one who told me to grab life with both hands and enjoy the ride."

"Is there room for me in your ride?"

"Oh yeah."

He nodded and stroked a hand down her arm to entwine her fingers with his. "I know this is early, but I think it's only fair to warn you, I'm hoping for room for a wedding ring in that ride too."

Happiness had her grinning from ear to ear. "I've got a space all picked out for that. How about you?"

"Yeah." He cleared his throat. "I figure we could have an outdoor wedding in Dead End. Maybe invite the town too."

"That," she told him as she kissed him, "is the best idea I've ever heard."

TO LOOK FOR YOU

Alina Adams

Kosovo, 1999

By the third week of NATO's self-proclaimed humanitarian bombing of Yugoslavia, nineteen-year-old Alyssa Gordon, a United States Army medic assigned to the outskirts of the Macedonian border, no longer had any idea if the waves of patients constantly arriving at her makeshift field hospital were the Albanian refugees on whose behalf this military action had allegedly been launched, Serbian civilians whom the UN most sincerely assured were not the intended targets, or the actual Yugoslav soldiers their air strikes were aimed to flush out. All Alyssa knew was that the wounded and the shell-shocked and the cold and the hungry kept coming, and that it was her job – along with the dozen other equally overwhelmed and sleep-deprived US medics – to sort out who was who. It was also their job to decide who should be referred to a refugee center, who to surgery, who to the morgue.

Truth be told, by this point, Alyssa felt relieved to come across a body with no pulse, lying outside, exposed to the elements. It meant that all she had to do was tag it and move on to the next patient and the next and the next. It meant she didn't have to do anything useful. She didn't have to rack her brain trying to figure out how to keep someone alive long enough for a stretcher to show up and transport them to the actual hospital just a few yards behind her. The one that was so filled to the rafters they'd been forced to perform their initial triage on the wooded grounds around it. All the training they'd learned during their sixteen weeks of combat medic training had – in any case – been useless.

Alyssa was about to classify a young man with a gaping, bleeding chest wound and no detectable pulse as simply Dead On Arrival, when her overdeveloped sense of responsibility forced her to dutifully go through the checklist as she'd been taught. Only to discern that her patient, though lacking a pulse, was still breathing. That meant that he, most likely, was suffering from cardiac tamponade. A sharp object of unknown origin ricocheting through the air with the speed of a bullet had penetrated his heart, filling the tough membrane around it with blood, and preventing the heart from beating. But, he was still breathing. This man could still be saved. With surgery. Unfortunately, the time it would take her to summon a stretcher and get him carried to the hospital, not to mention queued and prepped, would also be the time it took to kill him. Alyssa had no idea how long he'd already been lying there without a pulse. But she knew making him wait any longer was out of the question.

She looked around desperately, willing a stretcher to appear out of nowhere. The nearest available one was on the far side of the field. Alyssa frantically waved it over, knowing all the while that they would be too late.

"I help you?" What did appear out of nowhere was a high-pitched voice just below Alyssa's elbow. It had been there for over a week now, ever since Alyssa had cleaned and wrapped some third-degree burns on the arm of a remarkably stoic little boy – he was roughly the size of a nine-year-old, but his ultra-serious demeanor suggested he might have been a few years older – and, as a result, ended up with a permanent shadow.

She'd tried to shoo him away. A few days earlier, she'd even personally taken him to the US refugee camp where kids like him – she had no idea if he was Albanian or Serb or what, but he was definitely on his own – were commanded to go. He ran away before nightfall and turned up back at the US base, looking for her, with his combination of broken English, deliberate charm, and gritty perseverance. Alyssa had thought maybe he wasn't comprehending the situation, and made the mistake of trying to speak to him in Russian, since he appeared to understand that language better – despite her own vocabulary freezing at the level of the ten-year-old she'd been upon emigrating to America from Moscow. But all that seemingly did was pin him to her side even more.

Alyssa had pretty much accepted the boy dogging her every move, to the point where she'd forgotten he was even there. Except that right now, his perennial question of "I help you?" had suddenly become relevant.

Alyssa had one chance to save the figure lying in front of her. And she definitely needed an extra pair of hands to so much as try.

"You want to help me, Leo?" Alyssa turned around so quickly that the boy nearly leapt in the air with surprise.

He recovered remarkably though, bobbing his head insistently up and down and assuring, "Yes. Yes, I help you."

"All right. This is what I am going to need you to do." She opened her medical kit, pulling out a thoracic scalpel, a large-blade instrument solid enough to slice through flesh, ribs, and muscle. It took all of Alyssa's strength. She practically had to lie down on the scalpel in order to bluntly cut the fat between the fifth and sixth ribs. "You." She indicated the spot to Leo with a sharp jerk of her chin. "You shove down on the center of his chest – yes, right there, perfect. I'm going to count, and every time I say a number, you're going to push, hard as you can, do you understand?"

Leo nodded and, with the same self-possession that had kept him biting down on his lip and not making a sound even as she removed his own charred flesh – a procedure so reportedly painful, Alyssa had witnessed combat soldiers break down and scream – did exactly as Alyssa ordered.

She counted off the chest compressions in rhythm, even as she sliced through layer after layer of muscle until her knife had perforated the chest cavity. Grateful that she'd just put on a pair of fresh gloves, Alyssa stuck her hand directly into the wound, probing deftly until she found the precise spot where her patient's heart had been nicked, immediately covering the point of entry firmly with her thumb to keep any more blood from draining out.

She waited, holding her own breath even as she ordered Leo to keep their man breathing.

A beat. And then, right there against her palm, the heart muscle contracted.

Alyssa exhaled in exhilaration and relief. "We've got a pulse," she said.

Just in time for the stretcher to make its timely appearance, complete with a two-man crew who promptly took over for Alyssa and Leo, prepping the patient for his trip to the hospital – and surgery in slightly less primitive conditions.

As they took the wounded man away, Alyssa slumped to the ground, her chin practically between her upraised knees, the surge of adrenaline draining away as quickly as it had come, leaving her utterly spent and unable to look at another body. Not right now. Maybe not ever again. Her hands were coated in blood up to the elbows, as was the front of her olive-green fatigues. Crimson specks dotted the dog tags thumping against her chest where her heart was now beating quickly enough to make up for the time her patient had lost earlier.

She felt a hand patting her shoulder. "You good?"

"No," Alyssa told him honestly, choking on a bitter laugh that came out more like a sob. "Not good. Not good at all."

Leo gave the declaration some thought, then optimistically proposed, "You better soon?"

"Well." She considered his prediction, clinging to the one fact that had kept her going the past few months. "I'm going home next week. That's good."

"Home?" he sounded like he didn't know what the word meant. And like he knew precisely.

"Not exactly home," she conceded. "But back to America. Away from here."

"Home," he repeated slowly, this time clearly not liking what he'd heard.

"Yeah." She craned her neck to get a good look at him, finding Leo's face in that moment utterly inscrutable. About the only emotion she could clearly discern was anger. But about what? Her? Was he honestly . . . What gave him the right to be mad at her? She certainly hadn't promised . . . It wasn't her responsibility . . . She didn't owe this boy anything, after all, not a damn thing. Who did he think he was? Didn't he know what Alyssa had been through already?

"No," Leo suddenly blurted, reaching out abruptly and,

before Alyssa could stop him, grabbing her dog tags, yanking hard enough to rip them off her neck.

"Hey, wait a minute!" Her hand went to her throat in shock. She attempted to grab the tags back, but Leo was too fast for her.

Before Alyssa had managed to stagger to her feet, swaying sickeningly from light-headedness, Leo was turning and running away from her, ducking stretchers and leaping over prostrate bodies in a manner Alyssa's weary legs couldn't hope to match.

And so she didn't even bother trying.

New York City, 2013

For Dr Alyssa Gordon, five years in an Upper Manhattan Emergency Room had turned even literal life-and-death scenarios into a predictable, downright comforting routine. She moved efficiently from asthma attacks to broken bones to heart failures to overdoses to gun and knife wounds. She'd delivered babies in the distance from the parking lot to the Emergency Room doors, and talked down addicts ready to throttle her for a fix.

When the dispatch call arrived regarding an incoming ambulance transporting an elderly Caucasian male presenting with symptoms of kidney stones, Alyssa ordered her team to get the spiral CT scan ready, as well as an IVP X-ray. She told the lab to be on the lookout for a urine sample and a blood chemistry screen, and she ordered a normal saline IV that could also serve to dispatch pain medication as necessary.

Everything was ready by the time the patient arrived, and Alyssa proceeded to give him her full, practiced attention. Except for the fact that, even as she went through the prescribed motions, Alyssa couldn't help being briefly distracted by the paramedic who had brought the old man in.

He had to be new. At least to Alyssa's shift. Otherwise, she was sure she would have noticed him earlier. Not that Alyssa was frequently distracted by the paramedics on duty. But there was something about this one that particularly drew her attention. And it wasn't just the fact that he stood well over six feet tall, with shoulders so muscular and broad she could easily imagine him lifting an entire gurney, complete with victim, all on his own. While administering the appropriate first aid. And steering the ambulance.

It also wasn't just the sandy hair, cropped closely, almost military style – the better to emphasize the constantly shifting hazel of his eyes, or the way his entire face looked like it had been not carved, but forcibly ripped from a block of concrete.

And it wasn't even his hands, surprisingly long and limber, especially considering the width of his forearms, almost as if each individual finger had been blessed with an extra joint, making them more nimble and sensitive as a result.

It was more all of those things put together. And, at the same time, none of them.

Alyssa told herself there was nothing wrong with looking – discreetly. She was engaged, after all, and had been for the past three years. She wasn't suffering from central corneal ulceration.

And besides, it was not like Alyssa was even attracted to this new medic. It was more that he seemed . . . familiar somehow. Maybe he'd worked at the hospital before, or maybe she'd met him during residency or internship, though that was unlikely. He appeared to be in his mid-twenties and, at age thirty-three, Alyssa doubted there were a lot of places they could have crossed paths professionally.

Not to mention, he didn't look like the type of guy easy to forget.

"Yo, Leo!" His partner, already standing by the Emergency Room door, yelled. "Come on, let's go, we've got another call!"

Alyssa's head jerked up at the name. "Leo . . .?" Her mouth formed the sounds, but considering how loudly her heart suddenly began beating in response, she couldn't be sure he'd even heard her.

He must have. Because when Alyssa called his name – "Leo! Leo!" – he looked up, met her eyes, and smiled.

Right before taking off without a word.

Again.

She waited for two hours after her own shift was over just so she could catch Leo as he was leaving the hospital. When he saw her standing by the exit to the Emergency Room, he didn't appear surprised. Well, that made one of them.

"Leo?" she repeated, as if this still might be a case of mistaken identity. Just two men of roughly the same age with the same name. And the same way of looking right through her.

He nodded with a half-smile, tapping his chest with an open palm, eyes still boring into hers.

"You've . . . grown," she babbled, realizing how inane she sounded even as she utterly lacked any ability to stop.

He nodded again.

Funny, Alyssa didn't remember him being so agreeable as a kid. Well, he wasn't a kid any more, was he? Alyssa guessed he must be . . . "How old are you?" she asked.

"Twenty-five," was his answer, the pipsqueak voice Alyssa recalled from fourteen years ago deeper and more raspy now. And a lot less accented.

"What are you doing here?" Alyssa posed the one other query that came to mind. No, that wasn't true. She had dozens of questions running through her head. This was merely the one that sounded least self-centered.

In one smooth swoop, Leo pulled the silver chain from under his shirt that had been hanging around his neck for, from the looks of it, years now.

He pressed the necklace into her palm, wrapping Alyssa's fingers around it. Her dog tags. The ones for which she'd had to compose an official report explaining how they'd been lost. She'd blamed it on the heat of battle. Declining to mention that a United States Army medic had, in effect, been mugged by a wounded, eleven-year-old refugee.

"I came to look for you," Leo explained, just before fading away into the night.

"'I came to look for you'? That's what he said? 'I came to look for you'?" Alyssa's fiancé, John Mason, leaned back against the headboard, looking down at Alyssa with bemused, yet languid interest. One of the benefits to living with a fellow doctor was that John's schedule was as atypical as hers, so both could still be in bed at the crack of noon, dissecting Alyssa's interesting night at the ER.

"That's what I think he said." To be honest, the entire encounter was starting to feel more and more like a fever dream.

"How come you never told me about this kid before?"

"You don't like it when I talk about Kosovo."

"I don't like it when you talk about how miserable you were there. What guy would like that? But, this is interesting. Some little kid gets a crush on the brave, heroic American medic . . ."

"He didn't have a crush on me. He was an eleven-year-old boy in the middle of a war zone. He was hurt, he was scared."

"I don't know, he sounds pretty fearless to me. There's a reason I went into anaesthesiology – so I would never have to cut a guy open in the middle of a field."

"You went into anaesthesiology because it pays well and has regular hours."

"And doesn't involve making my patients bite down on sticks while I slice and dice them. You're a better man than I am, Dr Gordon, that's well established. Hell, the fact that you even considered going to medical school after what you saw in Kosovo . . ."

"I only joined the Army so I could pay for college. What would have been the point of quitting after the hard part was over?"

"Most people think of medical school, and internship and residency as the hard part."

"Yeah, well, frame of reference, you know?"

"Like I was saying. You're a badass. What little boy wouldn't fall in love with you under those circumstances?"

"How did we get from crush to in love?"

"Same thing to a kid."

"He's no kid any more," Alyssa pointed out.

"Oh, come on. He's eight years younger than you. That's always going to be a kid."

"You're eight years older than me," Alyssa pointed out. "Do you see me as a kid?"

John scrunched his face. "I refuse to answer the question on the grounds that it may incriminate me. If I say yes, you'll accuse me of not respecting you. If I say no, you'll claim I've called you old. It's a lose-lose for me."

"Since when have I ever acted like that?"

"There's always a first time for everything," John noted.

"What say we break our pattern here?" Alyssa proposed the next time she made a point of seeking out Leo, now while he was in the cafeteria on a break. She took the metal chair in front of the door, so that if he made another run for it, he'd have to get through her first.

The look on Leo's face, however, suggested he had no idea why she was acting so cautiously. He would never consider running from her, the look said. Especially not when he had his delicious helping of hospital-issued red Jell-O and whipped cream to leisurely spoon into his mouth.

God, had he been this infuriatingly unshakable as a kid? Alyssa didn't remember. Then again, she'd barely known him a week, and most of the time they'd been knee-deep in injured soldiers, civilians, and refugees. They hadn't exactly had much opportunity for in-depth acquaintance. Alyssa might have even thought she'd made up the whole thing, blown their battlefield camaraderie way out of proportion due to the intensity of the war. Except there was the . . .

"Why did you hold on to these?" Alyssa pulled the dog tags out of her pocket and laid them on the table between them like a bridge between then and now.

Leo turned the tags over, treating them with the same sort of delicacy Alyssa could imagine him employing to probe an elderly person's broken hip or when inserting an emergency IV into the fragile vein atop the skull of a prematurely born infant.

"Your name." He pointed at the heavily weatherworn and scuffed tags.

"You kept them because they had my name?"

He nodded. "And this number. I did not know what it was."

"That's my social security number," Alyssa explained. "And that's the branch of service."

"Yes. I know. Now."

"What did you need my name for?"

"To look for you," he reminded her, surprised that she'd forgotten. Hadn't he been perfectly clear the night before? "The number, it helped, also."

"Why?" she asked, flabbergasted. "I mean, why did you bother?"

Leo didn't say anything. He merely put down his Jell-O spoon on the plastic tray and leaned back in his chair, studying her from beneath half-mast eyelids. Alyssa had previously learned not to read too much into that particular expression. Lots of people at the hospital looked at her like that. It didn't mean much beyond that they were likely sleep-deprived. But Leo's gaze didn't come off as sleep-deprived. It came off as composed, and controlled, and knowledgeable. It came off like not only did he know what he was thinking, but she knew what he was thinking. And he knew that she knew. So what was there left to say?

Quite a bit, actually. Mainly because Alyssa had no idea what she was thinking. Maybe he'd consider filling her in?

No. That would be a very, very bad idea.

Especially since Leo looked like he might be gearing up to do precisely that.

So Alyssa cut him off at the pass. She said, "You . . . This . . . This is a bad idea."

"I am a bad idea?" he repeated quizzically, stymied either by the sentiment or the syntax.

"I'm engaged," Alyssa said. Which wasn't any kind of answer to his question, at all. Except in her head. There, it made perfect sequential sense.

"Married?" he asked.

"Kind of. Almost. Soon." That sounded kind of defensive, didn't it? Alyssa figured she'd best switch to offense, and quickly. "You shouldn't have . . . Why would you . . . Did you get your job here because of me?"

Just saying the words out loud made Alyssa squirm. It sounded so egotistical, as if she honestly believed the entire world revolved around her, and that a kid – well, a man now – she knew a lifetime ago would purposefully relocate himself from one continent to another, following the path of a pair of old dog tags like some sort of Holy Grail.

"Yes," he said simply, using far fewer words than she had to express the same thing.

"That's . . . Oh . . . I . . . You shouldn't have done that."

"I am a good paramedic," he insisted. "I completed my training in America."

"I'm sure you're great! In fact, I know you're great. I watched you the other night with the kidney stone that came in."

"I learned from you," Leo said. "I wanted to be like you."

Oh . . . So . . . Had she misunderstood? Had she just made a complete fool of herself? Alyssa was pretty good at both, barring standardized tests or on-the-spot diagnostics. Had she assumed all sorts of things about Leo's motives based on her own ego?

Had Leo merely meant that, "You mean you wanted to be a medic, like me?"

"Yes."

Well, that was certainly a relief. (Wasn't it?) Alyssa felt like she could breathe again. So John been right, after all – to a point. The little wounded boy had been inspired by the American soldier who'd dressed his wounds and allowed him to come along and even help with her work. Alyssa had inspired Leo to go into medicine, to help others. She'd given him a purpose and a goal, both so vital in a time of war and chaos. That's what he'd meant. That's why he'd come looking for her. To tell Alyssa that . . .

"I love you," Leo added.

"He sounds like a stalker," John said, no longer nearly as amused by her tale as he'd been the day before.

"You're exaggerating."

"Uh, let's see." John stood in front of the closet, peeling off his work clothes in order to change into the gym shorts he wore to play basketball. "He stole your personal identifying information . . ."

"He didn't even know what those dog tags were when he grabbed them."

"So he says." John slipped on his T-shirt. "He used them to track you down, and get a job at the same place you work."

"He's a paramedic. I'm an Emergency Room doctor. We tend to work at the same places."

"And now he just told you he loves you. In between scoops of Jell-O."

"He was done by then."

"Yesterday, you thought I wasn't taking this guy seriously. Now who's whistling past a graveyard?"

"He's harmless. You were right. It's a little kid crush."

"And you were the one who told me he wasn't a little kid any more."

"I'm sorry, did you have a court stenographer in our bedroom?"

"Remind me and I'll bring one in next time, so you'll remember what you said."

"He's had fourteen years to build up an idealized image of me in his head. Give him a week in my ER, and that'll be blown to smithereens. Along with any leftover hero worship."

"You should report him to the Chief of Staff."

"For doing what?"

"He's a stalker. He could be dangerous. What? Don't look at me like that. He's got all the markers of PTSD."

"Having a crush on me is a sign of post-traumatic stress disorder?"

"Do the math, Alyssa. War-torn childhood, injury, he was probably orphaned. You don't know how he might have been abused in those UN refugee camps before he grew big enough to defend himself. Likely a history of hunger, too, which can lead to all sorts of developmental delays, both physical and mental. He's the poster boy for PTSD. And now he's become fixated on you as his saviour. Well, what if you're right? What happens if one week in the ER with you really does shatter his delusions? What happens then? What if he snaps? You don't want to protect yourself? Fine. How about your patients? What happens if, as a result of his psychotic break, he takes a few innocent people down with him?"

"I need to understand." After prying the address out of Human Resources, Alyssa had shown up at Leo's apartment unannounced. He didn't seem surprised to see her. Then again, as Alyssa was beginning to learn, Leo rarely seemed surprised by anything. At least, he didn't express it. She wondered if that destroyed John's long-distance diagnosis of post-traumatic stress disorder, or merely confirmed it.

Alyssa tried to subtly search for other signs even as she accepted Leo's invitation to come in. The one-room studio at the top of a five-floor walk-up – despite Leo presumably not expecting company – was impeccably neat, almost hospital spotless, if Alyssa did say so herself. No dust on the television, no dirty dishes in the sink, a thin but obviously laundered navy blue spread tucked all around the bed in the corner. There was, in fact, nothing to indicate that this place belonged to a twenty-something bachelor.

Except for, you know, the twenty-something bachelor standing in the midst of it.

Because he hadn't been expecting company, Leo was a bit more disheveled than she'd seen him at work. He was barefoot, wearing an army surplus pair of shorts and a T-shirt that was also obviously recently laundered – having shrunk in the wash to the point where it clung to him just a bit more tightly than Alyssa suspected the manufacturer had intended. She could see the outline of his abdominal muscles, each ab a coil of rope that served to keep him standing so straight, towering over Alyssa, so that she was forced to look up to make eye contact. From that angle, she had a particularly good view of the stubble beneath his chin, and had to hold the wrist of one hand down with the other to keep from reaching out and brushing her fingers against it, just to see what it might feel like. Soft? Rough? And what might that say about the rest of him?

No. Alyssa forced her gaze – and wayward limbs – away from Leo and planted it firmly onto a neutral object. Would you just look at the hospital corners on that bed? Excellent work. She briefly recalled the sort of conditions Leo had been forced to endure during the few days she'd known him, and who knew for how long thereafter? The UN refugee camp was such a squalid madhouse of disorder, disease and corruption, with the few precious resources like clean water, fresh food and mattresses not covered in human fluids and lice going to either the strongest or those capable of offering the biggest bribe. Leo wasn't the only internee who preferred to take his chances out in the surrounding open woods rather than expose himself to the dubious mercy of humanitarian aid. Alyssa knew that her own exposure to such conditions – even with the knowledge that she was eventually getting the hell out of there – had instilled in her a love for order, hygiene, and indoor plumbing.

"How long have you lived here?" Alyssa realized that as the one who'd dropped by unexpectedly, the responsibility for explaining her presence and making general conversation fell on her shoulders.

"First of the month," Leo said.

"You mean you just moved in?"

"Yes."

"Here, or to New York, in general?"

"Yes," he repeated, with a touch of a twinkle in his eyes that suggested Leo knew how infuriating he was being. And that he was getting a kick out of it.

Alyssa realized that should make her like him less. Unfortunately, it only made her like him more. It was good to see his spirit still intact, playful even. It made everything so much easier. And so much more difficult.

"You just moved to New York this month? Where were you before?"

"Wisconsin."

"Wisconsin? What were you doing in Wisconsin?"

"University," Leo explained. "I requested a list of American universities, and I presented a letter to each one, explaining my situation and asking if there is please any way in which I might study there for no cost? Wisconsin responded. They helped me to get my student visa and many other details. I am most grateful to Wisconsin."

"Your situation," Alyssa repeated, realizing this was the largest number of words he'd ever spoken to her. She wondered if they were finally making progress. And she might finally be able to get some real answers. "What . . . What was your . . . situation? I mean, after I . . . we . . . after the American troops withdrew?"

He shrugged, as if the story was both not worth telling, and way too long to even try. "Bad," was as far as Leo would go. "Difficult. Not only for me. For everyone. It was bad for everyone. But I am lucky."

"You mean, because of getting the chance to go to school here? That wasn't luck. That was obviously your hard work and—"

"No. I am lucky, because I always knew where I wanted to be."

"America?" she guessed somewhat desperately.

"Yes." Leo nodded his head slowly. Making it clear that was not what he'd been talking about at all. But if it made Alyssa more comfortable . . . okay then.

She said, "You know, you had my dog tags. You had my name and my social security number. You could have tracked me down a long time ago. Asked me for help or . . . anything. I would have helped you." At least, Alyssa hoped that might be true.

"I did not want help," he clarified.

"Then what do you want?"

"You."

"Well, you can't have me." Alyssa all but stomped on his assertion with the heel of her boot. "You can't, do you understand? While you were getting your life together, I was trying to do the same thing. Now, I'm not going to pretend that what I went through over there was even a fraction of what you did. But it was still hard to get back into the swing of regular life. I finished my tour of duty and I came back to the States and I went to college. With a bunch of eighteen-year-old, middle-class kids who thought ending war was just a matter of lighting a bunch of candles and marching around with them while singing 'Give Peace a Chance'. Gee, why didn't any of us over in Kosovo think of that? I tried to tell them. I tried to explain how the world really works. But, eighteen-year-olds think they know everything. Especially when the worst thing that ever happened to them was that a guy didn't call when he said he would. I went through college being treated like a freak. Medical school was hardly better. I didn't start feeling like I belonged anywhere until after I started my residency. I thought I wanted nothing to do with the Emergency Room. I'd had enough. But, in the end, it was the only place I fit in. I'm good at it. I'm really good at my job."

"Yes. I know. I see."

"And do you know why I'm good at it? Because an Emergency Room is the most predictable place in the hospital. Yeah, I get it. That's not how most people think. But it is. You know exactly what's going to happen in an Emergency Room. Patient comes in, you evaluate him, you deal with whatever the issue is, and then you move on to the next one. And the next, and the next. Everything is constant. There's an equilibrium."

"Like in the ambulance," Leo said, clearly not just agreeing but understanding.

"Exactly! That's what I want in my life. In the Emergency Room, I'm in charge. I know that I can handle anything that gets thrown at me. Even if I lose a patient – and that happens, I'm not perfect; no one is perfect. But, even when that happens, it's okay, because I just move on to the next one. I can anticipate the future. I hate surprises, Leo. Have I mentioned that? I like predicting what's going to happen, because I like planning my response in advance. It's great in an Emergency Room. Not so great anywhere else."

"I am a surprise," Leo said, chewing on each word she'd said and trying to put it in context with her outburst.

Alyssa hadn't meant it like that exactly. Except now she realized that she had.

"Yes," she agreed with a sigh. And then she felt compelled to explain further. "My fiancé, his name is John Mason. Except that's not really his name. When he was a kid, his name was Rolling Stone. Yeah. Really. Not because he was Native American or anything like that. But, because his parents were these peace, love, and rock and roll hippies who had him on a commune. A bunch of communes, actually. They moved from place to place because they'd either get bored or the pot would run out or the law would catch up with them for shoplifting or whatever they'd done most recently to stick it to the man. They named John after their favorite band, and then they didn't even stick around much to take care of him. They kept dumping him on other people. Growing up, when John woke up in the morning, he didn't know where he'd be or who he'd be with or if there'd be anything to eat. When he was a teenager, he found out his parents were just playing at being poor and living off the land. Whenever things got really rough, they went back to their rich parents, taking their money while they made fun of them for being boring and bourgeois. Well, boring and bourgeois sounded pretty damn nice to John. Soon as he could, he ran away and went to live with his grandparents. Changed his name – Mason from Stone, you know, and John because, well, because he thought it would piss off his mom and dad the most. He finally went to school – had to do some ridiculous catching up, it's not like he'd been taught to read or write or, God forbid, calculus. Then medical school. Now he's an anaesthesiologist. Because it's steady and regular and boring and bourgeois. It's why we're together. We both don't like surprises. We both like knowing what's coming up tomorrow. We both like to be prepared."

"I am sorry."

"What?" It was the last response she'd been expecting. "For me? You feel sorry for me?"

He nodded. "I am sorry you are so scared all the time."

She opened her mouth to deny it as a matter of course. Then realized what he said was the absolute truth.

"I don't have to be," Alyssa said. "As long as my life stays the way I like it. I . . . Remember what I told you a long time ago? About how I wasn't born in America? How I came from Moscow when I was little? Well, again, I'm not saying what I went through was anything close to what you suffered. But I also have some idea of what it feels like to have your life just flipped upside down on you with no warning. My parents never got over it. They're the ones who wanted to come here, but . . . My mother was a college chemistry professor back in Russia, but her English wasn't good enough here, so she ended up working in some lab. My dad didn't even try to get a job. All he did was sit in Section eight housing, collect welfare checks, do odd jobs for cash so he didn't have to report it, and talk about how dumb and easy to scam all Americans were. I hated it. I told myself, that wasn't going to be me. At least, if you stick to the straight and narrow, that's one monkey you can get off your back."

Leo smiled. This was his first smile that Alyssa didn't feel confused or discomfited by. Maybe because it seemed so genuine. Or maybe because it made him look so damn cute. "Today then, you have come here to tell the monkey that is me to get off your back."

Again, she wanted to say no. Except that he'd hit the nail on the head perfectly. Even before she herself was aware of it.

She said, "I can't have this . . . you . . . in my life. Not like this. You don't . . . fit."

"I am sorry."

"It's not your fault. I mean, my issues, they aren't your fault."

"I am sorry," he repeated. "I will not bother you again."

"You're not bothering me!" This had all gone so easily, Alyssa didn't know how to react. "I don't blame your for anything. You took me by surprise, that's all. You're a very good paramedic. I hope we can continue working together. I . . . we . . . the hospital . . . we need you."

"This would not make you uncomfortable?" he asked.

Now it was Alyssa's turn to smile. "Not if I know it's coming."

The next time Alyssa saw Leo, he was bringing a little boy into the Emergency Room who'd fallen out a window. Alyssa was about to start issuing her traditional set of orders, when she realized that Leo had already implemented half of them. With a quick smile of gratitude, she jumped straight in, pleasantly surprised to find him anticipating her actions, almost as if he were reading her mind. Alyssa barely had to ask for pertinent diagnostic information before it was rattled off to her. She moved to start an IV only to find that Leo had beaten her to it.

He finished his duties and deftly stepped aside, letting the Emergency Room nurses pick up where he had left off.

"Nice job," Alyssa called at his departing figure.

He winked. "You may depend on me."

He wasn't kidding. Transfer went just as smoothly with the next patient he brought in, and the one after that. Within a week, Alyssa and Leo had developed a reputation as the most efficient team at the hospital. They didn't even have to speak. They predicted each other's actions, moving in synch and with mutual understanding to the point where Alyssa could have her back to him and still know where Leo was at any given moment, and how she should react accordingly. His inexperience compared to her wasn't a problem. The slight ongoing language barrier wasn't a problem. The only thing that proved a problem was how Alyssa felt every time she saw Leo stride in through the Emergency Room doors.

She felt great.

Which was a problem.

All Alyssa needed was to hear from the dispatcher the number of the ambulance that was scheduled to bring in her next patient, and her heart would begin beating faster. She found herself looking forward to a crisis, feeling genuinely happy that someone had been hurt badly enough to require medical care. She doubted that would be interpreted as a positive development.

And then there was just seeing Leo. It didn't matter what lay between them – a heart attack, a hemorrhaging ectopic pregnancy, a stabbing, a fractured skull; hell, even projectile vomiting wasn't an adequate deterrent – as soon as Alyssa saw Leo, he became the most important person in the room to her.

Not that Alyssa ignored her patients; by any means. If anything, her work had actually improved since Leo started showing up. In Leo's presence, all of her senses were heightened. She could see better, hear better, feel better, even diagnose better. It was as if being around Leo made her invincible. And even if she wasn't, just feeling that way for the first time in her life was pretty nice, too.

For his part, Leo remained utterly and completely professional. She could definitely depend on him for that. He obeyed Alyssa's directions and he kept a respectful distance at all times. Of course, in the controlled chaos of an Emergency Room, that respectful distance might, periodically, be less than a hair's breadth away. They brushed against each other moving from station to station. Her gloved fingers sometimes caressed his as Leo efficiently passed over an IV bag or BVM Resuscitator. Were a pair of gloved hands meeting for a split second supposed to trigger a spark powerful enough to make Alyssa turn towards the EKG machine, certain that the spike must have registered?

Did Leo feel any of the same things she was feeling? Alyssa had no idea. As per his word, their interactions now were strictly and utterly professional. He was polite and he was thorough and he was brilliant. While remaining suitably distant. Which was exactly how Alyssa wanted it.

Why exactly was it how Alyssa wanted it, again?

Oh, right. Because it made her life easier.

Sure didn't feel like it at the moment.

Luckily, life in the Emergency Room didn't leave Alyssa a lot of time to dwell on the irony of it all. And it made a great excuse as to why she hadn't done anything about it yet. Much easier to focus on the stabbing victim that Leo and his partner had just brought in than to stop and ponder the state of her own heart.

"No pulse," Leo reported, and Alyssa nodded to indicate she'd heard.

They went through the standard litany of recovery techniques. No response. He was breathing, but likely not for long.

"Cardiac tamponade," Alyssa mumbled, more to herself than anyone else. They needed an available operating room, stat.

She turned to tell Leo to get the patient quickly prepped for surgery. Their eyes met and, for a split second – no more than that, truly – she wavered. He had this way of looking at her, like a perennial question that only she had the answer to. He'd looked at her that way as a child and he continued to as an adult. Only the effects were markedly different. Back then, she'd been so tired and overwhelmed and scared that all she'd wanted to do was shout "No" to anything and everything that came her way. Now, the question in his eyes was completely different. And all Alyssa could think of to say was, "Yes."

She nodded. It was a practically imperceptible gesture. And it didn't mean a damn thing, not really.

Except that Leo apparently thought otherwise.

Before Alyssa even realized what has happening, he'd grabbed a scalpel off a nearby tray and proceeded to slice their patient open, sticking his hand in the chest cavity in order to plug up the massive bleeding coming from the heart – exactly the same way she'd done fourteen years earlier, stranded in a Kosovo field.

Stunned by what he'd done, Alyssa nevertheless acted on instinct, supporting his efforts, calling for the nurses to join them, to provide blood and oxygen, anything to keep the patient stable just long enough to get him to the operating room.

But, it all proved for naught. He died on the elevator, between floors.

And when the Chief of Staff heard about had happened, she requested to see Alyssa and Leo. Immediately.

"Do you realize how much trouble we could all be in?" the Chief of Staff demanded, looking from Alyssa to Leo as if expecting them to come up with a quantifiable number. "By what stretch of the imagination could what the two of you did today be considered acceptable procedure for the treatment of cardiac tamponade?"

"In the field—" Alyssa began.

Only to be cut off with the reminder, "This isn't the Alamo, Dr Gordon."

Duly noted.

The Chief of Staff continued, "Did you authorize this procedure, Doctor?"

"No," Leo burst in to answer before Alyssa had the chance. "No. She did not."

"You decided to perform it on your own?" All attention focused on the young paramedic.

"Yes," Leo said without a moment's hesitation.

The Chief of Staff paused, and then pronounced, "You are both hereby placed on suspension, pending a formal review. The next time you come here, you may wish to bring your lawyers with you."

"But, you didn't authorize it," John insisted for what felt like the umpteenth time, speaking slowly, as if to a particularly dim child. "You said yourself, this guy went cowboy on you. Which, may I add, for the record, I warned you about weeks ago. Why are you beating yourself up over a mistake he already admitted making?"

"First of all, I'm not certain it was a mistake. It may very well have been the patient's only chance."

"Well, now we'll never know, will we?"

"And second of all, Leo thinks I gave him the okay."

"The Mysterious Nod of Mystifying Mystery?"

She really wished he wouldn't call it that. But . . . "Yes."

"A head twitch. You're willing to throw away your entire career on a head twitch?"

"He thought he was acting on my orders."

"Which, once again, brings us to: He screwed up, not you."

"Because of me. It happened because of me. Any other doctor . . . Let's just say it wouldn't have happened with any other doctor."

"He's got a lot less to lose than you do," John pointed out. "He's only been on the job, what? A couple of weeks? He hasn't been anywhere long enough to build a reputation. He'll go somewhere else and start fresh. He won't even need to mention this."

"Criminal charges could be filed," Alyssa pointed out. "He could go to jail. At best, he might be deported."

"You could go to jail," John countered. "And you might not be deported, but you'll lose everything you spent years building. Good luck finding another position at a respectable hospital. You'll be a pariah now. Say goodbye to any sort of professional or financial stability. Anywhere you go, you'll spend half your time waiting for your past to catch up with you, and the other half wondering what will happen when it finally does. Because it will. And you'll be right back where you started. Everything will be gone again. Only that time, it'll be even worse. Is that really how you want to live the rest of your life?"

"You know it isn't," she snapped. Wondering what was so great about being with a person who knew you so well, when all that meant was they had more ammunition to throw back in your face when everything was falling apart?

"Then why are we even discussing this? Jesus Christ, Alyssa, I thought you were somebody I could count on here."

She blinked, as if abruptly plucked from one conversation and deposited into another. "You? What does this have to do with you?"

"It has to do with me feeling like, when the chips are down, I can't trust you to have my back."

"But that's exactly what I'm trying to do with Leo now."

"This Leo guy is a total stranger. You're choosing a total stranger over yourself. That doesn't speak of very good judgement on your part. I've got to admit, it scares me. If you're this ready to throw your own hard-earned career under a bus, how do I know you won't do the same with mine one day in the name of an equally lost cause?"

"I am taking responsibility for my actions. It's the right thing to do."

"You didn't authorize the procedure," John continued as if Alyssa hadn't spoken. "The kid went off half-cocked, and he owned up to it. Oh, and here's one more thing to think about.

You're sure you gave that nod, but even you have no idea what you were doing. Maybe it didn't really happen. Maybe you just think it did. Maybe the Mighty Medic isn't falling on his sword for you. Maybe he's just telling the truth, and you've got nothing to think about. Or ruin your career over."

"What did you think I meant," Alyssa asked Leo, this time not just barging into his apartment, but calling ahead and taking a seat on one of two chairs that flanked his rickety table, "when I nodded my head at you?"

Leo turned the other chair around, straddling it backwards, resting his elbows on the back, tapping his fingers nervously against the wood. "I . . . I do not know," he confessed.

"You mean, you didn't think I was telling you to go ahead and perform the procedure?" Alyssa leapt on his statement with hope. And despair.

"I believed you said yes, to go and do it. But, if you say you did not . . ."

"If you thought I'd really said it, then why did you lie?"

"You were scared." Leo did not budge from where he was sitting. And yet, suddenly, Alyssa felt as if the fingers tapping the chair had reached forward and begun to caress her face. "I did not wish you to be scared."

"You are not responsible for taking care of me!" She bristled. Strangely delighted.

"You took care of me," Leo reminded, shifting his arm so that Alyssa could see the scars still left from the long-ago burns she'd dressed. "You. No one else."

"I was just doing my job."

"Me, too," he told her, leaving the rest unsaid.

"Well, Dr Gordon?" The Chief of Staff waited expectantly.

Alyssa did not say a word. As her superior had advised earlier, she'd brought a lawyer with her to this follow-up meeting. And it was the lawyer who now coolly and efficiently explained, "My client's statement at this time is that, in the incident under discussion, she did not in any way grant permission for the procedure that transpired."

* * *

"That's my girl!" John swept Alyssa off the floor and spun her around. When he set her down, she felt vaguely nauseated. Or was that just the taste of self-loathing? "Nothing to it, just like I told you. See, the truth really will set you free!"

"I didn't tell the truth," Alyssa corrected.

"Yes, you did," he insisted. "You did not authorize the procedure. You can't be held responsible for what goes on in the head of some inexperienced MD wannabe. Come on, if that were the case, none of us would keep our medical licenses past six months!"

"Leo took the blame for me."

"Leo took the blame because Leo deserves the blame. But, why are we still even talking about this? We should be celebrating! Or, better yet, planning. I've been thinking, enough is enough. What do you say we finally go ahead and set the date? Let's get our life together started!"

She blinked at him in confusion. "What brought that on all of a sudden?"

"What are we waiting for?"

"What have we been waiting for the past three years?"

"Well, obviously, for the time to be right."

"And the time is right now?"

"You had some growing up to do, Alyssa."

"So committing perjury is, what, a bar mitzvah?"

"You didn't commit perjury. But you did make the right decision. I couldn't be more proud of you."

"Leo's been fired," she said.

John shrugged. "He should have been more careful."

"You would have been more careful," Alyssa guessed.

"Hell, yes. I'm not about to throw my life away on some ridiculous Hail Mary pass procedure. Especially not one most Emergency Rooms deliberately avoid using."

"You would have been too scared to take the chance."

John shrugged, unoffended. "I'd have been more sensible, damn right."

"Even if it cost your patient his life?"

"Guy's dead anyway. Why drag innocent people down with him?"

Alyssa said, "I can't marry you, John."

There was something he hadn't seen coming. And John prided himself on being able to see everything coming. Especially where Alyssa was concerned.

"Excuse me?"

"I can't marry you."

"You're kidding." He appeared poised for the follow up "gotcha". That never came. "I urge you to do the right thing, I pull your ass out of a fire you seem determined to stick it in, and this is the thanks I get?"

"This isn't about that," Alyssa said softly, wondering how she could make him understand.

"Right. You change your mind about marrying me after your precious pet, Leo, gets in trouble because of Big Bad John. It's all just a coincidence."

"I don't blame you for what happened with Leo."

"Gee, thanks."

"The blame lies with me, no one else."

"So how come I'm the one getting the boot here?"

"I can't." Alyssa's hands rose, as if to illustrate a point. "I won't go on like this. I've done it for too long as it is."

"What? Ramble incoherently?"

She dropped her hands to her sides. "You're scared all the time, John. Scared of losing what you've got, scared of ending up with nothing, scared of what might come next. It's okay. I'm exactly the same way."

"You know, some people might consider that a good thing. On both our parts. Remember the idiots you told me you went to college with? Idiots like my parents? We used to point out that they had no idea what the world was like out there beyond the safe confines of their risk-free rebellion. You and I, we knew better. We were a team. We were going to make it, not end up lost and broken like them."

"Weren't we doing the same thing though? We were hiding from the world, just as much as anyone."

"And doing a damn good job of it, too. Look, Alyssa. Look around you. This is everything you ever wanted. We're not living like your parents; we're not living like my parents. We're educated, we're successful, and we're safe. Do you know what ninety-nine per cent of the globe would give to end up like us?

Ask your precious Leo. Isn't this what he came to America for? This safety? This security? This life?"

"Leo's not scared." Alyssa realized that she would never be able to make John understand. That the words were now more for her sake than his. She needed to hear what they sounded like outside of her head. She needed to see if they were truly something she could live with. "He has better cause to be scared than you and me and pretty much everyone we know. But he's not scared. He knows that if everything goes away again, he'll be okay. He'll adjust. He'll make it. He'll survive."

"To each their own," John shrugged dismissively.

"Yes." Alyssa turned to pick up her purse, heading towards the door. "It is."

When Leo opened the door, Alyssa didn't say anything. This was a change, wasn't it? Leo standing there, a questioning look on his face, and Alyssa the one silent, biding her time.

But not for too long.

She leaned in, cupping his face between both of her hands, pulling him closer and kissing him, catching first his upper lip between both of hers, then his lower. It took him a split second to respond. And then it seemed to take him another second to truly believe this was actually, in fact, happening. She opened her mouth to his tongue, inhaling him, moving her palms down to his shoulders. At the same time, Leo's arms moved around her waist, then up to tangle in her hair. They took turns gulping for air, managing to stay pasted to each other all the while. His knee slipped between her thighs and she melted into him, only opening her eyes and looking up at him long enough to explain – in case there was still any doubt, "I came to look for you."

WHAT THE DOCTOR DIDN'T TELL HER

Jacqueline Diamond

"Finally, it's Friday!" declared receptionist Edda Jonas, short red hair framing her round, freckled face as she clicked off her computer terminal and grabbed her purse from behind the counter. "Anyone else going to the Orange County Fair this weekend?"

Dr Sarah Matthews listened to a chorus of agreement from the office nurses. But when they turned toward her, Sarah said, "I have on-call duty all three nights. I'm not going anywhere except home to bed."

Although her usual schedule involved only one or two nights of delivering babies per week, one of the obstetricians had recently left for a position in nearby Los Angeles. Being single and still owing on medical school loans, Sarah had volunteered to fill in. Despite her debts, she wasn't sure how much longer she could keep up the pace.

"But the fair only comes once a year," Edda protested. "I love that booth where they'll deep-fry almost anything. Pastries, cereal, sandwiches. I can't wait to find out what they're frying this summer."

"Maybe next year."

Missing out on zany activities didn't bother Sarah nearly as much as the fact that she had no one to share them with. As her mother kept reminding her, how could she meet men when she spent all her time in an obstetrical practice?

"I heard that Dr McKay and Dr Van Dam interviewed someone by Skype," Edda said. "Maybe we'll have a new doctor soon."

"That would be wonderful."

From her private office on the corridor, Dr Jane McKay popped out, phone to her ear. "Next week would be more than acceptable," she said into her mobile. "Did the rental agent find you a place? Terrific! As for a babysitter, I may know someone available for overnights."

"Sounds like we're in luck," Edda observed, trailing the nurses toward the rear exit. "Have a good weekend!"

"You too," Sarah replied.

As the rest of the staff departed, Jane stuck the phone in the pocket of her white coat. "Sarah, do you suppose your mother would be willing to babysit a little girl a couple of nights a week?"

Sarah's mother ran a licensed day-care center in their home a few blocks from the office. Although Betsy usually tended children from 7 a.m. to 7 p.m., she was flexible, and she'd been concerned about Sarah's extra on-call shifts.

"For a new doctor, probably." Pricked by curiosity, Sarah added, "Is it anyone I might know?" While that seemed unlikely, doctors occasionally crossed paths during their training and at medical conferences.

"He said you did your residencies together."

Sarah caught her breath. There'd been quite a few residents who'd trained with her. It couldn't be . . .

"Does the name Daniel Durand ring a bell?" Jane asked.

A vise clamped onto Sarah's throat. She saw him instantly: dark hair tumbling across his forehead, warm brown eyes transfixing hers, and a spontaneous joy in the bedroom that had swept her away. She'd imagined herself in love. Too bad he hadn't been honest about his own feelings.

"If you want my opinion, he's an egotistical jerk," she snapped.

"Sarah . . ."

"Don't let the good looks fool you." She struggled to keep the bitterness from her voice. "He's full of himself."

Jane coughed. What was wrong? Then she lifted the phone from her pocket, and Sarah realized every word she said had been transmitted to – where was it Daniel had moved? – a small town in northern Arizona, she recalled.

"So you think your mother might be available a few nights a week?" Jane accompanied her words with a shrug, as if to say, *Let's pretend this didn't happen.*

Heat stung Sarah's cheeks. "Most likely."

As Jane returned to her office, talking into the phone, Sarah wondered why Daniel was moving back to southern California. But then, she'd never understood why a physician skilled in advanced surgical techniques had joined a small-town clinic far from a major hospital.

Apparently he had a daughter. Was he married? But with a wife in the picture, why the need for an overnight sitter?

Jane came back. Fortyish and angular, she went straight to the point, as usual. "Is Daniel likely to be a problem?"

"I'm sorry I spoke so harshly."

The older doctor waved off the apology. "Luke and I should have consulted you." Her husband, Dr Van Dam, was also her business partner.

"It's water under the bridge. It'll be fine," Sarah assured her.

"You didn't sound like it was fine."

She might as well explain. "We had an affair and he dumped me."

Jane winced. "Oh dear. Was it the let's-just-be-friends sort of dumping?"

"No, it was the eat-my-dust kind of dumping." Sarah had had trust issues with men ever since. "We made wild sock-flinging love. The next thing I knew, he stopped returning my emails and texts, except to say how busy he was. And he became very good at ducking around corners whenever he saw me." She couldn't resist adding, "I guess he must be married now."

"You mean the child?" Jane said. "She's his five-year-old niece. Her parents died about a year ago, and he's adopted her."

Not every single male would take responsibility for a child, Sarah conceded with reluctant respect. "Here's my mother's phone number." She jotted it down.

"Thanks." Jane took the slip of paper. "Are you okay for tonight? Not too tired?"

"No, but I think I'll go home and take a nap." Sarah's on-call shift began in a couple of hours at the North Orange County Medical Center, a block from the office.

"Good idea."

A catnap should cure her sleepiness. In the meantime, Sarah resolved to put Daniel out of her mind.

With experience born of long practice, Sarah fell asleep the moment she lay down. An hour later, the alarm dragged her into wakefulness.

That, and the fact that her mother was sitting on the bed.

"Good, you're awake." Betsy Matthews reached over to shut off the alarm. "I promised Jane I'd babysit the little Durand girl a few nights a week. Is that okay with you?"

"Absolutely." Scooting around her mother, Sarah moved to the dressing table to brush her hair. It was fine-textured and light brown, about the same shade as her mom's but without the traces of grey, she noted in the mirror.

"It'll be good to see Daniel again," said Betsy from behind her. "I always liked him, right up until he showed such poor judgement about my daughter."

"He's charming," Sarah said dryly. "I'm sure half his patients will fall in love with him."

"Look on the bright side," Betsy said. "Now that he's coming to Orange County, maybe you'll finally receive an explanation."

"Always a rainbow after the storm, right?" That was one of her mother's favorite sayings. While appreciative of the upbeat attitude, Sarah considered the image corny.

Her mother stood up. "Come eat some soup. The children helped make it, so it may have a few odd bits in it."

Realizing she had barely forty-five minutes to dress and eat before her shift, Sara shot to her feet. "What kind of odd bits?"

"Come find out."

While she ate, her mother thumbed through a flyer that advertised kitchen appliances. "I need to replace the stove. It's nearly thirty years old and it's getting temperamental. What do you think, black, white or beige?"

"Anything but that metallic industrial look. It's ugly." Sarah peered at two lumps in her spoon. "Mom, there are walnuts in my soup."

"That was the kids' contribution. There used to be a saying that a complete meal went from soup to nuts," Betsy said. "We've combined them in one bowl."

Sarah knew better than to object further. If she did, no doubt her mother would remind her that until presented with a grandchild, she was entitled to bestow her indulgence on other people's children.

Betsy had only grudgingly accepted Sarah's decision during her residency to donate eggs to an infertile couple. Later, she'd mentioned that she felt cheated of the baby or babies that might have been born. Betsy also worried that, with Sarah approaching her mid-thirties, time was running out.

"A grandchild would mean the world to me," she'd once said.

A scary thought hit Sarah. She hoped her mother wasn't fantasizing about a renewed romance with Daniel. Never again would Sarah expose herself to such a cruel betrayal.

"The soup's delicious, Mom." It had been, even the nuts.

"And healthy, too."

Right on cue, the phone rang. It was the hospital, reporting several women in labor. "I'm on my way," Sarah said.

She wished her mom a good evening and went out into the lingering July heat.

Two weeks later, Sarah arrived at the hospital at 7.30 in the morning. Scheduled for surgery, she'd made sure to get plenty of rest. Fortunately, with a new doctor on staff, she'd been able to reduce her on-call shifts.

For the past week, since Daniel joined the office, she'd escaped all but the briefest contact. He'd acknowledged their first meeting with a searching gaze, holding her hand longer than necessary when they shook. However, braced by the presence of Jane and Luke, Sarah had slipped her hand free and excused herself to get ready for the next patient.

As she had anticipated, Daniel's masculine presence had created a stir. Edda Jonas's adoring looks followed him everywhere, while patients who'd initially been hesitant to see a new physician now readily accepted, even raved about Dr Durand. Such a good listener! Such a reassuring manner!

And such a louse, underneath it all.

He'd arranged for his niece to join Betsy's day-care center. For Sarah, that meant having to duck him before and after work, too.

She didn't regret her mother's decision to babysit the little girl, though. Nina was a cutie with light-brown hair and green eyes. Although shy around Betsy and the other children, she'd given Sarah a hug right away.

The child's timidity wasn't entirely due to the change of location. Apparently the five-year-old had narrowly escaped the fire that had engulfed her home and killed her parents. When she had a nightmare during her first sleepover, she awakened both Sarah and her mother.

Sarah had rushed in to hold and reassure the little girl. Something about Nina's distress tore at her heart, although she'd never experienced any strong maternal instincts before.

She gave Daniel credit for doing his best in a difficult situation. That didn't ease her concerns about today, though.

After working in a small town, Daniel had expressed a desire to brush up on his microsurgery skills. Luke had responded that Sarah was the best surgeon on their staff, and volunteered her to supervise.

Now she hurried along the hall toward the surgical suites, hoping to scrub in before he did. That way, she could confine their interaction to the operating room.

The familiar scent of spice and pine soap alerted her a few seconds before he rounded a corner, and she had to sidestep quickly. Daniel steadied her, his strong hand catching her shoulder.

"Sarah." His voice caressed her name. "Are you all right?"

"I'm . . . fine."

She felt foolish, standing frozen, while electricity tingled through her traitorous body. She ought to paste on an impersonal smile and brush past.

"Thank you for agreeing to mentor me," Daniel said, releasing her. The two of them fell into step, heading for the operating room.

"You're a terrific surgeon," Sarah responded honestly. "I'm surprised you let your skills lapse."

Daniel's mouth tightened. "There were reasons for moving to Arizona. Good reasons. But never mind that."

"None of my business, I suppose," she returned.

"That's not what I meant."

Too late for clarification. They'd reached the surgical suite, and nurses were waiting to assist them with scrubbing in, gowning and masking.

Sarah felt as acutely aware of Daniel's nearness as she had six years ago. During their residency, being around him hadn't served as a distraction; instead, it had strengthened her love of medicine. Discussing procedures had been valuable for them both, and when they'd made love, they'd been keenly attuned to each other.

She had to admit, she'd been the first to back off, but only because, months after being approved as an egg donor, she'd finally been chosen by a couple. After treating so many infertile women and seeing their desperate longing for a family, Sarah had been happy to volunteer. Spending a few months taking hormones, coordinating cycles with the recipient – who'd remained anonymous – and undergoing the egg transfer had seemed little enough to sacrifice in order to give life.

She'd been forbidden to have intercourse during that period, due to the risk of accidentally becoming pregnant with multiple babies. Had the awareness that she was undergoing this process proved a turn-off for Daniel? If so, he'd been cowardly not to tell her. Also, what a poor bet as a future husband and father, if he were that finicky.

Steeling herself, Sarah went into the operating room just ahead of him. With their hair hidden beneath sterile caps, neither of them was likely to make anyone's heart beat faster, she thought with a smile.

The procedure was a reversal of a woman's tubal ligation, so that she could have children with her second husband. Sarah spoke briefly to the patient, assuring her that they had a high likelihood of success. When she introduced Daniel as a skilled surgeon whom they were lucky to have with them today, the woman gazed at him gratefully.

Once the anaesthesia took effect, Sarah made the first incision. An operating room was a busy place, with the anaesthesiologist, scrub nurses, technicians and a circulating nurse, but she was mostly aware of Daniel across from her.

It was a painstaking procedure that involved opening the blocked ends of the Fallopian tube segments that had previously been tied off. They then threaded in a stent to hold them open, drew the tubal openings together and sutured them. The stitches had to be precisely aligned.

She and Daniel coordinated their tasks smoothly. Because they'd trained together and often thought alike, they were able to hand off tasks. At first, since he was out of practice with the surgical microscope and specialized tools, his motions were slower than usual, but he quickly regained his confidence.

Sarah felt a wave of exhilaration. She loved the challenge of surgery, and this procedure gave the woman an eighty per cent chance of having a successful pregnancy in the future.

Above his mask, excitement shone in Daniel's face. "I'm glad to be back."

"I'm glad you are, too." Sarah hoped he didn't misinterpret her words as anything more than professional respect. "Well, I'll leave you to finish. I have to prepare for another surgery."

"Thanks." He stayed focused on the task.

Outside the OR, Sarah saw that they'd been inside less than two hours. Since the surgery had been uncomplicated, that was typical for the procedure.

She stretched, took a short break, and went to her next surgery. With back-to-back procedures, a surgeon required plenty of stamina and steady nerves. Sarah had both those qualities, as did Daniel.

He had patient consults for the rest of the morning, she'd seen on the office schedule. Around 2 p.m., when she finally arrived at the hospital cafeteria for lunch, she was surprised to find him sitting in the nearly empty room. When he waved, Sarah realized he'd come on purpose to see her.

They might as well talk. This morning had broken the ice, and besides, they had to function as colleagues. Not to mention that dodging him at her house was wearing thin.

She selected a pastrami sandwich with a side salad and joined him at the table. "Good job this morning." It seemed a safe topic.

"I'm glad to be back in civilization." He grinned, and then grew serious. "Listen, I didn't mean to be rude when you asked why I moved to Arizona."

"It really isn't my business." Sarah tackled her sandwich hungrily.

"The truth is . . ." He paused. "Let's start with part of the truth. Neither of us has all day."

"Fair enough," she mumbled.

Daniel leaned back, his long legs bumping Sarah's. With his dramatic dark coloring and soulful air, he was almost painfully handsome, she thought. She shifted so they were no longer accidentally touching.

"Shortly after Nina was born, my brother Fred got laid off his job," he began.

What did that have to do with moving to Arizona? Sarah wondered, but kept quiet. No doubt he'd explain.

"He started binge drinking," he went on. "When he got a job managing a motel in northern Arizona, Misty – my sister-in-law – wasn't thrilled, but she went along."

A couple of nurses carried their trays to a table that gave them a good view of Daniel. He didn't appear to notice.

"When I learned that the local clinic had an opening for an obstetrician, I decided to take the post for a year to keep an eye on things," he went on. "I hoped my brother would stay sober now that he had a job and a baby."

"I gather he didn't."

Daniel gave a resigned headshake. "He and Misty quarreled frequently, and then she started drinking heavily, too, especially on weekends. I took care of Nina whenever I could."

All these years, he'd been sacrificing for his niece. "She's a sweetheart. But that must have been hard on you and her."

"I tried to get them into Alcoholics Anonymous," he said. "They wouldn't even acknowledge there was a problem. Then one night . . ."

They'd died in a fire, Sarah recalled. "What happened?"

"One of the motel guests heard Nina screaming and pulled her out of the manager's apartment before the firefighters arrived." He clenched his hands on the table. "Fred and Misty died from smoke inhalation."

"That's awful." And horrifying for the little girl. "What caused the fire, if you don't mind my asking?"

"The investigator said it started in the kitchen. Possibly unattended cooking equipment." Daniel's chest heaved. "My niece has blocked that whole night. She doesn't remember anything, except for having nightmares. I hired a therapist, hoping to help Nina face what happened so she can heal, but it didn't work."

"You stayed there another year?"

"Until the adoption was final. Then I heard about this job and it seemed perfect."

He still hadn't said why he'd withdrawn from their relationship. If it had to do with his brother's problems, there'd be no reason to keep it secret.

Sarah wondered if she'd been too hard on him. Or were his good looks clouding her judgement?

That afternoon, Luke Van Dam called Sarah's name as she walked past his private office. When she stopped in the doorway, he said, "Thanks for supervising Daniel today. My wife tells me you two had some issues. If I'd been aware of that, I wouldn't have volunteered you."

"No problem." Since he didn't appear reassured, Sarah added, "We've put that behind us."

"It's great that your mom's able to watch his little girl." Luke was a striking man in his own right, despite a slightly crooked nose from an old football injury. "I remember how hard it was when Zoey was a kid, after the divorce. My ex-wife travels – she's a singer, and that involves a lot of touring. Until I married Jane, I struggled to find good sitters."

"Doesn't seem to have hurt Zoey." Their twelve-year-old had sailed into adolescence with considerable self-assurance. She was popular, athletic and a good student.

"Kids need a mom, especially girls." Luke gave her a wry grin. "Despite my medical specialty, there are some areas of Zoey's development that I'm happy to turn over to Jane. The way women react to Daniel, he should have no trouble finding a new mom for Nina."

"You think it's that simple?" Sarah asked sharply. "Just find the right interchangeable mother and . . . Sorry, Luke. It's been a long day."

"I did make it sound like that, didn't I?" he said. "Came out wrong."

Instantly, Sarah realized she was protesting too much. Best to change the subject. "My last two patients canceled, so I'm off early."

"Thanks again."

With a wave, she stepped out. Down the hall lay the receptionist's counter, behind which Edda Jonas leaned forward, beaming at Daniel. They were both chuckling, apparently over a shared joke.

He should have no trouble finding a new mom for Nina. Luke's words sent a pang through Sarah.

Catching Daniel's eyes on her, she mustered a polite nod and hurried off. So what if he was flirting?

The walk cleared Sarah's thoughts, and she got home in a cheerier mood. She found her mom and Nina emptying the dishwasher. The little girl solemnly placed silverware in a drawer, matching forks to forks and spoons to spoons.

Eight years ago, after Sarah's father died of a heart attack, Betsy had been left with enough insurance money to pay her bills but little more. To bring in extra, she'd started babysitting for acquaintances. Discovering that she enjoyed caring for other people's children, as well as earning extra income, she'd turned this into a steady business.

It required flexibility to accommodate the schedules of different families, Sarah knew. Some children came before and after school, while others showed up later in the morning and left in the early afternoon. There was a mixture of ages, from babies up to ten-year-olds. Although the license allowed Betsy to care for as many as six children at one time, she rarely had more than four.

Betsy stifled a yawn as she regarded her daughter. "You're home early."

"Patient cancellations." Although she'd meant to lie down, Sarah could see her mom was tired. "Why don't you rest before dinner? I'll take care of Nina till her dad gets here. I can fix dinner, too."

"That would be lovely, if it's okay with Nina." Betsy turned to the little girl. "What do you say?"

"Yes!" Dropping the last spoon into place, Nina ran to Sarah and held up her arms for a hug. Flattered, Sarah scooped her up, and the five-year-old clung to her.

"She doesn't do that with me," Betsy said. "What's your secret?"

"My charming personality, naturally." Sarah lowered the little girl gently.

Nina took her hand. "Can we play Go Fish?"

"Sure." Card games were instructive as well as fun. Sarah got out a deck of cards and they sat at the table. "Do you know how many cards we start with in our hands?"

Nina frowned as if fearful of making a mistake.

"With just two players, we deal seven cards each." Sarah shuffled the deck, flipping them in the air as her father had showed her years ago. The little girl watched in fascination. "Can you help me count them?"

Eagerly, the little girl joined in, counting to seven along with Sarah as she laid out their hands, face down. Picking them up, Nina arranged the cards by herself.

"You know your numbers already. You're in good shape to start kindergarten." School would begin in a month. "Do you know your alphabet, too?"

"Uncle Danny taught me."

They'd played three rounds of Go Fish, two of which Nina won, when Sarah heard a noise from the living room. Glancing up, she met Daniel's brown eyes.

"You're good with her." He went to his niece. "Did you have fun, sweetie?"

"Yes! Can Sarah come with us to the fair on Saturday?" the little girl asked. "Please, please, please!"

Daniel made a silent appeal to Sarah before saying, "I traded overnights with Jane so I'm free this weekend. If you don't have plans on Saturday, we'd love for you to join us."

Sarah had planned to catch up on her sleep and do a little shopping before her Sunday on-call shift. But this was the fair's last weekend.

"It'll be crowded," she warned. "But yes, let's go!"

As uncle and niece departed, Betsy emerged from her bedroom. "Seems like he's as keen on you as Nina is."

"You were listening!" Sarah pretended to glare. "Anyway, it was his niece who invited me, not him."

"I didn't hear him objecting," her mother murmured.

"He could hardly do that, could he?" All the same, Sarah was glad to be going.

It had been years since Sarah visited the Orange County Fair. As a teenager, she'd gravitated to the big-name concert acts and the rollercoaster-style rides that drew up to a million guests during the event's month-long run.

She hadn't appreciated its old-fashioned, child-friendly side until today. Nina adored the miniature pig races, with little pink piglets jumping over tiny hurdles. After that, they took in a magic act and a performance by acrobats, then toured the model farm with its lambs, baby goats and chicks.

"I can't believe this place," Daniel said as they watched a demonstration of camel milking at the Oasis Camel Dairy. "A petting zoo and a dog show I might expect, but this is unusual."

"Have you seen the collections?" asked a young woman next to them, hanging on to twin boys.

"Collections?" Sarah echoed.

The woman pointed to the crafts building. "People collect all sorts of weird things."

"Sounds like fun," Daniel said. "Thanks."

Nina broke in. "I'm hungry!"

"And no wonder." Her uncle checked his watch. "It's been hours since lunch."

They bought chicken and pineapple kebabs. Those seemed healthy and not too fattening, but they couldn't resist following up with such fair specialties as chocolate-covered bacon and deep-fried ice cream bars.

"And we're doctors," Daniel murmured as they staggered toward the crafts building, stuffed with cholesterol-laden foods.

"Keep your voice down, okay?" Sarah teased.

Nina gave a little skip. "This is cool!"

Above her, Daniel eyed Sarah appreciatively. "I'm glad you came with us."

"So am I."

"Do you spend much time with children?" he asked suddenly.

"Only when I'm helping my mom. Why?"

"You're good with Nina," Daniel noted.

"I hope so." The conversation puzzled Sarah. However, they'd reached the crafts building, and there were other things to talk about.

The collections, they discovered, consisted of anything that people chose to amass. There were wrapped moist towelettes from restaurants around the country, unusual canned goods, vintage bottle caps, and a display of Bermuda shorts. Although Sarah had assumed those garments came from the island of the same name, she'd never realized they originated with the British Army for use in hot climates.

"You learn something new every day," she observed.

"Especially here." Daniel patted Nina as she leaned against him. "Tired, little one?"

"Wore out," she said.

Reaching down, he lifted her against his shoulder. "Let's go home. Okay, Sarah?"

"Sure."

It was nearly seven, and the sunlight was dimming. In the back seat, Nina fought to stay awake. "When we get home, Sarah has to read me a night-night story."

"We have to drop Sarah off at her house on the way," Daniel said.

Turning, Sarah saw the little girl's jaw set stubbornly. Exhausted, Nina obviously had no emotional reserves, and Sarah hated to spoil the day. "You only live a few blocks from us." Daniel had mentioned how lucky he was to rent an apartment so close to work. "I can walk from there."

"Are you sure?" He regarded her with concern before returning his attention to the freeway traffic. "Your feet must be sore."

They'd probably traipsed the equivalent of ten miles today, Sarah reckoned. "Thank heaven for athletic shoes."

"You're a good sport."

"I enjoy reading picture books too," she responded lightly. Also, she was curious to see where he and Nina lived.

The apartment turned out to be a charming one-story unit surrounded by flowering bushes. "This is pretty," Sarah observed as Daniel unlocked the door.

"Best I could find, and you can't beat the location."

The carpet might be a bit worn and the front room furnishings plain, but Nina's room came from another realm. A princess-pink canopy bed, a white bureau stenciled with fairy-tale characters, and a shelf overflowing with picture books transformed it into a fantasy.

"It's beautiful," Sarah said.

Beaming, Nina took out a pink nightgown. "You stay here while I brush my teeth."

"You bet." While Nina was gone, Sarah knelt by the shelf to select a story.

Lingering near the door, Daniel looked big and masculine amid the frills. "You fit right in."

"Did her parents buy all this?" Then she recognized her error. "I forgot about the fire."

"I tried to replace things as best I could." He ran his hand over the soft fur of a teddy bear. "She never said much about it."

"It must have felt strange to her at first." Book in hand, Sarah sat by the bed in the glow of a lamp. "To you, too."

Shadows obscured Daniel's eyes. "I was familiar with her routine because she'd slept on my cot one or two nights a week. Becoming a single dad, well, I'm still adjusting. We both are."

Nina returned and snuggled under the covers. While Sarah read, the little girl yawned, and, by the last page, she'd fallen asleep.

Sarah kissed her cheek. "Sleep well, sweetie." As they exited, Daniel switched off the lamp.

"She really doesn't recall anything?" Sarah asked in the living room.

"Only in her nightmares." Daniel ran his hand through his hair. Already mussed from the day's activities, it sprang up at odd angles.

Without thinking, Sarah reached to smooth it. As her palm caressed the soft texture, she heard his quick intake of breath.

His large hand covered her smaller one, bringing it to his cheek, which was roughened by a day's growth of beard. As Daniel moved closer, his male scent mingled with aftershave lotion, sending heat surging through her body.

His hand at her waist eased her against him, length for length, feeling his strength and his longing. Rising on tiptoe, Sarah touched her lips to his.

Then she was hard against him, her mouth yielding, his tongue exploring while his arms caged her. A low moan tore from her, pent-up need flooding to the surface.

She was lost, flying outside herself. Melting into this man who meant so much, even more now that they'd both learned, lived, grown.

Daniel lifted his head, his heart thudding so fast she could feel it through their clothing. "I've missed you terribly."

"Me, too," she whispered.

His hands cupped her face and they were kissing again, slower and deeper. Sarah's palms found Daniel's ribcage, then his back. How well she remembered those taut muscles and powerful hips. She wanted more of him, much more.

With a sigh, he released her. "We have a lot to discuss."

At a time like this? "Daniel, what's this about?"

"I have something to ask you." A flicker of hesitation, and then he said, "How would you feel about being a mother?"

Startled, Sarah said, "What?"

"You and Nina have bonded." He seemed to be searching for words. "She needs a mom."

Disappointment knotted in Sarah's stomach. "That's why you're interested in me? So your niece can have a mother?"

"I didn't put that very well."

"How else would you put it?" She couldn't believe she'd let herself fall for him again. He'd played on her feelings and her attachment to Nina, when all he wanted was a stand-in wife to shoulder some of his burden. Maybe not even a wife, just a convenient housemate. "I guess it would be handier to have me on the premises, is that it?"

"No, of course not." His tone was pleading, his manner distraught. What a great actor. "I wish things weren't so complicated."

"Never mind." She refused to stand here while he figured out the most effective lie. "I'll see you at work."

Sarah strode out without glancing back. If she did, she was afraid she might be tempted to grant Daniel another chance.

Her cheeks flamed as she recalled how she'd responded to his advances. What a gullible fool she was. By next week, no doubt he'd be putting the moves on Edda, or some other sucker.

Sarah's heart squeezed. The cool evening, typical of southern California's dry climate even after a hot day, gradually dried the tears. Even so, it took a long while before she felt calm enough to face her mother.

For the next week, Sarah spoke to Daniel as little as possible, and deleted his texts and emails. All he did was apologize for his clumsiness and repeat that the two of them had to talk. Why? So he could formulate a more effective plan to manipulate her?

At home, Betsy watched her anxiously, but didn't pry. All Sarah had said, on returning home Saturday night, had been, "Daniel isn't what he seems."

The following Friday night, when Nina stayed over while Daniel worked a labor and delivery shift, Sarah heated precooked turkey sausage in the microwave and fixed a salad. The stove wasn't working properly; her mother had ordered a replacement to be installed on Monday.

Betsy kept casting sad glances in Sarah's direction. For goodness sake, did her mother have to fall for Daniel, too? He sure knew how to turn on the charm when it suited him.

After watching an animated film with Nina curled on her lap, Sarah put the little girl to bed. She'd grown too attached to distance herself from the child.

In her own room, Sarah tossed and turned. When Daniel learned of the opening at Jane and Luke's practice, why had he been so eager to join the staff? Surely he had plenty of other opportunities.

Mentally, she replayed their last encounter. What exactly had he said? Could she have misjudged him, or were her doubts simply another sign of how susceptible she was?

Sarah fell asleep at last, only to be awakened by the shrill ring of the phone. It was the charge nurse in labor and delivery.

"There must be something in the water," the woman said apologetically. "We've had a rush of women in labor, and Dr Durand's performing an emergency Caesarian section. I know it isn't your night, but can you please come in?"

Sarah checked the clock – 3 a.m. "I'll be right there."

Leaving a note for Betsy in the living room, she hurried out. At this hour, she drove, arriving at the hospital barely in time to deliver a baby. The mother, who already had four children, gave birth easily and quickly. Two more uncomplicated births followed.

A new patient was admitted, a woman six weeks before her due date, carrying twins. Although it would have been preferable to delay the births, labor had progressed too far. To complicate matters, the first baby was in the breech position, with feet first, which posed additional dangers.

After a phone consultation with the patient's obstetrician, who was out of town for the weekend, Sarah called for an operating room. Fortunately, Daniel was almost finished with his surgery and could take over the other patients.

She was about to begin when Daniel poked his head into the room. "I apologize for interrupting your night off."

"That's hardly your fault."

He glanced at the other staff and the parents, who couldn't help overhearing. "How about breakfast in the cafeteria as soon as we're done?"

Might as well get that discussion over with. "Fine," Sarah said.

As soon as he left, the patient, who had only a local anaesthetic, grinned at her. "He's cute."

"Hey!" her husband teased. "You're taken."

"Yeah, like I'm going to flirt in this condition!" she tossed back.

"A girl can't help looking," said one of the nurses, and they all chuckled.

Amused in spite of herself, Sarah resumed the operation. The mom was strong and the twins did their bit: both proved in good shape, able to breathe on their own and weighing in at more than four pounds each. The pediatrician cleared them for the intermediate care nursery rather than neonatal intensive care.

Tired but elated, Sarah went home. The day shift had arrived, and Daniel was nowhere in sight.

She checked her voicemail. A couple of frantic messages, one from him and one from her mother, sent Sarah racing to her car.

* * *

"I had no idea there was any danger." In the early morning sunshine, Betsy huddled in a blanket. "The firemen think one of the gas pipes might have leaked and caused the fire."

The scene felt surreal: fire trucks, a paramedic unit and a police car filled the street, while neighbors stood around gawking. Sarah had hurried home, terrified of what she might find. Even now, her pulse was pounding and she felt shaky. She could only imagine what awful memories this must have stirred in Nina.

Paramedics, having determined that neither Nina nor Betsy required emergency treatment, had released the little girl to her uncle's care. Meanwhile, the fire, confined to the kitchen, had been extinguished.

"The important thing is, no one's hurt." Sarah glanced at Daniel, kneeling nearby on the grass with his arms around Nina. "Still, this must be traumatic."

Betsy shivered. "Just when she was starting to heal."

Sarah wished she had a view of Nina's face. In Daniel's expression, relief mingled with weariness.

"You're worried about her, aren't you?" Betsy asked. "Go on over. I'll be along shortly."

"You're sure?"

"I just want to catch my breath."

Sarah picked her way across the lawn, stepping over the fire hoses. When Nina turned, Sarah braced for tears.

Instead, the little girl beamed. "I saved her!" Nina jumped up and ran to Sarah. "I saved your mommy."

Sarah hugged her. "I was scared for you."

Daniel brushed off his slacks. "Nina woke up and smelled smoke a few minutes before the alarm sounded."

"I shook Betsy," Nina said earnestly. "I saved her."

"You certainly helped." Sarah wasn't sure a minute or two had made much difference. "I'm glad we had the alarm, too."

"Even a few seconds is important where a fire's concerned," put in a nearby firefighter. "More people die from smoke and carbon monoxide poisoning than from flames."

"I woke up Betsy," Nina reaffirmed as the fireman continued collecting the hoses.

"Yes, you did." Sarah's mother came to join them. "Thank you."

"My parents didn't wake up."

A shiver ran through Sarah. "Nina, did you try to save your parents?"

The girl nodded.

"What do you remember?" Daniel asked.

Nina pressed close to Sarah. "Mommy told me to watch the cooking. Only the pot boiled over and the flames jumped up to the curtains. I ran to get Mommy, but she and Daddy were sleeping too much."

"She left you alone with food on the stove?" Sarah asked in dismay.

A tear slid down the girl's cheek. "She said I was big enough."

"No, you weren't," Daniel answered with a trace of anger. "Your mommy made a mistake."

"This fire must have brought everything back," Betsy murmured. "I'm so sorry."

"Don't be," Daniel told her. "This is a major step. She'd blocked the memories, and no wonder. It seems that she felt responsible for what happened."

"Nina, it isn't your fault they didn't wake up," Sarah said. "The fire wasn't your fault, either."

Nina's mouth trembled. "It wasn't?"

What a burden of guilt this child had been carrying. "No. It's grown-ups' job to protect children, not the other way around."

Daniel crouched to face his niece. "Sweetheart, do you recall one night when I picked you up, when Mommy and Daddy had been drinking?"

Her nose wrinkled. "That nasty-smelling stuff."

"Your mommy was asleep and your daddy could hardly talk to me," Daniel went on. "I got mad and said angry things to them, remember?"

"Yes."

"I loved them and they loved you, but when they drank like that, they couldn't take care of you or themselves. I think that's what happened the night of the fire."

"You tried to help them," Sarah put in. "You were brave."

"And this morning," Betsy added, "you saved me."

"I'm glad." Nina's eyebrows drew together. She had a lot to think over, but with luck she was on the right path now, Sarah reflected.

Maybe this fire hadn't been such a bad thing, after all.

A neighbor generously invited Sarah and Betsy to stay in her guest room and, over the next few days, the father of several day-care youngsters worked his construction crew extra hours to put his children's sitter back in business. To cause as little disruption as possible, Betsy continued to babysit Nina, to the delight of their hostess, who was a long-distance grandmother.

Nina had been in a surprisingly upbeat mood. However, the fire had dealt an emotional blow to Betsy, who struggled to regain her usual good cheer.

"Life feels so fragile," she told Sarah one evening as they prepared for bed. "It's brought back memories of your father's sudden death. We never know where the next blow will come from."

"You always tell me to look for the rainbow after a storm," Sarah pointed out.

"I'm trying." Betsy wrapped her arms around herself. "It's just hard to believe life has happy things in store."

Sarah patted her mother's arm. "I'm still here."

Betsy smiled lovingly. "Yes, you are. And maybe one of these days . . ." Her gaze drifted to a photo collage on the wall, showing their neighbor's grandchildren. "Never mind."

Not much I can do about that, Sarah thought, and changed the subject.

Although her path and Daniel's crossed frequently, nearly a week passed before they were able to reschedule their breakfast. She arrived at the hospital cafeteria early, and claimed a corner table.

A few minutes later, Daniel showed up. Across the large room, she felt the impact of his dark, intense presence.

If only she knew where she stood with him. Since the fire, their interactions had been friendly but impersonal. She'd felt him holding back, yet he showed no interest in any other woman. What was it he planned to tell her?

Carrying an omelet and toast, he strode to her table. "Oh, I didn't see the waffles." He looked at her plate enviously. "I might go back. No, I won't." He took a seat.

Why was he so nervous?

To Sarah's frustration, he dug into his food. To break the silence, she asked, "How's Nina been sleeping?" There'd been no overnights with Betsy since the fire.

"Like a log." From little plastic tubs, Daniel spread butter and jam on his toast. "She's been fine."

"It's amazing," Sarah said. "She's so chatty, she's like a different person."

"She isn't a different person – she's the happy kid she used to be." He set down his fork. "She's been talking to me about her parents, remembering the good times. It's as if a big weight lifted from her."

"If only I'd known she carried such a load of guilt," Sarah said.

"How could you, when I didn't?"

It was hard to explain. "There's a connection between Nina and me. I don't think I'm imagining it."

Daniel's gaze held hers. "Sarah, there's something I need to tell you."

Here it comes. Her stomach clenched. "What is it?"

"I may be breaking some ethics rule or other, but I don't care. You have a right to know."

At a loss, Sarah waited for him to continue.

"Six years ago, when you donated eggs, I accidentally found out that the person you donated them to was my sister-in-law."

Astonished, she simply stared at him.

"I started suspecting it while you were coordinating your cycles. Misty was quite talkative about what was going on, and so were you," Daniel explained. "When she had the egg transfer the same week you donated, I realized what it meant."

In the process of egg donation, both the donor and the recipient synchronize their monthly cycles using birth control pills and other hormones, so the mother-to-be's body is ready at the right point. When mature, the eggs are retrieved from the donor through a minor surgical procedure, examined by an embryologist and, if healthy, fertilized in a laboratory using the male partner's sperm. About three days later, when they have grown to eight cells, the healthiest embryos are transferred into the recipient's womb. With luck, one or two implant and grow.

While some women choose to meet the donor, the recipient of Sarah's eggs had preferred anonymity. Her medical records were kept strictly private, but that hadn't prevented Daniel from guessing.

Sarah's mouth felt dry and overhead the lighting hummed loudly. "There might have been more than one transfer that week."

"The timing was spot on." A group of nurses strolled by, and Daniel waited to speak again until they were out of earshot. "I couldn't risk revealing what I knew."

"That's why you stopped seeing me." Sarah had never considered a reason like this.

"Yes. I handled it badly, but I couldn't figure out what else to do." He reached for her coffee cup. "How about a refill?"

"Yes, please." As Sarah waited for him to return from the coffee station, she wished that he hadn't let her believe the worst. Yet if they'd continued dating, the truth might have slipped out. If not, keeping such a secret would have created a wedge between them.

Daniel returned. "Where was I?"

"Dumping me."

"I kept hoping we'd find each other again." Regret tinged his words. "Then my brother lost his job and started drinking."

Sarah recalled his earlier account. "You moved to Arizona for Nina's sake."

"She was helpless and vulnerable." Daniel's dark eyebrows drew together. "And I kept seeing you in her."

The light-brown hair. The green eyes. The shape of Nina's chin. She's my daughter.

The impact took Sarah's breath away. She'd tried not to think about the child who might have been born, the child who drew half her genetic heritage from Sarah. In the Los Angeles–Orange County metropolitan area, with a population of nearly eighteen million, their paths were unlikely to cross, nor would they have recognized each other should that happen.

Except under these extraordinary circumstances.

"You sacrificed your career for my daughter," Sarah marveled.

"I just dialed it down a few notches." Daniel regarded her with infinite gentleness. "Besides, how could I help it? She's such an angel."

"Yes, she is."

"If you want to be sure of the relationship, you should take a DNA test."

Sarah didn't need one. "Even if the test was negative, I love that little girl."

"I can tell," he said. "When I mentioned that she needs a mother, that was my clumsy way of working around to this explanation."

"I thought you were just looking for someone to bail you out," she answered ruefully.

"Someone I love."

Did he mean that? Could she trust the sincerity in his voice and the yearning in her heart?

"I didn't rush things because, well, you made no secret of your opinion of me," Daniel said. "And well deserved it was, too."

Embarrassed, Sarah recalled her remarks to Jane when she'd learned Daniel was joining the staff. "You heard that?"

"I believe the term 'egotistical jerk' entered into it." He slanted a smile at her. "Now I'm asking you to put all that behind us and give me another chance."

"What kind of chance?" If he was asking for mere friendship, they'd better clarify that now. *Before I dive into the deep end again.*

"You're the only woman I've ever loved, Sarah, and I plan to marry you." Daniel leaned across the table. "However, I believe that, legally, you do have some say in the matter."

Her last reservation dissolved. "You'll have to court me properly."

"Flowers? Jewelry?" he asked. "Coming right up."

"Kisses and loving words." Everything she'd missed.

"Long walks, laughter, making love," Daniel contributed.

"Playing cards with Nina." Since that seemed anticlimactic, she added, "Making love a few more times."

"A few?"

"Many."

They were beaming at each other in front of the entire cafeteria, Sarah realized. "Maybe we should skip the courtship part. We've wasted long enough."

"Is that a yes?" Eagerness lit Daniel's expression.

"It is." Before he could make a general announcement, she added, "But we have to save the news until we tell my mom and Nina."

"Let's do it together." He picked up his tray.

"Agreed."

By the end of the day, Sarah felt as if she might burst with her news. At six o'clock, when the last patient had gone and the last report was entered into the computer, she nearly ran to join Daniel.

Her fiancé. Her soon-to-be husband. How incredible.

As she rode home with him, Sarah tried to rehearse her announcement. She was still working on that when they halted in front of the neighbor's house. Their own home still wasn't quite ready to occupy.

On the porch steps, Nina was playing with a kitten. Sarah's mother watched the little girl with an unguarded expression of pure, aching love, touched with longing.

When the car pulled up, two faces turned to look at them. Betsy and Nina wore almost identical expressions of curiosity. Grandmother and granddaughter. How could anyone miss the resemblance?

Hand in hand, Sarah and Daniel strolled up the walkway. The right words came to her at last.

"Mom," Sarah said with a catch in her throat, "I just found your rainbow."

THE BABY WHISPERER

Abbi Wilder

Chapter One

Dr Tiberio "Ty" Ross surveyed the crowd of more than two hundred people filling Kensington Hospital's auditorium and bit back the anticipation that was making him antsy.

Where was she?

Back at his home base of Bedford, Michigan, after more than two years away, his colleagues and the community greeted him with open arms. Not exactly what he'd expected from a place he'd turned his back on, but not totally unexpected either.

A small rush of relief came over him as cameras flashed from the row of reporters in the bay below the stage. One quest for forgiveness complete; one more to go.

There was one person he'd hoped to be front and center in the crowd, eagerly taking in his every word. The same individual who'd remained in his thoughts since he'd left her almost two years ago.

Dr Lily Finley.

But she wasn't there.

While speaking and answering moderated questions for almost an hour, Ty forced himself not to let his own anticipation ruin the show. As he spoke, he used every available chance to scan the crowd for the face etched in his memory.

Lily refused to join him when he'd accepted the talk show job in California. And, now, it seemed, she'd chosen to be just as stubborn about letting the past go. She'd refused to appear.

What had started as a simple calling to help sick infants turned into a national phenomenon. Since the end of the first season of the talk show – now broadcast in fifty different countries – he'd been on an eighteen-week publicity tour. Tokyo. San Francisco. London. Qatar. Countries from all over the world requested his expertise. The small town of Bedford was his second to last stop before he returned to California.

The only thing keeping his sanity intact was knowing he'd be certain to see Lily – and soon. He'd promised himself that during this visit he'd focus on two things: his clients and, of course, the love of his life. As the world-famous Baby Whisperer, he could pretty much ask for – and get – whatever he wanted. Hospitals clamored for his appearances.

"I think that concludes our Q and A session with Dr Ross. I know many will be looking for him when he visits this week but we'd like to remind you the doctor is here to work. Please respect his privacy as well as that of the patients and families on the unit."

Two security guards escorted Ty, the moderator and the gaggle of VIPs who'd joined him off the stage and down a thin, pale corridor. When they reached a small conference room, applause could still be heard faintly from the audience.

The room, to Ty's displeasure, was empty. His anticipation changed to dissatisfaction. Maybe they hadn't taken his request seriously. "There seems to be something missing here," he said.

"I think we've set things up just as you asked." The moderator must've noticed Ty's unhappiness. The stout man fidgeted as if a little uncomfortable.

"I've had a long tour and I'd like to get as much done as possible in the two days I'm here. But I can't do that without someone to help me."

"I guess it's a good thing I'm here then."

Ty turned toward the familiar voice and his anger quickly dissipated. Lily looked more stunning than ever. She'd let her auburn hair grow out and it cascaded over her shoulders. She still dressed to kill, wearing a form-fitting business suit, with heels that emphasized her shapely calves.

A few seconds later, Ty got his breath back. "Hello, Lily."

"Doctor Finley. Hello, Dr Ross."

He guessed that her sharp tone meant he was still in trouble.

So much for forgiveness number two. Still, he was in Michigan for two days.

A lot could happen in forty-eight hours.

He stared at Lily for a few moments, trying to remember exactly why he felt it had been necessary to leave her. After the initial media frenzy, the offers started pouring in. The opportunity from CBS to host his own daytime talk show from California – called *The Baby Whisperer* – had been too good to pass up.

But Lily hadn't seen it that way. She refused to even consider giving up her job and moving with him.

And now look at him. His fame had skyrocketed. He had everything he could ever want.

Everything but Lily.

Did the price of leaving her outweigh all the wealth and fame? He still hadn't figured that one out. Seeing her now, though, he was beginning to doubt it.

Lily dismissed the moderator and, after another round of handshakes with the VIPs, she herded them out of the office, closing the door behind them.

Once they were alone, Lily didn't waste time. She crossed her arms over her chest and planted herself solidly in front of him. "So, why don't you tell me what's really going on here?"

He took a breath and tried to keep his voice steady. "I agreed to visit Kensington Hospital. Seems there's some children here that need my expertise."

"We all know that. But I know you. What else are you up to?"

She didn't pull any punches, did she? One of the things he adored about this woman was her ability to get straight to the point. "Well, there is one other reason why I'm here." He cleared his throat, nervous. She looked ready to chew him up and spit him out.

Lily spoke through gritted teeth. "I knew it! Out with it, Tiberio."

He flinched at the use of his full name. Whatever happened to her fondness for calling him Ty?

"While it's true that I'm here to help Kensington Hospital, I'm also here for you, Lily-belle."

He heard her sharp intake of breath.

"I intend to convince you to come back with me to California."

* * *

Dr Lily Finley didn't know how to respond. Conflicting emotions tore at her. Her stomach didn't help matters either. If it rolled one more time at the sight of Ty's beautiful green eyes, she'd have to lock herself in her office and try to calm down.

He'd left her for fame and fortune. Love and family wasn't enough for this man. And now he said he was here for her? Right. The Baby Whisperer was, indeed, the most appropriate moniker for him. His skill with sick babies was legendary. His skill with her heart? Not so much.

She glared up at the striking six foot two man who'd managed to mesmerize the entire world with his abilities. Was this really the man she'd shared a bed with two years ago? His blond hair still had that rakish look as if he didn't care if or how he styled it: a brush or his fingers would do. His face had thinned like he'd lost some weight.

Clothes were the same though. Faded blue jeans, button-down dress shirt and ages-old leather jacket. He dressed more as the rebel MD than the billionaire physician revered for his bedside manner with babies.

When she'd agreed to act as Ty's hospital liaison for his visit, she'd decided it would be on her terms. She wasn't about to let him directly care for a baby in the care of her hospital without questioning his orders and double-checking the safety of them. This was her unit, her area of expertise. He might be the miracle worker, but she was the one in charge around here.

And now how was she supposed to respond to his declaration? With a yes? Her body wanted that, of course, but her mind knew it would be a huge mistake. She wasn't about to let Ty Ross get under her skin. "Baby Girl Dombrowski has been with us for almost a week now." She'd decided to simply ignore his declaration and move straight on to the task at hand.

"Baby Girl Dombrowski?"

"She's the sick baby you're here to help."

He cocked his head. "As I already told you," he smirked, "she's one of the reasons I'm here."

His smile always made her melt. But when her body began to thaw to the velvety sound of his voice, she pushed it all aside. "Why don't we keep our minds on our work right now. We have a very sick little girl on our hands. She could use your undivided attention, Ty."

She led Ty to a small room at the back of the pediatric ICU. "We moved her to a quieter area yesterday to allow the family some privacy. Since it's been leaked that you're going to be working on her, there were too many people hanging around, hoping to catch a glimpse of you."

Baby Girl Dombrowski's new room had a homey feel to it. Her parents had left stuffed animals along the windowsill, and a family picture taped to her warmer. Classical music played on a portable CD player.

Each time she entered a child's hospital room, all Lily could think was how unfair these situations were. Children shouldn't suffer. That was one thing she was sure of.

As much as she hated to admit it, Ty was doing some good work.

"So what can you tell me about this little one?" Ty was looking into the warmer at the sleeping little girl.

Lily breathed a short sigh of relief. Finally. No more talk about them. Getting down to business was all she wanted to do. "Baby Girl Dombrowski. Sixteen days old. Perfectly healthy at birth until she started having trouble breathing."

"No precursors to the distress?"

"If you mean did she show any signs of more problems? No."

Ty stood beside her. She tried to ignore how much her body liked the closeness. "We ruled out pulmonary hypertension, heart failure, pretty much everything imaginable."

"And that's why you asked me here." Ty was kneeling by the warmer now.

"No, that's why the hospital administrators asked you here." As she started to open the warmer, Ty put his hand up to stop her.

"Keep it closed. She needs to stay warm." He didn't even look at her when he said this, as if the little girl was the only thing in the room at that moment.

He had always been dedicated. As a doctor at Kensington, all those years ago when they'd been together, his patients were devoted to him.

She wanted to fight back with another smart comment, but all she could think about was the warmth from his touch. Ty's hands still had a roughness to them from his years as a construction worker trying to pay his way through medical school. The roughness of his skin only added to the sensations.

Ty pulled his hand away from her. "Try not to open the warmer unless you really need to," he continued. "I can assess her without opening the doors."

Her voice hardened. "How can you possibly do that without touching the baby?" The whole Baby Whisperer phenomenon had a certain mystic quality that rubbed her the wrong way. She'd seen the show, of course. Ty was a natural host, and his charm and sincerity with his guests, some going through the pain of a sick child themselves, made an hour of programming seem like ten minutes. She could see why he was so popular.

But his ideas about "sensing" a baby's illness as a way to diagnose them, seemed all a bit flaky to her.

Ty gave her a mysterious smile, so Lily stopped talking and just watched him work, tamping down emotions she didn't quite understand.

Maybe it was just jealousy, not professional but personal. She hadn't wanted to share Ty with anyone after he started becoming a huge success. And he had been taken away from her in a heartbeat.

Lily had been visiting a friend in Reno when the twin babies who'd gone almost a week without sleep ended up at Kensington Hospital. The family had already been to five hospitals in five different states, searching for a cure. They were on their way to a university-based hospital in the area to see a specialist when one of the twins started projectile vomiting.

So the family stopped at Kensington and Ty had a look at the twins. Overnight, seemingly effortlessly, he'd diagnosed an overactive thyroid. The twins were sleeping within twenty-four hours of their admission.

And how did he do it? Well, that was the secret to his success right there.

Before arriving at Kensington, the twins' story had been picked up by local and some national media. It was a heartfelt story of a desperate mother, fighting against all odds for her children. But when the mother spoke to the press about the young doctor at Kensington Hospital who solved her children's deadly sleeplessness by seeming to only whisper to them during the night, the story took on epic proportions and was beamed around the globe.

Within two weeks of her return, CBS had offered Ty the talk show, and other hospitals with sick babies were begging for his assistance.

Amid the whirlwind of notoriety, Lily and Ty never got a chance to discuss their future. It seemed Ty didn't have a moment when someone in the media didn't want to talk to him. One day he was here, the next he was in California. And eventually, the long-distance phone calls just petered out. It was just easier for her to try to forget him. She wasn't part of his life any more.

Ty lifted the handcrafted blanket from the top of the Plexiglas warmer and looked down at the baby. "No notable nasal flaring. Breathing seems calm, unlabored."

Despite her attempt to remain silent, Lily's emotions got the best of her. "You're ignoring my question. How can you assess her without touching her?"

"I've seen a lot of babies. Experience generates knowledge." He smiled at her, and she had to fight the feeling that he was mocking her, just a little.

She stubbornly pushed on. "So have I, but I still need to listen to their lungs, hear how clear they are. Don't you even want to look at an X-ray? I'm sure there's an inch-thick file and a disk drive full of research somewhere that you could review."

"I've been doing this for a while, remember?"

Lily almost harrumphed, her impatience bordering on frustration. "Yes, but—" She stopped mid-sentence.

"And this is how I always start – observing. Isn't that part of the basis of our practice?" He smiled again. No, he wasn't mocking her. She was just being paranoid.

Stop it, Lily! He's a great doctor and he's here to help. You should feel lucky.

"Okay, point taken. But I still think you should look at her medical records."

She stepped back and let Ty do his work. His technique might be different, a little unorthodox, but it had worked for countless other babies. And she needed answers if they were going to help this little girl. She and her team had been stumped by the baby's problems for days. It was dangerous to let this continue. They needed Ty.

After a couple minutes, she shifted position. Her foot was falling asleep. How long was he just going to stare? What could he possibly see that couldn't be discovered with a stethoscope or lab results?

She coughed. "Whenever you're ready to move on, just let me know."

Ty wasn't listening to her any more. He was off in another world. She'd never seen him like this. His eyes seemed to have clouded over. She fought the urge to wave her fingers in front of his face to snap him out of it.

Where was the energetic, talkative doctor she remembered? In the past, their conversations were dynamic, sometimes heated, but there was always an interaction between them. They talked to each other when they discussed cases. That's how they found solutions. Now, he was shutting her out.

"The problem seems to be respiratory on the surface . . ." He lowered his voice and he walked over to the other side of the warmer, stooping down to look at the baby from another angle. From his new stance he was almost eye to eye with the little girl.

"I agree." Lily watched Ty with curiosity. "So any other thoughts?"

Noise from across the unit distracted her. When she looked up, she saw a group of doctors and staff watching them through the window. They pointed and waved. She was certain they had come to see Ty – the infamous Baby Whisperer – at work.

"Your fan club has found you."

Ty looked up from the baby again and waved at them. He broke into a huge smile. "It seems I have some visitors to attend to. Care to join me?" He held out his hand to her.

Lily wanted to take it, to touch him again. But she couldn't. She couldn't fall for him again and then watch while he packed his bags and returned to his life of fame and popularity in California.

"No thanks," she said. "I'll wait here."

"Suit yourself," he said, jogging over to his admirers, who enveloped him in a swarm, harassing him for autographs, handshakes, photographs. And through it all he just smiled and laughed, eating it up. She would never be enough for him. That much was certain. He needed the adoration of the crowd as if it were oxygen. He couldn't survive without it.

Ty was always happiest when he was entertaining a crowd. He craved the recognition and attention yet she never quite understood why. She only required a comfortable, cosy home and some soft slippers at the end of the day. It was one of the differences they'd recognized early on in their relationship.

During his absence, however, she realized she wanted Ty too. Home and slippers sometimes just weren't enough. But what could she do? She couldn't leave Bedford, at least not permanently. This was her home.

She sighed. He hadn't changed. She was disappointed in herself for thinking he ever could.

Chapter Two

"Stop any fluids on Baby Girl Dombrowski." Ty's order to a nearby nurse broke Lily out of her thoughts.

What did he think he was doing?

"Keep a close eye on her and restart fluids when she's more alert." Ty told the nurse, who nodded.

"What are you doing?" Lily stormed over to him. How could he be giving orders without consulting her?

"I know what's wrong, " Ty said. "It suddenly came to me. She needs more sodium. If sodium levels are too low, it impairs breathing and she can't get enough oxygen. I'm going to stop the fluids and possibly start a hypertonic solution."

It felt like a logical solution but . . . "Wait a minute. Don't you want to at least check the labs first? If I recall correctly, her sodium levels have been normal since admission. "

"That doesn't mean there's nothing wrong. It takes time for sodium levels to drop in babies. You know the research."

She did but she wasn't ready to rush. Another one of the differences between them was that he'd jump off a cliff without hesitation. Lily preferred to assess the situation, and check out the jagged rocks below first.

The door was open and the staff were paying attention to every word they said. A young man in glasses was even taking notes. His decision would be taken seriously. After all, it was considered that he was the little girl's best hope.

Lily breathed deeply to calm herself, and then she strode over to the open door, shutting it against the audible dismay of Ty's hangers-on. Privacy was what she needed.

Okay. She'd give Ty the benefit of the doubt. Stopping fluids for a short time wouldn't hurt Baby Girl Dombrowski. And if he was right, it would be a huge step in the right direction. "How about we start a slow infusion while we go over the medical records together?"

He put up his hands in a show of mock deference. "You win, Dr Finley. We can review the materials together. Lead the way."

They took the back exit out of the room so they could avoid the crush of fans. They could hide away in her office and look at the records, have a coffee and relax without any undue attention.

But was it really a good idea to be alone with Ty? Or was that exactly what she wanted?

As they walked down the hall outside the pediatric ICU, Ty realized he'd made a mistake. It wasn't a good idea to have Lily as his escort. Her constant presence proved to be too much of a distraction for his mind and body.

If it wasn't her familiar scent of jasmine and violet assaulting his senses, it was her voice and unrelenting will that was giving his concentration a run for its money.

When he'd left two years ago, he'd thought it was for the best. Lily had wealth and a blue-blooded pedigree in her background. Most of her family graduated from Harvard. He was just a small-town pediatrician from a working-class family. So when fame and fortune called, he couldn't say no. This was a chance to prove himself at last, not only to Lily but to himself.

Lily stopped in front of her office door and pulled out her keys. Ty looked at the brass nameplate and smiled.

Lily Finley, MD Chief, Pediatric ICU

"Congratulations seem to be in order," he said.

"Thank you."

"Never thought chief was something you wanted to pursue." At least she'd never mentioned it during the time they were together. "Eats up a lot of free time to maintain a position like that."

"I've had a lot more free time on my hands lately." She shrugged her shoulders. "Work seemed like the best place to use it."

Was she referring to his absence?

"What about climbing?" he asked.

Lily was an avid climber. She'd spend her off-hours scaling the local mountains. "Weren't you planning to climb in Acadia National Park last year?"

She turned to look at him, and the disappointment in her expression jarred his resolve. "We were planning on climbing in Acadia, if I remember correctly, but you decided to leave."

Regret gnawed at his gut. He almost welcomed the voice that piped up behind them.

"Dr Finley, I've been looking for you." A portly doctor in glasses stopped in front of Lily.

"Hello, Dr Enright. So nice to see you—"

But Dr Enright didn't let Lily finish. "I've been waiting for your summary on Baby Girl Dombrowski. What is taking so long?"

"I'm sorry, Doctor. Baby Girl Dombrowski is everyone's priority. Mine especially. And I've had a lot of requests. All of them are being answered as they're received."

"My requests should take priority over any others." Enright raised his voice. Lily remained stalwart throughout the tongue-lashing. The only noticeable clue of her rising anger was the shade of red slowly crawling up her face. It took every bit of Ty's patience not to say anything.

Unfortunately, Ty didn't have very much patience to begin with. "Is this how you talk to all of your staff, Doctor?"

"Excuse me?"

Ty edged closer to make his point. He was a good six inches taller than Dr Enright. "I'm what you'd call new here so I'm wondering if this is how all staff are treated."

"You're new here? Maybe Dr Finley can apprise you on the proper protocol when addressing physicians." Dr Enright gave Ty the once-over, obviously looking for a name tag or some form or identification.

Ty put his hand out. "I'm Dr Ty Ross."

Enright looked at Ty's hand as if it were covered in mud. "Well, Dr Ross, it seems I haven't had the pleasure." Before Ty could respond, though, Enright's face took on a look of sheer shock. "Dr Ross, I'm sorry, I didn't recognize it was you."

"I'm glad you didn't. Seems to me there needs to be a discussion with administration about your unpleasant attitude toward senior staff."

"I don't think that's necessary," Lily said. She stepped between the two doctors.

"Yes, well . . ." Dr Enright tried to make light of the situation. "Hope to see more of you, Dr Ross. I've heard a lot of good things about your work."

As Dr Enright walked away, Lily opened her office door. "Sometimes he can be a bit overbearing."

"A bit? I was ready to throw him across the hall."

"Not necessary but greatly appreciated." She smiled to emphasize her gratitude.

What a smile. He liked being the one who had put it on her face. In the past, he wouldn't have been able to stand up for her like that. The doctor would have been his senior, and may have fired him on the spot. But now, as the world-famous Baby Whisperer, he had the power to be himself and do what he thought was right.

Lily's office was very chic. How couldn't it be? He recognized the large stone paperweight. It was one of the flattest stones he'd ever seen. He'd been going to skip it across the lake but Lily wanted to keep it. And she did.

Beside it was a picture of them.

Ty took this as a positive. He remembered the day all too well. They'd been near the bay skipping rocks when they asked someone to snap a photo. Lily loved skipping rocks as much as he did. It was one of the things he missed when he was away from her.

"Okay, here are the files," Lily said, tapping her fingers on the thick stack. She pulled up a chair and signaled for him to sit beside her. Ty hesitated at first, not sure if being this close was a good idea.

"Can I ask a question?" Lily asked.

"Shoot."

"Why?"

Ty stared into her blue eyes. His instincts worked wonders on infants and children but didn't do squat when it came to understanding women, and Lily especially. "I'm afraid you're going to have to be a little more explicit."

She smiled. "You didn't have to listen to me. You could've gone ahead and ordered the sodium drip without my approval."

Ty leaned back in his chair and put his hands behind his head. "I guess that's true, but I value your opinion. I'm usually right, you know, but I'm glad you stood up for Baby Girl Dombrowski instead of just giving in to me."

She blushed, reminding Ty why he'd originally fallen in love with her. Lily had a tendency toward unabashed honesty. And she didn't hide her embarrassment about it. "I wasn't trying to second guess you," she said. "I just wanted to make sure the correct steps were being followed."

He wanted to touch her but he didn't dare. If only he wasn't here for such a short time. If only . . .

"Do you really think it's your calling then? This whole Baby Whisperer thing?" Lily asked, locking her office door again as they ventured back out into the hallway after finishing with the records.

"I can't really explain it, but I think it is. All I know is I can help these babies. It's a feeling I have. It guides me to a way to help them."

"Okay, now you're losing me. I'm sorry to be so infuriatingly pragmatic but I'm your everyday, run-of-the-mill, conventional doctor." Maybe she needed to be more open. Maybe he could teach her a thing or two. "So tell me, Ty, where is this 'feeling' you talk about?"

Ty took Lily's hand and placed it on his chest.

"Here. In my heart."

Lily closed her eyes. She could feel his heartbeat. She was afraid that if she opened her eyes again, she might start crying.

"I've missed you," Ty whispered.

Lily whispered back, her eyes still closed. "I've missed you too."

She opened her eyes and saw that he was close enough to kiss her. But he held off. He kissed her hand instead.

"Dr Ross! Dr Ross!" At the end of the corridor, a group of nurses yelled his name, waving digital cameras for pictures. "Dr Ross, over here!"

Lily narrowed her eyes in disgust as a smile broke over his face and he smirked at his adoring audience.

"Duty calls," he said, smirking at her like a teenager.

Now? He was leaving now? Just when they were getting somewhere? When they might finally have a talk about their future?

"Ty, don't go. We need to talk." Lily appealed to him with her eyes, trying to get him to stay, but he kept backing away from her, down the corridor. Was he frightened by what almost occurred between them? By the fact that he had almost kissed her?

"We can talk more soon. I have a press conference in the lobby in ten mintues, so . . ." Ty checked his watch. "Gotta go."

She was exasperated. "You're leaving? Now?" There was an edge of utter disbelief in her voice. "But . . ."

"My fans, you know. I can't keep them waiting." He flashed her a cheeky smile, turned and ran down the corridor. A cheer went up from the nurses as he reached them.

Infuriating! Lily spun on her heels and stormed away. She wanted to throw something at him.

Chapter Three

Lily discovered a handwritten invitation on her office door a few hours later. She recognized Ty's scribble before she even read the contents.

Your presence is required for dinner.
Tonight, 8 p.m., Bucky's.
Formal engagement. Formal attire required.

Great. Ty was giving another show for his admirers and she had to be part of it. Part of her – the part just wanting to go home and relax – didn't want to go. The other part wanted to spend as much time with Ty as possible before he left. No matter how much it hurt.

Being with him today left her conflicted. She wanted to be selfish, give him an ultimatum and, hopefully, force him to stay. But she wasn't sure that he would. She was worried that he loved the world more than he loved her now. He wouldn't be happy here.

Since Bucky's was only a few blocks away from her apartment, though, Lily decided to go. The night air helped clear her thoughts. If only it'd shoo away some of her anxiety and frustration.

The entrance to Bucky's was unusually calm. In fact, she was the only person at the front door. Usually, at this time of night, there'd be a bustling crowd waiting to grab a seat.

Ty startled her when he opened the door just as she reached for the handle. "Welcome." He wore an immaculate tuxedo and his hair was slicked back. He looked beyond dashing.

"Where is everyone?" Lily asked, as they entered the visibly empty restaurant.

"We are everyone," he said, adjusting his bow tie. "I commandeered the whole restaurant tonight. They are closed to everyone but us."

"No cameras?"

"Why would there be cameras?"

"Your invitation indicated this was a formal event. I thought for sure there'd be cameras."

"Not a single one in sight as you can clearly see. It's just you and me." Ty took her hand.

They were here alone. This was a surprise. "I . . . I don't know what to say."

"No words are required. Dinner is served."

They chatted over filet mignon, twice-baked potatoes and French-fried corn.

"I want you to come back to California with me."

"Ty, we've been over this before."

He took her hand in his. "I've missed you, Lily-belle. Forty-eight hours here with you isn't going to cut it. Come back with me. Stay with me. Live with me."

Lily had a "yes" inside her fighting to pop out. But, sacrifices needed to be made on both sides. If she left, she'd be sacrificing everything and Ty nothing.

"Why not stay here?"

"There's nothing here for me." Ty took a sip of his champagne.

His words hurt worse than a dozen wasp stings. "I'm here. Doesn't that mean anything to you?"

"You know that's not what I meant."

She picked up her champagne flute. "There's plenty here for you and it's not just me. This whole hospital has missed you."

"My contract with the network stipulates I have to remain in California. Even if I wanted to return, I couldn't."

"Really?"

"If I read the fine print one more time, my eyes will cross, Lily-belle."

The band had started to play, and Ty extended his hand to her. "Would you do me the honor?"

She laughed. How could she be mad at him? It was impossible. She took his hand and he led her onto the empty dance floor.

As he held her tight, she snuggled into his chest, feeling safe and warm.

"What is it you want, Lily?" He murmured in her ear. "What can I get you? Anything. I can fly you to Rome, take you on a Mediterranean cruise. I can do this now for you. Name anything. I want to make you happy."

Lily's smile grew at his words. "A kiss, you silly devil. All I ask for is a kiss."

Ty dipped his head down and kissed her. His lips were as smooth and enticing as ever. His hand moved to the back of her neck and pulled her closer. She remembered this. She remembered him.

The hooting and clapping took her totally by surprise. Seems they weren't alone any more after all. A huge crowd, arrayed in formal attire, had gathered around the dance floor. She had been so preoccupied with being in his arms and with his kiss that she hadn't noticed them multiplying.

Then the flashbulbs started going off.

Lily frowned. "I thought you said it was only us tonight."

"It's just a few people, and some journalists who hadn't been able to get to the hospital for my official visit. It's okay that they're here, no? Let's go say hi." Ty grabbed her hand and began pulling her off the dance floor toward his waiting legion of fans.

"No, Ty. Stop it. I don't want to." She tried to pull her hand out of his grasp, but he was too strong for her.

"Come on. Just ten minutes. I'll answer some questions and then we'll go." Ty was already waving to a few people he seemed to recognize.

She summoned the last of her strength and ripped her hand from his. He stared back at her, shocked. "I'm going home. I will not be part of your circus any longer!"

All eyes were on her as she marched out of the restaurant but nobody seemed too bothered. She heard Ty behind her, yelling her name, but by the time she reached the door, he had given up and gone back to the party, she guessed. She waited for him outside for a few minutes, but when he didn't appear, she knew that she had been waiting in vain.

It started to rain as she walked home, and the hem of her formal gown ripped under her heel. Oh well. The perfect end to the perfect evening.

Chapter Four

His plan wasn't working and it was killing him. Twenty-four hours after his initial assessment of Baby Girl Dombrowski, his call for increased sodium had failed.

Add last night's disaster with Lily to this, and he was officially depressed. After she had run out, he'd tried to follow her, had yelled for her to stop, but soon the crowd descended on him and slowed his progress.

They were everywhere. All clamouring for his attention. He'd never felt scared or claustrophobic when presented with a large group of fans before, but this time they pressed on him and seemed to pry the breath right out of his lungs. He panicked a little. When he tried to push past, he couldn't. It was as if they held him there.

It was another hour before he was able to leave. And only then because he played ill and said he had a headache. When he got outside into the fresh air, Lily was nowhere in sight. She'd headed home, of course. Could he blame her?

Not only had Lily rejected him but Baby Girl Dombrowski seemed to be too. She refused to listen to him and get better. Why wasn't this baby responding to the sodium like she should?

"Little girl, you're testing my resolve." He touched the Plexiglas lightly. "You're too young to be doing this."

"A woman is never too young to challenge a man." He spun around and saw Lily standing in the doorway, a small smile on her lips.

"She's really working to breathe," Ty said.

"Maybe she's dry," Lily said. "We could give her some fluid."

"She can't take any more fluid." Ty ran his fingers through his hair. "I thought I had this. Even the labs supported my theory."

The baby's sodium levels were still within normal limits but they were dropping. What could he have missed?

"What about genetic testing?" Lily asked.

Ty's elbows now rested on top of the warmer, his hands covering his face. "We've done that. There aren't any matches to anything. I have no clue what's going on."

It was midnight when Ty walked back into the pediatric ICU. He'd spent the rest of his afternoon with Lily going over Baby Girl Dombrowski's medical records again. And again.

At 11 p.m., he told Lily to go home and get a good night's sleep. Now he was all alone. At midnight, the pediatric ICU was almost deserted. The nurses on duty flitted by occasionally like ghosts and paid him no mind. He felt like he could breathe easily for the first time since he'd arrived at his old hospital.

It was Lily. She was on his mind. Hell, she was always on his mind. He knew he needed to make a decision about their future once and for all. Then why couldn't he sit down and talk with her about it? Why was he always running away?

Life had become too much. He couldn't think straight. The flashbulbs, the media, the adoration. It had all gotten stale. And a little scary, to tell the truth.

The hospital tonight was so quiet. No one around. He took a deep breath.

The lights were dim when he walked into the little girl's room. Peaceful. He pulled the rocking chair close enough to the warmer so he could see her face.

"So, little girl," he said, keeping his voice at his trademark whisper. "What's it gonna be? Do we need to find another direction here? Or do you just need more time?"

He opened the Plexiglas door and reached in. The baby's hand was warm, and she clasped her little fingers around his pinkie finger though her eyes were closed. It was the first time he'd seen any real sign of movement in her since he'd arrived.

He smiled to himself at her gentle touch. This was what he was good at. Why was he doubting himself?

It was obvious what the little girl needed. It was exactly what he needed himself.

Time.

He took a deep breath and laughed softly. They both just needed a bit of time.

Lily was dressed in scrubs and a traditional white lab coat for Ty's last visit to Kensington Memorial.

Last visit, at least for now.

Ty's prediction about low sodium levels was right on the mark. Baby Girl Dombrowski had started to improve by the next day. The little girl's response had taken longer than expected. But she was doing well now. Her parents had now officially named her, and everything was getting back to normal.

It was time for Ty's big, ceremonial goodbye to Kensington Hospital. The film crew had set up in an open area outside Taylor Dombrowski's room and waited for Ty to arrive. It was quiet now, except for the humming of video cameras and the isolated pop of a few flashbulbs.

The warmer had been removed from the room and a proper crib was now in place.

"Not sure I believe this is happening." The tears streaming down Kate Dombrowski's face reflected Lily's own anguish. But Taylor's mother wasn't feeling the same torment as she was. Kate Dombrowski's daughter would be going home soon. All Lily knew was that she'd be losing a part of her heart soon.

Thank the stars I can cry now and it will only be seen as happiness.

Lily stood up from the chair and set the little girl in her mother's arms.

"I'm not sure what to do next." Kate clutched her daughter closer and kissed her forehead.

"I have some suggestions." Ty walked in the room, and looked down at the bundled baby.

"It's good to see you here, Dr Ross," said Kate.

"Looks like little Taylor will be wearing ribbons in her hair and climbing trees in no time," he said.

When Ty walked out of the room, Lily followed him. "Is that it?"

"I'm sorry about last night."

"There's nothing to be sorry about."

"Yes, there is. I need to take some time. A little time to get my life in order. It's been so crazy. Maybe too crazy. I need to find some balance, you know?"

"I know," Lily said.

"For the time being, I have to leave. I'm leaving now for us." He lifted her chin so he could look into her eyes. "I will make one promise. I promise I will come back, and when I do there will be plenty of time for us."

As she watched him leave, Lily broke her own promise to herself. She cried over him. Again.

Lily avoided going home that evening. Like when Ty left before, Lily wanted to put all her energy into work. Even when she felt drained of all her energy, she pushed herself to work harder. It was the only way to forget and to move forward. There was nothing worth putting her efforts into any more.

After her staff shoved her out the sliding glass door and into her car, telling her to get some rest, she drove home slowly. What was the rush?

She found a note and gift box waiting for her outside her apartment door. Inside the box was a map of Acadia National Park. The best areas to climb were highlighted.

Ty left a note, too, tucked inside the map.

Don't give up on your dreams. And, more importantly, don't give up on me. I'll always be there for you. I expect to hear about Acadia.

Epilogue

Kensington Hospital's annual 'Healthy Baby' celebration was in full swing by early evening three months later. The evening gathering celebrated the health of all the children who'd been treated. This year parents took time off to help prepare for the day and others came just to share in the joy.

The pediatric ICU had good reason to celebrate this year. The recovery of Taylor Dombrowski had been one of the hospital's high points. All thanks to Ty.

Since he'd left Kensington, he hadn't tried to contact her. Lily hadn't forgotten his promise to return but she didn't hold out much hope.

She scanned the crowd and soaked in the happiness. As she laughed at two children doing an impromptu skit, an approaching figure caught her attention. She couldn't see who it was because of the crowd of people gathering around them.

Before too long, his swagger gave him away. He approached like a cowboy on a mission. His attire had changed: faded blue jeans and a polo shirt – no leather jacket.

By the time Ty reached her, he'd managed to lose some of the crowd. She didn't know what to say. Her heart beat so fast she focused on trying to calm down. But how could she? Ty was here. And he was smiling.

Yes, she was excited to see him. The three months had seemed much longer than the two years. But was he here for good?

They stared at each other as if the silence was their way of communicating.

"What are you doing here?" she asked.

Ty smiled and pressed a kiss to her lips. "I thought I'd come get reacquainted."

She looked at him quizzically. "With me?"

He laughed. "With you. And with the hospital. I haven't worked here in two years. If I'm going to be head of the pediatric department I'm going to have learn the ropes here all over again."

Lily shook her head to try to clear it. Had she heard him correctly? "You're staying?"

"It seems that taping the show here wouldn't be that much different from taping it in California. A studio is a studio, you know?" He kissed her lips again. "The only attention I want in the future is yours. I promise. No more leaving."

She took a deep breath. Could this really be happening?

"But there is something I need to confirm." Ty tucked a wayward hair behind her ear. Her insides did a double flip.

"What's that?"

"At the end of the day, when our jobs are done, we shut out the world and pretend it's just you and me. No cameras, no VIPs, no throngs of followers." He winked at her. "I know how much of a problem that can be for you."

She laughed, and then threw herself into his arms. It was only the two of them now.

That's exactly how she liked it.

WAKE ME WHEN IT'S OVER

Cynthia D'Alba

Chapter One

"Great job with the board interview," Dr Troy Monroe said as he lowered himself into a large, leather desk chair. "Anderson sure was flattering about your clinical skills."

Dr Jack Bequette took the chair across from the St Michael's Hospital Chief of Staff. "Thanks. I wasn't that worried about the board. Hell, I've played golf with every single one of them at one time or the other. Now, Dean Anderson? He had me a little worried. Those questions about my interest in research had me sweating."

Troy laughed. "Yeah. I noticed, but you did fine. Besides, when was the last time we did any research here? We're just an adjunct clinical location for the med school."

Jack leaned forward, his elbows braced on his knees. "What do you think my chances are?"

"Pretty good, I think." Troy shrugged. "But remember, there's still one more guy to interview."

"What do you know about him?"

"Nothing beyond what's on his CV. Good education. Good work history. But we're such a tight hospital when it comes to the work environment. He'd have to fit in to make it. You know what I mean. He could look great on paper but be a real dick in person. May be the reason he's looking to relocate after only three years at his current place."

"Okay then. I'll hope he's a major SOB."

Troy laughed again. "Hey, one more thing before you go." He opened a drawer and plopped a stack of files crammed with papers on his desk. "I've continued to do all the anaesthesia department paperwork. Since you're the leading candidate to replace me as chief, probably time you took it over."

Jack's brows pulled into a frown. "What kind of paperwork?"

Troy laid an arm on top of the files. "Weekly production reports. Monthly drug stats. Personnel issues handled, like counseling on job performance. Morbidity and morality reports." He flipped a couple of files until he pulled one from the stack. "And my personal favorite – the monthly report to the board that summarizes everything else." He put the file back on the stack. "I'll be so glad to get rid of this extra paperwork. You have no idea."

No kidding. Jack had no idea there'd be so many different written reports he'd have to file. For the past eight months, he'd done all the surgery scheduling, the resident reviews, the medical student reviews as well as the drug usage monitoring. And there were more forms he needed to do? Crap. "Sure," he said with more enthusiasm than he felt. "You should have clued me in a long time ago."

"Here." Troy pushed the towering stack of files across the desk. "Take them. You might as well get familiar with all of it."

"Gee, thanks," Jack said with a grimace. "Didn't know you cared."

A knock stopped Troy's reply. "Yes?"

The door eased open and Marcie Gamble's head popped in. "Dr Stone's here," Troy's secretary announced.

Troy nodded. "Thanks, Marcie. Ask him to have a seat. I'll be right there."

Jack stood when Troy rose. "Thanks for your support, Troy."

Troy came around to slap him on the back. "It'll be great to have you in the job on a permanent basis. Want to meet for a drink later?"

"Water's Edge?" Jack picked up the file stack.

"See you there."

"Have fun with Dr Stone."

Troy rolled his eyes. "Thank God this is the last interview."

The two men walked into the reception area. A curvy redhead dressed in an olive-green business suit stood admiring the drawing of the proposed hospital expansion.

"Dr Stone. Dr Monroe is ready to see you now."

The statuesque woman turned when Marcie spoke. She smiled and Jack's gut tugged as though it'd been stitched too tightly. The air left his lungs in a rush when she took a step toward them.

"Good morning," she said. "Which one of you is Dr Monroe?"

Troy held out his hand. "I'm Troy Monroe. Nice to meet you, Dr Stone." He gestured toward Jack. "This is Dr Jack Bequette."

Dr Stone, who had to be close to six feet tall, extended her hand. "Dr Bequette. Nice to meet you. I'm Tommye Jo Stone."

Jack took her hand. An immediate sizzle of lust zinged through his system. His gaze rolled across an oval face with a straight nose and full lips. High cheekbones accentuated a pair of sparkling emerald-green eyes. "It's a pleasure," he said. He decided he may have held her hand a little longer than he intended when Troy coughed. Jack smiled and let go.

"You're on staff here?" she asked, her voice exuding a husky roughness that made Jack want to spend hours listening to her speak.

"I'm the Interim Chief for the Department of Anaesthesia."

Her face lit up. "Oh, that's wonderful. I have a lot of questions I can't wait to ask you."

"If you're ready, Dr Stone," Troy said, sweeping his hand toward the open office door. "We've only got a short while to visit before you're due to meet with the hospital board of directors."

"Of course." She looked at Jack. "Nice to meet you, Dr Bequette. I look forward to speaking with you further."

She and Troy walked into his office and shut the door.

"You should see your face," Marcie said. "You look stunned."

Jack shook his head. "I am. That's the last candidate for my job, right?"

She nodded.

"I thought she was a guy."

Marcie grinned. "We all did. Apparently we were all wrong."

"Damn," Jack muttered as he walked off. "Just damn."

Later that afternoon, Jack headed over to the Water's Edge, the bar located at Lake Waterton Yacht Club. Since his houseboat was parked in slot two, he found himself at the Water's Edge often. He knew everyone there and they knew him.

After retrieving his laptop and the stack of Troy's files from the passenger seat, he hit the lock button on his car and headed inside. His usual table, the rounded lakefront booth, was vacant and waiting. He waved at the bartender, an older man who'd been there for as far back as Jack could remember. Sam, the bartender, nodded, poured a bourbon over ice and walked it over to Jack's table.

He set the drink on a fresh napkin. Gesturing to Jack's laptop computer, the old man shook his head. "You're getting old, Jack. I remember the days when you'd bring a woman or two with you in here. Now you bring your laptop."

Jack laughed. "Thanks for the drink, Sam. I've got a little work to do and I'd rather be doing it with a bourbon in my hand."

"Just seems sad to be wasting good bourbon on work instead of a beautiful woman."

Jack grinned as he raised his glass in a salute. "You got that right."

He powered up his laptop and loaded the medical student and anaesthesia resident schedules for the next two weeks. Since St Michael's had become an adjunct clinical rotation for the medical school, he'd found himself doing as much teaching and observation as actual medical practice. He'd never viewed himself as a teacher and was surprised when he discovered not only did he like it, but he was good at it. Going over the assigned cases didn't take but a couple of minutes. He made a couple of changes, and forwarded the revised schedule to the chief resident to disseminate. Then he pulled the first file off the stack.

For the next couple of hours, Sam kept him supplied in fresh drinks as Jack read through page after page of administrative reports, graphs, statistics, and other headache-producing minutia associated with the position he sought on a full-time basis. Nothing was terribly mind-blowing or difficult. He could do it, but the number of trees sacrificed to produce this many reams of paper should be criminal.

The cell phone on his belt chirped. "Dr Bequette."

"Not gonna make it down to Water's Edge after all," Troy Monroe said in way of a greeting.

"No sweat. Problem?"

"No, not really. Just family stuff. Oh, one thing of interest. Charlie Bobbett got sick during the interview. Looking like a gall bladder attack. We've got him in the ED running tests, but Dr Stone's interview with the board was cut short. They've asked her to stay until Monday so they can pick up where they left off."

"So what does that mean?"

"No idea, really. Just that she'll be here a couple of days longer than intended. Aw, damn. That means I need to get Marcie to adjust her hotel and flight arrangements. Gotta run. Catch you later."

Jack checked the time on his cell phone. Where had the last four hours gone? He glanced around the bar. Sam had been replaced by Frank, the night bartender. The evening waitresses had come on duty. The sun had dropped low enough in the sky to be sending long orange daggers over the water's waves. The glass on his table was empty but for the life of him, he couldn't remember how many drinks he'd had. Sam had alternated between bourbon and water, and Jack drank whatever had been close at hand. He didn't feel drunk. In fact, he didn't even have a buzz. He smiled to himself. Sam probably put more water on the table than bourbon. It'd be just like the old bartender to think he needed to temper Jack's intake.

"This seat taken?" a southern female voice drawled.

Jack grinned and looked up. "Depends. Did you finally get smart and dump the sheriff for me?"

Dr Tess Sweeny slid into the booth. "You wish," she said with a laugh.

She had no idea how accurate that statement was. Jack had taken Tess Sweeny out a couple of times and he'd really liked her. He'd thought she might be the one for him until she hooked up with the local sheriff, Kyle Monroe. Now Tess and Monroe were so tight that a strand of dental floss couldn't be passed between them.

"So where's our county sheriff?" Jack looked around the bar. "He's got a gun. I want to make sure we're done making out before he gets here."

Tess playfully slapped his arm. "He's meeting me here. He said he had to run by and talk to his brother about some family thing."

Kyle Monroe, Tess's beau, was the twin brother of Troy Monroe. The two men were identical twins. The only way to tell them apart was haircuts. Sheriff Monroe kept his sheared short. Chief of Staff Monroe wore his a little longer.

"Besides, I told him I wanted to talk to you about the interview. You did great, by the way."

"Thanks. You meet today's candidate?"

"Dr Stone? Sure. I was on her interview schedule for this afternoon."

"What did you think?"

Tess signaled the waitress over. "Bring me a chardonnay."

"You got it. Doc? Another bourbon?"

Jack looked at the empty glass. "No. Bring me a Coke instead."

The waitress left and Jack looked at Tess. "Stop stalling. She that good?"

Tess pulled a frown. "Yes. She's that good, Jack. I still think you've got the inside track since you know everybody and you're already in the job, but she'd be a hell of an addition to the staff. Anderson was drooling over her research dollars."

Jack sighed. He picked up all the folders on the table. "See these?"

Tess nodded. "Sure. Looks like the stack I have on my desk. I am so behind on my monthly reports. That what you're working on this afternoon?"

"Hell, Tess. I didn't even know these existed until this afternoon. Troy continued to do these even after he took on Chief of Staff. Said he didn't want to train two different people to do them so he waited until his replacement was hired. He handed me all these this afternoon and told me to read them."

"And?"

Jack rubbed the headache behind his eyes. "I need some aspirin."

Tess handed him a couple of tablets from her purse at the same time the waitress set their drinks on the table.

"Put hers on my tab," Jack said.

"Thanks."

Jack threw back the pills and downed them with a gulp of soft drink. "So, go on. Tell me about Dr Stone."

"Thirty-six. Divorced. Everybody calls her T. J. or Jo. Has a mother living in the same town, a younger sister and a couple of younger brothers. Not sure where the siblings live at the moment. I didn't ask, but I felt downright petite standing next to her. Nice eyes, though. Did you notice?"

Jack huffed out a breath. "I mean, tell me about her work history."

Tess grinned. "Oops. My bad. But she is gorgeous and here for the weekend."

"Stop trying to play matchmaker, Tess. I don't need help getting a date."

She laid a hand on his arm. "I know that, Jack. It's just that I want you to be happy."

At one time, her touch would have sent his heart racing and desire surging through his blood. He was still attracted to her, but she'd made it clear they could be good friends and medical associates but nothing beyond that. Take it or leave it. He'd decided to take it, but sometimes he found himself quite jealous of the county sheriff.

"Bequette. You moving in on my woman?" The question came from a deep, gruff male voice. Jack didn't bother to look up. He knew the voice.

"You snooze, you lose, Monroe."

Tess playfully nudged Jack's arm with a chuckle then turned toward Kyle Monroe. "Hey, babe." She scooted over for Kyle to slide into the booth. They exchanged a quick kiss.

"Knock it off," Jack growled. "I haven't had dinner yet and you two are killing my appetite."

"Jealous, Bequette?" Kyle said with a grin. He waved the waitress over. "Bring me a beer. Whatever you've got on tap is fine." After she left, he turned back to the table. "So what's the discussion?"

"I was just telling Jack that I think he'd be great as permanent chief of anaesthesiology. Don't you?"

Kyle Monroe stretched an arm out along the back of the booth behind Tess. "Sure. But that's my brother's business. I stay out of his and he stays out of mine."

The waitress set an icy mug on the table along with a bowl of mixed nuts.

"So what was the family emergency?" Tess asked.

Kyle swallowed about half of the mug of beer in one long draw. "Mother. She's decided to move back to Waterton."

Tess frowned. "But that's good, right?"

"My dad doesn't think so."

Jack grabbed a handful of nuts from the bowl. "Your folks have been divorced for what? Fifteen years?"

"More like twenty. Mom waited until Troy and I were out of high school before she moved to Fayetteville to go back to college. I don't think they've been in the same town since." He swallowed the rest of his beer. "Gonna be an interesting fall. That's all I can say."

"Hello."

All three heads turned in the direction of the voice.

Tess spoke first. "Dr Stone. How are you? Please join us. Scoot over, Jack."

Dr Stone still looked as fresh as she had that morning. Her suit unwrinkled. Not a hair out of place. The pink of her cheeks still evident. How does a woman do that? Stay looking as though she just started her day when he knew she'd been talking to people for hours.

His heart pounded like a fist against his chest wall. Breathing became difficult as a band tightened around his torso. Blood flowed from his brain to below his waist. How could he think with no oxygen feeding his brain?

So unfair. The first woman he'd been attracted to in months and she turns out to be his worst nightmare.

"Jack," Tess said, snapping her fingers in front of his face. "Scoot over."

"Oh! Right." He slid toward Tess, opening up a space for his competition. "Dr Stone. How nice to see you again."

The smile she gave him lit up her face. "Thank you, Dr Bequette."

"Jack."

She nodded. "Jack." She looked across the table. "Tess. Dr Monroe. Good to see you again. Thank you for letting me join you." A worried expression flashed. "I'm not in someone's seat, am I?"

"Not at all," Tess said with a smile Jack recognized so well. Damn woman was going to play matchmaker. "And this is Sheriff Kyle Monroe, Troy Monroe's twin brother."

Embarrassed at her gaffe, a flush rushed up Dr Stone's face. "Oh my. I'm so sorry." She gave a little laugh. "But I did wonder about the drastic haircut since this morning. You look just like your brother, Sheriff Monroe."

Kyle smiled. "I've heard that. And it's Kyle."

"Call me Jo."

"I hate to run, but Tess and I have dinner plans."

Tess looked at Kyle in surprise. "We do?"

"I do." He grinned. "I've got your pontoon boat outside. I thought we could have one of our dinners-on-the-lake."

Jack looked at the two lovers, envious of their obvious devotion to each other.

"Well, that sounds like fun," Jo said.

Tess and Kyle slipped from the booth. "Nice to meet you, Jo," Kyle said. "Later, Bequette."

"Bye, y'all," Tess said.

Jack and Jo watched the couple walk off arm in arm.

"Well," Jo said on a long exhale. "This is awkward."

Jack looked at her. "How so?"

She lifted one eyebrow. "I'm here to get your job, and you want to make sure I'm not successful."

Jo studied her competition for head of the anaesthesia department. She'd known somebody who'd known somebody who'd been able to give her information on the inside candidate for the job before she arrived in Waterton, Arkansas. Every desirable job had at least one inside candidate, so she'd done her research.

Jacques Bequette, aka Jack Bequette, was thirty-nine, divorced, and a workaholic. He'd been educated at the University of Arkansas, gone to medical school at Baylor School of Medicine and had done his residency and fellowship at Emory in Atlanta. A southern-born, southern-raised, southern-educated insider. That was a lot for a northern female to overcome.

But the worst of the report was that he was a damn fine doctor who was developing a reputation as a first-class instructor. The residents respected him and the medical students hung on his every word, or at least that's what she'd heard. Now that she'd met him, she suspected a few single nurses were hanging on his every . . . whatever.

A tall man with hair that had turned a sexy silver and piercing blue eyes, Jack Bequette was a walking, talking erotic dream. With his cherry-red Corvette and houseboat-living arrangements (her spy had been quite thorough), he should have had a reputation as a ladies' man, but he didn't and that just didn't make sense to her.

"You think I'm your roadblock to head of anaesthesia?" Jack asked with a charming smile and a twinkle in his eyes.

She shrugged. "That's the rumor."

"You know hospitals. There's always the rumor of the day."

"It's the same everywhere, isn't it? The hospital grapevine. More news than you can get in the daily paper."

This time he laughed, his straight white teeth flashing between full, kissable lips.

No, no, no. She shouldn't be thinking that. It was wrong . . . so very wrong. This man had the power to wreck her carefully constructed plan. She shouldn't like him. The best plan would be to spend enough time to find his weakness then exploit it.

She glanced at her watch. Almost five. "Have you eaten?" she asked. "I'd love to buy you dinner and pick your brain. If you don't mind dining with the enemy."

"You know what they say. Keep your friends close and your enemies closer."

His deep-throated chuckle combined with just the right amount of roughness and southern drawl in his voice made her want to shut her eyes to close out any other stimulation and just listen to him talk. One of the bad aspects of not getting this job would be not getting to know this sexy southern man with a drawl that made her dizzy with lust.

"I hope we won't be enemies." She shifted uncomfortably on the seat. Somehow she knew Jack Bequette would not be a good man to have against you. "Frienemies, maybe."

That delicious chuckle vibrated from him again and she had the inane urge to lean over and put her head against his chest to soak in the sensation.

"Wish I could take you up on the dinner offer, but . . ." He lifted a stack of files off the seat next to him. "Got a little light reading for tonight and an early surgery tomorrow, so I'd better get going. Thanks for the offer. The food here is great. Try the filet mignon. I highly recommend it."

She tried to keep the disappointment from her face, but she'd never been good at hiding her feelings. She forced a smile. "Great. I'll give it a try. Dr Monroe invited me to observe the surgeries scheduled for tomorrow. I'm sure we'll run into each other."

He slid from the booth. "Great. See you then." After collecting his laptop and files, he gave her a lift of his chin in goodbye and walked off.

She ate a little regret with her filet mignon for dinner.

Early the next morning, Tess Sweeny was waiting in the circular driveway outside Jo's hotel when she walked out. Tess tapped the horn and waved. Jo opened the car door and leaned in.

"You here for me?"

"I sure am. Troy had a breakfast meeting that's running late. Called and asked me to give you a ride to the hospital. Observing in surgery today?"

She got in and fastened her seat belt. "I am." She held up her large satchel. "I brought scrubs. I wasn't sure how hard they might be to come by at St Michael's."

Tess wheeled out of the hotel drive and into the street. "Not bad if you wear an extra-small petite. Otherwise, the shelves can get a little bare."

"No different from any hospital I've ever worked in." Jo set the bag back on the floor. "You have anything interesting on your schedule this morning?"

"Well, let's see. I've got a gall bladder removal first thing. After that, I've got a patient with cholangiocarcinoma."

"Doing a Whipple? We've had a lot of success with that at Johns Hopkins in the last few years."

Jo's back cramped at the thought of standing at an OR table for the seven-hour Whipple operation. Removal of the gall bladder, the head of the pancreas, part of the bile duct and duodenum all in one surgery was exhausting for the surgery team.

However, in the hands of a skilled surgeon, the Whipple procedure gave the patient excellent long-term prognosis.

"Yep. I think it'll give the patient the best chance. Besides, it's a relatively young grandmother. Only fifty. I want her to have time with her new grandbabies."

Jo smiled. "You do many Whipples?"

"Quite a few. I get a lot of referrals because I'm just one of a few doctors locally who do."

"I'd like to come in on that if you don't mind."

"Glad for you to. Jack Bequette is doing the anaesthesia. He'll probably have a resident and med student with him, but I'm sure he won't mind your being in the room."

At the mention of Jack's name, Jo's stomach dipped. She placed her hand over it as though that could stop the feeling. No such luck.

Tess parked in a reserved spot in the hospital garage. She showed Jo to the female physician lounge.

"Once you're dressed, I'll introduce you to the surgery staff and turn you loose. That work for you?"

"Perfect," Jo said.

Once both women were clad in sky-blue scrubs, Tess led Jo over to a short, cute blonde woman also dressed in the standard hospital scrub attire. Given the visible sun damage Jo could see through the woman's tan, she estimated the woman's age at about thirty.

"Dr Stone. This is Kelly Franco. Kelly, this is Dr Stone." She looked at Kelly. "Dr Stone is here interviewing for Chief of the Anaesthesiology Department. She'll be observing in the OR today. I've assured her the staff would be happy to accommodate her."

Jo got the distinct impression that Tess's last statement was a warning of some type. A warning that the staff had better be friendly. After meeting Jack Bequette, she suspected a large number of the female OR nurses would line up behind Jack over her.

"Of course," Kelly replied with enthusiasm. "Don't hesitate to ask me or my staff for anything you might need, Dr Stone."

Tess looked at Jo. "Kelly is head nurse over the OR staff and does a damn fine job. We're lucky to have her."

Jo held out her hand to Kelly. "Nice to meet you, Kelly. I'm looking forward to spending time with your staff."

"You too, Dr Stone."

"I've got to get ready for my own case. I'll see you on Mrs Gate's Whipple," Tess said and walked off.

Once Tess was gone, Kelly smiled, and although the smile was on the woman's mouth, it never reached her stormy, green eyes. "Over here's the case board for today." She pointed to Grace Gate's name. "This is the Whipple Dr Sweeny was talking about. Why don't I give you a tour of our little area?"

Kelly was cordial and professionally friendly, introducing Jo to nurses, OR techs and a couple of residents. Just when she was beginning to question whether this was a good idea, a deep, southern drawl rocked her world.

"Well, well, well," Jack said. "Dr Stone. What a nice surprise."

"Good morning, Dr Bequette," she said as she wheeled around.

Nothing on earth had prepared her for the intensity of lust that punched her gut. Jack wore pressed blue scrubs and a scrub hat printed with images of Scooby-Doo. When he smiled at her, she almost staggered from the impact.

"Good morning, Dr Bequette," Kelly said, lowering her head to look at him from hooded eyes. The pose was so practiced, Jo was sure Kelly had worked on this move in the mirror more than once.

"Oh, good morning, Kelly," Jack said and then turned back to Jo. His blue eyes were bright and alert as he looked at her. "Did you have a good meal at the Water's Edge?"

"I did. So what's on your schedule this morning?"

"Nothing until the Whipple. I'll be rotating through the operating suites checking on my residents. Lucky for me, I have third and fourth years, so nobody is green. Want to come along?"

"I'd love to. Thanks." Jo glanced toward the head of the unit. "Thank you, Kelly, for showing me around. I appreciate your hospitality."

"Glad to," Kelly snapped back.

Oh dear. Apparently another victim of the Bequette charm, and unfortunately for Kelly, Jack didn't seem to notice the infatuation or didn't care.

"We'll head down to OR one. Dr Pollard is getting the patient ready for an umbilical repair. Should be fairly straightforward. Hour max."

They walked down the hall, Jack speaking to each person, introducing Jo simply as "Dr Stone, who is visiting today".

When they entered the operating suite, the patient was on the table, arms positioned out to the side on padded armboards. Dr Pollard, the resident Jack had come to check on, was making a notation in the patient chart.

Jo stood back to observe the interaction between Jack, as supervising staff, and the resident in anaesthesiology, Dr Pollard. Jack's tone as he asked questions was calm but commanded respect. Dr Pollard didn't appear to be bothered by Jack questioning him and gave detailed answers.

A scrub-clad female stood pressed against the wall as though in terror. Jo walked over.

"Hello. I'm Dr Stone. You are?"

The girl's hazel's eyes looked even darker than normal surrounded by her ashen skin tone. "Becky. Becky Clark."

"First surgery?"

Becky nodded. "I'm in nursing school. My teacher put me in here to observe. Do you think it's okay?"

Jo smiled. She remembered the first time she'd observed surgery. She'd been so nervous that ten minutes in, she'd had to leave the room and break scrub to rip her gloves off so her hands could breathe. She patted Becky's back. "You'll be fine."

The fine hairs on the back of her neck stood at attention. Without looking, Jo knew Jack was close.

"Problem?" he asked, maintaining that calming voice he'd used while questioning the resident.

"Nope," Jo replied. "This is Becky's first time to see a surgery so we were just chatting."

Becky and Jack briefly discussed what the hernia repair would involve. Becky's eyes were the size of a full moon.

"We'll be right back," he said to Jo and walked Becky over to where the anaesthesia resident stood. After a short conversation, he was back, leaving Becky at the head of the table.

"It'll be good for Henry to explain what's going on to her. He's an excellent doctor, but he could stand to work on his people skills and nothing will be better than a wide-eyed nursing student who thinks Henry knows everything."

"I bet he had to decide between anaesthesia and pathology for his residency."

Jack looked surprised then laughed. "Probably. Let's move on."

There were seven operating rooms, but each room wasn't in use yet. However, Tess Sweeny was standing at the table in OR five. Since she and Jack had already covered their heads with scrub caps, both donned masks and Jack pushed open the door.

"How's it coming, Tess? We going to be on schedule?"

Tess didn't look from where she was moving laparoscopic instruments in the patient's abdomen. "Should be. No snags here. You seen Dr Stone this morning?"

"As a matter of fact . . ." Jack began.

"I'm here, Tess. Jack has been kind enough to take me along with him on his OR rounds."

"Great. Give me a little more light to the left," she said to the OR tech. "Perfect."

Jack pointed to the door with his chin and Jo followed him outside.

"Why don't you roam around and check out the unit. I'm going to head to pre-op and check on Mrs Gate."

Jo admired Jack's backside as he walked off toward the end of the hall.

Frienemies. She had to remember that. She really needed this job. If that meant she had to step over Jack Bequette to get it, then just sit back and watch her high-step.

She looked around. Time to go make nice with the staff.

Chapter Two

Jack headed toward pre-op. He didn't need to check on Grace Gate. He'd already been there and she was ready. He needed to get away from Jo Stone before he dragged her into an empty call room and kissed her senseless. When she was nearby, the last thing on his mind was work.

Frustrated, he jerked off his scrub cap and ran his hand through his hair. Was he fascinated with Jo Stone because she was his competition? Or had he made a beeline for her because she was so damn pretty? It'd been a long time between women for him. Was that the problem?

Right now, none of that mattered. He'd scheduled himself for Mrs Gate's Whipple procedure – six to eight exhausting hours of surgery – and the patient came first, not his attraction to Dr Stone, regardless of how luscious he found her.

The pre-op door swung open and the gurney with Grace Gate rolled through. He tied his scrub hat back around his head and followed the team into the OR.

The first two hours of surgery went without a hitch, meaning Jo Stone was nowhere in the area. But he knew his luck couldn't last. His anaesthesia resident took a bathroom break, leaving him flying solo, so of course this was the exact time Jo slipped into the room. She moved to the head of the table to stand beside him.

"How's it going?" Her voice was muffled through the blue surgical mask.

When he looked up to answer, he momentarily lost his train of thought in her emerald-colored gaze over the rim of the mask. Beautiful. Stunning. Breathtaking.

"Is something wrong?" she asked, a frown puckering her brow.

"No. Not at all."

"How many hours in are you?"

He glanced at the big wall clock. "A little over two hours."

His resident, Wilma Strong, rejoined them.

"Wilma," Jack said. "This is Dr Stone. Jo, this is Dr Strong."

Jo gave a quick head nod. "Nice to meet you." She turned her attention back to Jack. "Have you massaged her shoulders and neck?"

Now it was Jack's turn to frown. "Excuse me?"

"I've read about that," Wilma Strong interjected. She looked at Jack. "Research is showing that massaging the neck and shoulders of patients during long surgeries keeps the blood from pooling, leading to less pain in the post-op period."

"Exactly," Jo said, pleased someone had read her research. "Follow-up massages in post-op and recovery can reduce the need for large amounts of pain relievers like morphine. Pain can be controlled with smaller doses."

Jack's skepticism must have been reflected in his eyes.

"You don't believe it, right?" Jo said.

He shrugged. Her suggestion sounded like new-age bull crap. Plus he didn't like her coming in and making it appear he wasn't up on whatever the latest anaesthesia trend was, even if he thought it was stupid. That was a good way to make his resident question his opinion.

"Do you mind if I try it, Dr Bequette?" his resident asked. "I've been reading the research results and have been interested in giving it a go."

Jack stood. "All yours." He looked at Jo. "Can I have a word?"

They walked outside the OR into the empty sink area. "I'd rather you didn't question my techniques in front of the residents."

"I didn't. I . . . I wouldn't do that," Jo sputtered.

"You just did. You're welcome to observe, but I'd rather you not get the residents off the routine we have established."

Her eyes took on the green of the ocean right before a storm. Around the edges of her mask, the muscles in her jaw flexed in tension. She gave a short nod. "Got it. Anything else?"

He spoke without thinking. "Will you have dinner with me tonight?"

Her eyebrows arched. "Maybe. I'll think about it."

Behind his mask, he grinned. "You do that. I'm going back in. Coming?"

She shook her head. "Dr Madison invited me to observe on his case. I'll head down there." Whipping around, she marched down the hall.

Jack snorted. Guy Madison. Handsome, or at least according to the nurses. He personally didn't have an opinion on Madison's appearance. But he did recognize a player and Guy Madison was definitely a player. Should have known Guy would have spotted a beautiful woman like Jo and make his move on her. Had Guy already invited Jo out tonight and that's why she couldn't give him an answer about dinner?

He headed back into the Whipple procedure and rolled his eyes when he saw his resident kneading the neck and shoulder muscles of their patient. He just shook his head and left the room.

He didn't see Jo again until lunch. The Whipple procedure for Mrs Gate's cholangiocarcinoma was on schedule. As usual Tess Sweeny had the surgery in hand, Dr Strong had taken a break, so Jack felt comfortable heading for the doctors' lounge for a quick lunch.

As he walked in, he heard a sexy laugh and his heart skipped a beat or two. Looking toward the sound, he saw Jo sitting at a table sharing a sandwich with Guy Madison. The prick. Guy's moves on Jo were so obvious Jack could see them clear across the room. The best option would be to ignore them.

Never let a woman see you sweat.

After hitting the coffee pot for a fresh cup, he found a sandwich in the refrigerator. He paid for the food and looked around the room for a place to sit, preferably away from Jo and Guy.

"Jack," Guy called. "Come join us."

Unfortunately, the room was fairly full and unless he wanted to sit with the gastroenterologist he couldn't bear, Guy and Jo were his only option.

"Hey," he said, dropping into the chair. "How's your morning been going?"

"Me or her?" Guy asked with a grin.

"Both. Either," Jack said.

"Mine has been great," Guy said. "Dr Stone, er, Jo, has had some excellent suggestions on ways we could track drug usage more easily."

Jack felt one eyebrow go up. "Really?" He bit into his turkey and cheese sandwich.

"It's nothing terribly unique," Jo protested. "Johns Hopkins has been using it for years."

And once again she implied that St Michael's wasn't up-to-date. First with massages for surgery patients and now with their drug documentation.

"Hmmm," Jack said in a deliberate uninterested tone. The last thing he wanted was to sit here and be critiqued like a medical student in front of Guy Madison. The man was the world's worst gossip; unfortunately his gossip was usually true.

"So, what are your plans for the weekend?" he asked Guy, intentionally moving the conversation away from medicine. "You get the motor replaced on your boat?"

Guy's pride and joy was his rebuilt, Chris-Craft inboard boat. Built in 1955, the boat was constructed of all mahogany wood with solid brass fittings. The original engine had blown a month ago and Guy had been working on finding a replacement. Jack's question provoked exactly what he'd intended. Guy's attention left medicine and went to his boat. He turned to Jo and began a long, detailed description of his boat, the work done, and what was left to do. Jack had stifled a laugh at the expression on Jo's face when Guy pulled out his wallet to show her pictures, much as a new father would flash baby pictures. Jack sat back and let Guy bore Jo to death with boats.

Mrs Gate rolled into the recovery room at 3 p.m. Jack found Tess standing at the nurses' station rolling the stiffness out of her shoulders.

"Any problems?"

She shook her head. "Smooth as silk. I really liked your resident, Dr Strong."

"I hope you told her."

"I did. Don't worry."

"Plans for the weekend?"

"Yes. I plan to sleep until Monday morning."

Jack laughed. "Tired?"

"I usually am after a seven-hour surgery. Unfortunately, I've got to make hospital rounds before I can head home to crash. You?"

"Not sure. I've invited Jo Stone out to dinner."

Tess whipped around to look at him. "Really?" she said, her voice tinged with both interest and amusement.

"Down, Molly Matchmaker. Nothing going on. Just thought she'd enjoy dinner with a colleague instead of dinner alone."

Tess patted his shoulder. "You're a good man, Jacques Bequette," she said in a French accent.

"*Oui, mademoiselle.*"

His cell phone buzzed. The number was a long-distance number he didn't recognize.

"Jack Bequette."

"Hi, Jack," Jo's creamy voice purred. "Is your dinner invitation still good?"

At the sound of her voice, his heart leapt into his throat. "Absolutely."

"Excellent. What time and where?"

"How about seven and my house? I'll cook."

"Seriously? I'd love it."

"I'll pick you up at your hotel about seven. Does that work?"

"Why don't I just take a taxi to your house?"

"Absolutely not. I'll pick you up."

"See you then."

He clicked off the phone.

"You're cooking?" Tess asked, her grin betraying her amusement. "I'm jealous. I love your cooking."

He shrugged. "What can I say? You picked Monroe's gun over my cooking."

She laughed. "He does have a very nice gun."

He rolled his eyes. "TMI, Tess."

Jo wasn't sure why she was so nervous as she dressed for dinner. It was just dinner with a professional colleague.

Yes, and the Grand Canyon is just a hole in the ground.

She slipped a pair of black bikini panties up her legs and hated herself for not having a thong. Not that anyone would ever see her underwear tonight. It was the thought that counted.

Right, just like you're putting on the matching bra for nobody too.

Pulling a freshly pressed pair of black pants from a hanger, she let her gaze run through her options for her upper half. Almost every piece of clothing she had with her screamed, "Professional. Do not touch."

And she had mixed emotions about that message tonight. Did she want this dinner to be more than a meal with another doctor? Would they talk shop all night? God, she hoped not.

June in Arkansas was warm, so she wouldn't need a jacket. Her gaze roamed again until it fell on a cream-colored, silk, sleeveless shell she'd brought to wear under her blue suit. She ripped it off the hanger and over her head, tucking the hem into the waistband of her slacks. Turning around a full circle in the mirror, she was content with the outfit. Friendly without being overtly sexy.

Her room phone rang. "Hello?"

"Dr Stone. This is Jerome at the front desk. Dr Bequette is downstairs."

"Thank you." She hung up and looked for her shoes. She finally located her black sandals on the shelf in the closet. After grabbing a black sweater off the back of a chair, she paused to press her hand against her queasy stomach. She took a few deep breaths to calm her nerves and headed down.

She almost wished he'd grown a big wart on the end of his nose since lunch. Maybe that could quell her growing fascination.

No such luck.

The elevator door opened. Jack stood there, legs spread, hands shoved in his pants pockets. His face brightened with a smile as soon as their gazes met.

"Hey there, Jo. You are looking fine this evening."

Jo felt the heat of her blush rush up her neck to her cheeks. It was high school and a date with the football captain all over again.

Jack wore dark jeans that fit nicely over trim thighs. His blue polo shirt stretched over wide shoulders and a flat abdomen. After all her concern about her footwear, he was sporting a worn pair of deck shoes. His wavy hair was windblown, which is how she imagined it might look after someone – her? – ran her fingers through it. All in all, he looked like an ice cream cone on a hot summer day . . . delicious and waiting to be licked all over.

She shook herself, reining in her wildly inappropriate thoughts. She tried for a casual smile, but wasn't sure if it worked or if she looked like a badger baring its teeth.

She had to bear in mind she was here for a job, not a man. She didn't need – or want – those complications.

"Good evening," she said, the rock in her throat making it hard to speak. She cleared her voice. "I appreciate your coming into town to pick me up."

"On a night like this, Little Red demands to be set free."

"Little Red?"

He laughed. "That's what my niece calls my car."

They walked outside to a cherry red convertible Corvette parked in the hotel's circle drive. The car's top was down. The red leather seats shone in the drive's overhead lights

"Little Red, I presume," Jo said with a grin.

He lovingly stroked his palm along the side of the car. Suddenly, Jo was jealous. Of a car.

"This is her. Isn't she a beauty?"

Having a couple of younger brothers, Jo understood the relationship a man had with his car. She also understood a woman should never put herself between a man and his car. So, instead, she traced her hand along the side of the car in the same path he did.

"She is that, Jack. A real beauty."

He opened the passenger door, allowing her to glide into the seat as gracefully as one could when climbing down into a vehicle almost on the ground. Having no roof to contend with helped make the entry less awkward. He reverently closed her door and hurried around to the driver's side. He sat with the expertise of someone used to a low ride.

"Okay to leave the top down?" he asked.

"Sure. What's a little windblown hair?" Nothing except she'd spent thirty minutes getting it to look exactly like what she wanted.

He grinned, started the car, threw it into drive and flew from the hotel's circular driveway. The ride was fast, curvy, and windy. It was riding on the back of her high school boyfriend's motorcycle – lots of noise and wind and impossible to carry on a conversation. She extended her arms above the rooftop, laughing as they danced in ripples of air.

She looked at Jack. "Do I have bugs in my teeth?"

He hooted. "You are just not what I expected when I met you yesterday morning."

"Is that good or bad?"

"Good. Definitely good."

She returned his smile. Giving up on her coiffure, she ran her fingers through her long hair, loosening the hairspray, and let the strands flow in the wind behind her. She felt young. Carefree. Desirable.

Her spy had mentioned he kept a houseboat at the Lake Waterton Yacht Club. As she neared the parking lot, she wondered if he lived on the boat full time. However, instead of the parking lot, he turned on a paved street that ran adjacent to the yacht club. The street ended at a pair of wrought iron gates. He pressed a button on the visor and the gates began to swing forward. As soon as he could wedge the small car in, they shot through the opening until he pulled into a circular drive. It was only afterwards that she realized they hadn't been on a road but on his driveway the entire time.

Jo gasped in delight. Situated on a high cliff overlooking the area lake, the house had been built from natural stone, wood, and glass. Soft lighting spilled from downstairs windows.

As the Corvette neared the house, bright outside lights flashed on, illuminating the drive and the plush green grass in the front yard. Jack bypassed the four-car garage and pulled into the driveway.

He turned off the engine and looked at her. "Welcome to Chez Bequette."

Jo's jaw dropped. "Wow, Jack. This is incredible."

"Thanks. I can't take credit. I inherited this place from my grandparents. I've done a little updating, but the design was all my grandfather. He was an architect and this place was his pride and joy." He slammed his door and raced around the front of the car to open hers. "Come on in and I'll show you around."

She'd dated a guy in college who'd driven a Corvette, and if there was one thing she remembered, it was that it was difficult to exit from this kind of car with poise. Jo swung her feet out of the door, but to stand straight up was impossible since she was technically climbing out of a roll cage. She had the options of pushing off the seat, or taking Jack's hand and letting him help her. No contest.

She took Jack's assistance to standing. Again, the missing convertible top was instrumental in making her appear more graceful than she felt.

She expected him to drop her hand once she was on her feet. Luckily, she was wrong. They walked up the massive stone steps to the glass front door. Jack threw the door open.

"Here it is. My grandparents' pride and joy."

The house had been built to capture and reflect the natural surroundings. Lake views filled every window. The internal wood supports as well as the hardwood floor gleamed from years of polish.

When she stepped through the door, her feet were cushioned by a thick rug. She was sure her head was rotating in all directions like Linda Blair as she tried to take it all in. Finally she gave up and looked at Jack. "I'm speechless. The beauty of your home overwhelms me."

He grinned. "And I haven't even shown you around."

"How big is this place?"

"A little over six thousand square feet. Since there are three levels including the basement, the actual footprint of the house is smaller."

"And you live here alone?"

"Yup. All by my lonesome. Come on to the back. I need to check on the sauce I left simmering."

As soon as he mentioned food, she noticed the aroma of tomatoes, basil and oregano.

"Smells wonderful," she said, as she followed him down the hall to the large, old-fashioned kitchen. The room had obviously been redone though, since it boosted granite countertops and stainless steel appliances.

"Hope you like Italian."

She snorted quietly. "Are you kidding? I love it. What's on the menu?"

"Home-made Caesar salad, baked ziti, fresh Italian bread with olive oil and an Italian cream cake for dessert."

She groaned in pleasure. "All my hot buttons."

He opened a bottle of wine, filled two thin crystal wine globes and handed her one. "I propose we drink to no medical talk tonight."

She clinked his glass. "I'll drink to that."

The wine was a rich merlot that had her taste buds sighing in ecstasy.

"Delicious," she said setting her glass on the granite counter. "What can I do to help?"

"Nothing, really. It's ready. Grab your wine and the bottle and follow me."

He led her into the formal dining room where fine china and sterling flatware glittered in the low light of the overhead chandelier. After setting the salad on the table, he pulled back a cherrywood chair.

"Sit," he said, so she did.

He tossed the salad and served each of them.

"Okay, I give up. How do you know how to cook?"

He lifted his wine glass and took a swallow. "My father's parents were French. My mother's parents were Italian. I grew up in a home with lots and lots of cooking. What's amazing is that I don't weigh three hundred pounds."

"Speaking of your family, do they live here?" She stabbed a leaf of romaine and put it in her mouth.

"Both sets of grandparents are deceased," he said, as he transferred a slice of hot bread to his bread plate. "My parents have a smaller house here on the property. They bought one of the huge motorhomes and have been traveling around the US for the past couple of years. They come home from time to time, but I guess they're gone at least nine months out of the year." He took a bite of salad.

"No siblings?"

"Two sisters. Both younger. One moved back here when her husband was killed in Afghanistan last year. The other is trying to make it in New York as a model, or maybe it's an actress this week." He shrugged. "I can't remember."

"I'm sorry to hear about your brother-in-law. We've lost a lot of fine men over there."

He nodded. "And he was one of the finest."

"Does your sister live here on the grounds also?"

"No. Believe it or not, she lives next door to Tess Sweeny."

Jo chuckled. "Small world. How come your parents don't live here in the big house?"

"Didn't want to. They lived here while I was growing up, but once I came home to set up practice, they left here for the small place they'd built. I think they were tired of the upkeep. Now, what about you?"

"Dad's deceased. Mom's still alive but battling some health issues, like any older adult, I guess. I have a sister, Risa, who's younger and a bit of a hellion. Right now, she's in Nashville trying to get a break in the country music world."

"That's a tough gig, I hear."

"That's what she's finding out. I've also got a set of twin brothers a couple of years younger than Risa but they're fraternal, not identical. They're in college. I have no idea what they'll end up doing. Right now, life's a party."

"That'll change."

"No kidding. Anyway, that's it for family. Tell me about growing up here in Waterton. Seems like a nice place."

She didn't go into her mother's medical condition or her reason for wanting to move her mother to Arkansas. He didn't press for more details about her family so she kept it brief.

As the meal progressed, they shared stories about growing up, their college years, medical school woes, and comparisons of the worst things they'd ever seen as doctors. Both of them agreed gross-out stories didn't count as medical talk.

She dragged her last corner of bread through the olive oil and spice mixture. She leaned back in her chair and moaned as she chewed. "I'm so stuffed. The food was wonderful."

"Too full for cake and coffee?"

"Are you kidding? Never. But just a small piece, please."

"Let's have coffee and dessert in the great room."

While he sliced the cake, she made a couple of cups of coffee, leaving his black like he'd had it at lunch.

The great room had a glass wall that bowed out over the lakeside, providing a panoramic view of the area. The majesty of the view was limited by the night, but the full moon afforded enough light to allow Jo to appreciate the scene.

"I don't know how you leave here every day for work. I wouldn't want to tear myself away."

Jack set his cake plate and mug on a coffee table in front of a plush leather sofa and joined her in front of the window.

"Sometimes I forget to stop and enjoy. That's what's nice about having you here. You're seeing things I've been taking for granted."

The warmth from his closeness wrapped around her. Momentarily, she shut her eyes and floated in his scent and heat. She didn't want this attraction to him. Wanted to fight it. Tried to fight it. Knew she was losing the battle with herself. How could she not? Jack was funny, self-deprecating, and a damn good cook.

She didn't think tonight's dinner was about the job, and she hadn't been invited out of some warped sense of professional courtesy. Today, she'd seen him watching her when he didn't think she was aware.

Jack laid his hand on her shoulder and pointed through the window at a boat in the distance. "That's a dinner cruise that goes out every night. Food kind of blah, but the cruise is pretty nice. You might like this lake at night. Quiet. Calm. Stress-reducing."

His hand was large, his fingers thick. Having him touch her certainly wasn't calming and stress-reducing. Her skin felt two sizes too small as though she might explode at any minute.

If she tilted her head even a fraction, her cheek would brush his fingers. Would that shock him? Frankly, the thought was a little shocking to her. She'd never been the aggressor in a relationship, the very few she'd been in. She'd always waited for the guy to make the first move.

"Jack." She looked over at him. "Your home is lovely. Thank you for inviting me over."

"That's what frienemies do, right?" He smiled. "Come on. You have to try the cake."

They found seats on the sofa, sitting close to each other. She took a bite and groaned. "Do not tell me you made this cake."

He chuckled. She was really loving his chuckles.

"No. Local bakery."

He turned on some soft music while they finished the cake and coffee. Jo set her empty plate and cup on the table and leaned back into the soft sofa. She closed her eyes and sighed loudly.

"I think this may be the best meal I've had in a long time."

She felt his heat first, then his breath on her cheek.

"Stop me now if you don't want me to kiss you," he said.

Slowly opening her eyes, she stared into a pair of hot blue irises. She cupped his cheek in the palm of her hand.

He brushed a soft kiss across her lips.

Her heart leapt.

He brushed another kiss, just a brush of his lips on hers.

Her stomach clenched.

The third time, he pressed firmly against her mouth, angling his head for maximum contact. The tip of his tongue licked the corner of her mouth, ran along the seam between the lips, finally finding its way into her mouth.

The taste of Jack mixed with the Italian cream cake and coffee sent heat and arousal flooding to the area between her thighs.

This was such a bad idea, but right at this moment, she couldn't make herself give a damn.

Chapter Three

Jack caressed Jo's thigh through her linen slacks. Firm. Lean. She felt like a runner. Was she a runner? Hell, he didn't know anything about her beyond the fact the hard, rapid pulse in her carotid arteries meant she was just as affected by their kisses as he was.

When he pulled back, she looked up at him with dilated, aroused eyes.

"Why are you here? What do you want, Jo?"

She leaned away from him. "What do you mean?"

"Here. My house. Waterton. Why?"

She pushed away from him. "I'm interviewing for a job, Jack. I'm sorry it's the one you want, but . . ." She shrugged. "There it is. The elephant in the room. We both want the job. Only one of us will get it."

"Why do you want it? Why leave Maryland for Arkansas?"

She stood. "It's late. I need to be getting back to my hotel. I'll be glad to call a cab so you don't have to get out."

He stood, insulted that she would think he would let a date call a cab. "Don't be ridiculous. I'll drive you back."

The drive back was nothing like the drive over. Where she'd been happy and carefree with her arms riding the air currents earlier, she was quiet and withdrawn now. He pulled into the hotel drive and stopped.

"Thank you for dinner, Jack." She opened her door. "Don't get out," she said when he opened his door. "No need. Thanks again." She got out and shut his door, entering the hotel without looking back.

* * *

Saturday, Jack went through all the administrative reports Troy had heaped on him Thursday, making notes to himself on what was recorded on each report. He tried to keep Jo out of his thoughts, which became harder with each passing hour. What had she done with her day? What was she doing this evening? Should he call? And if he did call, what would he say? She was the one who'd gotten terse and ended the night. He'd replayed the evening over and over and he still didn't really understand what went wrong.

Finally at five, he called her hotel. Her room phone went to voicemail.

"Jo. This is Jack. I, um, wanted to . . . Just wanted to make sure you were okay. I'd like to see you tomorrow. Call me. Five-oh-one, five-five-five, two-three, two-two."

By the time he turned off his lights at midnight, she still hadn't called. Disappointment and failure infiltrated every dream that night.

Pulling the bedcovers over his head, Jack groaned and rolled away from the sun pouring through the bedroom curtains he'd forgotten to close the night before. As much as he'd love another hour of sleep, once he was awake, he was up. On the bedside table, his phone began to buzz. He snatched it up.

"Hello?" The roughness of his voice divulged his not-quite-awake state.

"Jack? This is Jo Stone."

He slid up until his back rested against his headboard. He cleared his throat. "Good morning."

"Am I calling too early? Sorry. I'm still on Eastern time."

"No, no." He glanced at his bedside clock – 8 a.m. "I'm up," he lied. "Just still have morning voice. Did you have a good day yesterday?"

Her snort surprised him. "Does Arkansas have a law against a man marrying his boat because I'm pretty sure Guy Madison would marry his if he could."

"You were with Guy yesterday?"

"Well, I was there in the boat, but I'm pretty sure I ran a distant second to his new inboard motor."

Tension eased around Jack's heart.

"Don't get me wrong," she continued. "Guy is a great, um, guy, if you know what I mean. But I didn't want to share my cake and coffee with him."

He grinned. "Really? You ought to see what I can do with an omelet."

"I think I'd like that."

"Pick you up in an hour?"

"No. Let me come to you. Don't argue. I'll grab a cab. Give me ninety minutes, okay?"

"Yeah. I'll see you then."

About 9.45, his house phone gave three short rings. He picked up.

Jack pushed the button to open the gate and shortly, a yellow cab rolled to a stop in front of his house. Jo climbed from the rear seat, her bare legs looking pale but shapely and toned. She wore khaki shorts, a soft white pullover top, and white sandals. He opened the door before she could ring the bell.

"Nice legs," he said, waggling his eyebrows suggestively.

She grinned. "Thanks. I was actually out shopping for some shorts and cooler clothes when you called. I didn't plan to be here this long. Then I went to the movies. It was late when I got back to the hotel and I didn't want to wake you up. "

"I'm glad you did," he said. The words slipped out before he could stop them but he meant them. He stepped back to let her in the foyer.

"Me, too. Now, I think there was some mention of food."

He took her arm. "Right zis way, mademoiselle," he said in a French accent.

They talked about the lake, his love of fishing, her confusion over fishing, and other mindless topics, while he prepared omelets. Once they were seated to eat, she picked up her fork, and then set it down again. She blew out a heavy breath.

"Do you want to talk about the job today?"

He shook his head. "Nope. The board, Troy and Dean Anderson will make their decision. Nothing we say to each other will make a difference in that."

"Except the possibility of losing our friendship."

He reached over and squeezed her fingers. "That's not going to happen." He laced their fingers. "You happen to be not only qualified for the job, but maybe, and just maybe, you might be more qualified."

She lifted their joined hands to her lips. "For today, no job battle. No work talk."

"Agreed. How about we take my houseboat out?"

She rolled her eyes. "Depends on your marital status."

"Divorced that hag last year when she needed her kitchen overhauled."

Jo laughed. "Lucky for me I bought a new bathing suit yesterday and shoved it in my bag before I left this morning."

"Damn," Jack said. "I was going to propose strip poker followed by skinny-dipping."

"Eat your breakfast, Jack."

Monday morning, Jo woke in her hotel room, wishing she'd taken Jack up on his offer to stay overnight on his boat. But she felt herself getting in too deep, too fast. This wasn't like her. She was the cautious one. A person who lived by a plan, a calendar, a budget. Suddenly she was treading in unfamiliar territory. She wished she could back out of these interviews, withdraw from consideration for this position, but after her mother's last medical report, withdrawing was no longer an option.

The University of Arkansas Medical Center housed the world-renowned Myeloma Institute for Research and Therapy, aka MIRT. MIRT was founded and headed by the national physician of the year, awarded based on his groundbreaking research and treatment modalities. Jo's mother's multiple myelomas required more attention than she could get where she lived but she wouldn't come to Arkansas for treatment without Jo.

Jo owed her mother everything. She'd always been there for Jo and supported her, financially and emotionally, even when both assets were in short supply.

Besides, moving the family to Arkansas would put them all closer to Risa in Nashville.

She had no choice. She needed this job for its excellent salary and benefits and its ideal geographical location. She hoped Jack would understand when she explained.

She'd almost told him yesterday while they were floating on Lake Waterton but she couldn't bear his sympathy or pity. What scared her most was she believed him the type of man who would pass on a job if someone needed it more. She didn't want to put him in the situation where he might consider it.

Today, she'd give her finest interviews and hope for the best.

The day passed in a blur of faces, names and questions. Troy Monroe found her sitting alone in the doctors' lounge drinking her fifth cup of coffee while resting her feet from the high-heels-from-hell. He got a cup and joined her at the table.

"Dogs barking?"

"Excuse me?"

He pointed to her feet. "That's how we Southerners describe our feet hurting."

She laughed. "Then I'd say my dogs are howling."

He nodded. "Well, you'd better get used to our Southern ways, Dr Stone."

She leaned forward, her heart beating a tango between her lungs. "What are you saying, Dr Monroe?"

"The board loved you. Dean Anderson was very impressed with your research and publications. Guy Madison and Jack Bequette both spoke highly of your comments and suggestions during Friday's visit to the OR. We'd like to offer you the position."

Jo found it hard to breathe. She fought the tears of relief amassing. "Thank you, Dr Monroe."

He held out a hand. "Troy. We'll be working closely together."

She shook his hand.

"You look a little surprised, Jo," he said, using her informal name for the first time.

"A little surprised about Jack's recommendation. I mean, he wanted this job as much as I did."

Troy shook his head. "Damnest thing. Jack withdrew his name from consideration this morning."

Jo leapt from her seat, shoving it noisily backwards. "What? Why? Where is he?"

"I'll let him explain. He's in his office. Fifth floor. Five-thirty-five."

Jo tapped her toe as she waited for the elevator. Damn man. How dare he withdraw his name so she'd get the position of

Anaesthesiology Department Chief. Now she was even more glad she'd not told him about her mother. But damn! Even without telling him, somehow he figured out she needed this job.

The elevator creaked to a stop and she charged off. She headed to her left, realized she'd gone the wrong way, and whipped around. She ran into a hard surface. Looking up, she peered into a set of familiar blue eyes.

She slapped his chest. "Damn you. Why did you drop out?"

He smiled and caught her hand. "Got a better offer. Come on. I'll explain." He led her into a private office with a desk, a couple of chairs and computer. A long sofa ran along one wall. He sat on the sofa and pulled her down next to him.

"Now, what better offer?" she said, squinting her eyes. But then they popped open wide at a thought. What if he'd quit? Taken a position somewhere else? Acid ate at her gut. "Tell me you're not leaving."

He put his arm around her and pulled her against him. "I'm not leaving." He kissed her, sending her emotions on another rollercoaster ride.

She pushed him away. "Spill."

"Dean Anderson asked the board to establish a position for Director of Medical Education here at St Michael's. It'll be an adjunct appointment to the College of Medicine. I'd be working with each departmental chairman at the college to ensure the residents get the experience they need."

"Oh, Jack. It sounds perfect for you."

He hugged her close. "It is. Plus my paperwork will be less than half what you have to file."

She laughed, then caught his face between her hands. She pulled him down for a long, deep kiss.

"I have a confession, Jack."

He lifted an eyebrow. "Oh?"

"I don't cook. I don't clean. And I couldn't iron a shirt if my life depended on it."

"I cook. I have a housekeeper. And there's an excellent dry cleaners within a mile drive of my house."

She settled against him. "Sounds perfect."

"I don't know what our futures hold, Jo. I just know I want to spend mine getting to know you better."

"Another perfect plan." She looked up into his handsome face and knew in her heart, some things are just meant to be. "Kiss me, Director of Medical Education."

He smiled and her heart swelled. "Always, Anaesthesia Department Chief."

PAGING DR RESPONSIBLE

Patti Shenberger

Chapter One

22 December 2007

Abby set the gift box on the table. She couldn't wait to give Ethan his present. This year things would be very different.

The doorbell chimed and Abby opened the front door, and then took a step back in surprise.

Ethan stood on her doorstep. His wavy dark hair was shaved, and he wore Army fatigues.

"I'm sorry, but I can't stay. My unit's been called up, we ship out tomorrow."

"I don't understand." Abby grabbed the door frame to try to steady herself.

"It's the chance of a lifetime. Being in the Special Forces is what I've dreamed of my entire life. But I didn't want to leave without letting you know in person."

"When will you be back?"

"I don't know, and if I did, I'm not at liberty to say."

"I see." But she didn't.

Ethan looked at his watch and frowned. "I've got to go. We have a company briefing at oh-nineteen-hundred. Merry Christmas, Abby, take care of yourself." Ethan hugged her hard.

Abby wanted to stay wrapped in his embrace, to talk about this a little before he just walked out of her life. Before she could say a word, he was gone.

She felt sick. Her world was yanked out from under her.

"I'm pregnant with your baby," she whispered. But it didn't matter. Of all the scenarios she'd run through in her mind, this one never came up.

Wrapping her arms over her stomach, she tried to keep the tears at bay. She never planned on getting pregnant, but it happened. Now she'd be left to deal with the consequences on her own. The enormity of her situation consumed her. Just when Abby thought it safe to open her heart and take a chance on Ethan, fate played the same cruel trick it had in the past, and once more she was alone.

December 2012

Ethan bolted upright in the bed, searching the darkened room, sweeping his gaze over the corners. Thank God he was alone. Sweat beaded his brow, and the mangled bed sheets were clenched tight in his fists. His breathing was loud and harsh in the quiet as Ethan willed the memories to stop. But they didn't and he doubted they ever would. He was trapped in the same nightmare and every time it ended the same way. The deafening noise of the grenades going off, the constant rat-tat-tat of gunfire, and people screaming in agony. As soon as he'd tended to one patient another would take his place, their anguished cries reverberated through his head, begging for help. In the beginning, he awoke to the sound of his own screams. Now, only his hoarse cries roused him from sleep.

The past was the past and he planned to keep it that way. Was it any wonder he never had a woman spend the night? Who in their right mind would want to wake up with some fool screaming his head off in the bed beside them? It was better to part ways at the end of the night, plead long hours of work as his excuse, rather than suffer the consequences of having his secret exposed.

One day at a time, one hour, one minute. Get through the next day and the rest would follow. It was a mantra that had served him well over the past years.

Chapter Two

The small car fishtailed and Abby held tight to the wheel. Entering the intersection, she caught a blur of red out the corner of her eye. The vehicle was headed straight for them. She wrenched the wheel to the right to avoid the approaching car.

The sickening crunch of metal filled Abby's ears. The window shattered, yet her seat belt caught and held, the only thing preventing her from striking the windshield and being ejected from the car. With a loud whoosh, the airbag deployed – a bone-jarring jolt that sucked the air from her lungs.

The small car spun on the ice. Within seconds, a second car struck her from behind. Abby hit her head and stars danced across her vision. The car came to a sliding halt against a metal guard rail. Max's wails from the back seat grew louder with each passing second.

She couldn't see him in the rear-view mirror, couldn't catch her breath to ask if he was all right.

"Mommy, I hurt."

"Mommy's here." Her words came out hoarse and raspy. The pain in her side tore at her as she fumbled for the seat belt.

Abby heard voices at her window, telling her help was on the way. She heard Max calling out to her. But she couldn't go to him because the seat belt was stuck, couldn't tell him everything would be all right because she couldn't seem to get her breath. If anything happened to her, what would become of Max? He'd be alone.

Abby refused to even consider that, and clenched her eyes shut against the pain.

"Three kids under the age of ten would scare the crap out of me." Ethan aimed his words at the reality show playing on the television in the doctors' lounge. "I'm happy with my life the way it is."

At one point, the idea of having a wife and kids had meant the world to Ethan.

But, thanks to the past, things were now much different.

"Doctor Gregory, we've got a multiple vehicle crash with five victims en route. Four adults, one child. ETA ten minutes."

"Call Pediatrics and get Doctor Gates down here, stat. Let's not take any chances with this one." Ethan downed one last bite of his lukewarm Chinese takeout before heading back out into the ER department.

Seven minutes later, the Emergency Room doors burst open. Paramedics came in bearing two stretchers, the occupants covered in heavy blankets, as snow swirled across the floor.

"Talk to me, guys." Ethan followed the first gurney into Exam Room One.

"Mother's twenty-eight and the child is four. His name is Max. Blood pressure's stable and he was responsive and crying when we arrived. No sign of trauma, slight contusion to the left cheek. Witnesses tell us, she had the green; the other guy ran the red and T-boned her. Both mother and child were wearing seat belts. Impact spun the car and another vehicle hit them from behind."

Ethan looked down at the small child. "Hey, Max, I'm going to listen to your chest, okay?"

The little boy nodded and sniffled.

Ethan pulled the stethoscope from his neck. Clear with no sounds of fluid or rattles. He flashed his penlight in the boy's eyes, noting no sign of trauma. Moving on, he ran his fingers across the little boy's ribs. Amazingly, the child came through the accident remarkably well.

"Becky, run a CBC on the mom, tell the lab it's a rush, and get the son up to X-ray as soon as Doctor Gates examines him. Also prepare an ice pack. Let's get some of the swelling down on his cheek."

"I'm on it." The nurse's movements were practiced and efficient.

"Where's the mother?" Ethan asked.

"Exam Room Three. Initial assessment shows contusions to the left temple, multiple bruising to the chest. She complained of pain in her lower right side. Vitals indicate an elevated BP and rapid pulse. We started an IV at the scene."

"Great job, guys." Ethan stepped into the exam room, accepting the chart from the nurse.

Another nurse did her best to soothe the frantic woman on the gurney in front of him. "I promise to keep you posted every step of the way."

Ethan noted her elevated blood pressure, and with her current agitation level, he could see why. She also had a fever, which was not consistent with the rest of her symptoms per the EMT's examination.

"Ethan?"

Ethan's head snapped around suddenly to the blanket-clad figure. "Abby?"

What the hell was she doing in his hospital?

Confusion furrowed her brow as she stared at him. From her shocked look, it seemed that Abby hadn't expected to see him either.

"Ethan, where's Max?" Her voice barely above a whisper, as pain clouded her features. "Is he okay? Please tell me he wasn't hurt."

"Max is being examined by our pediatric specialist. He's in good hands, Abby. I need you to relax and let me assess you."

She shook her head. "I have to see him, to make sure he's all right. Ooh . . ." Abby clutched at her side and moaned.

Ethan gently explored her ribcage, then lower still to her side. "Abby, show me where it hurts."

The way Abby held her lower right quadrant made Ethan suspect appendicitis. Once he saw the X-rays, he'd have a clearer picture of her injuries.

"I'm sending you for a CT scan. We need to know what's going on in there."

Abby's fingers plucked at his sleeve. She looked at him with tear-filled eyes. "Ethan, if anything happens, I need you to take care of our son. Take care of Max."

For a second, Ethan forgot to breathe. The shock of hearing Abby say these words blind-sided him. A blow he never saw coming.

Everyone faded from view as Ethan drank in the sight of the woman he'd never been able to forget. And now here she was. Announcing they had a son.

"Take care of our son."

For a split second, panic filled him as his neat and tidy life flashed before his eyes.

He had a son?

No. Abby did.

If he had a child, Ethan would've known.

She was confused. Or lying. Or both.

The kid was not his. Some paternal instinct would have kicked in. Wouldn't it?

"Get a CT scan of the chest and abdomen. Call Doctor Tanner; tell him I've got a possible ruptured appendix with contusions to the ribcage. Soon as she's out of Radiology, get her prepped for surgery."

Against his better judgement, Ethan opened the door to Exam Room One and stepped inside. While he didn't doubt Abby was shaken up from the accident, it wouldn't hurt to take one more look at the kid.

The little boy stared up at him.

Nothing about the boy looked familiar. His hair color was different from Ethan's, the color of his eyes was different, in fact everything about him was different.

"Is my mommy okay?"

"She's going to be fine. She's having X-rays taken like you did."

"Doctor Gregory, Radiology's on line one." Becky leaned around the door.

A few minutes later, Ethan hung up the phone and headed to the third floor. The waiting room outside the surgical pre-op was empty, except for surgeon Jack Tanner, who would be operating on Abby. "I'm keeping Max overnight for observation. I don't expect anything to turn up with his mother in surgery, but considering the circumstances this is the best place for him at present."

"The nurses haven't been able to locate any family?" asked Jack.

Ethan shook his head. "I told them not to bother, she doesn't have anyone."

"And you would know this how?"

The look on Jack's face prompted Ethan to explain. "I met Abby when I was at Fort Polk. I know for fact she doesn't have any family."

"You okay?"

What Ethan wanted to say was "You won't believe what Abby did. She tried to pass off her son as mine." But he couldn't, not yet.

"Yeah, I'm fine."

"When's she's in Recovery you can tell me the whole story. Until then, stay the hell out of my OR, understood? The last thing I need is you hovering, asking all sorts of stupid questions."

Jack Tanner was the best general surgeon the hospital had, so Ethan knew Abby was in good hands. Even though she was part of his past, Ethan cared enough to make sure she got the best treatment.

The last time he'd seen Abby was in Louisiana, when he was about to deploy to Afghanistan. Ethan still remembered the stunned look on her face when he gave her the news.

The look stayed with him, lingering at the back of his mind during deployment. Walking away from her was the hardest thing Ethan had done in his life. They shared something special. If she'd been there when he returned . . . Well, there was no way of knowing where they'd be at this point in their lives.

Part of his past. That's what Abby was. A very big part. But a part of a life he could never go back to.

What happened in Afghanistan changed the future forever.

Since he'd been back, he hadn't been a monk and never claimed otherwise. Only a few women made it more than two weeks with him, thanks to his busy work schedule and his disappearing act at the end of the evening. When they learned he wasn't interested in putting down roots and calling the preacher, some were downright testy.

Abby hadn't been like that.

They met by accident when Abby was a civilian contractor working at the base hospital. He'd asked her out that very night and she accepted. Going into the relationship, they agreed it was one day at a time; enjoy each other's company in and out of bed.

In retrospect, it turned out to be something completely different.

Tomorrow he'd talk to Abby. She'd been through so much tonight that he could almost forgive her for randomly selecting him as a father figure for her son. Right now, she needed her rest.

* * *

Abby opened her eyes and looked around the room. The glare of the fluorescent lights caught her unaware. This definitely wasn't her apartment.

"Hey, how're you feeling?"

The woman's face swam in and out of view before her. "Like I've been hit by a train. Where am I?"

"You're in Brickfield General. Actually, you're in Recovery. Any nausea? How's your pain on a scale of one to ten?"

Abby oriented herself to her surroundings. "No nausea. Pain's about a five. Where's my son? Where's Max? Is he okay?"

"Max is in the Pediatrics ward. He's fine, a few bumps and bruises. The doctor thought it best to keep him overnight till you were discharged."

"Why am I here?"

"Do you remember the car accident?"

Abby nodded. "Some spots are vague."

"Your appendix ruptured, Doctor Tanner did the surgery. If the pain medications aren't doing the trick, let me know. In about thirty minutes, we'll move you to a room. Tomorrow we'll get you and your son out of here."

When she was brought in, Abby was positive Ethan had been in the ER. She was sure she heard his voice, reassuring her that Max was fine.

The nurse reappeared by her bedside. "Before I forget, Doctor Gregory asked to be notified when you were awake."

"Ethan Gregory?"

"Yes, he's the head of the ER department. You're lucky he was on duty tonight."

Lucky didn't begin to cover how Abby felt at the moment.

It was his voice she'd heard, his face she'd seen. The face of a man she never expected to see again. Abby closed her eyes and let the pain medication do its job.

Chapter Three

The next time Abby opened her eyes, sunlight spilled into the room. She squinted at the clock on the wall. Half of a day had passed. So much time away from Max. She had to find him, and make sure her son was all right. Running her hand across the top of the bed sheet, Abby searched for the call button.

"Relax. Everything's under control, Abby."

His voice hit her like a frozen stethoscope against the skin. Abby's heart leapt into her throat as she realized who it was.

Ethan.

Then an entirely different panic filled her body. "Where's Max?"

"Max is up in Pediatrics. He's fine."

"Can I see him?"

Ethan shook his head. "You concentrate your energies on getting better. Later, when you're up, dressed and looking more normal, you can see Max."

Abby knew Ethan was right. She shifted in the hospital bed, unable to contain the hiss of air that escaped her lips.

Ethan checked the bandage on her stomach. Satisfied, he raised his gaze to her face, examining the lump over her right eye.

She anticipated his question before being asked. "About an eight in severity for my side, a five for my head."

"Let me get you something." He exited the room and within minutes was back, injecting pain medication into her IV.

"That should bring down the pain. If you're still uncomfortable, I'll order something stronger."

He looked good. As much as Abby didn't want to notice, it was hard not to stare. Just thinking about their shared past made her heart skip a beat. Not smart when hooked up to a heart monitor.

Ethan was drop-dead gorgeous in every sense of the word. The hint of stubble that graced his jaw did nothing to detract from his deep blue eyes. Abby felt the warmth flood her cheeks at the memories. All the anxiety she felt seeing him in the ER was quickly replaced with emotions so strong they left her completely unprepared. She tried not to notice how well he filled out the lab coat. There were a lot of things Abby didn't want to notice about the man, but couldn't help it.

It was the instantaneous pull of attraction that drew her to Ethan in the past. The chemistry was there from the start and hadn't eased over time. If Abby were brutally honest with herself, she hoped it never would.

For the previous five years, Abby envisioned what it would be like to come face to face with her past. She'd thought about the things she'd say to Ethan, yet never imagined she'd be the patient and Ethan the doctor. Now the words escaped her.

She thought back to Fort Polk, working on base until the day she ran into Ethan in the hospital cafeteria. That day was the start of something wonderful, something magical, right up until the moment, ten months after they met when Ethan announced he was being deployed. Then everything quickly went sour.

How foolish she'd been to believe it would work out. Naive was a better way to put it. Abby refused to see the truth, never allowing her doubts to creep in until it was too late.

Learning she was pregnant was a huge shock. The plus sign on the pregnancy test stick brought everything home in a big way. Because it meant she was alone. She pushed away the negative thoughts and put all her energy into focusing on the man in front of her.

He wasn't an illusion. Abby never planned on telling Ethan about Max. If it weren't for the accident, they would never have run into one another again.

"I was surprised to see you in the ER. What are you doing in town?" Ethan scanned her chart before looking up.

"I've taken a job in Rochester, working as a physician's assistant at the Main Street Clinic."

Ethan was quiet, so unlike the man she remembered from five years prior.

"I'm sorry about the way it all happened."

Ethan looked at her oddly. "Hey, things happen that are out of our control. Just like I never thought I'd see you again."

Abby stared at him, confusion swirling about her brain. Why was he acting so nonchalant? Was he really going to stand there and ignore the fact he had a son? Especially after she blurted out the truth the previous night. No matter how Ethan reacted, she'd handle the fallout.

"We need to talk about our son. We need to talk about Max."

His brow furrowed as he stared at Abby, and she saw the confusion on Ethan's face. As the seconds passed, Abby watched the confusion turn to shocked realization.

"Are you telling me I really am Max's father?"

"Yes. That's what I said."

Her words were like a two by four to the midsection. He couldn't have heard Abby correctly. He simply couldn't have. Stunned, Ethan dropped down in the chair. "You mean you were serious?"

"You thought I was lying?"

Right now Ethan didn't know what to think. "How did this happen?"

Beside him, Abby let out an exasperated sigh. "You're a doctor. Do you really want me to explain it to you?"

"That's not what I meant." Right now he didn't know what he meant.

"I realize this comes as a big shock to you."

"You have no idea." He couldn't even bring himself to lift his head and look at her.

"This wasn't how I meant for you to find out," Abby continued.

Ethan wrapped his fingers around the arms of the chair, the wood biting into the palm of his hands. Abby was in no condition to face the anger Ethan currently felt. She needed to recuperate, get back on her feet before he started peppering her with questions.

"I never meant to intrude on your life. I never meant to . . ." Her words trailed off as Ethan lifted his head.

"You never meant to tell me at all." His voice was cold. She'd never planned on telling him. If it weren't for the accident, he'd never have known.

"I . . . I won't keep him from you."

Her words set alarm bells ringing in his head as panic filled Ethan's body. Keep him from Ethan? The words bounced around his brain like a ping-pong ball.

"I wanted to tell you, but there was no way to get in contact with you. I tried your commanding officer, but he could only help with a general post office box address in Afghanistan. I did everything I could to get word to you."

She must have thought his stunned look implied he thought she was after money. "I don't want anything from you. Max and I are fine."

Interesting way to put it, Ethan thought. "How do you expect me not to take responsibility?"

She flinched at his tone. Ethan knew this wasn't what she wanted to hear. If she thought he was going to drop to one knee and declare undying love, think again.

The shock of it all filled his body. He didn't want to hear any more, and definitely didn't want to debate her motives for doing what she did.

Ethan pushed to his feet and headed for the door. "This conversation isn't finished, Abby. Not by a long shot. I'll check on you later."

His meetings over for the morning, Ethan agreed to meet Jack Tanner for lunch.

"I want to thank you again for doing the surgery last night."

"Glad I could help. So, you haven't seen her for four years and now she ends up in your ER? What are the chances? More importantly, how come that never happens to me?" Jack leaned back in the chair.

"Closer to five years. Abby's due to start work as a PA at the Main Street Clinic the week after Christmas. She's in town, looking for a place to live."

"She's the one you were in a relationship with that ended when you went off to Afghanistan, right?"

Ethan nodded. "It wasn't going to be anything serious or permanent. We were . . . I don't know what we were, but now I find out I have a son."

Jack's chair legs hit the floor with a loud thud. "You're kidding?"

"You heard me. Max is my son. Abby dropped the bomb right before she went into surgery. I didn't believe her, but she swears it's the truth."

"I don't know what to say. Congrats or sorry to hear it. That explains a lot about last night. That had to have hit you like a ton of bricks."

"It's too fresh for me to even come to terms with." Ethan let out a shaky breath.

"What are you going to do?"

"I'm not ready for any of this. It's the last thing I want or need in my life."

"You're serious, aren't you?"

Ethan nodded. "She made it clear they're doing great on their own. If it weren't for the accident, none of this would have come out. You know being assigned to the Special Forces Unit was everything I wanted in life."

"We all have regrets, but the best we can do is to push through. Are you going to tell her what happened?"

Ethan shook his head before speaking. "What the hell am I supposed to say? If you hear someone screaming in the middle of the night, it's me. Yeah, that's going to go over real big. It'd scare the hell out of both of them."

"Hey, don't belittle what happened to you. What you went through was literally hell on Earth. And you got an up close and personal view."

Very few people knew what happened in Afghanistan, Jack being one, his family another. "That's a bridge I'll cross when I have to."

"Not that I want to put a damper on this momentous occasion, but before you get in too deep, have you given any thought to running a paternity test?"

It had weighed heavy on Ethan's mind since Abby had told him.

"It wouldn't hurt to make sure. I've got a friend in the lab who owes me a favour. We'll keep your name off the report." Jack took a sip of his beer.

Ethan frowned. He didn't know what he wanted, but the test was a good idea. Abby had never lied to him in the past, but things change, people change. "I'll let you know."

Ethan walked down the hallway toward Abby's room. The last time they spoke was five years ago. And now . . .

Now she was telling him he had a son.

Ethan heard his name being called. He turned, seeing Jack heading in his direction.

"I'm glad I caught up with you. We've got a problem. Peds wants to alert Social Services since Abby has no place to stay, and feel it's best for Max to spend a night or two in foster care, at least until she's out of the hospital," Jack said.

"I thought she had a place already?"

"No, just a hotel, but with the accident, everything changed. I thought you'd want to know. Under normal circumstances it wouldn't matter and I'd have approved the request, but with Max being your . . ." Jack's words trailed off.

"Thanks for letting me know before you said anything to Abby."

Jack nodded. "I figured you'd want to be the one to tell her."

"It might be better," Ethan agreed.

While it wasn't his problem to solve, Ethan felt a sense of responsibility. He was the only one she knew in town, and they had a history. He hated to see the kid end up away from his mother and in another strange place. It wouldn't do either of them any good to be separated. Anyone with eyes could see Abby's first and foremost concern was Max. And if he was her first priority, then how could Abby focus her attention on getting better? It was a catch-22 at best.

Thanks to his unwavering sense of duty, Ethan knew what was necessary. He'd offer up his house for the time being. It was the least he could do. Ethan would sleep at the hospital as he'd done too many times before to count. Catch a nap all hours of the day or night, and then head home in the morning to change when there would be no way Abby or Max would hear him in the throes of a nightmare. Now all he had to do was convince Abby that this was a good plan.

Chapter Four

Ethan walked into her hospital room. He didn't want to notice how sexy Abby looked. Her long blonde hair hung loose about her shoulders. Abby nervously licked her lips and desire slammed into him.

"How are you feeling?" Ethan busied himself with the bedside monitor, noting her BP, pulse and oxygen levels. All holding steady.

"Much better."

"How's the pain?"

"It's under control."

His thoughts slid to Max, up in Peds. On his last visit, Max had been coloring a picture for Abby. His face scrunched in thought, his gaze locked on the page, his brow furrowed in concentration. For a brief moment, Ethan thought he was looking at a miniature version of himself from thirty years ago. All the same characteristics, or were they? A niggling of doubt snuck into his brain and Ethan quickly pushed it aside.

Pulling his thoughts back to the present, he looked at Abby.

She was uncharacteristically quiet. So unlike the sexy, vibrant woman Ethan shared his bed with in Louisiana. That woman had no trouble telling him exactly what she did and didn't want. The chemistry between the two of them had been so potent, an all-consuming case of lust. The flames all but torched them into cinders. But when his orders came through, they parted ways and never looked back.

Until now.

Giving himself a mental shake, Ethan brought himself to the task at hand. Call him good old Doctor Responsible.

"Abby, we have to talk about Max."

"Ethan, I don't know what you want me to say. I told you, Max is your son. I wasn't lying."

"That's not what I want to discuss."

The look on Ethan's face raised red flags for Abby. "Is Max all right? Where is he?"

"He's fine. He's watching cartoons up in Peds," Ethan told her. "The doctor determined he's ready to be discharged. But with you still recovering from surgery, they feel it best to call in Social Services."

"What? Why?" The words Social Services made Abby's skin crawl. This was the worst thing she could think of.

"It'd be for one night, two at the most. And no one has made the call yet." Ethan tried to reassure her, but she wasn't listening.

"My child is not going into foster care, not even for one night. No, discharge me right now." She pushed back the covers on the bed and made to rise before clutching her side. The effort made Abby sag weakly against the pillows.

Ethan stepped forward to still her progress.

"I won't let them take Max." She knew only too well about foster care, and the words brought up an ugly memory. One she'd never been able to erase from her mind.

Abby thought of her mother and tried to squash the swell of panic that accompanied the memory. She'd waited for her mother to come back and get her. She would stare at the front doors of all the foster homes she'd been placed in and wait. Wait for a visit, a letter, a phone call. Until one day Abby realized it was never going to happen. That was the day she swore she'd never be that type of parent.

When she turned sixteen, Abby left for good. Years of hard work, and long hours of studying and waiting tables followed to get her where she was today. With her medical degree in hand, Abby knew she finally escaped her past.

"Since you and Max need to heal, the best solution would be to move into my home for the time being."

"No." Her denial was swift and emphatic.

"Hear me out. You have no place to live, no vehicle and those two things alone are enough to justify Social Services getting involved."

There was no way Abby was going to even consider his offer. "It's sweet of you, but not necessary. I'll find a place before the day's out. Get my discharge papers ready, please. Max and I will be fine. We've managed before and we'll do it again."

Ethan lifted his hand to halt her refusal, the line of his mouth firm and drawn. "You won't be fine. You've had major surgery. How are you going to take care of Max? Have you given any thought to that?"

She hadn't, but wasn't about to let Ethan know.

"Don't you care what people will say? What they'll think about Max and me in your home? Out of the blue, you suddenly offer up your house to two strangers who ended up in your ER."

Abby watched Ethan shrug off her concerns.

"It's none of their business what I do. All they need to worry about is that I perform the job they hired me to do and I do it well. Besides, I'll sleep at the hospital. I won't be at the house."

She didn't expect the man to move out of his own home. But considering the lack of options, she knew the right move was to stay, take advantage of Ethan's hospitality, let him get to know his son, then ease her and Max into their own new life. But she wouldn't sleep with him. Not that the option had even presented itself but . . . She was determined to stay strong, even though her heart beat faster whenever Ethan came near.

Reluctantly, Abby agreed to the idea.

Abby had envisioned a house full of chrome and glass, but when Ethan opened his front door, she found herself in a ranch-style home crammed with pieces of overstuffed furniture, every end table topped with medical books.

"I'll show you the guest rooms." Ethan picked up their two suitcases and headed down the hall.

Abby snuck a glance in the master bedroom – at the massive king-size bed, the curved brown leather headboard and foot-board. The room was done in shades of brown and tan. She imagined waking up in his bed, wrapped in those sheets, in Ethan's arms, as they started the new day.

"Abby?"

"Hmm." She tore herself from her indecent thoughts and hurried to catch up. She needed to focus on getting well, not playing house with Ethan. The past was over and done with, and Abby had no desire to repeat it.

"I left my cell number on the fridge. There's bread and lunch-meat in there too. If you'd rather, I can order in something for you and Max."

"Sandwiches are fine." Abby was too tired to care.

Ethan dug in his pocket and pulled out a key. "Here's a house key. If you need anything else, let me know."

"Thank you." She closed her fingers around it, the metal still warm from his touch. It's as if he can't get out of the house fast enough, she thought.

She could have kicked herself for even considering staying there. But there was no way was she going to let Social Services take her child, not even for a night.

Chapter Five

A week in Ethan's house had already flown by. Abby looked down at her son, sleeping peacefully in Ethan's guest bedroom. She was feeling better and stronger, and would be ready to set out on her own soon.

The last time Ethan called to check on them had been two days ago and the conversation was stilted and strained. Anything she asked Ethan was answered with a single yes or no answer and he never asked how Max was or even what he was doing to pass the time. Abby knew she shouldn't care, but she did. She hated the fact Ethan wasn't accepting his role as a father. More importantly, she hated the fact she still had feelings for the man.

Living in Ethan's home only intensified the memories. Memories Abby preferred dead and buried. She had no right to be thinking the things bouncing around in her head. Ethan showed no signs of wanting their relationship to start anew.

His cell phone rang and Ethan grabbed it on the first ring, noting the caller. "Ethan Gregory."

"Ethan, it's Abby. I apologize for bothering you, but wondered if you might have time to take Max and I to the grocery store. If you're too busy, I understand."

"No, it's not a problem. If you'd prefer, text me a list and I'll stop at the store when I get off work and drop it off. That way you won't have to go out in the snow," Ethan volunteered.

He heard the hesitation in her voice at his offer. "Actually, it might be better if you just took me. I'd hate to have you wandering all over the store trying to find the things Max likes."

"My shift ends in about an hour. I'll drop by then."

"Thank you."

He dropped the phone into his pocket and headed for the ER.

"Mommy, I'm hungry," Max said from the back seat.

Abby shifted to glance at her son. "We'll eat as soon as we get back to Doctor Dan's."

"If you're up for it, we could grab a bite now," Ethan offered.

She looked at Max and knew a mini-meltdown was fast approaching. "Yes, why don't we."

After ordering for Max and herself, Abby put down the menu while Ethan placed his order.

"How was your day? Is your side giving you any more trouble this afternoon?" Ethan asked.

"We had a quiet morning. As to my side, it's fine."

"I watched *Mickey Mouse Clubhouse* this morning, Doctor Dan. Want me to sing the song?" The little boy bounced up in his chair.

"Maybe later, Max," Abby said.

"Then I saw *Finding Nemo*. I like Dory best."

"Dory?"

"Dory is a fish who helps Nemo find his way home in the movie," Abby told Ethan.

"When it was over, I watched *Happy Feet*." Max jumped out of his chair and started hopping around the table. "See Doctor Dan, they dance like this.

"Then I saw *Fraggle Rock*. They live under a man's house and nobody knows they're there," Max explained. "And the man has a big dog, this big." Max flung his arms open wide and caught the rim of the glass.

Abby watched orange liquid cascade over the edge of the glass, and down over Ethan's lap.

"What the hell . . ." Ethan jumped to his feet, trying to get away from the cold, sticky drink, but it was too late.

Max quickly climbed up on his chair, his lower lip quivering.

"It's okay, Max, it was an accident. Doctor Dan knows you didn't do it on purpose." Abby grabbed a handful of napkins and covered the wet spot on the table.

She looked at Ethan, seeing the frown on his face.

He did know this was an accident, didn't he?

"I'm sorry," Max whispered.

"I know, sweetie. So does Doctor Dan. You were excited to tell him about your morning." She gave Max a smile, and then looked at Ethan, her pointed stare conveying the need to reassure Max that Dan did understand.

Ethan's gaze dropped back to the floor and Abby watched him draw in a deep breath before he looked back up.

Somehow Ethan didn't look convinced.

"Yeah, sure. It was an accident. No problem, Max."

"Let me help you." Abby reached over and started blotting the orange drink off Ethan's pants, squeezing the material to soak up the excess.

"I can do it." Ethan practically growled the words as he grabbed the napkins out of her hand and stepped out of reach.

"I was only trying to help." Her temper flared.

"Don't. Touch. Me."

The three words were a bullet to her heart. The man was seconds from losing his cool.

Maybe stopping to eat wasn't such a good idea after all, Abby thought.

Ethan stepped into the shower. The press of Abby's hand against his pants had felt like a live wire touching his skin. At any second, Ethan expected to see sparks shoot from the contact. After they finished grocery shopping, Abby had insisted he come and use the shower at his house before going back to the hospital for the night. He'd reluctantly agreed.

He leaned against the tile wall and ducked his head under the stinging spray, feeling the hot water pound at his tense muscles. As soon as he was finished, Ethan was going to throw some more clothes in his duffel bag and get the hell out of the house.

Ethan turned off the water, and reached for a towel. He still didn't understand why Abby suddenly got angry and demanded they leave the restaurant.

How was he to know lunch would turn out to be such a disastrous event? He never should have suggested it, but hearing Max whine in the back seat had taken its toll on Ethan's sanity. The lack of sleep was grating on his last nerve and Abby and Max had paid the price.

How was he supposed to react when the kid dumped soda on him? Smile and say everything was fine? It wasn't. It was a sticky mess that left his pant legs stuck to him like a second skin.

Maybe he had reacted badly. But it came to a head when Abby pressed the wad of napkins to his leg. The heat of her touch seared him, reaching places Ethan didn't want it to.

A small of part of him wanted to explain so he wouldn't end up hurting Abby once again. But, no, it was safer not to form an attachment, not to care for her. In the end, no one would be disappointed when everything fell apart. Maybe it was better to keep his mouth shut and let her assume whatever she wanted. Ethan rubbed his hand across the steam-covered mirror and stared hard at the man reflected there.

The bigger problem was imagining they could have what they once shared again. For a brief second Ethan wondered what it would be like if things were returned to normal. He knew if he took that giant leap of faith, it meant opening his heart and letting someone in, and that scared the living daylights out of him. Because if he failed, he would let everyone down.

Chapter Six

Abby had received her final clearance from her surgeon, Jack Tanner. Her newly repaired car sat in Ethan's driveway and she could barely contain her excitement. She could finally start apartment hunting.

Abby clutched Max's hand as they entered Santa's Kingdom at the mall. "Are you sure this is a good idea?" While she was thrilled Ethan suggested they take Max to see Santa, the crush of people was making her nervous.

"The line isn't going to get any shorter, Abby. With less than ten days until Christmas, it'll get longer. We'll be out of here in no time. Besides, Max and I want to see Santa," Ethan told her.

Max bounced up and down. "I see him, I see him. Look Mommy, there's Santa." Max pointed toward the front of the line, to the giant white igloo with the oversized throne in which Santa sat.

About twenty feet from the front of the line, Abby's cell phone rang. She dug in her purse, and then lifted it to her ear. "Hello."

A smile crossed her face. "That'll be perfect. I'll meet you there." She snapped the phone shut and dropped it back in her purse. "That was the realtor. She's found some apartments to show me the day after tomorrow."

"What time are you meeting?" Ethan asked.

"Noon."

"Is Max going with you?"

She nodded. "I thought it might be nice for him to get out of the house."

"I've got the day off and could watch him if you'd like. I'm not sure Max wants to be dragged around all afternoon looking at empty apartments."

"I wouldn't want to impose on you any more than we have." This was the first time Ethan mentioned spending any time alone with Max.

She thought about his offer for a few minutes before answering. It would be easier without Max along. And Max would be able to spend time with Ethan, which was a plus.

"If you're sure, then yes, I accept."

"Good. Why don't you go and do your Christmas shopping? That way Max won't see what you're getting him."

"That's a good idea. I'll run over to the toy store, then the children's shop. I'll be back before you even get up to see Santa."

"We'll be waiting." Ethan smiled at her.

The man could be over-the-top charming and now was one of those times.

"Max, you stay with Doctor Dan. I'll be back in a few minutes." She kissed the top of his head.

"Okay Mommy. Look Doctor Dan, I can see Santa."

Once inside the toy store, she quickly gathered up a selection of Max's favorites. A little later, she walked out of the kids' clothes store, her arms laden with packages. Abby headed across the mall back toward Santa's Village looking for Ethan and Max.

Max raced up the steps to get to Santa, and immediately climbed on his lap, waving at Dan all the while. Ethan couldn't help chuckling. He heard Santa laugh and listen attentively to everything Max said. His cell phone rang and Ethan lifted the phone to his ear.

"Ethan Gregory."

He listened intently to the voice on the other end.

"Start an IV, and put Doctor Tanner on alert. My feeling is gall bladder. Do an ultrasound, rush the results and get those to him as well."

"Doctor Dan, look at me. I got a candy cane." Max had finished with Santa and was now pulling at Ethan's pant leg.

Ethan waved at Max before turning his attention back to the call. "If you can't get him stabilized in ten minutes, get him up to surgery and call whoever is on duty. Don't wait."

"Ethan, where's Max?" Abby appeared on his left.

A quick glance at Santa's throne showed Max was not there. Where could that kid have gone? Ethan watched as Abby frantically searched the crowd. She was starting to panic.

"I've got to go to the hospital. He was right there . . ." Ethan's words trailed off. The boy was nowhere to be seen.

"What were you thinking, turning your back on him?" Abby rushed to the other side of the aisle.

"I didn't turn my back. I've been here the whole time. Relax, Abby; he's probably hiding behind the igloo waiting for us to find him."

"Max doesn't do things like that, Ethan. He knows better than to hide in a crowded place. Oh my God, we've got to find him!"

Ethan stepped over the velvet ropes and maneuvered his way through the line.

"I never should have left you alone. What if something's happened to him? What if someone took . . . ?" Abby's voice dropped to a frightened whisper.

Ethan scanned the crowd, looking for Max. But it was impossible to distinguish one child from another in the sea of child-size bodies waiting for Santa. Abby clutched at his sleeve, panic evident on her face.

A cold sweat broke out on his body, but Ethan refused to let himself get sucked in. They would find Max. Ethan wouldn't let himself think differently. Abby was on the verge of a meltdown when Ethan grabbed her hands. He needed her to trust him if they were going to find Max.

"Abby, I need you to breathe. We'll find Max; we will find him. You have my word."

Ethan didn't want to think about the consequences. Too much time had passed. He needed to alert the authorities and put out an Amber Alert. Ethan dialed 911 and was about to hit send when he lifted his head and searched the area once more.

He took off at a dead run. "There, I see him. Come on."

Max was at the other end of the mall, pointing at a display of reindeer. "Look, this is Santa's reindeers."

Ethan grabbed the young boy. His first reaction was to hug him; his second was to administer a sound spanking.

If this was what it felt like to be a parent, Ethan didn't think he'd be able to survive. The gut-wrenching sensation of not being able to find Max was akin to facing enemy fire. The thought of losing his son did something to Ethan he didn't think he'd be able to overcome.

"You're squishing me, Doctor Dan."

Ethan begrudgingly loosened his hold on Max.

"Max, you can't leave without telling Mommy or me where you're going. We were very worried." The words came out harsher than Ethan intended.

Tears filled Max's eyes. "I wanted to see Santa's reindeer."

"We know, sweetheart, but you scared us. If you ever do that again, you will be punished," Abby told him.

"Does this mean Santa won't come to Doctor Dan's house now?"

"Santa will come, don't worry." Abby led Max toward the mall exit.

Ethan stared after them. It was his fault for taking his eyes off Max. How could he have been so stupid? If anything had happened, Ethan would have had only himself to blame.

The strange surge of love he felt for Max at that second terrified him.

"What's wrong with you? You never take your eyes off a child in a crowd." Abby kept her voice low on the drive home.

"Crisis averted, he's safe."

"Don't you think your attitude's a little cavalier? This is a little boy we're talking about, your little boy. Even you should know the dangers of taking your eyes off a child for one minute. Something you would have known if you'd spent any time with Max."

"What's that supposed to mean?"

"It means you've been avoiding your son."

"I haven't been avoiding him. It's complicated." Ethan pulled the car into the driveway and turned to face her.

"You still think I'm lying to you, don't you?"

"I didn't say that."

"You never say the words aloud, but they come through crystal clear. What do I have to do to convince you? Have a paternity test done?"

The look on his face told Abby everything. "You're wasting

your time and money. Max is your son. But it won't change the way you've been treating him." Or me, Abby thought.

For a brief second, Abby thought they had made some headway. But instead of moving forward, it seemed they were stuck in neutral.

The night after the incident with Max, Ethan opened the front door of his house and came to an abrupt halt. There, lined up neatly, sat two pairs of boots.

A small pair and a larger pair. Realization slammed him hard.

Damn it! Abby and Max were here. How the hell could he forget something like that? He was so tired from the busiest day they'd had in the ER for months, the fact that he had house guests totally slipped his mind.

Ethan skirted a plastic tub of toys and sat down on the sofa, sleep now the farthest thing from his mind. He really needed to avoid waking them up at midnight and scaring the hell out of them.

He started to walk towards his bedroom. All of a sudden, a sharp pain radiated across the bottom of his foot.

"What the hell?" Hopping on one foot, Ethan dislodged the small piece of plastic from his sock. Barely an inch square, the green building block was no bigger than his thumbnail, but more painful than if he stepped on a rock.

He closed his fingers around the tiny weapon. When he'd offered his home to Abby and Max somehow miniature weapons of mass destruction scattered intermittently on the floor never entered his mind.

Reaching in his pocket, he fingered the slip of paper Jack had given him. The number of the lab for the paternity test. Ethan had called them last week and started the ball rolling. He knew he wouldn't be satisfied until he had proof. Being in the military taught him that actions had consequences. And consequences forced you to step up to the plate to take responsibility.

While he didn't deny he and Abby had had sex, he hadn't been able to wrap his head around the fact Max might actually be his. All he could do was to wait until he knew for sure.

If Max were his son, it wasn't as though Ethan was going to offer up his heart on a platter to Abby. It changed nothing.

Now that Abby knew about the paternity test, it should have made things easier. The hurt he saw reflected in her eyes stayed with him long after they'd gotten out of the car.

All week long Ethan had been waiting impatiently for the results to come in, but the incident the previous day had changed all that. When Max disappeared, it brought home every fear Ethan could imagine. Whether he knew how to parent or not wasn't the issue. The issue was whether Ethan was willing to learn.

Something horrible could have happened that day. So horrible there would have been no turning back and it would have been his fault. The thought hit home like a jackhammer.

He should have been watching Max like a hawk. Ethan felt sick. It was his responsibility no harm came to Max.

But did it go deeper than that? Did he care?

Care was a scary word. He hadn't allowed himself to care about anyone or anything in a very long time. He wasn't father material, but Ethan knew he would step up, if only financially.

Every time he tried to push Abby from his mind, she snuck back in, creeping around the fringes of his consciousness.

He tiptoed into his bedroom so as not to wake them. He'd just sleep for a couple of hours, and then get out first thing in the morning and they'd never be the wiser. Ethan sat down on the bed, closing his eyes against the headache that was starting to form behind them.

Chapter Seven

Abby lifted her head and listened. Then she heard it again, muffled yelling from down the hall.

She looked at the bedside clock. Midnight.

The sound was coming from Ethan's bedroom.

She raced from her bed. When she opened Ethan's bedroom door, the moonlight through the opened blinds gave off enough light for Abby to see Ethan thrashing back and forth on the bed. His hoarse cries filled the room. He was drenched in sweat, and tugging at the bed sheets with every cry.

Ethan was caught in the throes of a horrific nightmare. Without conscious thought, Abby climbed into the bed and pulled Ethan into her arms. She held him, murmuring his name, trying to get him to awaken.

"Ethan, it's okay. Wake up," she spoke softly. She willed him to come back, to leave behind whatever was holding him in its clutches.

"Abby?" Ethan's voice was groggy. "What are you doing here?"

"You're having a nightmare."

"I'm sorry. I forgot you were here. We had a hectic day at the hospital. I didn't mean to wake you." He shoved his hand through his hair. Confusion clouded his features. "I must have fallen asleep."

"Do you remember what you were dreaming about? You were pretty frantic." She hovered, unsure whether to leave.

He let out a harsh sound. "I know exactly what it was. The same nightmare I've had for the past five years."

"Tell me."

"You don't want to know."

"Try me."

His voice was raw with agony. "The mission to Afghanistan was tough. I don't know what I expected, but it was more than I imagined. From the minute we landed, we were surrounded by casualties. The base had been under heavy attack for weeks. They were performing surgery in the mess hall since the surgical facilities had been leveled by enemy fire. We salvaged everything, did the best we could."

He paused. "This is what I wanted to do my whole life, and yet I . . . I couldn't. My job was to put them back together so they could get out there again and fight for our freedom. There were times I didn't think I'd make it out alive. Nights when the mortar attacks were so close my teeth would rattle with each blast."

Her heart sank, knowing how much the revelation cost Ethan. "War is something we can't control. All we can do is pray for a safe and speedy resolution to the conflict. You did everything humanly possible for those soldiers."

"There was one soldier I couldn't help. He was barely nineteen and joined for the college money. My unit tried to help him, show him the ropes. One day he came into the tent with his arms full of letters and packages. When he got to me, he handed over a packet of letters. They were all pink."

Abby sat up, listening.

"His name was Grady Summers. He had this goofy grin on his face. 'These are for you,' he said. 'Looks like somebody's sweet on you, sir.' I hate that I remember this so clearly."

He looked at Abby. "I reached out to take the letters and a mortar hit. There wasn't time to take cover. One minute he was there, the next he was gone. So much blood and so many wounded and dying and I couldn't help them."

Ethan covered his face with his hands, his breathing harsh and ragged. "He was a kid. Somebody's child. There wasn't enough left to send home to bury. I promised myself if I got out alive, I'd be the best damn doctor I could. This was all I ever wanted and I failed. I failed to save the people I'd been sent over there to help."

"Ethan, you didn't fail; you did your job to the best of your ability, under unthinkable conditions. No one blames you for anything."

"Abby, this is why I couldn't stay here with you. I couldn't risk you or Max hearing my screams. I'm sorry you heard it tonight. I'm so sorry."

All her hurt about the past fluttered away with his words. This was why he wasn't staying here, with them. Not because he didn't want to, but because he was trying to protect them. Protect them from something that wasn't his fault to begin with.

His expression was sad . . . vulnerable . . . fragile.

A thought struck and Abby knew she'd have to ask. The pink envelopes. The letters she'd sent telling him she was pregnant. The letters he never received. She thought he ignored her, didn't have the decency to answer. But he'd never gotten the letters.

"Ethan, those pink envelopes were from me. I wrote every week for the first three months telling you I was pregnant. You never answered, so I thought . . ."

"You thought I didn't care," Ethan finished.

Abby nodded. "Yes."

As much as the news thrilled Abby, she felt sad for Ethan and even worse for the loss of his friend. She slid to the edge of the bed and moved to stand.

"Don't go. Stay with me tonight." Ethan caught her wrist in his hand.

"I don't know if that's such a good idea."

"Probably not. Spend tonight with me in my bed. I need you, Abby."

She knew she should walk away before her body convinced her otherwise. She was insane for even considering this. How easy it would be to say yes.

Either way Abby knew her life would never be the same again. If she said no, she'd regret it the rest of her days.

"Yes," she said softly, just before his lips captured hers in a kiss.

Abby squinted at the sunlight streaming through the window. Ethan's bedroom window.

Worse yet, she was in Ethan's bed. And she was alone.

Her heart lodged in her throat. The events of the night before came rushing back. She wished she spoke a foreign language, or two, or better yet twenty. Because then she'd have more ways to call herself an idiot.

Abby thought they'd established their old connection. But she was wrong. What had she been thinking? More to the point, not thinking. Knowing what he'd been through gave her a clearer picture of his life. While she felt sorry for him, it didn't change the fact Ethan hadn't accepted Max into his life. She couldn't live with someone who swung from acceptance to rejection overnight.

Climbing from the bed naked, she tugged her nightgown over her head, abandoned at the foot of the bed. After checking on Max, Abby shut her bedroom door behind her.

Ethan was a drug to her system, an itch she couldn't satisfy. No matter how much it hurt, things were never going to be any different and she better get used to the fact.

Ethan was furious with himself. He'd bolted back to the hospital right after Abby had fallen asleep. After they'd made love for the first time in forever. What was she going to think of him? But he couldn't stay, cuddled there beside her in his bed. He couldn't be what she needed, could he? Was he ready for all this? He thought back to the scene at the mall when he'd lost Max. Was he even able to be a proper father?

"Hey, you okay?" Jack walked into the room.

"I lost Max at the mall a couple of days ago."

"What happened?"

"He wandered away to see the reindeer while I was on the phone."

"Let me get this straight. You took a call and stopped watching Max in a crowded mall? What were you thinking?"

Ethan lifted his hands up in surrender. "Not the things I should have been. Abby already chewed me up and spit me out every which way possible and then some."

"Good for her. I'd hate to think what could have happened."

"I haven't been able to stop reliving it. I should've paid closer attention. I should've been watching my son, not worrying about work."

Somehow Ethan doubted a good parent would do something like that. A good parent would know exactly how to act. Considering Ethan had no idea how to be that parent, maybe it was best he started with small steps. The sooner the better.

Abby refused to call Ethan. After what happened the night before, she didn't even know if he was going to show up to watch Max while she went apartment hunting. For all Abby knew, Ethan might have made other plans. If he didn't show, she'd take Max with her. Ten minutes before she was ready to leave, Abby heard the front door open.

"Ethan." She turned to get her coat, and headed into the living room.

He grabbed her arm, halting her steps. Abby looked down at his fingers loosely holding her elbow.

"Abby, we need to talk. I want to apologize for last night. I shouldn't . . ."

She pasted on a smile that didn't reach her eyes. "We're both consenting adults and we knew exactly what we were getting into. We had an itch that needed to be scratched. It happened, now it's over."

As hard as it was to say the words, Abby knew it was for the best. If he were apologizing, the night was most certainly another accident she didn't want to repeat.

"Max will be up in a bit from his nap. There are movies on the coffee table he likes, his favorite books are in the red storage tub in the bedroom, and he'll need lunch. I'll be back as soon as I can."

Moving day couldn't come soon enough for Abby. She held back the tears until she reached the car.

Chapter Eight

"I'm hungry, Doctor Dan."

"How about a peanut butter and jelly sandwich with a glass of milk?"

"I love peanut butter and jelly sandwiches," Max said, hot on Ethan's heels.

Ethan made the meal, and then carried it to the dining room table. "Here you go, Max."

Max looked down at the sandwich, and then slumped back in his chair.

"What's the matter?"

"It's wrong. I can't eat it like that." Max's lower lip started to quiver.

"What's wrong? Its peanut butter and jelly, like you wanted."

"But it's wrong." Two fat tears rolled down his cheeks. "Mommy makes it different. I want it the way Mommy makes it."

Ethan didn't know what to do. He'd used the last two pieces of bread to make the sandwich.

"I want Mommy."

Just then, the front door opened and Abby walked in. Max ran into the living room, and wrapped his arms around her. "Mommy, Doctor Dan made my sandwich wrong. The peanut butter is on the bottom. It has to be on top, like you make it."

Abby hugged him. "Let me see what I can do."

She looked at the sandwich, and then smiled at Max.

"Okay, climb back up onto your seat, and I'll fix it for you." Abby took the plate and walked into the kitchen, where Ethan watched her flip the sandwich over and then walk back to the dining room.

"Here you go. Eat your lunch while I talk to Doctor Dan for a minute."

Max beamed up at her. "This is how I like it."

Of all the things Ethan tried, flipping the sandwich wasn't one. If the peanut butter is on the bottom, flip it over so it's on the top. Why hadn't he thought of that? Parenting was definitely a skill he had yet to master.

The next day, during a break in the ER, Ethan pulled out the small white envelope from his pocket that he'd received by internal hospital mail. The paternity test results. He needed to open it and get the damn thing over with.

What was he so afraid of?

The fear Max wasn't his son? Or that he was?

"What the hell am I waiting for?" He started to rip into the envelope.

Would it really make a difference whether Max was his son or not? After knowing the boy for less than a month, could Ethan just turn and walk away? He didn't need a piece of paper to tell him what he already knew.

He opened the letter carefully and took a deep breath.

For the first time in a very long while, Ethan could clearly see just how stupid he'd been. The minute Max was born, everything changed whether Ethan had been there or not.

He wadded up the letter and threw it in the trash receptacle.

Now that he knew the truth, what was he going to do about it?

The last box had been deposited in her new apartment, and Abby closed the door behind the movers.

Though she was eager to move into her own place, she was sad to be leaving Ethan's home. Everything he'd done made life a lot easier since the accident. For that, she owed him a big debt of gratitude. Now settled in her new home with Max, Ethan could go back to sleeping in his bed, instead of at the hospital.

But it didn't stop the way she felt about Ethan. Despite her best intentions, she'd been unable to shut off her feelings for him. She was still in love with him and she always would be.

Yup, everything was working out perfectly, Abby thought with a heavy heart.

"Good morning, I'm Abby Baxter. Is Doctor Ledford available?" Abby stepped up to the reception desk and smiled at the nurse.

"Abby, I hate to do this to you on your first day, but we're swamped. One doctor called in sick due to a severe case of the flu. Do you feel comfortable seeing patients on your own?" Doctor Jerome Ledford came around to greet her.

"Sure, as long as you don't have any objections?"

"Holler if you need help." He passed the chart to Abby.

"Piece of cake," Abby said, thumbing through the intake sheet.

"Hi, I'm Emily Cunningham, one of the RNs. Rest rooms are past the desk, turn right at triage for the vending machines, and the break room is down that way. Anything you need, let me know."

"Abby Baxter, PA. Thanks."

Abby reviewed the chart as she walked into the exam room.

"Hello, Maggie, I'm Abby Baxter, the physician's assistant here at the clinic. I've looked over your chart, but I'd like for you to tell me why you're here?"

"I did a home pregnancy test and it came out positive." The girl looked to be about eighteen years old and a little frightened.

"So you saw the nurses here when you first came in and they drew blood for an HCG test – a pregnancy test, right?"

"Yes."

"Can you remember the date of your last menstrual cycle?"

"October ninth, I think. But I haven't told my family. Right after I took the test, I called my boyfriend. He said it couldn't be his. He was the only guy I'd ever slept with and . . ." Maggie dissolved into tears as Abby pressed a handful of tissues into the girl's hand. "Every morning I'm sick. Can you give me something so I can take my mid-terms? Otherwise they're going to fail me."

"The less medication in your system for the next nine months, the better. Anything you take is going to pass to the baby. It can cause serious complications. But I can give you suggestions on what to eat and drink to help."

Emily stuck her head in and handed the lab results to Abby. "Okay, the blood test confirms you are pregnant."

Abby heard the young girl choke back a sob.

"When's the last time you ate, Maggie?"

"I had some chicken last night."

"How about ginger ale and crackers? Think you could hold those down?"

"I can try."

"Why don't you look over this list, and I'll be right back."

Abby headed toward the break room. Within minutes, she was back with a can of soda and some crackers.

"Thank you."

"Maggie, you need to tell your parents you're pregnant."

"I can't. They'll kill me."

"They won't kill you, Maggie. Talk to them. Take these pamphlets with you and have everyone at home read them. Bring your parents back with you to your next visit."

Abby walked her to the front desk. "You're going to need the support. This isn't something you want to do alone."

She watched the young girl walk out the door and pushed away a twinge of sadness. Yes, Abby had done it alone. Not that it was the right thing to do. If she had it to do all over again, she would have made sure she'd found some way to tell Ethan the truth. Whether that meant running out the door after him and telling him she was pregnant, or something else entirely. Abby wasn't sure. She just knew she'd have done things differently.

Abby grabbed the next chart and headed into the exam room.

"Mr Carpenter, I'm Abby Baxter. Let's see what we've got."

Abby pulled on a pair of latex gloves and approached a man in his mid-sixties, seated on the gurney. She pulled back the blood-soaked kitchen towel and examined the wound.

"Let me guess, snow blower?" The flesh was sliced open across the man's left palm. She pressed a clean piece of gauze to the wound, and then examined the rest of his hand.

Tom Carpenter nodded. "Best I can figure is I clipped the edge of the blade."

"I'm afraid we're looking at stitches." Abby pulled off her gloves. "I'm going to have Emily clean the wound. Then we'll numb you, stitch it up and get you home."

An hour later, Abby handed him a script for pain medication. "Now remember, anything out of the ordinary, I want to know."

"Thanks, Doc."

All in all Abby's first day on the job had gone swimmingly, despite the thoughts of Ethan that wouldn't stop intruding.

"Doctor Gregory, patient in Exam Room Three."

Ethan read the chart, hoping he missed something in the symptoms presented. "Any viral or bacterial infections in the past month?"

The boy's mother nodded. "A sore throat. Our pediatrician gave him penicillin."

Ethan sat so that he was eye level with the boy. "Hey, Bobby, I'm Doctor Dan. I'm going to check you out."

"I don't feel good," the little boy whispered.

"Let's see if we can make you feel better." Ethan looked in Bobby's eyes, and then ran his hands down the sides of Bobby's neck, feeling the swollen lymph nodes.

"I'd like to order a CBC, a complete blood count, to rule out a couple of things. Tonsils aren't causing this." Ethan pressed the button to summon a nurse.

A few seconds later, Becky popped her head around the door.

"Get a CBC and tell the lab stat."

"Hi, Bobby, I'm Nurse Becky and I'll be drawing your blood today. Have you ever had this done before?"

The little boy shook his head.

"Well then, you're going to get a big gold sticker since it's your first time."

"Will it hurt?"

"It might, but that'll go away quick. I need you to hold real still for me."

"It's okay, son, I'm right here. You squeeze my hand and I'll take the pain away. We'll do it together." Bobby's dad moved to the bed and wrapped his arm around the small boy.

"You were so good; I think you should have two stickers." Becky peeled two off the roll and stuck them to the front of Bobby's hospital gown.

Ethan lifted the sheet and looked at the boy's legs, noting bruising on the shins. "Does he bruise easy?"

"No more than a normal boy," Bobby's mom said.

"Is there something we should know about, Doctor Gregory?" Bobby's dad spoke up.

"I'd like to keep Bobby overnight for observation. Run a few more tests and see how he's doing tomorrow. I can have two cots sent up so you can stay. Give me a few minutes to make the arrangements and we'll get Bobby upstairs."

"Once the results come back, I want Doctor Gates and Doctor Ramani called in for a consult," Ethan told Becky in the hallway.

"I've seen that look on your face before. It isn't good, is it?"

"No, I'm afraid it isn't."

Chapter Nine

The next morning, Ethan made his way up to Pediatrics. Colin Gates met him at the door with a grim look on his face. Then Ethan watched Doctor Ramani finish his examination of the boy before turning to Bobby's parents, who instinctively reached for each other's hands.

"Mr and Mrs Corcoran, what we're seeing are signs of A.L.L., acute childhood leukemia. Most children are between two and eight years old when diagnosed, with an age peak of four years old."

"That's Bobby's age," Bobby's mom said, her voice barely above a whisper.

A suffocating sensation squeezed Ethan's throat. The exact same age as Max.

"The white blood cells are defective in children with leukemia. They saturate the bloodstream, making the body unable to protect itself. Your son may have been experiencing anaemia, which explains the bruising. Because the disease affects bone marrow production of red blood cells, children tend to be pale, tired, short of breath, and bruise easily. Everything we're seeing in Bobby."

"We thought it was his tonsils." Bobby's mother shook her head.

"We need to determine whether the leukemia has spread and we can do that with a lumbar puncture. It's done under anaesthesia so Bobby won't feel a thing. Once we know what we're up against, we'll know best how to treat it."

Doctor Ramani closed the chart. "The cure rate is very good. With proper treatment, children can be free of the disease without having a reoccurrence again."

"I'll do whatever it takes," Bobby's dad spoke up. "Nothing's more important than my family. If it means taking a leave of absence to be here, I'll do it. Whatever you ask of me."

The words resonated within Ethan. He couldn't imagine the agony Bobby's parents were experiencing. What if it were Max? Ethan didn't know how he would've handled the news. He couldn't bear it if anything happened to Max or to Abby.

Everything was becoming crystal clear. He'd immersed himself in his work, but for what? He had no close friends except for Jack. He saw his family once a month for Sunday dinner when he wasn't working.

Family.

A family depended on one another through thick and thin. Ethan now had the family he'd always wanted, but didn't know what to do with it. Ever since he'd gotten the paternity results, all he'd done was think of how he could change things, to make them right.

Could he be a father who'd be there when times got tough? Slipping his hand in his pocket, Ethan fingered the small green piece of plastic that had nearly taken his foot off last week. He felt the raised edges press against his skin. So small, and yet a huge reminder of what he was missing.

He was ready to be the father Max needed. The man Abby could count on for the rest of her life.

What he felt for Abby wasn't friendship; it was more than that. It was love. She made him understand that while war had taken the lives of people he was close to, there wasn't a damn thing he could have done about it.

It was time to say everything that needed to be said. So much had transpired in the past weeks. Would Abby be willing to take a chance on him again?

Ethan needed to see her. He couldn't waste another minute. He glanced at the clock. One more hour until his shift ended.

Jack walked in the room. "Highway's closed until morning, no more en route. You okay?"

"I will be once I get out of here and go talk to Abby, let her know how I feel about her and Max."

"I wondered how long it would take you to realize that." Jack poured a cup of freshly brewed coffee and took a sip.

Ethan smiled. "I'm a first-class idiot and a slow learner where women are concerned."

"No argument from me."

"Code blue, Exam Room Four. Code blue, Exam Room Four." The loudspeaker blared and Ethan and Jack hit the door running, their hot coffee now forgotten. His day in the ER wasn't over yet.

Abby had just shut off the nightly news when she heard the doorbell. She turned on the porch light to see him standing there.

Ethan.

Opening the front door, she asked, "Can't this wait till tomorrow?"

"No."

Abby motioned him to come in, closed the door and waited.

Ethan looked awful. His clothes were wrinkled, dark circles rimmed his eyes.

"Did something happen?"

He looked up at Abby with tears in his eyes and she forgot to breathe.

"I had a patient, a little boy. He'd been having sore throats, infections that wouldn't go away, bruises, fatigue and no appetite. His parents thought it was tonsillitis . . ."

"But it wasn't, was it?" Abby dreaded where this was going.

Ethan shook his head. "No, much worse. It's acute lymphocytic leukemia. He's Max's age. I was there when the oncologist gave them the news. The father was willing to take a leave of absence, give up his job, and drain the bank account, all so his little boy could get better."

He paused before speaking. "Abby, I lied to you when I said my feelings were casual. I was afraid because I didn't think it fair to ask you to wait for me to return from Afghanistan." Ethan stood and paced the living room. "You were right. I was scared that if I never joined the Special Forces Unit then I'd never get the chance again. When I came home, I went to your apartment. You'd moved on."

Ethan drew in a raspy breath. "Up until you walked back into my life, work consumed me."

He dropped to his knees. Abby's gaze widened when he took her hands in his. "I get it if you don't want me around. But I'll do whatever it takes to earn your trust and love. I love you and Max."

Abby shook her head. "Ethan, you're only saying this because of that little boy in the hospital. You're exhausted, go home and go to bed."

"No, I'm saying it because it's true. I'll make mistakes, but I'm willing to do whatever it takes to spend the rest of my life with you and Max. I don't know how I'd survive without the two of you. If you want to wait, I get it. But you won't get rid of me that easy. I love you, Abby Baxter, and I love Max. I want to spend the rest of my life proving it."

Abby couldn't stop the tears that ran down her face.

"I should have stayed in Louisiana, waited for you. I should . . ." Abby tried to speak through her tears, to say the words she should have said years ago.

"Abby, will you marry me? Forever isn't enough time to show you how much I love you."

This is what she'd always wanted. She wiped at her eyes. "Yes, I'll marry you."

Ethan lowered his lips to hers. The touch of his mouth erased all thoughts from her head.

TOGETHER FOREVER

Tina Beckett

Chapter One

Cade Rivers lay face down on the exam table and prayed for death. Or at least a good, stiff drink.

He got neither.

Instead, the curtain behind him swished open and a metal chart clattered. "Okay, so tell me, Mr Ri—"

A familiar husky tone threaded its way through his senses before fading away in shock, and Cade knew his worst fears had just been realized. Not only would he not die, but his wife was going to be the one to keep him alive – or ex-wife, if she had her way. That's what he got for spending his first day back in town spreading horse manure on his father's field: a cut the size of Wyoming above his butt and one heck of a welcome home party.

"Yeah, yeah, it's me. So just give me the shot of anaesthetic and let's get this over with."

She appeared in front of him, stethoscope dangling around her neck, lips parted in . . . horror?

Mirabella Rivers made his breath lodge in his throat, just as she had the first time he laid eyes on her in grade school, her blonde pigtails brushing the high ridge of her collarbone, expressive blue eyes giving away her every thought. And her thought du jour was consternation . . . and maybe even a hint of anger.

Why are you back?

He could almost hear the question. One to which he had no answer.

One minute he'd been an up-and-coming orthopedist specializing in sports medicine. The next, he'd been approached to work with one of the hottest football teams in the country. Taking the job meant half a year of travel and relocating to Dallas on a permanent basis. He'd accepted.

Mira had opted to stay in Raven's Gap.

He'd left last spring, only realizing he'd crossed some imaginary line when the divorce papers arrived two weeks ago, the courier taking one look at his face and saying, "Sorry, dude."

And coming in for sutures? Yeah, not exactly the place he'd hoped to have their first face-to-face meeting in a year. Especially since the spot she'd be looking at was nowhere near his face.

"What happened?" She hauled a swivel stool from the other side of the room and planted herself in front of him, her eyes meeting his for the first time.

"I told the lid of a rusty can it could kiss my ass." His lips twisted. "It decided to take me up on the offer."

She glanced toward the area where his hospital gown barely covered one of his mom's blue-flowered towels. "You never did know when to quit, did you?"

The muscles in his jaw tightened. "And you never knew when to hang in there."

Her eyes closed for several long seconds before looking at him again.

"I did hang in there, Cade. For almost a year. Until it became obvious we wanted different things out of life."

No, they'd wanted the same things. To practice medicine and help people. They just disagreed as to venue. Cade wanted to see the things he'd missed out on as the son of a small-town veterinarian, while Mira was perfectly happy remaining in the town she'd been born and raised in.

She'd specialized in emergency medicine. She could work anywhere in the country. Not so for him. There wasn't much call for a sports doctor in an agricultural town. The choice of who should do the compromising seemed obvious to him.

Mira hadn't seen it that way.

She sighed. "I'm going to take a look and see what you've done to yourself. Does it need more than suturing?"

Was she talking about his heart, or his butt?

Because if she was talking about that leaky, pumping organ inside of him, it was currently on life support and not expected to make it.

"I would have asked Dad to do it, but his hands are a little shaky nowadays."

Gerald Rivers was in the early stages of Parkinson's. While he still practiced veterinary medicine, he'd begun referring some of the more delicate surgical procedures to vets in neighboring towns. In Cade's mind, maybe it was time for his dad to hire a vet student who could take over the business a couple of years down the road. But that wasn't up to him.

She smiled. "You're just worried your dad'll leave you with an ugly scar."

He already had one. Invisible to the naked eye, but there nonetheless. "Can we just get this over with as quickly and painlessly as possible?"

"That's what I'm trying to do, believe me." Her soft voice said they were no longer talking about his rear end, but about something else entirely.

Mira tried to corral her racing thoughts as she pushed the needle into the vial of lidocaine and measured out the correct dosage. Gerald and Esther hadn't mentioned their son coming to town for a visit. If they had, she'd have taken a few weeks off to visit relatives in Cheyenne or something. The last thing she'd needed was a confrontation. She just wanted a divorce so she could move on with her life. The sooner, the better.

Setting the vial on the countertop, her thumb traveled to her ring finger to rub over the hard gold band, only to find empty skin instead. She'd taken the ring off last week. Cade, on the other hand, still wore his. A beacon of love that no longer gave off any glow.

She should call in another doctor and let them take care of her soon-to-be ex, but the Emergency Room was currently short-staffed. And the sutures shouldn't take long to do. She could make it out of the room with her heart still intact.

She hoped.

Clicking the protective cap onto the needle and placing it on a small wheeled instrument tray, along with the other items she'd need, she made her way over to the bed. Stiffening her spine, she drew the edges of the gown away from Cade's backside. The dainty towel beneath had a dark spot where his blood had seeped through.

She hesitated. Somehow exposing a butt you were intimately acquainted with was a whole lot harder than uncovering a stranger's body, although she had no idea why that would be so. "Does your mama know you ruined one of her good hand towels?"

He didn't answer, something she was glad of at the moment. Snapping on some surgical gloves, she went to pull the towel back, only to find it was stuck in place. The already firm muscles of his backside tightened further as the fabric pulled on the wound.

"Sorry," she murmured, reaching for the squirt bottle of sterile saline and dousing the towel. Unfortunately, she'd need to let it sit a minute or two to soften the dried blood enough to remove the towel. So much for making a quick exit.

She decided to get to the question she'd been avoiding. "Why are you here?"

"I brought the divorce papers."

Her quick intake of breath seemed to echo through the room. "You've already signed them?"

She'd half expected a fight, and was deflated that he wasn't here to give her one. She was the one who'd initiated the proceedings, so why did it sting so much that he'd already brought the paperwork to her? Was he hoping to rub her nose in it?

Her heart contracted. Or maybe he'd already met someone else and wanted to be rid of her as quickly as possible.

The silence that followed filled the room, lasting an uncomfortable amount of time. Mira shifted in her seat, not sure what else he expected her to say.

"No, they're not signed." He rose onto his elbows, his body twisting sideways as his eyes met hers, the dark depths swirling with an emotion that threatened to pull her under. "I have no intention of signing anything, darlin', until you and I sit down and have a little talk."

⋆ ⋆ ⋆

Mira felt like she was floating above her body looking down at herself as she slogged through the rest of her work day. In the back of her mind were Cade's enigmatic words. Did he mean he wasn't going to sign the papers at all? Or did he just want to work out the details before he did? He'd refused to say anything else. Because no one – he said – could have a rational conversation while his butt was on full display.

That wasn't exactly true. There'd been plenty of talking in bed. How rational those conversations had been was a matter of opinion. The fact that she didn't remember much outside of the way he made her body feel was telling.

She shook free of her thoughts and concentrated on the wife of her next patient.

"Yes, Mrs Bentley, I think your husband's still in surgery, but I'll check."

The victim of a drunken brawl, Hal Bentley had made it home, only to pass out on the sofa. Thinking he was asleep, his wife had awoken in the night and come down to pull a blanket over him. She'd called 911 the next morning when she found his face was "out of whack", as she'd put it. Out of whack was right. He'd had a dent where his left cheek should have been and a deformed eye socket. He thought he might have been hit in the face with a crowbar, but he couldn't exactly remember.

Mira called the nursing station in the OR with an inward sigh. She'd bet Cade didn't see many cases like this. Well, maybe he did. Football was a pretty rough and tumble sport.

Yeah? Well, so was marriage.

Luckily, Hal Bentley would survive his injuries, which was more than she could say for her marriage to Cade. She drew a slow, careful breath, wondering how a relationship filled with so much joy and hope had ended up being a thing of despair.

And now he was back in Raven's Gap.

All Mira wanted was to get on with her life. Cade was evidently going to make her scratch and claw and scrabble for every inch of ground along the way. But she would get her divorce, one way or the other.

Managing to get through her last two patients without bursting into tears, Mira slid into her car and drove the three miles to her house, an ancient two-story farmhouse with Wedgwood-blue siding and crisp white trim. She and Cade had bought it from her parents, who'd moved into one of the outbuildings they'd remodeled into a small guest-house. As soon as she turned into the long driveway and saw the Rivers's beat-up green truck parked out front, she tensed.

If he'd let himself into the house, she was going to flip.

Although she'd never changed the locks, and they were still married . . . so he technically wouldn't be considered a trespasser.

Not until the papers were signed.

She frowned as she climbed out of the car. There was no sign of him in the truck. And going into the house, she called his name and got silence for her trouble.

"Cade?" This time her voice held a tinge of impatience. How had he driven over here with those ten stitches in his backside, anyway? The lidocaine should have worn off a long time ago.

Okay, he wasn't here. Then why was his truck in the . . .

She gulped as a sudden thought came to her. Oh no. He wouldn't dare play that dirty. Would he?

Going through the back door, she headed across the field at a quick pace. Her eyes clipped the pasture, where Ozzie and Harriet, her two Appaloosas, were grazing as if they hadn't a care in the world. Two saddles were slung over one of the wooden rails, making her stomach twist. The tack served as a confirmation that he was here. And she had a feeling she knew exactly where.

Chapter Two

Cade took another sip of his coffee, a rueful smile coming to his lips when Mira slammed through the door, her face pink with anger. Right on cue.

Her mother, Grace, a carbon copy of her daughter, and a good indicator that Mira would only grow lovelier with age, uncurled her legs from the couch and stood. "What on earth, Mira? Is something wrong?"

Oh, something was wrong all right. But was she actually brave enough to tell her parents she'd filed for divorce? Right here, right now? He didn't think so. After all, they'd given him no indication that they knew anything. Why? Unless she wasn't as sure about ending their marriage as she seemed.

A forced smile came to her face. "No, everything is fine. I just . . . just wanted to—"

"She just didn't realize I was coming to visit. I wanted to surprise her."

And he'd done that and more.

Her parents had welcomed him back with open arms, her dad asking when he was moving back to town. At that question, he'd swallowed hard. He knew they didn't understand why he'd specialized in something that would carry him far from Raven's Gap and from their daughter. Cade himself didn't have an answer, only that the town had made him claustrophobic and edgy, the feeling growing more intense as he'd worked his way through medical school. Originally he'd specialized in orthopedics just because he'd always had an interest in kinesiology – the way the human body moved. Sports medicine was the perfect marriage of the two. He'd never in his wildest dreams thought of working with a sports team. Until one of his teachers had given a lecture on the subject. By then, he and Mira had already married and were happily settled in her family home.

He never thought she'd refuse to go with him, until he broached the subject. She hadn't merely balked, but had stubbornly dug in her heels. She'd forced him to choose between her and his career.

And now he was thinking he'd made the biggest mistake of his life.

Mira moved a couple of steps closer, to where he was leaning against the wall. The pain pills he'd downed hours ago were still working. Enough to get him through this, anyway.

She glared at him. "Mind telling me why there are two saddles draped over my fence?"

"I thought we might go for a short ride."

Her brows went up. "Do I need to remind you that you have stitches and could pull them out?"

Mira's dad's head whipped around. "You have stitches, son? What'd you do?"

"Cade fell off a tractor and landed on a tin can, isn't that right, honey?" That last word came out with all the sweetness of a dill pickle.

Her mom and dad sent each other a look, and Grace's hand went to her mouth to hide her sudden smile.

He grinned back. He could see the humor of the situation. "You know as well as I do, the stitches are high enough that I won't be sitting directly on them. And I'll hold Ozzie to a walk. Or I'll walk myself and lead him."

Which seemed silly, but Mira would know exactly what he meant. Because unless things had changed drastically in the year he'd been gone, Harriet wouldn't go out alone, not without her long-time equine companion. And Cade was all for practicing a little emotional blackmail: taking her down by the creek where they'd first made love as seniors in high school.

Whatever it took to make her reconsider.

She might be ready for a divorce, but he wasn't. Not until he saw with his own eyes that there was no hope for them. Because right now, he was just not convinced. Not after the flicker of yearning he swore he saw in her gaze when he was lying on that exam table. And despite the pain of his laceration, her touch still held the same power over him. He'd been lucky he was face down because she'd have seen the hard evidence of that fact.

"So, what do you say?" He crossed one booted foot over the other. "Those horses look pretty fat and lazy out in that field. When was the last time you had them out?"

Since her folks no longer rode, Cade bet he knew the answer to that question. It had been a year since either of those horses had done much more than graze in that pasture. Why she kept them around, he had no idea. Harriet was as buddy sour as they came. Even if Mira wanted to take her out, the horse would have refused to leave without Ozzie. And Ozzie let no one but Cade on his back.

She shrugged, giving him his answer. "I'm thinking about letting them go."

"Mira!" Her mother's shocked voice was no match for the rock that settled in the pit of his stomach.

Mira loved those horses. If she was thinking of selling them, then she really was serious about ending things between them.

The fact that he'd driven up to the house with the intent of seeing if she still had them was telling. Because those horses were useless on their own. They needed each other. And they needed Mira and Cade, working together as a team, to be able to ride them. His heart had leapt when he spied them in that pasture. It meant there was hope.

Only now she was talking about selling them.

Maybe he was fooling himself. Still he had to try or he'd never rest easy. "Come on, Mira. Take them out with me." He mustered every bit of coaxing he could find and put it into that request.

"I'm tired. I've worked a long day. And I haven't ridden Harriet outside of the pasture since you left."

"Just down by the river. We won't go far."

He saw her swallow. Knew she was remembering. "I really don't think that's a good idea," she murmured.

"I've missed it. And it'll be a good place for us to talk." The stone in his stomach got heavier. Would their relationship end at the very place it began? Well, he knew one thing. He was going to make her face what she was throwing away. She'd have to look him in the eye in the midst of all those memories and tell him she no longer wanted to be with him.

Hadn't he done the same thing by leaving Raven's Gap?

No, because he'd always felt one of them would eventually give in and move to be with the other. Neither had. And, in trying to give her time and space, Cade wondered if he'd waited too long to try to patch things up between them.

The unwelcome thought barreled back through his mind, poking him with an angry finger. Maybe there really was someone else.

Something he didn't want to think about right now.

Shoulders sagging, Mira gave a quick nod. "Okay, but I want to be back before dark."

Harriet trailed along behind Ozzie, just as she always did, head bobbing as she made her way down the once familiar path. Mira rolled her eyes at the old mare and leaned over to stroke the side of her neck. "You'd get out more, if you weren't so stubborn, you know that?"

Glancing ahead at Cade, she searched for any sign that the back and forth motion was doing a number on his stitches. But he sat high and proud in the saddle, just like he always had, boot heels pressed firmly down in the stirrups. He was right. Thinking back on the location of his stitches, they were about three inches above the saddle line, angled up toward his right hip. But still they had to be pretty tender. Sitting would compress the area, combined with the rhythmic motion of Ozzie's gait. As slow as it was, it had to be pulling on them with each and every hoof beat.

But, oh, he looked so right in that saddle. Like he was meant to be there.

God, the man was handsome. That he still did it for her was obvious from the way her insides twisted with anticipation when she saw him on the exam table. But that crazy attraction wasn't enough to make a marriage work. And certainly not from nine hundred miles away. Wyoming and Texas might as well be in different countries.

She couldn't believe she'd told Cade she was thinking of getting rid of the horses, though. They'd been with her ever since she was a kid. Ozzie had been her father's horse, until the arthritis in his back had made it too painful to ride. She thought he'd wind up as a pasture ornament, since he wouldn't let anyone but her father mount him – shying and balking whenever anyone else tried. No one had been more surprised than Mira when Cade saddled him up and trotted him around the field on his very first try. It was like the two of them were meant to be.

Like Cade and Mira?

No. It wasn't the same thing at all.

She squeezed her legs against Harriet's sides to keep her moving. Neither Ozzie nor Cade looked back to make sure they were still following them, probably because they were both supremely confident that they were irresistible. Hmph. If she could sweet talk Harriet into turning around and heading back to the barn without the other horse, she would. But she already knew it would be an exercise in futility. Not even the promise of grain would tempt her into leaving Ozzie's side.

Besides, they were only about two minutes away from the river.

Mira was surprised the trail was not more overgrown than it was, since she hadn't been out here since Cade left for Dallas. Then again, it had only been a year.

A year.

Funny how that length of time could mean two totally different things. Not enough time to let a trail become overrun with weeds, but long enough to kill what had once been a healthy, happy marriage.

Or maybe that had been wishful thinking on her part.

Why hadn't Cade talked to her, been honest about wanting to leave Raven's Gap?

Maybe he had, and she'd just been too deaf to hear him. Had she stopped up her ears and refused to face the truth: that Cade was desperately unhappy in their hometown?

Mira heard it before she saw it – the bubbling rush of water that signaled they were close to the creek. The treeline before them opened up, and there it was. About six feet across at the moment, the little river changed size depending on the season and the amount of precipitation they'd had over the winter. She reined Harriet to a stop and sucked a breath of moist, clean air deep into her lungs.

Cade glanced at her and swung his leg over Ozzie's back to dismount. As soon as the familiar sound of his boots hitting the ground washed over her, she shivered. A bevy of memories danced in the trees, murmured in the river, whispered by on warm air currents.

Too late, she realized her mistake. This was the last place she should have come with Cade.

Chapter Three

The old log was still there. As were those damned initials he'd carved into it.

They picketed the horses, and Mira noticed Cade moving with care. "I told you not to ride. Are you sure you haven't ripped your stitches open?"

"I'm fine. Just sore. That fall off the tractor banged me up a bit."

She hadn't even thought to check him for other injuries in the Emergency Room, assuming that ugly laceration was the only damage he'd done to himself. "Where else do you hurt?"

He gave a quiet laugh. "Don't worry, darlin'. I'll live, although it would make it easier on you if I just keeled over, I imagine."

"That's a terrible thing to say." Just the thought of Cade not being here any longer . . . She might not want to be married to him any more, but she certainly didn't want him dead.

"Yes, it was." His eyes softened, and he reached out to trace the line of her cheek. "Sorry."

She moved away, toeing a pebble into the river. "So, what did you want to talk about?"

"The papers. Custody issues. Division of property."

"Custody issues? We don't have any children."

Cade nodded at the horses. "Not children, but we have others who are dependent on us."

What was he talking about? Yes, he sent money every month for their feed and pine shavings, but Ozzie and Harriet had always been part of her family. He had no claim to them. "The horses are mine. They couldn't stand to be separated, and you know it."

"I want to keep paying for their care. No matter what happens."

"There's no need. I only accepted the money you sent because I always thought we'd . . ." She gulped back the rest of the sentence, realizing she'd already said too much.

"You always thought we'd what?"

"It doesn't matter." She lifted her eyes and took a step closer. "I need you to sign those papers, Cade. Please. I . . . I can't keep living like this."

He reached out and encircled her wrist, tugging her forward until she was against him, her hands splayed on his chest. "I'm not asking you to. Come back with me."

His warm scent washed over her, drugging her, as his hands cupped her face.

"Cade . . . don't." Even as she whispered the words, her eyes fluttered shut, branding her a liar. She wanted him to. Desperately.

And he didn't let her down, slowly lowering his head, lips sliding over hers.

The familiar touch took her by storm, crashing through a year's worth of defenses. Her hands fisted in the soft fabric of his T-shirt, and she went up on tiptoe in an effort to get closer.

The second her tongue touched his, a low, pained sound rumbled up from his chest and his arms came around her, crushing her against him, his head angling to deepen the kiss to levels she'd once thought impossible.

And she let him – reveled in the all-too-obvious reaction of his body against hers, the heady knowledge that he wanted her as much as she wanted him. There was no rhyme or reason to her response, it just was. Even now, on the brink of a painful and permanent separation, Cade Rivers had the power to reduce her legs to mush, her heart to a quivering mass of jumbled emotion. Just like when they were teenagers and she'd straddled him as he sat on the log just behind them. Or when they'd brought blankets and picnics in on the backs of these very same horses.

Surely it was okay to have this one last memory. To have to face exactly what she was willing to give up. Surely it couldn't hurt worse than it already did.

When Cade's right leg swung over the log, Mira found herself mirroring his move. And when he slowly lowered himself, she followed, her bottom coming to rest on the tattered bark of the fallen tree.

Her fingers went to the top button of her blouse and popped it open.

"Mira . . ." He pulled away, combing his fingers through her hair and pulling it back in a ponytail, eyes seeking hers.

"Shh, it's okay." She moved on to the second button, which slid free of its hole as well. "This is why you brought me here, isn't it?"

"No. Yes. Maybe . . ." He put his hands on hers, stopping her. "But not if you're not sure."

Harriet nickered at Ozzie, who answered with a soft whinny.

The sound crystallized things in Mira's head. She needed Cade, and he was here. For now, at least. And if she let this opportunity pass her by, something told her she'd regret it for the rest of her life.

She scooted forward on the log, until she was on his lap, her legs on either side of his muscular thighs. She leaned toward him with a slow, meaningful smile. "I am sure, Cade. Very, very sure."

Cade swallowed back his disappointment. He'd been so certain that being with her here would change everything. Had counted on it. So when they'd finally untangled themselves, rearranging clothing and dusted themselves off, he'd reached for her, only to have her sidestep him with a tight smile.

"We need to get back to the house before my folks worry."

Mira was an adult, and her folks had seen them ride off together, so he was pretty sure this excuse was a lie. "Are you okay?"

"Fine." She looked anywhere but at him, though.

He could almost feel her slipping further away with each passing second. Not physically, but emotionally. If he couldn't figure out a way to stop her, she'd be handing him a pen and demanding he sign those papers in another second.

"Slow down. I have my cell, we can call your parents."

She untied Harriet and tried to swing into the saddle. She didn't quite make it, and came back down with a quick curse.

He knew exactly how she felt. His legs were a little shaky as well, and the low fire in his backside was ramping up again, a sure sign that his pain pills were beginning to wear off.

Cade went up behind her and planted his hands on her butt without a word. With his help, she boosted herself into the saddle. "Thanks." Just like her smile, the word was strained.

"We still need to talk."

"That's what you said before we came on this little outing, and look where that got us."

That wasn't fair, and she knew it. He'd tried to slow things down and get the talking out of the way first, but he figured if she was willing to have sex with him, she was willing to hear him out afterwards. And he could pretty much bet the woman still cared about him. No one made love with that kind of intensity without feeling something.

"I'm not the one champing at the bit to get out of here. You are."

And from the looks of it, Harriet was in no more of a hurry to leave than Cade was. She stood with her head down, looking like she'd just as soon sleep.

"Well, I'm kind of stuck here, until you get Ozzie moving." As if to illustrate her point, she nudged her heels into Harriet's sides. The mare's head twisted around, looking back at her with a you've-got-to-be-kidding glare. *I don't lead. Ever.*

Her brows went up. "So if you'll do the honors . . ."

With an irritated shake of his head, Cade untied Ozzie and stuck his foot into the stirrup and mounted. At least he'd made it up on the first try, although there was a sick pulling sensation in his back as he did. He was definitely going to have to check his stitches after they got back. That's all he needed, to wind up back in the Emergency Room to have his sutures redone. Could he not escape with a few shreds of dignity intact?

He wheeled Ozzie around, which ended up looking more like the turning of a slow-moving barge than a well-trained barrel horse. Pulling up beside Mira, he waited for her to look at him.

"I have two weeks until I'm expected back in Dallas. Don't expect me to sign anything before they're up."

Chapter Four

This was how he won her over?

A week had gone by and she hadn't set eyes on Cade. Not once. She seesawed between relief and irritation. They'd had sex. Good sex. She thought that had been the first step in some crazy campaign to save their marriage. Or that he'd at least be in to have his stitches out.

But even though she hadn't spotted him in person during that time, his handiwork was everywhere, which made it even stranger that he hadn't tried to see her.

Three rotting boards on the round pen had been magically replaced, and she'd come home a few days ago to find both horses washed and groomed, Harriet's dark mane banded in an ornate continental braid. It must have taken hours. But instead of doing those chores while she was home, he seemed to have developed an uncanny knack for knowing when she wouldn't be here and planning his schedule accordingly. He reminded her of those sneaky little elves who did the shoemaker's work while he slept.

She'd even found fresh bales of hay neatly stacked in the barn. The fact that he was doing heavy lifting with those stitches didn't make her feel any better.

But it did make her feel cared for.

And that was the last thing she wanted. He could do those things all he wanted, but they weren't going to keep him here on a permanent basis. He'd be going back to Dallas, back to his hotshot job with the football team, and leaving Raven's Gap – and her – behind once again.

You could go with me.

His whispered request had come back to haunt her many a night. Yes, she could go with him, and she was probably selfish not to, but she loved this place. Loved knowing she was providing a valuable medical service. Not every doctor was willing to come to a small town and work. She glanced around the emergency exam area with its curtained-off cubicles and basic equipment. Any of the more serious trauma cases had to be medevacked to the hospital in Cheyenne, because Raven's Gap Memorial just wasn't up to dealing with them.

A bigger hospital would give her more experience, but at what cost?

What would her parents do? They couldn't take care of the house and land on their own any more; they'd have to hire someone or sell the place, something she didn't want to contemplate. Then there was Ozzie and Harriet to consider. Yes, she'd mentioned letting them go, but in her heart of hearts she didn't think she'd really be able to. They'd spent almost their entire lives with her family. How fair was it to uproot them and ship them off to another home? If she could even find someone to take them. Ozzie was not the easiest gelding to deal with.

"Dr Rivers, you have a patient."

She tilted her head at the nurse in question. She hadn't seen Hannah lead anyone back to the exam area. "I do?"

"Um . . . he actually says he's your husband, and that you'll know what he's here for." Hannah gave her a look as if maybe they were planning some kind of scandalous tryst in one of the nearby exam rooms. "Is someone pranking you?"

No. No prank, unfortunately.

"Stitches." She cleared her throat when the word came out shaky, her heart already pounding in her chest at the thought of seeing him again. "He's here to have his stitches out."

The other woman's eyes rounded. "So it's true? I'm sorry, I didn't even know you were married."

Glancing down at her empty finger, Mira sighed. She could say something snarky, like "Not for long," but that didn't seem appropriate. Why did things have to be so complicated?

Why had Cade had to leave in the first place?

She was no fool. As much as she'd hoped her crazy emotions might simply vanish with time, seeing him again made her realize they hadn't. They probably never would.

She loved him. And in all honesty, he was a good man.

Not a monster. Not irresponsible.

They just lived in two different universes. Cade preferred life in the fast lane, while she just wanted to take life at a slow and easy pace.

He'd outrun her years ago, and there was no way she could catch up, even if she wanted to.

So she said the only thing she could think of. "It's a long story. Which room is he in?"

"Three." Hannah leaned closer. "You're so lucky. He's a looker, isn't he?"

She couldn't stop the smile. "Yes. He is that."

Before the nurse could think of a reply, Mira turned with a wave and headed to the designated room.

Once there, she took a deep cleansing breath and slid the curtain aside. Cade turned at the swish of sound and gave her a quick grin that made her heart squeeze.

"I figured I couldn't put it off much longer."

Couldn't put what off much longer? Having his stitches removed or facing her after what they'd done on their little jaunt into the woods?

If it was the latter, she could see why he'd hesitated. Because seeing him again knocked the wind from her lungs and made her wish for things that could never be. Why oh why hadn't he just signed those divorce papers and sent them back to her? Did he have to go and open up old wounds? She was pretty sure she wasn't the only one scarred by their past.

Bolstering her courage, she went and ripped a pair of gloves from the holder and snapped them on, realizing how ridiculous it was to do so. She'd touched this man intimately a mere week ago. Had held his weight in her hands and guided him . . .

She closed her eyes, trying to blot out the rush of memories that threatened to lay her bare before him.

"How does it feel?" she asked, gathering her tools and trying to avoid looking at him any more than necessary.

"A little tender at the moment."

Lord, why did she keep putting meanings to things that weren't there? "Let me see how it's doing. Our, er, riding probably didn't do it any good."

"I beg to differ," he muttered.

There she went again. "Do you want a gown? Or do you just want to drop your pants and let me go to work?" The second the words were out of her mouth, she groaned aloud. "Okay, so that didn't come out quite right."

He had the gall to laugh. "You think?"

"You're impossible." She held up the scissors and opened and closed them a couple of times. "You know what they say. Snip, snip and we're all done."

He paled, and it was Mira's turn to laugh.

"Let's confine our snipping to the stitches, shall we?"

"Anything you say." She swirled the scissors toward his lower region. "Pants?"

He turned his back and undid his jeans, tugging them to just below his hips, exposing just the sutured area.

Her smile widened. Those jeans remained well above the waterline, she noticed.

Plopping onto her stool and wheeling closer, she inspected the site, trying to keep her thoughts clinical and not dwell on the tight muscles of his buns. The scar was still red, but there was no inflammation or swelling. Nothing to suggest the skin hadn't sealed shut. Horizontal stitches on the back were notorious for pulling apart, even when things looked good, though.

"You realize you'll have to keep an eye on this for a week or so. I think I'll butterfly it, just in case." She'd had a teenaged patient a year or so ago that had gone camping right after having similar stitches removed, only to have her cut pull apart as she sat around the campfire. The doc on duty had glued it shut again, but it hadn't been pretty.

"Yes, Doctor." The sarcasm was unmistakable, but there was a playfulness behind the words that took the sting out of them.

She rolled her eyes and grabbed hold of the first knot with her tweezers and pulled it out far enough to slip her scissors behind. Snip.

She tugged on the knotted end and the suture slid free. Pausing, she again checked the cut to make sure it was holding. "Looks good."

"Thanks."

"Your wound." She emphasized the word.

"Color me disappointed."

Jerk.

Despite the thought, she realized they were falling back into their old rhythm of give and take that had won her over all those years ago. Hardening her heart and shutting her mouth, she put her mind to the task at hand and left out the chit-chat.

Snip and tug. Snip and tug.

Three stitches down, seven more to go.

Just as she pulled the last suture free, her cell phone began to chirp. Dropping the stitch into the basin, she blinked. "Back in a sec." She rolled over to the counter and glanced at the readout where a familiar number blinked.

Her dad. She frowned. Since when did he call her at work? A frisson of alarm trickled down her spine.

"Hello?"

Her dad's worried voice came over the line. "Hey, honey. I think we have a little problem down at the barn."

"Oh? What is it?" Her dad's idea of a little problem and hers were worlds apart, and that made her all the more worried.

"It's Ozzie. He's in the paddock." There was a pause. "He's down, Mira."

Down. The word no horseperson ever wanted to hear.

Her heart scrabbled into her throat, jamming it shut for several seconds, while a flood of questions rushed up seeking a way out.

Finally she got her voice working. "Is he colicking?"

"I don't know. Harriet's standing over him whickering, trying to get him back on his feet. He tried a time or two, but . . . it's not looking good."

The snick of a zipper said Cade knew something was wrong. His hand gripped hers as she fought the sudden rise of tears. She squeezed his hand, needing something solid to keep her on her feet. "Did you call Cade's daddy?"

"As soon as I saw what'd happened. Gerald's finishing up another case and said he should be here in around fifteen minutes or so."

She covered the mouthpiece and glanced at Cade's face, knowing he could only hear her side of the conversation. "Something's wrong with Ozzie."

"I'll go and meet Dad at your place."

Relief swamped her, even as she said, "I still need to put that butterfly on you."

"Later."

She didn't argue. At least her father wouldn't have to be there by himself. She still had another three hours to her shift. And a part of her was dying inside. She couldn't lose Ozzie. Not now.

She stiffened her shoulders. "Cade is on his way too, okay, Dad?"

"Okay. He can help me get Harriet out of the paddock."

"Wait for him to get there. Please don't try to move her on your own." The last thing she needed was to hear her father had gotten injured trying to get Harriet to cooperate. The mare was so attached to her buddy that it would probably take more than one person to get her out of there.

"I won't." There was another pause. "What do you want me to do, if it's bad?"

"I . . . I don't know, I don't want him to suffer, but . . ."

Cade dropped a kiss on her cheek before grabbing his wallet and keys off the exam table. "I'll call you once I've seen him," he murmured.

She nodded and then went back to her father on the telephone. "Let's cross that bridge once Cade and his dad have looked him over." The door closed behind her husband, and all Mira wanted to do was race after him and climb in the passenger's seat. But she had responsibilities here at the hospital.

"Thanks for calling, Daddy. Try not to worry."

"I know how special those horses are to you."

He did, but he had no idea that seeing those horses together had somehow come to symbolize her and Cade. Together forever – just like the inscription in that log down by the river. It was almost as if the universe wanted to show her how much it was going to hurt to lose him. She'd feel just like Harriet did right now. Only Harriet would never willingly leave Ozzie's side, whereas she . . . she was willing to take the scissors she'd just used on Cade's back and sever the now-frayed ribbon that connected the two of them.

She had no choice. Unlike Harriet, she couldn't follow Cade to the ends of the earth. She had her own life to lead. Didn't her needs matter at all?

For the next hour or so, she focused on her work, while waiting on a call from her father or Cade. But her phone remained eerily silent.

She checked patients and tended to paperwork. When the next doctor came on duty, the Emergency Room was empty. He saw her face and put a hand on her shoulder. "You okay?"

Was it that obvious?

"One of my horses is sick, and I—"

"Hey. Go home." He nodded toward the vacant space out front. "I'll call you if anything urgent comes in."

"Are you sure?"

"Yes. You only have another hour to go anyway."

She removed the stethoscope from her neck and rolled the cord around her hand. "Thanks so much, Richard. I appreciate it."

"No problem. I hope things turn out okay."

"Me too." She grabbed her sweater and headed toward the doctor's lounge to get her purse and keys.

They'd gotten him on his feet, but Ozzie wasn't out of the woods.

Cade and his dad had taken turns walking the big gelding in

fifteen-minute shifts. His dad – ever the strong silent type – hadn't said much, but Cade could tell he was worried. They'd gotten a good dose of laxatives into Ozzie, hoping the problem was trapped gas, rather than a twisting of the intestines or a blockage that could require surgery. If a large section of bowel died, the horse could either be condemned to a life of debilitating diarrhea or have to be put down.

Gerald came over and laid his palm on the horse's side, where, despite the pain medication, the animal's skin quivered at the contact. But at least the gelding wasn't reaching around and biting at his flanks any more.

Poor Harriet, now confined to her stall, could be heard frantically whinnying from time to time. It was reaching the point that she'd need a sedative to calm her. Hell, Cade might need one himself by the time this was all over.

Crunching gravel signaled a car had pulled into the driveway. He braced himself, knowing Mira had gotten off work early to see to her beloved friend.

"Come on, Ozzie," he whispered, leaning his head against the horse's neck, "you can do this. She needs you right now."

He carefully led the horse around so he was facing the gate, just as Mira climbed out of the vehicle.

Ozzie tossed his head as he recognized her.

Mira's blue eyes met Cade's, and she shook her head, warning him not to say anything until she got herself under control. Instead, she hurried to the wooden post of the round pen and climbed onto the lowest rung. Her cheek rubbed against that of the stricken horse. She whispered to him, and although Cade couldn't hear the words, the communication between animal and human tore at his insides. Then both their fathers were there, Mira's dad putting an arm around her waist to steady her as she continued to talk to her horse.

She took a deep breath and finally lifted her head, giving Cade a tremulous smile before turning her attention to Cade's dad. "How bad is it?"

"I've seen worse. But we won't know for sure for a couple more hours. I think it's gas, rather than impaction. Has he been cribbing again?"

Cribbing, where the horse sinks his front teeth into the nearest solid object – usually his feed box or a fence rail – and gulps air, could cause all kinds of problems. Colic being one of the worst.

"Only when he's confined to his stall, and I put the cribbing collar on him when he has to be."

She kicked off her low pumps, and then climbed the rest of the way over the fence. Cade's arm automatically hooked around her waist and caught her as she dropped down onto the other side. He pulled her snug against him, unable to resist the contact. Ozzie's neck craned around and nudged against Mira's shoulder, as if pushing her closer still to Cade.

Cade started to drop a kiss onto the top of her head like he would have in happier days, but noticed both the men's eyes on him. Not a good idea to let them think things were permanent, especially since Mira had made it clear she wasn't going back to Dallas with him.

As if reading his thoughts, she pulled away and held her hand out for the lead rope. "I'll walk him for a while." Her glance skimmed Cade's face. "Thank you for coming, though. I don't know what I would have done if you hadn't . . ."

She didn't finish the phrase because they both knew shc would have gotten by had he not been there, just like she'd had to do from the day he left Wyoming.

He let her take Ozzie, watching as she started circling the round pen, keeping the horse on the rail. Her bare feet sank into the sandy footing with each step. She probably didn't even realize she still had on her lab coat, the coiled outline of her stethoscope clearly visible in the right pocket.

Three hours later, Ozzie appeared on the brink of turning a corner, as evidenced by repeated bouts of noisy flatulence – strange that something like gas could cause celebratory whoops from the humans surrounding him. Even from Mira's mother who'd brought out glasses of icy lemonade and warm brownies, when she realized no one was leaving the horse's side until there was some change.

As soon as they'd finished the lemonade, they led Harriet out of the barn, but didn't let her enter the pen, until it was obvious that Ozzie was strong enough to withstand her worried nuzzles.

Cade's dad removed his cowboy hat and slapped it against his thigh, wiping his brow with a forearm. "I'd say we're out of the woods at this point. His sides aren't heaving like they were, and his ears are pricking at Harriet. Why don't you set him loose, and we'll let Harriet join him."

Mira stroked his coat and unclipped the lead line from his halter. The second that Harriet passed through the gate, Ozzie nickered softly and shuffled toward her, touching his nose to hers. The mare huffed out a breath, nostrils flaring as if in relief to finally be with her companion again. "Does this mean he's going to be all right?"

"I think so. Keep an eye on him." He glanced at Cade. "Go ahead and put his cribbing collar on just to make sure he doesn't swallow more air when no one's around, and I'll be back to check on him in the morning."

Cade's dad looked exhausted all of a sudden. Mira must have noticed it too, because she went to him and put her arms around him, hugging him tight. "Thank you so much. I'll take you home."

Cade shook his head. "I'll take him. You stay with Ozzie." He had some thinking to do and this would give him the chance to do that.

Once at his folks' house, he went to his room and opened his suitcase. Inside was the manila envelope containing the divorce papers. Sitting on the bed, he opened it and read the contents. Really read them this time, trying to allow his mind and heart to absorb what they meant. The finality of what signing them would mean.

This is what Mira wanted, otherwise she wouldn't have gone down this particular road. But was it what he wanted?

Hell no.

But staying bound to her by a legal document while he lived in a state almost a thousand miles away wasn't what marriage was all about. There was no way he could be a real husband to her like that. Was it fair to expect her to put her life on hold, expect her to have no other relationships while he lived out his dreams elsewhere?

No. It wasn't.

And he realized that coming back to Raven's Gap this time had been all about him, rather than about her. He loved her, would always love her, and he didn't want to lose her. Only when he'd come back here, he'd had no intention of quitting his job for her.

What exactly had he expected her to do? Quit hers and move to Dallas with him?

Yes, that was precisely what he'd hoped.

It was finally time to think about what was best for Mira, even if doing so ripped his gut apart as surely as Ozzie's insides had twisted and turned in unrelenting spasms. This was about doing what was right, not what was comfortable.

Carrying the stack of papers over to the antique secretary desk, he rummaged around for a pen. For several long minutes, he stared at the blank space that would soon hold his signature. Then, before he could change his mind, he scribbled his name and shoved the papers back into the folder.

Chapter Five

Mira opened her back door early the next morning so she could go out and check on Ozzie. She had the morning off and planned to spend it caring for the old guy. The gelding seemed none the worse for wear after his bout with colic, but she'd done as Cade's dad had suggested and kept the cribbing collar on him overnight. Just as she put her hand to the screen door, something crinkled beneath her right foot. She glanced down, and her chest froze mid-breath. A manila envelope with the return address of her lawyer's office caught her eye. Clenching her fingers around the envelope, she sent up a silent prayer, although she had no idea what she was really asking for.

After the time spent with Ozzie yesterday, when they'd stood side by side – Cade's arm slung around her waist – she'd been struck by how right it had felt being with him again. She could have sworn he'd leaned down once to plant a kiss on her head, but he never did. And then everything else had been swallowed up by Ozzie's crisis.

Maybe he'd returned the papers unsigned. He'd as much as said he'd come home to work things out, although he never gave any indication as to exactly what that meant. Maybe in her heart of hearts she'd hoped he'd return to Wyoming, and they'd live the idyllic life she'd always envisioned.

Going back into the house, she debated leaving the envelope on the table until after she'd seen to Ozzie, but something inside her urged her to look. She flipped it over, noting he'd sealed the back flap. Sliding her thumbnail beneath it, she loosened it then tipped it upside down, until the contents spilled out onto the kitchen table's wooden surface.

Her eyes filtered out the legal jargon and zeroed in on the space at the bottom of the main document. She put a hand on the table to keep herself from sinking to the floor in a puddle. There, in the space provided, was Cade's familiar signature, the script firm and decisive.

Unwavering.

He was giving her the divorce. And suddenly, it was the last thing Mira wanted.

"Her right ear looks a little inflamed, and her throat is definitely red." She stroked the two-year-old's hair as she turned to face the child's worried mother. "I'll send the nurse in to swab her throat to make sure it's not strep."

"Thank you."

After reassuring the woman she'd be back in a few minutes, Mira went to the nurses' station and relayed her instructions. She'd gone about her shift like an automaton, caring for her patients and writing up paperwork, but her mind was somewhere else. All she could think about was Cade kissing her while they sat on that old fallen log. Making love to her.

Don't leave. Please don't leave.

But that's exactly what would happen. There were no other options.

Her teeth came down on her lower lip. Well, there was one. But she'd never even considered it.

Until now.

Maybe she could talk to him. They could figure out something, even if it was just meeting somewhere on the weekends. Or maybe she really could consider moving to Dallas to be with him. It wasn't the end of the world.

But losing him again would be . . . at least the end of hers.

Once she'd finished with her patient, she slid into the doctors' lounge and scrolled through the numbers on her phone until she found the listing for Cade's parents. His dad answered and she immediately heard the question in his voice.

"Ozzie was fine this morning," she said. "He ate his breakfast just like he always does. In fact he seems to have forgotten all about what happened yesterday."

"Good, good. I plan to stop by to check on him a little later."

"Thank you. I appreciate it." She licked her lips and reached for a dose of courage. What if Cade didn't even want to talk to her? Well, she wouldn't know unless she asked. "Listen, Dad, is Cade there? I'd like to speak to him, if I could."

There was silence over the line and she thought she heard him talking to someone in the background. Cade, maybe?

Then a female voice came on the line. "Mira, this is Mom, honey. Didn't you know? Cade left for the airport a few hours ago. He's heading back to Dallas."

Esther Rivers' voice seemed to come from a long way off as Mira struggled to process the information. "Cade left? Already. He said he'd be here for two weeks."

"He said he'd been called back early."

That explained why he'd left the envelope without a word. He probably didn't want a scene or to have to explain why he didn't want to stay in Raven's Gap. It was over. He'd finally accepted it.

Well, she hadn't. She knew now that she'd sent those papers to force him to come home. To help her find a solution.

And he was damn well going to sit still while she had her say, even if she had to chase him all the way back to Texas to do it. She'd made a mistake last time he left and suffered in silence, but this time, she was going to fight for what she wanted.

And what she wanted was Cade, just like she always had.

She asked Cade's parents for a favor and then hung up, drawing a deep breath as she thought about her next step.

There was about an hour left until the end of her shift, and then she was off duty tomorrow. She had a few personal days saved up, maybe now would be a good time to cash them in.

As soon as she could, she called her mom, telling her that she was going away for a couple of days and that Cade's dad had offered to come by and pick up Ozzie and Harriet and keep them at his place until she got home. Then she went to the hospital administrator and asked for some personal time. There were a few tense minutes as phone calls were made and schedules were juggled. Mira glanced at the door just needing to be gone. Maybe she could still catch Cade before his flight left. But if he'd already left hours ago . . .

Finally they worked something out, and Mira drove quickly

home and shoved a few things into an overnight bag. Tossing it into the back seat, she climbed back into her car and spun the wheels on the gravel as she headed for the country road in front of her house. Just as she started to pull out, another car came out of nowhere, laying on its horn and pulling in front of her, effectively blocking her in.

Idiot!

The figure that leaped out of the car, however, didn't belong to an idiot. It belonged to her husband. And he looked furious!

Her eyes widened as he stalked over to her door and yanked it open. Reaching inside, he unclicked her seat belt and hauled her out of the car.

Well, at least she'd finally have her say.

"Cade, listen, I . . . I don't want you to—"

His hard mouth came down on hers, cutting off her words mid-sentence, his body pivoting to press her against the side of the car. The door handle dug into her back, but she didn't care.

God!

She met the kiss with a matching desperation, arms wrapping tight around his neck, unsure whether this was hello or goodbye and not really caring. All she knew was that this was where she belonged. In his arms. Whatever they had to do to make it work would be worth it.

If necessary, she could take Ozzie and Harriet with her and board them somewhere in Dallas. Somehow. Just as long as they were together.

He lifted his head and looked into her eyes for a long moment, both struggling to catch their breath. "Don't go to work today."

"I just left work. I was headed to the airport."

He leaned further away from her and blinked. "You were? Why?"

"To ask if that invitation to come with you was still open."

His eyes closed and his palms came up to gently cradle her head, thumbs stroking along her cheekbones. "Sorry, Mira. It's not."

Shock rolled through her system. It wasn't? Then why had he come all this way, dragging her out of the car and kissing her like there was no tomorrow?

Because maybe there wasn't one.

Maybe he really did mean for this to be goodbye.

Tears rose and balanced on her lower lashes, waiting for a single good blink to launch them on their way. "I— it's not?"

"No. Because I'm coming back to Wyoming. I was hoping to find that envelope I'd left and shred the contents before you found it."

Hope rose in her stomach. "You signed them." The words came out as a whispered accusation.

"Yes." He put his finger over her lips when she would have said something more. "But only because I didn't think it was fair to hold you to a marriage that was all one-sided. I knew I'd never stop loving you, but you . . ." He swallowed. "You're still young. You have your whole life ahead of you. You could find someone else. Start a family."

"I don't want to start a family with someone else."

"Yeah, well I decided I couldn't stand that thought, either. So I'm back. For good."

Her eyes widened. "But what about Dallas? The team?"

"There are other teams here in Wyoming. I realized how little it all means if I can't share my life with you."

She laughed, then drew a deep breath and laid her head on his chest. "I'd just decided the same thing. Decided Ozzie and Harriet could get used to city life, and so could I."

"You did?"

"I love you too. And being with you again made me realize how much I missed you. How much I wanted to be with you on a permanent basis."

"Then I can move back into the house?"

She nodded, pushing against him so she could retrieve something out of the car. "As soon as you take care of one little item."

"And what's that?"

She handed him the envelope containing the divorce papers. "Tearing these up and never mentioning them again."

Cade sent her a smile that had her body warming in all the right places. He ripped the papers – envelope and all – in two and let the pieces spiral to the ground. When he reached for her again, he took a moment to smooth her hair back from her temples and stroke long fingers down the side of her jaw. When he finally kissed her, his lips were warm and tender, holding all the promise of a bright tomorrow.

BIOGRAPHIES

Alina Adams
New York Times bestselling author of soap opera tie-ins (*Oakdale Confidential, The Man From Oakdale, Jonathan's Story*), mysteries (*Murder on Ice, On Thin Ice, Axel of Evil, Death Drop, Skate Crime*), and romances (*Annie's Wild Ride, Counterpoint*). She is currently in the process of turning her entire backlist, including her medical romance, *When a Man Loves a Woman*, into enhanced eBooks.
www.alinaadamsmedia.com

Tina Beckett
Award-winning author, three-times Golden Heart® finalist and author of medical romances for Harlequin Mills & Boon. Fluent in Portuguese, she divides her time between the United States and Brazil, and loves to use exotic locales as the backdrop for many of her stories.
www.tinabeckett.com

Sam Bradley
A paramedic for more than thirty years, she is also a multi-published freelance writer for EMS related journals, online publications and textbooks, who trains firefighters, does disaster work and takes photographs in her spare time. She is currently working on a medical romance trilogy (Partners, *Odyssey of the Phoenix*).

Karen Elizabeth Brown
A retired registered nurse, she has also published fantasy (*Medieval Muse* and *Dragon Kind*).
www.karenelizabethbrown.com

Lucy Clark

While working full time in a hospital as a medical secretary for two busy orthopedic surgeons, she decided to try her hand at writing medical romances. Almost twenty years, and fifty-seven medical romance books (and counting) later, she holds a Graduate Certificate in Professional Writing and will soon complete her Master of Arts in Writing and Literature.
www.lucyclark.net

Cynthia D'Alba

After seventeen years as a Registered Nurse, she began writing romantic fiction on a challenge from her husband, and discovered she enjoyed falling in love and having imaginary sex with lots of hunky heroes. She is now an award-winning, bestselling author of contemporary romance. Her series, Texas Montgomery Mavericks, is popular with readers and reviewers alike.
www.cynthiadalba.com

Cassandra Dean

Bestselling author of historical romances, including her popular Diamond series and the upcoming Silk series. She lives in Adelaide, South Australia.
www.cassandradean.com

Jacqueline Diamond

A bestselling author of more than ninety novels, including medical romances, romantic suspense, fantasy, mystery and Regency romances, she is the recipient of a Career Achievement Award from *Romantic Times*, and a former reporter and TV columnist for the Associated Press in the Los Angeles bureau. She writes the Safe Harbor Medical mini-series for Harlequin American Romance.
www.jacquelinediamond.com

Dianne Drake

In 2001, after seven successful non-fiction books, and a career in magazine journalism for such publications as *Ladies' Home Journal*, *Better Homes and Gardens*, *Family Circle*, *Parenting* and *Seventeen*, her first medical romance novel, *The Doctor Dilemma*,

was published. Thirty-five books later, she's still thrilled to be writing medical romance for Harlequin Mills & Boon.
www.dianne-drake.com

Fiona Lowe
A Rita® and multi-award-winning author with Harlequin and Carina Press, her books feature small towns with big hearts, and warm, likeable characters that make you fall in love.
www.fionalowe.com

Janice Lynn
A bestselling medical and contemporary romance author with over twenty published books, her novels have won the prestigious National Readers' Choice Award, the Golden Quill for Best First Book and for Best Short Contemporary Romance, the American Title, and the Holt Medallion Award of Merit.
www.janicelynn.net

Sue MacKay
Harlequin Mills & Boon medical author of deeply emotional stories set in New Zealand.
www.suemackay.co.nz

Wendy Marcus
Writer of hot, sexy, fast-paced medical romances for Harlequin Mills & Boon, her first book, *When One Night Isn't Enough*, was a 2011 finalist for Best First Book in the National Readers Choice Awards.
www.wendysmarcus.com

Lynne Marshall
A multi-published and award-winning author for Harlequin Special Edition, Mills & Boon Medicals, and single title romance for Wild Rose Press, her stories include a dose of medicine and romance, and always come straight from her heart.
www.lynnemarshall.com

Julie Rowe
With a first career as a med lab tech in Canada, she loves to include medical details and a lot of adventure in her romance

novels. She has three books published with Carina Press (*Icebound*, *North of Heartbreak* and *Saving the Rifleman*), and her writing has appeared in magazines such as *Today's Parent*, *Reader's Digest* and *Canadian Living*. She lives in northern Alberta.
www.julieroweauthor.com

Patti Shenberger

A freelance magazine journalist and romantic fiction writer, she previously worked in the pathology and medical records departments at a large hospital in Michigan, where she learned everything she needed to know about writing medical romance.
www.pattishenberger.com

Abbi Wilder

An ICU nurse for more than twenty years, she has served as editor of the Washington, DC/Baltimore Metro edition of *Nursing Spectrum*, and has been published in newspapers nationally. She is the founder of a website celebrating nurses who write fiction at www.nursesinlit.com.
www.abbiwilder.com